select
editions

___

Reader's
Digest

Reader's Digest

The condensations in this volume are published with the consent of the authors and the publishers © 2011 Reader's Digest, Inc.

www.readersdigest.co.uk

Published in the United Kingdom by Vivat Direct Limited (t/a Reader's Digest), 157 Edgware Road, London W2 2HR

For information as to ownership of copyright in the material of this book, and acknowledgments, see last page.

Printed in Germany
ISBN 978 1 78020 022 4

select
editions

THE READER'S DIGEST ASSOCIATION, INC.

contents

What was the catalyst that led Jack Reacher to give up his career as a major in the US military police for life as a drifter and one-man vigilante? In this high-voltage action thriller, Lee Child provides the back story to his heroic series character.

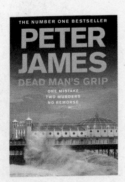

When a young cyclist loses his life in a road traffic accident, a terrifying chain of events is set in motion. For the cyclist had lethal connections who won't rest until all involved in the fatal accident are dead. A sinister and riveting crime story.

one summer
david baldacci

Jack Armstrong is losing his battle with a fatal disease when his beloved wife, Lizzie, is tragically killed. Now, with three children about to become orphans, what Jack needs is a miracle. An emotional departure for thriller writer Baldacci.

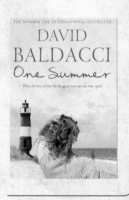

gamble
felix francis

A fast-paced mystery from the Dick Francis franchise. A murder at the races, a cryptic note and a shocking will, lead ex-jockey Nick Foxton, now a financial adviser, to turn sleuth as he tries to uncover why his colleague was killed.

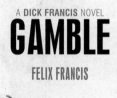

LEE CHILD
THE AFFAIR

March 1997. Major Jack Reacher, US Military Police, has been sent undercover to a small town in Mississippi. His mission: to find out whether anyone at the nearby army base is implicated in the murder of a local woman.

But why has he been ordered to shadow a colleague who is already checking out the base? And why has the local sheriff's investigation drawn a blank?

As Reacher hitches a lift into Carter Crossing, he starts to wonder what might lie ahead of him in this remote, deserted place . . .

ONE

The Pentagon is the world's largest office building, six and a half million square feet, 30,000 people, more than seventeen miles of corridors, but it was built with just three street doors, each opening into a guarded pedestrian lobby. I chose the southeast option, the main concourse entrance, the one nearest the Metro and the bus station, because it was the busiest and the most popular with civilian workers, and I wanted plenty of civilian workers around, for insurance purposes, mostly against getting shot on sight. Arrests go bad all the time, sometimes accidentally, sometimes on purpose, so I wanted witnesses. I remember the date, of course. It was Tuesday, March 11, 1997, and it was the last day I walked into that place as a legal employee of the people who built it.

A long time ago.

March 11, 1997 was also exactly four and a half years before the world changed, and so, like a lot of things in the old days, the security at the main concourse entrance was serious without being hysterical. Not that I invited hysteria. I was wearing my Class A uniform, clean, pressed, polished and spit-shined, covered with thirteen years' worth of medal ribbons, badges, insignia and citations. I was thirty-six years old, standing tall and walking ramrod straight, a totally squared away US Army Military Police major, except that my hair was too long and I hadn't shaved for five days.

Back then Pentagon security was run by the Defense Protective Service, and from forty yards I saw ten of their guys in the lobby, which I thought was far too many, which made me wonder whether they were all theirs or whether some of them were actually ours, working undercover, waiting for me. Most of our skilled work is done by warrant officers. They impersonate colonels, generals and enlisted men and they're good at it. I didn't recognise any of them, but they would have chosen men I had never met before.

I walked on, part of a broad wash of people heading across the concourse to the doors, some men and women in uniform, and some men and women obviously military but out of uniform, in suits or work clothes, and some obvious civilians, all of each category slowing as the crowd narrowed to a single file, as folks got ready to stream inside. I lined up behind a woman with pale hands and ahead of a guy in a suit that had gone shiny at the elbows. Civilians, both of them, probably analysts. It was close to noon. There was sun in the sky and the March air had a little warmth in it.

I waited in line. Way ahead of me two DPS guys were manning an enquiry counter and two were checking official badge holders and then waving them through a turnstile. Two were standing behind the glass inside the doors, looking out, scanning the approaching crowd. Four were hanging back in the shadows behind the turnstiles. All ten were armed.

It was the four behind the turnstiles that worried me. Back in 1997 the Department of Defense was seriously overmanned in relation to the threats we faced, but even so it was unusual to see four on-duty guys with nothing to do. Most commands at least made their surplus personnel look busy.

The line shuffled along. The two guys behind the glass noticed me about ten yards out. Their gaze moved off the woman in front of me, rested on me a beat longer than it needed to, and then it moved on to the guy behind.

Then it came back. Both men looked me over quite openly, up and down, side to side, four or five seconds. They didn't say anything to each other. Didn't say anything to anyone else, either. No warnings, no alerts. Two possible interpretations. One, best case, I was just a guy they hadn't seen before. Or maybe I stood out because I was bigger and taller than anyone within 100 yards. Or because I was wearing a major's gold oak leaves and ribbons for some heavy-duty medals including a Silver Star, but because of the hair and the beard I also looked like a caveman, which visual dissonance might have been enough reason for the long second glance.

Or two, worst case, they were confirming to themselves that some expected event had indeed happened, and that all was going according to plan. Like they had prepared and studied photos, and were saying to themselves: *OK, he's here, right on time, so now we wait two more minutes until he steps inside, and then we take him down.*

Because I was expected, and I was right on time. I had a twelve o'clock appointment with a colonel in a third-floor office in the C ring, and I was certain I would never get there. To walk head-on into an arrest was a blunt tactic, but sometimes if you want to know for sure whether the stove is hot, the only way to find out is to touch it.

The guy ahead of the woman ahead of me stepped inside the doors and held up a badge that was attached to his neck by a lanyard. He was waved onwards. The woman in front of me moved and then stopped short, because right at that moment the two DPS watchers chose to come out from behind the glass. The woman let them squeeze in front of her. Then she resumed her progress and stepped inside, and the two guys stopped and stood exactly where she had been, but facing in the opposite direction, towards me.

They were looking right at me. I was pretty sure they were genuine DPS personnel. Their uniforms had stretched and moulded themselves to their individual physiques over a long period of time. These were not disguises.

In front of me the guy on my right said, 'Sir, may we help you? Where are you headed today?'

'Do I need to tell you that?' I asked.

'No, sir,' the guy said. 'But we could speed you along a little, if you like.'

Probably via an inconspicuous door into a small locked room, I thought. I said, 'I'm happy to wait my turn. I'm almost there, anyway.'

The two guys said nothing in reply. Stalemate. To try to start the arrest outside was dumb. I could push and shove and turn and run and be lost in the crowd in the blink of an eye. And they wouldn't shoot. Not outside. There were too many people on the concourse. Better to wait until I was inside the lobby. The two stooges could close the doors behind me and form up shoulder to shoulder in front of them while I was getting the bad news at the desk. I could turn back and fight my way past them again, but the four guys with nothing to do could shoot me in the back.

And if I charged forward they could shoot me in the front. And where would I go anyway? To escape *into* the Pentagon was no kind of a good idea. Five floors. Two basements. Seventeen miles of corridors. There are ten radial hallways between the rings, and they say a person can make it between any two random points inside a maximum seven minutes, which was presumably calculated with reference to the army's official quick-march pace of four miles an hour, which meant if I was running hard I could be anywhere within about three minutes. But where? So I waited.

The DPS guy in front of me on my right said, 'Sir, you be sure and have a nice day now,' and then he and his partner moved past me.

The door was right in front of me. It was open. I took a breath and stepped into the lobby.

The woman with the pale hands was already deep into the corridor beyond the turnstile. She had been waved through. Straight ahead of me was the enquiry desk. To my left were the two guys checking badges. The open turnstile was between their hips. The four spare guys were still clustered together beyond it, quiet and watchful. I stepped up to the counter.

The desk guy on the left looked at me and said, 'Yes, sir.' Fatigue and resignation in his voice. A response, not a question, as if I had already spoken. He looked young and smart. Genuine DPS, presumably.

I said, 'I have a twelve o'.clock appointment with Colonel Frazer.'

The guy leafed through a book the size of a telephone directory and asked, 'Would that be Colonel John James Frazer? Senate Liaison?'

I said, 'Yes.'

To my left the four spare guys were watching me. But not moving.

The guy at the desk didn't ask my name. Partly because he had been briefed, presumably, and shown photographs, and partly because my Class A uniform included my name on a nameplate, worn as per regulations on my right breast pocket flap, exactly centred, its upper edge a quarter of an inch below the top seam.

Seven letters: REACHER. Or, eleven letters: Arrest me now.

The guy at the enquiry desk said, 'Colonel John James Frazer is in 3C315. You know how to get there?'

I said, 'Yes.' Third floor, C ring, nearest to radial corridor number three, bay number fifteen. The Pentagon's version of map coordinates, which it needed, given that it covered twenty-nine whole acres of floor space.

The guy said, 'Sir, you have a great day,' and his guileless gaze moved to the next in line. I stood still for a moment. The general common law test for criminal culpability is expressed by the Latin actus non facit reum nisi mens sit rea, which means, roughly, 'Doing things won't necessarily get you in trouble unless you mean to do them.' They were waiting for me to step through the turnstile. Which explained why the four spare guys were on their side of the gate. Crossing the line would make it real. Maybe there were jurisdiction issues. Maybe lawyers had been consulted. Frazer wanted my ass gone for sure, but he wanted his own ass covered just as much.

I crossed the line and made it real. I walked between the two badge checkers and squeezed between the cold flanks of the turnstile. The bar was retracted. I stepped out on the far side.

I was looking at the four spare guys, and they were looking at me. I looped round them and headed deeper into the building. I used the E ring counter-clockwise and turned left at the first radial hallway.

The four guys followed. They stayed about sixty feet behind me, close enough to keep me in sight, far enough back not to crowd me. I figured there would be another crew waiting outside 3C315, or as close to it as they decided to let me get. I was heading straight for them. Nowhere to run, nowhere to hide.

I used some stairs on the D ring and went up two flights to the third floor. I changed to a clockwise direction, just for the fun of it, and passed radial corridor number five, and then four. The D ring was busy. People were bustling from place to place with armfuls of files. I dodged and sidestepped and kept on going. I stopped at a water fountain and bent down and took a drink. Sixty feet behind me the four spare DPS guys were nowhere to be seen. But then, they didn't need to tail me. They knew where I was going.

I straightened up and got going again and turned right into radial number three. I made it to the C ring. I looked left and right. There were people in the corridor, but no big cluster outside bay fifteen. Maybe they were waiting for me inside. I was already five minutes late.

I turned without breaking stride and headed for bay fifteen.

THE DOOR WAS OPEN. I knocked on it once and then I stepped inside. Frazer's billet in 3C315 was a small, square space with a window without a view, and a rug on the floor, and photographs on the walls, and a metal desk, and a chair with arms and two without. It was entirely empty of people, apart from Frazer in the chair behind the desk. He looked up at me and smiled. He said, 'Hello, Reacher.'

I looked left and right. No one there. No one at all. There was no private bathroom. No large closet. No other door of any kind.

Frazer said, 'Close the door.'

I closed the door.

Frazer said, 'Sit down, if you like.'

I sat down.

Frazer said, 'You're late.'

'I apologise,' I said. 'I got hung up.'

Frazer nodded. 'This place is a nightmare at twelve o'clock. Lunch breaks, shift changes, you name it.' He was about five foot ten, maybe 200 pounds, wide in the shoulders, red-faced, black-haired, in his mid-forties. Plenty of old Scottish blood in his veins, filtered through the rich earth of Tennessee, which was where he was from. He had been in Vietnam as a teenager and the Gulf as an older man. He had combat pips all over him like a rash. He was an old-fashioned warrior, but unfortunately for him he could talk and smile as well as he could fight, so he had been posted to Senate Liaison, because the guys with the purse strings were now the real enemy. He said, 'So what have you got for me? Good news, I hope.'

'No news,' I said. I had nothing to say. I hadn't expected to get that far.

'You told me you had the name. That's what your message said.'

'I don't have the name.'

'Then why say so? Why ask to see me?'

I paused. 'It was a short cut. I put it around that I had the name. I wondered who might crawl out from under a rock, to shut me up.'

'And no one has?'

'Not so far. But ten minutes ago I thought it was a different story. There were four spare men in the lobby. In DPS uniforms. They followed me. I thought they were an arrest team. I lost them on the stairs.'

Frazer smiled again. 'You're paranoid. I told you, there are shift changes at twelve. They come in on the Metro, they shoot the breeze for a minute or two and then they head for their squad room on the B ring. They weren't following you. There are always groups of them hanging around. We're seriously overmanned. Something is going to have to be done. That's all I hear about on the Hill. We should all bear that in mind. People like you, especially.'

'Like me?' I said.

'There are lots of majors in this army. Too many, probably. Was I on your list of things that might crawl out from under a rock?'

You were the list, I thought. 'No,' I lied.

He smiled again. 'Good answer. If I had a beef with you, I'd have you killed down there in Mississippi. Maybe I'd come on down and take care of it myself.'

I said nothing. He looked at me for a moment and said, 'You look terrible. There are barbershops here. You should use one.'

'I can't,' I said. 'I'm supposed to look like this.'

FIVE DAYS EARLIER my hair had been five days shorter, but still long enough to attract attention. Leon Garber, who at that point was once again my commanding officer, summoned me to his office, and because his message read in part *without repeat without attending to any matters of personal grooming* I figured he wanted to dress me down right then, while the evidence was still in existence, right there on my head. And that was exactly how the meeting started out. He asked me, 'Which army regulation covers a soldier's personal appearance?'

I thought this was a pretty rich question, coming from him. Garber was the scruffiest officer I had ever seen. He could take a brand-new Class A coat and an hour later it would look like he had fought two wars in it.

I said, 'I can't remember which regulation covers a soldier's personal appearance.'

He said, 'Neither can I. But I recall that the hair policies are in chapter one, section eight. This section tells us that hair-grooming standards are necessary to maintain uniformity within a military population. It mandates those standards. Do you know what they are?'

'I've been very busy,' I said. 'I just got back from Korea.'

'Do they have barbers in Korea?'

'I'm sure they do.'

'Chapter one, section eight says the hair on the top of the head must be neatly groomed, and that the length and the bulk of the hair may not present a ragged, unkempt, or extreme appearance. It says that the hair must present a tapered appearance, where the outline of the soldier's hair conforms to the shape of his head, curving inwards to the base of his neck.'

I said, 'I'll get it taken care of.'

'These are mandates, not suggestions. Would you not describe your current hairstyle as ragged, unkempt, or extreme?'

'I'll get it taken care of,' I said again.

Then Garber smiled, and the tone of the meeting changed completely.

He asked, 'How fast does your hair grow, anyway?'

'I don't know,' I said. 'Same as anyone else probably. Why?'

'We have a problem,' he said. 'Down in Mississippi.'

Garber said the problem concerned a twenty-seven-year-old woman named Janice May Chapman. She was a problem because she was dead. She had been unlawfully killed a block behind the main street of a town called Carter Crossing.

'Was she one of ours?' I asked.

'No,' Garber said. 'She was a civilian.'

'So how is she a problem?'

'I'll get to that,' Garber said. 'It's the back of beyond down there. Northeastern corner of the state, near the Alabama line and Tennessee. There's a north–south railroad track, and a little road that crosses it east–west near a place that has a spring. The locomotives would stop there to take on water, and the passengers would get out to eat, so the town grew up. But since the end of World War Two there've only been two trains a day, both freight, no passengers, so the town was on its way back down again.'

'Until?'

'Federal spending. Washington couldn't let large parts of the South turn into the Third World, so we threw money down there. Carter Crossing got an army base called Fort Kelham. Ground was broken in about 1950. It could have ended up as big as Fort Hood, but ultimately it was too far east of I-55 and too far west of I-65 to be useful. You have to drive a long way on small roads just to get there. Or maybe Texas politicians have louder voices than Mississippi politicians. Either way, Hood got the attention and Kelham withered on the vine until it was turned into a Ranger school.'

'I thought Ranger training was at Fort Benning in Georgia?'

'The 75th sends their best guys to Kelham for a time. It's not far.'

'The 75th is a special ops regiment. Are there enough special ops Rangers in training to keep a whole town going?'

'Almost,' Garber said. 'It's not a very big town.'

'So what are we saying? An Army Ranger killed Janice May Chapman?'

'I doubt it,' Garber said. 'It was probably some local hillbilly thing.'

'Then why are we even talking about it?'

At that point Garber got up and came out from behind his desk and crossed the room and closed the door. He was worried. It was rare for him to close his door. He sat down again. 'Have you ever heard of a place called Kosovo?'

'Balkans,' I said. 'Like Serbia and Croatia.'

'There's going to be a war there. Apparently we're going to try to stop it. Apparently we'll probably fail and we'll end up just bombing the hell out of one side or the other instead.'

'OK,' I said. 'Always good to have a plan B.'

'The Serbo-Croat thing was a disaster. A total embarrassment. We're going to try to do Kosovo right.'

'Well, good luck with that. Don't come to me for help. I'm a policeman.'

'We have already had people over there, intermittently, in and out over the past twelve months.'

I asked, 'Who?'

Garber said, 'Peacekeepers.'

'What, the United Nations?'

'Not exactly. Our guys only.'

'I didn't know that.'

'You didn't know because nobody is supposed to know.'

'We've been deploying ground troops to the Balkans in secret for a whole year? Who did we send?'

Garber said, 'Army Rangers.' He told me that Fort Kelham was still operating as a Ranger training school, but was also being used to house two full companies of Rangers, handpicked from the 75th Ranger Regiment, designated Alpha Company and Bravo Company, who deployed covertly to Kosovo on a rotating basis, a month at a time. Kelham's isolation made it a perfect clandestine location.

I asked, 'Does Carter Crossing have a police department?'

Garber said, 'Yes, it does.'

'So let me guess. They're getting nowhere with their homicide investigation, so they want to go fishing. They want to list some members of Alpha and Bravo Company in their suspect pool, and they want to ask them all kinds of questions.'

Garber said, 'Yes.'

'But we can't afford to let them ask anyone any questions, because we have to hide all the covert comings and goings.'

'Correct.'

'Do they have probable cause?'

'Slightly circumstantial. The timing is unfortunate. Janice May Chapman was killed three days after Bravo Company got back from Kosovo, after their latest trip. They fly in direct from overseas. Kelham has an airstrip. I told you, it's a big place. They land under cover of darkness, for secrecy's sake. Then a returning company spends the first two days locked down and debriefing. On the third day they get a week's leave.'

'And they all go out on the town. Including Main Street and the blocks behind.'

'That's where the bars are.'

'And the bars are where they meet the local women.'

'As always.'

'And Janice May Chapman was a local woman.'

'And known to be friendly.'

I said, 'Terrific.'

'So what would you do, down there in Mississippi?'

I said, 'We can't shut out the local police department. But we can't assume any expertise or resources on their part, either. So we should offer some help. We should send someone down there. We can do all the work on the base. If a Kelham guy did it, we'll serve him up on a platter. That way justice is done, but we can hide what we need to hide.'

'Not that simple,' Garber said. 'It gets worse. Bravo Company's commander is a guy called Reed Riley. You know him?'

'The name rings a bell.'

'And so it should. His father is Carlton Riley.'

I said, 'Shit.'

Garber nodded. 'The senator. The chairman of the Armed Services Committee. About to be our best friend or worst enemy, depending on which way the wind is going to blow. And you know how it is with guys like that. Having an infantry captain for a son is worth a million votes to him. Having a hero for a son is worth twice that. I don't want to think about what happens if one of young Reed's guys turns out to be a killer.'

I said, 'We need someone at Kelham right now.'

Garber said, 'That's why you and I are having this meeting.'

'When do you want me there?'

'I don't want you there,' he said.

Garber told me his top pick for the Kelham job wasn't me. It was a newly minted MP major named Duncan Munro. Military family, Silver Star, Purple Heart, and so on. He was currently doing some great work in Germany. He was five years younger than me, and from what I was hearing he was exactly what I had been five years in the past. I had never met him.

Garber said, 'He's flying down there tonight. ETA late morning.'

'Your call,' I said. 'I guess.'

'It's a delicate situation,' he said.

'Evidently,' I said. 'Too delicate for me, anyway.'

'Don't get your panties in a wad. I need you for something else.'

'What?'

'Undercover work,' he said. 'That's why I'm happy about your hair. Ragged and unkempt. There are two things we do very badly when we're undercover. Hair and shoes. Shoes, you can buy at Goodwill. You can't buy messy hair at a moment's notice.'

'Undercover where?'

'Carter Crossing, of course. Off post. You're going to blow into town like some kind of aimless ex-military bum, the kind of guy who feels at home there, because it's the environment he's familiar with. You're going to develop a relationship with local law enforcement, and you're going to use that relationship in a clandestine fashion to make sure that they and Munro are doing this thing absolutely right.'

'You want me to impersonate a civilian?'

'It's not that hard. We're all members of the same species, more or less.'

'Will I be actively investigating?'

'No, you'll be there to observe and report only. My eyes and ears.'

'OK,' I said. 'When do I leave?'

'Tomorrow morning, first light.'

I WENT BACK to my quarters and took a shower, but I didn't shave. Going undercover is like method acting, and Garber was right. I knew the type. Towns near bases are full of guys who washed out for some reason and never got further than a mile. Some stay, and some move on, and the ones who move on end up in some other town near some other base. It's what they know. They retain some ingrained military discipline, but they abandon regular grooming. Chapter one, section eight no longer rules their lives. So I didn't shave and I didn't comb my hair either. I just let it dry.

Then I laid stuff out on my bed. I didn't need to go to the Goodwill for shoes. I had a pair that would do. About twelve years previously I had been in the UK and I had bought a pair of brown brogues. They were big, heavy, substantial things. They were well cared for, but a little worn and creased. Down at heel, literally.

I put them on my bed. I had no other personal clothing. None at all. I found an old army T-shirt in a drawer, olive drab, cotton, originally of a hefty grade, now washed pale and as thin as silk. I figured it was the kind of thing a guy might keep around. I put it next to the shoes. Then I hiked over to the PX and poked around the aisles. I found a pair of mud-coloured canvas trousers and a long-sleeved shirt that was maroon, but it had been pre-washed so that the seams had faded to a kind of pink. I wasn't thrilled with it, but it was the only choice in my size, and it looked civilian. I had seen people wearing worse things.

I chose white underwear and khaki socks and then found a kind of half-size travel toothbrush in the toiletries section. I liked it. The business end was nested in a clear plastic case, and it pulled out and reversed and clipped back in, to make it full-length and ready to use. It was obviously designed for a pocket. It would be easy to carry and the bristle part would stay clean.

I sent the clothing straight to the laundry, to age it a little, then I walked off post to a hamburger place for a late lunch. I found an old friend in there, an MP colleague, a guy called Stan Lowrey. We had worked together many times. He was sitting at a table in front of a tray holding the wreckage of a half-pounder and fries. I got my meal and slid in opposite him. He said, 'I hear you're on your way to Mississippi.'

I asked, 'Where did you hear that?'

'My sergeant got it from a sergeant in Garber's office. He said you're going as second fiddle and the lead investigator is some kid.'

I nodded. 'I'm baby-sitting.'

'That sucks, Reacher. That blows big time.'

'Only if the kid does it right.'

'Which he might.'

I took a bite of my burger and a sip of my coffee. 'Actually I don't know if anyone could do it right. There are sensitivities involved. It could be that Garber is protecting me and sacrificing the kid.'

Lowrey said, 'Dream on, my friend. You're an old horse. A new star is about to be born. You're history.'

'You too, then,' I said. 'If I'm an old horse, you're already waiting at the glue-factory gate.'

'Exactly,' Lowrey said. 'That's what I'm worried about. I'm going to start looking at the want ads tonight.'

NOTHING MUCH HAPPENED during the rest of the afternoon. My laundry came back, a little bleached and battered by the giant machines. I left it on the floor, piled neatly on my shoes. Then my phone rang, and a switchboard operator patched me into a call from the Pentagon, and I found myself talking to a colonel named John James Frazer. He said he was currently with Senate Liaison. Then he said, 'I need to know immediately if there's the slightest shred of a hint or a rumour about anyone in Bravo Company. Immediately, OK? Night or day.'

'There already are hints and rumours. The timing is suggestive.'

'The timing could be entirely coincidental.'

'Could be,' I said. 'Let's hope it is.'

Frazer said, 'I need to know immediately if there's anything Captain Riley could have, or should have, or might have, or ought to have known. Anything at all, OK? No delay.'

'Is that an order?'

'It's a request from a senior officer. Is there a difference?'

'OK,' I said.

'Anything at all,' he said again. 'My ears only. Night or day.'

'OK,' I said again.

Then Frazer said, 'But I don't want you to do anything that makes you feel uncomfortable.'

I went to bed early, my unshaven face scratchy on the pillow, and the clock in my head woke me at five on Friday, March 7, 1997. The first day of the rest of my life.

TWO

I showered and dressed in the dark, socks, boxers, trousers, my old T, my new shirt. I laced my shoes and put my toothbrush in my pocket with a pack of gum and a roll of bills. I left everything else behind. No ID, no wallet, no watch, no nothing. Then I headed out. I walked up the post's main drag and got to the guardhouse and Garber came out to meet me. Six o'clock in the morning. Not yet light.

Garber said, 'You don't have a bag?'

I said, 'Why would I have a bag?'

'For your spare clothing.'

'I don't own spare clothing. I had to buy these things especially.'

'What are you going to do when those clothes get dirty?'

'I don't know. Buy some more, I suppose.'

'How are you planning to get to Kelham?'

'I figured I'd walk into town and get a Greyhound bus to Memphis. Then hitchhike the rest of the way.'

Garber paused a beat and asked, 'Did John James Frazer get you on the phone yesterday? From Senate Liaison?'

'Yes, it sounds like we're in trouble unless Janice May Chapman was killed by a civilian. Is Frazer in my chain of command?'

'Probably safest to assume he is.'

'What kind of a guy is he?'

'He's a guy under a whole lot of stress right now. Five years' work could go down the pan, just when it gets important.'

'He told me not to do anything that makes me feel uncomfortable.'

'Bull,' Garber said. 'You're not in the army to feel comfortable.'

I said, 'What some guy on leave does after he gets drunk in a bar is not a company commander's fault.'

'Not in the real world,' Garber said. 'But this is politics we're talking about.' Then he went quiet, as if he had many more points to make. But in the end all he said was, 'Well, have a safe trip, Reacher. Stay in touch, OK?'

DURING THE WALK to the Greyhound depot I was passed by a few vehicles. None of them stopped to offer me a ride. They might have if I had been in uniform. Off-post citizens are usually well disposed towards their military neighbours. I took their neglect as proof that my civilian disguise was convincing. I had never posed as a civilian before. I had never even been a civilian. I suppose technically I was, for eighteen years between birth and West Point, but those years had been spent living inside a blur of Marine Corps bases, because of my father's career. So that morning's walk felt fresh and experimental to me. The sun came up behind me and the air went warm and dewy and a ground mist rose off the road to my knees.

There was a coach diner a half-mile short of downtown and I stopped there for breakfast, then I walked on to where the Greyhounds came and went. I bought a ticket and thirty minutes later I was in the back of a bus.

The ride took six hours. The view out of the window changed so slowly it seemed never to change at all, but even so the landscape at the end of the journey was very different than at the beginning. Memphis was a slick city, laced with wet streets, boxed in by low buildings, heaving and bustling with furtive, unexplained activity. I got out at the depot and stood in the bright afternoon. Then I walked south and east on a wide road leading out of town.

I fuelled up at a greasy-spoon café and then went looking for a corner with a big green rectangle road sign, marked with an arrow and OXFORD or TUPELO. In my experience a guy standing under such a sign with his thumb out left no doubt about what he wanted and where he was going. No need for a driver to stop and ask, which helped a lot. People are bad at saying no face to face. Often they just drive on by to avoid the possibility.

I found such a corner and such a sign after a thirty-minute walk, on the edge of a leafy suburb. I figured I would be mobile within an hour.

And I was. Twenty minutes later an old pick-up truck eased to a stop next to me and the driver told me he was heading out past Germantown. He told me if I rode with him I would end up outside of the urban tangle with a straight shot into northeastern Mississippi ahead of me. So I climbed aboard and another twenty minutes later I was alone again, on the shoulder of a dusty two-lane that headed in the direction I wanted to go. A guy in a sagging Buick sedan picked me up and we crossed the state line. He drove forty miles east and twenty miles south. He let me out on a minor road at what he said was the turn I wanted. It was late in the afternoon and the sun was heading for the far horizon, pretty fast. The road ahead was straight, with low forest on both sides. I figured Carter Crossing straddled that road, thirty or forty miles to the east. Once I got there, I would need to make contact with the local cops, which might be harder. There was no reason for a transient bum to pal up with people in police uniforms.

But both objectives were achieved in one fell swoop, because the first eastbound car I saw was a police cruiser heading home. I had my thumb out and the guy stopped for me. He was a talker and I was a listener, and within minutes I found out that some of what Garber had told me was wrong.

The cop's name was Pellegrino, like the sparkling water. It was no surprise he stopped for me. Small-town cops are always interested in strangers heading into their territory. The easiest way to find out who they are is simply to ask, which he did. I told him my name and said I was recent ex-military, heading to Carter Crossing to look for a friend who might be living there. I said the friend had last served at Kelham and might have stuck around. Pellegrino had nothing to say in response. He just took his eyes off the road for a second and looked me up and down, and then he nodded and faced front again. He was short and overweight, with black hair buzzed short and olive skin. He was somewhere between thirty and forty.

I finished saying my piece and he started talking, and the first thing I found out was that he wasn't a small-town cop. Garber had been wrong, technically. Carter Crossing had no police department. Carter Crossing was in Carter County, and Carter County had a County Sheriff's Department, which had jurisdiction over an area close to 500 square miles. But there wasn't much inside those 500 square miles except Fort Kelham and the town, which was where the Sheriff's Department was based. Pellegrino was indisputably a deputy sheriff, not a police officer.

I asked him, 'How big is your department?'

'Not very. We got the sheriff, who we call the chief, we got a sheriff's detective, we got me and another deputy in uniform, we got a civilian on the desk, we got a woman on the phones, but the detective is out sick long-term with his kidneys, so it's just the three of us, really.'

I asked Pellegrino, 'How many people live in Carter County?'

'About twelve hundred,' he said.

Which I thought was a lot, for three functioning cops. 'You guys must be busy, twelve hundred citizens, five hundred square miles.'

'Right now we're real busy,' he said, but he didn't mention Janice May Chapman. Instead he talked about a more recent event. Late in the evening the day before, someone had parked a car on the train track. Garber was wrong again. He had said there were two trains a day, but Pellegrino told me there was only one. It rumbled through at midnight, a mile-long giant hauling freight from Biloxi on the Gulf Coast. That midnight train had smashed into the parked vehicle, wrecking it, hurling it up the line, bouncing it into the woods. The train had not stopped. Pellegrino thought it was possible the engineer hadn't even noticed. So did I. Thousands of tons against one, moving fast, no contest. Pellegrino said, 'Who would park a car on the train track? And why?'

'Kids?' I said. 'For fun?'

'Never happened before. And we've always had kids.'

'No one in the car?'

'No, thank God. As far as we know, it was just parked there.'

'Stolen?'

'Don't know yet. There's not much of it left. We think it might have been blue. It caught fire. Burned some trees with it.'

'No one called in a missing car?'

'Not yet.'

I asked, 'What else are you busy with?'

At that point Pellegrino went quiet and didn't answer, and I wondered if I had pushed it too far. But it turned out Pellegrino's hesitation was based purely on courtesy and old-fashioned Southern hospitality. He said, 'Well, I don't want to give you a bad impression, seeing as you're here for the first time. But we had a woman murdered two days ago.'

'Really?' I said. 'Murdered how?'

It turned out that Janice May Chapman's throat had been cut.

Pellegrino said, 'Ear to ear. Real deep. One big slice. Not pretty.'

I said, 'You saw it, I guess.'

'Up close and personal. She was all bled out. It was real bad. A good-looking woman, all dressed up for a night out, neat as a pin, just lying there on her back in a pool of blood. She was raped, too. The doctor found that out when he got her on the slab. Unless you could say she'd been into it enough to throw herself down and scratch up her ass on the gravel. Which I don't think she would be.'

'You knew her?'

'We saw her around.'

I asked, 'Who did it?'

'We don't know. We think it was probably a guy off the base.'

'Why?'

'Because those are who she spent her time with.'

I asked, 'If your detective is out sick, who is working the case?'

Pellegrino said, 'The chief.'

'Does he have much experience with homicides?'

'She,' Pellegrino said. 'The chief is a woman.'

'Really?'

'It's an elected position. She got the votes.' There was a little resignation in his voice.

'Did you run for the job?' I asked.

'We all did,' he said. 'Except the detective. He was already sick.'

Up ahead the evening gloom had gone. Pellegrino's headlights lit the way fifty yards in front. Beyond that was nothing but darkness. The road was straight, like a tunnel through the trees. I saw a faded tin sign on the shoulder, advertising a hotel called Toussaint's, promising a convenient Main Street location and rooms of the highest quality.

Pellegrino said, 'She got elected because of her name.'

'The sheriff? Why? What's her name?'

'Elizabeth Deveraux. Her daddy was sheriff before. We think some folks voted out of loyalty. Or maybe they didn't know he was dead and thought they were voting for him. Things take time to catch on, in certain quarters.'

I asked, 'Is Carter Crossing big enough to have quarters?'

'Halves, I guess. Two of them. West of the railroad track, or east.'

'Right side, wrong side?'

'Like everywhere.'

'Which side is Kelham?' I asked.

'East. You have to drive three miles. Through the wrong side.'

'Which side is Toussaint's Hotel?'

'Won't you be staying with your friend?'

'When I find him. If I find him. Until then I need a place.'

'Toussaint's is OK,' Pellegrino said. 'I'll let you out there.'

We drove out of the tunnel through the trees and the road broadened and the forest died back to saplings. The road became an asphalt ribbon that led through a right turn to a straight street between low buildings. Main Street, presumably. We passed a building marked Carter County Sheriff's Department, and then a vacant lot, and then a diner, and then we arrived at Toussaint's Hotel. It had green paint and trim and iron railings on the first-floor balconies. A faded signboard hung outside.

Pellegrino eased the cruiser to a stop and I thanked him for the ride and got out. He pulled a wide U-turn behind me and headed back the way we had come, presumably to park in the Sheriff's Department lot. I used a set of wormy wooden steps and crossed a bouncy wooden verandah and pushed in through the hotel door. I found a small square lobby and an unattended reception desk. There was a matrix of pigeonholes on the wall behind the desk. Four high, seven wide. Twenty-eight rooms. Twenty-seven of them had their keys hanging in place.

There was a bell on the desk. I hit it twice, and a polite *ding ding* echoed around for a spell, but it produced no results. There was a closed door next to the pigeonholes, and it stayed closed. A back office, I guessed. Empty, presumably. I saw no reason why a hotel owner would deliberately avoid doubling his occupancy rate.

A door on the left of the lobby opened to an unlit lounge that smelled of damp and dust. There were humped shapes in the dark that I took to be armchairs. No people. I stepped back to the desk and hit the bell again.

No response.

I called out, 'Hello?'

No response.

So I gave up for the time being and went back out. There was nothing much to see. Across Main Street was a long row of low buildings. Stores, presumably. All of them were dark. Beyond them was blackness. The night air was dry and faintly warm. March, in Mississippi. I could hear the breeze in distant leaves. I could hear an extractor fan in the wall of the diner up the street. Beyond that, nothing. No human sounds. No revelry, no traffic, no music. Tuesday night, near an army base. Not typical.

I had eaten nothing since lunch in Memphis, so I headed for the diner. Inside the front door was a payphone on the wall and a register and a hostess station. Beyond that was a long straight aisle with tables for four on the left and tables for two on the right. The only customers in the place were a couple about twice my age. They were face to face at a table for four. The guy had a newspaper and the woman had a book. They were settled in, like they were happy to linger over their meal. The only staff on view was a waitress. She was close to the swing door that led to the kitchen at the back. She saw me step in and she hustled the whole length of the aisle to greet me. She put me at a table for two, about halfway into the room.

'Something to drink?' the waitress asked me.

'Black coffee,' I said. 'Please.'

She went away and came back, with coffee in a mug and a menu.

I said, 'Quiet night.'

She nodded, unhappy, probably worried about her tips. She said, 'They closed the base. They locked it down this afternoon.'

'Kelham? Does that happen a lot?'

'Never happened before.'

'I'm sorry,' I said. 'What do you recommend to eat?'

'Here? It's all good.'

'Cheeseburger,' I said.

'Five minutes,' she said. She went away and I took my coffee with me and headed past the hostess station to the payphone. I dug in my pocket and found three quarters, which were enough for a short conversation, which was the kind I liked. I dialled Garber's office and a duty lieutenant put him on the line and he asked, 'Are you there yet?'

I said, 'Yes.'

'Got a place to stay?'

'Don't worry about me. I've got seventy-five cents and four minutes before I eat. I need to ask you who briefed you on this.'

Garber paused. 'I can't tell you that,' he said.

'Well, whoever it was, he's kind of hazy about the details.'

'That can happen.'

'And Kelham is locked down.'

'Munro did that when he got there. There's a risk of bad feeling between the town and the base. It was a common-sense move.'

'It was an admission of guilt.'

'Well, maybe Munro knows something you don't. Don't worry about him. Your only job is to eavesdrop on the local cops.'

'I'm on it. I rode in with one. I need you to find out if anyone from Bravo Company owns a blue car. The cop said someone parked a blue car on the railroad track. The midnight train wrecked it. Could have been an attempt to hide evidence.'

'He'd have burned it out, surely?'

'Maybe it was the kind of evidence that burning wouldn't conceal.'

'How would that relate to a woman getting carved up in an alley?'

'She wasn't carved up. Her throat was cut. That was all. Deep and wide. One pass, probably.'

Garber paused a beat. 'That's how Rangers are taught to do it. But how would that relate to a car?'

'I don't know. Maybe it doesn't relate. But let's find out, OK?'

'There are two hundred guys in Bravo Company. Law of averages says there's going to be about fifty blue cars.'

'And all fifty of them should be parked on the base. So, let's find out if one isn't.'

'This is Munro's investigation,' Garber said. 'Not yours.'

I said, 'And we need to know if someone got a gravel rash. Hands, knees and elbows, maybe. From the rape. The cop said Chapman had matching injuries.'

'This is Munro's investigation,' Garber said again.

I saw the waitress push in through the kitchen door. She was carrying a plate with an enormous burger in a bun and a tangle of shoelace fries. I said, 'I have to go, boss,' and I hung up and carried my coffee back to my table. The waitress put my plate down.

'Thanks,' I said.

'Can I get you anything else?'

'You can tell me about the hotel,' I said. 'I need a room, but there was nobody home.'

The waitress half turned and gestured to the old couple settled in at their table for four. She said, 'They usually sit a spell in here and then go back. That would be the best time to catch them.'

Then she went away and left me to it. I ate slowly and enjoyed every bite.

LATER THE WAITRESS CAME back and picked up my plate and offered me dessert. She said she had great pies. I said, 'I'm going to take a walk. I'll look in again on my way back and if those two are still here, then I'll stop in for pie. I guess there's no hurrying them.'

'Not usually,' the waitress said.

I paid for the burger and the coffee and added a tip that didn't compare to a roomful of hungry Rangers, but it was enough to make her smile a little. Then I headed back to the street. The night was getting cold. I turned right and strolled past the vacant lot and the Sheriff's Department building. Pellegrino's car was parked outside and there was a glow in one window suggesting an interior room was occupied. I kept on going and came to the T where we had turned. To the left was the way Pellegrino had brought me in, through the forest. To the right that unlit road continued east into the darkness. Presumably it crossed the railroad line and then led onwards through the wrong side of town to Kelham. There were deep ditches on either side of it. There was a thin moon in the sky and a little light to see by. I turned right and walked on into the gloom.

Two minutes and 200 yards later I found the railroad track. First came the warning sign on the shoulder of the road, two diagonal arms bolted together at ninety degrees, one marked RAILROAD and the other marked CROSSING. There were red lights attached to the pole and somewhere beyond it there would be an electric bell in a box. Twenty yards farther on the ditches on either side of the road ended and the track was up on a hump, two parallel rails running north and south, looking old and worn. I stood on a tie between the rails and looked first one way and then the other. Twenty yards to the north, on the left, was the shadowy bulk of an old water tower.

I turned a full 360 in the dark. There was absolute silence everywhere. I could smell charcoal, maybe from where the blue car had burned the trees to the north. I could smell barbecue faintly in the east, where I guessed the rest of the township was, on the wrong side of the tracks. But I could see only the suggestion of a hole through the woods, where the road ran, and then nothing more.

I turned back the way I had come, thinking about pie, and I saw headlights, coming straight at me, moving slow. At one point it looked ready to make the turn into Main Street, and then it seemed to change its mind. Maybe it had picked me up in its beams.

It was a cop car. I could make out the silhouette of a light bar on the roof. At first I thought it was Pellegrino out on patrol, but when the car got closer it killed its lights and I saw a woman behind the wheel, and Mississippi suddenly got a lot more interesting.

THE CAR CAME OVER into the wrong lane and stopped alongside me. It was an old Chevy Caprice police cruiser painted up in the Carter County Sheriff's Department colours. The woman behind the wheel had an unruly mass of dark hair, tied back in an approximate ponytail. Her face was pale and flawless. I pegged her at somewhere in her middle thirties, old enough to show some mileage, young enough to still find some amusement in the world. She was smiling slightly and the smile was reaching her eyes, which were big and dark and liquid and seemed to have a glow in them. Although that might have been a reflection from the Chevy's instrument panel.

She wound down her window and looked at me, with nothing but frankness in her gaze. I stepped in closer to give her a better look, and to take a better look. She was more than flawless. She was spectacular. She had a revolver in a holster on her right hip and a shotgun stuffed muzzle-down in a scabbard between the seats. There was a radio slung under the dash on the passenger side, and a microphone in a clip near the steering wheel.

She said, 'You're the guy Pellegrino brought in.' Her voice was quiet but clear, warm but not soft, and her accent sounded local.

I said, 'Yes, ma'am, I am.'

She said, 'You're Reacher, right?'

I said, 'Yes, ma'am, I am.'

She said, 'I'm Elizabeth Deveraux. I'm the sheriff here.'

I said, 'I'm very pleased to meet you.'

She paused a beat and said, 'Did you eat dinner yet?'

I nodded. 'But not dessert,' I said. 'As a matter of fact I'm heading back to the diner for pie right now.'

'Do you usually take a walk between courses?'

'I was waiting out the hotel people. They didn't seem in a hurry.'

'Is that where you're staying tonight? The hotel?'

'I'm hoping to.'

She nodded in turn. 'I need to talk to you,' she said. 'Find me in the diner. Five minutes, OK?'

'OK,' I said. 'Five minutes.'

She wound up her window and reversed and drove away. She turned into Main Street. I followed on foot.

When I got to the diner I found Elizabeth Deveraux's cruiser parked outside. She was at the same table I had used. The old couple from the hotel had decamped. The place was empty apart from Deveraux and the waitress.

Deveraux used one foot under the table to shove the facing chair out a little. An invitation. Clearly, she had already ordered. I asked the waitress for a slice of her best pie and another cup of coffee. She went to the kitchen and silence claimed the room.

Up close Elizabeth Deveraux was a seriously good-looking woman. Truly beautiful. She was tall, and her hair was amazing. There must have been five pounds of it in her ponytail alone. She had all the right parts in all the right proportions. She looked great in her uniform. But best of all was her mouth. And her eyes. Together they put a wry, amused animation into her face, as if whatever happened to her she would stay calm and collected, and then she would find a quality in it to make her smile. There was still light in her eyes. Not just a reflection from the Caprice's speedometer.

She said, 'Pellegrino told me you've been in the army.'

I paused a beat. Undercover work is all about lying, and I hadn't minded lying to Pellegrino. But for some unknown reason I found myself not wanting to lie to Deveraux. So I said, 'Six weeks ago I was in the army,' which was technically true.

'What branch?'

'I was with an outfit called the 110th, mostly,' I said. Also true.

'Infantry?'

'It was a special unit. Combined operations.' Which was true.

'Who's your local friend?'

'A guy called Hayder,' I said. An outright invention.

'He must have been infantry. Kelham is all infantry.'

I nodded. '75th Ranger Regiment,' I said.

'Was he an instructor?' she asked.

'Yes,' I said.

She nodded. 'They're the only ones who are here long enough to want to stick around afterwards. I've never heard of him.'

'Then maybe he moved on. How long have you been sheriff?'

'Two years. Long enough to get to know the locals, anyway.'

'Pellegrino said you'd been here all your life.'

'Not true,' she said. 'I haven't been here all my life. I was here as a kid, and I'm here now. But there were years in between.'

I asked her, 'How did you spend those years?'

'I had a rich uncle,' she said. 'I toured the world at his expense.'

And at that point I suspected I was in trouble and my mission was about to fail. Because I had heard that answer before.

THE WAITRESS BROUGHT OUT Elizabeth Deveraux's main course and my dessert together. Deveraux had ordered the cheeseburger and the nest of fries. My pie was peach and the slice I got was bigger than the dish it was in. My coffee was in a tall mug. Deveraux had plain water in a glass.

It's easier to let a pie go cold than a cheeseburger, so I figured I had a chance to talk while Deveraux had no choice but to eat and listen and comment briefly. So I said, 'Pellegrino told me you guys are real busy. A wrecked car and a dead woman.'

She nodded and chased an errant pearl of mayonnaise back into her mouth with the tip of her little finger. She had short nails, nicely trimmed and polished. She had slender hands. Good skin. No rings. None at all. Especially not on her left ring finger.

I asked, 'Any progress on any of that?'

She swallowed and smiled and held her hand up like a traffic cop. *Stop. Wait.* She said, 'Give me a minute, OK? No more talking.'

So I ate my pie. The crust was sweet and the peaches were soft. She ate the burger and fries, her eyes on mine most of the time. She was a slim woman. She must have had a metabolism like a nuclear reactor. She took occasional long sips of water. I drained my mug.

She asked, 'Doesn't coffee keep you awake?'

I nodded. 'Until I want to go to sleep. That's what it's for.'

She took a last sip of water and left a rind of bun and six fries on her plate. She laid her napkin next to her plate. Dinner was over.

I asked, 'So are you making progress?'

She smiled and looked me over again, slowly. She said, 'You're pretty good. Nothing to be ashamed about, really. It's not your fault.'

I asked, 'What isn't?'

She leaned back in her chair. 'My daddy was sheriff here before me. He won twenty consecutive elections. He was firm, but fair. And honest. But I didn't like it here much. Not as a kid. I mean, can you imagine? It's the back of beyond. I knew there was a big world out there. So I had to get away.'

I said, 'I don't blame you.'

She said, 'But some ideas get ingrained. Like public service. Like law enforcement. It starts to feel like a family business.'

I nodded. She was right. Kids follow their parents into law enforcement far more than most other professions.

She said, 'So look at it from my point of view. What do you think I did when I turned eighteen?'

I said, 'I don't know,' although I was pretty sure I did know.

She said, 'I went to South Carolina and joined the Marine Corps.'

I nodded. Worse than I had expected. For some reason I had been betting on the air force. I asked her, 'How long were you in?'

'Sixteen years.'

Which made her thirty-six. Eighteen years at home, plus sixteen as a jarhead, plus two as Carter County Sheriff. Same age as me.

I asked her, 'What branch of the Corps?'

'Provost Marshal's office.'

I looked away. 'You were a military cop,' I said. 'Terminal rank?'

'CWO5,' she said.

Chief Warrant Officer 5. An expert in a specific specialised field. The sweet spot, where the real work was done.

I asked her, 'Why did you leave?'

'Rumblings. The Soviets are gone, reductions in force are coming. I figured it would feel better to step up than be thrown out. Plus my daddy died, and I couldn't let an idiot like Pellegrino take over.'

I asked her, 'Where did you serve?'

'All over. Uncle Sam was my rich uncle. He showed me the world.'

The waitress came back and took away our empty plates.

'Anyway,' Deveraux said. 'I was expecting you. It's what we would have done under the same circumstances. A homicide behind a bar near a base?

Some big secrecy *on* the base? We would have put an investigator on the post and sent another into town, undercover. The undercover guy would keep his ear to the ground and stop the locals embarrassing the Corps. It was a policy I supported back then, naturally. But now I *am* the locals, so I can't support it any more.'

I said nothing.

'Don't feel bad,' she said. 'You were doing it better than some of our guys did. I love the shoes, for instance. And the hair. You're fairly convincing. You ran into bad luck, that's all, with me being who I am. You shouldn't have said the 110th. I know about the 110th. You were nearly as good as we were. But really, Hayder? Far too uncommon a name.'

'I didn't want to lie,' I said. 'Didn't seem right. My father was a Marine. Maybe I sensed it in you.'

'He was a Marine but you joined the army? Was that mutiny?'

'I don't know what it was,' I said. 'But it felt right at the time.'

'How does it feel now?'

'Right this minute? Not so great.'

'Don't feel bad. You gave it a good try. What rank are you?'

I said, 'Major.'

'Still with the 110th?'

'Temporarily. Home base right now is the 396th MP. The Criminal Investigation Division.'

'How many years in?'

'Thirteen. Plus West Point.'

'I'm honoured. Maybe I should salute. Who did they send to Kelham?'

'A guy called Munro. Same rank as me. Are you making progress?'

She said, 'You don't give up, do you?'

'Giving up was not in the mission statement. You know how it is.'

'OK, I'll trade. One answer for one answer. And then you ship back out. You hit the road at first light. Do we have a deal?'

What choice did I have? I said, 'We have a deal.'

'No,' she said. 'We're not making progress.'

'OK,' I said. 'Thanks. Your turn.'

'Obviously it would give me an insight to know if you're the ace, or if the guy they sent to Kelham is the ace. As in, do the army think the problem is inside the gates or outside? Are you the big dog? Or is the other guy?'

'The honest answer is I don't know,' I said.

ELIZABETH DEVERAUX PAID for her burger and my pie and coffee, so I left the tip, which made the waitress smile again. We stepped out to the sidewalk together and stood next to the old Caprice. The moon had got brighter. I said, 'Can I ask you another question?'

Deveraux was immediately guarded. She said, 'About what?'

'Hair,' I said. 'Ours is supposed to conform to the shape of our heads. Tapered, they call it. Curving in to the base of the neck. What about yours?'

'I wore a buzz cut for fifteen years,' she said.

I looked at her in the moonlight. I pictured her with a buzz cut. She must have looked sensational. I said, 'Good to know. Thanks.'

'The regulation for women in the Corps said your hair could touch your collar, but it couldn't fall below the bottom edge. You were allowed to pin it up, but then I couldn't get my hat on.'

'Sacrifices,' I said.

'It was worth it,' she said. 'I loved being a Marine.'

'You still are,' I said. 'Once a Marine, always a Marine.'

'Is that what your daddy said?'

'He never got the chance. He died in harness.'

She asked, 'Is your mom still alive?'

'She died a few years later.'

'Mine died when I was in boot camp. Cancer.'

'Really? Mine too. Cancer, I mean. Not boot camp.'

'I'm sorry.'

She nodded and put her hand on the Caprice's door. I said, 'OK, good night, Chief Deveraux. It was a pleasure meeting you.'

I turned left and walked towards the hotel. I heard the Chevy motor start up and then the car passed me, pulled a U-turn across the width of the street and stopped, just ahead of me, facing me, at the kerb next to the hotel. I walked on and got there as Deveraux opened her door and got out. I assumed she had something more to say to me, so I stopped walking.

'I live here,' she said. 'Good night.'

She had gone upstairs before I got into the lobby. The old guy I had seen in the diner was behind reception. He took eighteen dollars of mine and in return he gave me the key to room twenty-one. He told me it was on the first floor, at the front of the building, overlooking the street, which he said was quieter than the back, which made no sense until I remembered the railroad.

On the first floor the staircase came up in the centre of a long corridor. It had eight doors off the back side and nine off the street side. There was a bar of yellow light showing under room seventeen's door, which was on the street side. Deveraux, presumably, getting ready for bed. My room was four doors farther north. I unlocked it, went in and turned on the light. It was a rectangular space with a high ceiling and what would have been pleasant proportions, except that a bathroom had been shoehorned into one corner. The window was a pair of glazed doors that gave onto the iron balcony I had seen from the street. There was a bed, a chair and a dressing table.

I unpacked, which consisted of assembling my new toothbrush and propping it in a glass in the bathroom. I had no toothpaste. An army dentist I had known swore that the mechanical action of the brush's bristles was all that was needed for perfect oral health. And I had chewing gum for freshness.

The clock in my head said it was twenty after eleven. I had been up early and was tired, but not exhausted. And I had things to do and limited time to do them in, so I waited long enough to let an average person get off to sleep and then I went out to the corridor.

There was no light showing under Deveraux's door. I crept downstairs to the lobby. I went out to the street and turned left.

I looked at Main Street. It ran on south for about 200 yards, as straight as a die, and then it meandered and became residential. The west side of the straight downtown stretch had stores and commercial operations, punctuated with narrow alleys. Those stores and commercial operations were matched by similar establishments on the east side of Main Street, and their matching alleys linked through to a one-sided street built parallel to and behind Main Street. I guessed that street had been the whole point of the town in the early days.

It ran north and south and had a long line of establishments that faced the railroad track across nothing but a blank width of beaten earth. I imagined old passenger trains wheezing to a stop, with their panting locomotives next to the water tower a little way up the line. I imagined restaurant staff and café owners running across the beaten earth and placing wooden steps below the train doors. I imagined passengers stepping down, dry and hungry from their long haul, eagerly crossing the width of earth, and then eating and drinking their fill. I imagined the train whistles blowing, the passengers returning, the trains moving onward, the wooden steps being retrieved, then stillness returning until the next train eased in.

That single-sided street had powered the local economy, and it still did.

The passenger trains were long gone, and so were the cafés and the restaurants. They had been replaced by bars, and auto parts stores, and bars, and loan offices, and bars, and gun shops, and bars, and the trains had been replaced by streams of cars coming in from Kelham. I imagined the cars parking on the beaten earth, and small groups of Rangers-in-training spilling out. A captive market, miles from anywhere like Garber had said.

I found the spot where Janice May Chapman had been killed easily enough. Pellegrino had said she had bled out like a lake, which meant sand would have been used to soak up the spill. I found a fresh pile of it, three or four inches deep, in an alley near the rear left-hand corner of a bar called Brannan's. Brannan's was in the centre of the one-sided street and the alley in question ran along its left flank, before dog-legging twice and exiting on Main Street between a pharmacy and a hardware store.

The spot was not overlooked. Brannan's rear door was about fifteen feet away, and the bar had no side windows. The back of the pharmacy was a blank wall. Brannan's neighbour was a loan office, and its right flank had a window at the rear, but the place would have been closed. No witnesses.

I stepped out of the alley and walked to the railroad track. The moon was still high and the sky was still clear. I stepped over the first rail and turned left and hiked north, walking on the ties. I passed over the road crossing and I passed the old water tower.

Then the ground began to shake.

Just faintly at first, a mild constant tremor. I stopped walking. The tie under my feet trembled. The rails on either side of me started to sing. I turned round and saw a pinpoint of light in the distance. The midnight train, a couple of miles south of me, coming on fast.

I stood there. The rails hummed and keened. The gravel under the ties clicked and hopped. The ground tremors deepened to big bass shudders. The distant headlight twinkled like a star.

I stepped off the track and looped back to the old water tower and leaned against a tarred wooden upright. It shook against my shoulder. The ground shook under my feet. The rails howled. The train whistle blew, loud and forlorn in the distance. The warning bells at the roadside started ringing. The red lights started flashing.

The train kept on coming towards me, for a long time resolutely distant, then all of a sudden right next to me, right on top of me, huge and impossibly loud. The ground shook so hard that the old water tower next to me danced mutely in place and I was bounced up and down whole inches. The locomotive flashed past, and then began an endless sequence of cars, ten, twenty, fifty, a hundred. I clung to the tarred pole for a whole minute, sixty long seconds, deafened by squealing metal, beaten numb by the throbbing ground. Then the train was gone and silence came back.

The first thing I did was change my mind about how far I was going to have to walk to find the wreckage of the blue car. I had assumed it would be close by. But after that awesome display of power I figured it might be somewhere in New Jersey. Or Canada.

THREE

In the end I found most of the car about 200 yards north. It was preceded by a debris field that stretched most of the intervening distance. There were pebbles of broken windshield glass, glistening and glinting in the dew and the moonlight. There was a chrome bumper, torn off and folded capriciously in half. It had embedded itself in the ground.

I guessed the car had been parked on the track about twenty yards north of the water tower. That was where the first of the glass was located. The locomotive had hit the car and it had flown fifty or more yards through the air. I guessed the initial impact had more or less disassembled it and flung its parts all over the place. Including its fuel, which had ignited. There were narrow black tongues of burnt scrub all over the last fifty yards, and what was left of the vehicle itself was nested against the trees in a starburst of blackened trunks and branches.

Pellegrino had seen the car in daylight and called it blue. In the moonlight it looked ash-grey to me. I couldn't find an intact painted surface. I couldn't find an intact anything larger than a square inch. If someone's intention had been to conceal evidence, then that someone had succeeded.

I GOT BACK to the hotel at one o'clock exactly and went straight to bed. I set the alarm in my head for seven in the morning, which was when I guessed Deveraux would be getting up. I figured her day would start at eight. Clearly she was not neglectful of her appearance, but she was a Marine and a pragmatic person, so she wouldn't budget more than an hour to get ready. I reckoned I could match her shower time with my own, and then I could find her in the diner for breakfast. I wasn't sure what I was going to say to her.

But I didn't sleep until seven. I was woken at six. By someone knocking on my door. I rolled out of bed and pulled on my trousers and opened up.

It was the old guy. The hotel keeper. He said, 'Mr Reacher? You have a phone call from your uncle.'

'My uncle?'

'Your uncle Leon Garber. He said it was urgent.'

I put my T-shirt on and followed the guy downstairs, barefoot. He led me through a side door into the office behind the counter. There was a worn desk with a phone on it. The handset was off the hook.

The old guy said, 'Please make yourself at home,' and left, closing the door on me. I sat in his chair and picked up the phone.

I said, 'What?'

Garber said, 'You OK?'

'I'm fine. How did you find me?'

'Phone book. There's only one hotel in Carter Crossing. Everything going well?'

'Terrific.'

'You sure? Because you're supposed to check in every morning at six.'

'Am I?'

'That's what we agreed.'

'We didn't agree we'd talk at six every day. What do you want?'

'You're cranky this morning.'

'I was up late last night looking around.'

'And?'

'There are a couple of things,' I said. 'Matters of interest.'

Garber said, 'Munro is getting nowhere at Kelham. Not so far.'

I didn't answer that. Garber was quiet for a beat. 'Wait,' he said. 'What do you mean, matters of interest? And why were you looking around in the dark? Why didn't you wait for first light?'

I said, 'I met the chief here. Different from what you might expect.'

'How?' Garber asked. 'Is he honest?'

'He's a she,' I said. 'Her father was sheriff before her.'

Garber paused again. 'Don't tell me. She figured you out.'

I didn't answer.

'How long did it take her?' he asked. 'Ten minutes? Five?'

'She was a Marine MP,' I said. 'One of us, practically. She knew all along. She was expecting me. To her it was a predictable move.'

'Is she going to shut you out?'

'Worse. She wants to throw me out.'

'She can't throw you out. It's a question of civil rights. The First Amendment, or something. Free association. Mississippi is part of the Union, same as anywhere else. So stay there, OK?'

I hung up. I didn't go back to bed. I showered and got fully dressed. Then I stood by my window and watched the dawn. I saw fields and forest extending in every direction. Then I sat in my chair to wait. I figured I would hear Deveraux go out to her car. I was right above where it was parked.

I HEARD DEVERAUX LEAVE the hotel at twenty past seven. First the street door creaked open and slammed shut, and then her car door creaked open and slammed shut.

I went downstairs and out to the sidewalk. The morning air was fresh and cold. I looked up the street and saw that Deveraux's car was parked again, right outside the diner. I walked in that direction and pushed in through the door. There were six customers, including Deveraux. The waitress was the same woman as the night before. She was busy toting plates of food, so I just walked up to Deveraux's table and said, 'Mind if I join you?'

She was sipping coffee. She didn't have her food yet. She smiled and said, 'Good morning.' Her tone was warm.

I said, 'Yes, good morning.'

She said, 'Have you come to say goodbye? That's very polite.' She did her thing with her foot again, under the table, and kicked the facing chair out. I sat down. She asked, 'Did you sleep well?'

I said, 'Fine.'

'The train didn't wake you at midnight?'

'I was still up,' I said.

'Doing what?'

'This and that,' I said.

'Inside or out?'

'Out,' I said.

'You found the crime scene?'

I nodded.

'And you found two things of note,' she said. 'So you thought you'd stop by and make sure I appreciated their significance before you got on your way. That's very public-spirited of you.'

The waitress came by and put a plate of French toast on the table. Then she turned to me and I ordered the same thing, with coffee. After she was gone, I said, 'I'm not going.'

She smiled again. 'Are you going to give me your civil rights speech now?'

'Something like that.'

'I'm all for civil rights,' she said. 'And certainly there's room at the inn, as they say. So sure, by all means, please stay. Enjoy yourself. Do whatever you want to. Just don't get between me and my investigation.'

I asked her, 'How do you explain the two things?'

'I can't trust you. You're here to steer me wrong, if you have to.'

'No, I'm here to warn the army if things start to look bad. But we're a long way from any sort of a conclusion here. It's too early to steer anybody anywhere, even if I was going to. Which I'm not.'

'We?' she said. '*We're* a long way from a conclusion? What is this, a democracy?'

'OK, you,' I said.

'Yes,' she said. 'Me.'

At that point the waitress came back with my meal. And my coffee. I sniffed the steam and took a long first sip. Nothing better than just-made coffee, early in the morning. Across the table Deveraux continued eating.

She said, 'OK, time out. Convince me. Tell me about the first thing, and spin it so it looks bad for the army. Which it does, by the way.'

'Have you been on the base?'

'All over it.'

'I haven't. Therefore apparently you know what I'm only guessing at.' I looked straight at her. 'Janice May Chapman was not raped in that alley.'

'Because?'

'Because Pellegrino reported gravel abrasions on the corpse. And there's no gravel in that alley. Nor anywhere else that I could see. It's all dirt or blacktop or smooth paving stones for miles around.'

'The railroad track has gravel,' she said.

'Not really gravel,' I said. 'Pieces of granite, bigger than a pebble, smaller than a fist. The injuries wouldn't look like gravel rash.'

'So?'

'Kelham is for the elite,' I said. 'It's a finishing school for the 75th, which is special ops support. They must have all kinds of terrain. Sand, to simulate the desert. Concrete, like the frozen steppes. I'm sure they have plenty of gravel there, for one reason or another.'

Deveraux nodded again. 'They have a gravel running track. For endurance training. Ten laps is like ten hours on a road surface.'

I said nothing.

Deveraux said, 'She was raped on the base.'

I said, 'Not impossible.'

I started to eat my breakfast just as she finished hers. She said, 'The second thing is more problematical, though. I can't make it fit.'

'Really?' I said. 'Isn't it basically the same as the first thing?'

She looked at me, blankly. She said, 'I don't see how.'

I stopped eating and looked back at her. 'Talk me through it.'

'How did she get there? She left her car at home, and she didn't walk. She was wearing four-inch heels and no one walks anywhere any more. She wasn't picked up from home either. Her neighbours are busybodies. They swear no one came calling on her. She just materialised in that alley.'

I was quiet for a second. Then I said, 'That wasn't my second thing. Your two things and my two things are not the same two things. Which means there are three things in total.'

'So what's your second thing?'

I said, 'She wasn't killed in that alley, either.'

I FINISHED MY BREAKFAST before I spoke again. French toast, maple syrup, coffee. Protein, fibre, carbohydrates. And caffeine. All the essential food groups. I put my silverware down and said, 'There's really only one obvious way to cut a woman's throat. You stand behind her and use one hand in her hair to pull her head back. You expose her throat and you put some tension in the ligaments and the blood vessels. Then you get busy with the blade.'

Deveraux said, 'I'm assuming that's what happened in the alley. But suddenly, I hope. So it was all over before she realised it was happening at all.'

I said, 'It didn't happen in the alley. It can't have. One benefit of doing it from behind is you don't get covered in blood. And there's a lot of blood.'

'I know. I saw it. She was all bled out. As white as a sheet. I assume you saw the sand. That's how big the pool was. It looked like a gallon or more.'

'You ever cut a throat?'

'No.'

'You ever seen it done?'

She shook her head. 'No,' she said.

'The blood comes out like a fire hose, spraying everywhere, ten feet or more, splattering all over the place, like someone took a paint can and threw it around. There would have been blood all over the alley. Not a neat pool right underneath her. That's just not possible. She wasn't killed there.'

Deveraux linked her hands on the table and bowed her head over them. She breathed in, breathed out, and five seconds later she looked up again and said, 'I'm an idiot. I just didn't see it.'

'Don't feel bad,' I said. 'You never saw it happen.'

'No, it's basic,' she said. 'I'm an idiot. I've wasted days.'

'It gets worse,' I said. 'There's more.'

She didn't want to hear about how it got worse. She was still beating herself up for missing the thing with the blood. I had had that kind of reaction many times. She frowned at herself, and then she shook her head and came up with a brave smile. She said, 'OK, tell me more. But not in here.'

So we paid for our breakfasts and stepped out to the sidewalk. She said, 'Let's go back to the hotel. We can use the lounge.'

We walked back down the street, and up the shaky steps, and across the old verandah. We went in and used the door on the left of the lobby. In the daylight the humped shapes I had seen in the dark turned out to be armchairs, as I had thought. We took a matched pair.

I asked her, 'Why do you live here?'

'I thought it would be a month or two. But it extended.'

'What about your old man's house?'

'Rented,' she said. 'The lease died with him.'

'You could rent another one. Or buy one.'

'I looked at some. Couldn't pull the trigger. I hadn't decided how long I was going to stay. Still haven't, really. No doubt it will turn out to be the rest of my life, but I guess I don't want to admit that to myself.'

I thought about my pal Stan Lowrey and his want ads. There was a lot more to leaving the service than getting a job. There were houses, cars, clothes. There were a hundred strange, unknown details, like the customs of a remote foreign tribe, glimpsed only in passing and never fully understood.

Deveraux said, 'So let's hear it.'

I said, 'Her throat was cut, right? We're clear on that?'

'Definitely. Unmistakably.'

'And that was the only wound?'

'The doctor says so.'

'So wherever it was actually done, there's blood all over the place. In a room, maybe, or out in the woods. It's impossible to clean up properly. This woman's throat was cut, blood sprayed everywhere and she died. Then she was dumped in the alley. But whose blood was she lying in? Not her own, because she'd left it all back in the unknown location.'

'Don't tell me the guy collected it and brought it with him.'

'Possible,' I said. 'But unlikely. It would be tricky to cut someone's throat while dancing around with a bucket, trying to catch the spray.'

'So what are you saying? Whose blood was it?'

'An animal's, possibly. Maybe a deer.'

'A hunter?'

'That's my guess.'

'It could have been fake blood from a joke store. Or it could have been hers. Someone might have figured out a way to collect it.'

'Still a hunter,' I said.

Deveraux said, 'Why are you fixated on hunters?'

'Pellegrino told me she was all dressed up for a night out, as neat as a pin, just lying there on her back in a pool of blood.'

Deveraux nodded. 'That's exactly what I saw.'

'What was she wearing?'

'A dark blue sheath dress with a white collar. Underwear and pantihose. Dark blue shoes with spike heels.'

'Clothes in disarray?'

'No. They looked neat as a pin. Like Pellegrino told you.'

'So she wasn't put into those clothes post-mortem. Clothes never go on a corpse just right. So she was still dressed when she was killed. Was there blood on the white collar? At the front?'

Deveraux said, 'No, it was immaculate.'

'Was there blood anywhere on her front?'

'No.'

'OK,' I said. 'So her throat was cut in an unknown location, while she was dressed in those clothes. But she got no blood on her until she was dumped on her back in a pool that was separately transported. Tell me how that isn't a hunter.'

'Tell me how it is. If you can.'

'Tell me how you cut a woman's throat without getting a drop of blood on her front.'

'I don't know how.'

'You string her up on a deer trestle. By her ankles. Upside down. You tie her hands behind her. You haul her arms up until her back is arched and her throat is presented as the lowest point.'

We sat in the shadowed silence for a minute, not saying a word. I guessed Deveraux was picturing the scene. I sure was.

Deveraux asked, 'Do you really think that's how it was done?'

I nodded. 'Any other method, she wouldn't have bled out all the way. Not white as a sheet. She would have died, and her heart would have stopped pumping, and there would have been two, three pints left inside her.'

'The ropes would have left marks, wouldn't they?'

'What did the medical examiner say? Have you had his report?'

'We don't have a medical examiner. Just the local doctor.'

Not a democracy. I said, 'You should go and take a look for yourself.'

She said, 'Will you come with me?'

We walked back to the diner and took Deveraux's car from the kerb and U-turned and headed back down Main Street, past the hotel again, and onwards to where Main Street turned into a wandering rural route. The doctor's place was half a mile south of town. It was a clapboard house, painted white, with a shingle next to the mailbox at the end of the driveway. The name on the shingle was MERRIAM and it was lettered crisply in black over a rectangle of white paint that was brighter and newer than the surrounding surface. A new arrival, not long in town, new to the community.

The house had its ground floor given over to the medical practice. The front parlour was a waiting room, and the back room was where patients were treated. We found Merriam in there, at a desk. He was a florid man close to sixty. New in town, perhaps, but not new to doctoring. His greeting was languid and his pace was slow. I got the impression he regarded the Carter Crossing position as semi-retirement.

Deveraux told the guy what we wanted to see and he led us to what might have been a kitchen. It was tiled in cold white and it had medical-style sinks and cupboards and a stainless-steel mortuary table. On the table was a corpse. The light over it was bright.

The corpse was Janice May Chapman. She was naked. Deveraux had called her as white as a sheet, but by that point she was pale blue and light purple. She had been perhaps five feet seven inches, and she might have weighed a hundred and twenty pounds. She had dark hair bobbed short. Pellegrino had called her pretty, and it didn't require much imagination to agree. The flesh on her face was collapsed, but her bone structure was good. Her teeth were white. Her throat was laid open from side to side. I could see a single horizontal score mark on it.

Deveraux said, 'We need to examine her wrists and ankles.'

The doctor made a *have at it* gesture.

Deveraux took Chapman's left arm and I took her right. The skin lying over her wrist bones had no abrasions. No rope burns. But there was faint residual marking. There was a two-inch-wide band that was slightly bluer than the rest. Almost not there at all. And very slightly swollen, compared to the rest of her forearm.

I looked at Merriam and asked, 'What do you make of this?'

'The cause of death was exsanguination through severed carotid arteries,' he said. 'That was what I was paid to determine.'

'How much were you paid?'

'The fee structure was agreed between my predecessor and the county.'

'Was it more than fifty cents? Because fifty cents is all that conclusion is worth. Cause of death is obvious. So now you can earn your corn by helping us out a little.'

Merriam said, 'I don't like your attitude.'

I said, 'And I don't like twenty-seven-year-old women lying dead on a slab. You want to help or not?'

The guy sighed and stepped forward. He looked at Janice May Chapman's wrist closely. He asked, 'Do you have a hypothesis?'

I said, 'I think she was tied up. Wrists and ankles. The bindings started to bruise her, but she didn't live long enough for the bruises to develop. A little blood leaked into her tissues and it stayed there when the rest of it drained out. Which is why we're seeing compression injuries as raised welts.'

'Tied up with what?'

'Not ropes,' I said. 'Something wide and flat. Maybe silk scarves. Something padded, perhaps. To disguise what had been done.'

Merriam moved past me to the end of the table and looked at Chapman's ankles. He said, 'She was wearing pantihose when she was brought in. The nylon was undamaged. Not torn or laddered at all.'

'Because of the padding. Maybe it was foam rubber. Something like that. But she was tied up.'

Merriam was quiet for a moment. Then he said, 'Not impossible.'

'How do you explain the complete exsanguination?'

'She could have been a haemophiliac.'

'Suppose she wasn't?'

'Then gravity would be the only explanation. She was hung upside down.'

'Turn her over,' I said. 'I want to see the gravel rash.'

'You'll have to help me,' he said, so I did.

The human body is a self-healing machine and it doesn't waste time. Skin is crushed or split or cut and blood immediately rushes to the site, the red cells scabbing and knitting a fibrous matrix to bind the parted edges together, the white cells seeking out and destroying germs and pathogens below. The process is under way within minutes and it lasts as many hours or days as are necessary to return the skin to its previous unbroken integrity.

Janice May Chapman's back was peppered with tiny cuts, as was the whole of her butt, as were her upper arms above her elbows. The cuts were small, thinly scabbed incisions, surrounded by small areas of crushing. The cuts were inflicted in random directions, as if by loose and rolling items of similar size and nature, small and hard and neither razor-sharp nor completely blunt. Classic gravel rash.

I asked Merriam, 'How old do you think these injuries are?'

He said, 'I have no idea.'

'Come on, Doctor,' I said. 'You've treated cuts and grazes before.'

'Four hours,' he said.

I nodded. I figured four hours was about right, judging by the scabs, which were more than nascent, but not fully mature. They had been developing steadily, and then their development had stopped abruptly when the throat was cut and the heart had stopped.

I asked, 'Did you determine the time of death?'

Merriam said, 'That's very hard to know. Impossible, really. The exsanguination interferes with normal biological processes.'

'Best guess?'

'Some hours before she was brought to me. More than four. Fewer than twenty-four. That's the best I can do.'

'No other injuries. No bruising. No sign of a defensive struggle.'

Merriam said, 'I agree.'

I asked him, 'Did you do a vaginal examination?'

'Of course. I judged she had had recent sexual intercourse.'

'Any bruising or tearing in that area?'

'None visible.'

'Then why did you conclude she was raped?'

'You think it was consensual? Would you lie on gravel to make love?'

'I might,' I said. 'Depending on who I was with.'

'She had a home,' Merriam said. 'With a bed in it. And a car, with a back seat. Any boyfriend would have a home and a car, too. And there's a hotel in town. No one needs to conduct a tryst out of doors.'

'Especially not in March,' Deveraux said.

The small room went quiet until Merriam asked, 'Are we done?'

'We're done,' Deveraux said.

'Well, good luck, Chief,' Merriam said. 'I hope this one turns out better than the last two.'

Deveraux and I walked down the doctor's driveway to the sidewalk, where we stood next to Deveraux's car. I knew she was not going to give me a ride. This was not a democracy. Not yet. I said, 'Did you ever see a rape victim with intact pantihose?'

'You think that's significant?'

'Of course it is. She was attacked on gravel. Her pantihose should have been shredded.'

'Maybe she was forced to undress first. Slowly and carefully.'

'The gravel rash had edges. She was wearing something. Pulled up, pulled down, whatever, but she was partially clothed. And then she changed afterwards. Which is possible. She had four hours.'

'This guy had himself an all-day session. He had access to her clothes. He made her change. This was all highly premeditated.'

'Possible,' I said.

'They teach effective tactical planning in the army.'

'True,' I said. 'But they don't give you a day off very often. Not in a training environment. Not usually.'

Deveraux said, 'But Kelham is not just about training, is it? There are a couple of rifle companies there. In and out on rotation. And they get leave when they come back. Days off. Plenty of them. All in a row. You should call your CO. Tell him it's looking bad.'

I said, 'He already knows. That's why I'm here.'

She paused a long moment. 'I want you to do me a favour. Go and look at the car wreck again. See if you can find a licence plate or identify the vehicle. Pellegrino got nowhere with it.'

'Why would you trust me?'

'Because you're the son of a Marine.'

I asked, 'What did Merriam mean, when he wished you better luck with this one than the other two?'

Her beautiful face fell a little and she said, 'Two girls were killed last year. Same MO. Throats cut. I got nowhere with them. They're cold cases now. Janice May Chapman is the third in nine months.'

ELIZABETH DEVERAUX CLIMBED into her Caprice and drove away, back to town. I set off walking. Ten minutes later I was through the last of the rural meanders and the road widened and straightened. Some daytime activity was starting up. The stores were opening.

I walked on the right-hand sidewalk and passed the hardware store, and the pharmacy, and the hotel, and the diner. Deveraux's car was not parked in the Sheriff's Department lot.

I made it to the T-junction and turned right. The road speared straight ahead of me. Narrow shoulders, deep ditches. The traffic lanes banked up and over the rail crossing and then the shoulders and the ditches resumed and the road ran onwards through the trees.

I heard a car on the road behind me. I waited and it swept past. It was a black town car. Urban. Dark windows. It thumped up the rise, pattered across the tracks, and thumped down again. Then it kept on going straight. An official visitor, heading to Kelham.

I walked on to the railroad track, where I turned left on the ties and headed north. I traced the wreck's debris field from its beginning. The smaller and lighter pieces had travelled shorter distances. Less momentum, I supposed. The smaller beads of glass and the smaller flakes of metal were the first to be found. It had been a fairly old car. There were flakes of rust, from the underbody.

An old car, with significant time spent in cold climates where they salt the roads in winter. Not a Mississippi native. A car that had been hauled from pillar to post, six months here, six months there.

A soldier's car, probably.

I tried to picture a licence plate, bursting free of its bolts, sailing through the night-time air. I tried to figure out where it might have landed. I couldn't see it anywhere. Then I remembered the howling gale that had accompanied the train, and I widened my search.

In the end I found it still attached to the chrome bumper I had seen the night before. The bumper had folded up just left of the plate, and made a point, which had half buried itself in the scrub. I rocked it loose and pulled it out and turned it over, and saw the plate hanging from a single black bolt.

It was an Oregon plate. I memorised the number and reburied the bent bumper in its hole. Then I walked on to where the bulk of the wreck had burned against the trees.

By bright daylight I agreed with Pellegrino. The car had been blue. I found enough unblemished paint to be sure. There was an overspray stripe under melted plastic trim inside one of the doors. Not much else had survived. No personal items. No paperwork. No hairs, no fibres. No ropes, no belts, no straps, no knives.

I walked back the way I had come. I saw another black car with black window glass coming towards me from the west, fast and purposeful. It blew past me, thumped up over the rail line, thumped down again, and rushed on towards Kelham. I started walking again. I was hungry, so I headed for the diner. The same waitress was on duty. She asked, 'Is your name Jack Reacher?'

I said, 'Yes, ma'am, it is.'

'There was a woman in here an hour ago, looking for you.'

The waitress was a typical eyewitness, unable to describe the woman who had been looking for me. Tall, short, heavy, slender, old, young, she had no recollection. All she could remember was a smile and the question. Was there a new guy in town, very big, answering to the name Jack Reacher?

I thanked her for the information and she sat me at my usual table. I ordered a piece of pie and a cup of coffee and I asked her for coins for the phone. She opened the register and gave me a roll of quarters in exchange for a five dollar bill. She brought my coffee and told me my pie would be right along. I walked to the phone by the door and split the roll with my thumbnail and dialled Garber's office. He answered the phone himself.

I asked, 'Have you sent another agent down here?'

'No,' he said. 'Why?'

'There's a woman asking for me by name.'

'Who?'

'I don't know who. She hasn't found me yet. And I saw two cars heading for Kelham. Limousines. Lawyers or politicians, probably.'

'Is there a difference?'

'I got the licence plate off the wreck. Blue car, from Oregon.' I recited the number from memory and I heard him write it down.

He said, 'Call me back in ten minutes. Don't speak to a soul before that.'

I ignored the letter of the law by speaking to the waitress. I thanked her for my pie and coffee. She hung around a beat longer than she needed to. Turned out she was worried she might have got me in trouble by telling a stranger she had seen me. I told her not to worry. By that point I was pretty sure who the mystery woman was. Who else had the information and the imagination to find me?

The pie was good. Blueberries, pastry, sugar and cream. It hit the spot. I took the full ten minutes to eat it, a little at a time. I finished my coffee. Then I walked over to the phone again and called Garber.

He said, 'We traced the car.'

I said, 'Whose is it?'

'I can't tell you. Classified information, as of five minutes ago.'

'Bravo Company, right?'

'I can't tell you that. Where's the plate?'

'Where I found it.'

'Who have you told?'

'Nobody.'

'OK,' Garber said. 'Here are your orders. Firstly, do not, repeat, do not give that number to local law enforcement. Secondly, return to the wreck and destroy that plate immediately.'

FOUR

I obeyed the first part of Garber's order, by not immediately rushing round to the Sheriff's Department and passing on the news. I disobeyed the second part, by not immediately rushing back to the debris field. I just sat in the diner, drank coffee and thought. I wasn't even sure how to destroy a licence plate. Burning it would conceal the state of origin, but not the number itself, which was embossed. In the end I figured I could fold it twice and stamp it flat and bury it. But I didn't go and do that. I figured if I sat in a diner long enough, drinking coffee, my mystery woman would surely find me.

Which she did, five minutes later.

I saw her before she saw me. I was looking out at a bright street, and she was looking in at a dim room. She was wearing black trousers and black leather shoes, a black T-shirt, and a leather jacket. She was carrying a brief-case. She was lean and lithe and limber. Her hair was still dark, still cut short, and her face was still full of fast intelligence and rapid glances. Frances Neagley, First Sergeant, United States Army. We had worked together many times, tough cases and easy. She was as close to a friend as I had, back in 1997, and I hadn't seen her in more than a year.

She came in and saw me at my table. No surprise in her face. She knew the state and she knew the town, and she knew I drank a lot of coffee.

I used my toe and poked the facing chair out, like Deveraux had twice done for me. Neagley sat down. She put her briefcase on the floor. No salute, no handshake, no peck on the cheek. There were two things people needed to understand about Neagley. Despite her personal warmth she couldn't bear to be physically touched, and despite her considerable talents she refused to become an officer.

'Ghost town,' she said.

'The base is closed,' I said.

'I know. I'm up to speed. Closing the base was their first mistake. It's as good as a confession.'

'Story is they were worried about tension with the town. So, seen any-thing else?'

'Everything. I've been here two hours.'

'What do you need?'

'Nothing,' she said. 'It's you that needs. You need to get a clue. This is a suicide mission, Reacher. Stan Lowrey called me. He's worried. So I asked around. And Lowrey was right. You should have turned this thing down.'

'I'm in the army,' I said. 'I go where I'm told.'

'I'm in the army too. But I avoid sticking my head in a noose.'

'Kelham is the noose. Munro is the one risking his neck.'

'I don't know Munro. But dollars to doughnuts he'll do what he's told. He'll cover it up and swear black is white. But you won't.'

'A woman was killed. We can't ignore that.'

'Three women were killed.'

'You know about that already? How did you find out?'

'I met the sheriff. Chief Deveraux herself. She dropped by her office. I was there, asking for you.'

'And she told you stuff?'

'I gave her the look.'

'What look?'

Neagley looked up at me, her eyes open wide and serious and sympathetic and understanding and encouraging, her whole demeanour astonished and marvelling at how bravely I was bearing the heavy burdens my lot in life had brought me. She said, 'This is the look. Works great with women. Like we're in the same boat?'

It was a hell of a look. But I was disappointed that Deveraux had fallen for it. 'What else did she tell you?'

'Something about a car. She's assuming it's critical to the case and that it belonged to a Kelham guy.'

'I just found the plate. Garber ran it and told me to sit on it.'

'And are you going to?'

'I don't know. Might not be a lawful order.'

'See what I mean? You're going to commit suicide. I'm going to stick around and keep you out of trouble. That's why I came.'

'Aren't you deployed?'

'I'm in D.C. At a desk. They won't miss me for a day or two.'

I shook my head. 'No. I don't need help. I know what I'm doing.'

At that point the waitress came out of the kitchen. She saw me, saw Neagley, recognised her from before, saw that we weren't tearing each other's eyes out, and her guilt evaporated. She refilled my coffee mug. Neagley ordered tea. Then the waitress went away again and Neagley said, 'Chief Deveraux is a very beautiful woman.'

I said, 'I agree.'

'Have you slept with her yet?'

'Certainly not.'

'Are you going to?'

'I guess I can dream. Hope dies last, right?'

'Don't. There's something wrong with her. She's got three unsolved homicides and her pulse is as slow as a bear in winter.'

'She thinks a Kelham guy did it, and she has no jurisdiction.'

'Whatever, there's a bad vibe there. Trust me.'

'Thanks, but I don't need a big sister on this occasion.'

'Last chance,' Neagley said. 'Do I stay or do I go?'

'Go,' I said. 'This is my problem, not yours.'

'Parting gift,' she said. She leaned down and opened her briefcase and came out with a slim green file folder. It was printed on the outside with the words *Carter County Sheriff's Department*. She laid it on the table. She said, 'You'll find this interesting.'

I asked, 'What is it?'

'Photos of the three dead women. They've all got something in common.'

'Deveraux gave this to you?'

'Not exactly. She left it unattended. I borrowed it. You can return it when you're done. I'm sure you'll find a way.' She slid the file across to me, she stood up, and she walked away. She pushed out through the door, turned right on Main Street and disappeared.

I opened the file. Three women. Three victims. Three photos.

Janice May Chapman's photograph was a waist-up colour shot taken at what looked like a party. She was looking directly into the lens, smiling in the first seconds of spontaneity. A well-timed click.

Pellegrino had been wrong. He had called her real pretty, but that was a serious underestimate. In life Chapman had been absolutely spectacular.

I looked at the second woman. She had died in November 1996. Four months ago. A note pasted to the bottom corner of the photograph told me so. The photograph was one of those rushed, semi-formal colour portraits like you see from a college service at the start of the academic year. The woman in the picture was black, probably in her middle twenties, and was every bit as spectacular as Janice May Chapman. She had flawless skin and the kind of eyes that start wars. Dark, liquid, radiant.

The third woman had died in June 1996. Nine months ago. She was also black, young and spectacular. She had been photographed in a yard, with late-afternoon light coming off a white clapboard wall and bathing her in its glow. She had liquid eyes and a shy smile.

I laid all three pictures side by side on the table. *They've all got something in common*, Neagley had said. They were all roughly the same age. But Chapman was white and the other two were black. Chapman was economically comfortable, judging by her dress and her jewellery. The first black woman looked less so, and the second one looked close to marginal, in a rural way, judging by her clothes and by the yard she was in.

Three lives, lived in close geographic proximity, but separated by vast gulfs. The women may never have met or spoken. They may never have even laid eyes on each other. They had absolutely nothing in common.

Except that all three were amazingly beautiful.

I REPACKED THE FILE and tucked it in the back of my trousers under my shirt. I paid my bill and left a tip. I figured I would walk up to the Sheriff's Department. Time for an initial foray. A toe in the water. Not a democracy, but it was a public building. And I had a legitimate reason to be there. I had lost property to return.

Deveraux's car was in the lot. I walked past it, opened a heavy glass door and found myself in a dowdy, beat-up lobby. An enquiry desk was facing me, with an old guy behind it. As soon as he saw me he said, 'End of the corridor on the right. She's expecting you.'

I walked the corridor and got a glimpse through a half-closed door of a stout woman at a telephone switchboard, and then I arrived at Deveraux's billet. Her door was open. I knocked once, went in.

It was a plain square space, full of stuff bought cheap at the end of the last geological era. Desk, chairs, filing cabinets, all plain and municipal and well out of date.

At first glance, not a wonderful room. But it had Deveraux in it. I had pictures of three stunning women digging into my back, but she held her own with any of them. She looked small in the desk chair, lithe and relaxed. As usual, she was smiling.

She asked, 'Did you ID the car for me?'

I didn't answer that question, and her phone rang. She picked it up and listened for a moment, and then she said, 'OK, but it's still a felony assault. Keep it on the front burner.' Then she put the phone down and said, 'Pellegrino,' by way of explanation.

I said, 'Busy day?'

'Two guys were beaten up this morning by someone they swear was a soldier from Kelham. But the army says the base is still closed. I don't know what's going on. First tell me about your friend, Frances Neagley. I'm guessing she's your sergeant.'

'She was my sergeant once. Many years, on and off.'

'I'm wondering why she came.'

'She came to warn me. Apparently I'm in a lose-lose situation. She called it a suicide mission.'

'She's right,' Deveraux said. 'She's smart. I liked her. She does this thing with her face, a special look, all collegial and confiding. I bet she's a great interrogator. Did she give you the photos?'

'You meant her to take them?'

'I hoped she would. I left them accessible and ducked out for a minute. I wanted you to see them, alone and on your own time. No pressure. I wanted a completely unguarded first impression.'

'Is this a democracy now?'

'Not yet. So what was your first impression?'

'All three of them were amazingly beautiful.'

Deveraux nodded. 'I agree.'

I leaned forward to let my back clear the chair, and I pulled the file out of my waistband. I laid it on the desk.

She slid the file closer and ran her palm over it, and her hand came to rest at one end. She asked, 'Did you ID the car?'

She looked straight at me. Her question hung in the air. *Did you ID the car?* In my head I heard Garber's emphatic squawk in my ear: *Do not, repeat, do not give that number to local law enforcement.*

I said, 'Yes.'

'And?'

'I can't tell you. Classified information, just minutes after I called it in.'

She didn't respond.

I said, 'Well, what would you do in this situation?'

'As a Marine I would have done exactly what you're doing.'

'I'm glad you understand.'

She nodded. 'I didn't tell you the whole truth before. About my father's house. It wasn't always rented. He owned it. But when my mother got sick, they found out they didn't have insurance. It was supposed to come with the job. But the county guy who was responsible had run into trouble and had been stealing the premiums. Just a two-year hiatus, but that happened when my mother got sick. After that, it was a pre-existing condition. My father refinanced, things got worse and he defaulted. The bank took the title, but they let him live there as a renter. I admired both parties. The bank did the right thing, as far as it could, and my daddy kept on serving his community, even though it had kicked him in the teeth. Honour and obligation are things I appreciate.'

'*Semper Fi*,' I said.

'You bet. And you answered my question anyway, as I'm sure you intended. If the ID is classified, then it's a Kelham car.'

'Only if there's a connection between the car and the homicide. I'm sorry about your father.'

'Me too. He was a nice man and he deserved better.'

I said, 'What happened to those civilians who got beaten?'

'The incident took place more than twelve miles away. Almost past Kelham's northern limit. Two guys were out taking a walk. They could see the woods around Kelham's fence. A guy came out of the woods, they got hit. They claim the guy that hit them was a soldier.'

'Was he in uniform?'

'No. But he had the look, and he had an M16 rifle. It's like they're establishing a quarantine zone.'

'Why would they? They've already got a million acres.'

'I don't know why. But what else are they doing? They're chasing anyone that gets anywhere near the fence.'

Just at that point, phones started ringing in the building and I heard urgent radio chatter coming from the switchboard. Ten seconds later the stout woman appeared in the doorway. 'Pellegrino is calling in from near the Clancy place. Near the split oak. He says we got another homicide.'

BOTH DEVERAUX AND I glanced instinctively at the file folder on her desk. Three photographs. Soon to be four.

Then Deveraux glanced at me. *Not a democracy.* I said, 'I need to see this. I need to know what I'm committing suicide over.'

She hesitated, and then said, 'OK,' and we ran for her car.

The Clancy place was more than ten miles north and east of the town. We crossed the railroad and headed towards Kelham. Out there the road had no shoulders and no ditches. Flat fields full of dirt came up to the edge of the blacktop. I saw old frame houses, low barns, and tumbledown shacks. I saw old women on porches and raggedy kids on bikes. Every face I saw was black. Then Deveraux turned north and left the dwellings behind us.

Where we were going turned out to be a large stretch of uncultivated land with a battered house in its centre. We turned up a two-rut driveway that became a plain farm track as it passed the house. Deveraux blipped her siren as a courtesy. I saw an answering wave from a window. An old black man. We headed on across flat barren land. In the distance I could see a lone tree, chopped vertically by lightning down two-thirds of its height. Each half was leaning away from the other. The split oak, I assumed. Near it was parked a police cruiser. Pellegrino's, I assumed.

Deveraux put her car next to it and we got out. Pellegrino was fifty yards away, at ease, facing us, with his hands behind his back.

Ten yards farther on was a shape on the ground.

We hiked across the dirt. Far to my right I could see a line of trees, thick in parts and thin in others. Through the thin parts I could see a wire fence. Kelham's northwestern boundary, I guessed.

Halfway to Pellegrino I could see a back, facing towards me. A brown jacket. A suggestion of dark hair and white skin. The empty slump of a corpse. The stillness of the recently dead. Unmistakable.

Deveraux walked past Pellegrino, looping around wide and approaching the collapsed shape from the far side. I stopped five yards short and hung back. Her case. *Not a democracy.*

She shuffled closer to the shape, slowly and carefully, watching where she put her feet. She squatted down with her hands clasped together. She looked right to left, at the head, the torso, the arms, the legs. Then she looked left to right, the same sequence again, but in reverse. Then she looked up and said, 'What the hell is this?'

I followed the same loop Deveraux had used. I squatted next to her. I clasped my hands together. I looked, right to left, and then left to right. The corpse was male. And white. Forty-five years old, maybe a little less, maybe a little more. Maybe five-ten, a hundred and eighty pounds. Dark hair. Two or three days' stubble. A green work shirt, a brown canvas jacket. Jeans. Brown engineer boots, creased and cracked and caked with dirt.

I asked Deveraux, 'Do you know him?'

She said, 'I never saw him before.'

He had bled to death. He had taken a high-velocity rifle round through his right thigh. His trousers were soaked with blood. Almost certainly the round had torn his femoral artery. The femoral artery is a high-capacity vessel. Absolutely crucial. Any significant breach will be fatal within minutes, without prompt and effective emergency treatment.

But what was extraordinary about the scene in front of us was that prompt and effective emergency treatment had been attempted. The guy's trouser leg had been slit with a knife. The wound was partially covered with a military field dressing.

Deveraux stood up and backed away until she got ten feet from the corpse. I did the same thing and joined her. She talked low, as if noise was disrespectful. 'What do you make of that?'

'There was a dispute,' I said. 'A warning shot went astray.'

'Why not a killing shot that missed?'

'Because the shooter would have tried again. But he didn't. He tried to help the guy. And saw that he was failing. So he panicked and ran away.'

'The shooter was a soldier.'

'Not necessarily.'

'Who else carries GI field dressings?'

'Anyone who shops at surplus stores.'

Deveraux turned round. She raised her arm and pointed at the horizon on our right. A short sweep of her arm. 'What do you see?'

I said, 'Kelham's perimeter.'

'I told you,' she said. 'They're enforcing a quarantine zone.'

Deveraux headed back to her car for something and I looked at the ground. The earth was soft and there were plenty of footprints. The dead guy's looped and staggered, ending where he lay. Around the lower half of his body were round depressions from knees, where his assailant had knelt to work on him. Those marks were at the head of a long straight line of partial prints, mostly toe, not much heel, all widely spaced. The shooter had run in fast. A reasonably tall person. Not especially heavy. There were identical prints facing the other way, where the shooter had run away. I didn't recognise the tread patterns. They were unlike any army boot I had ever seen.

Deveraux came back from her car with a camera. While she took crime-scene pictures, I followed the panicked running prints away from the area. They petered out on a broad vein of bone-hard dirt. I kept going straight, hoping to pick up the prints again, but within fifty yards the ground became matted with weeds that shaded into the brush that had grown at the base of Kelham's fence.

I turned back and took a step and saw a glint of light to my right. Metallic. Brassy. I bent down and saw a cartridge case lying on the dirt. Bright and fresh. Long, from a rifle. Best case, it was a .223 Remington, made for a sporting gun. Worst case, it was a 5.56 mm NATO round, made for the military. Hard to tell the difference with the naked eye. The Remington case has thinner brass. The NATO case is heavier. I picked it up and weighed it in my palm. Dollars to doughnuts, it was a military round.

I looked ahead at Deveraux and Pellegrino and the dead guy. They were about 140 yards away. Practically touching distance, for a rifleman. The 5.56 NATO round was designed to penetrate a steel helmet at 600 metres. The dead guy was more than four times closer than that. An easy shot. And the kind of guy that gets sent from Benning to Kelham for finishing school isn't the kind that misplaces a round at point-blank range. This was clearly an unintentional hit. The bandage proved it. But the kind of guy that gets sent from Benning to Kelham puts his warning shots high and wide.

I put the brass in my pocket and hiked back. Deveraux had snapped a whole roll of film. She took it out of her camera and sent Pellegrino to the pharmacy to get it printed. She told him to bring the doctor back with him, with the mortuary wagon. He departed on cue and Deveraux and I were left standing together in 1,000 acres of emptiness.

I asked, 'Did anyone hear a shot?'

She said, 'Mr Clancy is the only one who could. Pellegrino talked to him already. He claims not to have heard anything.'

'A single NATO round far away and outdoors might not be loud.'

'You accept it was a NATO round now?'

I put my hand in my pocket and came out with the shell case. 'I found it a hundred and forty yards out, twelve feet off the straight vector. Exactly where an M16 ejection port would have put it.'

Deveraux said, 'It could be a Remington .223,' which was kind of her. Then she took it from me. Her nails felt sharp on the skin of my palm. It was the first time we had touched. She weighed the brass in her palm. 'NATO for sure. I've fired a lot of these, and picked them up afterwards.'

'Me too,' I said.

'I'm going to raise hell,' she said. 'Soldiers against civilians, on American soil? I'll go all the way to the Pentagon, if I have to.'

'Don't. You're a county sheriff. They'll crush you like a bug.'

THE GUY WAS FINALLY PRONOUNCED dead thirty minutes later, at one in the afternoon, when the doctor showed up with Pellegrino. Pellegrino was in his cruiser and the doctor was in a fifth-hand meat wagon that looked like something out of a history book. It was a riff on a 1960s hearse, but built on a Chevrolet platform and devoid of viewing windows. It was like a half-height panel van, painted dirty white.

Merriam checked pulse and heartbeat and poked around the wound. He said, 'This man bled out through his femoral artery. Death by gunshot.'

I helped Merriam put the guy on a canvas gurney and then we loaded him in the back of the truck. Merriam drove him away and Deveraux sent Pellegrino about his business. She spent five minutes on the radio in her car. Then she got out of her car again.

'Butler claims no one came out of Kelham's main gate this morning.'

I said, 'Who's Butler?'

'My other deputy. Pellegrino's opposite number. I've had him stationed outside the base. I wanted a quick warning, in case they cancel the lockdown. There's going to be tension. There must be more gates. Or holes in the fence. It's got to be, what? Thirty miles long? Someone came out somewhere.'

'And went back in,' I said. 'If you're right, that is. Someone bloody to the elbows, with a dirty knife and at least one round short in his magazine.'

'I am right,' she said.

'I never heard of a quarantine zone before,' I said. 'Not inside the United States, anyway.' I paused a beat and asked, 'Have you spoken to Munro yet? The guy they sent to the base?'

She nodded. 'He called and left a message when he arrived. First thing. As a courtesy. He gave me a number to reach him.'

'Good,' I said. 'Because now I need to speak to him.'

We drove back together, across Clancy's land, out of his gate, south along the road, then west through the black half of town, towards the railroad. I saw the same old women on the same front porches.

'Tell me about the first two women,' I said to Deveraux.

Her response to that was to brake sharply and back up twenty yards. Then she nosed into the turning she had just passed. It was a dirt track, lined on both sides with what might once have been slave shacks. Deveraux passed by the first ten or so, and then she turned into a yard I knew from the third photo I had seen. The poor girl's house. I recognised the white clapboard wall that had reflected the setting sun softly into her face.

We parked on a patch of grass and got out and knocked on the back door. It was opened by a woman not much older than Deveraux and me. She was tall and thin. She smiled a resigned smile at Deveraux and shook her hand, and asked her, 'Any news about my baby?'

Deveraux said, 'We're working on it. We'll get there in the end.'

The bereaved mother was too polite to respond. She just smiled her wan smile again and turned to me. 'I don't believe we've met.'

I said, 'Jack Reacher, ma'am,' and shook her hand.

She said, 'I'm Emmeline McClatchy. I'm delighted to meet you, sir. Are you working with the Sheriff's Department?'

'The army sent me to help.'

'Now they did,' she said. 'Not nine months ago. I have some deer meat in the pot. Would you two care to join me for lunch?'

Deveraux said, 'Emmeline, I'm sure that's your dinner, not your lunch. We'll be OK. We'll eat in town. But thanks anyway.'

The woman smiled again and disappeared into the gloom behind her. We walked to the car. Deveraux backed out to the street and we drove away. We threaded through a matrix of dirt streets. I saw an abandoned construction project. Building materials were scattered around the lot in untidy piles. There were surplus cinder blocks, there were bricks, there was a pile of sand, there was a stack of bagged cement.

There was also a pile of gravel.

Deveraux drove on and turned left into a broader street. Bigger houses, bigger yards. She eased to a stop outside a place twice the size of the shack we had just left. A decent one-storey house. But shabby. There was a boy in the yard, maybe sixteen years old. He was standing still, watching us.

Deveraux said, 'This is the other one. Shawna Lindsay was her name. That's her baby brother right there, staring at us.'

The baby brother was no oil painting. He was nothing like his sister. He had fallen out of the ugly tree, and hit every branch. He had a head like a bowling ball and eyes like the finger holes.

I asked, 'Are we going in?'

Deveraux shook her head. 'Shawna's mom told me not to come back until I could tell her who slit her first-born's throat. I can't blame her.'

The boy was still staring. Quiet, baleful and patient.

'So let's go,' I said. 'I need to use the phone.'

DEVERAUX LET ME USE the phone in her office. She dialled the number Munro had left, and she told whoever answered that Sheriff Deveraux was on the line for Major Duncan Munro. Then she handed the receiver to me and vacated her chair and the room.

I sat behind her desk with nothing but dead air in my ear. A minute later a handset was scooped up off a desk. A voice said, 'Sheriff Deveraux? This is Major Munro. How are you?'

The voice was hard, and brisk, and hyper-competent, yet it had an undertone of good cheer in it. But then, I figured anyone would be happy to get a call from Elizabeth Deveraux.

I said, 'Munro?'

He said, 'I'm sorry, I was expecting Elizabeth Deveraux.'

'Well, sadly you didn't get her,' I said. 'My name is Reacher. I'm using the sheriff's phone right now. I'm with the 396th, currently TDY with the 110th. We're of equal rank.'

Munro said, 'I've heard of you, of course. How can I help you?'

'Did Garber tell you he was sending an undercover guy to town?'

'No, but I guessed he would. That would be you, right? Tasked to snoop on the locals? Which must be going pretty well, seeing as you're calling from the sheriff's phone. How can I help you, Reacher?'

'There was a guy shot to death this morning, close to your fence, northwestern quadrant. Probably a military round, and definitely an attempt to patch the fatal wound with a GI field dressing.'

'What, someone shot a guy and then gave him first aid? Sounds like a civilian accident to me.'

'How do you explain the round and the dressing?'

'Remington .223 and a surplus store.'

'And two guys were beaten up before that, by someone they swear was a soldier.'

'Not a soldier based at Kelham.'

'Really? How many Kelham personnel can you vouch for? In terms of their exact whereabouts this morning?'

'All of them. We've got Alpha Company overseas as of five days ago, and I've got everyone else confined to quarters. I guarantee no one left the base this morning. Or since I got here, for that matter.'

'Is that your standard operating procedure?'

'It's my secret weapon,' Munro said. 'Sitting down all day, no reading, no television, no nothing. Sooner or later someone talks, out of sheer boredom. Never fails. My arm-breaking days are over.'

'Tell me again,' I said. 'This is very important. You're absolutely sure no one left the base this morning? Or last night? Not even under secret orders, maybe local, or from Benning, or maybe even from the Pentagon? I'm serious here.'

'I'm sure,' Munro said. 'I guarantee it. Who was the dead guy?'

'No ID at this time. Civilian, almost certainly.'

'Near the fence?'

'Same as the guys that got beat up. Like a quarantine zone.'

'That's ridiculous. That's not happening. I know that for sure.'

'What else do you know for sure? Let's play Twenty Questions.'

'Let's not.'

'The short version. Two questions. Yes or no answers.'

'Don't put me on the spot, OK?'

'We're both on the spot already. We've got a mess here. Either it's in there with you or it's out here with me. Sooner or later one of us is going to have to help the other. We might as well start now.'

Silence. Then: 'OK, two questions.'

'Did they tell you about the car?'

'Yes.'

'Did they tell you about two other dead women?'

'No. What other dead women?'

'Last year. Local. Same MO. Cut throats.'

'Jesus. No, nobody said a word.'

I asked, 'You making any general progress there?'

No answer.

I asked, 'How long does it normally take for your secret weapon to work?'

He said, 'It's usually much faster than this. Listen, Reacher, this is hardly worth talking about, because you're just going to think well, what else would I say, because we both know I was sent here to cover someone's ass. But I'm not like that. From what I know, none of our guys killed any women. That's how it looks right now.'

I put the phone down on Munro and Deveraux came back into the office. Maybe she'd been watching a light on the switchboard. She said, 'Well?'

'No quarantine patrols. No one's left Kelham since Munro arrived.'

'He would say that, though, wouldn't he?'

'He's not smelling anything. He thinks the perp is not on the base.'

'Ditto.'

I nodded. Smoke and mirrors. Politics and the real world. Utter confusion.

I excused myself and went to the bathroom down the hall. When I got back I said, 'You want to get lunch?'

'I already have a lunch date,' she said. 'Major Duncan Munro just called and asked me to dine with him in the Kelham Officers' Club.'

DEVERAUX LEFT FOR KELHAM in her car and I was left alone on the sidewalk. I walked past the vacant lot to the diner. I ordered the cheeseburger again and then stepped over to the phone by the door and called the Pentagon. Colonel John James Frazer. Senate Liaison. He answered on the first ring. I asked him, 'What genius decided to classify that plate number?'

He said, 'I can't tell you that.'

'Whoever, it was a bad mistake. All it did was confirm the car belongs to a Kelham guy. It was practically a public announcement.'

'We had no alternative. Journalists would have got it five minutes after local law enforcement. We couldn't allow that.'

'You're telling me it belonged to a Bravo Company guy?'

'I'm not telling you anything. But, believe me, we had no choice. The consequences would have been catastrophic.'

'Right now you're making it sound like it was Reed Riley's own vehicle.'

'I can't confirm or deny,' Frazer said. 'And don't ask again. And don't use that name again, either. Not on an unsecured line.'

'Does the officer in question have an explanation?'

'I can't comment on that.'

I said, 'This is getting out of control, Frazer. You need to rethink. The cover-up is always worse than the crime. You need to stop it.'

'Negative on that, Reacher. There's a plan in place.'

'Does the plan include an exclusion zone around Kelham?'

'What the hell are you talking about?'

'I've got circumstantial evidence of boots on the ground outside Kelham's fence. Part of the circumstantial evidence is a corpse.'

'Who's the corpse?'

'A scrappy middle-aged guy.'

'A journalist?'

'I don't know how to recognise a journalist by sight alone.'

'No ID on him?'

'We haven't looked yet. The doctor hasn't finished with him.'

Frazer said, 'There is no exclusion zone around Fort Kelham.'

I hung up with Frazer, ate my burger and drank some coffee and then I set out to do what Garber had ordered me to do mid-morning, which was to return to the wreck and destroy the licence plate. I turned east on the Kelham road and then north on the railroad ties. I passed the old water tower and headed for where I had seen the half-buried bumper.

The half-buried bumper was gone. It had been dug up and taken away. The hole its lance-like point had made had been filled with earth, which had been stamped down by boot soles and tamped flat by the backs of shovels.

I walked deeper into the debris field. It had been sifted and examined and turned over, and evaluated. Almost 200 linear yards. Maybe 1,000 fragments had been displaced. A lot of work. Slow and painstaking. Six men, I figured, working with great precision. With military precision.

FIVE

I walked back the way I had come. I got to the middle of the railroad crossing and decided to walk east, towards the black part of town. There were things over there that I wanted to see again.

I made the turn Deveraux had made in her car, on the dirt road between the ditches and the slave shacks. At walking speed I was seeing different things than from the car. Poverty, mostly, up close. There were patched clothes on lines and chickens in some of the yards. There were duct-tape and baling-wire fixes to electric lines, to rain gutters, to plumbing outlets. I passed Emmeline McClatchy's place and the abandoned work site and its pile of gravel. It was waiting to be made into concrete, I assumed. It was about the size of a queen bed.

I walked on and found the wider street where Shawna Lindsay had lived. The second victim. The middle-class girl, comparatively. Her baby brother was still in his yard. About sixteen years old. The ugly boy. Watching me approach. I came to a stop face to face with him. I said, 'How's life, kid?'

He said, 'My mom's out.'

'Good to know, but that wasn't what I asked. I need to talk to you.'

'Why? You earning a whitey merit badge? You need to find a black person to talk with today?'

'I'm in the army,' I said. 'Which means half my friends are black, and it means half my bosses are black. I talk to black people all the time, and they talk to me. So don't give me that ghetto crap.'

The boy asked, 'What part of the army are you in?'

'Military Police.'

He asked, 'What do you want to talk about?'

'A hunch,' I said. 'My guess is no one ever talked to you about your sister's death. Normally with a homicide victim, they talk to everyone who knew her. They ask for insights and opinions. They want to know what kinds of things she did, where she went, who she hung with. Did they ever talk to you about that kind of stuff?'

'No,' he said. 'Nobody ever talked to me.'

'They should have,' I said. 'I would have. Because brothers know things about sisters. I bet you knew things about Shawna that no one else did. I bet she told you things she couldn't tell your mom. And I bet you figured out some stuff on your own.'

The kid shuffled in place a little. Bashful, and a little proud. Like saying: Yeah, maybe I did figure some things out. Out loud he said, 'No one ever talks to me about anything.'

'Why not?'

'Because I'm deformed. They think I'm slow, too.'

'Who says you're deformed?'

'Everybody.'

'Even your friends?'

'I don't have any friends. Who would want to be friends with me?'

'They're all wrong,' I said. 'You're not deformed. You're ugly, but you're not deformed. There's a difference.'

He smiled. 'That's what Shawna used to tell me.'

I said, 'You should join the army. You'd look like a movie star compared to half the people I know.'

'I'm going to join the army,' he said. 'I talked to Shawna's last boyfriend about it. He was a soldier.'

THE KID INVITED ME INSIDE. His mom was out, and there was a jug of iced tea in the refrigerator. The kid told me his name was Bruce. We took glasses of tea and sat at the kitchen table.

Up close and personal the kid was no better looking than he had been outside. But if you ignored his head, then the rest of him was in pretty good shape. Deep down he seemed patient and cheerful. I liked him, basically.

He asked me, 'Would the army really let me join?'

'Do you have felony convictions? An arrest of any kind?'

'No, sir.'

'Of course they'll let you in. They'd take you today if you were old enough.' I sipped my tea. 'So, who do you think killed your sister?'

The boy took a breath and then he started in on everything he had been thinking. It tumbled out, fast, coherent and thoughtful. He said, 'Her throat was cut, so we need to think about who is trained to do that kind of thing, or experienced with that kind of thing.'

I asked, 'So who fits the bill?'

'Soldiers. And ex-soldiers. Fort Kelham is field training for special ops guys. They know those skills. And hunters.'

I asked, 'When and where did you last see Shawna alive?'

'It was the day she was killed. It was a Friday in November. She left here about seven. After dark, anyway. She was all dressed up.'

'Where was she going?'

'To Brannan's Bar, probably. That's where she usually went.'

'Who did Shawna go with that night?'

'She left on her own. Probably she was going to meet her boyfriend.'

'Did she ever get to the bar?'

'No. She was found two streets from here. Where someone started to build a house.'

'The place with the gravel pile?'

The boy nodded. 'She was dumped right on it.'

I said, 'Tell me about Shawna's last boyfriend.'

'First white boyfriend she ever had.'

'Did she like him?'

'Pretty much.'

'Did they get along?'

'Pretty good.'

'Did he kill her?'

'He might have.'

'What was his name?'

'Reed. That was all Shawna ever said. Reed this, Reed that.'

'Last name?'

'I don't know.'

'We wear name tapes,' I said. 'Battledress uniform, above the right breast pocket.'

'I never saw him in uniform. He wore jeans and T-shirts to town.'

'Officer or enlisted man?'

'I don't know.'

'You talked to him. Didn't he say?'

The kid shook his head. 'He said his name was Reed. That's all.'

'What did he tell you about joining the army?'

'He said serving your country was a noble thing to do. He said I could learn a skill. He said they would explain it all at the recruiting office. He said there's a good one in Memphis.'

'Don't go there,' I said. 'Recruiting offices are shared between all four branches of the service. The Marines might grab you first.'

'So where should I go?'

'Go straight to Kelham. There are recruiters on every post. As soon as you've got something in your hand that proves you're eighteen years old, they'll let you in and never let you out again.'

'What's wrong with the Marines?'

'Nothing. It's a traditional rivalry. They say stuff, we say stuff.'

'Sheriff Deveraux was a Marine.'

'Is a Marine,' I said. 'They never stop being Marines, even after they leave. It's one of their things.'

'You like her,' the kid said. 'I could tell. I saw you riding in her car.'

'She's OK,' I said. 'Did Reed have a car? Shawna's boyfriend?'

The kid nodded. 'He had a 1957 Chevy Bel-Air two-door hardtop. Not really a classic. It was kind of beat up.'

'What colour was it?'

The kid said, 'It was blue.'

THE KID SHOWED ME his sister's room. It spoke of loss and bewilderment, and lack of energy. The bed was made and small piles of clothes were neatly folded. There was none of Shawna's personality on display. There were no posters on the walls, no souvenirs, no diary. She had owned some clothes and two books. That was all. One book explained how to become a notary public. The other was an out-of-date tourist guide to Los Angeles.

'Did she want to be in the movies?' I asked.

'No,' the kid said. 'She wanted to travel, that's all.'

'Did she have a job?'

'She worked part-time at the loan office. Next to Brannan's Bar. She could do her numbers pretty good.'

'What did she tell you that she couldn't tell your mom?'

'That she hated it here. That she wanted to get out.'

'What else do you know about Shawna?'

The kid started to say something and then he stopped. He moved towards the centre of the plain square space and stood there, as if he was soaking something up. He said, 'I really miss her.'

I left a few minutes later. Shawna's brother resumed his position near the fence, just standing there, watching the street. I waved to him, and he waved back. I hiked back to the Kelham road and turned left for town. I got some of the way towards the railroad and heard a car behind me, and a siren. I turned and Deveraux pulled up alongside me. A moment later I was in her front passenger seat, with nothing between us except her holstered shotgun.

The first thing I said was, 'Long lunch.'

She said, 'Jealous?'

'Depends what you ate. I had a cheeseburger.'

'We had rare roast beef and horseradish sauce. It was good.'

'How was the conversation?'

'Challenging.'

'In what way?'

'First tell me what you've been doing.'

'I went back to the wrecked car. I was under orders to destroy the licence plate. But it was gone. The debris field had been picked clean, very methodically. So I think you're right. There are boots on the ground outside Kelham's fence. They're operating an exclusion zone. They were diverted to the clean-up because someone at the Pentagon didn't trust me to do it. Then I took a long walk.'

Deveraux asked, 'Did you see the gravel pile?'

'I saw it this morning,' I said. 'I went back for a closer look.'

'Thinking about Janice May Chapman?'

'Obviously.'

'It's a coincidence,' she said. 'Black-on-white rapes are incredibly rare in Mississippi. No matter what folks want to believe.'

'Shawna Lindsay's body was found there. I talked to her brother.'

'It's a vacant lot. That's where bodies get dumped.'

'Was she killed there?'

'I don't think so. There was no blood at the scene or inside her.'

'What do you make of that?'

'Same guy,' she said. 'Addiction to risk. June, November, March, the bottom of the socio-economic scale, then the middle, then the top. He started safe and got progressively riskier. No one cares about poor black girls. Chapman was the first really visible victim.'

'What was the McClatchy girl's name?'

'Rosemary.'

'Where was her body found?'

'In the ditch near the crossing. West of the tracks.'

'Any blood?'

'None at all.'

'Was she raped?'

'No.'

'Was Shawna Lindsay?'

'No.'

'So Janice May Chapman was another kind of escalation. Did Rosemary McClatchy have a connection with Kelham?'

'Of course she did. You saw her photo. Kelham guys were lining up at her door. She stepped out with a string of them.'

'Black guys or white guys?'

'Both.'

'Officers or enlisted men?'

'Both.'

'Any suspects?'

'I had no probable cause even to ask questions. She wasn't seen with anyone from Kelham for at least two weeks before she was killed. My jurisdiction ends at Kelham's fence. They wouldn't have let me through the gate.'

'They let you through the gate today. What is Munro like?'

'Challenging,' she said again.

WE THUMPED UP over the tracks and parked just beyond them, with the ditch where Rosemary McClatchy had been found on our right and the turn into Main Street ahead and on our left.

Deveraux said, 'Obviously I started out with the baseline assumption that

Munro would be lying. Job one for him is to cover the army's ass. I understand that. He's under orders, the same way you are. I asked him about the exclusion zone. He denied it.'

'He would have to,' I said.

She nodded. 'But then he tried to prove it to me. He toured me all over. He's running a very tight ship. Every last man is confined to quarters. The armoury is under guard. The logs show no weapons in or out for two days. I assumed I was getting conned big time. And sure enough, there were two hundred empty beds. I assumed they've got a shadow force bivouacked in the woods. But Munro said that a full company's deployed elsewhere for a month. He swore blind. And I believed him because I've heard the planes come in and out, and I've seen the faces come and go.'

I nodded. Alpha Company, I thought. Kosovo.

'So in the end it all added up. Munro showed me a lot of evidence and it was all very consistent. So there is no exclusion zone. I was wrong. You must be wrong about the debris field. It must have been kids, scavenging.'

'I don't think so,' I said. 'It looked like a very organised search.'

She paused a beat. 'Then maybe the 75th is sending people from Benning. Maybe they're living in the woods around the fence. All Munro proved is that no one is leaving Kelham.'

'What did he say about Janice May Chapman?'

'He gave me what appeared to be a very expert summary of what appeared to be a very expert investigation, which appeared to prove no one from Kelham was ever involved with anything. He made it clear that it's the army against the local sheriff. He wants the world to think the bad guy is on my side of the fence.'

'So let's find out the truth and go and talk to Janice May Chapman's nosy neighbours.'

'No,' she said. 'I can't let you turn against your own people.'

'Maybe I wouldn't be turning against my own people,' I said. 'Maybe I would be doing exactly what my own people wanted me to do all along. Because maybe I would be helping Munro, not you. Because he might be right. We still have no idea who did what here.'

She said, 'But what's your best guess?'

I thought about the limousines scurrying in and out of Fort Kelham, perhaps carrying expensive lawyers. I thought about the exclusion zone, and about the panic in John James Frazer's voice on the phone from the

Pentagon. Senate Liaison. I said, 'My best guess is it was a Kelham guy.'

'You sure you want to take the risk of finding out for sure?'

'Talking to a man with a gun is a risk. Asking questions isn't.'

I believed that then, back in 1997.

JANICE MAY CHAPMAN'S HOUSE was 100 yards from the railroad track, one of three dwellings on a dead-end lane a mile south and east of Main Street. It was facing two other houses, as if it was nine o'clock on a dial and they were two and four. Clearly this was Carter Crossing's middle-class enclave. Lawns were green and weed free. Driveways were paved and uncracked.

Chapman's house had a full-width front porch, roofed over for shade and equipped with a pair of white rocking chairs. Both her neighbours had the same thing, the only difference being that both their porches were occupied, each by a white-haired old lady sitting in a rocker and staring at us.

Deveraux rolled forward and parked. We got out of the car.

'Which one first?' I asked.

'Doesn't matter,' Deveraux said. 'Whichever, the other one will be right over within about thirty seconds.'

Which is what happened. We chose the right-hand house, the one at four o'clock, and before we were three steps onto its porch the neighbour from the two o'clock house was right behind us. Deveraux made the introductions. She gave the ladies my name and said I was an army investigator. The ladies welcomed me. They were from a generation that liked the army.

Deveraux ran through what she had already discussed. No, neither of the ladies had seen Chapman leave her house on the day she died. Not on foot, not in her car, not in anybody else's car.

The next question was tactically difficult, so Deveraux left it to me. I asked, 'Were there intervals when something could have happened that you didn't see?' In other words: *Just exactly how nosy are you? Were there moments when you weren't staring at your neighbour?*

Both ladies saw the implication, of course, and they clucked and fussed for a minute, but the gravity of the situation meant more to them than their wounded feelings, and they admitted that no, they had the situation pretty much sewn up round the clock. Both liked to sit on their porches when they weren't otherwise occupied, and they tended to be otherwise occupied at different times. Both had bedrooms at the front of their houses, and both were light sleepers, so not much escaped them at night, either.

I asked, 'Was there usually much coming and going over there?'

The ladies conferred and launched a long, complicated narrative. I started to tune it out until I realised they were describing a fairly active social calendar that about half a year ago had settled into a month-on, month-off pattern, first of social frenzy, and then of complete inactivity. Chapman was either never out, or always out, first four or five weeks in one condition, and then four or five weeks in the other.

Bravo Company, in Kosovo. Bravo Company, at home. Not good.

I asked, 'Did she have a boyfriend?'

She had several, they said primly. All polite young men with short hair, all in what they called dungaree trousers and undershirts.

Jeans, T-shirts. Soldiers, obviously, off duty. Not good.

I asked, 'Was there anyone in particular? Anyone special?'

They agreed that three or four months earlier, the parade of suitors had been replaced by a lone young man, again described as polite, short-haired, but inappropriately dressed. In their day, a gentleman called on his belle in a suit and tie.

I asked, 'What did they do together?'

They went out, the ladies said. Probably to bars. There was little in the way of alternative entertainment in that corner of the state. The couple tended to come back late, sometimes after midnight. Sometimes the suitor would stay an hour or two.

I asked, 'When was the last time you saw her?'

The day before she died, they said. She had left her house at seven o'clock in the evening with the suitor.

'Did her friend show up in his own car?' I asked.

Yes, they said, he did. It was a blue car.

WE LEFT BOTH LADIES on one porch and crossed the street to take a closer look at Chapman's house. We stood on the porch and I looked in a window and saw a small, square living room, full of furniture that looked pretty new. The living-room door was open and I could see part of a narrow hallway beyond. I shifted position and craned my neck for a better look.

'Go inside if you want,' Deveraux said, behind me. 'The door is unlocked. It was unlocked when we got here.'

'Is that usual?'

'Not unusual. We never found her key.'

'Not in her pocketbook?'

'She seems to have left her pocketbook in the kitchen.'

'Is *that* usual?'

'She didn't smoke,' Deveraux said. 'She certainly didn't pay for drinks. Why would she need a pocketbook?'

'Make-up?' I said.

'Twenty-seven-year-olds don't powder their noses halfway through the evening. Not like they used to.'

I opened the front door and stepped inside the house. It was neat and clean. The floors and the paint and the furniture were all fresh, but not brand new. There was a kitchen across the hall from the living room, with two bedrooms behind, and presumably a bathroom.

'Nice place,' I said. 'You could buy it.'

Deveraux said, 'With those old biddies across the street, watching me all the time? I'd go crazy inside a week.'

I smiled. She had a point.

Then she said, 'Actually I couldn't buy it even if I wanted to. We don't know who the next of kin is. I wouldn't know who to talk to.'

'No will?'

'She was twenty-seven years old. We haven't found one so far.'

'No mortgage?'

'Nothing on record with the county.'

'No family?'

'No one recalls her mentioning any.'

I walked from room to room. There were minor examples of disarray, the kind of things that would have been tidied away before an expected guest's arrival, but on the whole it was bland and soulless. All the furniture matched. It looked like it had been selected from the same manufacturer, all at the same time. All the rugs went well together. All the paint was the same colour. There were no pictures on the walls. No books. No prized possessions.

The bathroom was clean. The medicine cabinet contained toothpaste, tampons, dental floss and shampoo. The main bedroom had a bed in it, which was made, but not well. The second bedroom had a narrower bed.

The kitchen was fitted out with a range of useful stuff, but I doubted that Chapman had been a gourmet cook. Her pocketbook was stowed neatly on the counter. It was a small leather pouch, navy-blue in colour. I opened it. Inside was a slim leather wallet, a pack of tissues, a pen, some coins and a car key. The car key had a black plastic head, embossed with a letter H.

'Honda,' Deveraux said, beside me. 'A Honda Civic. Bought new three years ago from a dealer in Tupelo.'

'Where is it?' I asked.

Deveraux pointed to a door. 'In her garage.'

I took the wallet out of the bag. It had nothing in it except cash money and a Mississippi driver's licence, issued to Chapman three years before. I put it back in the bag and opened the door Deveraux had pointed out. Behind it I found a tiny boot room that had two more doors in it, one to the back yard, the other to the garage. The garage was empty apart from the Honda, which was silver in colour, clean and undamaged.

I opened the door to the back yard and stepped out. Deveraux followed me and asked, 'So, was there anything in there I should have seen?'

'Yes. There were things in there anyone should have seen.'

'So what did I miss?'

'Nothing,' I said. 'That's my point. We should have seen certain things, but we didn't. Because certain things were missing.'

'What things?' she asked.

'Later,' I said, because by that point I had seen something else.

The back yard was not maintained to the same standard as the front yard. In fact it was basically weed, not grass. At the far end was a low panel wood fence with the centre panel fallen out and laid aside.

What I had seen from the door was a faint narrow path through the mown weeds. It was almost imperceptible. Only the late afternoon sun made it visible and showed a ghostly trail, where the weeds were a little crushed and bruised. The path led straight to the hole in the fence.

I walked along it and Deveraux followed me. The path led through the gap and into an abandoned field. At the far edge of the field was the railroad track. Beyond the field was a dirt road that ran east and west. The field had tyre tracks across it. They came in and ran straight towards the gap in Chapman's fence. They ended close to where I was standing, in a wide looping triangle, where cars had backed up and turned, for the return trip.

'She got sick of the old biddies,' I said. 'Sometimes she came out the front and sometimes she came out the back.'

Deveraux cursed. 'But it makes their evidence meaningless. Now we don't know when she came and went on that last day.'

I looked around. Nothing to see. No other houses, no other people. Total privacy. Then I looked back at the weed patch that passed for a lawn. 'She bought this place three years ago?' I asked.

'Yes,' said Deveraux.

'She was twenty-four at the time. Is that usual? Twenty-four-year-olds owning real estate with no mortgage?'

'Not very usual. But what has that got to do with her yard?'

'She wasn't much of a gardener. And the previous owner wasn't much of one either. He or she didn't like mowing the lawn, so chose to dig it up and replace it with something else.'

'With what?'

'Go take a look.'

She backtracked through the gap in the fence and walked halfway along the path and squatted down. She dug her fingers beneath the weeds. Then she looked up at me and said, 'Gravel.'

The previous owner had opted for raked stones. Like a Japanese garden. But the gravel had not been a total success. It had been laid thin. The subsoil had been full of weed roots. Applications of herbicide had been needed.

Janice May Chapman had not continued the herbicide applications. That was clear. No hosepipe in her garage. Those weeds had come boiling up like madmen. Some boyfriend had brought over a mower and hacked them back. Some nice guy who didn't like disarray. A soldier, almost certainly.

Deveraux asked, 'So what are you saying? She was raped here?'

'Maybe she wasn't raped at all. Think about it. A sunny afternoon, total privacy. They're sitting out the back because they don't want to sit on the front porch with the old biddies watching every move. They're feeling good, they get right to it.'

'On the lawn?'

'Wouldn't you?'

She looked right at me and said, 'Like you told the doctor, it would depend on who I was with.'

I pressed my forearm down on the gravel and simulated the throes of passion. I came up with plenty of green chlorophyll stains and a smear of dry stony mud. When I wiped off the dirt we both saw the same kind of small red marks we had seen on Janice May Chapman's corpse.

'We need to go inside again,' I said.

We found Chapman's laundry basket in the bathroom. On top of the pile inside was a short sundress. It was printed with red and white pinstripes. It was rucked and creased at the waist. It had grass stains on the upper back.

'Rosemary McClatchy wasn't raped,' I said. 'Nor was Shawna Lindsay. Escalation is one thing. A change in MO is another.'

Deveraux stepped into the hallway. She looked all around. She asked, 'What did I miss here? What should be here that isn't?'

'Something more than three years old,' I said. 'She moved here from somewhere else and she should have brought things with her. Books, maybe. Or photos. Maybe a favourite chair or something.'

'Twenty-four-year-olds aren't very sentimental.'

'They keep some little thing. She showed up here three years ago out of the blue and brought nothing with her. She bought a house, a car and got a local driver's licence. She bought a houseful of new furniture. All for cash. She doesn't have a rich daddy or his picture would be next to the TV in a frame. I want to know who she was.'

'She was already here when I got back to town. I never thought about it. I mean, people come and go all the time. This is America.'

'Did you ever hear anything about her background?'

'Nothing.'

'Did she have a job?'

'No.'

'Accent?'

'The Midwest, maybe. I only spoke to her once.'

'Did you fingerprint the corpse?'

'No. Why would we? We knew who she was.'

I nodded. By now Chapman's skin would be sloughing off her fingers like an old glove. 'Do you have a fingerprint kit in the car?'

She shook her head. 'Butler does the fingerprinting.'

'You should get him here. He can take prints from the house. He should start with the tampon box.'

'She won't be on file anywhere. Why would she be? She was a kid. She didn't serve and she wasn't a cop.'

I said, 'Nothing ventured, nothing gained.'

Deveraux used the radio in her car. She had chess pieces to move. Pellegrino had to replace Butler at Kelham's gate. She came back in and said, 'Twenty minutes. I have to get back. You wait here. But don't worry. Butler should do it right. He's reasonably smart.'

I asked, 'Will you have dinner with me?'

She said, 'I have to work pretty late. Nine o'clock, maybe.'

'Nine would be fine.'

'Are you paying?'

'Absolutely.'

She paused a beat. 'Like a date?' she asked.

'We might as well,' I said. 'There's only one restaurant in town. We'd probably end up eating together anyway.'

'OK,' she said. 'Dinner. Nine o'clock. Thank you.' Then, just before she left, she said, 'Don't shave, OK? You look good like that.'

I WAITED ON Janice May Chapman's porch. Deputy Butler showed up just inside twenty minutes. He took a black box out of his car and walked up Chapman's driveway towards me. I held out my hand. I said, 'Jack Reacher.'

He said, 'Geezer Butler.'

I led him inside. I said, 'The challenge is to get her prints and no one else's.'

'To avoid confusion?' he said.

No, I thought. To avoid a Bravo Company guy lighting up the system. Better safe than sorry. I said, 'Yes, to avoid confusion.'

'The chief said I should start in the bathroom.'

'Good plan,' I said. 'Toothbrush, toothpaste, tampon box, personal things like that. Things that were boxed up or wrapped in cellophane in the store. No one else will have touched them.'

I watched him pretty carefully. He was extremely competent. He took twenty minutes and got twenty good prints, all small neat ovals, all obviously a woman's. We agreed that was an adequate sample, and he packed up his gear and gave me a ride back to town.

I got out of Butler's car outside the Sheriff's Department and walked to the hotel, where I stood and wrestled with a dilemma. I felt I should go and buy a new shirt, but I didn't want Deveraux to feel that dinner was supposed to be more than just dinner. Or in reality I did want her to feel dinner could be more than just dinner, but I didn't want her to feel pushed into anything.

In the end I decided a shirt was just a shirt, so I hiked across to the other side of Main Street and looked at the stores. Most of them were about to close. I found a men's outfitters, so I went in and looked at the shirts.

Eventually I chose a white button-down made of heavy cotton, which was about my size. I hauled the shirt to the old guy behind the counter and paid for it. It cost me less than the pink shirt from the PX. I planned to dump it in my room. I made it into the hotel lobby in time to see the owner setting off up the stairs in a hurry. He turned when he heard the door, and saw it was me and stopped. He said, 'Your uncle is on the phone again.'

I took the call alone in the office. Garber was tentative, which made me uneasy. His first question was, 'How's it going there?'

'Bad,' I said.

'With the sheriff?'

'No, she's OK.'

'Elizabeth Deveraux, right? We're having her checked out.'

'Why?'

'Maybe we can get you something you can use against her. We might need leverage at some point.'

'Save your effort. She's not the problem.'

'So what is?'

'We are,' I said. 'Or you are. The army, I mean. They're patrolling outside Kelham's fence, shooting people.'

'That's categorically impossible.'

'I've seen the blood. And the car wreck has been sanitised.'

'That can't be happening.'

'It's happening. And you need to stop it happening. Because right now you've got a big problem, but you're going to turn it into World War Three. There are two guys beat up and one guy dead down here.'

'Dead? How?'

'He bled out through a gunshot wound to the thigh. There was a half-assed attempt to patch it up with a GI field dressing. And I found a NATO shell case at the scene.'

'That's not us. I would know.'

'Would you?' I said. 'Or would I? I'm down here looking.'

'It's not legal.'

'Tell me about it. Worst case, it's a policy decision. Best case, someone's gone rogue. You need to find out which and stop it.'

'How?' Garber said. 'You want me to walk up to a random selection of senior officers and accuse them of an egregious breach of the law? I'd be locked up before lunch and court-martialled the next morning.'

I paused. Asked, 'Are there names I shouldn't say on an open line?'

Garber said, 'There are names you shouldn't even know.'

'This whole thing is drifting out of control. Two black women were killed here before Chapman. Did you even know that? We ignored them and then our heads exploded when a white woman got killed. The officer in question needs to be pulled out and redeployed.'

'That's not going to happen. Not as long as Kosovo is important. This guy could stop a war single-handed and all by himself.'

'He's one of four hundred men, for God's sake.'

'Not according to the political ad campaigns two years from now. Think about it. He's going to be the Lone Ranger.'

'He's going to be locked up in Leavenworth.'

'Munro doesn't think so. He says the officer in question is likely innocent.'

'Then we should stop patrolling outside the fence.'

'We're not patrolling outside the fence.'

I gave up, ended the call, and then I carried my new shirt upstairs and left it on my bed. I started to think about dinner with Elizabeth Deveraux. Three hours to go, and one more thing to do beforehand.

SIX

I came out of the hotel and looped through the dog-leg alley between the pharmacy and the hardware store and came out the other end between the loan office and Brannan's Bar. Where Janice May Chapman's body had been found. The sand pile was still there. I stepped round it and checked activity on the one-sided street. Not much was going on. Some of the bars were closed, but Brannan's was open. I went in and found two guys that looked like brothers. Mid-thirties, maybe two years apart.

I said, 'My name is Jack Reacher and I'm an MP with a dinner date coming up, which means that usually I'd hang around all night and weasel stuff out of you in the course of conversation, but I don't have time for that, so we'll have to rely on a question-and-answer session, OK?'

They got the message. Base-town bar owners worry about MPs. Easiest thing in the world to put an establishment on a local no-go list, for a week, or a month. They introduced themselves as Jonathan and Hunter Brannan, brothers. They ran the best bar in town, so they couldn't deny they saw everybody from time to time.

'Janice Chapman came here,' I said. 'The woman who got killed.'

They agreed that yes, she did. Everyone comes to Brannan's.

I asked, 'With the same guy every recent time?'

They agreed that yes, that was the case.

I asked, 'Who was he?'

Hunter Brannan said, 'His name was Reed. Don't know much about him, but he was a big dog. You can always tell by the way the others react.'

'Was he in here that night?'

'That's a tough question. This place is usually packed, but I would say he was. For the early part of the evening, at least.'

'What car does he drive?'

'Some old thing. Blue, I think.'

I asked, 'How long has he been coming here?'

'A year or so, I guess. But he's one of the in-and-out guys.'

'What does that mean?'

'They've got a couple of squads over there. They go somewhere, and then they come back. A month on, a month off.'

'Did you see him with previous girlfriends?'

Jonathan Brannan said, 'A guy like that always has arm candy.'

'Black or white?'

'Both. He's pretty much an equal opportunities type of guy.'

'Remember any names?'

'No,' Hunter Brannan said. 'But I remember feeling pretty jealous a couple of times.'

I went back to the hotel. Two hours until dinner. I spent the first hour taking a nap, because I was tired. I woke myself up at eight o'clock and took a long hot shower. I put on my new shirt. I put my shoes on and shined them one at a time against the backs of my calves.

I dumped my old shirt in the trash can and left my room. I pushed in through the diner door at a minute after nine and found the place empty apart from the waitress and the old couple from Toussaint's. The woman had a book, the man had a paper. Deveraux wasn't there yet. I told the waitress I was expecting company. She set me up at a table near the front and I was about to sit down when Deveraux stepped in through the door.

She wasn't in uniform. She was wearing a silver silk shirt and a black skirt. High-heeled shoes. A silver necklace. The shirt was open at the top. The skirt sat at her waist. Her legs were bare. And slim. Her hair was wet from the shower. It was loose on her shoulders. As she walked to the table she was smiling, all the way up to her amazing eyes.

We sat down facing each other.

She said, 'You didn't shave.'

'You told me not to.'

'I know,' she said. 'I like you like that.'

'You look great too.'

'Thank you. I decided to quit early. I went home to change.'

The waitress came by. Deveraux asked for the cheeseburger. So did I, with coffee to drink. The waitress made a note and went away.

I said, 'You had the cheeseburger yesterday.'

Deveraux said, 'I have it every day.'

'Really? How do you stay thin?'

'Mental energy,' she said. 'I worry a lot.'

'About what?'

'Right now about a guy from Oxford, Mississippi. That's who got shot in the thigh. The doctor brought his personal effects to my office. There was a wallet and a notebook. The guy was a journalist.'

'Big paper?'

'No, freelance. Struggling, probably. His press pass was two years old.'

The waitress came with my coffee and a glass of water for Deveraux.

I said, 'My CO still denies there are boots on the ground outside the fence.'

Deveraux asked, 'How does that make you feel?'

'I don't know. If he's lying to me, it will be the first time ever.'

'Maybe someone's lying to him. Does it make you angry?'

'I never get angry. I'm a very placid type of a guy. Except when I'm talking to the Pentagon.'

The waitress brought our meals. Two big cheeseburgers, two big tangles of fries. I had had the same thing for lunch. I hadn't remembered that. But I ate. And I watched Deveraux eat.

She said, 'What else did your CO tell you?'

'That he's having you checked out.'

She stopped eating. 'Why would he?'

'To give me something to use against you.'

'There's not much there. I was a good little jarhead. But don't you see? They're proving my case for me. The more desperate they get, the more I know for sure it's a Kelham guy.' She began eating again.

We ate in silence and finished up. Meat, bread, cheese, potatoes, all gone. Deveraux was half my size. Or less. I didn't know how she did it.

When the waitress returned, we ordered peach pie and coffee, for both of us, which I took to be a good sign. Deveraux wasn't worried about being kept awake. Maybe she was planning on it. The old couple from the hotel got up and left. The clock in my head hit ten in the evening.

The pies arrived and so did the coffee. I didn't pay much attention to either. I spent most of my time looking at the third button on Deveraux's shirt. It was the first one that was done up. Therefore it was the first one that would need to be undone. It was a tiny mother-of-pearl thing, silvery grey.

The waitress put the bill on the table, face down. I flipped it over. Not bad. You could still eat well on a soldier's pay in 1997. I put some notes on it and looked at Deveraux. 'Can I walk you home?'

She said, 'I thought you'd never ask.'

MAIN STREET WAS DESERTED. Deveraux was taller in her heels. We walked close enough for me to hear the whisper of silk on skin.

We got to the hotel. I held the door for her. The old guy was behind the counter. We nodded good night to him and headed for the stairs. At the top Deveraux paused and said, loud and clear, 'Well, good night, Mr Reacher, and thanks again for your company at dinner.'

I just stood there. She crossed the corridor. She took out her key.

She put it in room seventeen's lock. She opened the door. Then she closed it loudly, tiptoed back to me, stretched up, put her lips close to my ear and whispered, 'That was for the man downstairs. I have to think about my reputation. Mustn't shock the voters.'

I breathed out. I took her hand and we headed for my room.

We were both thirty-six years old. All grown up. Not teenagers. We didn't rush. We took our time, and what a time it was.

We kissed as soon as my door was closed. It was a great kiss. I had one hand in her hair and one on the small of her back. She was jammed hard against me and moving. Her eyes were open. So were mine. We kept that first kiss going for whole minutes. Five of them, or maybe ten. We took it slow. I think we both understood that the first time happens only once.

Eventually we came up for air. I took my shirt off. I have a big shrapnel scar low down on my front. Ugly white stitches. Deveraux ignored it. She was a Marine. She had seen worse. Her hand went to her top button.

I said, 'No, let me.'

She smiled. 'That's your thing? You like undressing women?'

'More than anything in the world,' I said.

I took her left hand and got her to hold it out, palm up. I undid her cuff button. I did the same with her right hand. The silk fell back over slim wrists. I moved on to the button on the front of her shirt. It was small. And slippery. My fingers are big. But I got the job done. The button popped open. I moved down to the fourth button. Then the fifth. I eased the silk out of the waistband of her skirt slowly and carefully. She was looking at me and smiling. I eased the shirt off her shoulders and it parachuted to the floor. She was wearing a bra. A tiny black thing with lace and delicate straps. Her breasts were fantastic. I kissed the curve where her neck met her shoulder. She put her head back and her hair spilled everywhere. I kissed her throat.

'Now your shoes,' she said, and her throat buzzed against my lips.

She pushed me back and sat me down on the bed. She knelt in front of me. She untied my right shoe, and then my left. She eased them off. She peeled down my socks.

'PX for sure,' she said.

'Less than a dollar,' I said. 'Couldn't resist.'

We stood up and kissed again. By that point in my life I had kissed hundreds of girls, but I was ready to admit Deveraux was the finest of them all. She was spectacular. She was strong, but gentle. Passionate, but not aggressive. Hungry, but not demanding.

We finished undressing each other and I sat down on the bed again. Her legs were long, smooth and toned. She was wearing tiny black panties, just a wisp of dark fabric. Bra, panties, shoes. She climbed into my lap. I lifted her hair away and kissed her ear. I could feel her cheek against mine. I could feel the smile. We spent twenty minutes learning every contour above our necks, then we moved lower. I unsnapped her bra, then I lifted her off my lap and rolled her on her back on the bed. It was time. We started tenderly. Long and slow. Deep and easy. Then faster.

'Wait,' she said. 'Not now. Not yet. Slow down.'

Long and slow, long and slow.

'OK,' she said. 'OK. Now. Now. Now!'

The room began to shake.

Just faintly at first, like a mild tremor, like the edge of a distant earthquake. The French door trembled. A glass rattled on the bathroom shelf.

My shoes hopped and moved. The floor shook hard. The walls boomed. The bed shook and bounced and walked tiny fractions across the moving floor.

Then the midnight train was gone and so were we.

AFTERWARDS WE LAY side by side, breathing hard, holding hands. I stared up at the ceiling. Deveraux said, 'I've wanted to do that for two whole years.'

I said, 'If I ever buy a house it's going to be next to a railroad track. That's for sure.'

She snuggled next to me. We lay quiet, and spent, and satisfied.

We had a languid conversation about whether she should go back to her own room. Reputations. Voters. I said the old guy had come upstairs for me when Garber had called. He had got a good look inside the room. She said if that happened again I could delay a second and she could hide in the bathroom. We said nothing more about voters or reputations. We fell asleep, in each other's arms, in the still silence of the Mississippi night.

I WOKE AT SEVEN O'CLOCK in the morning.

Elizabeth Deveraux was sitting upright in bed. She was facing me, back straight, legs crossed. She was very beautiful. She said, 'They must have had something else in common. Those three women. Beauty is too subjective. It's just an opinion.'

'It's not just an opinion,' I said. 'Not with those three.'

'Then we're looking for two factors. Two things that interacted. They were beautiful and they were also something else.'

'Maybe they were pregnant,' I said.

We examined the proposition. It was a base town. These things happen. Mostly by accident, but sometimes on purpose. Sometimes women think that moving from one base town to another with a baby is better than living alone in the base town where they were born.

I said, 'Shawna Lindsay was desperate to get out, according to her brother.'

Deveraux said, 'But I can't see why Janice May Chapman would have been. She wasn't born here. She chose this place. And she wouldn't have needed a guy to get her out. She could have just sold up and driven away.'

'Accident, then,' I said. 'With her, anyway. Did Rosemary McClatchy want to get out of town?'

'I don't know. Probably. Why wouldn't she?'

'Did the doctor test for pregnancy?'

'No,' Deveraux said. 'Merriam signed the certificate and gave us the cause of death, that's all.'

I said, 'Would Rosemary McClatchy have told her mother?'

'I can't ask her,' Deveraux said. 'Absolutely not. No way. I can't put that possibility into Emmeline's mind.'

'There was something Shawna Lindsay's brother wasn't telling me. You should talk to him. He wants to join the army, by the way.'

'Not the Marines?'

'Apparently not. He seems drawn towards the military. You're a Marine and a sheriff. Approach it right and he might salute.'

'OK,' she said. 'Maybe I'll try it. Maybe I'll go and see him today.'

'All three of them could have been accidental,' I said. 'The big decisions might have come afterwards. About what to do, I mean. They might have been persuaded.'

'Abortion? Where would they get an abortion in Mississippi? You'd have to drive north for hours.'

'Which is maybe why Janice Chapman got dressed up before she was murdered. Maybe her boyfriend was driving her to an appointment.'

'We'll never know for sure. Unless we find the boyfriends.'

'Or the boyfriend, singular. It might have been the same guy.'

'But it makes no sense. Why would he set up an appointment at an abortion clinic for them and then murder them before they got a mile down the road? Why not just go through with the appointment?'

'Maybe he's the kind of guy who can't afford either a pregnant girlfriend or an association with an abortion clinic.'

'He's a soldier. Not a preacher. Or a politician.'

I said nothing.

'Or maybe he's got preachers or politicians in the family. Maybe he has to avoid embarrassing them.'

There was a creak from a floorboard outside in the hall, and then a soft knock on my door. I recognised the sound immediately. The same as the morning before. The old guy.

Deveraux cursed.

Now we were like teenagers. Deveraux rolled off the bed and grabbed an armful of clothing, which happened to include my trousers, so I had to wrestle them back from her, which spilled the other garments all over the place. She tried to collect them and I tried to get my trousers on. She made it to the bathroom but left a trail of underwear. I got my trousers more or less straight and the old guy knocked again. I limped across the floor and kicked clothes towards the bathroom as I went. Deveraux darted out and collected them. Then she ducked back in again and I opened the door.

The old guy said, 'Your fiancée is on the phone for you.'

I PADDED DOWNSTAIRS barefoot, wearing only my trousers. I took the call in the back office. It was Frances Neagley, my old colleague.

I asked, 'Why did you have to say you were my fiancée?'

She asked back, 'Why, did I interrupt something?'

'Not exactly. But she heard.'

'Elizabeth Deveraux? You two are getting it on already? You need to take care there, Reacher. Deveraux is being checked out, big time.'

'I know that,' I said. 'Garber already told me. Waste of time.'

'I don't think so. It all suddenly went quiet.'

'Because there's nothing there.'

'No, because there is. You know how bureaucracy works. It's easy to say no. Silence means yes.'

'What would they find if they checked you out?'

'Plenty.'

'Or me?'

'I hate to think.'

'So there you go. Nothing to worry about. What else?'

'A friend of a friend got into the Kosovo files, and they're plenty thick right now. Two local women disappeared without a trace.'

Neagley told me that over the last year two Kosovan women had simply vanished. There was no local explanation. No family troubles. Both were unmarried. Both had been within range of the US Army's local footprint. Both had fraternised.

'Good-looking?' I asked.

'I didn't see photographs.'

I asked, 'Was there an investigation?'

'Under the radar. They flew a guy in from Germany. As a patriotic American you'll be glad to hear that every last member of the US armed forces was as innocent as a newborn baby.'

'Who was the investigator?' I asked.

'Major Duncan Munro.'

I FINISHED THE CALL with Neagley and went upstairs. Deveraux wasn't in my room. I padded back to hers and found the door locked. I heard the shower running. I knocked but got no response. So I showered and dressed and went back fifteen minutes later and found nothing but silence. I walked up to the diner, but she wasn't there either. Her car was not in the department lot.

I loitered on the sidewalk for half of that hour, then headed into the diner for breakfast. A woman who ate like Deveraux did couldn't stay away for long. I chose eggs and was halfway through my third cup of coffee when she came in. She was in uniform again and her hair was tied back. Her face was a little set in place. A little immobile. She looked wonderful.

I took a breath and kicked the facing chair out. She didn't react. I saw her eyes move as she considered her options and looked at all the tables. Most of them were unoccupied. But evidently she decided that to sit on her own might cause a scene. She was worried about voters. Worried about her reputation. So she came over to me. She sat down, knees tight together, hands in her lap.

I said, 'I don't have a fiancée. I don't have any other girlfriend.'

She didn't answer.

I said, 'It was my former sergeant, Frances Neagley, on the phone. They're all playing a game with the undercover thing. Apparently it amuses them. My CO calls himself my uncle.'

'I'm hungry,' she said. 'This is the first time in two years I've missed breakfast. If you had a fiancée, would you cheat on her?'

'Probably not,' I said. 'But I'd want to, with you.'

She went quiet. I saw her thinking. *Last night*. She waved to the waitress and ordered French toast.

'I called Bruce Lindsay,' she said. 'Shawna's little brother. I'm heading there this afternoon. I think you're right. He has something to tell me.'

Me. Not us.

I said, 'It was a fellow officer's lame joke. That's all.'

She said, 'I'm afraid there's a problem with the fingerprints. From Janice Chapman's house, I mean. My own fault, as a matter of fact.'

'What kind of problem?'

'Butler has a friend at the Jackson PD. From when he took the course. I encourage him to get her to do our processing for us, on the quiet, to save ourselves the money. But she got her file numbers mixed. Chapman's data went to a case about a woman called Audrey Shaw, and we got Audrey

Shaw's data. Unless Audrey Shaw was the previous owner of Chapman's house, in which case it was Butler's screw-up.'

'No, Butler did a good job. Those prints weren't from a previous owner, not unless she sneaked back in and used Chapman's toothbrush in the middle of the night.'

'Tell me again,' she said. 'About that phone call.'

'It was Frances Neagley with information for me. That's all.'

'And the fiancée thing was a joke?'

'Don't tell me the Marines are better comedians, too.'

Deveraux went quiet again. I could see a decision coming. And I was pretty sure it was going to turn out OK. But I didn't find out then what the decision was. Because before she could speak the woman from the department's switchboard room crashed in through the diner door. She was out of breath. She had run all the way. She called out, 'There's another one.'

SEVEN

Deputy Butler had been on his way to relieve Pellegrino for the watch at Fort Kelham's gate. A mile out he had glanced to his left, and he had seen a forlorn shape in the scrub 100 yards north of the road. Five minutes after that he had been on the horn to HQ, and ninety seconds after taking the message the dispatcher had made it to the diner. Deveraux and I were in her car twenty seconds after that. She put her foot down hard and drove fast all the way.

We parked behind Butler's car and got out. We were on the main east–west road, two miles beyond Carter Crossing, one mile short of Kelham, out in an open belt of scrubland, with the forest that bordered Kelham's fence well ahead of us. It was the middle of the morning and the sky was clear and blue.

I could see what Butler had seen. It was dark, slightly humped, slightly elongated, deflated. It was unmistakable. Judging its size was difficult, because judging the exact distance was difficult. If it was eighty yards away, it was a small woman. If it was 120 yards away, it was a large man.

Butler was standing out in the scrub, halfway between the dark shape and us. We set out walking towards him, and then we passed him without a word. I figured the overall distance was going to be close to dead on 100 yards, which made the shape either a tall woman, or a short man. Or a teenager, maybe. Then I recognised the distorted proportions. And I started to run. At ten yards out I was certain. It was Bruce Lindsay. Shawna's little brother. He was on his front. His giant head was turned towards me.

Deveraux and I rolled the corpse over and found an entry wound on the left side of the rib cage. The bullet had shredded the heart.

I scanned the horizon. If the kid had been walking east, he had been shot from the north, almost certainly by a rifleman who had exited Kelham's fence-line woods and had been patrolling the scrub. The quarantine zone.

Deveraux said, 'I talked to him this morning. Just an hour ago. We had an appointment at his house. So why was he here?'

'He had a secret to keep. About Shawna. He knew you'd get it out of him. So he decided to be somewhere else this afternoon.'

'Where? Where was he going?'

'Kelham,' I said.

'If he was heading for Kelham he would have been on the road.'

'He was shy about strangers seeing him. Because of the way he looked. I bet he never walked on the roads.'

'If he was shy with strangers, why would he go to Kelham?'

I said, 'He went because I told him it would be OK. I told him soldiers would be different. I told him he'd be welcome there.'

The kid had on a jacket that had fallen open when we rolled him. I saw folded paper in the inside pocket. I said, 'Take a look at that.'

Deveraux slid the paper out of the pocket. It looked like an official document, heavy stock, folded three times. It looked old, and I was sure it was. About sixteen years old, almost certainly. Deveraux unfolded it and scanned it and said, 'It's his birth certificate.'

I nodded and took it from her. The State of Mississippi, a male child, family name Lindsay, given name Bruce, born in Carter Crossing. Born eighteen years ago, apparently. It might have withstood a hasty glance, but not further scrutiny. Two digits had been carefully rubbed away, and then two others had been drawn in to replace them. The ink matched well, and the style matched well. Only the breached surface of the paper gave it away.

'My fault,' I said. 'My fault entirely.'

Go straight to Kelham, I had said. There are recruiters on every post. As soon as you've got something in your hand that proves you're eighteen, they'll let you in and never let you out again.

I had meant he would have to wait. But the kid had gone ahead and made himself eighteen years old. He had manufactured something to have in his hand. I started walking back towards the road. Deveraux came after me.

I told her, 'I need a gun.'

She said, 'Why?'

I stopped and looked east. Fort Kelham was a giant rectangle north of the road and its fence ran through a broad belt of trees that extended 200 yards each side of the wire. Easy enough for a small force to stay concealed among them, slipping outwards into the open belt of scrub when necessary, then slipping back inwards and on through the fence for rest or resupply.

I started walking again. I said, 'I'm going to find this quarantine squad that everyone claims doesn't exist.'

'I can't let you do that.'

'They shouldn't have shot the kid, Elizabeth. That was way out of line. They opened the wrong door there. That's for damn sure.'

'You don't even know where they are.'

'They're in the woods.'

'In camouflage with binoculars. How would you get near them? They're shooting people, Reacher.'

'They're shooting the people they see. They won't see me.'

'I'll give you a ride back to town.'

'I want a ride in the other direction. And a firearm.'

She didn't answer.

I said, 'I'm prepared to do it without either thing if necessary.'

She said, 'Get in the car, Reacher.'

We got in the car. Deveraux took off towards Kelham. The right direction, as far as I was concerned. We covered most of the last mile. I said, 'Head off across the grass. To the edge of the woods.'

She slowed, turned the wheel and thumped down off the road onto hard-packed dirt. Two hundred yards north of it Kelham's trees ran away from us in a gentle curve. Deveraux made a wide turn and came to a stop with the flank of the car next to the woods.

I said, 'Gun?'

'This is illegal on so many levels,' she said, pulling the shotgun from its scabbard. It was an old Winchester, forty inches long, seven pounds in weight. It could have been fifty years old, but it seemed well looked after. Even so, I worry about guns I have never fired. Nothing worse than pulling a trigger and having nothing happen.

I asked her, 'Does it work?'

She said, 'It works perfectly.'

I asked, 'Is it loaded?'

She smiled. 'There are six in the magazine and one in the breech. I have spares in the trunk. It was my father's gun. Take care of it.'

'I will.'

We got out of the car and she stepped round to the trunk and opened the lid. It was a messy trunk. There was dirt in it. But I wasn't worrying about tidiness, because there was a metal box bolted to the floor behind the seat back bulkhead. For a woman built like Deveraux, it was long way forward. She went up on tiptoes and bent forward at the waist and leaned in. The manoeuvre looked fabulous from behind. She flipped up the lid of the box and came back out with fifteen twelve-gauge shells. I put five in each trouser pocket and five in my shirt pocket. She watched me do it.

'You have a great ass, by the way,' I said.

'Thank you.'

'We good now? You and me?'

She smiled. 'We always were. I was just yanking your chain.'

'Glad to hear it,' I said. 'I'll see you later.'

'Make sure you do, OK? We have a train to catch tonight.'

I smiled and nodded once, and then I stepped into the trees.

AT FORTY INCHES the Winchester was too long for easy transport through a forest. I carried it two-handed, in front of me.

It was March in Mississippi and there were enough new leaves on the trees to deny me a clear view of the sky. So I navigated by guesswork. The vegetation was dense, but not impossible. There was some underbrush and a lot of leaf litter. The tree trunks were of various thicknesses and mostly three or four feet apart. There were no paths. No sign of recent disturbance.

I had one circumstance working in my favour and two against. The negatives were that I was making a lot of noise, and I was wearing a bright white shirt. No camouflage. No silent approach. The positive was that I had to be approaching them from their rear. They had to be hunkered down just inside the edge of the woods, looking outwards for unexplained strangers. Anyone walking towards them was fair game. But I would be coming from behind.

And I figured I wouldn't be dealing with too many guys at once. Minimum of two, maximum of four men in each unit. They would be looking out past the growth into the bright daylight and the units would be widely scattered. Thirty miles of fence is a lot of ground to defend. You could put a full-strength company in those woods, and one four-man unit would end up 1,000 yards from its nearest neighbour. And 1,000 yards in a wood is the same thing as 1,000 miles. No possibility of immediate support or reinforcement. No covering fire.

After advancing 200 paces roughly north and west, I figured I must be approaching the first obvious viewpoint, inside a bulge that commanded a sweeping view west and south. Almost certainly it was the viewpoint that Bruce Lindsay had been seen from.

I moved cautiously through the trees, almost to the edge of the wood, then stopped. I found myself to be partly right and partly wrong. Where I was standing was indeed an excellent viewpoint, but it was unoccupied. The field of view was wide and wedge-shaped. The road to Carter Crossing ran across it. Nothing was moving on it, but if something had been I would have seen it. There were cigarette butts stamped into the earth. There was a chocolate-bar wrapper. There were clear footprints, similar to the ones I had seen alongside the bled-out journalist on old man Clancy's land. I wasn't impressed. Army Rangers are trained to leave no sign behind.

I backed away and moved north. I stuck to a route fifty yards inside the edge of the wood. I detoured again 200 yards later, back to where the trees thinned, to a spot with a worse view of the road but a better view of the fields. Again, an excellent vantage point. Again, unoccupied.

I moved deeper into the woods and got halfway back to my original line when I heard footsteps and voices, ahead on my left. I moved west and got behind a tree. I leaned my left shoulder on it, levelling the shotgun.

There were three men coming. Slow, relaxed, undisciplined. I heard ragged scuffling from their feet in the leaves. I heard their voices. This was not an orderly advance. These were not first-rate infantry soldiers. The men seemed to be tracking south. No question that they were heading back to one of the viewpoints I had already scoped out. I couldn't see the men but I could hear them. They were about thirty yards away, to my left.

I didn't follow them. Not immediately. I wanted to be sure there were no more coming. I stayed where I was, standing still and listening hard. But I was hearing nothing except the three guys wandering south. I let the three guys get about thirty yards down the track and then I moved after them.

I let myself get within twenty yards of them. Still no visual contact, but I could hear them clearly. There were three of them. One was older than the others, by the sound of it. One wasn't saying much, and the third was nasal and hyped up. I followed them to the first viewpoint. The place where Bruce Lindsay's killers had been hiding out, almost certainly.

I heard them stop just inside the edge of the wood, where the chocolate wrapper, the footprints and the cigarette butts were. I moved towards them, three yards, five, and then I stopped. I heard one of them belch, and I guessed they had moved north for a meal, and were now back on station. I heard rifle barrels parting eye-level branches as they peered out at the open land. I heard the clunk of a Zippo lighter and I smelled tobacco smoke.

I took a breath and moved closer, the Winchester in front of me. I could sense the three guys ahead of me, standing still, looking outwards. I moved up one tree closer to them, then another. Finally I got my first sight of them.

There were three men, as I had thought. They had their backs to me. One was grey-haired and heavy, wearing Vietnam-era olive fatigues and carrying an M16 rifle. I could see a Beretta M9 semiautomatic pistol in a holster on his belt. Standard US army issue, as was the M16. He had paratrooper boots on his feet and no hat.

The second guy was younger and a little taller. He was sandy-haired and wearing Italian army combat fatigues. Similar to ours, but better cut. He was carrying an M16. He was wearing black sneakers. No hat.

The third guy had on 1980s-issue US army camouflage BDUs. He was maybe five feet six, 140 pounds. He was carrying an M16. Civilian shoes, no sidearm. He was the smoker. There was a lit cigarette in his left hand.

The Italian battledress made me wonder if they were a weird NATO force. But the first guy's Vietnam fatigues didn't fit with any current 1997 scenario and neither did the third guy's street shoes, nor did their collective lack of combat headgear, or their lack of portable lunch rations, or their unprofessional behaviour. Then finally I figured it out: they were amateurs.

The Mississippi backwoods, next to Tennessee and Alabama. Civilian militias. Pretend soldiers. Men who like to run around in the woods with guns, but like to say they're defending some vital thing or other. Men who like to buy their guns at certain country gun stores near military bases. A steady stream of M16s and Berettas is written off every year as lost or damaged or otherwise unusable, whereupon it is destroyed—except it isn't. It's hustled out of the back door in the dead of night and an hour later it's under the counter at the gun shop.

I have arrested many people, though I have never been good at it. But I had with me the greatest conversation-stopper ever made: a pump-action shotgun. At the cost of one unfired shell, I could make the most intimidating noise ever heard.

Crunch-crunch.

My ejected shell hit the leaves at my feet. The three guys froze solid.

I said, 'Now the rifles hit the deck.' Normal voice, normal tone.

The sandy-haired guy dropped his rifle first. Then went the older guy and last of all came the wiry one. Their arms came up.

I said, 'And now you take three big paces backwards.'

They complied, all three guys taking exaggerated stumbling steps.

I said, 'And now you turn around.'

The older guy was on my left. He was a little pouchy and worn. The guy in the middle was the sandy-haired one. Just a guy, a little soft and civilised. The third guy was what you get when you eat squirrels for four generations. Smarter than a rat, tougher than a goat, and jumpier than either one.

I was holding the Winchester one-handed. I aimed it less than perfectly at the guys on the right. But it was a twelve-gauge shotgun. My aim didn't need to be perfect. I looked at the older guy. 'Now take out your sidearm and hand it to me. Here's how to do it. You're going to pull it out of the holster with one finger and one thumb, and then you're going to juggle it around and reverse it in your hand, and you're going to point it at yourself, OK?'

No response.

I said, 'Second prize is I shoot you in the legs.'

No response. I thought about pumping the gun again, but I didn't need to. The old guy wasn't a hero. He did the finger and thumb thing, and he got the gun reversed in his hand, and he pressed its muzzle to his belly.

I said, 'Now find the safety and set it to fire.'

It was hard to do backwards, but the guy succeeded.

I said, 'Hold the barrel with your thumb and first two fingers. Get your ring finger back there in the trigger guard. Press on the trigger.'

The guy did it.

I said, 'Any struggle, you get a bullet in the gut. You understand?'

The guy nodded.

I said, 'Now move your arm and bring the gun slowly towards me. Keep it pointing at yourself. Keep your ring finger on the trigger.'

The guy did it. He got the gun a couple of feet out from his centre mass, and I stepped in and took it from him. I stepped back and he dropped his arm and I swapped hands. The Winchester went to my left and I held the Beretta in my right. And breathed out. And smiled.

I looked at the old guy and asked, 'Who are you people?'

He swallowed twice and he said, 'We're on a mission, and it's the kind of mission civilians should stay away from.'

'Are you military personnel?'

The old guy said, 'Yes, we are.'

I said, 'No, you're not. You're a shower of make-believe.'

He said, 'It's a mission authorised by our commander.'

'Who authorised him?'

The guy started to hem and haw. He started talking and stopped a couple of times. I pointed the handgun at the guy. I wasn't sure it worked. But it felt right. And the guy was flinching pretty good. He should know whether the piece worked. Because it was his. I laid my finger hard on the trigger.

Then the sandy-haired guy spoke up. The soft one. He said, 'He doesn't know who authorised the mission, and he's too embarrassed to admit it. That's why he isn't saying anything. Can't you see that? None of us knows who authorised anything. Why would we?'

I asked, 'Where are you from?'

'First tell me who you are.'

'I'm a commissioned officer in the United States Army,' I said. 'Which means that if your so-called mission was authorised by the military, then you must currently be under my command, as the senior officer present. Right? That would be logical, wouldn't it?'

'Yes, sir.'

'Where are you from?'

'Tennessee,' the guy said. 'We're the Tennessee Free Citizens. We got word that we were needed here.'

'How many of you came?'

'There are sixty of us.'

I asked, 'What instructions did you get when you got here?'

'We were told to keep people away, however we had to do it.'

'Why did the nation's military need your help?'

'We weren't told why.'

'Did you kill that kid this morning?'

Silence for a long, long moment.

Then the runt on my right said, 'You mean the black boy?'

I said, 'I mean the African-American teenage male, yes.'

The guy with the sandy hair glanced urgently at his buddies. He said, 'None of us should answer questions about that.'

I said, 'At least one of you should.'

The old guy said, 'This mission is authorised at the very highest level. Whoever you are, mister, you are making a very big mistake.'

I said, 'Shut up.'

The sandy-haired guy looked at the runt. 'Don't say anything.'

I looked at the runt. 'Say what you like. No one will believe you anyway. Everyone knows a guy like you is just there for the ride.'

The runt said, 'I shot the black boy.'

I asked him, 'Why?'

'He was acting aggressive.'

'I saw the corpse. The bullet hit high under his arm. No damage to the arm. I think he had his hands up. I think he was surrendering.'

The runt sniffed. 'I suppose it could have looked that way.'

I pointed the handgun at the little guy. 'Tell me about yesterday.'

He said, 'We were north of here yesterday, and I guess you could say I'm two for two this season.'

'Who applied the field dressing?'

The sandy-haired guy said, 'I did. It was an accident.'

I turned back to the runt and said, 'Tell me again. About sighting in on a sixteen-year-old boy with his hands up.'

The guy grinned. 'I suppose he might have been waving.'

I pulled the trigger. The gun worked fine. Just fine. The sound of the shot cracked and hissed and rolled. Birds flew up in the sky. The spent case ejected and bounced off a tree. The runt went down vertically and then he bounced slackly and spilled over in the kind of boneless tangle only the recently and violently dead can achieve.

I looked at the two survivors and I said, 'Your alleged mission has been terminated. And the Tennessee Free Citizens has been disbanded. You two run along and spread that news. You've got thirty minutes to haul your asses out of my woods and an hour to get out of this state. All fifty-nine of you.

Any slower than that, I'll send a Ranger company after you. Now beat it.'

The two survivors just stood there for a second, pale and shocked and afraid. Then they came to. And they ran. I listened to them go until their noise faded away to nothing. I knew they wouldn't be back.

I clicked the safety on the Beretta and put it in my trouser pocket. I untucked my shirt and let the tails hide it. Then I headed back the way I had come, with the Winchester in front of me.

Elizabeth Deveraux was waiting exactly where she had left me, right next to her car. I stepped out of the woods right in front of her and she jumped a little, but then she gathered herself quickly. I guessed she didn't want to insult me by being surprised I had made it. Or she didn't want to show that she had been anxious. I kissed her, handed back the Winchester, and she asked, 'What happened?'

I said, 'They're some kind of a citizens' council from Tennessee. Some kind of an amateur backwoods militia. They're leaving now.'

'I heard a handgun.'

'One of them was so overcome with regret he committed suicide.'

'Who brought them here?'

I said, 'That's the big question, isn't it?'

I returned her spare ammunition from my pockets. She made me put it in the trunk myself. We drove back to town. When we pulled in to the Sheriff's Department's lot, she said, 'Go and get a cup of coffee. I'll be back soon.'

'Where are you going?'

'I have to give Mrs Lindsay the news about her son.'

I watched her drive away and then I headed to the diner for coffee. And for the phone. I kept my mug close at hand on the hostess station and dialled Stan Lowrey's office. He picked up. I said, 'You're still there. You've got a job. I don't believe it.'

'I think that I'm safer than you are right now. What do you want?'

'I want you to check some names for me. In every database you can find. Mostly civilian, including government. Call the D.C. police and try to get them to help. The FBI too. If there's anyone there still speaking to you.'

'On the up and up or on the quiet?'

'On the very quiet.'

'What names?'

'Janice May Chapman,' I said.

'That's the dead woman, right?'

'One of several. And Audrey Shaw,' I said.

'Who is she?'

'I don't know. That's why I want you to check her out.'

'What else?'

I asked, 'How far away is Garber's office from yours?'

'It's on the other side of the stairwell.'

'I need him on the line. So go and get him and drag him over.'

'Why not just call him direct?'

'Because I want him on your line, not his.'

No answer, except a thump as he put the phone on his desk. Then silence. Minutes passed. Then I heard the phone lift up off the desk and a familiar voice asked, 'What do you want?'

'I want to talk to you,' I said.

'So call me. We have switchboards now. And extensions.'

'They're listening to your line. I think that's obvious, isn't it? You're a pawn, the same as me. Therefore someone else's line is safer.'

Garber was quiet for a beat. 'Possible. What have you got for me?'

'The boots on the ground outside Kelham were a local citizens' militia, part of some weirdo network of true patriots. Apparently they were here to defend the army from unjustified harassment.'

'Well, Mississippi,' he said. 'What do you expect?'

'They were from Tennessee, actually. They weren't just passing by on a whim. They were deployed here. They have a contact who knew exactly when, exactly where, exactly how, and exactly why they would be needed. Who would have that information?'

'Someone who had all the facts from the get-go.'

'And where would we find such a person?'

'Somewhere high up.'

'I agree,' I said. 'Any idea who?'

'None at all.'

'OK, go back to your office. Five minutes from now I'm going to call you. You can ignore what I say, because it won't mean much. But stay on the line long enough to let the tape recorders roll.'

'Wait,' Garber said. 'There's something I have to tell you. News from the Marine Corps. There's an issue with Elizabeth Deveraux.'

'What kind of issue?'

'I don't know yet. They're playing hard to get, making a big deal about access. The file she's in is apparently some highest category, biggest deal in the world. Word is there was a big scandal five years ago. Deveraux got a Marine MP fired for no good reason. Rumours say it was personal jealousy.'

'Five years ago is three years before she quit. Was she honourably discharged?'

'Yes, she was.'

'Voluntary separation or involuntary?'

'Voluntary.'

'Then there's nothing there,' I said. 'Don't worry about it. Five minutes. Be back at your desk.'

The waitress freshened my cup and I drank most of the new brew while I counted 300 seconds in my head. Then I stepped back to the phone and dialled Garber. He answered and I said, 'Sir, this is Major Reacher reporting from Mississippi. Can you hear me?'

Garber said, 'Loud and clear.'

I said, 'I have the name of the individual who ordered the Tennessee Free Citizens to Kelham. That order became part of a criminal conspiracy in that it resulted in two homicides and two felony assaults. I have an appointment I need to keep at the Pentagon the day after tomorrow, and then I'll return to base immediately and I'll get Judge Advocate General's Corps involved.'

Garber was on the ball. He caught on fast and played his part well. He asked, 'Who was the individual?'

'I'll keep that to myself for forty-eight hours, if you don't mind.'

Garber said, 'Understood.'

I dabbed the cradle to end the call and then I dialled a new number. Colonel John James Frazer's billet in the Pentagon. The Senate Liaison guy. I got his scheduler and made a twelve o'clock appointment with him, in his office, for the day after next. I didn't say why, because I didn't have a real reason. I just needed to be somewhere in the giant building. As bait in a trap.

Then I sat at a table and waited for Deveraux. She came in thirty minutes later, looking pale and drawn. She sat down.

'Bad?' I asked.

She nodded. 'Terrible. That woman is going to take a midnight stroll on the railroad tracks. I guarantee it.'

'Has that happened before?'

'Not often. But the train is always there, once a night. Like a reminder that there's a way out if you need one.'

I said nothing. I wanted to remember the midnight train in a happier context.

She said, 'I want to ask you a question, but I'm not going to.'

'What question?'

'Who put those idiots in the woods?'

'Why aren't you going to ask it?'

'I'm assuming there's a bunch of interconnected things here. Some big crisis on the base. A part answer wouldn't make sense. You'd have to tell me everything. I don't want to ask you to do that.'

'I don't know everything. If I knew everything I wouldn't be here any more. The job would be done and I'd be back on post doing the next thing.'

'So who put those idiots in the woods?' she asked.

'I don't know,' I said. 'Kelham is a pie and there are lots of folks with their fingers in it. Any of them could feel threatened in some way bad enough to pull a stunt like this.'

'But you're going to nail the person responsible?'

'Of course. Day after tomorrow, I hope. I have to go to D.C. for a night.'

'Why?'

'I got on a line I knew to be tapped and said I knew a name. So now I have to go and hang out up there to see what comes out of the woodwork.'

'You made yourself the bait in a trap?'

'Same difference if I go to them or they come to me.'

'I agree. It's time to shake something loose. If you want to know if the stove is hot, sometimes the only way to find out is to touch it.'

'You must have been a pretty good cop. So when did you stop enjoying being a Marine?'

'For years I laughed off the small things, but they came so thick and fast that eventually I realised an avalanche is made up of small things. Suddenly the small things were big things.'

'No single specific thing?'

'No, I got through fine. I had some minor bumps here and there. I dated the wrong guy once or twice. But nothing worth talking about. I made it to CWO5, which is as high as it goes for some of us.'

'You did well.'

'Not bad for a country girl from Carter Crossing.'

'We should have lunch now.'

'That's why I came in.'

DEVERAUX'S LUNCH STAPLE was chicken pie. We ordered a pair and were halfway through eating them when the couple from the hotel came in. The old guy saw me and detoured to our table. He told me my brother-in-law Stanley had just called. Something very urgent.

'OK,' I said. 'Thanks.'

The old guy shuffled off and I said, 'Major Stan Lowrey. A friend.'

I started eating again, but she said, 'You should call him back if it's very urgent, don't you think?'

I put my fork down. 'Probably,' I said. 'But don't eat my pie.' I went back to the phone for the third time and dialled.

Lowrey answered on the first ring. 'Are you sitting down?'

I said, 'No, I'm standing up. I'm on a payphone in a diner.'

'Hold on tight. I have a story for you. About a girl called Audrey.'

I leaned on the wall next to the phone. Lowrey's stories were usually very long. He liked background. And context.

He said, 'Audrey is a very ancient name, apparently.'

The only way to knock Lowrey off his discursive stride was to get your retaliation in first. I said, 'Audrey was an Anglo-Saxon name, a diminutive of Aethelthryt or Etheldreda. It means noble strength. There was a St Audrey in the seventh century. She was the patron saint of throat complaints.'

'How do you know stuff like this? I had to look it up. My point is, it's no longer a common name. If you search for Audreys you don't get many hits.'

'So you found Audrey Shaw for me?'

'I think so,' Lowrey said. 'She's an American citizen, Caucasian female, born in Kansas City, Missouri, went to college at Tulane in Louisiana. She was a party girl. Middling grades. After graduation she used family connections to get an intern's job in D.C.'

'What kind of intern's job?'

'Political. In a Senate office. Working for one of her home-state Missouri guys. She was beautiful, apparently. She made strong men weak at the knees. So guess what happened? She had an affair. With a married man.'

'Who was the guy?'

'The senator himself. The record gets a little hazy from that point onwards, because the thing was covered up like crazy. But between the lines it was a torrid business. People say she was in love.'

'Where are you getting this from, if the record is hazy?'

'The FBI,' Lowrey said. 'Plenty of them still talk to me.'

'How long did the affair last?'

'Senators have to run for re-election every six years, so generally they spend the first four rolling around on the couch and the last two cleaning up their act. Young Ms Shaw got the last two of the good years and then she was patted on the butt and sent on her way.'

'And where is she now?'

'This is where it gets interesting,' Lowrey said. I looked over at Deveraux. She was eating what was left of my pie. Lowrey said, 'I've got rumours and hard facts. The rumours come from the FBI. The hard facts come from the databases. Which do you want first?'

'The rumours,' I said. 'Always much more interesting.'

'OK, the rumours say Ms Shaw felt very unhappy about being discarded. She began to look like the kind of intern that could cause trouble. That was the FBI's opinion. But the parties must have reached some mutual accommodation. Everything went quiet. The senator was re-elected and Shaw was never heard from again.'

'Where is she now?'

'This is where you ask me what the hard facts say.'

'What do the hard facts say?'

'They say Audrey Shaw isn't anywhere. The databases are blank. No taxes, no purchases, no cars or houses or boats or trailers, no warrants or judgments or arrests or convictions. It's like she ceased to exist three years ago.'

'How old was she then?'

'She was twenty-four. She'd be twenty-seven now.'

'Did you check the other name for me? Janice May Chapman?'

'You just spoiled my surprise. You just ruined my story.'

'Let me guess,' I said. 'Chapman is the exact reverse. There's nothing there more than three years old.'

'Correct.'

'They were the same person,' I said. 'Shaw changed her identity. Part of the deal, presumably. A big bag of cash and a stack of new paperwork. Like a witness protection programme.'

'And now she's dead. End of story. Anything else?'

There was one last question. But I hardly needed to ask it. I was sure I knew the answer. I asked, 'Who was the senator?'

'Carlton Riley,' Lowrey said. 'Mr Riley of Missouri. The man himself. The chairman of the Armed Services Committee.'

EIGHT

I got back to the table as the waitress was putting down two slices of peach pie and two cups of coffee. Deveraux started eating immediately. She was a chicken pie ahead of me and she was still hungry. I gave her a lightly edited recap of Lowrey's information. Everything except for the words Missouri, Carlton and Riley.

She asked, 'What made you give him Audrey Shaw's name?'

'Flip of a coin,' I said. 'A fifty-fifty chance. Either Butler's buddy screwed up her case numbers or she didn't.'

'Does this stuff help us?'

I said, 'It might narrow things down. If a senator has a problem, which of the chains of command is going to react?'

'Senate Liaison,' she said.

'That's where I'm going. The day after tomorrow.'

'Wait,' she said. 'Why would the army get involved if a senator had a problem with a girl? That's a civilian matter. I mean, Senate Liaison doesn't get involved every time a politician loses his car keys. There would have to be a military connection. And there's no military connection between a civilian senator and his civilian ex-girlfriend, no matter where she lives.'

I didn't answer.

She looked at me. 'Chapman wasn't in the army and there aren't any senators in the army. Did Chapman have a brother in the army? Is that it? Jesus, is her *father* in the army? Was Chapman a general's daughter?'

I said nothing.

She said, 'Or maybe the senator is the one with a relative in uniform.'

'You're missing the point,' I said. 'If Janice May Chapman was a sudden short-term problem who required a sudden short-term solution, why was she killed in exactly the same way as two other unconnected women six and nine months previously?'

'Are you saying it's a coincidence? Nothing to do with the senator connection? Then why the big panic?'

'Because they're worried about blowback. In general. They don't want any kind of taint coming near a particular unit.'

'They weren't worried about blowback six and nine months ago?'

'They didn't know about six and nine months ago. Why would they? But Chapman jumped out at them. She had two kinds of extra visibility. Her name was in the files and she was white.'

WE FINISHED OUR DESSERTS. Deveraux told me she had work to do. I asked her if she would mind if I went to see Emmeline McClatchy.

'Why?' she asked.

'Boyfriends,' I said. 'Apparently both Lindsay and Chapman were stepping out with a soldier who owned a blue car. I'm wondering if McClatchy is going to make it a trifecta.'

'That's a long walk.'

'I'll find a short cut,' I said. I was beginning to piece together the local geography in my head. No need to walk three sides of a square, first north to the Kelham road, then east, then south again to the McClatchy shack. I figured I could find a way across the railroad track well short of the official crossing. A straight shot east. One side of the square.

Deveraux said, 'She's very upset. Don't say anything about pregnancy.'

'I won't,' I said.

I headed south on Main Street, in the general direction of Dr Merriam's office, but about 300 yards before I got there I turned east. I saw a dirt road nested in the trees. I found a house 100 feet later. It was a tumbledown, swaybacked affair, but it had people living in it. The fourth house I came to was abandoned, its mailbox hidden by tall grass. Its driveway was overgrown. It had brambles against the door and the windows. It was standing alone in a couple of acres of what might have been meadow or pasture but was now nothing more than a briar patch crowded with sapling trees about six feet tall. The place must have been empty for a long time. A couple of years, maybe. But it had fresh tyre tracks across its turn-in.

Seasonal rains had left a smooth puddle of mud in the dip between the road and the driveway. Seasonal heat had baked the mud to powder. A four-wheeled vehicle had crossed it twice, in and out. The marks were recent.

I jumped over the dip and fought through a tangle of waist-high weeds. I could see where the tyres had crushed the weeds. There were broken stalks. Whoever had rolled down the driveway had not entered the house. None of the rampant growth round the doors or windows had been disturbed. I walked past the house, out to the space behind.

There was a belt of trees ahead of me, and another to my left, and another to my right. It was a lonely spot. I moved on to an abandoned vegetable garden. Beyond was a long high mound of something green and vigorous. An old hedge, maybe, run to seed. Behind it were two structures. The first structure was an old wooden shed, rotting and listing.

The other structure was a deer trestle.

THE DEER TRESTLE was built in an A-frame style from solid timbers. It was at least seven feet tall. I guessed the idea was to back up a pick-up and dump a dead animal onto the dirt between the A-frames, and then to tie ropes to the animal's hind legs and to flip the ropes up over the top rail, and then to use the pick-up to haul the animal up in the air so that it hung vertically and upside down, ready for the butcher's knife.

The trestle could have been fifty years old. Its timbers were seasoned and solid. The dirt between its legs had been disturbed recently. The top two or three inches had been dug up and removed, leaving a shallow pit about three feet square. The shed next to the trestle was empty.

I walked back down to the road, stopped at the mouth of the driveway and parted the grass around the mailbox. It was standard size, flecked with rust. There had been a name on the box, spelled out in stick-on letters printed on forward-leaning rectangles. They had been peeled off, but they had left dry webs of adhesive residue behind, like fingerprints.

There had been eight letters on the box.

I jumped the ditch and continued east. The road narrowed, burrowing into a wall of trees. I pressed on. Fifty paces later I came out on the other side and found the railroad track blocking my path. At that location it was up on a raised earth berm about a yard high.

I scrambled up the yard of earth and crunched over the ballast stones and stood on a tie. To my right the track ran all the way south to the Gulf. To my left it ran north. I could see the road crossing in the distance, and the old water tower. Ahead of me were more trees, and beyond them was a field, and beyond the field were houses.

I heard a helicopter, somewhere east and a little north. I scanned the horizon and saw a Black Hawk in the air, about three miles away. Heading for Kelham, I assumed. I listened to the *whap-whap-whap* of its rotor, and I watched it come in to land. Then I scrambled down the far side of the earth berm and headed on through the next belt of trees.

I hiked across the field that came after that and stepped over a wire and found myself on a street I figured was parallel with Emmeline McClatchy's. But between it and me were other houses. I walked through their yards and heard the Black Hawk again, taking off from Kelham. A short visit for somebody, or a delivery, or a pick-up. I saw it rise above the treetops, a distant speck, nose down, accelerating north.

I looped past a ramshackle bar building and out to the street. And saw an army Humvee easing to a stop outside the McClatchy house.

A HUMVEE is a very wide vehicle, and it was on a very narrow dirt road. It almost filled it, ditch to ditch. I walked towards it and it came to a stop and the motor shut off. The driver's door opened and a guy climbed down. He was in woodland-pattern BDUs. Since before the start of my career, battle-dress uniform had been worn with subdued name tapes and badges of rank, and they were unreadable from more than three or four feet away. The result was I had no idea who had just got out of the Humvee.

But I had a clear premonition about who the guy was. Who else was authorised to be out and about? He even looked like me. Same kind of height, same kind of build, similar colouring. It was like looking in a mirror, except he was five years my junior.

He watched me approach, curious about who I was, a white man in a black neighbourhood. I let him gawk until I was six feet away. My eyesight is good, and I can read subdued tapes from farther than I should. His tapes said: *Munro. US Army.* He had little black oak leaves on his collar, to show he was a major.

I stuck out my hand and said, 'Jack Reacher.'

He took it and said, 'Duncan Munro.'

I asked, 'What brings you here?'

He said, 'Let's sit in the truck a spell.'

A Humvee is equally wide inside, but most of the space is taken up by a gigantic transmission tunnel. The front seats are small and far apart. It was like sitting in adjacent traffic lanes.

Munro said, 'The situation is changing. The officer in question has been relieved of his command.'

'Reed Riley?'

'We're not supposed to use that name.'

'Was that him in the Black Hawk?'

Munro nodded. 'He's on his way back to Fort Benning. Then they're going to move him on and hide him away somewhere.'

'Why?'

'There was some big panic two hours ago. The phone lines were burning up. I don't know why.'

'Kelham just lost its quarantine force, that's why.'

'That again? There never was a quarantine force. I told you that.'

'I just met them. Bunch of civilian yahoos. I chased them away.'

'So then someone felt he had to withdraw Riley. You're not going to be popular.'

'I don't want to be popular. I want to get the job done.' I looked out of my window at the McClatchy place. 'Why did you come here?'

'Same reason you chased the yahoos away,' Munro said. 'I'm trying to get the job done. I checked out the other two women you mentioned. There were FYI memos in the XO's files. Then I cross-referenced information I picked up along the way. It seems like Captain Riley is something of a ladies' man. It's likely both Janice Chapman and Shawna Lindsay were on the list. I want to see if Rosemary McClatchy will make it three for three.'

'That's why I'm here, too. Did you bring his picture?'

He unbuttoned his right breast pocket, just below his name. He pulled out a slim black notebook and opened it and slid a photograph from between its pages. He handed it to me.

Captain Reed Riley. The first time I had seen his face. The photo was in colour. He looked to be in his late twenties. He was broad but chiselled. He was tanned. He had brown hair buzzed short, and wise empty eyes creased at the corners. He looked steady, competent and hard. He looked like every infantry captain I had ever seen.

I handed the picture back. 'We'll be lucky to get a definitive ID. I bet all Rangers look the same to old Mrs McClatchy.'

'Only one way to find out,' Munro said, and opened his door. I got out on my side. He said, 'I'll tell you something else that came up with the cross-referencing. Sheriff Deveraux is a notch on Riley's bedpost too. Apparently they were dating less than a year ago.'

And then he walked ahead of me, to Emmeline McClatchy's door.

She opened up after Munro's second knock and greeted us with polite reserve. She remembered me. After Munro introduced himself, she invited us inside, to a small room that had two wooden chairs on either side of a fireplace and a rag rug on the floor. There were three framed photographs on the wall. One was Martin Luther King, and one was President Clinton, and the third was Rosemary McClatchy, from the same series as the picture I had seen in the Sheriff's Department's file.

Emmeline and I took the chairs by the fireplace and left Munro standing on the rug. He took the photograph from his pocket again and held it face down against his chest. He said, 'Mrs McClatchy, we need to ask you about your daughter Rosemary's friends. In particular one young man from the base she might have been seeing.'

'Let me see the picture.'

Munro bent down and handed it over. She studied it. She asked, 'Is this man suspected of killing the white girl?'

Munro said, 'We're not sure. We can't rule him out.'

'Nobody brought pictures to me when Rosemary was killed. Nobody brought pictures to Mrs Lindsay when Shawna was killed. Why is that?'

Munro said, 'Because the army made a bad mistake. There's no excuse for it. All I can say is it would have been different if I had been involved back then. Or Major Reacher here. Beyond that, all I can do is apologise.'

She looked at the picture again and said, 'This man's name is Reed Riley. He's a captain in the 75th Ranger Regiment.'

'So they were dating?'

'Almost four months. She was talking about a life together.'

'Was he?'

'Men will say anything to get what they want.'

'When did it end?'

'Two weeks before she was killed.'

'Why did it end?'

'She didn't tell me.'

'Did you have an opinion?'

Emmeline McClatchy said, 'I think she got pregnant. She acted different. She looked different. At first she was happy, and then later she was miserable. I didn't ask her anything. I thought she would come to me on her own. But she didn't get the chance.'

Munro asked, 'Do you think Captain Riley killed her?'

'Rosemary said his father was an important man. Politics, perhaps. Something where image matters. I think a black girlfriend was a good thing for Captain Riley, but a pregnant girlfriend wasn't.'

EMMELINE MCCLATCHY wouldn't be pushed any further. We said our good-byes and walked back to the Humvee. Munro said, 'This is looking bad.'

I asked him, 'Did you speak to Shawna Lindsay's mother too?'

'She wouldn't say a word to me.'

'How solid is the information about Sheriff Deveraux?'

'Rock solid. They dated, he ended it, she wasn't happy. Then Rosemary McClatchy was next up, as far as I can piece it together.'

'Was it his car that got wrecked on the track?'

'According to the Oregon DMV it was. Via the plate you found.'

'Did he have an explanation?'

'No, he had a lawyer.'

'Can you prove he was Janice Chapman's boyfriend too?'

'Not beyond a reasonable doubt. She was a party girl. She was seen with a lot of guys. She can't have been dating all of them.'

'Did you know she wasn't really Janice Chapman?'

'What do you mean?'

'She was born Audrey Shaw. She changed her name three years ago.'

'Why?'

'Politics,' I said. 'She was coming off a two-year affair with Carlton Riley.'

I LEFT HIM with that information and walked away south. He drove north. Five minutes later, I was inside the Sheriff's Department in Deveraux's office. She was behind her desk.

I said, 'We need to talk.'

Deveraux looked up at me. She said, 'Talk about what?'

I asked her, 'Did you ever date a guy from the base?'

'Of course not. Are you crazy? You know how it is between a military population and local law enforcement. It would have been the worst kind of conflict of interest. Why are you asking?'

'Munro was at the McClatchy place. Rosemary McClatchy and Shawna Lindsay seem to have dated the same guy. Janice Chapman also, probably. Munro heard you had dated the guy too.'

'That's bull. I haven't dated a guy in two years. Couldn't you tell?'

I sat down. 'I had to ask,' I said. 'I'm sorry.'

'Who was the guy?'

'I can't tell you.'

'You have to tell me. McClatchy and Lindsay are my cases. Therefore it's relevant information. And I have a right to know if some guy is taking my name in vain.'

'Reed Riley,' I said.

'Never heard of him,' she said. Then, 'Wait a minute. Did you say Riley?'

I didn't answer.

'Carlton Riley's son? He's at Kelham? That explains a lot.'

I said, 'It was his car on the railroad track. And Emmeline McClatchy thinks he got Rosemary pregnant. I didn't ask her. She came out with it.'

'I need to talk to him.'

'You can't. They just choppered him out of there.'

'To where?'

'What's the most remote army post in the world?'

'I don't know.'

'Neither do I. But a buck gets ten that's where he'll be tonight.'

'Why would he say he dated me?'

'Ego,' I said. 'Maybe he wanted his pals to believe he had collected the four most beautiful women in Carter Crossing.'

'His father probably knows the guy Janice Chapman had the affair with. They're in the Senate together.'

I said nothing.

She looked right at me. She said, 'Oh, no.'

I said, 'Oh, yes.'

'The same woman? Father and son?'

'Munro can't prove it. Neither can we.'

'Whatever, you can't go to D.C. It's far too dangerous. You'll be walking around with a target on your back. Senate Liaison has got a lot invested in Carlton Riley. They won't let you screw things up.'

Deveraux's phone rang. She picked up and listened for a minute. She covered the mouthpiece and said, 'I have to take this call.'

Then she got busy with unrelated police matters. I wandered out of her office and I didn't talk to her again until dinner at nine o'clock.

AT DINNER WE TALKED about her father's house. She ordered her cheeseburger and I got a roast beef sandwich and I asked her, 'What was it like growing up here?'

'It was weird,' she said. 'Obviously I didn't have anything to compare it to, and we didn't get television until I was ten, and we never went to the movies, but even so I sensed there had to be more out there. We all did.'

Then she asked where I grew up, so I went through as much as I could remember. Conceived in the Pacific, born in West Berlin when my father was assigned to the embassy, a dozen different bases before elementary school, education all over the world. Then West Point, and a restless, always-moving career of my own.

'Where was your house?' I asked.

'South on Main Street until it curves, and then first on the left. A little dirt road. Fourth house on the right.'

'Is it still there?'

'Just about. My dad was sick before he died and he let the place go.'

'All overgrown, with slime on the walls and a cracked foundation? A big old hedge at the back? Eight letters on the mailbox?'

'How do you know all that?'

'I was there. I passed by on my way to the McClatchy place.'

She didn't answer.

I said, 'I saw the deer trestle. And I saw the dirt in the trunk of your car. When you gave me the shotgun shells.'

The waitress came by and picked up our empty plates and took our orders for pie. She went away and Deveraux was left looking at me. A little embarrassed, I thought.

'I did a stupid thing,' she said. 'I hunt. Just for fun. Deer, mostly. I give the meat to the old folks, like Emmeline McClatchy. They don't eat well.'

'I remember,' I said. 'Emmeline had deer meat in the pot when we were there the first time. She offered us lunch. You declined.'

'I got that deer a week ago. I couldn't take it back to the hotel. So I used my dad's place. That's a good trestle. But then you came up with your theory about Janice Chapman. I thought you might get on the phone to HQ. I had visions of Black Hawks in the air, finding every trestle in the county. So I sent you off to ID the wrecked car so you would be out of the way for an hour, and I went over and dug up the blood.'

'Tests would have proved it came from an animal.'

'I know,' she said. 'But how long would that have taken? I don't even know where the nearest lab is. Atlanta, maybe. It could have taken two weeks. I can't afford to be under a cloud for two weeks. This is the only job I have. I don't know where I'd get another one.'

'OK,' I said. 'But it was a fairly dumb thing to do.'

'I know it was. I panicked a little bit.'

'Do you know other hunters? And other trestles?'

'Some.'

'Because I still think that's how those women were killed. Sooner or later we might need to get those Black Hawks in the air. But first I'll see what comes out of the woodwork the day after tomorrow.'

'I'll have Pellegrino drive you to Memphis.'

We ate our pie slowly. We had time to kill. At that point the midnight train was probably just easing out of Biloxi.

DEVERAUX WAS STILL WORRIED about the old man in the hotel, and she didn't want to repeat her charade at the top of the stairs, so I gave her my key and we left the diner separately, ten minutes apart, which left me with the bill. Then I strolled down the street and nodded to the guy behind the desk and headed upstairs and tapped on my own door. Deveraux opened up and I stepped inside. She had taken her shoes and her gun belt off.

We slowly undressed each other, and then we set my shower running and climbed into the tub together and pulled the curtain. We grabbed soap and shampoo and washed each other.

We stayed in the shower until Toussaint's tank ran cool, and then we grabbed enough towels to make sure we wouldn't put puddles in my bed, and then the serious business began. We were very patient. I figured the midnight train was maybe forty miles and forty minutes away.

And forty minutes is a long time. Halfway through it there was little we didn't know about each other. I knew the way she moved, what she liked, and what she loved. She knew the same about me. We began a long slow build-up, with a certain time in mind. Eventually the glass on my bathroom shelf began to tinkle. The French doors shook, the floorboards vibrated, the bedhead beat on the wall in a rhythm not our own.

The midnight train. Right on time. But this time it was different.

The train's sound was not the same. Its pitch was low. Its distant rumble was overlaid with the grinding howl of brakes. Deveraux slipped out from under me and sat up, listening hard. The grinding howl kept going, mournful, primitive, impossibly long, and then it started to fade, partly because the train's momentum had carried it far beyond the crossing, and partly because it was almost at a stop.

By my side Deveraux whispered, 'Oh, no.'

WE DRESSED FAST and were out on the street two minutes later. Deveraux took two flashlights from her trunk. She lit one up and gave one to me. We used the alley between the hardware store and the pharmacy, past Janice Chapman's sad pile of sand, between the loan office and Brannan's Bar.

Deveraux walked ahead of me. She was going to the railroad track. She scrambled up the packed stones and stepped over the bright steel onto the ties. She turned south. I figured the engineer would be twenty minutes behind us. His train weighed about 8,000 tons. Sometimes MPs are traffic cops and our traffic includes tank trains, which weigh about 8,000 tons. It takes a tank train about a mile to stop. And it takes a man twenty minutes to walk a mile, so we would get there twenty minutes before the engineer did.

We were headed to where I had walked twice that day, where the field to the east crossed the track before heading into the woods to the west. Deveraux started playing her flashlight beam left and right.

I did the same thing, and it fell to me to find it. All that was left. It was a human foot, amputated just above the ankle. The black shoe was still in place. A polished black item, plain and modest, with a low heel. The stocking was still under it. Under its beige opacity was ebony skin.

'Those were her church shoes,' Deveraux said. 'She was a nice woman at heart. I am so, so sorry this happened.'

'I never met her,' I said. 'She was out. That was the first thing the kid ever said to me. "My mom's out," he said.'

We sat on a tie and waited for the engineer. He joined us fifteen minutes later. There wasn't much he could tell us. Just the lonely glare of the headlight, and the briefest subliminal flash of a white lining inside a black coat falling open, and then it was all over.

The engineer and Deveraux exchanged reference numbers and names and addresses, per regulations, and Deveraux asked him if he was OK or wanted help, but he brushed the concerns aside and set off walking north again, a mile back to his cab.

We went back to Main Street, to the Sheriff's Department. Deveraux called Pellegrino and told him to come back in on overtime, and she called the doctor and told him he had more duties to perform. They arrived almost together within a matter of minutes. Maybe they had heard the train too.

Deveraux sent them off to collect the remains. They were back within half an hour. The doctor left again for his office and Deveraux told Pellegrino to drive me to Memphis.

I DIDN'T GO BACK to the hotel. I left directly from the Sheriff's Department, with nothing except cash in one pocket and the Beretta in the other. We saw no passing traffic. No big surprise. It was the dead of night, and we were far from anywhere. Pellegrino didn't talk. He just drove. We arrived at the bus depot in Memphis before dawn.

Fifty minutes later I was in the back of a bus, heading north and east. I watched the sun come up through the window on my right, and then I slept for the rest of the six-hour ride. I got out at the depot on the edge of the town close to the post where I was based. I was back on post and in my quarters before two o'clock in the afternoon.

The first thing I did was take a long hot shower. I dried off and dressed in full-on Class A uniform, soup to nuts. Then I called Stan Lowrey and asked him for a ride back to the bus depot. I reckoned I could get to D.C. by dinner time. I told Lowrey to make no secret of where I was going. I figured the more people who knew, the better chance things would have to come crawling out of the woodwork.

WASHINGTON D.C. at seven o'clock on a Monday evening was going quiet. A company town, where the company was America, and where work never really stopped, but where it moved into quiet confidential locations after five in the afternoon. Salons, bars, fancy restaurants, those locations were unknown to me, but I knew the neighbourhoods most likely to contain them. So I skipped the kind of distant chain hotels a low-paid O4 like me would normally use, and I headed for the brighter lights and the cleaner streets and the higher prices south of Dupont Circle. Not that I was intending to pay for anything. Legend had it there was a fancy place on Connecticut Avenue with a glitch in its back office, whereby uniformed guests were automatically billed to the Department of the Army.

I walked there slowly, in the centre of every sidewalk I used. I used store windows as mirrors. No one paid me any attention. I got to the hotel and checked in, and the legend held up. I was asked for no deposit. All I had to do was sign a piece of paper.

I rode the elevator to my room and called down and asked for dinner to be delivered. Thirty minutes later I was eating a sirloin steak, which would also be billed to the Pentagon.

I went to bed in my luxurious room, and I waited to see what would happen the next day, Tuesday, March 11, 1997.

NINE

I woke up at seven and let the Department of the Army buy me a room-service breakfast. By eight I was showered and dressed and out on the street. I figured this was when the serious business would begin. A noon appointment at the Pentagon for a guy based as far away as I was made it likely I would have stayed in town the night before, and Washington hotels were easily monitored. It was that kind of city. So I half expected opposition in the lobby, or right outside the street door. I found it in neither place. It was a fresh spring morning and the sun was out.

I bought a *Post* and a *Times* at a kiosk, went to a coffee shop and sat at an outside table. No one looked at me.

By ten o'clock I was full of coffee and had read the ink off both broadsheets and no passer-by had shown any interest in me. I began to think it likely the opposition would be focusing on the end of my journey, not a stop along the way. Which meant they would be waiting for me in or around the Pentagon, at or before twelve o'clock.

I walked south on 17th Street, past the Executive Office building next to the White House and on to the Mall. I looped left of the Abraham Lincoln Memorial and found my way onto the Arlington Memorial Bridge and stepped out over the waters of the Potomac. I stopped halfway across, leaned on a rail. But there was no one behind me. So I moved on again and I arrived in Virginia. Ahead of me was Arlington National Cemetery.

I detoured to pay my respects to the Unknown Soldier, then walked to the cemetery's south gate. There it was: the Pentagon. Six and a half million square feet, but just three street doors. I joined the stream of people coming in to the southeast entrance from the Metro station. I wanted witnesses. Arrests go bad all the time, sometimes accidentally, sometimes on purpose.

But I got in OK, despite a little uncertainty in the lobby. What I thought was an arrest team turned out to be a new watch coming on duty. So I made it to 3C315 unmolested. John James Frazer's office. Senate Liaison. There was no one in there with him. He told me to close the door. I did. He told me to sit down. I did.

He said, 'So what have you got for me?'

I said nothing. I hadn't expected to get that far.

He said, 'Good news, I hope.'

'No news,' I said.

'You told me you had the name. That's what your message said.'

'I don't have the name.'

'Then why say so? Why ask to see me?'

I paused a beat. 'It was a short cut,' I said.

And right there the meeting died. Frazer put on a big show of being tolerant. He called me paranoid. He laughed a little. Then he looked concerned. He said, 'You look terrible. There are barbershops here, you know. You should use one.'

'I can't,' I said. 'I'm supposed to look like this.'

'Because of the undercover role? But you're not really undercover. I heard the sheriff rumbled you. Anyway, I expect you'll be withdrawn now. Matters appear to be resolved in Mississippi. The shootings outside Kelham were clearly a case of an excess of zeal from an unauthorised paramilitary force from another state. The authorities in Tennessee will take care of that.'

'They were ordered there.'

'No, I don't think so. Those groups have extensive underground communications. We think it will prove to be a civilian initiative.'

'What about the three dead women?'

'The perpetrator has been identified, I believe.'

'Who is it?'

'I don't have all the details.'

'One of ours?'

'No, I believe it was a local person. Anyway, thank you for coming in. This meeting is over, Major.'

I said, 'No, Colonel, it isn't.'

THE PENTAGON WAS BUILT because World War Two was coming, and it was built without much steel. Thus the giant building was a monument to the strength and mass of concrete. The result was extreme solidity. And silence. There were 30,000 people the other side of Frazer's closed door, but I couldn't hear any of them. I couldn't hear anything at all.

Frazer said, 'Don't forget you're talking to an officer senior to you.'

I said, 'Don't forget you're talking to an MP authorised to arrest anyone from a newborn private to a five-star general.'

'What's your point?'

'The Tennessee Free Citizens were ordered to Kelham. That's clear. And, I agree, they acted with an excess of zeal when they got there. But that's on the guy who gave the order, as much as it's on them.'

'No one gave any orders.'

'They were dispatched at the same moment I was. And Munro. We all converged. It was one single integrated decision. Because Reed Riley was there. Who knew that?'

'Perhaps it was a local decision.'

'What was your personal position?'

'Purely reactive. I was ready to handle the fallout. Nothing more.'

'You could have seen the danger coming and decided to defend Kelham's fence from pesky civilians asking awkward questions. But you couldn't ask the Rangers to do that themselves. No commander would recognise that as a legal order. So you could have called some buddies. From Tennessee, which is your home state.'

'No, that's ridiculous.'

'And then you could have decided to tap MP phones, to give yourself a warning in case things headed in the wrong direction.'

'That's ridiculous too.'

'Do you deny it?'

'Of course I deny it.'

I asked, 'How good is your short-term memory?'

'Good enough.'

'What was the first thing you said to me when I came in here?'

'I told you to close the door.'

'No, you said hello. Then you told me to close the door.'

'And then I told you to sit down.'

'And then we had talked about how busy this place is at noon. And then you asked me what news I had.'

'And you didn't have any.'

'Which surprised you. Because I had left a message in which I told you I had the name. What name?'

'I wasn't sure. It might have concerned anything.'

'In which case you would have said *a* name,' I said. 'Not *the* name. You slipped up. I didn't leave you a message. I made an appointment. With your scheduler. That was all. I didn't give a reason for it. I just said I needed to see you at noon today. The only time I mentioned anything about names and the Tennessee Free Citizens was on a separate call with General Garber. Which evidently you were listening to.'

Frazer said, 'Some things are too big for you to understand, son.'

'Probably,' I said. 'But I understand the Constitution of the United States pretty well. You ever heard of the First Amendment? It guarantees the freedom of the press. Which means any journalist is entitled to approach any fence he likes. The second human being your boys killed was an underage recruit. He was on his way to try to join the army. His mother killed herself the same night. I understand both those things. Because I saw what was left.'

No reply.

I said, 'And I understand you're doubly arrogant. First you thought I wouldn't figure out your genius scheme and then, when I did, you thought you could deal with me all by yourself. No help, no back-up. Just you and me, here and now. I have to ask, how dumb are you?'

'And I have to ask, are you armed?'

'I'm in a Class A uniform,' I said. 'No sidearm is carried with Class A uniform. That's in the regulations. You got a gun in your desk?'

'I have two guns in my desk.'

'You going to shoot me?'

'If I have to.'

'There are thirty thousand military personnel outside your door. They're all trained to run towards the sound of gunfire.'

'My neighbours won't hear. No one will hear a thing.'

'Why? You got suppressors on those guns?'

'I don't need suppressors. Or guns.'

Then he did a very strange thing. He stepped over and took a picture off his wall and laid it on his desk. Then he stepped back to the wall again and worried the nail out of the plaster with his fingertips.

'Is that it?' I said. 'You're going to prick me to death with a pin?'

He put the nail next to the photo. He opened a drawer and took out a hammer. He said, 'I was rehanging the picture when you attacked me. Fortunately I was able to grab the hammer, which was close at hand. It will be very quiet. One solid blow should do it. I'll say that I ordered you to leave but you attacked me.'

'You're insane,' I said.

'No, I'm committed,' he said. 'To the future of the army.'

HAMMERS ARE VERY EVOLVED. A heavy metal head and a handle. Frazer's was a claw design, maybe twenty-eight ounces. A big ugly thing. Total overkill for picture hanging. It made for a decent weapon, though.

He came at me with it cocked in his right hand. I scrambled up out of my chair pretty fast. Sheer instinct.

How this would go depended on how smart Frazer was. He had survived Vietnam, and the Gulf, and years of Pentagon bull. You don't do that without brains. He was in no danger of winning the Nobel Prize, but smarter than the average bear. Which helped me. Fighting morons is harder. You can't guess what they're going to do. But smart people are predictable.

He swung the hammer right to left, waist height. I arched back and it missed me. I figured next he would slash back the other way, left to right, and he did, and I arched back again and he missed again. He was breathing strangely. Ferocity, not a throat problem. He was a warrior at heart and warriors love the fight itself.

He swung the hammer a third time. I arched back and the hammer head buzzed by an inch from my coat. The momentum of the miss carried it way round. His shoulders turned ninety degrees and he twisted at the waist. He used the torque to come right back at me. With some arm extension this time. He forced me back. I ended up close to the wall.

The fourth swing aimed high, right at the side of my head. I saw a glint off the hammer's inch-wide striking face. Nearly two pounds in weight. It would have punched a very neat hole through the bone.

But it didn't, because my head wasn't there when it arrived.

I dropped onto bent knees, and I heard the rush of air above me, and I felt the miss drag him round in a wild part-circle, and I started back up. I was twisting as I rose and my elbow was already moving fast. It was a certainty I was going to hit him with it in the neck. But which part? The answer was, whichever part was there when the blow landed. Front, side, back, it was all the same to me. But for him, some parts would be worse than others.

The twenty-eight ounces had first pulled his arms away from his shoulders, in a kind of Olympic hammer-throwing way, and then they had pulled his trailing shoulder hard, in a kind of whip-cracking way, so he was well into a serious but uncontrolled spin. And my elbow was doing pretty well by that point. My weight was behind it, my foot was braced, and it was going to land very hard. He might survive if he took it on the side of the neck, but a blow on the back of the neck would be fatal.

So it was all about time, speed, and rotation. It was impossible to predict. At first I thought he was going to take it mostly on the side. Then I saw the twenty-eight ounces suddenly pulled him off in some new direction, and then there was no doubt he was going to take it on the back of the neck. No doubt at all. The guy was going to die.

Frazer went down by his desk, making a sound no louder than a fat guy sitting down on a sofa. Which was safe enough. No one calls the cops when a fat guy sits down on a sofa. There was carpet on the floor. Under the carpet would be underlay and under that was concrete. So sound transmission was strictly contained. I pulled the illicit Beretta from my Class A coat pocket and held it on him. Just in case. But he didn't move.

I left him where he was for the time being and was about to start scoping things out, when the door opened. And in walked Frances Neagley.

She was wearing latex gloves. She glanced round the room once, twice, and said, 'We need to move him near where the picture was.'

I just stood there.

'Quickly,' she said.

So I hauled him over to where he might have fallen while he was hanging the picture. He could have gone over backwards and hit his head on the edge of the desk. The distances were about right.

'But why would he?' I said.

'He was banging in the nail,' Neagley said. 'He flinched when he saw the claw coming at him on the backswing. Some knee-jerk reaction. He got his feet tangled up in the rug and over he went.'

'So where's the nail now?'

She took it off the desk and dropped it at the base of the wall. 'Time to go,' she said.

'I have to erase my appointment.'

She showed me diary pages from her pocket.

'Already in the bag,' she said. 'Let's go.'

Neagley led me down two flights of stairs and through the corridors at a pace somewhere between moderate and brisk. We used the southeast entrance to get outside and then we headed for the parking lot, where Neagley unlocked a large Buick sedan. It was a Park Avenue. Dark blue.

Neagley said, 'Get in.'

So I got in, onto soft beige leather. Neagley headed for the exit, through the barrier, and pretty soon we were on a six-lane highway heading south.

I said, 'The enquiry desk has a record of me coming in.'

'Wrong tense,' Neagley said. 'It had a record. It doesn't any more.'

'When did you do all that?'

'I figured you were OK as soon as you were one on one with the guy. Although you should have moved to the physical much sooner.'

'Why are you even here?'

'I got word of this crazy trap. From Sheriff Deveraux herself.'

'She called you?'

'No, we had a séance.'

'Why would she call you?'

'Because she was worried. As was I, as soon as I heard.'

'I don't think I told her what time the appointment was.'

'Her deputy told her what time he'd got you to Memphis, and so it was easy enough to figure out what bus you would take.'

'How did that help you this morning?'

'It didn't, but it helped me yesterday evening. I've been on you since you left the bus depot. Nice hotel, by the way.'

I said, 'Whose car is this?'

'It belongs to the motor pool. When a senior staff officer passes away, his department-owned car is returned to the motor pool. Where it is immediately road tested to determine what remedial work needs to be done before it can be reissued. This is the road test.'

'Who was the officer? Frazer?'

'It's easier for the motor pool to do the paperwork first thing in the morning. We were all counting on you.'

'I might have arrested him instead.'

'Same thing. Dead or busted, it makes no difference to the motor pool.'

'Where are we going?'

'You're due on post. Garber wants to see you.'

'That's three hours away.'

'Sit back and relax. This might be the last rest you get for a spell.'

'I thought you didn't like Deveraux.'

'Doesn't mean I wouldn't help her if she was worried.'

I said, 'I should try to call her.'

'I already tried from the scheduler's phone while you were talking to Frazer. I was going to tell her you were nearly home, but she didn't answer. A whole Sheriff's Department and no one picked up.'

'Perhaps they're busy.'

'Perhaps they are. Because there's something else you need to know. I checked a rumour from the sergeants' network. The ground crew at Benning says the Black Hawk that came in from Kelham on Sunday was empty. Apart from the pilots. No passenger, is what they meant. Reed Riley didn't go anywhere. He's still on the base.'

THE RIDE TOOK a lot less than three hours. The Buick was much faster than a bus. I was back on post by three thirty.

I went to my quarters and took off the fancy Class As and took a shower. Then I put on BDUs and went to see what Garber wanted.

Garber wanted to show me a confidential file from the Marine Corps. That was the purpose of his summons. But first came a short question-and-answer session. It didn't go well. It was very unsatisfactory. I asked the questions and he refused to answer them.

And he refused to make eye contact.

I asked, 'Who did they arrest in Mississippi?'

He said, 'Read the file.'

'Do they have a good case?'

'Read the damn file, Reacher.'

He stepped out of his office and left me alone with it.

It was cased in a khaki jacket, smooth and crisp, only a little scuffed by the passage of time. It had red chevrons on all four edges, presumably denoting some elevated level of secrecy. It had a label with a USMC file number printed on it, and a date five years in the past. It had a second label with *DEVERAUX, E* printed on it. Her name was followed by her rank, and CWO5, her service number.

The contents started with her photograph. It was in colour and maybe a little more than five years old. Her hair was buzzed very short, like she had told me. She looked very beautiful.

I laid the photograph face down on my left and looked at the first sheet of printed words. They were typewritten.

The file was a summary of an investigation conducted by a US Marine Corps brigadier general from their provost marshal's office, which oversaw their MPs. The one-star's name was James Dyer. A very senior man for what appeared to be a personal dispute between one Marine MP and two others. On one side of the issue were a woman named Alice Bouton and a man named Paul Evers, and on the other side was Elizabeth Deveraux.

The summary began with a bald narrative of events, written neutrally and patiently, without implication or interpretation. The story was fairly simple. Elizabeth Deveraux and Paul Evers were dating, and then they weren't, and then Paul Evers and Alice Bouton were dating, and then Paul's car got trashed, and then Alice got dishonourably discharged after a financial irregularity came to light.

Next came a digression into Alice Bouton's situation. Like a sidebar. Alice was indisputably guilty, in General Dyer's opinion. The facts were clear. The prosecution had been fair. The defence had been conscientious. The verdict had been unanimous. The amount in question had been less than $400. In cash, taken from an evidence locker. Proceeds from an illegal weapons sale, confiscated, bagged up, logged in and awaiting exhibition in a court-martial. Alice Bouton had taken it and spent it on a dress, a bag and shoes, in a store close to the base. The store remembered her. Some of the notes were in the store's register when the MPs came calling, and the serial numbers matched the evidence log.

Case closed. Sidebar over.

Next up was General Dyer's interpretation of the three-way turmoil. It was prefaced with a cast-iron guarantee that all conclusions were supported by data. Interviews had been conducted, information had been gathered, witnesses had been consulted, and anything supported by fewer than two independent sources had been omitted. A full court press, in other words.

I started in on the analysis. The story went like this: Elizabeth Deveraux had felt disregarded and insulted when Paul Evers dumped her for Alice Bouton. She was a woman scorned and her behaviour seemed determined to prove the cliché true. She victimised the couple by bad-mouthing them and by manipulating workloads to stop them getting downtime together.

Then she drove Paul Evers's car off a bridge.

Evers's car was nothing special, but it was essential to his social life. Deveraux had retained a key for it, and late one night had driven it away and steered it carefully beyond a bridge abutment and let it roll over a thirty-foot drop into a concrete flood sluice.

Then Deveraux had turned her attention to Alice Bouton.

She had started by breaking her arm.

General Dyer's two-independent-sources rule meant that the circum- stances were not described, because the attack had not been witnessed, but

Bouton said Deveraux had been the assailant, and Deveraux never denied it. Bouton's left elbow had been dislocated and both bones in her left forearm had been snapped. She was in a cast for six long weeks.

And Deveraux had spent those six long weeks pursuing the theft allegation with demonic intensity. Except that 'pursuing' was the wrong word, initially, because at the outset no one knew anything had been stolen. Deveraux had first inventoried the evidence lockers and audited the paperwork. Only then had she discovered the discrepancy. And then she had made the allegation and had pursued it, like an obsession, with the result being a court-martial and a guilty verdict.

There was a huge uproar in the Marine MP community, of course, but Bouton's guilty verdict had insulated Deveraux from any formal criticism. What would have looked like a vendetta, had the verdict been different, was left looking like a good piece of police work. But General Dyer had been in no doubt that the case involved major elements of personal retribution. And, unusually for such reports, he had attempted to explain why. Again, he confirmed that interviews had been conducted, information had been gathered. The participants in these new discussions had included friends and enemies, acquaintances and associates, doctors and psychiatrists.

The salient factor was held by all to be Alice Bouton's unusual physical beauty. Words quoted included gorgeous, stunning, knockout, incredible.

All the same words applied to Deveraux too, of course. All were agreed on that point also. The psychiatrists had concluded that therein lay the explanation. Deveraux couldn't stand not to be definitively the most beautiful woman on the post. So she had taken steps to make sure she was.

I read the whole thing one more time. Then I butted all the pages neatly together, closed the jacket, and Garber came into the room.

The first thing he said was, 'We just heard from the Pentagon. John James Frazer was found dead in his office. Looks like a freak accident. Apparently he fell and hit his head on the desk. He was doing something with a picture on the wall.'

'That's bad. This is not a great time to lose our Senate Liaison.'

'Did you read the file?'

I said, 'Yes, I did. Is this going to be the official line?'

'It's the truth. She was a Marine, Reacher. Sixteen years in. She knew how to cut throats. And the car alone proves it. She wrecks Paul Evers's car and she wrecks Reed Riley's. Same MO. Except this time she's one of four beautiful women. Munro says that Riley bragged to the men in Bravo Company that he dated her and dumped her for the other three in succession. So this time she's three times as mad and she goes beyond breaking arms. This time she has her own private deer trestle behind an empty house.'

'So what next?'

'It's purely a Mississippi matter now. Most likely nothing will happen. My guess is she won't arrest herself.'

'So we're going to walk away?'

'All three of them were civilians. They're nothing to do with us.'

'So the mission is terminated?'

'As of this morning.'

'Is Kelham open again?'

'As of this morning.'

'She denies dating Riley, you know.'

'She would, wouldn't she?'

'Do we know anything about General Dyer?'

'He died two years ago after a long and exemplary career. He never put a foot wrong. The man was stainless.'

'OK, I'll take steps towards wrapping up my involvement.'

'Your involvement is already wrapped up. As of this morning.'

'I have private property to recover.'

'You left something there?'

'My toothbrush. Will the DoD reimburse me?'

'For a toothbrush? Of course not.'

'Then I have a right to recover it. They can't have it both ways.'

'Reacher, if you draw one iota more attention to this thing there won't be anything I can do to help you. Right now some very senior people are holding their breath. We're one inch away from news stories about a senator's son dating a three-time killer. We'll probably get away with it. But we don't know yet. Right now it's in the balance.'

I said nothing.

He said, 'You know she's good for it, Reacher. A man with your instincts? She was only pretending to investigate. And she was playing you like a violin. First she was trying to get rid of you and then, when you wouldn't go, she switched to keeping you close so she could monitor your progress. The bus to Memphis is long gone, anyway. You'd have to wait until tomorrow now. You'll see things differently then.'

I asked, 'Is Neagley still on the post?'

He said, 'Yes, she is. I just made a date to have a drink with her.'

'Tell her she's taking the bus home. I'm taking the company car.'

He asked, 'Do you have a bank account?'

I said, 'How else would I get paid?'

'Where is it?'

'New York. From when I was at West Point.'

'Move it to somewhere nearer the Pentagon. Involuntary separation money comes through quicker if you bank in Virginia.'

'You think it will come to that?'

'The Joint Chiefs think war is over. There are big cuts coming. Most of them will fall on the army. People above us are making lists.'

'Am I on those lists?'

'You will be. And there will be nothing I can do to stop it.'

'You could order me not to go back to Mississippi.'

'I could, but I won't. Not you. I trust you to do the right thing.'

TEN

I met Stan Lowrey on my way off the post. My old friend. He was locking his car just as I was unlocking the Buick with the key I'd collected from the motor pool. I said, 'Goodbye, old pal.'

He said, 'That sounds final.'

'You may never see me again.'

'Why? Are you in trouble?'

'Me?' I said. 'No, I'm fine. But I heard your job is vulnerable. You might be gone when I get back.'

He just shook his head and smiled and walked on.

THE BUICK WAS an old lady's car, as soft as a marshmallow inside, but it had a big motor. And government plates. It was useful on the I-65, as I headed south, down the eastern edge of a national corridor, not down the western edge through Memphis. It was a straighter shot. And therefore faster. Five hours, I figured. I would be in Carter Crossing by ten thirty at the latest.

I went south through Kentucky in the last of the daylight and then it got dark pretty quickly as I drove through Tennessee. The broad road took me through the bright neon of Nashville. I crossed into Alabama. I would need to head west off an early Alabama exit and find the road that led past Kelham's gate to Carter Crossing.

Fort Kelham had been built in the 1950s, a time of big wars and mass mobilisations. And DoD planners have always been a cautious bunch. They didn't want some reservist convoy from New Jersey or Nebraska getting lost in unfamiliar parts. So they put discreet and coded signs here and there, marking the way to and from every major installation in the nation. Their efforts intensified after the Interstate system was begun. If those signs had not been trashed by locals, I could use them like homing beacons.

I found the first of the signs shortly after I entered Alabama. I came off the ramp and struck out west on a meandering rural route. There were trees and fields. There was a bright moon high in the sky. I drove on but saw no more DoD signs until I was in Mississippi, and only one more after that. It was a bold and confident arrow pointing straight ahead, with the number 17 embedded in the code below it, indicating just seventeen more miles to go.

TEN MILES OUT, I recognised the road to Kelham. I sensed the trees and the fence in the darkness. Kelham's southeastern corner.

The southern perimeter slid by my window and soon I drove by the gate. Physically it was stronger than anything I had seen outside a combat zone. It was flanked by fortifications and the guardhouse, which had nine personnel in it. The county's interests were represented by Deputy Geezer Butler, sitting in his car, in a kind of no-man's-land, where the county's road became the army's.

But the army's steel barriers were wide open and the army's road was in use. People were coming and going. Most were driving, but some were on motorbikes. More were coming than going, because it was close to ten thirty and there were early starts tomorrow. But some hardy souls were still venturing out. I braked behind two cars and someone came out of the gate and pulled in behind me. I found myself in a four-car convoy, heading for the other side of the tracks.

I saw Pellegrino in his cruiser, coming the other way, trying to calm the returning traffic with his presence. Then we were rolling through the black half of town, bouncing over the railroad track, pulling a tight left behind

Main Street, and then we were parking in front of the bars, the auto parts places, the loan offices, the gun shops and the secondhand stereo stores.

I got out of the Buick and stood halfway between Brannan's Bar and the lines of parked cars. There were guys in transit from one bar to another, and there were guys standing around talking.

And there were plenty of women, too. Some were paired off with soldiers, others were in mixed groups, and some were in groups of their own. I could see about 100 guys, and maybe eighty women, and I guessed there might be similar numbers inside. The men were from Bravo Company, I assumed. They were exactly what I would have expected to see. Good guys, well trained, by day performing at 100 per cent of their capacities, by night full of energy and high spirits. They were what a good infantry unit looks like when it comes out to play. There was plenty of buzz and noise going on, but I sensed no hostility. They didn't blame the town for their recent incarceration. They were just glad to get back to it.

Even so I was sure local law enforcement would be holding its breath. In particular I was sure Elizabeth Deveraux would still be on duty. And I was definitely sure where I would find her. She needed a central location, and a chair and a table and a window. Where else would she be?

The diner was almost completely full. There were eighteen customers. Sixteen were Rangers, in groups of four at four tables, big guys sitting tight together. They were talking loud, keeping the waitress busy. She was running in and out of the kitchen, but she looked happy.

Alone at the rearmost table for two was Major Duncan Munro. He was in BDUs and his head was bent over a meal. On the spot, just in case, even though his involvement in Kelham's affairs had been terminated hours before, presumably. He was a good MP. I guessed he was on his way back to Germany and was waiting for transport.

And Elizabeth Deveraux was there. She was at a table close to the window. On the spot, vigilant, just in case, not willing to let the mayhem filter out from behind Main Street onto Main Street itself. She was in uniform. She looked tired, but still spectacular. She looked up, saw me, smiled happily and kicked a chair out for me.

I paused, thinking hard, and then I stepped over and sat down opposite her. She looked me over, head to toe, maybe checking me for damage, maybe adjusting to the sight of me in uniform.

I said, 'Busy day?'

She said, 'Real busy since ten o'clock this morning. They opened the gates and out they came. Like a flood.'

'Any trouble?'

'None of them would pass a field sobriety test on their way home, but everything's cool. I've got Butler and Pellegrino out and about, just to show the flag. Just in case. So how did it go up there?'

'Inconclusive. Bad timing on my part. One of those freak things. The guy I went to see died in an accident. So I got nothing done.'

'I figured. I was getting updates from Frances Neagley until things got busy here. From eight until ten this morning you were drinking coffee and reading the newspaper. But somebody must have reached a conclusion about something around nine o'clock, because an hour later it all let loose. It was back to business as usual here.'

I nodded. 'I think new information was released this morning.'

'Do you know what it was?'

I said, 'By the way, thank you for worrying. I was very touched.'

'Neagley was just as worried as I was,' she said. 'Once I told her what you were doing, that is. She didn't need much persuading.'

'In the end it was safe enough. I got talking with a guy about you and a one-star called James Dyer. This guy said Dyer knew you.'

'Dyer?' she said. 'Really? I knew him, but I doubt if he knew me. He was a real big deal. Who was the guy you were talking to?'

'His name was Paul Evers.'

'Paul? You're kidding. We worked together for years. In fact we even dated once. He was a nice guy. But we didn't really click.'

'So you dumped him?'

'More or less. But we both knew it wasn't going to work. It was just a question of who was going to speak first. He wasn't upset.'

'When was this?'

She paused to calculate. 'Five years ago. Feels like yesterday.'

'Then he said something about a woman called Alice Bouton. His next girlfriend after you, apparently.'

'I don't think I knew her. I don't recall the name. Did Paul seem happy?'

'He mentioned something about car trouble.'

Deveraux smiled. 'Girls and cars,' she said. 'Is that all guys talk about?'

I said, 'Reopening Kelham means they're sure the problem is on your side of the fence, you know. They wouldn't have done it otherwise. That will be the official line. It's not one of us. You got any thoughts on that?'

'I think the army should share its information,' she said. 'If it's good enough for them, it would be good enough for me too.' She paused. 'Munro told me he got new orders. I suppose you have, too.'

I nodded. 'I came back to tie up a loose end. That's all, really.'

'And then you'll be moving on. To the next thing. Are you tired?'

I said, 'Not very.'

'I have to go and help Butler and Pellegrino. They've been working since dawn. And I want to be on the road when the last of the stragglers start to head home. They're always the drunkest.'

'Will you be back by midnight?'

'Probably not. We'll have to manage without the train tonight.' She smiled, a little sadly, and then she got up and left.

The waitress finally got to me and I ordered coffee and pie. I asked her how her day had gone. She said it had gone very well.

'No trouble at all?' I asked.

'None,' she said.

'Even from the other major at the back? I heard he can be a handful.'

She turned, looked at Munro. 'I'm sure he's a perfect gentleman.'

'Would you ask him to join me? Get him some pie, too.'

She delivered my invitation. Munro shrugged and got up. Each of the Ranger tables fell silent as he passed. Munro was not popular with these guys. He had had them sitting on their thumbs for four days.

He sat down and I asked him, 'How much have they told you?'

'Bare minimum,' he said. 'Classified, need to know, eyes only.'

'No names?'

'No,' he said. 'But I'm assuming that Sheriff Deveraux must have given them solid information that clears our guys. What else could have happened? But she hasn't arrested anybody. I've been watching her all day.'

'What has she been doing?'

'Crowd control,' he said. 'Watching for signs of friction. But it's all good. No one is mad at her or the town. It's me they're gunning for.'

'When are you leaving?'

'First light. I get a ride to Birmingham, Alabama, and then a bus to Atlanta, Georgia, and then I fly Delta back to Germany.'

'Did you know Reed Riley never left the base?'

'Yes,' he said.

'What do you make of that?'

'It puzzles me a little. He was still scheduled to leave when the Black Hawk departed Benning, but by the time it arrived at Kelham the orders had changed. Which means some big piece of decisive information came in literally while the chopper was in the air. Which was two days ago, on Sunday, right after lunch. But they didn't act on it in any other way until this morning, which is Tuesday.'

'Why wouldn't they?'

'I don't know. It feels to me like they were evaluating the new data for a few days, which makes no sense. If the new data was strong enough to make a snap decision to keep Riley on the post on Sunday afternoon, why wasn't it strong enough to open the gates on Sunday afternoon? It's as if they were ready to act privately on Sunday, but they weren't ready to act publicly until this morning. What changed?'

'Beats me.'

The waitress delivered our pies and I asked Munro, 'What are you doing in Germany? When you get back, what's on your desk?'

'Not very much. Why?'

'Three women were killed here,' I said. 'And the perp is running around free as a bird.'

'We have no jurisdiction.'

'Remember that picture in Emmeline McClatchy's parlour? Martin Luther King? He said all that needs to happen for evil to prevail is that good men do nothing.'

'I'm a military cop, not a good man. What do you want me to do?'

'I want you to stay here,' I said. 'One more day.'

Then I finished my pie and went looking for Elizabeth Deveraux again.

IT WAS ELEVEN THIRTY-ONE when I left the diner. I walked past the Sheriff's Department and I turned onto the Kelham road. There was a stream of traffic coming out from behind Main Street. I saw every single car except my Buick in motion. I kept walking, on the left-hand shoulder. Dust was coming up off the road, bright headlight beams were cutting through it and motors were roaring. Ahead of me cars were thumping over the railroad track and then accelerating into the darkness.

Deveraux was sitting in her car on the far side of the crossing, facing me. She was parked on the left shoulder of the road. I walked towards her. By the time I got there the stream of cars was thinning behind me. Deveraux opened her door and got out to meet me. She said, 'Five more minutes and they'll be gone. But I have to wait until Butler and Pellegrino get back. I can't go off duty before they do.'

I asked, 'When will they get back?'

'The train takes a whole minute to pass a given point. Which doesn't sound like much, but it feels like an hour when you've been working all evening. So they'll try to make it before midnight.'

'How long before midnight?'

She smiled. 'Five to, maybe. We wouldn't get home in time.'

I said, 'Pity.'

She smiled wider. She said, 'Get in the car, Reacher.'

She started the motor and waited as the last of the Bravo Company stragglers sped by. Then she eased off the shoulder and manoeuvred out to the road. She turned a tight right that left us up on the crossing, facing north up the railroad track. She put a light foot on the gas, steered carefully and got her right-hand wheels up on the right-hand rail. Her left-hand wheels were down on the ties. She drove past the water tower. Then she braked gently and came to a stop. Right where Reed Riley's car had waited for the train.

I said, 'You've done this before.'

She said, 'Yes, I have.'

SHE TURNED THE WHEEL hard to the left and just as the front right-hand tyre came down off the right-hand rail she hit the gas and the pulse of acceleration popped the front left-hand tyre up over the left-hand rail. The other wheels followed suit, and then she stopped again and parked in the dirt very close to and parallel with the track.

She said, 'I love this spot. No other way to get to it because of the ditch. But it's worth the trouble. I come here quite often.'

'At midnight?' I asked.

'Always.'

I turned and looked out of the back window. I could see the road. No traffic. Then a car flashed past, away from Kelham, towards town, moving fast. A big car, with lights on its roof and a shield on its door.

'Pellegrino,' she said. 'He was probably holed up a hundred yards away, and as soon as that last straggler passed him he counted to ten and high-tailed it for home.'

I said, 'Butler was parked right at Kelham's gate.'

'Yes, Butler is the one with a race on his hands.'

It was eleven forty-nine. Butler was three miles away and wouldn't hesitate to drive at sixty, which meant he could be home in three minutes. But he couldn't start until the last straggler got within headlight range of Kelham. My guess was Butler would be through in eleven minutes, which would be midnight exactly, and I said so.

'No, he'll have jumped the gun,' Deveraux said. 'He'll have moved off the gate five minutes ago. He might not be far behind Pellegrino.'

I got out of the car. The left-hand rail was gleaming in the moonlight. I figured the train was ten miles south of us.

Deveraux got out on her side and opened a rear door. She checked the back seat. She said, 'We might as well be ready.'

'Too cramped,' I said. 'Let's do it right here. On the ground.'

She smiled. 'Sounds good to me. Like Janice Chapman.'

I took off my BDU jacket and spread it out on the weeds.

I knelt down and put my ear on the rail. I heard a faint metallic whisper. The train, six miles south.

We watched the road. We saw a hint of a glow in the east.

Deveraux said, 'Good old Butler.'

We heard a straining engine. Then the glow changed to delineated beams and a second later Butler's car flashed left to right in front of us and thwacked over the crossing. Then he was gone.

Four minutes to go. We were neither refined nor elegant. We wrenched our shoes off and pulled our trousers down. Deveraux got comfortable on my jacket and I went on top of her and watched for the glimmer of the train's headlight in the distance. Not there yet.

From the first moment, we were anxious, desperate, insanely energetic. We were kissing and breathing both at the same time.

Then the ground began to shake.

As before, the same mild tremor. The stones in the rail bed next to us started to scratch and click. The rails started to sing. The ties jumped and shuddered. The ground under my hands and knees danced with big bass shudders. I looked up and gasped and blinked and squinted and saw the distant headlight. The ground beat on us from below. The rails screamed and howled. The train whistle blew, long and loud and forlorn. The warning bells at the crossing forty yards away were ringing. The train kept on coming, still distant, then right next to us, then right on top of us, insanely massive and impossibly loud.

The ground shook hard under us and we bounced whole inches in the air. A bow wave of air battered us. Then the locomotive flashed past, its giant wheels five feet from our faces, followed by the endless sequence of cars. We clung together, deafened by the squealing metal, beaten numb by the throbbing ground, scoured by dust from the slipstream.

Then the train was gone.

I turned my head and saw the cars rolling away from me into the distance. The earthquake quietened down and the night-time silence came back. We rolled apart and lay on our backs, spent, completely overwhelmed by sensations. My knees and hands were torn and scraped. I imagined Deveraux was in an even worse state. I turned my head to check and saw she had my Beretta in her hand.

THE MARINE CORPS never liked the Beretta as much as the army did, so Deveraux was handling mine with less than total enthusiasm. She said, 'I'm sorry. It was in your jacket pocket. I wondered what it was. It was digging into my ass. I'm going to have a bruise.'

'In which case it's me that's sorry,' I said.

She smiled at me and stood up and went in search of her trousers. She asked, 'Why did you bring a gun? Were you expecting trouble? It's just the two of us here.'

'As far as we know.'

'You're paranoid.'

'But alive,' I said. 'And you haven't arrested anyone yet.'

'The army must know who it was. They should tell me.'

I said nothing in reply, but staggered to my feet and picked up my trousers. We got dressed. Getting back to the road was no problem. Deveraux did it in reverse, backing up onto the track like parallel parking, then backing all the way to the crossing, before turning the wheel and taking off. We were in my hotel room five minutes later. In bed. She went straight to sleep. I didn't. I lay in the dark and stared at the ceiling and thought.

Mostly I thought about my last conversation with Leon Garber. My commanding officer. An honest man and my friend. *It's the truth*, he had said. *She was a Marine, Reacher. Sixteen years in. She knew how to cut throats.* Then he had got a little impatient. *A man with your instincts*, he had said, about me. Later I had pushed the issue. *You could order me not to go back to Mississippi*, I had said. *I could*, he had said. *But I won't. I trust you to do the right thing.*

The conversation replayed endlessly in my head.

In the end I fell asleep very late and completely unsure whether Garber had been telling me something, or asking me something.

THE NEXT MORNING Elizabeth Deveraux and I ate breakfast together in the diner, and then she went to work and I went to use the phone. I tried to call Frances Neagley at her desk in D.C., but she wasn't back. Probably still on an all-night bus somewhere. So I dialled Stan Lowrey instead. I said, 'I need you to do something for me.'

He said, 'No jokes today? About how you're surprised I'm still here?'

'I didn't have time to think of any. I wanted Neagley, not you. She's better than you at this kind of stuff.'

'Better than you, too. What do you need?'

'Fast answers. Statistically speaking, where would we be most likely to find US Marines and concrete flood sluices in close proximity?'

'Southern California,' Lowrey said. 'Statistically speaking, almost certainly Camp Pendleton, north of San Diego.'

'Correct,' I said. 'I need to trace a jarhead MP who was there five years ago. His name is Paul Evers.'

'I'm in the army, not the Marine Corps. I can't get into their files.'

'That's why you need to call Neagley. She'll know how to do it.'

I hung up with Lowrey and called the Kelham number Munro had given Deveraux. The call went through. Munro was still on post.

Munro answered and I said, 'Thank you for sticking around.'

'But what am I sticking around for? What do you need?'

'I need to know Riley's movements today. I want to ask him a question.'

'That could be difficult. He'll be pretty much tied up all day.'

'I need him to come to me. In town.'

'The mood has changed here. Riley's father is flying in for a visit.'

'The senator? Today?'

'ETA close to one o'clock this afternoon. It's billed as an off-the-record celebration of what the guys are doing in Kosovo.'

'How long will it last?'

'You know what politicians are like. The old guy is supposed to watch some training crap in the afternoon, but dollars to doughnuts he'll want to hang around all night drinking with the boys.'

'OK,' I said. 'I'll figure something out.'

'Anything else?'

'You could tell me about Kelham. As in, is there a good reason for Alpha Company and Bravo Company to be based there?'

'Kelham is pretty isolated. Helps with the secrecy thing.'

'That's what they told me, too. But I don't buy it. There are secrets on every base. But they chose Kelham a year ago. Why? Have you seen anything about Kelham that would make it the only choice?'

'No,' Munro said. 'It's adequate. But not essential. I assume it was about sending four hundred extra wallets to a dying town.'

'Exactly,' I said. 'It was political. One more thing. You're clear about how Janice Chapman ended up in that alley, right?'

'Based on what I saw last night, Chief Deveraux operates an exclusion zone in terms of Main Street. She makes sure the action happens between the bars and the railroad track. Therefore Main Street and the alley would have been deserted. The perp must have stopped on Main Street and carried the corpse in from that direction.'

'How long would it have taken?'

'Could have been a minute, could have been twenty,' Munro said.

'But why there? Why not somewhere else, ten miles away?'

'I don't know. Maybe the perp was constrained. Maybe he had company close by. Maybe he had to duck out and take care of it real fast. Maybe he couldn't be gone for long without somebody noticing.'

SENATOR RILEY'S IMPENDING visit kept the town quiet. I left the diner and found Main Street back to its previous torpor. My borrowed Buick was the only car parked on the block behind. I drove to the hotel, retrieved my toothbrush and settled my account. I got back behind the wheel.

I drove to the vacant lot between the diner and the Sheriff's Department. I headed south to Main Street, driving fast. I made the left into Deveraux's childhood street and hustled along to her old house. Total elapsed time, forty-five seconds.

I turned in and drove down the overgrown driveway, past the tumble-down house to the deer trestle. I popped the trunk and got out. Total elapsed time, a minute and fifteen seconds.

I mimed supporting a body's weight, cutting the wrist straps, cutting the ankle ties, carrying the body to the car, lowering it into the trunk. I fiddled around, taking off imaginary pads and straps and belts and scarves from two wrists and two ankles. I stepped back to the trestle and picked up an imaginary bucket of blood and wedged it in the trunk alongside the body. I closed the trunk and got back into the driver's seat. Total elapsed time, three minutes and ten seconds.

I backed up and turned and drove the length of the driveway again and headed back to Main Street. I drove the same 200 yards I had driven before and stopped on the kerb between the hardware store and the pharmacy at the mouth of the alley. Total elapsed time, four minutes and twenty-five seconds.

Plus one minute to put the blood in the alley.

Plus another minute to put Janice May Chapman in the alley.

Plus fifteen seconds to get back where I started.

Total elapsed time, six minutes and forty seconds.

I drove the Buick to the diner and went in. I made my way to the payphone and tried Neagley first and found her at her desk.

I said, 'I'm sorry about the bus. Did you talk to Stan Lowrey?'

'Yes, and I traced the name for you. Paul Evers died a year ago in an accident. A helicopter crashed at Lejeune. Two pilots and three passengers died, one of which was Evers.'

'The other name I want is Alice Bouton. She's been a civilian for five years. She was discharged from the Corps without honour.'

'Why are we doing this? Elizabeth Deveraux is guilty as sin.'

I said, 'Maybe she did it, maybe she didn't. We don't know yet.'

I hung up and then the phone rang again.

It was Munro, and he wanted to tell me he had talked to a steward about the day's festivities. Munro said the stewards expected to be busy until dinner, but no later than that, because the last time the senator visited he had hosted everybody in town, at Brannan's Bar, and no doubt he would do the same thing again.

'OK,' I said. 'That's good. Riley will come to me after all. And his father. What time will dinner finish?'

'Scheduled to be over by eight o'clock, according to the steward.'

'OK,' I said again. 'I'm sure father and son will leave the base together. I want you on them from the moment they drive through the gate. But unobtrusively. Can you do that?'

'Probably,' Munro said.

'Use this phone number as a contact if you need me,' I said. 'I'll be in and out of this diner all day long.'

I hung up, and I asked the waitress to answer the phone for me if it rang again. I asked her to write the callers' names on her order pad. Then it was all about waiting. For information, and for face-to-face encounters. I stepped out to the Main Street sidewalk and stood in the sun. The town was deserted. No hustle, no bustle, no traffic.

Until the goon squad from Kelham showed up.

There were four of them. They were Kelham's version of Senate Liaison, I guessed, preparing the ground the way a Secret Service advance team prepares the ground ahead of a presidential visit. They came out of the mouth of the alley. They were all officers. Two lieutenants, a captain and a light colonel. He was fiftyish and fat. He was the kind of soft staff officer who looks ludicrous in battledress uniform.

He saw me. I was in battledress uniform too. He spoke to one of the lieutenants. Too far to hear his voice, but I could read his lips. He said, Tell that man to get his ass over here double-quick.

The lieutenant approached. He stopped a respectful four feet away and saluted. 'Sir, the colonel would like a word with you.'

Normally I treat lieutenants well. But right then I wasn't in the mood for nonsense. I just said, 'OK, kid, tell him to step right up.'

The kid said, 'Sir, I think he would prefer it if you went to him.'

'You must be confusing me with someone who gives a damn what he prefers.'

The kid went a little pale, blinked twice and headed back. He must have spent the walk translating my response into acceptable terms, because there was no explosion. Instead the colonel set off waddling in my direction. He approached and I saluted him.

He returned the salute and asked, 'Do I know you, Major?'

I said, 'That depends on how much trouble you've been in, Colonel. Have you ever been arrested?'

'You're the other MP. You're Major Munro's opposite number. Why are you still here? I was told all issues had been resolved.'

'The issues will be resolved when I say they are. That's the nature of police work.'

The fat guy said, 'Well, stay out of sight tonight. The senator must not see a CID presence here. There are to be no reminders of recent suspicions. None at all. Is that clear?'

I said, 'Request noted.'

'It's more than a request.'

'Next up from a request is an order. You're not in my chain of command.'

The guy rehearsed a reply, but in the end he didn't come out with anything. He just waddled back to his pals. And at that point I heard the phone ring inside the diner, very faintly, and I beat the waitress to it by a step.

It was Frances Neagley on the line, from her desk in D.C. She said, 'Bouton is a very uncommon name, apparently. I am basing my conclusion on an hour's solid work, which turned up no Boutons, much less any Alice Boutons. I can't get any further than three years back with the Marines, which would miss her, and if she was dishonourably discharged she probably didn't get the kind of job or income that would show up in too many places. I have a call in to the FBI. And to a pal in USMC personnel command. I just wanted to let you know I'm on it. I'll have more tonight.'

'Before eight o'clock would be good.'

'I'll do my best.'

I hung up and decided to stay in the diner for lunch.

AND INEVITABLY DEVERAUX came in ten minutes later, in search of her own lunch, and, possibly, in search of me. She stepped inside and paused.

She saw me staring, and she started towards me. I kicked the opposite chair out an inch. She smiled. 'How was your morning?'

I said, 'No, how was yours?'

'Busy,' she said.

'Making any progress with your three unsolved homicides?'

'Apparently the army solved those homicides. I'll be happy to do something about them as soon as the army shares its information.'

'You don't seem very interested in finding out who did it. The army says it was a civilian. Do you know who it was?'

'Are you saying I do?'

'I'm saying I know how these things work. There are some people you can't arrest. Like Mrs Lindsay. Suppose she'd shot somebody. You wouldn't have arrested her for it.'

'Maybe. But I'd arrest anyone else, whoever they were. Any other issues, before we order?'

'Just one. Tell me again. You never dated Reed Riley, right?'

'Reacher, what is this?'

'It's a question.'

'No, I never dated Reed Riley.'

'Are you sure?'

'Reacher, please. I didn't even know he was here. I told you that.'

'OK,' I said. 'Let's order.'

She was mad at me, but she was hungry, too. More hungry than mad, clearly, because she stayed at the table. Changing tables wouldn't have been enough. She would have had to storm out and she wasn't prepared to do that on an empty stomach.

She ordered the chicken pie. I ordered grilled cheese.

She said, 'You know who it is.'

I said nothing.

'You do, don't you? You know who it is. So this wasn't about me knowing who it is. It was about you knowing who it is. Who is it?'

'I don't know who it is,' I said. 'Not for sure. Not yet.'

We finished our lunch without saying much more. The phone rang. Deveraux stared at it. I said, 'It's for me.'

I walked over and picked up. It was Munro. He said, 'I have the transportation details, if you're interested. Reed Riley doesn't own a car any more, as you know, so he's borrowing a plain olive drab staff car. He'll be driving with his father as his only passenger. The motor pool has been told to have the car ready at eight o'clock exactly.'

'Thanks,' I said. 'Good to know. Is there a return ETA?'

'There's an eleven o'clock curfew tonight. So people will be leaving town from ten thirty onwards. The senator's plane is scheduled to be wheels-up at midnight.'

'Good to know,' I said again. 'Thanks. Has he arrived yet?'

'Twenty minutes ago, in an army Lear.'

I hung up the phone and walked back to the table, but Deveraux was getting up to leave. She said, 'I have to get back to work. I have three homicides to solve.' She pushed past me, walked out the door.

Waiting. I spent the afternoon drinking coffee and eating pie. No one called, and no one came, and the town stayed quiet. At seven o'clock Main Street went dark, and at seven thirty the old couple from the hotel came in.

Then Stan Lowrey phoned and the evening began to unravel.

ELEVEN

Lowrey said he had just heard from an MP friend at Fort Benning in Georgia, where the 75th Ranger Regiment was based. Apparently a lieutenant colonel from their remote detachment at Kelham had phoned home and told his bosses there were still two criminal investigation majors on the scene, one on the post itself and one in town, the latter a prize pain in the ass, and because his bosses were determined that Senator Riley be shown nothing but a good time, they had dispatched a baby-sitting squad to muzzle the said CID majors for the remaining duration of the senator's visit. Just in case. Lowrey said the squad had left Benning in a Black Hawk helicopter some time ago, and therefore might well have arrived at Kelham.

'MPs?' I said. 'They won't mess with me.'

'Not MPs,' Lowrey said. 'Six regular Rangers. Real tough guys. Three for you and three for Munro, I guess.'

'Rules of engagement?'

'I don't know. What does it take to muzzle you?'

'More than three Rangers,' I said. I scanned the street outside the window and saw no vehicles, no pedestrians. 'Don't worry about me, Stan. It's Munro I'm concerned about. I need two pairs of hands tonight. It's going to make it harder if he gets hung up.'

'Which he will,' Lowrey said. 'You will too, probably.'

'Would you call him and give him the same warning? If they haven't got to him, that is.' I recited Munro's VOQ number. 'Could you also call Neagley and see if she has any results on that ex-Marine I asked her about? Tell her if I'm busy with the GI Joes when she calls she's authorised to leave a message with the waitress.'

'OK, and good luck,' Lowrey said, and hung up. I stepped out to the sidewalk. I guessed the Rangers would look for me first in one of the bars. Probably Brannan's. If I was planning to make trouble, that was where I would be. So I looped round through the dog-leg alley and scanned the acre of ground from deep in the shadows.

Sure enough, there was a Humvee parked right there. I guessed the plan was to frogmarch me over to it and throw me in the back and drive me out to Kelham, and then to stash me in whatever room Munro was already locked up in. Then the plan would be to wait until the senator's Lear plane left at midnight, and let us out again, and apologise most sincerely.

I eased out round the corner of Brannan's Bar and looked in through the window. Jonathan and Hunter Brannan were behind the bar. Three guys in BDUs were talking to them. They were Rangers. One of them was a sergeant and two of them were specialists.

I eased back into the shadows and headed back to the diner. There were three customers still in the place, the old couple from Toussaint's and a guy in a pale suit. Three was a good number and the demographics were close to perfect. Local business people, solid citizens, mature, easily outraged. And the old couple at least were guaranteed to stay for hours, which was good, because I might need hours, depending on Neagley's progress.

I came in the door and stopped by the phone and the waitress shook her head at me, to tell me there had been no incoming calls. I used the phone book and found the number for Brannan's Bar, and then I put a quarter in the slot and dialled. One of the Brannan brothers answered and I said, 'Let me speak to the sergeant.'

I heard a second of surprise and uncertainty and then I heard the phone being passed from hand to hand. A voice said, 'Who is this?'

I said, 'This is the guy you're looking for. I'm in the diner.'

No answer.

I said, 'This is where you put your hand over the mouthpiece and ask the barmen where the diner is, so you can send your guys to check while you keep me on the phone. But I'll save you the trouble. The diner is about twenty yards west of you and about fifty yards north. Send one guy through the alley on your left and the other out of the lot and round the Sheriff's Department building. You can come in through the kitchen door. That way you've got me covered in every direction. But I'm not going anywhere. I'll wait for you right here.' I hung up and walked to the rearmost table for four.

The sergeant was the first in. He came through the kitchen door slowly and cautiously. Then one of the specialists came in the front. From the alley, I assumed. A minute later the third guy was there. They stood there, filling the aisle, two to my right and one to my left.

'Sit down,' I said. 'Please.'

The sergeant said, 'Our orders are to take you to Kelham.'

I said, 'That isn't going to happen, Sergeant.'

The clock in my head showed a quarter to eight.

I said, 'Here's the thing, guys. To take me out of here against my will would involve a considerable amount of physical commotion. We would bust up at least three or four tables and chairs. There might be personal injuries. And the waitress will assume we're Bravo Company personnel. She knows Bravo's company commander is expected in Brannan's Bar any minute. So it would be natural for her to head there to complain. And to get that done she'd have to interrupt a moment of intimacy between father and son.'

No answer.

'Sit down, guys,' I said.

They sat down. The sergeant sat down face to face with me; the specialists sat across the aisle, one each side of a table for two, their chairs out at an angle, ready to intervene if I made a break.

'You should try the pie,' I said. 'It's really good.'

'No pie,' the sergeant said.

'You better order something, or the waitress might throw you out for loitering. You really can't afford to attract attention.'

The waitress came by and the sergeant shrugged and ordered three pies and three cups of coffee.

The sergeant said, 'We'll sit here all night, if that's what it takes.'

'Good to know,' I said. 'I'm going to sit here until the phone rings, and then I'm going to leave.'

'I can't let you communicate with anyone. Those are my orders. And I can't let you leave. Unless you agree to go to Kelham.'

I said, 'Didn't we just have this discussion?'

At eight o'clock the guy in the pale suit left. At five past eight I began to hear the sound of cars outside, as Bravo Company started to arrive in town. I assumed Reed Riley had led the parade in his borrowed staff car, with his father in the seat beside him. I assumed the old guy was at that moment stationed at Brannan's door, greeting his son's men, ushering them in, grinning like an idiot.

The three Rangers boxing me in had eaten their pies one at a time, with the other two always alert and watchful. The waitress collected their plates. She seemed to sense what was going on and she gave me a concerned look. There was no doubt whose side she was on.

The noise from outside continued to build. The phone didn't ring.

I thought about their Humvee. I knew that like every other Humvee it would weigh north of four tons, which would make it good for about sixty miles an hour, tops. Which I knew wasn't racing-car fast, but which I knew was fifteen times faster than walking, which I knew was a good thing.

Then, just after eight thirty, two things happened.

First, the old couple left. She closed her book, he folded his paper, and they got up and shuffled out of the door. Back to the hotel, presumably. Far earlier than ever before.

The waitress was in the kitchen, which left just four people in the room, one of which was me and three of which were my baby sitters.

The sergeant smiled. 'Just us now. No members of the public.' He was leaning forward across the table. Closer to me than before.

Then the second thing happened. The phone rang.

Halfway through the first ring all three Rangers were in motion. The guy to my left was instantly on his feet, putting big hands on my shoulders, pressing me down into my seat. The sergeant opposite me was leaning forwards, grabbing my wrists, pressing them into the tabletop. The third guy came up out of his chair, balled his fists and blocked the aisle, ready to hit me if I moved.

I offered no resistance. I just sat there. The phone rang on.

The waitress came out of the kitchen. She paused a beat, took one look and then she headed for the phone. She picked up and listened and glanced my way and started talking, looking at me the whole time, as if she was describing my predicament to someone.

To Frances Neagley, I assumed. Or I hoped.

The waitress listened again and then trapped the phone between her ear and her shoulder and took out her pad and her pen. She started writing. And kept on writing. She started a second page. Then she stopped writing, hung up the phone and tore out her two written pages. She took a step towards us. The guy behind me took his weight off my shoulders. The sergeant let go of my wrists. The third guy sat down. The waitress walked the length of the aisle, right into our little group, and she focused on the sergeant.

She said, 'I have a two-part message for you, sir: "First, whoever you are, you should let this man go immediately, for both your own sake and the army's, because second, whoever you are and whatever your orders, he's likely to be right and you're likely to be wrong. This message comes from an NCO of equal rank, with nothing but the army's interests at heart."'

The sergeant said, 'Noted.'

Neagley, I thought. Good try.

Then the waitress leaned forward and put her second handwritten page face down on the table and slid it towards me, fast and easy, the same way she had slid a million diner checks before. I trapped it under my left palm. The waitress walked back to the kitchen.

I used my left thumb and curled the top of the paper upwards, like a guy playing poker, and I read the first two lines of my message. The first word was a Latin preposition. Typical Neagley. *Per*. Meaning in this context *According to*. The next six words were *United States Marine Corps Personnel Command*. Which meant that whatever information was contained in the rest of the note had come from the horse's mouth. It would be definitive. It would be solid gold.

I let the top of the paper slap back down against the tabletop. I spread my thumb and my first two fingers and pincered them together, and folded the note, and jammed it in my right top pocket.

Ten minutes to nine in the evening.

I looked at the sergeant. 'OK, you win. Let's go to Kelham.'

We went out through the kitchen and used the diner's rear door, because that was the fastest route to their Humvee. The sergeant led the way. I was sandwiched between the two specialists. The area was jammed with parked cars. There were men in uniform, fifty yards to my right, clustered in around Brannan's Bar. Most had bottles of beer in their hands. The Humvee looked wide and massive in among the regular rides. Parked next to it was a flat green sedan. Reed Riley's borrowed car, I assumed.

When we reached the truck, the sergeant opened the left rear door and the specialists crowded behind me and left me no option but to get in. The sergeant waited until the specialists were on board, one of them in the front passenger seat, the other across the wide tunnel next to me in the back, both of them turned watchfully towards me. Then he climbed into the driver's seat and started the engine. He turned the headlights on, rolled forwards, towards the Kelham road, and prepared to turn right thirty yards ahead.

I asked, 'What are you guys trained for?'

He said, 'Man-portable shoulder-launch surface-to-air defence.'

'Not police work?'

'No.'

'I could tell,' I said. 'You didn't search me. You should have.'

I came out with my Beretta in my right hand. I reached forwards and bunched his collar in my left hand. I hauled him back hard against his seat. I jammed the muzzle of the gun hard into the back of his right shoulder. I said, 'Let's all sit still and stay calm.'

They all did both things, because of where I had the gun. His ear or his neck would not have worked. They would not have believed I would shoot the guy dead. Not one soldier against another. But a non-fatal wound to the right of his shoulder blade was plausible.

I said, 'Turn left.'

He turned left, onto the east–west road.

I said, 'Drive on.'

He drove on, into the die-straight tunnel through the trees, away from Kelham towards Memphis.

I said, 'Faster.'

He speeded up and the big truck was rattling and straining close to sixty miles an hour. It was nine o'clock in the evening. That road was forty miles long and the chances of meeting traffic on it were low.

Thirty minutes later we were at some featureless point thirty miles west of Carter Crossing and maybe ten miles short of the minor road that led up towards Memphis. I said, 'OK, let's stop here.'

The guy braked to a stop. He put the transmission in Park and took his hands off the wheel and sat there like he knew what was coming next, which maybe he did and maybe he didn't. I turned my head and looked at the guy next to me and said, 'Take your boots off.'

And at that point they all knew what was coming next, and there was a pause, like a mutiny brewing, but then the guy next to me bent to his task.

I said, 'Now your socks.'

The guy peeled them off and stowed them in his boots.

I said, 'Now your jacket.'

He took his jacket off.

I said, 'Now your trousers.'

There was another long pause, but then the guy hitched his butt up off the seat and slid his trousers down over his hips. I looked at the guy in the front passenger seat and said, 'Same four things for you.'

He got right to it and then I made him help his sergeant out. I wasn't about to let the guy fold forwards and away from me. Not at that point. When they were done I turned back to the guy next to me and said, 'Now get out of the truck and walk forward twenty paces.'

His sergeant said, 'You better hope we never meet again, Reacher.'

'Get out of the truck,' I repeated.

And a minute later all three of them were standing on the road in the headlight beams, barefoot, trouserless, in nothing but T-shirts and boxers. They were thirty miles from where they wanted to be, which under the best of conditions was a seven- or eight-hour walk, and going barefoot on a rural road was no one's definition of the best of conditions. And even if by some miracle there was passing traffic, they stood no chance of hitching a ride. No one in his right mind would stop in the dark for three wildly gesticulating bare-legged men.

I climbed into the driver's seat, turned round and headed back the way we had come. The clock in my head showed nine thirty-five, and I figured I would be in Carter Crossing at three minutes past ten.

TWO MINUTES SHORT of ten o'clock I pulled up and hid the truck in the last of the trees and walked the rest of the way.

Main Street was quiet. There was nothing to see except light in the diner's window and my borrowed Buick and Deveraux's Caprice parked nose to tail in front of it. I guessed Deveraux was keeping half an eye on the situation but not worrying too much about it. The senator's presence all but guaranteed a quiet and untypical night.

I stayed on the Kelham road and looped round behind Main Street. I kept myself concealed behind the last row of parked cars and walked level with Brannan's Bar. I could see a big crowd inside the bar. I moved closer, squeezing between parked cars and pick-up trucks.

As I eased between a twenty-year-old Cadillac and a beat-up GMC Jimmy, a soft voice right next to me said, 'Hello, Reacher.'

I turned and saw Munro leaning against the far side of the Jimmy, in the shadow, nearly invisible, relaxed and patient and vigilant.

'Hello, Munro,' I said. 'It's good to see you. Although I have to say I didn't expect to.'

He said, 'Likewise.'

'Did Stan Lowrey call you?'

He nodded. 'But a little too late.'

'Three guys?'

He nodded again. 'Mortar men from the 75th.'

'Where are they now?'

'Tied up with telephone wire, gagged with their own T-shirts, locked in my room.'

'Good work,' I said. Which it was. One against three, no warning, taken by surprise. I was impressed. Munro was nobody's fool.

He asked, 'Who did you get?'

'An antiaircraft crew.'

'Where are they?'

'Walking back from halfway to Memphis with no shoes and no trousers.'

He smiled. He said, 'I hope I never get posted to Benning.'

I asked, 'Is Riley in the bar?'

'First to arrive, with his dad. They're holding court big time.'

'Curfew still in place?'

He nodded. 'But it'll be a last-minute rush. The mood turned out to be pretty good. No one will want to be the first to leave.'

'OK,' I said. 'Your job is to make sure Riley is the last to leave. By a minute at least. Do whatever it takes to make that happen.'

With anyone else I might have sketched out ways to accomplish that goal, anything from puncturing a tyre to asking for the old guy's autograph, but I was beginning to realise Munro didn't need help. He would think of all the same things I could, and a few more besides.

He said, 'Understood.'

'And then your job is to go and sit on Elizabeth Deveraux. I need her to be under your eye throughout. Again, whatever it takes.'

'Understood,' he said again. 'She's in the diner right now.'

'Keep her there,' I said. 'Good luck. And thanks.'

I squeezed back between the Cadillac and the Jimmy and threaded through the rearmost rank of cars. Five minutes later I was just past the railroad crossing, hidden in the trees on the side of the road that led to Kelham, waiting again.

Munro's assessment of the collective mood turned out to be correct. No one left at ten thirty. Ten thirty-five came and went. Ten forty, likewise.

Then at ten forty-five the dam broke and they came in droves.

I heard noise like a muted version of an armoured division firing up and I saw headlight beams far in the distance as they all started funnelling out of the lot. Thirty seconds later the lead car thumped over the crossing and sped on by. It was followed by all the others in sequence. The cars kept on coming, heading home.

Ten minutes later the last vehicles were moving out. None of them was a flat green staff car. The final tail-end charlie was an old Pontiac. It thumped over the track on soft tyres and then it was gone.

I stepped out of the trees and saw a lone pair of headlights click on. I saw their beams bounce and swing, side to side, up and down, and I saw them lead the way north, out through the lot and swing towards me.

The clock in my head showed one minute to eleven.

I walked west, back over the railroad crossing towards town, and then I stopped on the road and raised my hand, palm out, like a traffic cop.

The headlight beams picked me up 100 yards out. Reed Riley lifted off the gas and slowed down. Pure habit. Infantrymen spend a lot of time riding in vehicles, and many of their journeys are enabled or directed by guys in BDUs waving them through or pointing them left or right or bringing them to a temporary standstill.

The flat green staff car came to a stop with its front bumper a yard from my knees. I could see Riley and his father side by side behind the windshield. Neither looked surprised or impatient. Riley looked exactly like his photo, and his father was an older version, a little larger in the ears and nose, a little more powdered and presentable.

I stepped round to Reed Riley's door and he wound his window down. He saw the oak leaves on my collar. He said, 'Sir?'

I didn't answer. I took one more step and opened the rear door and got in the back seat. I closed the door and shuffled over to the centre of the bench and both men craned round to look at me.

'Sir?' Riley said again.

'What's going on here?' his father asked.

'Change of plan,' I said.

I could smell beer on the breath, and smoke, and sweat in their clothing.

'I have a plane to catch,' the senator said.

'At midnight,' I said. 'No one will look for you before then.'

'What the hell does that mean? Do you know who I am?'

'Yes,' I said. 'I do.'

'What do you want?'

'Instant obedience,' I said. I took out the Beretta, I clicked the safety to fire, a small sound, but ominous in the silence.

The senator said, 'You're making a very serious mistake, young man. As of right now your military career is over.'

'Be quiet,' I said. I leaned forward and bunched Reed Riley's collar in my hand, like I had with the sergeant from Benning. But this time I put the muzzle of the gun in the hollow behind his right ear. 'Drive slowly. Turn left on the crossing. Head up the railroad line.'

Riley said, 'But the train is coming.'

'At midnight,' I said. 'Now hop to it, soldier.'

It was a difficult task. But he did OK. He rolled forwards and spun the wheel hard and crabbed diagonally up onto the rise. He lined it up and his right front tyre hit the groove in the road. He eased forward. His right-hand tyres stayed up on the rail. His left-hand wheels were down on the ties.

'You've done this before,' I said.

He didn't answer.

We rolled on, radically tilted, the right side of the car up and running smooth, the left side down and rising and falling over the ties. We rolled past the old water tower, then ten more yards. and then I said, 'Stop.'

He braked gently and the car stopped. I kept hold of his collar and kept the gun in place. Ahead of me through the windshield the rails ran straight north to a vanishing point far in the distance.

I said, 'Captain, use your left hand and open all the windows.'

'Why?'

'Because you guys already stink. And it's going to get worse, believe me.'

Riley scrabbled blindly with his fingers and first his father's window came down, then mine, then the one opposite me.

Fresh night air came in on the breeze.

I said, 'Senator, lean over and turn the lights off.'

It took him a second to find the switch, but he did it.

I said, 'Now turn the engine off and give me the key.'

He said, 'But we're parked on the railroad track.'

'I'm aware of that.'

The old guy leaned sideways, twisted the key, pulled it and held it out.

'Toss it onto the back seat,' I said.

He did so and it landed next to me and skittered down the slope of the cushion made by the tilt of the car.

I said, 'Now both of you put your hands on your heads.'

The senator went first, and I pulled the Beretta back to let his son follow suit. I let go of his collar and sat back in my seat. 'Either one of you moves a single muscle, you're either dead or crippled. Get it?'

No response.

I said. 'I need an answer.'

'We get it,' Riley said.

His father said, 'What do you want?'

'Confirmation. Captain, you lied to your men about dating Sheriff Deveraux, am I right?'

Riley's father said, 'Son, don't say a word to this man.'

I said, 'Captain, answer my question.'

Riley said, 'Yes, I lied about Deveraux.'

'Why?'

'Command strategy,' he said. 'My men like to look up to me.'

I said, 'Senator, why were Alpha Company and Bravo Company moved from Benning to Kelham?'

The old guy huffed and puffed, but in the end he said, 'It was politically convenient. Mississippi always has its hand out.'

'Not because of Audrey Shaw? Not because you thought your boy deserved a little gift to celebrate his new command?'

'OK, it was a side benefit. I thought it might be fun. But nothing more. Decisions of that magnitude are not based on trivialities.'

I said, 'Captain, tell me about Rosemary McClatchy.'

Riley said, 'We dated, we broke up.'

'Was she pregnant?'

'If she was, she never said anything to me about it.'

'Did she want to get married?'

'Major, you know any one of them would marry any one of us.'

'What was she like?'

'Insecure,' he said. 'She drove me nuts.'

'Now tell me about Shawna Lindsay.'

The old man said, 'That matter has been resolved, I believe. The Lindsay girl. And the other one.'

I said, 'Captain, tell me about the dead women in Kosovo.'

His father said, 'There are no dead women in Kosovo.'

I said, 'Seriously? What, they live for ever?'

'Obviously they don't live for ever. They were Kosovan women and it happened in Kosovo. It's a local matter, like this is a local matter. A local person has been identified.'

I said, 'Captain, how old are you?'

Riley said, 'I'm twenty-eight.'

I said, 'Senator, how would you feel if your son was still a captain at thirty-three?'

The old guy said, 'I would be very unhappy. No one stays five years at the same rank. You'd have to be an idiot.'

I said, 'That was their first mistake.'

'What? What do you mean "their"? Who are they?'

'When you turned to the Marine Corps's Senate Liaison for help they made a number of mistakes. Five years in the same rank? Deveraux is not the kind of person who spends five years in the same rank. Deveraux is not an idiot. My guess is she was a CWO3 five years ago and she got two promotions since then. But your Marine Corps boys wrote CWO5 on a file that was supposed to be five years old. They used an old picture but they didn't change her rank. Which was a mistake. They were in too much of a rush.'

'What rush?'

'Janice Chapman was white. Finally you had one people would take seriously. And she was linked to you. So you worked like crazy and teased us about access to give yourself more time. Finally you got the file done on Sunday. The word came through while the chopper was in the air. So it went back empty. But you waited until Tuesday before releasing it for public scrutiny. You needed two days to make it look old, by scuffing it around.'

'Are you saying that file was a forgery?'

'I know, you're shocked. Maybe you've known for nine months, or six, or maybe just a week or so, but we all know now.'

'Know what?' Reed Riley said.

I turned towards him. He was staring forward, but he knew I was talking to him. I said, 'Maybe Rosemary McClatchy was insecure because her beauty was all she had, so maybe she got jealous, and maybe that's where you got the idea for the vengeful woman. And she was pregnant, too, and you'd already checked out the local sheriff, because that's what an ambitious company commander does, so you knew about the empty house, so you took poor pregnant Rosemary McClatchy there and you butchered her.'

No response.

'And you liked it,' I said. 'So you did it again. And you got better at it. No more dumping them in the ditch by the railroad track. Maybe Shawna Lindsay had delusions of marriage, and she was talking about living in a little house together, so you dumped her on a construction site. And you dumped Janice Chapman behind a bar because she was a party girl. Maybe you set yourself an extra challenge that night. You snuck out from the guys you were with and did it in the time you needed to take a leak. Six minutes and forty seconds would be my guess. Which is not plausible for Deveraux. She couldn't lift a woman off a deer trestle. She couldn't carry a corpse to a car. That's where the alternative theory starts to falter. Someone thought up a neat little story. The jealous woman, the broken arm. The missing four hundred dollars. It was quite subtle. But they didn't want subtle. They wanted a flashing red light. So you included a car. Then you got on the phone and told your son to put his car on the train track.'

'That's crazy.'

'There was no other reason behind the stuff with the car. It served no other purpose. Other than to nail the lid shut on Deveraux.'

Senator Riley said, 'That file is genuine.'

'Then they went too far with the dead people. We could buy James Dyer, a senior officer. Health maybe not the best. But Paul Evers? Too convenient. Which brings us to Alice Bouton. Is she dead too? Or is she alive? In which case, what would she tell us if we asked her about her broken arm?'

'The file is completely genuine, Reacher.'

'Can you read, Senator? If so, read this for me.' I slid the folded diner bill from my pocket and tossed it in his lap.

He picked it up. It shook in his hand. He asked, 'Have you read this?'

I said, 'No, I haven't looked at it. I don't need to know. Either way I've got enough to nail you.'

He took a breath. He read out, '"Per United States Marine Corps Personnel Command, there was no Marine named Alice Bouton."'

I smiled. 'They invented her. She didn't exist. Very sloppy work. It makes me wonder if the car came first. Maybe it was Alice Bouton you wrote in at the last minute. Without enough time to steal a real identity.'

The old guy said, 'The army had to be protected.'

'It was your son you were protecting.'

'It could have been anyone in his unit. We'd do this for anyone.'

'Bull,' I said. 'This was about the two of you and no one else.'

I didn't want to shoot them. Not that there would be much left for the pathologist to examine, but a cautious man takes no unnecessary risks. So I dropped the gun on the seat and came forward with my right hand open, and I got it flat on the back of the senator's head, and I heaved it forward and bounced it off the dashboard rail. Pretty hard. The human arm can pitch a baseball at 100 miles an hour, so it might get close to thirty with a human head. And the seat-belt people tell us that an untethered impact at thirty miles an hour can kill you. Not that I needed the senator dead. I just needed him out of action for a minute and a half.

I moved my right hand over and got it under Reed Riley's chin. His hands came down off his head to tear at my wrist and I replaced them with my own left hand, open, jamming down hard on the top of his head, like a vice. Then I slid my right hand up over his chiselled chin until the heel of my hand lodged there and I clamped my palm over his mouth. I slid my left hand over his brow. I stretched down and clamped his nose between my finger and thumb.

He thought he was suffocating. He tried to bite my palm, but he couldn't get his mouth open. I was clamping too hard. I waited him out. He clawed at my hands. I waited him out. He stretched his head up towards me. I changed my grip, twisted hard and broke his neck.

It was a move I had learned from Leon Garber. The suffocation part makes it easy. They always stretch their heads up. Garber said it never fails, and it never has for me.

And it succeeded with the senator. He was weaker, but his face was slick with blood from where I had broken his nose on the dashboard rail, so the effort expended was very much the same.

I got out of the car and closed my door at eleven twenty-eight. I tossed the key into Reed Riley's lap and turned away.

And sensed a figure on my left. And another, on my right.

The figure on my right spoke. She said, 'Reacher?'

I said, 'Deveraux?'

The figure on my left said, 'And Munro.'

I said, 'What the hell are you two doing here?'

Deveraux said, 'Did you really think I was going to let him keep me in the diner?'

'I wish he had. I didn't want either of you to hear about this.'

'You made Riley open the windows. You wanted us to hear.'

'No, I wanted fresh air. I didn't know you were there. I didn't want you to know what they were saying about you. And I wanted Munro to go back to Germany with a clear conscience.'

Munro said, 'My conscience is always clear.'

Deveraux said, 'I'm glad I heard what they said about me.'

Eleven thirty-one. The train was twenty-nine miles south of us. We walked away, on the ties, between the rails, leaving the flat green staff car and its passengers behind us. We made it to the crossing and turned west. Deveraux's cruiser was parked on the shoulder. Munro wouldn't get in. He said he would walk down to Brannan's Bar, where he had left a car he had borrowed. He said he needed to get back to Kelham, to square things away with the captured mortar men, and then to hit the sack ahead of his early start the next morning. We shook hands and I thanked him for his help, and then he moved away and within ten paces he was lost to sight in the dark.

DEVERAUX DROVE ME back to Main Street and parked outside the hotel. Eleven thirty-six in the evening. I said, 'I checked out of my room.'

She said, 'I still have mine.'

'I need to make a phone call first.'

We used the office behind the reception counter. I put a dollar on the desk and dialled Garber's office. A lieutenant answered and said he was the senior person on duty. Night crew. I asked if he had paper and pencil handy. He said yes. I told him to stand by to take dictation and to leave the finished product on Garber's desk.

'Ready?' I asked him.

He said he was.

I said, 'A tragedy occurred last night in Carter Crossing, Mississippi, when a car carrying United States Senator Carlton Riley was struck by a passing train. The car was being driven by the senator's son, US Army Captain Reed Riley, who was based at nearby Fort Kelham, Mississippi. Senator Riley, of Missouri, was chairman of the Senate's Armed Services Committee, and Captain Riley, described by the army as a rising star, was in command of an infantry unit regularly deployed on missions of great sensitivity. Both men died in the accident. Carter County Sheriff Elizabeth Deveraux confirmed that local drivers regularly attempt to beat the train across the road junction, in order to avoid a long and inconvenient delay, and it is believed that Captain Riley, recently posted to the area and adventurous in spirit, simply mistimed his approach to the crossing.'

'Second paragraph,' I said. 'The senator and his son were returning to Fort Kelham after helping the nearby town celebrate Sheriff Deveraux's successful resolution of a homicide investigation. The killing spree had lasted nine months. The five victims included three local women in their twenties, a teenage boy and a freelance journalist. The male perpetrator, responsible for all five deaths, is described as a militia member from Tennessee. He was shot to death earlier in the week by local police, while resisting arrest.'

'Got that,' the lieutenant said again.

'Start typing,' I said, and hung up.

Eleven forty-two. The train was eighteen miles away.

WE SAT SIDE BY SIDE on her bed, a little shell-shocked, and she said, 'You did everything you could. Justice is done all round and the army doesn't suffer. You're a good soldier.'

I said, 'I'm sure they'll find something to complain about.'

'But I'm disappointed with the Marine Corps. They shouldn't have cooperated. They stabbed me in the back.'

'Not really,' I said. 'They were under tremendous pressure. They pretended to play ball, but they put in a bunch of coded messages. Two dead people and an invented one? That thing with your rank? Those mistakes had to be deliberate so the file wouldn't stand up. Same with Garber. He was ranting and raving about you, but really he was acting a part. He was challenging me to think.'

'Did you believe the file when you first saw it?'

'Honest answer? I didn't instantly reject it. It took me a few hours.'

'You asked me all kinds of weird questions.'

'I know,' I said. 'I'm sorry.'

She leaned over and kissed me. I went and washed the last traces of Carlton Riley's blood off my hands and then we made love. The room began to shake on cue, the glass on her bathroom shelf began to tinkle, her floor quivered, and her bed shook and bounced. And then the train was gone.

Afterwards I dressed and got ready to head home. Deveraux smiled bravely and asked me to drop by any time I was in the area. I smiled bravely and said I would. I left the hotel and walked up to the diner and climbed into the borrowed Buick and drove east. I drove past Fort Kelham's gate, onwards into Alabama, and then north, no traffic, night-time hours all the way, and I was on post before dawn.

I hid out and slept four hours and emerged to find that my hasty dictation to Garber's night crew had been adopted by the army as the official version of events. There was talk of a posthumous Distinguished Service Medal for Reed Riley, to recognise his time in an unspecified foreign country, and his father was to have a memorial service in a grand D.C. church.

I got neither medal nor memorial. I got thirty minutes with Leon Garber. He told me the news was not good. The fat staff officer from Kelham's PR squad had done the damage. He had made some calls to Benning, which had bounced around, mostly upwards, and then followed up with a written report. As a result I was on the involuntary separation list. Garber said he would gladly broker the deal to get me taken off. Then he went quiet.

I said, 'What?'

He said, 'But your life wouldn't be worth living. You'd never get promoted again. You'd be terminal at major if you lived to be a hundred. You'd be deployed to a storage depot in New Jersey.'

'I covered the army's ass.'

'And the army will be reminded of that every time it sees you.'

Garber's clerk gave me a paper explaining the procedure. I could do it in person at the Pentagon, or by mail. So I got in the Buick and headed for D.C. I had to return the car to Neagley anyway. When I got there I picked a bank at random and moved my account.

Then I headed over to the Pentagon. I got halfway to the main concourse door and then I stopped. The crowd carried on around me. I didn't want to go in. I borrowed a pen from a passer-by. I signed my form and dropped it in a mailbox. Then I walked out of the main gate to the tangle of roads between it and the river.

I was thirty-six years old, a citizen of a country I had barely seen, and there were places to go, things to do. There were cities, and there was countryside. There were mountains, and there were valleys. There were rivers. There were museums, and music, and motels, and clubs, and diners, and bars, and buses. There were battlefields and birthplaces, and legends, and roads. There was company if I wanted it, and there was solitude if I didn't.

I picked a road at random, and I put one foot on the kerb and one in the traffic lane, and I stuck out my thumb.

lee child

What led you to go back to Jack Reacher's early career for this latest book?

It had always been in the back of my mind that we should have a book about Reacher's last case in uniform. Readers have often wondered why he left the army all those years ago, and this year seemed like a good time to lay it out.

Have you ever put Reacher in a real bind and then worried that you might not be able to get him out?

All the time, but that's the fun of it. He has to work hard, and I have to work hard, and I think the readers find that convincing.

Do you think there are things about Jack Reacher that even you don't know yet?

Probably—he continues to surprise me.

What do you enjoy most about the time you spend in Manhattan?

I love New York City for its energy and its endless range of things to do. It's crowded but anonymous.

And what tells you it's time to head to your other home in the South of France, to spend time with family?

My wife and I travel back and forth unpredictably, so we're often together in both places. It's usually about commitments—if I need to be in Europe I head over there, and if I need to be in the States I come back.

What's your most treasured possession?

Honestly, I don't treasure any possessions. I guess I would be sad if I lost my library.

Reacher seems to thrive on not getting tied down. Do you think that, in today's world, it's actually a hard lifestyle to follow and that we need a solid home life more than ever?

I suppose some people do. Wandering has always been hard, but I don't think it has got any harder. Different strokes for different folks, I guess.

It's a little-known fact, perhaps, that you studied Law at university, although never with any intention of working as a lawyer. What appealed to you about the subject?

I was interested in history, politics, sociology, language, economics, psychology and so on, and it struck me that law is a snapshot of all of those things at the same time.

What do you think these days of the TV industry that you left in the 1990s?

Pretty bad, but not always awful. Which is a shame—British TV used to lead the world.

Are there any professions you'd like to have tried, had you not made it as a writer?

None that suit my meagre talents—I would love to be a musician, but that's a non-starter, unfortunately.

Reacher's motto: 'hope for the best, plan for the worst' is one that you've said you share. Does it still work for you, or have you become more hopeful or more cautious over the years?

I'm always hopeful and never cautious, but a plan B is a good thing to have.

What has been the happiest time of your life, or what brings you most joy?

My whole life has been happy. Probably the first ten years of parenthood was the most sustained period of fun and joy.

And what is your biggest regret, if any?

I have no real regrets.

If you could give your daughter, Ruth, one piece of advice that she should follow to the letter, what would it be?

Ignore all advice—find your own way.

And what would your wife change about you if she could, do you imagine?

She'd make me more romantic.

Do you feel you've become more American since you've lived in the States, or are you still easily recognisable as an Englishman at twenty paces? And, if so, why?

I think I've become a transatlantic person—there are thousands of us and, yes, we're recognisable.

Toast and Marmite or bagel with smoked salmon and cream cheese?

Toast and Marmite, probably.

A quiet night in with a good book or DVD to enjoy, or a lively party with lots of people—which appeals the most?

Both—and happily I get plenty of each.

What's your favourite indulgent treat?

Probably the quiet night in with a good book!

Has filming started yet for *One Shot*, the first of your movies to go into production in Hollywood? Are there any plans for you to visit the set or meet the stars?

Yes, shooting has started, and I have visited the set and met everybody, and I've got another few visits lined up. It's a lot of fun for me.

DEAD MAN'S GRIP

PETER JAMES

After Carly Chase is involved in a traffic accident in Brighton, in which a teenage cyclist is killed, she receives a chilling warning from Detective Superintendent Roy Grace of the Sussex Police informing her that the deceased young man had deadly connections—a family across the Atlantic who have sworn revenge at all cost. With the net closing in, Carly realises she must resort to desperate measures to save herself and her son from danger . . .

1

On the morning of the accident, Carly Chase had forgotten to set the alarm and overslept. She woke with a bad hangover, a dog crushing her and the demented pounding of drums and cymbals coming from her son's bedroom.

To add to her gloom, it was pelting with rain outside.

She lay still for a moment, gathering her thoughts. A client she loathed would be in her office in just over two hours. It was going to be one of those days, she had the feeling, when things just kept on getting worse.

Like the drumming.

'Tyler!' she yelled. 'For Christ's sake, stop that. Are you ready?'

Otis leapt off the bed and began barking furiously.

The drumming fell silent. 'What's for breakfast, Mum?' Tyler called out.

She staggered to the bathroom, found the paracetamols and gulped two down. She stared at herself in the bathroom mirror. Most of her forty-one-year-old face was shrouded in a tangle of blonde hair that looked like matted straw.

'Arsenic!' she called back. 'Laced with cyanide and rat poison.'

'I had that yesterday!' Tyler shouted back.

'Well, it didn't work, did it?'

She switched on the shower, waited for it to warm up, then stepped inside.

STUART FERGUSON sat high up in his cab, waiting impatiently for the lights to change. The wipers clunked away the rain as rush-hour traffic sluiced across Brighton's Old Shoreham Road below him. The engine of his sixteen-wheel Volvo fridge-box artic chuntered away, a stream of warm air toasting his legs. April already, but winter had still not relaxed its grip: he'd driven through snow at the start of his journey.

He yawned, then took a long swig of Red Bull. He put the can into the cup-holder, then drummed his hands on the steering wheel to the beat of 'Bat Out of Hell', which was playing loud enough to wake the dead fish behind him. It was the fifth can he had drunk in the past few hours, and that and the music were the only things that were keeping him awake.

He had driven through the night from Aberdeen, in Scotland. He'd been on the road for eighteen hours, with barely a break other than a stop for food at Newport Pagnell Services and a brief kip in a lay-by a couple of hours earlier.

The traffic lights changed and he rammed the gear lever forward. After an earlier stop at Springs, a salmon smokery a few miles north in the South Downs, he now had one final delivery to make. It was to a supermarket on the outskirts of Brighton. Then he would drive to the port of Newhaven, load up with frozen New Zealand lamb, snatch a few hours' sleep on the quay and head back up to Scotland.

Ordinarily on this run he would have taken a few hours out to get some proper kip—and comply with the law on driver hours. But the refrigeration was on the blink, with the temperature rising steadily, and he couldn't take the risk of ruining the valuable cargo of scallops, shrimps, prawns and salmon. He just had to keep going.

So long as he was careful, he would be fine. He knew where the vehicle check locations were, and by listening to CB radio he'd get warned of any active ones. That was why he was detouring through the city now, rather than taking the main road round it. Then he cursed. Ahead of him he could see red flashing lights, then barriers descending. The level crossing at Portslade Station. With a sharp hiss of his brakes, he pulled up.

'Bat Out of Hell' finished and, as the railway-crossing barrier began to rise again, he switched to an Elkie Brooks album. 'Pearl's a Singer' began to play.

'In one hundred yards turn left,' commanded the voice of the satnav.

'Yes, boss,' he grunted and glanced down at the left-angled arrow on the screen, directing him off Station Road and into Portland Road.

He indicated and changed down a gear, breaking well in advance, careful to get the weighting of the heavy lorry stabilised before making the sharp turn on the wet road.

TONY REVERE leaned down and kissed her, tasted her sleepy breath and inhaled it deeply, loving it. 'You're gorgeous, did I tell you that?'

'About a thousand times. You're gorgeous, too. Did I tell you that?'

'About ten thousand times. You're like a record that got stuck in a groove,' he said.

Suzy looked up at him. He was tall and lean, his short, dark hair gelled in uneven spikes. He was dressed in a padded anorak over a T-shirt and jeans, and smelled of the Abercrombie & Fitch cologne she really liked.

There was an air of confidence about him that had captivated her the first time they had spoken, down in the dark basement bar of Pravda, in Greenwich Village, when she'd been in New York on holiday with her best friend. Poor Katie had ended up flying back to England on her own, while she had stayed on with Tony.

'Come back to bed,' she said.

'I am so not coming back to bed. You know what's going to happen if I don't get good grades this semester?'

'Back to the States to Mummy.'

'You know my mom.'

'Uh huh, I do. Scary lady.'

'You said it.'

'So, you're afraid of her?'

'Everyone's afraid of my mom.'

He'd been smitten with Suzy since the first day they'd met. So much so that he had abandoned his plans to study for a business degree at Harvard and instead had followed her from New York to England, and joined her at the University of Brighton.

He kissed her again, then tugged a baseball cap onto his head, wheeled his mountain bike out of the apartment, down the stairs, and out into the cold, blustery April morning. As he closed the front door behind him, he breathed in the salty tang of the Brighton sea air, then looked at his watch.

Shit. He was due to see his tutor in twenty minutes. If he pedalled like hell, he might just make it.

'THAT NOISE is driving me nuts,' Carly said.

Tyler, in the passenger seat of her Audi convertible, was bent over his iPhone playing some game he was hooked on called Angry Birds. Why did everything he did involve noise?

'We're late,' he said, without looking up and without stopping playing.

'Tyler, please. I have a headache.'

He grinned. 'You shouldn't have got drunk last night. Again.'

She winced. 'Yep, well, you'd have got drunk last night, too, if you'd had to put up with that prat.'

'Serves you right for going on blind dates.'

'Thanks.'

'You're welcome. I'm late for school. I'm going to get stick for that.' He was still peering intently at the game through his oval, wire-framed glasses.

She stared through the windscreen at the red light and then at the clock: 8.56 a.m. With luck, she'd drop him off at school then arrive at the office in time to see her client, Mr Misery. No wonder his wife had left him. But hey, she wasn't paid to sit in judgment. She was paid to stop Mrs Misery from walking off with both of her husband's testicles, as well as everything else that she was after.

'It really hurts, still, Mum.'

'What does? Oh, right, your brace.'

Tyler touched the front of his mouth. 'It's too tight.'

'I'll call the orthodontist and get you an appointment with him.'

Tyler nodded and focused back on his game.

She reached out and ran her fingers through his tousled brown hair.

He jerked his head away. 'Hey, don't mess it up!'

She glanced fondly at him for an instant. He was growing up fast and looked handsome in his shirt and tie, red blazer and grey trousers. Not quite thirteen years old and girls were already chasing him. He was growing more like his late father every day; there were some expressions he had which reminded her of Kes too much. In unguarded moments that could make her tearful, even five years on.

Moments later, at a few minutes past nine, she pulled up outside the red gates of St Christopher's School. Tyler clicked off his seat belt and reached behind him to pick up his rucksack.

'Is Friend Mapper on?'

He gave her a 'Duh' look. 'Yes, it's on. I'm not a baby, you know.'

Friend Mapper was a GPS app on the iPhone that enabled her to track exactly where he was at any moment on her own iPhone.

'So long as I pay your bill, you keep it on. That's the deal.'

'You're overprotective. I might turn out to be emotionally retarded.'

'That's a risk I'll have to take.'

He climbed out of the car, then smiled hesitantly and slammed the door.

She watched him walk in through the gates. Every time he went out of her sight, she was scared for him. Worried about him. Tyler was right, she was overprotective, but she couldn't help it. She loved him desperately and, despite some of his maddening attitudes and behaviour, she knew that he loved her back, just as much.

She headed up towards Portland Road, driving faster than she should, anxious not to be late for her client.

Her phone pinged with an incoming text. When she reached the junction with the main road, she glanced down at it.

I had a great time last night—wld love to see you again XXX

In your dreams, sweetheart. She shuddered at the thought of him. Dave from Preston, Lancashire. Preston Dave, she'd called him. At least she had been honest with the photograph of herself she'd put up on the dating website.

Keeping her foot on the brake and leaning forwards, she deleted the text, decisively, returning the phone to the hands-free cradle with no small amount of satisfaction. Then she made a left turn, pulling out in front of a white van, and accelerated. The van hooted and flashing its lights angrily, closed up right behind her and began tailgating her. She held up two fingers.

There were to be many times, in the days and weeks ahead, when she bitterly regretted reading that text. If she hadn't waited at that junction for those precious seconds, fiddling with her phone, if she had made that left turn just thirty seconds earlier, everything might have been very different.

'BLACK,' GLENN BRANSON SAID, holding the golf umbrella over their heads. 'It's the only colour!'

Detective Superintendent Roy Grace looked up at him. At five foot ten inches, he was a good four inches shorter than his junior colleague and friend, and considerably less sharply dressed. Approaching his fortieth birthday, Grace was not handsome in a conventional sense. He had a kind face with a slightly misshapen nose that gave him a rugged appearance. His fair hair was cropped short and he had clear blue eyes that Cleo said resembled those of the actor Paul Newman.

Feeling like a child in a sweet shop, the detective superintendent ran his eyes over the rows of vehicles on the used-car forecourt. He was taking advantage of a quiet lunchtime to nip out of the office. A car he'd liked the look of on the Autotrader website was at this local dealer.

Detective Sergeant Branson shook his head. 'Black's best. You'll find that useful when you come to sell it—unless you're planning to drive it over a cliff, like your last one.'

'Very funny.'

Roy Grace's previous car, his beloved maroon Alfa Romeo 147 sports saloon, had been wrecked during a police pursuit the previous autumn, and he had been wrangling with the insurance company ever since. Finally, they had agreed a miserly settlement figure.

'You need to think about these things, old-timer. Getting near retirement, you need to look after the pennies.'

'I'm thirty-nine. Anyhow, black's wrong for an Italian sports car.'

'It's the best colour for everything.' Branson tapped his chest. 'Look at me. Black is the colour of the future.'

Roy Grace stared at him. 'I'm not allowed to discuss that under the Racial Equality Act. And anyway, as I'm so old I won't live long enough to see the future—especially standing here in the pouring rain. I'm freezing.' He pointed. 'I like that one,' he said, indicating a red two-seater convertible.

'In your dreams. You're about to become a father, remember? What you need is one of those.' Glenn Branson pointed across at a Renault Espace.

'Thanks, I'm not into people carriers. Anyhow, I'm not choosing anything without Cleo's approval.' He took a step towards a sleek silver two-door Alfa Brera and stared at it covetously.

'Don't go there,' Branson said. 'Two doors. How are you going to get the baby in and out of the back?' He shook his head sadly. 'You have to get something more practical now you're going to be a family man.'

Grace stared at the Brera. It was one of the most beautiful cars he'd ever seen. As he took a further step towards it, his mobile phone rang.

'Roy Grace,' he said.

It was Cleo, twenty-six weeks pregnant with their child, and she sounded terrible, as if she could barely speak.

'Roy,' she gasped. 'I'm in hospital.'

'TOSSER,' CARLY SAID, watching the white van that filled her rearview mirror. She kept carefully to the 30mph speed limit as she drove along the wide street, heading towards Station Road.

Immediately ahead of her was a van parked outside a kitchen appliance shop, with two men unloading a crate from the rear. It was blocking her view of a side road just beyond. She clocked a lorry that was coming towards her, a few hundred yards away, but she had plenty of space. Just as she started pulling out, her phone rang.

She glanced down at the display and saw to her irritation that it was Preston Dave calling. She was in no mood to speak to him. Then, as she looked back up at the road, a cyclist going hell for leather suddenly appeared out of nowhere, coming straight at her, over a pedestrian crossing on her side of the road, just as the lights turned red.

For an instant, in panic, she thought it must be she who was on the wrong side of the road. She swung the steering wheel hard to the left, stamping on the brake pedal, thumping over the kerb, missing him by inches, and skidded, wheels locked, across the wet surface of the pavement.

Empty chairs and tables outside a café raced towards her as if she was on a scary funfair ride, and she screamed as the nose of her car smashed into the wall beneath the café window. An explosion numbed her ears and she felt a terrible jolt on her shoulder, saw a blur of white, and smelled something that reminded her of gunpowder. Then she saw glass crashing down in front of the buckled bonnet of the car.

'Oh God!' she said, panting in shock. 'Oh God!'

Her ears popped and sounds became much louder. A baggy white cushion lay on her lap. The airbag, she realised. Still in shock, she shoved the car door open and tumbled out, her feet catching in the seat belt, tripping her, sending her sprawling painfully onto the wet pavement.

As she lay there for an instant, she heard a banshee wail above her head. A burglar alarm. Then she could hear another wailing sound. This time it was human. A scream. Had she hit someone?

Her knee and right hand were stinging like hell, but she hauled herself to her feet, looking first at the wreckage of the café and then across the road. She froze.

The lorry had stopped on the opposite side. A huge artic, slewed at a strange angle. The driver was clambering down from the cab. People were running into the road right behind it. Running past a mountain bike that had been twisted into an ugly shape, past a baseball cap and tiny bits of debris, towards what she thought was a roll of carpet lying further along the road, leaking dark fluid from one end onto the rain-lashed black tarmac.

All the traffic had stopped, and the people who had been running stopped too, suddenly, as if they had become statues. She felt she was staring at a tableau. Then she walked, stumbling into the road, the high-pitched howl of the siren almost drowned out by the screams of a young woman who was standing on the pavement, staring at that roll of carpet.

Fighting her brain, which wanted to tell her it was something different, Carly saw the laced-up trainer that was attached to one end.

And realised it wasn't a roll of carpet. It was a severed human leg.

She vomited, the world spinning round her.

PHIL DAVIDSON and Vicky Donoghue, dressed in their green paramedic uniforms, were chatting in the cab of the ambulance when they were interrupted by the high-pitched siren. The sound of a call-out. Vicky started the engine, switched on the blue lights and pushed her way carefully out over a red traffic light. She turned right and accelerated up the hill, past St Nicholas's Church.

By the time they reached Portland Road, Vicky could see that traffic had come to a complete halt in both directions. Phil pulled on his surgical gloves, mentally preparing himself for the task ahead.

A lorry was facing them, the driver's door open, and several people were gathered towards its rear offside. Vicky halted in front of the lorry and the two paramedics climbed out.

A short, stubby man in his mid-forties, in jeans and overalls, hurried towards them. From his pallid face, wide staring eyes and quavering voice, Vicky could see he was in shock.

'Under my lorry,' he said. 'He's under my lorry.' He turned and pointed.

They hurried through the rain towards the rear of the articulated lorry.

Both paramedics knelt down and peered under the vehicle. Vicky saw a young man with short, dark hair streaked with blood and a lacerated face, his body contorted. His eyes were closed. He was wearing a ripped anorak and jeans, and one leg was wrapped round the wheel arch. The other was just a stump of white bone surrounded by jagged denim. The anorak and layers of T-shirt round his midriff were ripped open and a coil of his intestines lay on the road.

Followed by her colleague, Vicky, who was smaller, crawled forwards, beneath the lorry, and seized the young man's wrist, feeling for a pulse. There was a very faint one. She knew there was very little chance of the victim's survival. Even if they got him to hospital still technically alive, infections would finish him off.

'Pulse?' Phil asked.

'Faint radial,' she replied. A radial pulse meant that he had enough blood pressure to maintain some of his organs.

'I'll get the kit.'

They couldn't move him because his leg was trapped. Although the victim's chances were slim, they would do all they could.

She heard Phil radioing for the fire brigade to bring lifting gear. She squeezed the young man's hand. 'Hang on in there,' she said. 'Can you hear me? What's your name?'

There was no response. The pulse was weakening.

'Hang in there,' she said. 'Just hang in there.'

ROY GRACE was shocked to see how pale Cleo looked. She lay in a high bed, in a room with pale blue walls that were cluttered with electrical sockets and apparatus. A tall man in his early thirties, with short, thinning brown hair, dressed in blue medical scrubs and plimsolls, was standing beside her, writing a measurement on a graph on his pad as Roy entered.

She gave Roy a wan, hesitant smile.

'I'm sorry,' she said meekly, as he took her hand and squeezed it.

He felt a terrible panic rising inside him. Had she lost the baby?

The registrar turned towards him. 'You are this lady's husband?'

'Fiancé.' He was so choked he could barely get the word out.

'Ah, yes, of course.' The registrar glanced down at her engagement ring. 'Well, Cleo is all right, but she's lost a lot of blood.'

'What's happened?' he asked.

Cleo's voice was weak as she explained, 'I'd just got to work—I was about to start preparing a body for post-mortem and I suddenly started bleeding, really heavily. I thought I was losing the baby. Then I felt terrible pain, like cramps in my stomach—and the next thing I remember, I was lying on the floor with Darren standing over me. He drove me here.'

Darren was her assistant in the mortuary.

Grace stared at Cleo, relief mingled with uncertainty. 'And the baby?' His eyes shot to the registrar.

'There are complications, but your baby is fine at the moment,' the registrar said, as he turned towards the door and nodded a greeting.

Grace saw a solidly built, bespectacled man enter.

'Mr Holbein, this is Cleo Morey's fiancé.'

'How do you do?' He shook Grace's hand. 'I'm Des Holbein, the consultant gynaecologist. I'm very glad you've arrived. We're going to have to make some decisions.'

Roy felt a sudden stab of anxiety.

'Cleo came in for a routine ultrasound scan five weeks ago, at twenty-one weeks. At that time the baby was a normal size.' The consultant turned to Cleo. 'Today's scan shows your baby has hardly grown at all. This is unusual and cause for concern. It signifies that the placenta is not working well enough to enable your baby to grow. And I'm afraid there's a further complication. It's a very rare condition known as placenta percreta—the placenta is growing much further into the wall of the uterus than it should.'

Roy's heart plunged. 'What does that mean?'

'I would advise waiting and monitoring the placenta very closely. The decision is yours, but my advice is that we keep you here, Cleo, for a few days, and try to support your circulation and hope that the bleeding settles.'

'If it does, will I be able to go back to work?'

'Yes, but not immediately, and no heavy lifting. And we'll have to keep a careful eye on you for the rest of the pregnancy. If there's a second bleed, I will insist on further reductions to your workload and, depending on how the percreta condition develops, I may require you to be hospitalised for the rest of your term. It's not only the baby that is at risk.' He looked at Cleo. 'You are, too.'

'To what extent?' Grace asked.

'Placenta percreta can be life-threatening to the mother,' the consultant said. He turned back to Cleo again. 'If there is a third bleed, there is no doubt about it. You'll have to spend the rest of your pregnancy in hospital.'

'What about damage to our baby?' Grace questioned.

The consultant shook his head. 'Not at this stage. The baby can lose some placenta without a problem. But if it loses too much, it won't grow well. And then, in extreme cases, yes, he or she can die.'

Grace squeezed Cleo's hand again and kissed her on the forehead, terrible thoughts churning inside him. 'It's going to be fine, darling,' he said, but his mouth felt dry.

Please be OK, my darling Cleo. I couldn't bear it if anything happened to you, I really couldn't.

2

In his eight years' experience with the Road Policing Unit, PC Dan Pattenden had learned that if you were the first car to arrive at a crash scene, you would find chaos. Even more so if it was raining.

He began slowing down as he approached and, sure enough, what he observed was a scene of total confusion. An articulated lorry facing away from him and an ambulance just beyond it. A small crowd gathered round the rear offside of the lorry. On the other side of the road, a black Audi convertible, with a buckled bonnet, was up against a café wall.

He halted the brightly marked BMW estate car at an angle across the road—the first step to sealing off the scene—and radioed for back-up. Then, tugging on his cap and his fluorescent jacket, he grabbed an accident report pad and jumped out of the car.

Pattenden sprinted over to the lorry and knelt beside the paramedics.

'What can you tell me?' he said.

The male paramedic shook his head. 'Not looking good. We're losing him.'

More emergency vehicles were arriving. He saw a second ambulance and a paramedic car which would be bringing a specialist trauma doctor. He saw a smartly dressed woman with rain-bedraggled hair standing near the Audi. She was staring, transfixed, at the lorry.

Hurrying over to her, he asked, panting, 'Are you the driver of this car?'

She nodded, eyes vacant, still staring over his shoulder.

'Are you injured? Do you need medical assistance?'

'He just came out of nowhere, came out of that side street, straight at me. I had to swerve, otherwise I'd have hit him.'

'Who?' Surreptitiously he leaned forwards, close enough to smell her breath. There was a faint reek of stale alcohol.

'The cyclist,' she said numbly.

'Were there any other vehicles involved?'

'A white van was right behind me, tailgating me.'

He had a quick look at the Audi. Although the bonnet was crumpled and the airbags had deployed, the interior of the car looked intact.

'Madam, would you mind getting back into your car for a few minutes?'

He waited as she climbed in, then with some difficulty pushed the door, which seemed to have a bent hinge, closed.

At this point, to his relief, came the reassuring sight of his inspector, James Biggs, accompanied by his duty sergeant, Paul Wood. At least now the buck no longer stopped with him.

CARLY SAT NUMBLY in her car, grateful for the rain that coated the windscreen and the side windows like frosted glass, at least giving her some privacy. Her chest was pounding. The image of what was going on underneath the lorry behind her was going round and round inside her head.

She picked up her phone, dialled her office and spoke to her secretary. Halfway through telling her that she did not know when she would be in, she broke down in tears.

She heard a tap on her window. A moment later, the door opened and the police officer who had told her to wait in her car peered in. He was a serious-looking man in his mid-thirties.

'Would you mind stepping out of the car please, madam?'

She climbed out into the rain, her eyes blurry with tears.

The officer asked her again if she was the driver of the car, and then for her name and address. Then, holding a small instrument in a black and yellow weatherproof case, he addressed her in a stiffer, more formal tone. 'Because you have been involved in a road traffic collision, I require you to provide a specimen of breath. I must tell you that failure or refusal to do so is an offence for which you can be arrested. Do you understand?'

She nodded and sniffed.

'Have you drunk any alcohol in the past twenty minutes?'

How many people had an alcoholic drink before 9 a.m.? she wondered. But then she felt a sudden panic. How much had she drunk last night? Not that much, surely. It must be out of her system by now. She shook her head.

'Have you smoked in the last five minutes?'

'No,' she said. 'But I need a fag now.'

Ignoring her comment, the officer asked her age.

'Forty-one.'

He tapped it into the machine, then made a further couple of entries before holding the machine out to her. A white tube protruded from it.

'I'd like you to take a deep breath, seal your lips round the tube and blow hard and continuously until I tell you to stop.'

Carly took a deep breath, then exhaled until she heard a beep.

He nodded his head. 'Thank you.'

He showed her the dial of the machine. On it were the words: Sample taken. Then he stepped back, studying the machine for some moments.

She watched anxiously as suddenly his expression hardened. He said, 'I'm sorry to tell you that you have failed the breath test.' He held the machine up so she could read the dial again. The one word on it: Fail.

She felt her legs giving way. Aware that a man was watching her from inside the café, she steadied herself against the side of her car. This wasn't possible. She could not have failed. She just couldn't have.

'Madam, this device is indicating that you may be over the prescribed limit and I'm arresting you for providing a positive breath sample. You do not have to say anything, but it may harm your defence if you do not mention when questioned something which you may later rely on in court. Anything you say may be given in evidence.'

She shook her head. 'It's not possible,' she said. 'I didn't . . . I haven't . . . I was out last night, but—'

A few minutes ago, Carly could not have imagined her day getting any worse. Now she was walking through the rain, being steered by the guiding arm of a police officer towards a marked car just beyond a line of police tape. She climbed lamely into the rear of the BMW and fumbled for the seat belt. The officer slammed the door behind her.

The slam felt as final as a chapter of her life ending.

THE VAGUELY ART DECO building that housed HQ CID for Sussex Police had always reminded Carly of the superstructure of a tired old cruise ship: ironically, she knew the building well from the start of her career, when she'd been a trainee solicitor.

She was taken inside to a large, brightly lit room dominated by a raised semicircular central station divided into sections. Behind each section sat men and women dressed in white shirts with black epaulettes and black ties. PC Pattenden steered her across to the console and up to the counter, which was almost head-high. Behind it sat a uniformed man in his forties.

She listened numbly as PC Pattenden outlined the circumstances of her arrest. Then the shirt-sleeved man spoke directly to her, his voice earnest, almost as if he was doing her a favour.

'I am Custody Sergeant Cornford, Mrs Chase. You have heard what has been said. I'm authorising your detention for the purpose of securing and preserving evidence and to obtain evidence by questioning. Is that clear to you?'

Carly nodded.

'You have the right to have someone informed of your arrest and to see a solicitor. Would you like us to provide you with a duty solicitor?'

'I'm a solicitor,' she said. 'I'd like you to contact one of my colleagues, Ken Acott at Acott Arlington.'

Carly got some satisfaction from the frown that crossed the sergeant's face. Acott was widely regarded as the top criminal solicitor in the city.

'May I have his number?'

Carly gave him the office number, hoping Ken was not in court.

'I will make that call,' the custody sergeant said. 'But I am required to inform you that although you have a right to see a solicitor, the drink-driving process may not be delayed. I am authorising you to be searched.' He then produced two green plastic trays and spoke into his intercom.

Carly's phone was handed to the sergeant. A young, uniformed woman police officer came over, snapping on a pair of blue gloves before patting her down, starting with her head and rummaging in each of her coat pockets. Then she asked her to remove her boots and socks, knelt down and searched between each of her toes. The woman then started emptying out her handbag. Carly said nothing, feeling utterly humiliated.

When the woman had finished, Carly signed a receipt, and PC Pattenden led her into a small side room, where she was fingerprinted and a swab of her mouth was taken for DNA.

Next, holding a yellow form, PC Pattenden escorted her out, past the console, up a step and into a narrow room that felt like a laboratory. There was a row of white kitchen units to her left, followed by a sink and a fridge, and a machine at the far end, with a video monitor on the top. To her right was a wooden desk and two blue chairs.

PC Pattenden pointed at a wall-mounted camera. 'OK, I must tell you that everything seen and heard in this room is recorded. Do you understand?'

'Yes.'

The officer then told her about the breath-test machine. He explained that he required her to give two breath specimens and that the lower of the readings would be taken. If the reading was above forty but below fifty-one she would have the further option of providing a blood or urine sample.

She blew into the tube, desperately hoping that she was now below the limit and this nightmare, or at least this part of it, would be over.

'I can't believe it. I didn't drink that much—really, I didn't.'

'Now blow again for the second test,' he said calmly.

Some moments later, he showed her the printout of the first test. To her horror it was fifty-five. Then he showed her the second reading. It was also fifty-five.

Roy Grace's phone rang in the hospital room. Releasing his grip on Cleo's hand he tugged the phone out of his pocket and answered it.

It was Glenn Branson, sounding in work mode. 'Yo, chief. How is she?'

'OK, thanks. She'll be fine.'

'We've had a call from Inspector James Biggs, Traffic. A fatal at Portland Road. Sounds like a hit and run. They're requesting assistance from Major Crime Branch as it looks like death by dangerous driving or possibly manslaughter.'

'OK, organise a crime scene manager for them, then go down yourself and see that they've got everything they need.'

'I'm on my way.'

As Grace put his phone back in his pocket, Cleo took his hand.

'I'm OK, darling. Go back to work,' she said. 'Really, I'm fine.'

He looked at her dubiously, then kissed her on the forehead. 'I love you.'

'I love you, too,' she said.

'I don't want to leave you here.'

'You have to get out there and catch bad guys. I want them all locked up before Bump is born!'

He stayed for another half-hour, then, after saying goodbye to Cleo and promising to return later in the day, he drove towards Portland Road and the accident. Portland Road, with its shops and cafés, was normally busy at most times of the day and night, but as Grace turned his car into it, it was as quiet as a ghost town. A short distance ahead he saw a Road Policing Unit BMW parked sideways in the middle of the road, with crime-scene tape beyond and a gaggle of rubberneckers, some snapping away with cameras and phones.

Beyond the tape was a scene of quiet, businesslike activity. He saw a large articulated lorry, its rear section screened off by a green tarpaulin. He noticed Darren Wallace, Cleo's assistant, standing with a colleague. Further along was another tape across the road, a Police Community Support Officer scene guard and more rubberneckers. He saw several police officers he recognised, including Glenn Branson, who was talking to Major Crime Branch Crime Scene Manager Tracy Stocker, and the uniformed Road Policing Unit inspector, James Biggs. The scene of crime officer photographer was working away methodically. Some officers were combing the road and taking notes. Unlike at most crime scenes, none of those present was wearing protective suits and overshoes. Collision, or RTC, sites were generally considered already too contaminated.

Before he had a chance to hail Branson, suddenly, materialising out of the ether—as he seemed to do at every crime scene Grace attended—was Kevin Spinella, the young crime reporter from the local paper, the *Argus*. In his mid-twenties, with bright eyes and a thin face, he was chewing gum with small, sharp teeth that always reminded Grace of a rat's.

'Good morning, Detective Superintendent!' he said. 'Nasty, isn't it?'

'The weather?' Grace said.

Spinella grinned. 'Na! You know what I'm talking about. Sounds like it could be a murder from what I hear—is that what you think?'

Grace was guarded, but tried to avoid being openly rude. The police needed the local media on their side as it could be immensely useful. But equally, he knew, it could at times bite you hard and painfully.

'You tell me. I've just arrived, so you probably know more than I do.'

'Witnesses I've spoken to are talking about a white van that went through a red light and hit the cyclist, then accelerated off at high speed.'

'You should be a detective,' Grace said.

'Think I'll stick to reporting. Anything you'd like to tell me?'

'Anything we find out, you'll be the first to know.' He nearly added, *You always are anyway, even if we don't tell you*. It was an ongoing cause of irritation to Roy Grace that Spinella had a mole inside Sussex Police, which enabled him always to get to the scene of any crime way ahead of the rest of the press pack.

For the past year he had been quietly digging away to discover that person's identity, but so far he had made no progress.

He turned away, signed his name on the log held by the scene guard and ducked under the tape to greet Glenn Branson. Then they both walked towards the lorry, safely out of earshot of the reporter.

'What have you got?' Grace asked.

'Young male under the lorry. They've found a student ID card. His name's Anthony Revere, he's at Brighton Uni. Someone's gone there to get his full details and next of kin. It seems like he came out of a side road—St Heliers Avenue—turned right, east, on the wrong side of Portland Road, causing that Audi travelling west to swerve onto the pavement. He was then hit by a white van that had gone through the red light, a Transit or similar, that was behind the Audi, also travelling west. The van flipped him across the road, under the wheels of the artic, which was travelling east. Then the van did a runner.'

Grace thought for a moment. 'Anyone ID the driver?'

Branson shook his head. 'There are a lot of witnesses. I've got a team covering the area for any CCTV footage. I've put an alert out to the Road Policing Unit to stop any white van within two hours' driving distance of here. With luck, we'll get the registration from a CCTV camera.'

'What about the drivers of the Audi and the lorry?'

'Woman Audi driver's in custody—failed a breath test. Lorry driver's in shock. Someone from the Collision Investigation Unit's had a look at his tachometer and he's way out of hours.'

'That's all looking great, then,' Grace said sarcastically. 'A drunk driver in one vehicle, an exhausted one in another, and a third who's scarpered.'

'We do have one piece of evidence so far,' Branson said. 'They've found part of a damaged wing mirror that looks like it's from the van. It has a serial number on it.'

Grace nodded. 'Good.' Then he pointed along the road. 'What's under the fluorescent jacket?'

'The cyclist's right leg.'

Grace swallowed. 'Glad I asked.'

SPECIALLY TRAINED family liaison officers were used whenever possible, but any member of the police force could find themselves delivering a death message. It was the least popular duty, and officers of the Road Policing Unit tended, reluctantly, to get the lion's share.

PC Tony Omotoso was a muscular, stocky, black officer with ten years' experience in the unit. Despite all the horrors he had seen, he remained cheerful and positive, and was always courteous, even to the worst offenders he encountered.

His first task had been to make next-of-kin enquiries from the information that he'd found in the victim's rucksack. The most useful item in it had been the deceased's student card from Brighton University.

A visit to the registrar's office at the university had revealed that Tony Revere was a US citizen, twenty-one years old, and cohabiting with another student, Susan Caplan, who was from Brighton. She wasn't due to attend any lectures until tomorrow, so it was likely that she was at home. The university had the contact details of Revere's family in New York, but Omotoso decided that Susan Caplan should be informed first. Hopefully, she would have more details about him and would be able formally to identify his body.

As much for moral support as anything else, Omotoso asked his regular shift partner, PC Ian Upperton, to join him.

They parked the car outside a semi-detached house on Westbourne Villas that looked surprisingly smart for student accommodation, then walked along the path to the front door. Both of them looked at the entry phone panel with its list of names. Number eight read: CAPLAN/REVERE.

PC Omotoso pressed the button.

There was a crackle of static, followed by a voice. 'Hello?'

'Susan Caplan?' he asked.

'Yes. Who is it?'

'Sussex Police. May we come in, please?'

There was a silence lasting a couple of seconds but it felt much longer. Then, 'Police, did you say?'

'Yes. We'd like to speak to you, please,' Omotoso said firmly.

'Uh, yuh. Come up to the second floor, door at the top. Are you calling about my handbag?'

'Your handbag?' he said, thrown by the question.

Moments later there was a rasping buzz, followed by a sharp click. Omotoso pushed the door open and they walked up the stairs. As they reached the top of the second flight, a door opened and a pretty girl, about twenty, greeted them with a smile.

'Don't tell me you've found it!' she said. 'That would be amazing!'

Both men courteously removed their caps.

Tony Omotoso said, 'Found what?'

'My handbag?' She squinted at them quizzically. 'The one someone stole at Escape Two nightclub on Saturday night.'

'No, Susan, we haven't come about your handbag. I don't know about that, I'm afraid. We're from the Road Policing Unit,' Omotoso said, registering her sudden look of confusion. 'According to the records from Brighton University, you are living with Tony Revere. Is that correct?'

She nodded, eyeing each of them with sudden suspicion.

'I'm afraid that Tony has been involved in a road traffic accident on his bicycle.' She stared at him, suddenly fixated. 'I'm sorry to say, Susan, that following the injuries he received he didn't survive.'

He fell silent deliberately. It had long been his policy to let the recipient of the message come out with the words themselves. That way, he found, it sank in better and more immediately.

'You mean Tony's dead?' she said.

'I'm very sorry, yes.'

She started reeling. PC Upperton caught her arm and guided her down onto a large sofa. She sat there in silence for some moments, while the two officers stood awkwardly. There was never an easy way. She fell silent and then started to shake, little tremors rippling through her body.

They remained standing. She was shaking her head from side to side now. 'Oh, shit!' she said suddenly. 'Oh, shit.' Then she seemed to collapse in on herself, burying her face in her hands. 'Tell me it's not true.'

The two officers glanced at each other. Tony Omotoso said, 'Do you have someone who could come round and be with you today? A friend? Any member of your family you'd like us to call?'

She looked up, then closed her eyes tight. 'What happened?'

'He was in a collision with a lorry, but we don't have all the details.'

There was a long silence. She hugged herself and began sobbing.

'Do you have a neighbour who could come round?' Omotoso asked.

'No. I . . . I don't . . . I . . . we . . . I . . . oh . . .'

'Would you like a drink?' Ian Upperton asked.

'I don't want a drink, I want Tony,' she sobbed. 'Tell me what happened.'

Omotoso's radio crackled. He turned the volume right down. There was another long silence before eventually he said, 'We're going to need to make sure it is Tony Revere. Would you be willing to identify the body later today? Just in case there's been a mistake?'

'His mother's the one you're going to have to speak to. She'll be on the first plane over from New York, I can tell you that.'

'Would you prefer her to identify Tony?'

She fell silent again, sobbing. Then she said, 'You'd better get her to do it. She hates my guts. She'd never believe me, anyway.'

DAN PATTENDEN'S expression was unreadable. 'I'm sorry, but I'm going to repeat the caution I gave you earlier at the collision scene, Mrs Chase.' He did so, finishing with, 'Anything you say may be given in evidence.'

Carly felt her throat constricting: her mouth was suddenly parched. 'The cyclist has died?' Her words came out almost as a whisper.

'Yes, I'm afraid so.'

'It wasn't me,' she said. 'I didn't hit him. I crashed because I was . . . because I avoided him. I swerved to avoid him because he was on the wrong side of the road. I would have hit him if I hadn't.'

'You'd best save all that for your interview.'

He propelled her across the custody reception floor, past the large central station and into a narrow corridor. They stopped at a green door with a glass panel. He opened it and, to her horror, ushered her into a cell.

'You're not putting me in here?'

'This is where you will have to wait until your solicitor gets here. I have to get back now, so I'm leaving you. OK?'

It was not OK. It was so totally not OK. But she was too shocked to argue. Instead she just nodded lamely. Then he shut the door.

SHORTLY BEFORE 5 P.M., Roy Grace sat in his first-floor office in the Major Crime Branch of Sussex CID, sipping a mug of tea.

His mountain of paperwork seemed to grow of its own accord, as if it was some fast-breeding organism, and it seemed that emails were pouring in faster than he could read them. But he was finding it hard to focus on anything other than Cleo. Since leaving the hospital that morning, he had made repeated calls to check on her.

Taking a break, Roy Grace leaned back in his chair and stared out of his window towards the south. The CID headquarters, Sussex House, was in an industrial estate on the outskirts of the city of Brighton and Hove. On a clear day, he could see the distant rooftops of Brighton and sometimes the blue of the English Channel.

The first two months of the year had been relatively quiet. But since the start of spring, the whole city seemed to be kicking off. Three of the average twenty murders that Sussex could expect annually had taken place during the past few weeks. In addition, there had been an armed robbery on a jewellery shop and the brutal rape of a nurse.

As a consequence, both the Major Incident Rooms at Sussex House were in use, so Grace had borrowed the office next door to his for the first briefing of Operation Violin, the name the computer had given to the hit-and-run fatality involving the cyclist in Portland Road.

Grace planned to keep the inquiry team small and tight. From his study of the evidence so far, it seemed a straightforward case. The van driver could have had any number of reasons for doing what he did—possibly he had stolen the vehicle, or had no insurance, or was carrying something illegal. Grace did not think it would be a hard job to find him. He had made Glenn Branson his deputy senior investigating officer.

He stood up and walked next door. DC Nick Nicholl was already sitting down at the long meeting table. He looked bleary eyed and zapped of energy. Since the birth of his son some months before, the young detective constable's focus tended to be elsewhere. He had recommended some books to Grace: *Fatherhood. From Lad to Dad. Secrets of the Baby Whisperer*. There was so much to take on board.

He was joined a few moments later by Bella Moy, carrying a box of Maltesers in one hand and a bottle of water in the other. The detective sergeant was in her mid-thirties, cheery-faced beneath a tangle of hennaed brown hair.

Next came DC Emma-Jane Boutwood. A slim girl with an alert face and long, fair hair scooped up into a ponytail, the DC had made a miraculous recovery after being nearly killed by a stolen van the previous year.

She was followed by the shambling figure of DS Norman Potting. Because of the pension system in operation for the police, most officers took retirement after thirty years' service: the system worked against them if they stayed on longer. But Potting wasn't motivated by money. He liked being a copper and seemed determined to remain one as long as he could. Thanks to the endless disasters of his private life, Sussex CID was the only family he had, although, with his old-school, politically incorrect attitudes, a lot of people—including the chief constable, Grace suspected—would have liked to see the back of him. However, much as he irritated people at times, Grace couldn't help respecting the man. Pot-bellied and with a comb-over like a threadbare carpet, Norman Potting was a true copper.

Roy Grace looked down at the briefing notes typed out by his assistant as he waited for Glenn Branson, who had just come in, to sit down. Glenn was followed by the cheery figure of the Road Policing Unit inspector, James Biggs.

'OK,' Grace said. 'This is the first briefing of Operation Violin, the inquiry into the death of Anthony Vincent Revere.' He paused to introduce Biggs, a pleasant-looking man with close-cropped fair hair, to his team. 'James, would you like to start by outlining what happened earlier today?'

The inspector summarised the morning's tragic events, placing particular focus on the eyewitness reports of the white van that had disappeared from the scene, having gone through a red light and struck the cyclist. So far, he reported, there were two possible sightings of the van from CCTV cameras in the area, but neither was of sufficient quality to provide legible registration numbers.

The first sighting was of a Ford Transit van, matching the description, heading fast in a westerly direction from the scene, less than thirty seconds after the collision. The second, one minute later, showed a van, missing its driver's wing mirror, making a right turn half a mile on. This was significant, Biggs told them, because of pieces of a wing mirror recovered from the scene. Its identity was now being traced from a serial number on the casing. That was all he had to go on so far.

'There's a Home Office post-mortem due to start in about an hour's time,' Grace said, 'which Glenn Branson will attend, along with Tracy Stocker and the Coroner's officer.' He looked at Glenn, who grimaced, then raised his hand.

Grace nodded at him.

'Boss, I've just spoken to the family liaison officer from Traffic who's been assigned to this,' he said. 'He's just had a phone call from an officer in the New York Police Department. The deceased, Tony Revere, was a US citizen, doing a business studies degree at Brighton University. Now, I don't know if this is going to have any significance, but the deceased's mother's maiden name is Giordino.' All eyes were on him. 'Sal Giordino. Does that name mean anything to anyone?' Glenn asked, looking at each of the faces.

They all shook their heads.

'Anyone see *The Godfather*?' Branson went on.

This time they all nodded.

'Marlon Brando, right? The Boss of Bosses? The Godfather, right?'

'Yes,' Grace said.

'Well, that's who the deceased's mother's dad is. Sal Giordino is the current New York Godfather.'

3

Detective Investigator Pat Lanigan, of the Special Investigations Unit of the Office of the District Attorney, was seated at his Brooklyn desk when the call from a detective in the Interpol office came through.

A tall man of Irish descent, with a pockmarked face, a greying brush-cut and a Brooklyn accent, Lanigan had the rugged looks of a movie tough guy and a powerful physique that meant few people were tempted to pick a fight with him. At fifty-four, he'd had some thirty years' experience of dealing with the Wise Guys—the term the NYPD used for the Mafiosi. He knew personally many of the rank and file in all the Mob families, partly helped by his having been raised in Brooklyn, where the majority of them lived.

Lanigan listened to the information that the Interpol officer relayed. He didn't like the hit-and-run part. Retaliation was a big part of Mob culture and each of the families had its enemies. He decided that the best way to see if that line of thought had any relevance would be to take a ride to East Hampton and check out the family himself. Delivering the shocking message just might make one of them blurt out a giveaway.

Thirty minutes later he was heading out to the parking lot with his regular work buddy, Dennis Bootle. Although two years older than his colleague, Bootle had hair a youthful straw-blond colour, styled in a boyish quiff. The two partners were chalk and cheese. They argued constantly. Yet they were close.

The early afternoon traffic on Long Island was light and it stayed that way during the next ninety minutes as they approached the Hamptons. Trees and shrub gave way to the outskirts of East Hampton with its large houses set well back from the road and then a parade of expensive-looking shops. As they headed along a leafy lane, Bootle broke twenty minutes of silence.

'This kid's mother, she's married to Lou Revere, right?'

'Uh huh.'

'He's the Mob's banker. You know that? Last election, rumour has it he gave the Republicans ten million.'

Pat Lanigan, an Obama man, grinned. 'All the more reason to bust him.'

The lane narrowed. On both sides there were trim hedges. The satnav stuck to the windshield told them they had arrived. Directly in front of them were closed, tall, grey-painted gates. A sign below a speaker panel said ARMED RESPONSE.

Pat stopped the car, lowered his window and reached out to press a button on the panel by the gates. The cyclops eye of a CCTV camera peered suspiciously down at them.

A voice speaking broken English crackled out: 'Yes, hello, please?'

'Police,' Pat said, holding up his shield for the camera to see.

Moments later, the gates swung slowly open and they drove through.

Ahead of them, beyond an expanse of lawn and plants straight from a tropical rainforest, rose an imposing modern mansion.

Pat pulled up alongside a gold Porsche Cayenne. They climbed out and took in the surroundings for a moment. Then, a short distance away, the front door opened and a uniformed Filipina maid stared out nervously.

They strode over.

'We're looking for Mr and Mrs Revere,' Pat Lanigan said, holding up his shield again. Dennis Bootle flashed his, too.

The maid ushered them through into a vast hallway with a grey flag-stone floor and a grand circular staircase sweeping up in front of them. Following her nervy hand signals, they walked after her through to a palatial, high-ceilinged drawing room, with a minstrel's gallery above them. The furniture was all antique: sofas, chairs, a chaise longue. A large picture window looked out over a lawn, with Long Island Sound beyond. It was a house to die for, and Pat was certain of just one thing at this moment: a lot of people had.

Seated in the room was an attractive but hard-looking woman in her mid-forties, with short, blonde hair and a made-to-measure nose. She was dressed in a pink tracksuit and bling trainers, holding a pack of Marlboro Lights in one hand and a lighter in the other. As they entered she shook a cigarette out, pushed it between her lips, then clicked the lighter.

'Yes?' she said, drawing on the cigarette.

Lanigan held up his shield. 'Detective Investigator Lanigan and Detective Investigator Bootle. Are you Mrs Fernanda Revere?'

'Why do you need to know?'

'Is your husband here?' Lanigan asked patiently.

'He's playing golf.'

'Will he be home soon?'

'I don't know,' she said. 'Two hours, maybe three.'

The officers exchanged a glance. Then Lanigan said, 'OK, I'm sorry to have to break this to you, Mrs Revere. You have a son, Tony, is that right?'

She was about to take another drag on her cigarette, but stopped, anxiety lining her face. 'Yes?'

'We've been informed by the police in Brighton, in England, that your son died this morning, following a road traffic accident.'

Both men sat down, uninvited, in chairs opposite her.

She stared at them in silence. 'What?'

Pat Lanigan repeated what he had said.

She sat, staring at them, an unexploded bomb. 'You're shitting me, right? Tell me you're shitting me.'

'I'm very sorry, Mrs Revere. I wish I was.'

Pat saw her hands trembling. Saw her stab the cigarette into the ashtray as if she was knifing someone. Then she grabbed the ashtray and hurled it at the wall. It struck just below a painting, exploding into shards of glass.

'No!' she said, her breathing getting faster and faster. 'Noooooo!'

She picked up the table the ashtray had been on and smashed it down on the floor, breaking the legs.

'Noooooooo!' she screamed. 'Noooooooo! It's not true! Tell me it's not true! Tell me!'

The two officers sat there in silence, watching as she jumped up and grabbed a painting off the wall. She then jerked it down hard over her knees, ripping through the face and body of a Madonna and child.

'Not my Tony. My son. Nooooooooooooo! Not him!'

She picked up a sculpture of a tall, thin man holding dumbbells and smashed its head against the floor.

'Get out!' she screamed. 'Get out, get out, get out!'

CLEO WAS ASLEEP in the hospital bed. The sleeve of her blue hospital gown had slipped up over her elbow, and Roy Grace, who had been sitting beside her for the past hour, staring at her face, thought how lovely she looked when she was asleep. Then his eyes fell on the grey plastic tag round her wrist and another coil of fear rose inside him.

He was scared, his mind all over the place. Sick with fear for her. He listened to her steady breathing. The possibility that they might lose their baby struck him harder each time he thought about it. Even worse was the unthinkable idea that, as the consultant had warned, Cleo might die.

It was 9.10 p.m. A crime show was on television, with the volume turned right down. His mind returned to the fatal accident this morning. He'd heard summaries of the first eyewitness accounts. The cyclist was on the wrong side of the road. If it was a planned hit, then the cyclist had given the van the perfect opportunity. But how would the van have known that he was going to be on the wrong side of the road? The hit theory didn't fit together at all. But the New York crime family connection bothered him, for reasons he could not define. He just had a really bad feeling about that.

People said that the Italian Mafia was a busted flush. But Grace knew otherwise. It was just a different organisation from in its heyday. Now, the established crime families were less visible, but no less wealthy, despite competition from the Russian Mafia. A major portion of their income came from narcotics—once a taboo area for them—fake designer goods and pirated films, while large inroads had been made into online piracy.

Before leaving the office that evening, he had Googled Sal Giordino and what he found did not make comfortable reading. Although Sal himself was languishing in jail, his extensive crew were highly active and as ruthless as any crime family before them in eliminating their rivals. Could their tentacles have reached Brighton?

Drugs were a major factor in the city. The current police initiative in this sphere, Operation Reduction, had been extremely effective in busting several major rings, but no matter how many people were arrested, there were always new players waiting to step into their shoes. The Force Intelligence Bureau had not to date established links to any US crime families, but could that be about to change?

Suddenly his phone rang. He stepped out of the room as he answered, not wanting to wake Cleo.

It was Norman Potting, still diligently at work in the Incident Room.

'Boss, I've just had a phone call from Interpol in New York. The parents of the deceased cyclist, Tony Revere, are on their way over in a private jet. They are due into Gatwick at 6 a.m. Thought you should know. They've booked a room at the Metropole in Brighton. Road Policing have arranged a family liaison officer to take them to the mortuary later in the morning, but I thought you might want to send someone from Major Crime as well.'

'Smart thinking, Norman,' Grace said, and thanked him.

After he had hung up, he dialled a number. Glenn Branson answered.

'How was the post-mortem?' Grace asked.

'It hasn't revealed anything unexpected so far. There was white paint on the boy's anorak on the right shoulder, consistent with abrasions on his skin. Probably where the Transit van struck him. Death from multiple internal injuries. Blood and other fluid samples have been sent off for drug testing.'

'All the witness statements say he was on the wrong side of the road.'

'He was American. Early morning. Might have been tired and confused. Or just a typical mad cyclist. There's no CCTV of the actual impact.'

Grace thought briefly, then said, 'You planning a lie-in tomorrow?'

'Why's that?'

'I need you back on parade at the mortuary.'

AT 7.15 A.M., just twelve hours after he had left the place, Glenn Branson parked the unmarked police car he was driving in the deserted visitors' parking area at the rear of the Brighton and Hove City Mortuary.

He waited as he heard a car approaching. Moments later, Bella Moy drove round the corner and parked beside him. She was here at Roy Grace's suggestion because she was a trained and highly experienced family liaison officer. He climbed out into the light drizzle and popped open his umbrella.

Politely, Glenn opened Bella Moy's door and held the umbrella over her as she climbed out. She thanked him, then they both turned at the sound of another car. It swung into view, pulling up next to them. Branson recognised the driver as PC Dan Pattenden from the Road Policing Unit. Beside him sat an arrogant-looking man in his early fifties, with slicked-back silver hair and a suspicious expression. As he turned his head, he reminded Branson of a badger. A woman sat behind him.

The badger climbed out and yawned, then peered round, blinking, with a weary, defeated expression. He was wearing an expensive-looking fawn Crombie coat with a velvet collar, a loud tie and brown loafers with gold buckles, and he sported an ornate emerald ring on his wedding finger. His skin had the jaundiced pallor of fake tan and a sleepless night.

Suddenly, the rear door of the car flew open as if it had been kicked. Branson breathed in a sudden snatch of perfume as the woman emerged.

She was a little taller than her husband, with an attractive but hard face that looked tight with grief. Her hair looked immaculate, and her camel coat, dark brown handbag and matching crocodile boots had a quietly expensive aura.

'Mr and Mrs Revere?' Branson said, with his hand outstretched.

The woman looked at him like he was air, like she didn't speak to black people, and tossed her head disdainfully away from him.

The man smiled meekly and gave him an even meeker nod. 'Lou Revere,' he said. 'This is my wife, Fernanda.' He shook Glenn's hand.

'I'm Detective Sergeant Branson and this is Detective Sergeant Moy. We're here to help you in any way we can, along with PC Pattenden. We are very sorry about your son. How was your journey?'

'Fucking awful, if you have to know,' the woman said, still not looking at him. 'They had no ice on the plane. You want to believe that? No ice. Now, do we have to stand out here in the rain?'

'Not at all. Let's get inside,' Glenn said, and indicated the way.

'Honey,' the man said. 'Honey—' he looked apologetically at the two detectives—'it was a last-minute thing. An associate had just flown in, luckily, and had the plane on the tarmac. Otherwise we wouldn't have been here until much later, if not tomorrow.'

'We paid twenty-five thousand dollars and they didn't have any fucking ice,' she repeated.

Glenn Branson was finding it hard to believe that anyone whose son had just died was going to be worried by something so trivial, but he responded diplomatically. 'Doesn't sound good,' he said, leading the way round to the front of the building. Then he stopped in front of the door and rang the bell.

It was opened by Cleo Morey's assistant, Darren Wallace, who was already gowned up in blue scrubs. He ushered them inside.

The smell hit Glenn Branson immediately, the way it always did. The sickly sweet reek of Trigene disinfectant could mask, but never get rid of, the smell of death that permeated the whole place.

They went through into a small office and were introduced to Philip Keay, the Coroner's officer. A tall, lean man, wearing a sombre dark suit; Keay's manner was courteous and efficient as he led the way to a small conference room. It had an octagonal table with eight black chairs round it, and two blank whiteboards on the wall. A clock on the wall read 7.28.

'Can I offer you any tea or coffee?' Darren Wallace asked, indicating for them to sit down.

Both Americans shook their heads and remained standing.

'I didn't know this was a goddamn Starbucks,' Fernanda Revere said. 'I've flown here to see my son, not to drink coffee.'

Darren Wallace exchanged a glance with the police officers, then the Coroner's officer addressed the Americans, speaking quietly but firmly.

'Thank you for making the journey. I appreciate it can't be easy for you.'

'Oh, really?' Fernanda Revere snapped. 'You do, do you?'

Philip Keay was diplomatically silent for some moments. Then, ignoring the question, he addressed the Reveres again.

'I'm afraid your son suffered very bad abrasions in the accident. I would recommend that you look through the glass of the viewing window.'

'I haven't flown all this way to look at my son through a window,' Fernanda Revere said icily. 'I want to see him, OK? I want to hold him, hug him. He's all cold in there. He needs his mom.'

There was another awkward exchange of glances, then Darren Wallace said, 'Yes, of course. If you'd like to follow me. But please be prepared.'

They all walked through to a spartan waiting room. The three police officers remained in there, as Darren Wallace led the Reveres and Philip Keay through the far door and into the narrow viewing room.

In the centre, dominating the viewing room, was a table on which lay the shape of a human body beneath a cream, silky cover.

Fernanda Revere began making deep, gulping sobs. Her husband put an arm round her.

Darren Wallace delicately pulled back the cover, exposing the young man's head. His bereavement training had taught him how to deal with almost any situation at this sensitive moment but, even so, he could never predict how anyone was going to react. He'd been present many times before when mothers had screamed, but never in his career had he heard anything quite like the howl this woman suddenly let rip.

It was as if she had torn open the very bowels of hell itself.

IT WAS AN HOUR before Fernanda Revere came back out of the viewing room, barely able to walk, supported by her drained-looking husband. They were taken back to the waiting room, where Darren guided each of them to a chair.

Lou Revere looked at each of the police officers in turn before speaking quietly but assertively, in his slight Brooklyn accent.

'My wife and I would like to know exactly what happened. How our son died. Know what I'm saying? What are you able to tell us?'

Branson and Bella Moy turned to Dan Pattenden.

'I'm afraid we don't have a full picture yet, Mr and Mrs Revere,' the road policing officer said. 'Three vehicles were involved in the accident. From witness reports so far, your son appears to have come out of a side road onto a main road, on the wrong side, directly into the path of an Audi car. The female driver appears to have taken avoiding action, colliding with the wall of a café. She subsequently failed a breathalyser test and was arrested on suspicion of drink driving.'

'Terrific,' Fernanda Revere said. 'Terrific.'

'At this stage we're unclear as to the extent of her involvement in the actual collision,' Pattenden said. 'A white Ford Transit van behind her appears to have travelled through a red stop light and struck your son, the impact sending him and his bicycle across the road, into the path of a lorry coming in the opposite direction. It was the collision with this vehicle that probably caused the fatal injuries.' Dan Pattenden paused, then added, 'We have established that the lorry driver was out of hours.'

'Meaning?' Lou Revere asked.

'We have strict laws in the UK governing the number of hours a lorry driver is permitted to drive before he has to take a rest. From our examination of the tachometer in the lorry involved in your son's fatal accident, it appears the driver was over his permitted limit.' He continued, 'We have a full alert out for the white van. We're hoping that CCTV footage will provide us with more information.'

'You *hope* that, do you?' Fernanda Revere rasped. Her voice was pure vitriol. She pointed through the closed door. 'That's my son in there.' She looked at her husband. '*Our* son. How do you think we feel?'

Pattenden looked at her. 'I can't begin to imagine how you feel, Mrs Revere. I'm deeply sorry for you and for all of your relatives. I'm here to answer any questions you may have and to give you assurances that we will do all we can to establish the facts pertinent to your son's death.' He passed her his card. 'These are my contact details. Please feel free to call me, any time, twenty-four-seven, and I'll give you whatever information I can.'

She left the card lying on the table. 'Have you ever lost a child?'

He stared back at her for some moments. 'No. But I'm a parent, too. I can't imagine what it would be like. I can't imagine what you are going through and it would be presumptuous to even try.'

'Yeah,' she said icily. 'You're right. Don't even go there.'

TOOTH AND HIS DOG, Yossarian, sat out on the deck area of the Shark Bite Sports Bar, overlooking Turtle Cove Marina, on Providenciales Island. Thirty miles long and five wide, Provo, as it was known to the locals, was the main tourist island in the Turks and Caicos archipelago. It was still mostly undeveloped and that suited Tooth: the day it got too developed, he planned to move on.

Tooth and Yossarian weren't so much friends as *associates*. Tooth had never had an actual friend in all his forty-one years. The dog was named after a character in one of the few books he'd read all the way through, *Catch-22*.

It was happy hour in the bar and the air-conditioned interior was full of expat Brits, Americans and Canadians who mostly knew each other and regularly got drunk together in this bar. Tooth never talked to any of them. He didn't like talking to anyone, content in the company of his associate. He lived in an apartment on the far side of the cove, and his cleaning lady fed the dog on the occasions, two or three times a year, when he was away on business.

The Turks and Caicos Islands were a British protectorate that sat strategically between Haiti, Jamaica and Florida and, because of that, they were a favoured stopover for drug runners and illegal Haitian immigrants bound for the USA. The UK government made a pretence of policing them but mostly left things to the corrupt local police force.

Tooth drank two more bourbons and then headed home along the dark, deserted road with Yossarian.

His first job had been as a warehouse man in New York City, then as a fitter in a Grumman fighter aircraft factory on Long Island. When George Bush Senior had invaded Iraq, Tooth had enlisted in the US Army. There he discovered that his natural calm gave him one particular talent: he was a very accurate long-range rifle shot. After two tours in that particular theatre, his commanding lieutenant had recommended he apply for the sniper school. That was the place where Tooth discovered his métier. A range of medals testifying to that hung on one wall of his apartment.

He walked out onto his balcony and lit up a cigarette, mentally calculating his finances. He had enough to last him for another five years, at his current cash burn, he figured. The $2.5 million he'd accumulated in his Swiss bank account gave him a comfort zone, but hey, he had to fuel his thirty-five-foot motor yacht, in which he went out hunting for food most days. He could do with another good contract.

GRACE CHANGED THE VENUE of the morning briefing to the conference room, to accommodate the extra people now attending. These included Paul Wood, the sergeant from the Collision Investigation Unit who had attended at the scene yesterday, and his own crime scene manager, Tracey Stocker, as well.

He had also brought in two additions to his inquiry team. The first was a young PC, Alec Davies. A quiet, shy-looking man, Davies was to be in charge of the Outside Inquiry Team of PCSOs, who were trawling every business premise within a mile of the accident in the hope of finding more CCTV footage. The second member was David Howes, a tall, suave DC in his mid-forties, who was a former prison liaison officer. Dressed in a pin-striped grey suit and checked shirt, with neatly brushed ginger hair, he could have passed muster as a stockbroker or a corporate executive.

On a large whiteboard next to a video screen, James Biggs had drawn a diagram of the position of the vehicles involved in the incident, immediately following the impact with the cyclist.

Reading from his notes, Roy Grace started the briefing. 'The time is 8.30 a.m., Thursday, April the 22nd. This is the second briefing of Operation Violin, the investigation into the death of Anthony Revere, conducted on day two, following his collision in Portland Road, Hove, with an unidentified van, then a lorry belonging to Aberdeen Ocean Fisheries. Absent from this meeting are DS Branson, PC Pattenden and DS Moy, who are attending the viewing of his body with his parents, who have flown over from the US.'

He turned to Sergeant Wood. 'Paul, I think it would be helpful to start with you.'

Wood stood up. 'We've fed all the information from the initial witness statements, skid marks and debris pattern into the CAD program we are using for accident simulation. We have created two perspectives of the accident. The first being from the point of view of the Audi car.'

He picked up a digital remote and pressed it. On the video screen appeared a grey road, approximating the width of Portland Road. The screen showed the white van tailgating the Audi, the cyclist emerging from a side street ahead and the articulated lorry some way ahead, on the other side of the road, approaching in the distance.

He pressed a button and the animation came to life. On the far side of the road, the lorry began to approach. Suddenly the cyclist began to move, swinging out of the side street, on the wrong side, heading straight for the Audi. At the last minute, the cyclist swerved to the left, towards the centre of the road, and the Audi swerved left onto the pavement. An instant later, the tailgating van clipped the cyclist, sending him hurtling across the far side of the road and straight underneath the lorry, between its front and rear wheels. The cyclist spun round the rear wheel arch as the lorry braked to a halt. When the animation stopped, there was silence.

Grace turned to the RPU inspector. 'James, from this simulation it doesn't look as if the Audi driver, Mrs Carly Chase, had any contact with Revere.'

'I would agree with that. But I'm not yet convinced we've heard the full story. It might be that she was unlucky to be breathalysed on a morning-after offence. But it's too early to rule out her culpability at this stage.'

Grace turned to the Major Crime Branch crime scene manager. 'Tracy, do you have anything for us?'

Tracy Stocker, a senior scene-of-crime officer, or SOCO, was one of the most respected crime scene managers in the force. She had a strong, good-looking face framed with straight, brown hair. She was dressed in civvies: a navy trouser suit with a grey blouse.

'Yes, chief. We have sent the serial number on the part of the wing mirror that was recovered at the scene to Ford. They will be able to tell us if it's from a Ford Transit and the year of manufacture.'

'It's going to be thousands of vans, right?' DC Nick Nicholl said.

'Yes,' she conceded. 'But most of them should have two wing mirrors. The mirror itself has been shattered, but I've requested fingerprint analysis of the casing. There's a good chance we'll get something off that.'

'Thanks. Good work, Tracy.'

Grace then turned to PC Alec Davies. 'Any luck so far from CCTV?'

The young PC shook his head. 'No, sir. We've looked at all the images taken, and the angles and distance don't give us enough detail.'

'OK, Alec, I think you should widen the net. If the van was travelling at thirty miles per hour, that's one mile every two minutes. Expand your trawl to a ten-mile radius. Let me know how many people you need to cover that and I'll authorise you.'

Norman Potting raised his hand and Grace signalled to him to speak.

'Boss, in view of the information that came to light yesterday, about the relationship of the deceased to the New York Mafia, should we be concerned that there is more to this than just a traffic accident?'

'It's a good point to raise, Norman,' Grace replied. 'I'm starting to think, from what I've seen so far, that this is unlikely to be some kind of gangland killing.' At that moment, Grace's phone rang. Excusing himself, he pressed the answer button. It was his boss, Assistant Chief Constable Rigg, saying he needed to see him right away. He did not sound in a happy mood.

4

Malling House, the headquarters of Sussex Police, was a fifteen-minute drive from Grace's office, on the outskirts of Lewes, the county town of East Sussex. Grace quite liked the new ACC, Peter Rigg—he was a far more benign character than his predecessor, the acidic and unpredictable Alison Vosper—but he always felt as if he was stepping on eggshells in his presence.

Peter Rigg was a dapper man in his mid-forties, with a healthy complexion, fair hair and a sharp, public school voice. Although several inches shorter than Grace, he had fine posture, giving him a military bearing that made him seem taller than his actual height.

He was on the phone when Grace entered his office, but waved to him cheerily to sit on one of the chairs in front of his huge rosewood desk. He put a hand over the receiver and asked Grace if he would like a drink.

'I'd love a coffee—strong with some milk, please, sir.'

Rigg repeated the order down the phone, to his assistant, Grace presumed. Then he hung up and smiled at Grace.

'I hear that your girlfriend's in hospital, Roy,' Rigg said.

Grace was surprised that he knew.

'Yes, sir. She has pregnancy complications.'

'Sorry to hear that,' Rigg said. 'If you need any time out, let me know.'

'Thank you, sir. She's coming home tomorrow, so it looks like she's out of immediate danger.'

As the assistant came in with Grace's coffee, the ACC looked down at a sheet of printed paper on his blotter, on which were some handwritten notes. 'Operation Violin,' he said pensively. Then he looked up with a grin. 'Good to know our computer's got a sense of humour!'

Now it was Grace's turn to frown. 'A sense of humour?'

'Don't you remember that film *Some Like It Hot*? Didn't the mobsters carry their machine guns in violin cases?'

Grace grinned. 'Ah, yes, of course. I hadn't made the connection.'

The smile slipped from the assistant chief constable's face. 'Roy, I'm concerned about the Mafia connection with this case. We are in terrain that we're not familiar with. I think it has the potential to go pear-shaped.'

'In what sense, sir?'

Rigg's face darkened. 'We're in the middle of a recession. Businesses in this city are hurting. Tourist trade is down. Brighton's had an unwarranted reputation as the crime capital of the UK for seven decades, and we are trying to reassure people that this city is as safe as anywhere on the planet to visit. The last thing we need is the Mafia headlining in the press here.'

'We have a good relationship with the *Argus*, so I'm sure we can keep that aspect under control.'

'You are, are you?' Rigg was starting to look angry. It was the first time Grace had seen this side of him. 'So what about this reward?'

The word hit Grace like a sledgehammer. 'Reward?' he asked. 'I'm sorry. I don't know what you mean, sir.'

Rigg waved a hand, summoning Grace round to his side of the desk. He leaned forward and tapped on his keyboard, and the *Argus* website appeared.

MAFIA BOSS'S DAUGHTER OFFERS $100,000 REWARD FOR SON'S KILLER

His heart sinking, Grace read on:

Fernanda Revere, daughter of New York Mafia Capo Sal Giordino, currently serving eleven consecutive life sentences for murder, this morning told our reporter Kevin Spinella that she is offering $100,000 for information leading to the identity of the van driver responsible for the death of her son, Tony Revere. Revere, 21, a student at Brighton University, was killed yesterday after his bicycle was in a collision involving an Audi car, a van and a lorry in Portland Road, Hove.

'You know what particularly I don't like in this piece, Roy?'

Grace had a pretty good idea. 'The wording of the reward, sir?'

Rigg nodded. 'As you'll know, the customary wording is "for information leading to the arrest and conviction". I'm not happy about this "leading to the identity" wording here. It's vigilante territory.' He turned to Grace. 'You told me you had this reporter, Spinella, in your pocket.'

'Not exactly, sir. I told you that I had forged a good working relationship with him, but I am concerned that he has a mole working somewhere inside Sussex Police.'

'It proves something to me, Roy.'

Grace looked at him, feeling very uncomfortable suddenly.

Rigg went on, 'It tells me that my predecessor was right. Alison said I should keep a careful eye on you.'

GRACE DROVE OUT of the police headquarters seething with anger. He dialled Kevin Spinella's mobile phone number on his hands-free. The reporter answered almost immediately.

'You've just blown all the goodwill you ever had with me and with HQ CID,' Grace said furiously.

'Detective Superintendent Grace, why, whatever's the matter?' Spinella sounded a tad less cocky than usual.

'You bloody well know what the issue is. Your front-page splash. I can't believe you've been so damned irresponsible.'

'We published it at Mrs Revere's request.'

'Without bothering to speak to anyone on the inquiry team?'

There was a silence, then Spinella said, 'I didn't think it was necessary.'

'What do you think you'll achieve with this? Do you want the streets of Brighton filled with vigilantes driving around in pick-up trucks with gun racks on their roofs? It may be the way Mrs Revere does things, but it's not how we do it here.'

'Sorry if I've upset you, Detective Superintendent.'

'You know what? You don't sound at all sorry. But you will be. This'll come back to bite you, I can promise you that.'

Grace hung up, then returned a missed call from Glenn Branson.

'What's happening?' he asked the detective sergeant.

'We got doorstepped outside the mortuary by that shit Spinella. I imagine there'll be something in the *Argus* tonight.'

'There's already something in the online edition,' Grace said. He told him the gist of the piece, about his dressing-down from ACC Rigg, and his subsequent conversation with the reporter.

'I'm afraid I couldn't do anything, boss. He was waiting right outside the mortuary, knew exactly who they were and took them aside.'

'Who tipped him off?'

'Must have been dozens of people who knew the parents were coming over. Not just in CID. Could have been someone in the hotel.'

Grace did not reply for a moment. Sure, it could easily have been someone at the hotel. But there was just too much consistency about Spinella always being in the right place at the right time. It had to be an insider.

'What kind of people are the parents?' Grace asked.

'The father's creepy but he's pretty sensible. Very shaken. The mother's poison. But, hey, she just identified her dead son, right? That's not a good place to judge anyone, so who can tell? But she wears the trousers, for sure, and I wouldn't want to tangle with either of them.'

Grace told him the ACC's concerns.

'What does he mean by "the potential to go pear-shaped"?' Branson asked.

'I don't know,' Grace answered truthfully. 'I think the chief constable's under pressure to get rid of Brighton's historic image of a crime-ridden resort. We need to find that white van fast and get the driver under arrest. That'll take the heat off everything.'

'You mean get him into protective custody, boss?'

'You've seen too many Mafia movies,' Grace said. 'You're letting your imagination run away with you.'

'One hundred grand,' Glenn Branson replied, 'That's an offer someone might not be able to refuse.'

'Put a sock in it.'

But, Grace thought privately, *Branson could well be right.*

LOU REVERE didn't like it when his wife drank heavily, and these past few years, since their three kids had got older and left home, Fernanda hit the bottle hard most evenings. The drunker she was, the more bad-tempered she became, and she would start blaming Lou for almost anything that came into her head. Often it was for allowing their younger son, Tony, to live with that 'piece of trash' in England.

'If you were a man,' she would shout at him, 'you'd have put your foot down and made Tony complete his education in America. My father would have never let his son go!'

Lou would shrug his shoulders and say, 'It's different for today's generation. You have to let kids do what they want to do. Tony's his own man and he needs his independence. I miss him, too, but it's good to see him do that.'

'Good to see him getting away from our family?' she'd reply. 'You mean, like, my family, right?'

He did mean that, but he would never dare say it. Privately, though, he hoped the boy would carve out a life for himself away from the clutches of the Giordinos. Some days he wished he had the courage himself. But it was too late. This was the life he had chosen. It was fine and he should count his blessings. Despite his wife's behaviour, Lou loved his wife. It was true also, of course, that her connections had not exactly done his career any harm.

Lou Revere had started out as an accountant, with a Harvard business degree behind him. Although related to a rival New York crime family, during his early years he'd had no intention of entering the criminal world. That changed the night he met Fernanda at a charity ball. He was lean and handsome then, and he'd made her laugh.

Sal Giordino had been impressed with Lou's quietly strategic mind and, within five years, Lou Revere had married his daughter and become the principal financial adviser to the Giordino family. Gradually, Revere had spread the family's ill-gotten income through smart investments into legitimate businesses.

Fernanda was drunk now. By the end of the seven-hour flight back to the US, she had finished one bottle of Grey Goose vodka and had made inroads into a second. She was still clutching a glass as the plane touched down at Republic Airport in East Farmingdale at 2.15 p.m. local time.

Lou helped her down the short gangway onto the tarmac at Republic Airport. They passed through immigration control and, fifteen minutes later, were in the limo driving the short distance home to East Hampton.

She was just sober enough to check that the glass partition to the driver's compartment was closed and the intercom was off, as she lifted the phone and tapped out a number.

'Who you calling?' Lou asked.

'Ricky.'

Her brother was a sleazebag. Lazy, smug and nasty. He'd inherited his father's ruthless violence, but none of the old man's cunning.

She must have got through to voicemail because she said into the phone, 'Ricky, it's me. Call me. I need to speak to you urgently.'

Lou looked at her. 'What's that about?'

'I'll tell you what it's about,' she slurred. 'It's about a drunk woman driver, a goddamn van driver who didn't stop and a truck driver who should not have been on the road. That's what it's about.'

'What do you want Ricky to do?'

She turned and glared at him, her eyes glazed, as hard as drill bits.

'My son's dead. I want that drunken bitch, that van driver and that truck driver who killed him, OK? I want them to suffer.'

READING FROM HIS prepared notes to the team assembled in the conference room of Sussex House, Roy Grace said, 'The time is 8.30 a.m., Saturday April the 24th. This is the sixth briefing of Operation Violin, the investigation into the death of Tony Revere, conducted at the start of day four.'

A major focus of the meeting was on damage limitation concerning the massive reward the dead boy's parents had offered. It had made headlines in many of the nation's papers, prompting any number of conspiracy theories. These ranged from Tony Revere being murdered by a Brighton crime family in a drugs turf war, to Tony being an undercover agent for the CIA.

Glenn Branson and Bella Moy took the team once more through the reactions of the dead boy's parents. It was agreed that there was no indication from them that their son's death might have been a targeted hit, or that he had any enemies. The only issue with the parents, DS Branson reported, had been their anger that they could not take their son's body home with them until after the results of the toxicology reports, and that it might be necessary to subject it to a second post-mortem.

'Are we having a full tox scan, Roy?' asked DC David Howes.

A full toxicology scan cost over £2,000. Ordinarily, Grace would have tried to save this money. The cyclist was clearly in the wrong. The woman in the Audi had been driving while over the limit, but she had not, they had decided, been a contributory factor in the accident. The van driver, however, had gone through a red light and, when found, would be facing serious charges. The toxicology report was not going to add anything to the facts as they stood, other than to explain the possibility of why the cyclist was on the wrong side. But it could feature in any defence case by the van driver.

'Yes, we are,' Grace replied, and briefly outlined his reasons for this to the team. Then, changing the subject, he said, 'I'm pleased to report a possible breakthrough this morning. A fingerprint taken from the damaged wing mirror found at the scene, and presumed to have snapped off the door of the Ford Transit van, has been identified. This was from a further fragment discovered during the continued search of the scene yesterday.'

All eyes were on the detective superintendent.

'The print is from Ewan Preece, a thirty-one-year-old convicted drug dealer serving his last three weeks of a six-year sentence in Ford Open Prison,' Grace said. 'He's on a day-release rehabilitation programme, working on a construction site in Arundel. On Wednesday, April the 21st, the day of the collision, he failed to return for evening lock-in.'

'I know that name,' Norman Potting said. 'Ewan Preece. Little bastard. Nicked him years ago for stealing cars. Used to be one of the Moulsecoomb troublemakers when he was younger.'

'Know anything about him now, Norman?' Grace asked. 'Where he might be? Why would anyone go over the wall with just three weeks left?'

'I know the people to ask, chief.'

'OK, good. If you can follow that up. I spoke to an officer at the prison just before this meeting. She told me Preece has been as good as gold there. He's applied himself, learning the plastering trade. She says she knows him well and feels it's out of character for him to have done this.'

Nick Nicholl interjected, 'Boss, might it be a good idea to get the word spread round the prison about the reward? It's likely someone in there will know what Preece was up to. All prisoners know each other's business.'

'Good point,' Grace said. 'You should go over there, Norman. See if any of the prisoners will talk to you.'

'I'll do that, chief. I know where to start looking in Brighton, as well. A bloke like Ewan Preece isn't capable of hiding for long.'

'Especially,' Grace said, 'when there's a hundred-thousand-dollar price tag on finding him.'

TOOTH WAS UP at dawn, as he was every morning, before the heat of the sun became too intense. He ran his regular ten-mile circuit up in the arid hills close to his home, then worked out in the gym in his small, air-conditioned spare room. While Yossarian waited patiently for his breakfast, Tooth went through his martial arts routine. Sometimes, when he had been behind enemy lines, using a gun wasn't practical. Tooth was fine with his bare hands. He preferred them to using knives. You could hurt people a lot more with your bare hands. And you didn't leave a trail of blood.

When he had finished in the gym, he showered, then set a bowl of dog food down on the balcony for Yossarian. A few minutes later he joined him and had his own breakfast, reading the *New York Times* on his Kindle.

Suddenly his phone rang. He looked at the black Nokia. The number was displayed. A New York State number, but not one he recognised. He memorised the number and killed the call, then waited for some moments, composing his thoughts.

Only one person knew how to contact him. That man had the number of his current pay-as-you-go phone. Tooth had five such phones in his safe. He would only ever take one call on a phone, then he would destroy it. It was a precaution that had served him well.

He removed the SIM card from the phone, then held it in the flame of his cigarette lighter until it had melted beyond recovery. Then he went to his safe, removed another phone from it, ensured that it was set to withhold the caller's number, and dialled.

'Yep?' said a male voice the other end, answering almost immediately.

'You just called.'

'I'm told you can help me.'

'You know my terms?'

'They're fine. How soon could we meet? Tonight?'

Tooth did a quick calculation of flight times. He knew the flights out of there to Miami and the times of the connecting flights to most capitals that concerned him. And he could always be ready in one hour.

'The guy who gave you this number, he'll give you another number. Call me on that at 6 p.m. and give me the address.' Then Tooth hung up.

He phoned the cleaning lady who took care of Yossarian when he was away, and then ordered a taxi. While he waited for it to arrive, he chatted to his associate and gave him an extra big biscuit in the shape of a bone.

Yossarian took it and slunk miserably away to the dark recess within the apartment where he had his basket. He knew that when he got a big biscuit, his pack leader was going away. That meant no walks. It was like some kind of a punishment, except he didn't know what he had done wrong. A few minutes later he heard a sound he recognised. Departing footsteps. Then a slam.

'DO YOU KNOW what I'm really looking forward to?' Cleo asked. 'What I'm absolutely craving?'

'Wild sex?' Roy Grace said hopefully, giving her a sideways grin.

They were in the car, heading home from hospital, and she looked a thousand times better. The colour had returned to her face and she looked more beautiful than ever. The rest in hospital had clearly done her good.

'Wild sex would be good,' she conceded. 'But at a risk of denting your ego, there is something I desire even more than your body right now, Detective Superintendent Grace.'

'And what might that be?'

'Something I can't have. A big slice of Brie with a glass of red wine.'

As he turned south into Grand Parade, with the Royal Pavilion ahead of him, he pouted in a mock-sulk and said, 'I'm going to arrest every sodding piece of Brie in this city.'

Grace was aware of a sudden feeling of euphoria. After all his fears for Cleo and their baby these past few days, everything suddenly seemed good again. Cleo was fine, back to her normal, cheery, breezy self. Their baby was fine. The bollocking from ACC Rigg suddenly seemed very small and insignificant in comparison. The two-bit petty crook van driver, Ewan Preece, would be found within days, if not hours, and that would put Rigg back in his box. The only thing that really mattered to him at this moment was sitting beside him.

ONE OF THE current inquiries at Sussex House had ended sooner than expected, which meant that Major Incident Room One had finally become available for Grace's 6.30 p.m. meeting. MIR-1 was an L-shaped space, divided up by three large workstations, each with room for up to eight people to sit, and several large whiteboards. One now had the diagram of the vehicles involved in the accident, which Inspector Biggs had produced earlier. Another had the family tree of Tony Revere, and on a third was a list of names and contact numbers of principal witnesses.

There was an air of intense concentration, punctuated by the constant warbling of phones.

Grace sat down at an empty workstation and placed his notes in front of him. 'Right!' he said, raising his voice to get everyone's attention. 'The time is 6.30 p.m., Saturday, April the 24th. This is the seventh briefing of Operation Violin.' He looked at Tracy Stocker, the crime scene manager. 'Tracy, I understand you have a development?'

'Yes, chief,' she replied. 'We've had a positive ID of the van type back from Ford, from their analysis of the serial number on the wing mirror. They've confirmed it was fitted to the '06 model. So, considering the time and location where the mirror-casing fragment was found, I think we can say with reasonable certainty it belonged to our suspect Ford Transit.'

'Do we know how many of the vans were made that year?' someone asked.

'Yes,' Stocker answered. 'Exactly 57,434 were sold in the UK in 2006. And 93 per cent of them were white, which means 53,413 vans fit our description.' She smiled wryly.

Sergeant Paul Wood of the Collision Investigation Unit said, 'One line that would be worth pursuing would be to contact all repair shops and see if anyone's brought a Transit in for wing-mirror repair.'

Grace made a note, nodding. 'Yes, I've thought of that. But he'd have to be pretty stupid to take the van in for repairs so quickly. More likely he'd tuck it away in a lock-up.'

'Ewan Preece doesn't sound like the sharpest tool in the shed,' Glenn Branson chipped in. 'I don't think we should rule it out, boss.'

'I'll put it down as an action for the Outside Inquiry Team.' Grace turned to Potting. 'Norman, do you have your update from Ford Prison?'

Potting pursed his lips. 'I do, chief,' he said. 'The good news is that word of this reward has spread round the prison, as you might imagine. Several inmates have come forward, offering suggestions where Preece might be, and I've got a list of six names and addresses to follow up.'

'Good stuff, Norman,' Grace said.

Potting allowed himself a brief smile before continuing, 'But there's some bad news, too. Ewan Preece had a friend in Ford Prison, another inmate—they go back years.' He checked his notes. 'Warren Tulley. The officer had arranged for Tulley to talk to me. Someone went to fetch him and found him dead in his cell. He'd hanged himself.'

There was a momentary silence while the team absorbed this.

David Howes asked, 'What do we know about Tulley's circumstances?'

'He had two months to serve. Married with three young kids. All fine with the marriage apparently. He was looking forward to getting out and spending time with his kids.'

'Not someone with any obvious reason to top himself?'

'Doesn't sound like it, no,' Potting replied.

'I'm just speculating, but what it sounds like to me,' Howes went on, 'is that possibly Warren Tulley knew where to find Preece.' He shrugged.

'Which might be why he died?' Grace said. 'Not suicide at all?'

'They're launching a full investigation,' Potting said. 'Seems a bit coincidental to them.'

'How hard would it be to hang yourself in Ford?' Glenn Branson asked.

'Being an open prison, the inmates have got much more freedom than in a higher-category place,' Potting said. 'And they have their own rooms. If you wanted to hang yourself, you could do so easily.'

'And equally easily hang someone else,' Howes said.

'One hundred thousand dollars is a lot of money to someone inside,' Glenn said.

'It's a lot to anyone,' Nick Nicholl replied.

5

Fernanda Revere sat restlessly on the edge of her green sofa. She gripped a glass in one hand and held a cigarette in the other, tapping the end impatiently, every few seconds, into an ashtray.

Outside a storm raged. Wind and rain were hurtling in from Long Island Sound, through the dunes and the wild grasses. There was a ball game on television that her brother shouted at intermittently.

She took another angry drag on her cigarette and puffed the smoke back out. 'So, where is he? You sure about this, Ricky?'

She stared suspiciously at her brother who was sitting opposite her, cradling a whisky and sucking on a fat cigar.

Lou looked at Ricky, his face suddenly hard, and said, 'He's going to show, right? He's reliable? You know this guy?'

'He's reliable. One of the best. He's in the car. Be here any moment.'

Ricky picked up the brown envelope he had prepared, checked its contents, then put it down again, satisfied, and returned to the game.

At forty, Ricky Giordino had the Italian looks of his father, but not the old man's strong face. His face was weak, a tad pudgy, like a baby's, and pockmarked. His black hair was styled into a quiff. He was dressed in a black cardigan and baggy blue jeans that concealed the handgun permanently strapped to his calf.

'You done business with this guy before?' Fernanda asked.

'He's recommended by an associate of mine. And knows this city, Brighton. He did a job there one time. He'll do what you want done.'

'He'd better. I want them to suffer. You told him that, didn't you?'

'He knows.' Ricky puffed on a cigar.

Fernanda drained her drink and got up to walk unsteadily towards the drinks cabinet as a series of sharp chimes came from the hall.

Ricky got to his feet. 'He's here.'

TOOTH SAT in the back of the limousine, dressed casually but smartly in a sports coat, open-neck shirt, chinos and brown leather loafers; the kind of clothes in which he could go anywhere without raising an eyebrow. His brown holdall lay on the seat beside him. Tooth never let it out of his sight. He never checked it in; it came inside the plane with him on every flight. The bag contained clean underwear, a spare shirt, pants, shoes, his laptop, four cellphones, three spare passports and an assortment of forged documents all concealed inside three hollowed-out paperback books.

Tooth never travelled with weapons, other than a quantity of the incapacitating agent 3-quinuclidinyl benzilate—BZ—disguised as two deodorant sticks, in his washbag. It wasn't worth the risk. Besides, he had his best weapons on the end of his arms: his hands.

In the beam of the headlights he watched the high, grey electric gates opening and the rain pelting down. Then they drove on, until ahead he could see the superstructure of a showy modern mansion.

The driver opened the rear door and Tooth stepped out into the rain with his bag. As they reached the porch, the front door of the house was opened by a Filipina maid in uniform. Almost immediately, she was joined by a mean-faced man in a black cardigan and jeans.

The man held out a fleshy hand covered in glinting rings, saying, 'Mr Tooth? Ricky Giordino. Y'had a good journey?'

Tooth shook the man's hand briefly, then released it as fast as he could. He didn't like to shake hands. Hands carried germs.

'The journey was fine.'

'Can I fix you a drink? Whisky? Vodka? We got just about everything.'

'I don't drink when I'm working.'

Ricky grinned. 'You haven't started yet.'

'I said I don't drink when I'm working.'

The smile slid from Ricky's face, leaving behind an awkward leer. 'OK. Terrific. We're good, then. All set. Come with me.'

Tooth, still holding his bag, followed him along a corridor furnished with a fancy antique table, on which sat ornate Chinese vases, and past a living room that reminded him of an English baronial hall in a movie he'd seen long ago. A bitch in navy velour was sitting on a sofa, smoking a cigarette, with an ashtray full of butts beside her, and a loser was sitting opposite her, watching a bunch of dumb assholes playing American football.

Ricky ducked into the room and reappeared almost immediately carrying a brown envelope. He led Tooth down the stairs and into the basement. Tooth followed the man through into a huge poolroom.

The man sucked on his cigar. 'My sister's pretty upset. She lost her youngest son. She doted on the kid. You gotta understand that.'

Tooth said nothing.

'You shoot pool?' the man said.

Tooth shrugged.

'Bowl?'

The man indicated him to follow and walked through into the room beyond. And now Tooth was impressed.

He was staring at a full-size, underground ten-pin bowling alley. It had just one lane, with polished wooden flooring. It was immaculate. Balls were lined up in the chute.

'You play this?'

As his reply, Tooth selected a ball and placed his fingers and thumb in the slots. He squinted down the length of the lane and could see that all the pins, white and shiny, were in place.

'Go ahead,' the man said. 'Enjoy!'

Tooth sent the ball rolling. In the silence of the basement it rumbled, like distant thunder. It clouted the front pin slightly off centre, and had the desired effect. All ten pins went down.

'Great shot! Gotta say, that's not at all bad!'

The man drew again on his cigar and hit the reset button, watching as the mechanical grab scooped up the pins and started to replace them.

Tooth dug his hand into his pocket, pulled out a pack of Lucky Strikes and lit one. After he had taken the first drag, the man suddenly snatched it out of his hand and crushed it out in an onyx ashtray on a ledge beside him.

'I just lit that,' Tooth said.

'I don't want that fucking cheap thing polluting my Havana. You want a cigar, ask me. OK?'

'I don't smoke cigars.'

'No cigarettes in here!' He glared challengingly at Tooth. 'You do business my way or you don't do it. I'm not sure I like your attitude, Mr Tooth.'

Tooth considered, very carefully, killing this man. It would be easy, only a few seconds. But the money was attractive. Jobs hadn't exactly been flooding in just recently. Even without seeing the house, he knew about the wealth of this family. This was a good gig. Better not to blow it.

He picked up another ball, hit another strike, all ten pins down.

'You're good, aren't you?' the man said, a little grudgingly.

Tooth did not respond.

'You've been to a place in England called Brighton, right?'

'I don't remember.'

'You did a job for my cousin. You took out an Estonian ship captain in the local port who was doing side deals on cargoes of drugs.'

'I don't remember,' Tooth said again, being deliberately vague.

'Six years ago. My cousin said you were good. They never found the body.' Ricky nodded approvingly.

Tooth shrugged.

'So, here's the deal. In this envelope are the names and all we have on them. My sister's prepared to pay one million dollars, half now, half on completion. She wants each of them to suffer, real bad. That's your speciality, right? We have a deal?'

'One hundred per cent cash up-front only,' Tooth said. 'I don't negotiate.'

'You know who you're goddamn dealing with here?'

Tooth, who was a good six inches shorter, stared the man hard in the eye. 'Yes. Do you?' He shook another cigarette out of the pack and stuck it in his mouth. 'Do you have a light?'

Ricky Giordino stared at him. 'You got balls, I tell you that.' He hit the reset button again. 'How can I be sure you'll deliver? That you'll get all three hits?'

Tooth selected another ball from the chute. He ran up, then crouched and sent the ball rolling. Yet again all ten pins scattered. He dug in his pocket and pulled out a plastic lighter. Then he held it up provocatively, willing the man to stop him.

Ricky Giordino surprised him by pulling out a gold Dunhill, clicking it open and holding up the flame to his cigarette.

'I think we're pretty close to understanding each other.'

Tooth accepted the light but did not reply. He didn't do understanding.

CARLY WAS CURLED UP on the sofa with a glass of red Rioja in one hand and *Top Gear* about to start on the television. The Sunday supplements were spread all around her. It was her first drink since the accident and she needed it, as she was feeling very depressed.

The *Argus* had been running stories on the accident every day. Her photograph had appeared on Thursday: **BRIGHTON SOLICITOR ARRESTED AT DEATH CRASH**. It had made the national press also, with a big splash in the tabloids, as well as being in that day's *Sunday Times*. It was big news that Tony Revere was the grandson of the New York Mafia capo Sal Giordino, and that a reward of $100,000 was being offered. She'd even had reporters phoning her at the office, but on the advice of Ken Acott, her colleague and solicitor, she had not spoken to them. She had badly wanted to, however—to point out that she had not caused the accident, or even collided with the cyclist.

A dark gloom swirled inside her. Sunday evenings had been hard for her since Kes had died. It had been around this time, five years ago, that two police officers had turned up at her front door and informed her that her husband was missing, presumed dead, in an avalanche while heli-skiing in Canada. It had been a further four days of anxious waiting, hoping against hope for some miracle, before they had recovered his body.

She often thought of selling the house and moving to a different part of the city. But she wanted to give Tyler some continuity and stability. Kes and Tyler had been close. They went to football together to support the Albion every home match during the season. In the summer they went fishing, or to the cricket, or more often than not to Tyler's favourite place in Brighton: the Booth Museum of Natural History.

After Kes's death, Tyler had become withdrawn. She had made a big effort, taking him to football and to cricket herself, and on a fishing trip on a boat out of Brighton Marina. They'd developed a certain closeness, but there was still a distance between them, a gap she could never quite close. It was as if the ghost of his father would always be the elephant in the room.

She drank some more wine and increased the volume on the remote.

'Tyler!' she shouted. '*Top Gear*'s starting!'

He'd had been in a strange mood these past few days, since her accident. It was almost as if he was blaming her for what had happened. But as she replayed those moments again, for the thousandth time, she still came to the same conclusion: she was not to blame. Even if she had not been distracted by her phone, and had braked half a second earlier, the cyclist would still have swerved out and been hit by the van. Wouldn't he?

Suddenly she heard the clack of the dog flap in the kitchen door, then the sound of Otis barking furiously out in the garden. What at? she wondered. Occasionally they had foxes, and she often worried that he might attack one and find he had met his match. She jumped up, but as she entered the kitchen, the dog came running back in, panting.

'Tyler!' she called out again, but still there was no answer from him.

She went upstairs, hoping he wasn't watching the programme on his own in his room. But, to her surprise, he was sitting on his chair in front of his desk, going through the contents of his father's memory box.

Tyler had an unusual ambition for a twelve-year-old. He wanted to be a curator of a natural history museum. His ambition showed in his bedroom, which was itself like a museum. His bookshelves were crammed with natural history reference books and models of reptiles, and the walls were covered with carefully selected and mounted photographs, wildlife and fossil prints, and some cartoon sketches of his own, all divided into sections.

'Tyler, *Top Gear*'s on,' she said.

He didn't stir. He was sitting in silence with the old shoebox that he had filled with items that reminded him of his dad in the months following Kes's death. She wasn't sure where he had got the idea of the memory box from, but she liked it.

He was laying the contents out on his desk. She saw him take out his father's spotted silk handkerchief, his glasses case, fishing permit, a Brighton & Hove Albion season ticket and a cartoon he had drawn, depicting Kes as an angel, flying past a signpost directing him up to heaven.

She went over and placed her hands on his shoulders.

'What's up?' she said tenderly.

Ignoring her, he removed his father's fishing knife. At that moment, there was a dark snarl from Otis. A second later, she heard again the bang of the dog flap, then Otis was out in the garden, barking furiously. Puzzled, she walked across to the window and peered down.

It wasn't fully dark yet and she could see Otis running round, barking furiously. At what? She could see nothing. But it unsettled her. This wasn't his normal behaviour. It was probably just a fox. Or had there been an intruder? She turned back and saw to her surprise that Tyler was crying.

She walked the few steps back over to him, knelt and hugged him.

'What is it, darling? Tell me?'

'I'm scared,' he said, eyes streaming behind his glasses.

'What are you scared of?'

'I'm scared after your crash. You might have another one, mightn't you?' He looked at her. 'I don't want to have to make another memory box, Mummy. I don't want to have to make one about you.'

Carly put her arms round him and gave him a hug. 'Mummy's not going anywhere, OK? You're stuck with me.' She kissed his cheek.

Out in the garden, Otis suddenly began barking even more ferociously.

Carly got up and moved to the window. She peered out again, feeling a deepening sense of unease.

THE PLANE LANDED HARD. All the stuff in the galley rattled, and one of the locker doors flew open. Flying didn't bother Tooth. Since his military days, he considered it a bonus to be landing any place where people weren't shooting at you. He sat impassively, thinking hard.

He'd slept fine, bolt upright in the same position for most of the six-and-a-half-hour flight from Newark. He could have charged the client for a business or first-class seat if he'd wanted, but he preferred the anonymity of economy.

He looked at his watch. It was 7.05 a.m. UK time. The watch had a built-in digital video recorder with the pinhole camera lens concealed in the face. It had its uses for clients who wanted to see his handiwork.

Like his current client.

He looked out across the grey sky and concrete, the parked planes and runway lights of Gatwick Airport. One civilian airport looked pretty much like another, in his view.

IT WAS DAY SIX of the inquiry, 8.30 a.m., and Roy Grace was sitting with his team in the Monday morning briefing. A wet, grey morning outside. A sense of frustration inside.

Grace turned to PC Davies. 'Anything to report, Alec?'

'Yes, chief. There were several CCTV sightings of what might be our van within the timeline.'

'Did any of the cameras get the licence plate number?'

Davies shook his head. 'No, but several are fairly positive sightings because you can see the wing mirror's missing. Its last sighting was on the road heading south towards Southwick.'

'Do any show the driver?' Glenn Branson asked.

Davies nodded. 'Yes, but not clearly enough to identify him. I've given the footage to the Imaging Unit to see if they can enhance it for us.'

'Good,' Grace said.

'I think he may have gone to ground somewhere in central Southwick,' Alec Davies said. He walked over to a whiteboard, on which was pinned a large-scale street map of the city. 'My reasoning is this: the vehicle was last sighted here.' He pointed. 'This CCTV camera is close to Southwick Green. So far there are no further sightings, yet there are a number of cameras in that area that would almost certainly have picked up the van if it had gone down to the harbour or doubled back along the Old Shoreham Road.' He looked directly at Grace. 'It could be an indication it's still within this area, sir.' He circled with his finger round Southwick and Portslade, taking in the northern perimeter of Shoreham Harbour.

'I agree,' Grace said. 'Map the area out and get the Outside Inquiry Team to do a street-by-street search. Get them to knock on the door of every house that's got an enclosed garage and ask permission to look inside. And see if there are any lock-ups in the area.'

Grace looked down at the next item on his list, then addressed Sergeant Paul Wood. 'Have we got any more information from the van's wing mirror?'

'I wasn't happy, because we hadn't recovered all the parts from the scene, chief,' Wood replied. 'So I had the Specialist Search Unit take a look down all the gutters and they found a bit I was missing. There's a clean break on the arm, which means it's probable the actual mountings for the mirror unit on the van are still intact. Replacing it would be a simple task of buying, or stealing, a replacement wing-mirror unit. It could be fitted by anyone in a few minutes with basic tools.'

Grace made a note, thinking that most spare parts depots would have been closed the day before, Sunday. He looked up at Norman Potting, who he could always rely on to be thorough. Nick Nicholl was a grafter, too.

'Norman and Nick, I'm tasking you to cover all places where you could obtain a new or secondhand wing mirror for this vehicle. And check to see if there have been any reports of wing-mirror thefts off similar vans in the Brighton and Hove area. If you need extra manpower, let me know. I want every possibility covered by this evening's briefing, if possible.'

Nicholl nodded like an eager puppy. Potting made a note, his face screwed up in concentration.

'What about eBay? That could be a likely port of call to replace something like this.'

'Good point, Norman. Give that to Ray Packham in the High-Tech Crime Unit. He'll know the most effective way to search it.' Grace returned to his list. 'OK, the last agenda item is Ford Prison. Glenn and Bella, I want you to go there and see what you can get out of any of the inmates who knew Preece or Warren Tulley. Your strategy should be to focus on Preece as someone who's gone missing, rather than as a suspect in the hit and run, and don't even refer to Tulley. If any of them open up, emphasise the reward ticket. Tell them Preece is going to be shopped by someone, so it might as well be them.'

TOOTH MADE HIS WAY from the car rental desk and found the Avis section of the car park at Gatwick, climbed into the Toyota Yaris he'd reserved and began a circuit of the airport. Then he went in through the entrance marked LONG TERM CAR PARK and drove up and down the lanes of cars parked there, looking for other Toyota Yaris models that were of the same year and colour as his own.

Within twenty minutes he had identified five. Three of them were parked in deserted areas, out of sight of any CCTV cameras. Working quickly, he removed each of their front and rear licence plates and put them in the boot of his car. Then, paying the minimum fee, he drove back out of the car park and headed towards the Premier Inn, one of the hotels close to the airport perimeter. There he requested a second-floor room, one with a view of the hotel parking area and the main entrance, and told the woman receptionist he was expecting delivery of a FedEx package.

He locked the door, placed his bag on the bed, opened it and took out the brown envelope Ricky Giordino had given him. Then he moved the wooden desk in front of the window, climbed onto it and taped over the smoke detector on the ceiling. He made himself an instant coffee and then studied once more the contents of the envelope. Three photographs. Three names.

Stuart Ferguson. A stocky man of forty-five with a shaven head and a triple chin, wearing a green polo shirt with the words ABERDEEN OCEAN FISHERIES in yellow. Carly Chase, forty-one, a passably attractive woman, in a chic black jacket over a white blouse. Ewan Preece, thirty-one, spiky-haired scumbag, in a dark cagoule over a grey T-shirt.

He had addresses for the first two, but only a phone number for Preece.

He took out one of his cellphones and inserted the UK pay-as-you-go SIM card he had purchased at Gatwick Airport, then dialled the number.

It answered on the sixth ring. An edgy-sounding man said, 'Yeah?'

'Ricky said to call you.'

'Oh, yeah, right. Hang on.' Tooth heard a scraping sound, then the man gave him the address. Tooth wrote it down on the hotel notepad, then hung up without thanking him. He removed the SIM card, burned it with his cigarette lighter until it started melting and flushed it down the toilet.

He unfolded the street map of the City of Brighton and Hove he had bought and searched for the address. It took him a while to locate it. Then he pulled out another phone he had with him, his Google Android, which was registered in the name of his associate, Yossarian, and entered the address into its satnav.

The device showed him the route and calculated the time. By car it was forty-one minutes from the Premier Inn to this address.

On his laptop, Tooth opened up Google Earth and entered Carly Chase's address. Some moments later, he was zooming in on an aerial view of her house. It looked like there was plenty of secluded garden round it. That was good.

He showered, changed and made himself some more coffee. Then, returning to Google Earth, he refreshed his memory of another part of the city, an area he had got to know well the last time he was there: the port to the west of Brighton, Shoreham Harbour. Seven miles of waterfront, it was a labyrinth with a large number of places where no one went.

Shortly after 11 a.m., the room phone rang. It was the front desk, telling Tooth that a courier was waiting with a package for him. He went down and collected it, took it up to his room and removed the contents, then placed them in his bag with the rest of his things.

He had already prepaid the room charge for a week, but he didn't yet know when he would return, if he returned at all.

CARLY DID NOT start the week in a good frame of mind. Her only small and bleak consolation was that, with luck, this week would be marginally less shitty than the previous one. Ken Acott had informed her that the court hearing was set for Wednesday of the following week. He was going to try to get her Audi released from the police pound as soon as possible, but the car was badly damaged and there was no likelihood of it being repaired within the next ten days. She was going to lose her driving licence for sure, hopefully only getting the minimum of one year's ban.

Clair May, another mother with a son at St Christopher's with whom she was friendly, had taken Tyler to school that morning and would bring him home in the evening. She had told Carly that she was happy to do it for as long as was needed, and Carly was grateful for that. It had never occurred to her quite how lost she would be without a car, but she was determined not to let it get her down. Kes used to tell her to view every negative as a positive. She was damned well going to try.

TOOTH WASN'T HAPPY as he turned into the residential street and drove over a speed bump. The road was wide and exposed, with little tree cover. A hard street to hide in. A little parade of shops and mixture of semidetached houses and bungalows. There was also a school some way down, and that wasn't good news, either. These days, people kept an eye on men in cars parked near schools.

He saw the house he had come to find, number 209, almost immediately. It was opposite the shops and had a garage. It was the house where he had been informed that his first target, Ewan Preece, was holed up.

He drove past, continuing along the street for some distance, then meandered along various side roads before returning to his target street five minutes later. There was an empty parking space a short distance from the house and he reversed into it.

It was a good position, giving him an almost unobstructed view of the house. It seemed to be in poor repair, and in the front garden there were black trash bags and a rusted washing machine that looked like it had been there for years. *People ought to have more self-respect*, he thought. *You shouldn't leave trash in your front yard*. He might mention that to Preece. They'd have plenty of time to chat. Or rather, Preece would have plenty of time to listen.

He pulled out the photograph of Ewan Preece and studied it yet again. Preece looked like an asshole. He'd recognise him if he left or returned to the house. Assuming the information was correct.

Then suddenly he stiffened. Two uniformed police officers came into view round the corner, at the far end of the street. He watched them strut up to the front door of a house and ring the bell. After some moments they rang again, then knocked on the door. One of them pulled out a notebook and wrote something down, before they moved on to the next house, nearer to him, and repeated the procedure.

This time the door opened and he saw an elderly woman. They had a brief conversation on the doorstep, she went back inside, then came out again with a raincoat on, shuffled round to the garage and opened the door.

It didn't take a rocket scientist to figure out what they might be looking for. But their presence there threw him totally. He watched as the two officers nodded, then turned away and walked down to the next house, moving closer still to him. He was thinking fast now.

Driving away was one option. But the police were so close, that might draw attention to him, and he didn't want them taking note of the car. He glanced over the road at the parade of shops. Better to stay here, remain calm. There was no law against sitting in your car, was there?

He sat watching them. They got no answer at the next house, had a brief conversation on the pavement, then split, one of them crossing the road, heading up the pavement and entering the first shop in the parade. His colleague was now knocking on the door of number 209.

Tooth watched the windows of the house as the policeman stood on the doorstep, his knock unanswered. Then he glimpsed an upstairs curtain twitch, just a fraction. There was someone in there. Someone who wasn't going to open the door to a cop. Good.

The officer knocked again, then pressed what Tooth assumed was a bell. After some moments he turned away, but instead of walking to the front door of the next house, he came over to the car.

Tooth remained calm. The policeman was bending, tapping on the passenger side window.

Tooth switched on the ignition and powered the window down.

The policeman was in his mid-twenties. He had sharp, observant eyes and a serious, earnest expression.

'Good morning, sir.'

'Morning,' he replied, in his best English accent. He could do a good English accent.

'We're looking for a white Ford Transit van that was seen driving erratically in this area last Wednesday. Does that ring any bells?'

Tooth shook his head, keeping his voice quiet. 'No, none.'

'Thank you. Just as a formality, can I check what you are doing here?'

Tooth was ready for the question. 'I'm waiting for my girlfriend. She's having her hair done.' He pointed at the salon, which was called Jane's.

'Likely to be a long wait, if she's like my missus.'

The officer stared at him for a second, then stood up and walked towards the next house. Tooth powered the window back up, watching him in the mirror. The cop stopped suddenly and turned back to look at his car again. Then he walked up to the front door of the house.

Tooth continued to watch him, and his colleague, working their way down the street, until they were safely out of sight. Then he drove off. There wasn't any point in hanging out in this street in daylight. He would return after dark. In the meantime, he had plenty of work to do.

6

Taking his seat at the workstation in MIR-1, coffee in hand, Roy Grace felt tired and a little despondent. Ewan Preece had gone to ground and tomorrow would be a whole week since the collision, without a single reported sighting of the man. Sooner or later Preece would make a mistake and be spotted, for sure—if he wasn't shopped first by someone. But in the meantime, there was a lot of pressure on Grace from ACC Rigg, who in turn was under pressure from the chief constable, to get a fast result.

'The time is 8.30 a.m., Tuesday, April the 27th,' Grace said, at the start of the briefing. He took a quick sip of coffee, and looked down at his notes. 'We have new information from Ford Prison about the death of Warren Tulley, Ewan Preece's mate.'

He looked at Glenn Branson, who said, 'I have the post-mortem report on Tulley, boss. He was hanging from a steel beam in his cell from a rope made out of strips of bedding sheet. The officer who found him cut him down and proceeded to perform CPR on him, but he was pronounced dead at the scene twenty minutes later by a paramedic. To summarise the report'—he held it up to indicate that it was several pages long—'there are a number of factors to indicate this was not suicide. The Assessment, Care in Custody and Teamwork report on this prisoner indicates no suicidal tendencies and, like Ewan Preece, he was due to be released in three weeks' time.'

Branson looked down at his notes. 'There was evidence of a struggle in Tulley's cell and several bruises have been found on his body. The pathologist says that it appears he was asphyxiated by strangling first and then hanged. He also found human flesh under some of his fingernails, which has been sent off for DNA analysis. With luck, we'll have a result back later today or tomorrow.'

He glanced down at his notes again, then went on. 'Apparently, Tulley had been shooting his mouth off about the reward money. He was boasting he knew where Preece was and was weighing up his loyalty to his friend against the hundred thousand dollars.'

'Did he genuinely know?' asked Bella Noy.

Branson raised a finger. 'Every prisoner in a UK jail gets given a PIN code for the prison phone, right? Well, listen to this recording on the prison phone of a call made by Tulley to Ewan Preece's number.'

There was a loud crackle, then they heard a brief, hushed conversation: two scuzzy, low-life voices.

'Ewan, where are you? You didn't come back. What's going on?'

'Yeah, well, had a bit of a problem, you see.'

'What kind of problem? You owe me. It's my money in this deal.'

'Keep yer hair on. I had a bit of an accident. I'm lying low for a bit. All right? Don't worry, I'll see you right.' There was a clank and the call ended.

Branson looked at Roy Grace. 'That was recorded at 6.25 p.m. last Thursday, the day following the accident. I've also checked the timing. Prisoners working on paid resettlement, which is what Preece was doing, are free to leave the prison from 6.30 a.m. and don't have to be back until 10 p.m. That would have given him ample time to be driving in Portland Road around 9 a.m.'

'Lying low,' Grace said, pensively. 'You need someone you can trust to be able to lie low.' He stood up and went over to the whiteboard where Ewan Preece's family tree was sketched out. Then he turned to Potting. 'Norman, you know a fair bit about him. Any ideas who he was close to?'

'I'll speak to some of the neighbourhood teams, boss. My guess is, since the van seems to have disappeared in Southwick, that he'll be there, with either a girlfriend or a relative.'

'Chief,' Duncan Crocker said, standing up. 'I've already been doing work on this.' DS Crocker had just been brought into the team as the intelligence manager. Now he went over to the whiteboard and said, 'Preece has three sisters. One emigrated to Australia with her husband four years ago. The second lives in Saltdean. I don't know where the youngest, Evie, lives, but she and Preece were pretty thick as kids. She was in his car when he was done for joyriding. She'd be a good person to look for.'

'And a real bonus if she happens to be living in Southwick,' Grace replied.

'I know someone who'll be able to tell us,' Crocker said. 'Her probation officer. She's on probation for handling and receiving. For her brother.'

'Phone the probation officer now,' Grace instructed.

Crocker went over to the far side of the room to make the call, while they carried on with the briefing. Two minutes later, he returned with a big smile on his face.

'Chief, Evie Preece lives in Southwick. Manor Hall Road.'

Suddenly Grace felt a surge of adrenalin. 'Good work, Duncan,' he said. He turned to Nick Nicholl. 'We need a search warrant, asap.'

The DC nodded.

Grace turned back to Branson. 'OK, let's get the Local Support Team mobilised and go and pay him a visit.' He looked at his watch. 'Perhaps we'll be in time to bring him breakfast in bed!'

AN HOUR AND A HALF LATER, Grace and Branson cruised slowly past 209 Manor Hall Road, Southwick. Branson was behind the wheel and Grace studied the house. Curtains were drawn, a good sign that the occupants were not up yet, or at least were inside.

Grace radioed to the other vehicles in his team, while Branson stopped at their designated meeting point, one block to the south, and turned the car round. The only further intelligence that had come through on Evie Preece was that she was estranged from her common-law husband and apparently lived alone in the house. She had police markers going back years, for assault, possession of stolen goods and handling drugs, while her three children—all by different fathers—had been taken into care by the Social Services. *She and her brother are two peas in a pod*, Grace thought.

An unmarked white minibus, containing eight members of the Local Support Team, halted alongside them, momentarily blocking the road. Two other marked police cars reported they were now in position at the far end of the street.

The team inspector looked in at them and Grace gave him the thumbs-up, mouthing, 'Rock 'n' roll.'

The officer pulled his visor down and the three vehicles moved forward, accelerating sharply with a sense of urgency now, then braking to a halt outside the house. Everyone bundled out onto the pavement.

Two sets of dog handlers ran up the side of the house to cover the back garden. The members of the Local Support Team, in their blue suits and military-style helmets, ran up to the front door. One of them carried a metal battering ram, known colloquially as the Big Yellow Door Key. Two others, bringing up the rear, carried the back-up hydraulic ram and its power supply, in case the front door was reinforced. Two more stood outside the garage to prevent anyone escaping that way.

The first members of the team to reach the door pounded on it with their fists, at the same time yelling, 'POLICE! OPEN UP! POLICE! OPEN UP!' It was a deliberate intimidation tactic.

One officer swung the battering ram and the door splintered open.

All six of them charged in, shouting, 'POLICE! POLICE!'

Grace and Branson followed them into a tiny hallway that stank of stale cigarette smoke. Grace's adrenalin was pumping. Like most officers, he'd always loved the thrill of raids, and the fear that went with it. You never knew what you were going to find. His eyes darted everywhere, warily, ever conscious of the possibility that someone might appear with a weapon.

The Local Support Team had split up inside. Some were bursting into different downstairs rooms and others were charging up the stairs, yelling menacingly, 'POLICE! STAY WHERE YOU ARE! DON'T MOVE!'

The two detectives stayed in the narrow, bare hallway and heard doors banging open above them. Heavy footsteps. Then a female voice called out, 'Sir, you'd better come in here!'

Followed by Glenn Branson, Grace walked through the open doorway to his right, into a small and cluttered sitting room. He noticed a wooden-framed settee; bottles of wine and beer littering a manky carpet, along with unwashed clothes; and a massive plasma TV screen on the wall.

Face-down on the floor was a writhing, moaning woman in a fluffy pink dressing gown, bound hand and foot with grey duct tape, and gagged.

Grace ran upstairs quickly, glanced into the two bedrooms and bathroom, then went back down and knelt beside the woman, as a female member of the team worked away the tape over her mouth, then the rest of the bindings.

The woman, in her mid-twenties, had a shock of short, fair hair and a hard face with a flinty complexion.

'What took you so long? What's the time?'

'Five past ten,' the woman officer said. 'What's your name?'

'Evie Preece.'

'Are you injured, Evie?' She turned to another officer and said, 'Call an ambulance.'

'I don't need no ambulance. I need a drink and a fag.'

Grace looked at her. He had no idea at this stage how long she had been there, but she looked remarkably composed for someone who had been tied and gagged. He wondered if it was a set-up.

'Where's Ewan?' Roy Grace asked her.

'In prison. Where you pigs put him.'

'So he hasn't been staying here?'

'I didn't have no one staying.'

'Someone's been sleeping in your spare bed,' Grace said.

'I want a solicitor.'

'You're not under arrest, Evie. You only get a solicitor if you are charged with something.'

'So charge me.'

'I will do in a minute,' Grace said. 'I'll charge you with obstructing a police officer. Now, tell me who slept in your spare room?'

She said nothing.

'The same person who tied you up?'

'No.'

Good, he thought. *That is a big step forward.*

'We're concerned about your brother,' he said.

'That's touching, that is. You've been nicking him since he was a kid, but now you're suddenly concerned about him? That's rich!'

AT THE EVENING BRIEFING, Grace brought his team up to speed on the raid. Evie Preece was unable to give any information about her assailant, but the fact that she consented, albeit reluctantly, to a medical examination was an indication to Grace that the attack on her had been real and not a put-up job by herself and her brother, as he had first suspected.

The police doctor's opinion was that some severe bruising to her neck was indicative of a sharp blow. She added that the side of the neck, just above the collarbone, was the place where someone experienced in martial arts would strike, if they wanted to render their victim instantly unconscious.

This was consistent with Evie's story that around eleven the previous night she had gone out into the garden to let her cat out, and the next thing she had found herself lying, trussed up, on her living-room floor. She was continuing to refute the allegation that her brother had been in the house and she denied vehemently that any vehicle had been in her garage recently, despite evidence to the contrary. The first piece of which was a pool of engine oil on the surface of the garage floor, which looked recent. The second and even more significant was the discovery of male clothing in the spare bedroom: a pair of trainers and jeans that were consistent with Ewan Preece's size, while a white T-shirt, also his size, was found in her washing machine.

Grace had ordered her to be arrested on suspicion of harbouring a fugitive. In addition, he had put an experienced search team into the property to see if they could find anything else in the house or garden.

So far, in addition to the oil and the clothes, they had come up with what they believed to be signs of a forced entry through patio doors at the rear of the house. It was very subtly done, with an instrument such as a screwdriver handled by someone with a good knowledge of locks; someone who was skilled not just in breaking and entering, but in assault and in bindings. They had found no fingerprints so far; nothing that might yield DNA, and no other clues. It was still early days, but it wasn't looking good.

DRESSED IN A heavy fleece jacket, thick jeans, a lined cap and rubber boots, David Harris began his workday as he had every day for the past forty-one years, by checking the rows of smokehouses where the fish had been curing overnight. He was in a cheery frame of mind: business was booming, despite the recession, and he genuinely loved his work.

He might have been less cheery had he known he was being watched, and had been since the moment he had arrived there that morning.

Springs Smoked Salmon was a household name throughout Europe, but its location, tucked away in a valley in the South Downs, close to Brighton, was an improbable one for a fish company. The place had an unprepossessing air: the ramshackle collection of single-storey buildings could have belonged to a tumbledown farm, rather than containing a business that had become an international legend.

He unlocked the padlock on the door of a cold-storage shed and pulled it open, revealing rows of headless Scottish salmon and trout hung on hooks suspended from overhead racks. He checked that the temperature was fine. Then he checked each of the next three sheds as well, before moving on to the smokery ovens. These were nearly fifty years old, but still going strong. Huge, grimy, brick and steel walk-in boxes, each had a wood-fired kiln in the base, and the ceiling covered with racks and hooks, on which hung rows of pink and gold-brown fillets of smoking fish.

When he had finished his inspections, he entered the shop where the staff were busy making up the orders that had come in overnight.

He went to his office and sat down at his computer, checking his stock. At that moment, the phone rang.

He answered and an American voice the other end asked, 'How quickly could you supply two thousand langoustines?'

'What size, and how quickly do you need them, sir?'

After a moment, the American said, 'The biggest available. Before the end of next week. We've been let down by a supplier.'

Harris asked him to hold for a moment, then checked on the computer. 'We are low on stock at the moment, but we have a delivery coming down from Scotland early Wednesday. If you want that quantity, I could get it added to the consignment. Would you like me to give you the price?'

'That won't be an issue. You can guarantee Wednesday morning?'

'We have a delivery from Scotland every Wednesday, sir.'

'Good. I'll come back to you.'

THE WEEK PROCEEDED without any significant progress being made by Roy Grace's team. This was despite the DNA from the flesh found under Tulley's fingernails producing a suspect within Ford Prison, a giant of a man called Lee Rogan. Rogan was serving out the final months of a sentence for armed robbery and grievous bodily harm, prior to release.

Rogan had been arrested on suspicion of murdering Warren Tulley but was claiming in his defence that they'd had a fight over money earlier the same evening Tulley had died. So far, the internal investigation had not unearthed any calls made by Rogan using his prison PIN code, or any mobile phone concealed in his cell. If he had been intending to claim the reward, they had no evidence of it as yet.

Evie Preece had been released on bail. Grace had put surveillance on her house, in case her brother returned. It was unlikely, he knew, but then Preece was stupid enough to do it.

On Friday morning, Grace was heading towards his office when his phone rang. It was Tracy Stocker, the crime scene manager.

'I think we've found Preece,' she said.

GRACE LET BRANSON DRIVE. Ever since gaining his green Response and Pursuit driving ticket, Branson had been keen to show his prowess. And every time he allowed Branson to take the wheel, Grace quickly regretted it. With the speedometer needle the wrong side of the 120mph mark at times, it was more by sheer good luck than anything he would want to attribute to driving skill that they finally ended up on the approach road to Shoreham Port with their lives, although not his nerves, still intact.

'What do you think of my driving, old-timer?' asked Glenn. 'I think I've nailed that four-wheel-drift thing now!'

'I think you need to be more aware about what other road users might do,' Grace replied diplomatically.

They drove straight over a mini roundabout and entered an industrial area. There was a tall, brick-walled warehouse to their right and a blue corrugated metal warehouse to their left. They passed a gap between two buildings, through which Grace caught a glimpse of the choppy water of the Shoreham Port canal. Then, immediately in front of them, was a marked police car, its lights flashing in stationary mode.

As they approached, they saw several parked vehicles, including the crime scene manager's. A line of crime-scene tape ran between the walls of two buildings and a PCSO stood guard in front of the car.

They climbed out of the car into the blustery, damp wind, walked up to her and gave their names.

'I need you both to suit up, please, sirs,' she said. 'CSM's request.'

They returned to the car and wormed their way into hooded blue paper oversuits before ducking under the tape and walking down to the quay. Grace looked around for CCTV cameras but couldn't see any, to his disappointment. Directly ahead of them was the rear of the large yellow mobile operations truck of the Specialist Search Unit.

He had always loved this part of the city. He took a deep breath, savouring the tangy smells of salt, oil, tar and rope that reminded him of his childhood and coming down here with his dad to fish.

As they rounded the corner, he saw a hive of activity. There were several police officers, all in protective oversuits, and he immediately picked out the short, sturdy figure of the crime scene manager, Tracy Stocker, and the lean figure of the Coroner's officer, Philip Keay.

Members of the search team stood around, dressed in dark blue fleeces, waterproof trousers, rubber boots and black baseball caps with the wording POLICE above the peaks. One of them was standing beside a coil of cable that ran from a box of apparatus and down over the edge of the quay into the water. Grace realised there was a diver below.

Sitting centre stage on the quay was a dull white, beat-up-looking Ford Transit van, its roof and sides streaked with mud. A steady stream of water poured from its doorsills. Grace could see that the driver's-side wing mirror was missing. Four steel hawsers ran vertically from its wheel arches high above to the pulley on the arm of a mobile crane parked beside it. But he barely gave the crane a second glance. All his focus was on the man hunched motionless over the steering wheel.

Tracy Stocker walked up to greet Grace and Branson. She was accompanied by a burly, rugged-looking man in his fifties.

'Hi, Roy and Glenn,' she said cheerily. 'This is Keith Wadey, the assistant chief engineer of Shoreham Port. Keith, this is Detective Superintendent Grace and Detective Sergeant Glenn Branson.'

They shook hands. Grace took an instant liking to Wadey, who exuded a friendly air of confidence and experience.

He turned back to Tracy. 'Have you run a check on the van's index?'

'Yes, chief. False plates. The serial number's been filed off the chassis, so it's almost certainly nicked, but that's about all we know.'

Grace thanked her, then spoke to Wadey. 'What do we have?' he asked, looking at the figure in the van again.

'Well, sir,' Wadey said. 'We carry out regular side-scan sonar sweeps of the canal, checking for silt levels and for any obstructions. Yesterday afternoon at around 4.30 p.m., we identified what looked like a vehicle about a hundred and twenty feet off the edge of this quay, in twenty-five feet of water.'

Grace nodded.

'I contacted the police dive team—our standard procedure—and we assisted them in recovering the vehicle from the water this morning. I'm afraid we found a poor sod in there. Dunno if he's a suicide—we get quite a few of them—because he doesn't seem to have made any effort to get out.'

Grace glanced at their surroundings: a large, rusting warehouse that looked derelict.

'What is this place?' he asked.

'It now belongs to Dudman, an aggregates company. They bought it a couple of months ago. It had been empty for several years. A bankruptcy.'

'Anyone working here? Any security guards?'

'No security guards or cameras, sir.'

A secluded spot, Grace thought. *Carefully chosen? It isn't the kind of place you find by accident.*

'Is it locked at night?'

'Padlocked with a chain, yes,' Wadey said. 'But it was open when we got here. Either someone unlocked it or picked the lock.'

Grace walked across to the driver's side of the van.

'How long has he been in the water?'

'My guess would be a maximum of three or four days,' the engineer replied. 'You can see some bloating, but he's intact. The fish and crustaceans like to wait for a week or so before they set to work.'

'Thanks.'

Grace peered in through the driver's window, which was down, as was the passenger's, he noted. To help the vehicle sink more quickly? he wondered. The rear doors were open, too. The immediate question in his mind was whether this was an accident, suicide or murder. His experience had taught him never to jump to conclusions.

Even though the body was bloated from gases, the face was still thin, streaked with mud, eyes wide open, staring ahead with a look of shock. In the flesh, Preece looked even paler than in his photographs, but his identity was still clear.

Grace looked at the dead man's hands. Preece was gripping the steering wheel as if with grim determination. As if he had thought that somehow, if he kept hold of it, he could steer himself out of trouble.

And that did not make sense.

'Dead man's grip,' said a female voice beside him.

He turned to see the sergeant in charge of the search team, Lorna Dennison-Wilkins. 'Lorna!' he said. 'How are you?'

She grinned. 'Understaffed, underappreciated and busy as heck. How about you?'

'Couldn't have put it better myself.' He nodded at the dead man. 'Dead man's grip?'

'Rigor mortis,' she said. 'It's the suddenness of immersion that brings it on very fast. If someone drowns and they're holding on to something at that moment, it's really hard to prise their fingers off it.'

He stared at Preece's fingers. Why was he holding on to the steering wheel? Had he frozen in stark terror? Grace knew that if he'd just driven off a harbour quay into water, he'd be doing everything he could to get out.

AFTER A PHONE DISCUSSION with him, the Home Office pathologist agreed with Grace that she should definitely see the body in situ, prior to its being taken to the mortuary. Unfortunately, she was finishing a job in London, which meant a long, cold wait for them all on the quay: Nadiuska estimated she would be there by about 2 p.m., and when Grace glanced at his watch it was only 12.30 p.m.

The good news was that of the two regular Home Office pathologists for this area, they had been allocated Nadiuska De Sancha, the one whom Grace and everyone else preferred to work with. As an added bonus to the fact that the statuesque, red-haired Spaniard was good at her job, and extremely helpful with it, she also happened to be very easy on the eye.

A Home Office pathologist, of which there were thirty in the UK, was always called in when there were grounds for suspicion following the discovery of a body. A standard post-mortem usually took less than an hour. A Home Office one could take from three to six hours, and sometimes more.

Grace phoned the Incident Room to tell them to call off the search for Ewan Preece and instead to concentrate on the immediate neighbours of Preece's sister, to see if anyone had seen or heard anything. He also wondered whether the dead man's sister might be sufficiently shocked into telling the truth about what had happened that night—if she genuinely knew.

An hour later, when Grace had completed an inspection of the surrounding area, a voice came through on his radio. It was the scene guard at the entrance. 'Sir, there's someone here to see you. Says you're expecting him. Kevin Spinella?'

Grace was expecting him, the way he would expect to see blowflies round a decomposing cadaver. He walked round the corner and up to the barrier. Spinella stood there, short and thin, collar of his beige mackintosh turned up in the clichéd fashion of a movie gumshoe.

'Good morning, Detective Superintendent!' he said.

Grace tapped his watch. 'It's afternoon, actually.' He gave the reporter a reproachful glance. 'Unlike you to be behind the times.'

'Ha ha,' Spinella said.

Grace stared at him quizzically, but said nothing.

'Hear you've got a body in a van,' the reporter said. 'What can you tell me about it? Don't suppose it's Ewan Preece, is it?'

An educated guess? Grace wondered. Or had one of the team there phoned Spinella?

'There is a body in a van, but the body has not been identified at this stage,' Grace replied.

'Could it be the van you are looking for?'

He saw Nadiuska De Sancha, gowned up, walking towards them.

'Too early to tell,' Grace said. He nodded a silent greeting at the pathologist, and she ducked under the tape, which Grace had lifted for her.

'Home Office pathologist?' Spinella said. 'Looks to me like you could have a murder inquiry going on.'

Grace turned to him. 'Makes a change, does it, being the last to know?'

He turned, with great satisfaction, and escorted Nadiuska De Sancha towards the quay and across to the right, out of the reporter's line of sight. Then, knowing that she liked to work alone, he went to join the rest of the team inside the warmth of the SSU truck.

HALF AN HOUR LATER, Nadiuska De Sancha came over. 'Roy, I think we can safely rule out accidental death. And I'm fairly confident we can rule out suicide, too,' she said.

Shrugging himself back into his anorak, Grace followed her to the white van. The pathologist stopped by the driver's door, which was open.

She pointed up at a small, cylindrical object Grace had not taken in before, clipped to the driver's-side sun visor. 'See that? It's a digital underwater camera and transmitter. And it's switched on, although the battery's dead.' Grace frowned. How the hell had he missed it? And what was it there for? Had Preece been filming himself? Then, interrupting his thoughts, she pointed at the man's hands and gave him a bemused look.

'Dead man's grip is caused by rigor mortis, right?'

Grace nodded. She reached in with a blue, latex-gloved hand and raised one of Preece's fleshy, alabaster-white fingers. The skin of the tip remained adhered to the steering wheel. It looked like a blister with tendrils attached.

'I'll need to do some more lab tests, but it looks to me as if the poor man's hands have been superglued to the steering wheel.'

7

Tooth sat at the desk in his room at the Premier Inn, in front of his laptop, sipping a mug of coffee and editing the video of Ewan Preece's last few minutes. The smoke detector in the ceiling was still taped up, and a pack of cigarettes lay beside the saucer that he was using as an ashtray.

He had used three cameras: the one on his wrist; the one he had fitted to the interior of the van; and one he had balanced on the edge of a skip. The film began with an establishing exterior shot of the van at night, at the edge of the quay. A time and date print at the top right of the frame showed it was 2 a.m., Tuesday, April 27. Preece could be seen at the wheel, apparently unconscious, with duct tape over his mouth.

Then it cut to the interior. There was a wide-angle shot of Preece, buckled into his seat. He was opening his eyes as if awaking from sleep, seemingly disorientated. Then he peered down at his hands, which were on the steering wheel, clearly puzzled as to why he could not move them.

He began to struggle, trying to free his hands. His eyes bulged in fear as he started to realise something was wrong. A hand appeared in frame and ripped the duct tape from his mouth. Preece yelped in pain, then turned his head towards the door, speaking to a person out of shot.

'Who are you? What are you doing?' The driver's door slammed shut.

The camera angle changed to an exterior shot. It showed the whole driver's side of the van and a short distance behind it. A figure, wearing a hoodie, his face invisible, drove a fork-lift truck into view, steered it right up to the rear of the van, rammed it a few inches forwards and began to push it steadily towards the edge of the quay. The van then suddenly lurched downwards, as the front wheels went over and the bottom of the chassis grounded on the stonework, with a metallic grating sound.

The film cut back to the interior of the van. Ewan Preece was bug-eyed now and screaming, 'No, no! What do you want? Tell me what you want! Please tell me! Tell me!' Then he visibly lurched forward, held by the seat belt, and his mouth opened in a long, silent scream, as if, in his terror, he could not get any more words out.

THE POST-MORTEM ROOM at the Brighton and Hove City Mortuary, with its tiled walls and stark, cold lighting, always gave Grace the creeps.

He shuddered as he took in the scene before him. At that moment, Ewan Preece was a surreal sight, lying on his back, in his jeans and T-shirt, on the stainless-steel PM table, his hands still gripping the black steering wheel, which Nadiuska De Sancha had requested be detached from the vehicle and brought with him to the mortuary. He looked, in death, as if he was driving some spectral vehicle.

Nadiuska was plucking delicately at the skin of one of Preece's fingers with tweezers. The SOCO photographer was steadily working his way round the body. Glenn Branson was in a corner, surreptitiously talking on his phone. The Coroner's officer, Philip Keay, was standing in a green gown, dictating into a machine.

Cleo and her assistant, Darren, stood by, ready to assist the pathologist, but at the moment they had nothing to do but watch.

The detective superintendent was thinking hard. Preece's hands glued to the wheel confirmed, beyond any doubt in his mind, that the man had been murdered. And the presence of that camera in the vehicle was bothering him a lot. Put there by a sadistic killer? Or was there an even darker aspect to this? The Mafia connection was weighing heavily on his mind. Could this have been a sadistic revenge hit?

The body had not yet been formally identified, but from the tattoos on his body and a scar on his face, Ford Prison had already confirmed Preece's identity beyond much doubt.

Grace stepped out of the PM room and made a call to Detective Investigator Pat Lanigan in America, to ask him whether, in his experience, the dead boy's parents were the kind of people who might be sufficiently aggrieved to go for a revenge killing.

Lanigan informed him that they had the money, the power and the connections and that with people like this, a whole different set of rules applied. He said that he would see what intelligence he could come up with, and promised to come back to Grace as soon he found out anything.

Grace hung up with a heavy heart. The notion of a Mafia-backed killing in the heart of Brighton was not something that would sit well with anyone —not the council, not the tourist board, not his boss, ACC Rigg, and not with himself, either. Lanigan had said a whole different set of rules applied. Well, not in his beloved city, they didn't.

'THE TIME IS 8.30 A.M., Saturday, May the 1st,' Roy Grace announced to his team in MIR-1. 'This is the eighteenth briefing of Operation Violin. The first thing I have to report is the positive identification of Ewan Preece.'

'Shame to have lost such an upstanding member of Brighton society, chief,' said Norman Potting.

There was a titter of laughter. Grace gave him a reproachful look.

'Thank you, Norman. Let's hold the humour. We have some serious issues on our hands.' Grace looked back down at his notes.

'It will be some days before we get the toxicology reports, but I have significant findings from the PM. The first is that there was bruising to the side of Preece's neck very similar to the bruising that was found on his sister, Evie, who is claiming to remember nothing immediately after going outside on Monday night to let her cat out. According to Nadiuska De Sancha, this is consistent with a martial arts blow with the side of a hand to cause instant loss of consciousness. This could be the way Preece was over-powered by his assailant.'

Grace looked down again. 'The sea water present in Preece's lungs indi-cates that he was alive at the time the van went into the water and he died from drowning. As his hands were glued to the steering wheel, it makes this extremely unlikely to have been suicide. Does anyone have a different view?'

'If he was unconscious, sir,' said Nick Nicholl, 'how did the van actually get into the water? It would have been difficult for someone to physically push it, because when the front wheels went over the edge of the quay, surely the bottom of the chassis would have grounded on it?'

'Good point,' Grace said. 'Dudman, the company that owns that particu-lar section of the wharf, say that their fork-lift truck had been moved. Anyone with a basic knowledge could have started the engine with a screw-driver and used it to push the van in.'

'Has the kind of glue been established?' asked DS Duncan Crocker.

'It has been sent for lab analysis. We don't have that information yet.'

'There was no tube of glue found in the vehicle?' Crocker asked.

'No,' Grace replied. 'The Specialist Search Unit did an extensive dive search round the area where the van was recovered, but so far they have found nothing. My sense is that they won't find anything, either.' Grace looked around at his team. 'I think we could be looking at an underworld hit here. It has all the hallmarks of a professional.'

'If it is a professional Mafia hit,' Nick Nicholl said, 'then whoever did this could already be back in America. Or wherever it is they came from.'

Grace nodded, thinking. 'Evie Preece does not have an internal door into her garage. If our man knocked Preece out, he would have had to carry him out of the house and into the garage on a street in a densely populated neighbourhood. When he got to Shoreham Harbour, he would have had to leave him in the van while he opened the gates. Then he would have had to glue his hands to the wheel, start the fork-lift truck and use it to push the van into the water. I want to ramp up those house-to-house enquiries in Evie's street and round the harbour. Someone must have seen something, and we have to find them.'

Grace turned to DC Boutwood and DC Nicholl, to whom he had delegated the line of enquiry regarding the camera found in the van.

'Do you have anything to report?'

Emma-Jane shook her head. 'Not so far, sir. The camera is a Canon model widely on sale here, at a price of around a grand, and overseas. There are seventeen retail outlets in Brighton that stock it, as well as numerous online stores. In the US there are thousands of retail outlets, Radio Shack, a national chain, being among the major discounters.'

'Great. So we're looking for a needle in a haystack?'

'That's about it, sir.'

'OK,' Grace made a note, then sat in silent thought for some moments. He could not put a finger on it, but he had a bad feeling. Copper's nose, they used to call it. Gut feelings. Instinct.

DRESSED ALL IN BLACK, with a black baseball cap pulled low over his face, Tooth knew he would be almost invisible outside the car. Tuesday night: 11.23 p.m. The motorway was dark and busy. Just taillights, headlights and occasional flashing indicators.

At long last, the lorry he had been following from Aberdeen was pulling into a service station. The driver had been going steadily for nearly five hours since he had stopped for a break just south of Lockerbie.

He followed the taillights of the truck along the slip road and up a slight incline. They passed signs with symbols for fuel, food, accommodation and another one for the goods vehicles' parking area.

Conveniently, as if obeying Tooth's silent wishes, the driver headed the articulated lorry past rows of parked lorries, and pulled into a bay several spaces beyond the last one, in a particularly dark area of the car park.

Tooth parked the car and switched off its lights. He had already disabled the Toyota's interior light. He jumped out and ran, crouching low. He couldn't see any CCTV cameras in this area. The lorry nearest to his target had its blinds pulled. The driver was either asleep or watching television.

INSIDE THE CAB of his sixteen-wheel, fridge-box artic, Stuart Ferguson reached down for the parking brake, then remembered it was in a different position from the one in the Volvo he normally drove. That vehicle was currently in a Sussex Police vehicle pound where it would remain until the inquest on the young cyclist was complete.

He switched off the engine and killed the lights. He was still badly shaken and had been having nightmares. He kept seeing the poor laddie tumbling across the road towards him, coming straight at him, still gripping the handlebars of his bike.

On top of that, he had been worrying this could be the end of his trucking career. Because he had been over his allotted hours, he had had the threat of a death by dangerous driving charge hanging over him. It had been a relief to hear the police were only going to prosecute him for the relatively minor and straightforward hours offence.

At least it felt OK being back behind the wheel again. He'd missed his regular journey to Sussex last Tuesday because the company did not have a spare vehicle available, so his boss had given him the week off. In fact, all things considered, the company was being very supportive to him, despite his pending prosecution. Driving out of hours was not something they could ever sanction officially, but everyone knew it went on.

He climbed down onto the footplate, and locked the door. As his right foot touched the tarmac, he felt a blow on his neck and his head filled with dazzling white streaks, followed by a shower of electric sparks. *Like a psychedelic light show*, he thought, in the fraction of a second before he blacked out.

TOOTH KNELT, holding the limp body of the short, sturdy man in his arms, and looked around him. He heard the hum of traffic on the motorway a short way away. The rattle of a diesel engine firing up.

He dragged the man the short distance to his car, the lorry driver's heavy-duty boots scraping noisily along the tarmac. He hauled him onto the rear seat, closed the doors, then drove a short way across the car park and pulled up in an area of total darkness, away from all the vehicles.

Next he tugged the man's polo shirt out of his trousers. With his thumbs he counted down from the top of the man's spine to C4. Then, using a movement he had been taught in the military for disabling the enemy without killing him, he swung him out of the car, lifted him up, and dropped him down hard, backwards, across his knees, hearing the snap. He manoeuvred him back into the car and set to work, binding the man's mouth and arms with duct tape. He jammed him down into the gap between the front and rear seats and covered him with a rug—in case he got stopped by the police for any reason—then he locked up.

He sauntered across to the service station cafeteria, pulling the baseball cap even lower over his face as he spotted a CCTV camera. He walked past, facing away, as he entered the building.

Tooth used the restroom, and bought himself a large black coffee and a custard Danish. He chose a table in a quiet section, ate his pastry and sipped the scalding coffee. He felt good. His plan was coming together, the way his plans always came together. He didn't do abortive missions.

'THE TIME IS 8.30 A.M., Wednesday, May the 5th,' Roy Grace read from his notes to his team in MIR-1. 'This is the twenty-sixth briefing of Operation Violin.' He felt like adding, *And we're not making any sodding progress*, but he refrained. There were flat spots like this in almost every inquiry.

He was in a bad and worried mood. His biggest worry was Cleo. She had almost fainted stepping out of the shower that morning. She insisted it was purely because the water had been too hot, but he had wanted to take her straight to hospital. She'd refused, saying that she felt fine, right as rain; they were short-handed at the mortuary and she needed to be there.

He was worried about this case, too. It was a full-on murder inquiry, yet he sensed a spark was missing. Although he had most of his trusted regulars in his team, there didn't seem to be the air of commitment and focus that he was used to feeling. He knew the reason. It was the wrong reason, but it was human nature. It was because the murder victim was Ewan Preece.

Despite the horrific nature of his death, no one from Sussex Police was going to be shedding a tear at Preece's funeral—although he would send a couple of undercover officers along, to keep an eye on who turned up, or lurked nearby. But regardless of however undesirable a character Preece was, he had been murdered. And Grace's job was not to be judgmental, but to find the killer and lock him up. To do that, he needed to get his team better motivated.

'Before we go through your individual reports,' he said, 'I want to recap on our lines of enquiry.' He stood up and pointed to the whiteboard, on which there were three numbered headings, each written in caps in red. 'In the first, we look into the possibility that there is no link between Preece's killing and the death of cyclist Tony Revere, clear? Preece was a man who made enemies naturally. We could be looking at a drugs turf war or something like a double-crossing.'

Duncan Crocker put up his hand. 'The camera's the thing that bothers me with that line of enquiry, chief. Why wouldn't they just kill him? Why chuck away an expensive camera like that?'

'There are plenty of sadists out there,' Grace replied. 'But I agree with your point about the camera. We'll come back to that. OK, right, the second line of enquiry is that Preece was killed by someone who was after the reward money.'

'Doesn't the same apply with the camera, boss?' asked Bella Moy. 'If they're after the reward, why chuck away a camera of that value?'

'It would be a good idea to remind ourselves of the wording of the reward,' Grace replied. 'The reward is for "information leading to the identity of the van driver" responsible for the death of Fernanda Revere's son.' He looked up. 'That's a big difference.'

'Do you think something might have gone wrong, Roy?' Nick Nicholl asked. 'Perhaps the killer was planning to get Preece to fess up into the camera and it didn't happen.'

'Maybe it did happen,' Glenn Branson said. 'The camera transmits—we don't know what was said or transmitted to whom.'

'I can't speculate on whether anything went wrong, Nick,' Grace replied to DC Nicholl. Then he pointed at the whiteboard again. 'Our third line of enquiry is whether, bearing in mind Revere's family's connection with organised crime, this was a professional revenge killing—a hit. So far, from initial enquiries I've made, there is no intelligence of any contract of any kind that's been put out regarding this, but we need to look at the US more closely.' He turned to Crocker. 'Duncan, I'm tasking you with getting further information on the Revere family and their connections.'

'Yes, boss,' the DS said, and made a note.

'I have a 3.30 p.m. meeting with the ACC. I need to take him something to show that we're not all asleep here.'

At that moment, his phone rang. Raising a hand apologetically, Roy Grace answered it. Kevin Spinella was on the other end, and what the *Argus* reporter told him suddenly made his bad mood a whole lot worse.

THAT WEDNESDAY was not promising to be one of the best days of Carly's life. She was due to meet her solicitor, Ken Acott, outside Brighton Magistrates' Court before her court appearance.

She was wearing a simple navy two-piece, a white blouse and a silk scarf, with navy court shoes. Ken had advised her to look neat and respectable.

As she stepped out of the taxi, Carly felt the warmth of the sun, but the promise of a fine day did little to relieve the chill inside her. She was nervous as hell. Acott had already warned her that a lot depended on which trio of magistrates she came in front of that morning. In the best-case scenario she would get a one-year driving ban and a hefty fine. But the magistrates might decide that even if the police were not going to prosecute her for death by careless driving, they would throw the book at her. That could mean a three-year ban, and a fine running into thousands.

Fortunately, money had not been a problem for her so far, since Kes's death, but the following year Tyler would move on to his public school, where the fees would be treble what she was currently paying at St Christopher's. She was going to be stretched. So the prospect of a three-year driving ban and all the costs of taxis involved, and a huge fine as well, quite apart from the fact that her conviction was bound to be splashed over the local news, was not leaving her in the best frame of mind.

Her iPhone pinged with an incoming text. She checked the display. It was Ken Acott, saying he'd be there in two minutes.

Then she flicked across the phone's applications screen to Friend Mapper, to check that her friend Clair had safely delivered Tyler to school. His mood was still upsetting her. He'd put a wall round himself and was even resenting putting Friend Mapper on each day. For the past two years, they had used this GPS app daily. A small blue dot marked her precise position on a street map and a purple one marked his. Each time either of them logged on they could see where the other was. It was like a game to Tyler, and he'd always enjoyed following her, sending her the occasional text when she was away from the office, saying: I can c u.

To her relief the purple dot was where it should be, near the corner of New Church Road and Westbourne Gardens, where St Christopher's School was located. She put the phone back in her bag.

TOOTH WAS TIRED but he had to keep going, keep up the pace. Speed was vital. Cut the police some slack and they could catch up with you very fast. He needed to keep two jumps ahead of them. He was running on adrenalin and catnaps, the way he used to in the military, when he was behind enemy lines. Five minutes' shut-eye and he was good to go again. He could function for days like that.

He peered out at the neighbourhood as he drove. People had to be well off to live there. Detached houses, nice lawns, smart cars. And the houses had big gardens. Gardens were urban jungles. He was good at urban jungles.

There was a big park on his left as he drove round the wide road. Tennis courts. An enclosed playground with kids in it and their mothers watching. Tooth scowled. This was the kind of safe neighbourhood that five centuries of winning wars against invaders bought you. The comfort zone of civilisation. The comfort zone Carly Chase inhabited, or so she thought.

He turned into her street. Hove Park Avenue. He'd already paid a visit there earlier, on his way back from Springs Smoked Salmon. This was going to be easy. His client would like it, a lot. He was certain.

GRACE WAS STILL SEETHING at the thought of his conversation with Kevin Spinella as he entered Peter Rigg's office punctually at 3.30 p.m. The ACC, looking dapper in a chalk-striped blue suit and polka-dot tie, offered him tea as he sat down, which he accepted gratefully. He hoped some biscuits might come along with it, as he'd had no lunch.

'So, how are we doing, Roy?' Rigg asked.

Grace brought him up to speed on his team's current lines of enquiry. Then he handed him a copy of the latest exhibits list and ran through the key points of that with him.

'I don't like the camera, Roy,' the assisant chief constable said. 'It simply doesn't chime.'

'With what, sir?'

Rigg's assistant brought in a china cup and saucer on a tray, with a separate bowl of sugar and, to Grace's delight, a plate of assorted biscuits.

Rigg said, 'We've seen plenty of instances of low-life filming their violent acts on mobile phone cameras, happy slapping, all that. But this is too sophisticated. Why would someone go to that trouble and, more significantly, that expense?'

'Those are my thoughts too, sir.'

'So what are your conclusions?'

'I'm keeping an open mind. But I think it has to have been done by someone after that reward. Which brings me on to something I want to raise. We have a problem with the crime reporter from the *Argus*, Kevin Spinella.'

'Oh?'

'I had a call from him earlier. Despite all our efforts at keeping from the press that Ewan Preece's hands were glued to the steering wheel of the van, Spinella has found out.' Grace filled him in on the history of leaks to the reporter during the past year.

'Do you have any view on who the mole might be?'

'No, I don't at this stage.'

'So is the *Argus* going to print with the superglue story?'

'No. I've managed to persuade him to hold it.'

'Good man.'

Grace's phone rang. Apologising, he answered.

It was Tracy Stocker, the crime scene manager, and what she had to say was not good news. Grace asked her a few brief questions, then ended the call and looked back at his boss.

'I'm afraid we have another body, sir,' Grace said.

ONE OF THE many things Roy Grace loved about Brighton was the clear delineation to its north between the city limits and stunning open countryside. There was no urban sprawl, just a clean dividing line made by the sweep of the A27 dual carriageway between the city and the start of the South Downs.

The part of that countryside he was driving towards now, the Devil's Dyke, was an area that never ceased to awe him, no matter how often he went there. He drove as fast as he dared, along the high top road, on blue lights and wailing siren. Open land stretched away on both sides, shimmering beneath the almost cloudless afternoon sky.

Springs Smoked Salmon was a Sussex institution. He passed a cluster of farm buildings and dwellings, then slowed as he went down a sharp dip. Rounding the next bend he saw the flashing lights of a halted police car, while several more police vehicles were pulled tightly into the side of the road. He drew up behind the last car, switched off his engine and climbed out. As he shrugged himself into his paper oversuit, he could see a line of blue and white police tape across the entrance to the smokery. A young constable, whom he did not recognise, was acting as scene guard. Grace showed his ID.

'Good afternoon, sir,' the young officer said, a little nervously.

Grace nodded to him as he pulled on a pair of gloves and walked towards a cluster of similarly attired people. One of them was Tracy Stocker.

'We can't go on meeting like this, Roy!' she said chirpily.

He grinned. 'So, what do we have?'

'Not the prettiest picture I've ever seen.'

She turned and led the way. Grace nodded to a couple of detectives he knew. He followed Tracy across to the first of a row of grey, single-storey sheds. The door of the building was open.

Tracy stepped aside, gesturing with her arm for him to enter. He felt a blast of air on his face and became aware of a very strong, almost over-powering reek of smoked fish. Straight ahead he saw a solid wall of large, headless, dark pink fish, hanging in four straight rows, suspended by sturdy hooks to a ceiling rack.

Almost instantly his eyes were drawn to the front of the third row. He saw what at first looked like a huge, plump animal, its flesh all blackened, hanging among the fish. *A pig*, he thought, fleetingly. Then, as his brain began to make sense of the image, he realised what it actually was.

Over the years, Roy Grace had seen a lot of horrific sights. Mostly, as he had grown more experienced, he was able to leave them behind, but every now and then, like most police officers, he would come across something that he took home with him. When that happened he would lie in bed, unable to sleep, unpacking it over and over again in his mind.

He was going to take the one in front of him home, he knew. It was horrific, but he couldn't stop looking, couldn't stop thinking about the suffering during this man's last moments. He hoped they were quick, but he had a feeling they probably weren't.

The man was short and stocky, with a buzz cut and tattoos on the backs of his hands. He was naked, with his clothes neatly folded on the ground. He was hung from one of the heavy-duty hooks, the sharp point of which had been pushed up through the roof of his jaw and was protruding just below his left eye, like a foul-hooked fish. It was the expression of shock on the man's face, his bulging, terrified eyes, that was the worst thing of all.

'You're not going to like what I have to tell you, Roy,' Tracy Stocker said breezily, seemingly totally unaffected.

'I'm not actually liking what I'm looking at that much, either. Do we know who he is?'

'Yes, the boss here knows him. He's a lorry driver. Makes a regular weekly delivery here from Aberdeen. Has done for years. According to Mr Harris, the guv'nor here, this is the driver involved in our fatal in Portland Road. Stuart Ferguson.'

Grace looked at her. Before the ramifications of this had fully sunk in, the crime scene manager was speaking again.

'And you need to see this, Roy.'

She took a few steps forward and Grace followed. Then she turned and pointed to the interior wall, a foot above the top of the door.

'Does that look familiar?'

Grace stared at the cylindrical object with the glass lens. Now he knew for sure that his worst fears were confirmed. It was another camera.

8

In the taxi on the way home from work that afternoon, Carly sat immersed in her thoughts. Ken Acott had been right about the magistrate. She'd got a one-year ban and a £1,000 fine, which Ken Acott said afterwards was about as lenient as it could get. She'd also accepted the court's offer for her to go on a driver-education course, which would reduce her ban to nine months.

She looked out of the window. They were moving steadily in the heavy rush-hour traffic along the Old Shoreham Road. She texted Tyler to say she'd be home in ten minutes, and signed it with a smile and a row of kisses.

When they came to a halt, she paid the driver and told him to keep the change. As she climbed the steps to her front door, she did not look back.

On the other side of the road, Tooth, in his rented grey Toyota, made a note on his electronic pad: Boy 4.45 p.m. home. Mother 6 p.m. home.

Then he yawned. It had been a very long day. He started the car and pulled out into the street. As he drove off, he saw a police car heading down slowly, in the opposite direction. He tugged his baseball cap lower over his face as they crossed, then he watched in his rearview mirror. He saw its brake lights come on.

CARLY COULD HEAR the clatter of dishes in the kitchen, which sounded like her mother clearing up Tyler's supper. There was a smell of cooked food. Lasagne. Sunlight was streaking in through the window. *Summer's coming*, Carly thought, entering the house with a heavy heart.

The realisation was hitting her that everything was going to be a hassle this summer with no driving licence. *But sod it*, she thought. She was determined to think positively. She owed it to Tyler, and herself, not to let this get her down. After her father died, four years ago, her mother told her, in the usual philosophical way she had of coping with everything, that life was like a series of chapters in a book and now she was embarking on a new chapter in her life.

So that was what this was, she decided. The Carly Has No Licence chapter. She would just have to get to grips with bus and train timetables, like thousands of other people. She was going to use her holidays to give Tyler exactly the same kind of summer he always had. Days on the beach. Treat days to the museums in London, particularly the Natural History Museum. Maybe she'd get to like travelling that way so much she wouldn't bother with a car again.

Maybe the skies would be filled with flying pigs.

As she walked into the kitchen, her mother came and gave her a hug.

'You poor darling, what an ordeal.'

Her mother had been there for her throughout her life. In her early sixties, with short, auburn hair, she was a handsome, if slightly sad-looking woman. She had been a midwife, and these days kept herself busy with a number of charities, including working part-time at a hospice in Brighton.

'At least the worst part's over,' Carly replied. 'How's Tyler?'

'He's fine. Upstairs, playing with that lovely friend of his, Harrison.'

'I'll go and say hi. Do you need to get off?'

'I'll stay and make you some supper. What do you feel like? There is some lasagne and salad left.'

'I feel like a large glass of wine.'

'I'll join you.'

The doorbell rang. Carly glanced at her watch. It was 6.15 p.m. She opened the front door and saw a tall, bald, black man in his mid-thirties, dressed in a sharp suit and snazzy tie, accompanied by a staid-looking woman of a similar age. She had a tangle of hennaed hair and wore a grey trouser-suit over a blouse with the top button done up, giving her a slightly prim air.

The man held up a small black wallet with a document inside it bearing the Sussex Police coat of arms and his photograph.

'Mrs Carly Chase?'

'Yes,' she answered, hesitantly.

'Detective Sergeant Branson and this is Detective Sergeant Moy from Sussex CID. May we come in? We need to speak to you urgently.'

His manner was friendly but he seemed uneasy. He threw a wary glance over his shoulder. His colleague was looking up and down the street.

Carly ushered them in, unsettled by something she could not put a finger on. She saw her mother peering anxiously out of the kitchen door.

'We need to speak to you in private, please,' DS Branson said.

Carly led them into the living room, signalling to her mother that all was fine. She followed them in and pointed to one of the two sofas, then shut the door, before sitting down on the sofa opposite.

'How can I help you?' she asked.

'Mrs Chase, we have reason to believe your life may be in immediate danger,' Glenn Branson said.

Carly blinked hard. 'Pardon?'

Then she noticed for the first time that he had a large, brown envelope in his hand. He was holding it in a strangely delicate way for such a big man.

'It's concerning the road traffic collision two weeks ago today, which resulted in the death of a young student, Tony Revere,' he said.

'What do you mean exactly by immediate danger?'

'There were two other vehicles involved, Mrs Chase, a Ford Transit van and a Volvo refrigerated lorry.'

'They were the ones that actually struck the poor cyclist, yes.'

'Are you aware of who the cyclist was?' he asked.

'I've read the papers. Yes, I am. It's very distressing to have been involved.'

'You're aware that his mother is the daughter of a man purported to be the head of the New York Mafia?'

'I've read that. And the reward she offered. I didn't even know they existed any more. I thought that the Mafia was something from the past.'

The DS exchanged a glance with his colleague, who then spoke. 'Mrs Chase, I'm a family liaison officer and I'm here to help you through the next steps you choose. You know the van that was just mentioned?'

'The one that was right behind me?'

'Yes. You need to know that the driver of that van is dead. His body was found in it on Friday, in Shoreham Harbour.'

'I read in the *Argus* that a body had been found in a van in the harbour.'

'Yes,' Bella Moy said. 'What you won't have read is that he was the driver we believe was involved in the collision, or that he was murdered.'

Carly frowned. 'Murdered?'

'Yes. I can't give you details, but please trust us, he was. The reason we are here is that just a few hours ago, the driver of the Volvo lorry involved in the death of Tony Revere was also found murdered.'

Carly felt a cold ripple of fear. The room seemed to be swaying. She put her right hand on the arm of the sofa, to hold on.

'I—' she began. 'I . . . I . . . I thought the reward that . . . that the mother had put up . . . was for the identification of the van driver.'

'It was,' Bella Moy said.

'So why would they be murdered?' A vortex of fear swirled inside her.

'We don't know, Mrs Chase,' Glenn Branson replied. 'This could just be a coincidence. But the police have a duty of care. The inquiry team have made a threat assessment and we believe your life may be in danger.'

This can't be happening, Carly thought. There was some kind of subtle entrapment going on. Her lawyer's mind was kicking in. They'd come in order to scare her into some kind of confession about the accident.

Then Glenn Branson said, 'Mrs Chase, there is a range of things we can do to try to protect you. One of them would be to move you away from here to a safe place somewhere in the city. How would you feel about that?'

She stared at him, her fear deepening. 'What do you mean?'

Bella Moy said, 'It would be similar to a witness being taken into protective custody, Mrs Chase—can I call you Carly?'

Carly nodded bleakly, trying to absorb what she had just been told. 'Move me away?'

'Carly, we'd move you and your family under escort to another house, as a temporary measure. Then, if we feel the threat level is going to be ongoing, we could look at moving you to a different part of England; change your name and give you a completely new identity.'

Carly stared at them, bewildered. 'Change my name? A new identity? Move to somewhere else in Brighton? Right now?'

'Right now,' Glenn Branson said. 'We'll stay here with you while you pack, and then arrange a police escort.'

Carly raised her hands in the air. 'Wait a second. This is insane! My life is in this city! I have a son at school here. My mother lives here. I can't just up sticks and move to another house. No way. Certainly not tonight.' Her voice was trembling. 'Listen, I wasn't part of this accident. OK, I know, I've been convicted of driving over the limit, but I didn't hit the poor guy, for Christ's sake! I can't be blamed for his death, surely? The traffic police have already said so. It was said in court today, as well.'

'Carly,' Bella Moy said, 'we know that, and the dead boy's parents have been given all the information about the accident, too. But as my colleague has said, Sussex Police has a legal duty of care to you.'

Carly tried to think clearly. She couldn't. 'The driver behind me, in the white van, you say he is dead, that he's been murdered?'

Glenn Branson looked very solemn. 'Yes, he has been murdered, Carly. And the lorry driver, too. No question about it. We've carried out intelligence as best we can on the dead boy's family and, unfortunately, they are fully capable of revenge killings such as this. Dare I say it, these things are part of their culture. It's a different world they inhabit.'

Carly sat still for a moment, thinking hard. 'Are you saying there's a hit man, or whatever they're called, hired by this family?'

'It's a possibility, Carly,' Bella Moy said gently. 'One hundred thousand dollars is a lot of money. It is indicative of the parents' anger.'

'But this is my home. This is our life here. Our friends are here! You seriously want me to go into hiding, with my son, tonight? And what if we do move house? If these people are for real, don't you think they're going to be able to find us? I'm going to spend the rest of my life in fear of a knock on the door, or a creak in the house, or the crack of a twig in the garden!'

'We're not forcing you to move out, Carly,' Bella Moy said. 'We're just saying that would be the best option in our view.'

'If your decision is to stay we will give you protection,' Glenn Branson said. 'We'll provide CCTV and a Close Protection Unit, but it will be for a limited period of two weeks.'

'Two weeks?' Carly retorted. 'Why's that? Because of your budget?'

Branson raised his hands. 'These are really your best two options.' Then he picked up the envelope and removed a document and pen from it. 'I need you to read and sign this, please.'

Carly looked at the heading: OSMAN WARNING: NOTICE OF THREAT TO PERSONAL SAFETY. She read the document and looked up at the two officers.

'Let me understand something. Are you saying that if I don't agree to move, that's it, I'm on my own?'

Bella Moy shook her head. 'No, Carly. As DS Branson explained, we would provide you with a round-the-clock police guard for a period of time —two weeks. And we would put in CCTV surveillance for you. But we cannot guarantee your safety. We can just do our best.'

'This isn't for me, is it, this signature? It's to protect your backsides. If I get killed, you can show you did your best. Is that about the size of it?'

'Look,' Glenn Branson said. 'All of us at Sussex Police will do what we can to protect you. But if you don't want to move away, and I can understand that, then what we can do is limited. We'll have to try to work together.' He placed his card in front of Carly on the coffee table. 'Detective Sergeant Moy will be your immediate contact, but feel free to call me twenty-four-seven.'

Carly picked up the pen. 'Great,' she said, as she signed it, sick with fear, trying hard to think straight.

GRACE LAY IN BED beside Cleo, tossing and turning, wide awake, totally wired. He'd been at the mortuary until 2 a.m., when the post-mortem on the lorry driver was finally completed. At least he'd managed to persuade Cleo to go home early, so she'd left shortly before midnight. He lived in fear that Cleo would have another bleed at any moment. Potentially a life-threatening one, for herself and for their baby.

The bright blue dial on the clock radio, inches from Grace's eyes, flicked from 3.58 a.m. to 3.59 a.m. Shit.

He faced a long, hard day in front of him, during which he would need to be on peak form to manage his expanding inquiry team, to cope with the inevitable quizzing from Peter Rigg, and to make important decisions on a revised press strategy. But, most importantly of all, the absolute number-one priority: he had to safeguard a woman who could be in imminent, life-threatening danger.

'I WANT YOU ALL to know,' said Grace at the start of the 8.30 a.m. briefing in MIR-1, 'that I am not a happy bunny.' Taking a sip of his coffee and looking down at his notes, he went on, 'Item One on my agenda is the ongoing series of leaks coming from someone to our friend Kevin Spinella at the *Argus*. OK?'

He looked up at thirty-five solemn faces. Yesterday afternoon's horrific discovery had shaken even the most hardened of this bunch. 'I'm not accusing any of you, but someone has leaked to him about Preece's hands being superglued to the steering wheel of his van. It is either a member of this inquiry team, or the Specialist Search Unit, or an employee at Shoreham Harbour, or one of the mortuary team. At some point, I'm going to find that person and, when I do, I'm going to hang them out to dry on something even more painful than a meat hook. Do I make myself clear?'

Everyone nodded. All those who worked with Roy Grace knew him to be even-tempered and placid. It startled them to see him in a temper.

He took another sip of his coffee. 'Our media strategy could be vitally important. We believe a professional contract killer is here in Brighton, in all probability hired by the Revere family in New York to avenge their son's death. We need to manage the media extremely carefully, both to try to get assistance from the public in finding this killer before he strikes again, and to avoid any possible impact on the community.'

'Was the Osman served on Mrs Chase, chief?' asked Duncan Crocker.

'Yes,' Glenn Branson replied on Grace's behalf. 'Bella and I served it yesterday evening just after 6 p.m. Mrs Chase was offered the opportunity to be moved out of the area, but she refused. Frankly, I think she's unwise. DS Moy spent the night in her house, pending the installation of CCTV equipment this morning, and a Close Protection Team unit have been in place outside her residence since 9 p.m. last night. So far without incident.'

'Is there any protection on her commute to work?' asked Norman Potting. 'And while she's in her workplace?'

'Today and tomorrow, and for the first part of next week, she will be driven to and from work in a marked police car. And I'm putting a PCSO in reception at her office. I want to send a clear signal to this killer, if he's out there and targeting this woman, that we are on to him.'

'What about Revere's family in New York?' said Nick Nicholl. 'Is anyone speaking to them?'

'I updated our NYPD contact, DI Lanigan, on the situation and they're on the case. He was going to go and see Mr and Mrs Revere last night and report back to me. But, frankly, I'm not expecting anything from them. And one thing Lanigan told me, which is not good news for us, is that intelligence on contract killers is very limited.'

'Boss, what information are you releasing to the press about the death of the lorry driver?' DC Emma-Jane Boutwood asked.

'For now, no more than that a man was found dead at Springs Smoked Salmon,' Grace said. 'Let people think that it was an industrial accident. I haven't yet decided what we should release beyond that. But I've no doubt someone will make that decision for me.'

He gave a challenging stare to his team, without looking at any specific individual. Then he glanced down at his notes again. 'According to his employers, Stuart Ferguson left the depot shortly after 2 p.m. on Tuesday. We need to find his lorry. We should be able to plot much of its journey fairly easily from an ANPR search.'

Automatic number-plate recognition cameras were positioned along many of the UK's motorways and key arterial roads. They filmed the registration plates of all passing vehicles and fed them into a database.

Grace then read out a summary of the post-mortem findings. After dealing with questions on that, he moved on to the next item on his list.

'OK, an update on lines of enquiry. The matter of the murder of Preece's friend Warren Tulley at Ford Prison is still ongoing.' He looked at DS Crocker. 'Duncan, do you have anything there for us?'

'Nothing new. A wall of silence from the other inmates.'

Grace thanked him, then turned to DC Nick Nicholl. 'The superglue on Ewan Preece's hands. Nick, anything to report?'

'The Outside Inquiry Team are continuing to visit every retail outlet in the Brighton and Hove area that sells superglue. It's a massive task, chief.'

'Keep them on it,' Grace said. Then he turned to Norman Potting. 'Anything to report with the camera?'

'We've covered every retailer that sells this equipment, chief. One of them checked the serial number on the one in the van. He reckons it's not a model sold in the UK. It can only be bought in the USA. I haven't had a chance to check the one found at Springs yet, but it looks identical.'

As the meeting ended, Glenn Branson received a call on his radio. When he had finished the conversation, he turned to Roy Grace.

'Mrs Chase is downstairs. Says she needs to see me urgently.'

TOOTH SAT in his room at the Premier Inn, with his laptop open on the desk in front of him. A Lucky Strike dangled between his lips as he stared at the screen, clicking through the images of Hove Park Avenue, where Carly Chase lived. Photographs of the front, back and sides of her house.

Early in the morning, after he had finished at Springs smokery, he had driven down this street, memorising the cars. A dog had started barking inside the house and an upstairs interior light came on as he was leaving. Last night he'd taken another drive down there and had spotted a parked dark-coloured Audi, with a shadowy figure behind the wheel. The Audi had not been there previously.

The police weren't stupid. He had little doubt there were others out there that he hadn't spotted. Some on foot, probably in the back garden or down the sides of the house.

He had already listened to the conversation inside the house that the minute directional microphones he had concealed in her garden, pointed at her windows, had picked up when the police had visited her yesterday evening. When she had told them she did not want to leave.

He looked down at his notes. The kid had been picked up in his school uniform at 8.25 a.m. by a woman in a black Range Rover, with two other kids in it. At 8.35 a.m., Carly Chase had left home in the back of a marked police car. At 9.05 a.m. he made a phone call to her office, masquerading as a client, saying he needed to speak to her urgently. He was told she had not yet arrived. A second phone call told him she had still not arrived at 9.30. Where was she?

CARLY CHASE sat down beside Glenn Branson at the small, round conference table in Roy Grace's office. Grace joined them.

'Nice to meet you, Mrs Chase,' he said, sitting down. 'I'm sorry it's not under better circumstances. Would you like something to drink?'

She felt too sick with fear to swallow anything. 'I'm OK, thank you. I wanted to talk to you,' she stammered nervously, looking at Grace. 'Detective Sergeant Branson and his colleague explained the situation to me yesterday evening. I've been thinking about it overnight. I'm not sure if you know, but I'm a solicitor specialising in divorce.'

Grace nodded. 'I know a fair bit about you.'

'I'm a great believer in compromise rather than confrontation. In my experience, dialogue is so often missing,' she said.

Grace stared at her. He had no idea what point she was leading up to.

'I lost my husband five years ago in a skiing accident. He was buried in an avalanche in Canada. My first reaction was that I wanted to get on a plane to Canada, find the guide who had taken him on that mountain, and who survived, and kill him with my bare hands. OK?'

Grace glanced at Branson, who gave him a helpless shrug back. 'Everyone has to deal with grief in their own way,' he replied.

'Exactly,' Carly replied. 'That's why I'm here.' She turned to Glenn Branson. 'You told me last night that my life is in danger from a revenge killing arranged by the parents of the poor boy who died on his bike. But I wasn't a guilty part of that. OK, I know I've been prosecuted for drink driving, but your traffic police confirmed in court that it wouldn't have made a damned bit of difference if I'd been stone-cold sober. It wasn't the van driver's fault either, even if he did do a hit and run, and it sure as hell wasn't the lorry driver's fault. The whole thing was caused by the poor kid himself, cycling on the wrong side of the road!'

Branson was about to reply, but Grace cut in on him. 'Mrs Chase, we're aware of that. But, as my colleague has explained, the Reveres come from a culture where differences are settled not in court, but by brutality. They have been informed that you did not collide with their son, and it may be that they've now finished with their terrible revenge, if that's what these two killings are about. But I have a duty of care to you.'

'But I can't live my life in fear! There's always a way through a problem and I think I have found a way through this one. I've decided I'm going to go to New York to talk to Mrs Revere. She's lost her son. I lost my husband. Both of us would like to try to blame other people to try to find some sense in our losses. But vengeance won't bring my husband Kes back or ease the pain of my loss. I have to find ways to move forward in life. She and her husband are going to have to do the same.'

'From what I know about this family,' Grace said, 'I don't think going to see them is a good idea, and it's certainly not something we could sanction.'

'Why not?' She glared at Grace with a sudden ferocity that startled him.

'Because we're responsible for your safety. I can protect you here in Brighton, but I couldn't look after you in New York.'

She turned to Glenn Branson. 'You told me last night that you could only guard me for a fortnight. I can't spend the next fifty years looking over my shoulder. I have to deal with this now.' She was silent for a moment, then she spoke again. 'Are you saying you'd stop me from going?'

Grace shook his head. 'I have no powers to stop you. But I cannot guarantee your safety if you go. I could send an officer with you, but frankly he wouldn't be able to do a lot out of his jurisdiction—'

'I'm going alone,' she said determinedly. 'I can look after myself. I can deal with it. I deal with difficult people all the time.'

'Mrs Chase, you don't know who you are dealing with here.'

'I've been Googling them,' she said. 'There's a lot of stuff about Sal Giordino, of course, but I've not found anything about his daughter.' She paused, then continued, 'But going on what you've told me about their world, isn't that all the more reason for me to go there and try to reason with them?' she said.

'These people don't reason,' Grace said. 'What about emailing or phoning Mrs Revere first, to see what reaction you get?'

'No, it's got to be face to face, mother to mother,' Carly replied.

The two detectives looked at each other.

'I can find the address out for you on one condition,' Roy Grace said.

'Which is?'

'You allow us to arrange an escort for you in New York.'

At 10.17 a.m., an alert pinged on Tooth's laptop. A voice file was recording. Which meant someone was speaking inside Carly Chase's house.

He clicked and listened in. She was on the phone to a woman, asking about flights to New York that day. It sounded like the woman was a travel agent. After some moments of checking availability, she booked Carly Chase on a 14.55 British Airways flight from London to Kennedy Airport, New York. Then they discussed hotels. The travel agent made a reservation at the Sheraton at Kennedy Airport.

Tooth glanced at his watch, double-checking the time and smiling. She was making this very easy for him. She had no idea.

Next, he heard Carly Chase speak to someone who identified herself as Sarah Ellis when she picked up. The woman sounded like a friend. Carly Chase explained to her that Tyler had a dental appointment at 11.30 the following morning. Ordinarily, his gran could have taken him, but she had a hospital appointment. She explained she had been planning to take Tyler herself, but something urgent had come up—would it be possible for Sarah to take him?

Sarah said that Justin, who was presumably Sarah's husband, had taken the week off to do some work on their new house and he could pick Tyler up. Carly Chase thanked her and gave her the dentist's address.

Tooth stared down at his notepad, on which he had written Carly Chase's flight details. She'd only booked one way, on an open ticket. He speculated about where she was going, and had a good idea. He wondered what she was like at ten-pin bowling.

Except he did not think she would get as far as the Reveres' bowling alley. He just hoped they wouldn't kill her. That would spoil all his plans.

9

Carly stood in a long, snaking queue in the crowded Immigration Hall at Kennedy airport. It was 5.30 p.m., which meant it was 10.30 p.m. in England. But it seemed like the middle of the night. She had a blinding headache and was feeling decidedly spaced out.

Finally, she reached a yellow line and was next. The immigration officer, a cheery-looking, plump black woman, summoned Carly forward. She handed over her passport. She was asked to look into a camera lens. Then she was told to press her fingers on an electronic pad.

Carly pressed hard and the red lights changed to green.

Frowning, the woman suddenly said, 'OK, I need you to come with me.'

Bewildered, Carly followed her through a door at the far end of the room. She saw several armed immigration officers standing chatting and some weary-looking people seated round the room.

'Mrs Carly Chase from the United Kingdom,' the woman announced loudly, seemingly to no one in particular.

A tall man in a checked sports jacket ambled over to her.

'Mrs Chase?' he said, in a Brooklyn accent.

'Yes.'

'I'm Detective Investigator Lanigan from the Brooklyn District Attorney's Office. I'm taking care of you while you're over here.'

She stared at him. In his fifties, she guessed, with a powerful physique, and a pockmarked face wearing a concerned but friendly expression.

'I understand you have the home address of Mr and Mrs Revere for me?' she said.

'Yes. I'm going to take you there.'

She shook her head. 'I have a car booked. I need to go alone.'

'I can't allow you to do that, Mrs Chase. That's not going to happen.'

Carly thought for a moment. 'Look, OK, follow me to their place, but at least let me go in alone. I can handle myself. Can I please do that?'

He stared at her for some moments.

'OK, we'll go in convoy. I'll wait outside, but here's what we're going to do. You're going to text me every fifteen minutes so I know you're OK. If I don't get a text, I'm coming in. Understand what I'm saying?'

'Do I have any option?'

'Sure, you do. I can have Immigration put you on the first available flight back to London.'

'Thanks,' she said.

'You're welcome, lady.'

IN THE BACK of the limousine it was dark and silent. Carly sat immersed in her thoughts. She'd phoned home again as soon as she'd got into the car, and her mother told her all was fine.

Her thoughts turned back to what she was going to say when she arrived at the Revere family's front door. If they even let her in.

Carly looked at her watch. It was 7.30 p.m. Her headache was worsening by the minute. As were her doubts. All the confidence she'd had earlier that day was deserting her, and she felt a growing slick of fear inside her. She tried desperately in her mind to reverse the roles. How would she feel in this woman's situation?

She simply did not know. She felt tempted, suddenly, to ask the driver to turn round and go to the hotel and forget all about this. But what then? Maybe nothing. Maybe those two killings had been coincidental? Maybe they'd been all the revenge the family wanted? But then, thinking more lucidly, she wondered how she would ever know that. How would she stop living in fear? And she knew that she could not, ever, without resolving this. Her determination became even stronger.

Suddenly—it seemed only minutes later—they were arriving in a town.

'East Hampton,' the driver informed her.

Carly's stomach tightened. Her nerves were in tatters now.

Her fear deepened as the car made a right turn and headed down a tree-lined lane. She took a few deep breaths to calm down. The car slowed, then halted. Directly in front of them were tall gates, painted grey, with spikes along the top. She noticed a speaker panel and a warning sign beside it.

Carly turned and peered through the rear window and saw that the detective was getting out of his car. She climbed out, too.

'Good luck, lady,' Lanigan said. 'Let's see if they let you in. If they do, I'll be waiting here.' He entered his number on Carly's phone and tapped in 'OK'. 'That's what you're gonna text me, every fifteen minutes. You don't forget that, right?'

She tried to reply, but nothing came out. Every shred of her confidence seemed to have deserted her. She nodded.

She pressed the square metal button. Instantly a light shone in her face. Above it, she could see a CCTV camera pointing down at her.

A voice speaking in broken English crackled. 'Yes, who is this?'

Carly stared straight back at the camera and forced a smile. 'I've come from England to see Mr and Mrs Revere. My name is Carly Chase.'

'They expect you?'

'No. I think they know who I am. I was in the accident involving their son, Tony.'

'You wait, please.'

The light went off. Carly waited, clutching her iPhone, her finger on the Send button. She turned and saw Detective Investigator Lanigan leaning against his car, smoking a cigar. He gave her a good-luck shrug.

A minute later, the gates began to swing open with a faint electric whirr. Sick with fear, she climbed back into the car.

CARLY STEPPED OUT into the silence of the night. Above her loomed the façade of a huge modern mansion. It looked dark and unwelcoming. Her nerves shorting out, she swallowed, then stared at the front door, which was set beneath an imposing portico. *Am I up to this?* she thought.

Before she had a chance to change her mind, the front door opened and a woman emerged, slightly unsteadily, dressed in a turquoise tracksuit and sparkly trainers. She held a Martini glass tilted at an angle. Her whole demeanour was hostile.

Carly took a few, faltering steps towards her. 'Mrs Revere?' She tried to put on the smile she had been practising, but it didn't feel like it was working.

The woman stared at her with eyes as cold and hard as ice. Carly felt as if she was staring right through her soul.

'You got balls coming here.' The words were slightly slurred and bitter. 'You're not welcome in my home. Get back in your car.'

The woman scared her, but Carly stood her ground. She had been preparing herself for a whole range of responses and this was one of them, although she had not factored in that Mrs Revere might be smashed.

'I've flown from England to talk to you,' she said. 'I just want a few minutes of your time. I'm not going to begin to pretend I understand what you must be going through—but you and I have something in common.'

'We do? We're alive, that's about all I can see we have in common. I don't believe we have much else.'

'May I come in? I'll leave the moment you want me to. But, please, let's talk for a few minutes.'

Fernanda Revere snorted contemptuously. Then, with her drink slopping over the rim of her glass, she gestured for Carly to enter.

Carly hesitated. This woman looked dangerously unpredictable. Glad now that DI Lanigan was sitting outside the gates in his car, she glanced at her watch. Thirteen minutes left before her first text.

She entered a grand hallway with a flagstone floor and a circular staircase, and followed the woman along a corridor furnished with antiques. They entered a palatial drawing room, with oak beams and tapestries hanging from the walls, alongside fine-looking oil paintings. Almost all of the furniture was antique, except for one item.

Seated in an incongruously modern leather recliner armchair was a man in his fifties with slicked-back grey hair, watching a ball game on television. He held a can of beer in one hand and a large cigar in the other.

The woman walked towards him, picked up the TV remote from the table beside him, and muted the sound.

'Hey, what the—' the man protested.

'We have a visitor, Lou.' Fernanda pointed at Carly. 'She's come all the way from England. How nice is that?' she said icily.

Lou Revere gave Carly a weak smile. Then, keeping his eyes on the silent players on the screen, he turned to his wife.

'This is kind of an important moment in the game.'

'Yeah, right,' Fernanda said. 'Well, this is kind of an important moment, too. Know who this bitch is? This is the bitch who killed our son.'

Carly watched him, her eyes swinging between them. She was trying to keep calm, but her nerves were in meltdown.

'What do you mean, hon?' the man said, his whole demeanour changing.

'This is the bitch who was arrested at the scene for drunk driving. She killed our son, and now she's standing here in front of us.'

There was now a sudden menace in Lou Revere's voice as he spoke. 'Just what the hell do you think you're doing? Turning up like this? Not satisfied you've caused us enough pain, is that it?'

'It's not that at all, Mr Revere,' Carly replied, her voice quavering. 'I'd just appreciate the opportunity to explain what happened.'

'We know what happened,' he said.

'You were drunk and our son died,' his wife added, bitterly.

Carly drew on all her reserves. 'I'm desperately sorry for your loss. But there are things about this accident that you need to know, that I would want to know if it was my child. Could we please sit down, the three of us, and talk this through? Please let me tell you how it actually happened.'

'We know how it happened,' Fernanda Revere said. Then she turned to her husband. 'Get rid of this bitch. She's polluting our home.'

'Hon, let's just hear her out,' he said, without taking his glare off Carly.

'If you don't tell her to go, I'm leaving,' she shouted. 'I'm not staying in this building with her. So tell her!'

'Hon, let's talk to her.'

'GET HER OUT OF HERE!'

With that Fernanda stormed out of the room and, some moments later, a door slammed.

Carly found herself facing Lou Revere, feeling awkward. 'Mr Revere, maybe I should go . . . I can come back in the morning if that's—'

He jabbed a finger at her. 'You came to talk, so talk.'

Carly stared at him, trying to think of the best way to calm him down.

'Mr Revere, I have a young son,' she began.

'Have?' he replied. 'Well, you're a lucky lady, then, aren't you? My wife and I had a young son, too, before a drunk driver killed him.'

'It didn't happen like that.'

Outside, through the window, Carly heard a car engine fire up.

'Oh, it didn't happen like that?' Lou Revere looked, at that moment, as if he was about to strangle her with his bare hands.

And Carly suddenly realised what it was that the two detectives in

Brighton had meant when they'd tried to explain the nature of these people to her. That they were different. That their whole culture was different. She had to stand her ground. Had to find a way through to this man. He was, she realised, her only chance.

FERNANDA REVERE accelerated past a car parked outside the gates, sped recklessly towards the T-junction by the gas station, and braked. She pulled a cigarette pack out of her purse, shook out a Marlboro Light and jammed it between her lips. Then she stabbed the cigarette lighter, made a left and accelerated down the highway.

Everything was a blur in her drunken fury. She overtook a slow-moving cab, her speed increasing steadily: 70 . . . 80 . . . 90mph. She flashed past a whole line of taillights, lit her cigarette and tried to replace the lighter, but it fell into the footwell.

She was shaking with rage. The road snaked away into the distance. Steering with one hand, she rummaged in her purse and pulled out her phone, then squinted at the display. It was a blur. She brought it closer to her face, scrolled to her brother's number and hit the dial button.

She had to get away. Just had to get away from the bitch polluting her home. After six rings, it went to voicemail.

'Where are you, Ricky?' she shouted. 'What's going on? The English bitch came to the house. She's there now. Do you hear me? The bitch who killed Tony is in my house. Why isn't she dead? What's going on here? You gotta deal with this, Ricky. Call me. Goddamn call me!'

She ended the call and tossed the phone down beside her on the passenger seat. She did not know where she was heading. Just away from the house and into the rushing darkness. She overtook another car. The night was hurtling past. Oncoming lights were a brief, blurred flash, then gone.

Tony was gone. Dead. Three scumbags had taken his life away. Some asshole in a van. Some asshole in a truck. And this goddamn bitch who had the nerve to come to their home.

The speedometer needle was hovering on 110mph. Or maybe it was 120: she could barely see it. A light began flashing on the passenger seat. Her phone was ringing, she realised. She grabbed it and held it up in front of her. The name was blurry but she could just about read it. Her brother.

She answered it, hurtling past another car, still steering with one hand towards a tight left curve. Tears were streaming from her eyes.

'Ricky, I thought you were dealing with this?' she said. 'How do you let this stupid bitch come to the house? How?'

'Listen, it's all cool!'

'Cool? She came to my house—that's cool? You wanna tell me what's cool about that?'

'We have a plan!'

She steered the car through the curve, then there was another curve to the right, even sharper. She was going into it too fast, she realised. She stamped on the brake pedal and suddenly the car began snaking left, then right, then even more violently left again.

'Shit.'

She dropped the phone. There were bright lights coming in the opposite direction, getting brighter and more dazzling by the second. She heard the blare of a horn. She jerked the wheel and suddenly it turned with such force it tore free of her hands, spinning like it had taken on a mind of its own.

The lights got brighter. The horn was blaring, deafening. She was spinning too now, like the wheel. Then a jarring impact and a clanging metallic boom like two giant oil drums swinging into each other.

In the silence that followed, Ricky's voice came through her phone. 'Hey, babe? Sis? Listen, we're cool. Listen, babe!'

But she could no longer hear him.

'YOU'VE REALLY UPSET my wife,' Lou Revere said. 'I don't know what you thought you'd achieve by coming, but we don't want you here. You're not welcome.' He stabbed his cigar at her. 'I'm gonna show you out.'

'Please just give me a chance,' Carly said, on the verge of tears.

'You had your chance, lady, when you were deciding whether to get into your automobile drunk or not. That's more chance than my son had.'

'It wasn't like that, Mr Revere. Please believe me. It wasn't like that.'

'Sure it wasn't like that, lady. We've had the toxicology report on our son. He had nothing in him. Not one drop of alcohol, not one trace of any drug.' He lowered his head like a bull about to charge. 'How was your toxicology report? Huh? Tell me. I'm listening.'

They faced each other in silence. Carly was trying desperately to find a way through to him. But he scared her. Outwardly, he might be playing the role of a grieving father, but there was something truly chilling about him. She had met difficult people in her time, but never anyone like Lou Revere.

It felt as if she was in the presence of total, inhuman evil.

'Maybe I should come back tomorrow,' she replied. 'Can I do that?'

He took another step towards her, quivering. 'You dare come within one hundred miles of my home, I'll tear you apart with these.' He held up his trembling hands. 'You understand?'

Carly nodded, her mouth dry.

He pointed. 'That's the way out.'

It seemed only moments after he had fallen asleep that Roy Grace was woken by the sound of his phone ringing and vibrating.

He rolled over, reaching towards the flashing display in the darkness. The clock beside it said 1.37 a.m.

'It's OK. I'm awake,' said Cleo, grumpily. He knew her pregnancy was getting to her. It was getting to both of them. Most of the time it was a shared joy, or a shared anxiety, but just occasionally it seemed like a growing wedge between them. She had been in a really grumpy mood last night.

He switched on his bedside light and grabbed the phone. 'Yurrr?'

It was Duncan Crocker. 'You awake, boss?'

A stupid question, Grace thought. 'What's up?'

'You asked me to let you know as soon as we found the lorry, boss.'

'You've found it? You're still at work?'

'Yes. I just had a call from Thames Valley Road Policing Unit. They found it in a parking area at Newport Pagnell Services on the M1. The last time it was logged by an automatic number-plate recognition camera was as it entered Bucks on the M1 on Tuesday night, so we asked the local police to check likely pull-ins.'

'Good stuff! Get them to check the CCTV cameras to see if Ferguson went into the service station. How long are you planning on staying up?'

'As long as you need me.'

'Ask them for copies of the videos from the time the ANPR clocked him to now, and get them down to us as quickly as possible.'

'Will do.'

'And make sure Ferguson's lorry is protected as a crime scene. If the driver was attacked, it's likely to have happened close to the vehicle. We need a search team on to it at first light. And we need the indexes of the vehicles either side of Ferguson's lorry on the motorway immediately before Newport Pagnell Services,' he said. 'Get everything up to five vehicles in front and twenty back. I want to know every one of the vehicles that went into the services at the same time as him, and where they went when they left afterwards. It's likely that Ferguson was in one of those. Willingly or otherwise. I think it is probably going to be a rental car, so look for late-model, small to medium saloons.'

'I'll get what I can, but it may take me a while to check out every vehicle. Is the morning briefing meeting soon enough?'

No, it isn't soon enough, Grace thought. But he needed to be realistic and Crocker sounded exhausted.

'Yes, that's fine. Do what you can, then get some sleep.'

CARLY SAT in the back of the limousine as they drove through the gates of the Revere home. A few yards on she could see Detective Investigator Lanigan standing by his car and told her driver to stop.

'So?' he asked, with an inquisitive but sympathetic stare.

'You were right,' she said, and gave a helpless shrug. She was still in shock from the way Lou Revere had spoken to her.

'It didn't go like you planned it?'

'No.'

'What's with Mrs Revere driving off like that? She was pissed at you?'

'She was drunk. She wasn't in a rational state of mind. I have to try again,' she said. 'Maybe tomorrow morning, when she's sobered up.'

'Lady, you've got guts, I'll give you that.' He smiled. 'You look like you could use a drink.'

Carly nodded.

'Let's get you to your hotel. We'll have a drink and you can talk me through what happened in there. Does your driver know where to go?'

'The Sheraton JFK Airport Hotel.'

'I'll follow you. I'll be right behind.'

She got back into the limousine and, as they drove away, she closed her eyes and prayed. She asked the God she had not spoken to in years to give her strength and a clear mind. Then she rummaged in her bag for her handkerchief and dabbed away the tears that were streaming down her cheeks.

Darkness slid by on either side of the car. They made a left turn and headed away from town. For several minutes it did not occur to her that it was strange that no headlights were coming in the opposite direction. But ahead she suddenly saw flashing lights and the taillights of traffic braking. The limousine slowed and they came to a halt behind a line of stationary vehicles.

The driver turned towards her. 'Looks like an accident up ahead.'

She nodded silently. Then she heard a rap on her window and saw DI Lanigan standing there. She pressed the button and lowered the window. He held a police radio in his hand.

'You want to come with me? Sounds like Mrs Revere's involved in a wreck up ahead. They've closed the road.'

'An accident? Fernanda Revere?'

The words flooded her with dread. She climbed out of the car and followed the detective past a line of cars towards a stationary police car that was angled across the road, its roof spinners hurling shards of red light in every direction. A row of traffic cones was spread across the road behind it.

An accident. The woman would be blaming her. Everyone would be blaming her.

A cacophony of sirens was closing in on them. Just beyond the patrol car now, she could see the mangled wreckage of a car partially embedded in the front of a white truck. Carly stopped. This wasn't just a minor bump, this was major. Massive. Horrific. She turned towards Lanigan.

'Is she OK?' Carly asked. 'Have you heard if she's OK? Is she injured?'

He strode on, through the cones, saying nothing. A cop was standing there, a young plump man wearing glasses and a cap that was too big for him. He looked about eighteen years old and waiting to grow into his uniform.

Lanigan held up his police shield and had a few quiet words with him. When he turned round again, his face was grim.

He walked back to Carly. 'She's dead,' he said.

She turned away, quaking in horror and shock. She staggered a few yards, then fell to her knees and threw up, her eyes blinded by tears.

A LARGE WHISKY at the hotel bar, followed by two glasses of Pinot Noir, helped calm Carly down a little, but she was still in shock.

Whatever her background had been, Fernanda Revere was still a human being. A mother capable of intense love for her son. No one deserved to end up the way she had. And Carly had caused it.

The detective investigator told her she should not think that way: Fernanda Revere had no business getting into a vehicle in the state she was in. She didn't have to drive away: that was her choice. She could, and should, have simply told Carly to leave. Driving away, and doing so drunk, was not a rational act. But Carly still blamed herself. She could not help thinking, over and over, that she had caused the accident. That if she had not gone to the house, Fernanda Revere would still be alive.

She felt utterly bewildered. How was Fernanda Revere's husband going to react? The other members of the woman's family?

'I think now, Carly, you're going to have to think pretty seriously and quickly about entering a witness protection scheme,' Pat Lanigan said. 'I'm going to see that you have someone guarding you all the time you're here, but people like the Reveres have long memories and a long reach.'

'Do you think I'd ever be truly safe in a witness protection scheme?'

'You can never say one hundred per cent, but it would give you your best possible chance.'

'You know what it means?' Carly stared at him. 'To move to another part of the country, just you and your child, and never see any of your family or friends again, ever. How would you like to do that?'

He shrugged. 'I wouldn't like it too much. But if I figured I didn't have any option, then I guess it would be better than the alternative.'

'What—what alternative?'

He gave Carly a hard stare. 'Exactly.'

The air-conditioning was too cold and too loud, but nothing Carly did to the controls in her hotel bedroom seemed to make any difference. She couldn't find any extra bedding either, so she ended up almost fully clothed, under the sheets, tossing and turning, a tsunami of dark thoughts crashing through her mind.

Shortly after 6 a.m. and wide awake, she slipped out of bed, walked across to the window and opened the blinds. Light flooded in from a cloudless dark blue sky. Her head was pounding again. She felt queasy and very afraid. The idea of walking away from her life and going into hiding, for ever . . . it wasn't going to happen. There had to be a better solution.

Suddenly her mobile phone rang. She hurried across and picked it off her bedside table, staring at the display. It simply said, INTERNATIONAL.

'Hello?' she answered.

'Hi, Carly?' It was Justin Ellis. His voice was sounding strange.

'Yes. You all right?' Carly replied, conscious her voice was strained.

'Well, not really,' he replied. 'I think there's been a mix-up over Tyler.'

'How do you mean? His dentist appointment? Have I screwed up?' She looked at the clock radio, doing a mental calculation. She always got the time differences wrong. England was five hours ahead. Coming up to 11.15 a.m. there. Tyler's appointment was for 11.30 a.m., wasn't it?

'What's the problem, Justin?'

'Well, you asked me to take him to the dentist. I'm at the school now to collect him, but they're telling me you arranged a taxi to take him there.'

Carly sat down on the side of the bed. 'A taxi? I didn't arrange any—'

A terrible, dark dread began to seep through her.

'A taxi collected him half an hour ago,' Justin said, sounding a little pissed off. 'Did you forget?'

'Oh God,' Carly said. 'Oh, my God. Tell me it's not true!'

'What do you mean?'

'This can't have happened! They must have made a mistake! Tyler has to be in the school somewhere. Have they checked?' Her voice was trembling with rising panic. 'Please get them to check. Tell them they have to check.'

'Carly, what's the matter? What is it?'

'Please let him be there. Please, Justin, you have to find him. Please go in there and find him. Please! Oh, my God, please.' She was sobbing and shouting in her desperation.

There was a brief moment of silence, then Justin said, 'What's the matter, Carly? Calm down! Tell me—what's the matter?'

'Justin, call the police! I didn't order a taxi!'

THE TRAFFIC JAM along the seafront was irritating Tooth. The noise behind him was irritating him too, but it was keeping the kid distracted while he drove, so that was a good thing. He watched him in the mirror. The boy, in his red school blazer and wire-framed glasses, was concentrating hard on some noisy electronic game.

Suddenly the kid looked up. 'Where are we going? I thought we were going to the dentist. This isn't the right way.'

Tooth spoke in his English accent. 'I had a message that the address got changed. Your dentist is working at his other clinic today in a different part of the city, over in Regency Square.'

'OK.'

They were getting closer. In a few moments he would make a left turn.

'What game are you playing?' Tooth asked, wanting the kid to feel OK, relaxed, normal, at least for the next couple of minutes.

'It's called Angry Birds. It's ace. Have you played it?'

Concentrating now, Tooth did not reply. The Skoda taxi made a sharp left turn off the seafront into Regency Square, driving past a terrace of Regency houses and into the entrance to the underground car park. Partway down the ramp he had a fit of sneezing. He halted the car, sneezing again and pulling a handkerchief out of his pocket. He sneezed once more into it.

'Bless you,' Tyler said.

The driver turned. Tyler thought the man was going to thank him, but instead he saw something black in the man's hand that looked like the trigger of a gun, but without the rest of the weapon. Then he felt a hard jet of air on his face and suddenly he found it hard to breathe. He took a deep gulp, while the air still jetted at him from the capsule.

Tooth watched the boy's eyes closing, then turned and continued down the ramp, lowering his window, then removing the handkerchief from his face. He carried on down to the car park's lowest level, which was deserted apart from one vehicle: his rental Toyota, with new licence plates.

He reversed into the bay alongside it.

10

At 11.25 a.m., Roy Grace was seated at his desk, making some adjustments to his statement, which he was due to read out at the midday press conference.

His phone rang: Tracy Stocker, calling from Newport Pagnell Services.

'Roy, we've found one item of possible interest so far. The stub of a Lucky Strike cigarette. I can't tell you if it is significant, but it's a relatively unusual brand for the UK.'

Grace knew Lucky Strikes were American. If, as he surmised, the killings of Preece and Ferguson were the work of a professional, it was a distinct possibility that a hit man, trusted by the Reveres, had been employed. He could be an American, sent over here.

'Did you manage to get a print from it, Tracy?' he asked.

'No. We can send it for chemical analysis, but we may have more luck with DNA. Do you want me to fast-track it?'

'Yes, fast-track definitely,' he said. 'Good work, Tracy. Well done.'

He asked her to keep him updated. Then, as he hung up, his phone rang again. It was Duncan Crocker.

'Boss, we've had two possible hits on cars at Newport Pagnell that arrived at the same time as Ferguson. One is a Vauxhall Astra and the other is a Toyota Yaris—both of them common rental vehicles,' the detective sergeant said. 'We've eliminated the Astra, which was being driven by a sales rep for a printing company. But the Yaris is more interesting.'

'Yes?'

'You were right, sir. It's a rental car—from Avis at Gatwick Airport. I put a marker on it and it pinged an ANPR camera on the M11 near Brentwood at 8 a.m. this morning. A local traffic unit stopped it. It was a young female driver who lives in Brentwood, on her way to work.'

Grace frowned. Was Crocker being dim?

'It doesn't sound like you got either of the right vehicles, Duncan.'

'I think it may do when you hear this, sir. When the young lady got out of the car, she realised they weren't her licence plates on the car. Someone had taken hers and replaced them with these.'

'While she was in the Newport Pagnell Services?'

'She can't swear that, sir—she can't remember the last time she noticed her number plates. To be honest, a lot of us probably don't.'

As Grace took down the licence plate details from Crocker, he thought for a moment. 'So it may be that our suspect has switched plates with hers. Have you put a marker out on her plates?'

'I have, sir, yes. So far nothing.'

'Good work. Let me know the instant anyone sees that car.'

'Of course, sir.'

'Have you sent someone down to Avis at Gatwick?'

'I've sent Emma-Jane Boutwood.'

'OK, good.'

As he looked up at the clock on his wall, Glenn Branson walked in and pulled up a chair.

'I've just had a call from Carly Chase in New York,' he said. 'Tony Revere's mother was killed in a car smash last night.'

Grace stared at him in stunned silence. Then he asked, 'What information do you have? How? I mean, what happened?'

'I'll come back to it. That's the least of our problems. At the moment, we have a much bigger one: Carly Chase's twelve-year-old son has gone missing.'

'Missing? What do you mean?'

'It sounds like he's been abducted.'

'When did this happen?'

'A friend of Carly's, called Justin Ellis, should have picked her son up from St Christopher's School at 11.15 a.m. to take him to a dental appointment. Ellis got there at ten past, to discover the boy had been collected twenty minutes earlier by a taxi. But Carly Chase is absolutely adamant she didn't order one.'

Grace stared at him, absorbing the information, trying to square it with the news he had just had about the licence plates from Duncan Crocker.

'She seemed in a pretty ramped-up state yesterday. Are you sure she didn't forget she'd ordered one?'

'I just came off the phone to her. She didn't order it, she's one hundred per cent sure.' Branson looked at his notes, then continued. 'One of his teachers at the school got a call that the taxi was outside. She knew he was being picked up, because his mum had already told them that was going to happen. She didn't think to query it.'

'Did she see the driver?'

'Not really, no. He was wearing a baseball cap. But she wasn't focused on him. Her concern was that Tyler got into the taxi safely and she watched him do that from the school gates. Apparently Tyler was regularly dropped off and picked up by taxis, so no one had any reason to question it.'

Grace sat in silence for some moments, thinking hard. He looked at his watch. 'The appointment is for 11.30 a.m.?'

'Yes.'

'Has anyone checked with the dentist to see if he's turned up?'

'Someone's on that now. He hadn't as of a couple of minutes ago.'

'Where's the dentist?'

'In Wilbury Road.'

'St Christopher's is on New Church Road, right?'

Branson nodded.

'That's a five-minute drive. Are you on to the taxi companies?'

Branson nodded again. 'I've got Norman Potting, Nick Nicholl and Bella Moy making calls right now.'

Grace thumped his desk in anger and frustration. 'Why wasn't I told about this dental appointment?'

Branson gave him a helpless look. 'We guarded her house with the boy and Carly's mother in it all night. And we had a friend of Carly Chase, who was doing the school run, tailed to make sure he got there safely. No one said anything about him having an appointment.'

Grace shook his head. 'She was vulnerable. That meant anyone close to her was vulnerable, too. We should have had someone at the school today.' He picked up a pen and began making notes on his pad, his brain going into overdrive. 'OK, do we have a photograph of this boy?'

'No. I have a description of him. He's five foot tall, looks a little like Harry Potter: floppy brown hair; oval, wire-framed glasses; and wearing a school uniform of red blazer, white shirt, red and grey tie, and grey trousers.'

'Good, that's fairly distinctive,' Grace said. 'We need a photo, asap.'

'We're on to that.'

'Has anyone spoken to the gran?'

'She's at an appointment at the Sussex County hospital. I have someone on their way there.'

Grace grabbed the phone and, as he dialled, said, 'Glenn, we need to plot an arc round the school. How far away someone could be in any direction now and in thirty minutes' time. We've got to get the make of vehicle. Is someone going to see the teacher?'

'Two officers should be at the school now.'

'We need more officers down at that school immediately, talking to everyone round it, in houses, walking their dogs, cats, goldfish . . .'

Grace dialled the number for Ops-1, gave the duty officer in the control room a quick summary and asked her who the Force Gold was that day. The Gold Commander was normally a superintendent or chief superintendent who would take control of any critical incident that happened on his watch.

He was pleased to hear it was Chief Superintendent Graham Barrington, the current commander of Brighton and Hove, an exceptionally able and intelligent officer. Moments later, he was on the line. Grace quickly brought him up to speed. Barrington said he wanted a detective as Silver and suggested Chief Inspector Trevor Barnes. He quickly reeled off the Bronzes to complete his command team, and concluded, 'I think because of the gravity we should have an assistant chief constable handle the media. ACC Rigg is on call today.'

Grace smirked. He liked the idea of Peter Rigg being given a role down the pecking order, beneath the chief superintendent.

'I think we should make your deputy SIO Investigations Bronze, as he'll be up to speed. Who is that?'

'Glenn Branson.'

'He's a DS?'

'Yes, but he's good,' Grace said, turning to his colleague and winking.

'OK.'

'I think our very first priority, Graham, is road checks.'

'Yes, we'll get them on all major routes. What do you think? Forty-five minutes' or one hour's drive away?'

Grace looked at his watch, doing a calculation. 'An hour's drive, to be safe. Can we scramble Hotel 900?'

Hotel 900 was the call sign for the police helicopter.

'Right away. Get me a description of the taxi as quickly as possible to give to them. What about utilising Child Rescue Alert?'

'Yes, definitely. I'm about to do that,' Grace said.

Child Rescue Alert was a recent police initiative, modelled on the US's Amber Alert, for getting descriptions of missing or abducted children circulated fast, nationwide. It included social-networking sites, news bulletins and posting descriptions on motorway signs. Its use always generated thousands of responses, each of which would have to be checked out. But it was a valuable resource and ideal for this situation.

'We need an all-ports alert out, too,' Grace said. 'No one's leaving this country with a young boy until we've cleared them. We need to throw everything we have at this.'

Grace hung up and turned back to Branson.

'OK, you're Investigations Bronze. Chief Superintendent Barrington will brief you shortly, but there are three urgent things you need to do.'

'Yes?'

'The first is to get the boy's computer—I assume he must have one—down to the High-Tech Crime Unit for analysis. Find out who he's been talking to and engaging with on Facebook, chat lines, email.'

Branson nodded. 'I'll access that via his gran.'

'The second is to get every inch of his house and garden searched, and his immediate neighbours'. You may be able to draft in some locals as volunteers to help search his entire home area.'

'Yep.'

'The third is to keep checking with the dentist and the school. I don't want egg all over my face if this kid turns up safe and sound because his mum forgot to tell you something.'

Branson nodded. 'Understood, but that's not going to happen. Not from what she's told me.' He got up to leave.

As the door closed, Grace grabbed his pad and scribbled down several more actions as they came into his head. Then he sat in silence for some moments, thinking. His phone rang. It was his assistant asking if he had the amended draft of his press statement ready for retyping. He told her he was going to have to rewrite it totally because of the latest development, and that the press conference might need to be delayed by half an hour.

He felt very afraid for this young boy. The man who had killed Preece and Ferguson was a cruel sadist. There was no telling what he had in mind for Tyler Chase, and all Grace's focus now was on how to get the boy safely out of his clutches. At least the timing of the press conference could hardly be better. Within the next hour, combining Child Rescue Alert and the press and the media, he could have nationwide coverage on the missing boy.

Then he picked up his phone and made the call that he was not looking forward to. ACC Peter Rigg answered on the first ring.

CARLY WALKED ROUND her hotel room in a black vortex of terror, tears streaming down her face. Her brain was jumping round all over the place and she was feeling physically sick. How could she have been so damned stupid leaving him at home, unprotected like that?

She had to get home. Someone helpful down at the front desk was looking into flights to England for her. She had to get back, somehow had to, *had to*. She had to think straight. But the only thing that came to her mind was the image of Tyler getting into a taxi. Driven by a monster.

She had her phone beside her, willing Tyler to ring. Desperately praying he would ring. And suddenly it began ringing. The display said, BLOCKED.

'Yes-hi-hello?' she blurted.

'Carly? It's DS Branson.'

'Yes?' she said, trying to mask her disappointment. But maybe he had news? *Please, please have news.*

'I need to ask you some questions, Carly.'

Her heart sinking, she rushed on, 'I was thinking: is it possible there was a mix-up at the school and the taxi was for another boy? Have they checked he's not somewhere at the school? He likes science, history, stuff like that.

He often just goes into the labs and works on his own. Did they check?'

'They're searching the school now. But the taxi was definitely there to collect your son, Tyler.'

'Did he turn up at the dentist? Do you have any news at all?'

'So far not, but we'll find him, don't worry. But I need your help.'

'DON'T WORRY? YOU'RE TELLING ME NOT TO *WORRY*?' she shouted at him.

'We're doing everything we possibly can, Carly.'

'I'm going to get the first flight home.'

'Let me know your flight details when you can and we'll meet you at the airport. We've heard about Mrs Revere.'

'This is just a nightmare,' she said. 'Please help me. Please find my son. Oh God, please help me.'

'One thing that could be significant: can you tell me who might have known about Tyler's dental appointment?'

'Who? Only his school, and my friends, Sarah and Justin Ellis. Justin was going to take him. I—I can't think of anyone else. Have you checked he didn't go home? He's very resourceful. He wouldn't have got into a car with a stranger, I know that.'

'We're keeping a round-the-clock watch on your home. There doesn't appear to be anyone in. But he definitely went off from his school in a taxi.'

'Please find him,' she said. 'Please find him.'

'We are going to find him, I promise. The whole nation's looking for him.'

Tears were stinging her eyes and everything was a blur. The detective's kind voice was making her weepy.

'The Revere family,' she sobbed. 'They can do anything they want to me. I don't care. Tell them that. Tell them they can kill me. Tell them to give me my son back and then kill me.'

He promised to call her back the moment he had any news. As she hung up, she crossed over to the window and stared out at the drab landscape. Christ, the world was a big place. How could you find someone? Where did you start looking? Suddenly she had a thought.

Wiping away tears, she stared down at the screen of her iPhone, and quickly fingered through the applications until she reached the one she was looking for. Then she tapped it hard. Moments later, she felt a sudden flicker of hope. She stared at it harder, brought it closer to her face.

'Oh, yes! Oh, you good boy, Tyler! Oh, you clever boy!'

GRACE CAME OUT of the press conference at 12.50 p.m., pleased with the solid performance ACC Rigg had delivered, and very relieved. Rigg had been sensible, keeping it tight and focused, and brief.

He was about to call the Gold Commander for an update, when his phone rang. It was Glenn Branson.

'We have a development with Tyler, boss.'

'Where are you?'

'MIR-1.'

'I'll be right there.'

When he got there, Glenn Branson was seated in the far corner of the room. Grace hurried across to him.

'Boss, have you used an iPhone?'

'No. Why?' Grace frowned.

'There's an app called Friend Mapper. It operates on GPS, just like a satnav. You and someone you know with an iPhone can both be permanently logged on to it. So if you and I are logged on to it, I'd be able to see where you are, anywhere in the world, and you'd be able to see me.'

Grace suddenly had a feeling he knew where this was going.

'Carly Chase and her son?'

'Yes! When Carly Chase got her son an iPhone, the deal was that he had to keep Friend Mapper on all the time he was out of her sight. And it's on now. We had a call from her twenty minutes ago. It's not moving, but there was a signal coming from Regency Square. We don't know whether it's been switched off or the battery's dead—or he could, as I suspect, just be in a bad reception area.'

'How old is this signal?'

'She can't tell, because she's only just checked. She says it looks like it's very near the entrance to the underground car park.'

Grace suddenly felt himself sharing Branson's excitement. 'If he's in the car park that could explain the lack of a signal!'

Branson smiled. 'Gold's got every unit in Brighton down there now. They're ring-fencing it, searching the place and any vehicle that leaves.'

'Let's go!' Grace said.

WITH HIS MEMORY of Glenn Branson's driving still too close for comfort, Grace took the wheel. As they blitzed through Brighton's lunchtime traffic, Branson said, 'Carly Chase is booked on a flight that leaves at 8.40 a.m.

New York time—1.40 p.m. UK time. She arrives at Heathrow at 8.35 p.m.'

'OK.'

Grace's phone rang. 'Could you answer it, Glenn?'

Branson took the call while Grace overtook a line of traffic waiting at a red light at the junction of Dyke Road and the Old Shoreham Road, blazing down the wrong side of the road.

When Branson ended the call he turned to Grace. 'That was Emma-Jane, reporting back from Avis. That Toyota Yaris was rented Monday morning of last week to a man called James John Robertson, according to his licence. The address he had given was fictitious and the information received back from the High-Tech Crime Unit was that the Visa credit card he paid with was a sophisticated clone. Avis gave a description of the renter, but it wasn't much to go on. A short, thin man with an English accent, wearing a baseball cap and dark glasses.'

The journey to Regency Square from Sussex House would normally have taken around twenty minutes. Grace did it in eight. He turned off the seafront, ignored a No Entry sign, and pulled up behind two marked cars that were halted by the car park entry ramp.

The entire square was teeming with uniformed police officers, and the statuesque figure of the Brighton and Hove duty inspector, Sue Carpenter, was heading over to greet them. In her early forties, she stood a good six feet tall, and the hat riding high on her head made her look even taller.

'Good afternoon, sir,' she said, then gave Glenn Branson a quick smile.

'How are you doing?' Grace asked.

'We've just found a taxi parked on the third level—the lowest. The vehicle is locked, sir. We've radioed Streamline, which it's registered with, to see if we can get any information.'

'Let's take a look,' Grace said. He glanced around. 'Presumably there's CCTV on the entrance and exit?'

'There are cameras, sir, and some inside. Every single one of them was vandalised last night. The timing seems a little coincidental.'

Grace cursed as he and Branson followed Inspector Carpenter down a concrete stairwell. Then they walked along the bottom level of the car park, which was almost deserted. Over to the right, partially obscured by a concrete abutment, he saw a Skoda saloon taxi that had been reversed into a bay and backed up tight against the rear wall. Two officers stood beside it.

As they approached, Grace noticed a few fragments of black plastic on the ground close to the car. He fished the gloves from his pocket and snapped them on. Then he knelt, picked the fragments up and put them in an evidence bag, just in case.

At that moment a controller's voice came through Inspector Carpenter's radio. Grace and Branson could both hear it clearly. Apparently the Streamline operator was concerned, as she'd not been able to get a response from the driver of the taxi since just after midnight the night before.

'Do we have a name?' Carpenter asked.

'Mike Howard,' the voice crackled back.

'Ask if she has a mobile phone number for him,' Grace said.

Still wearing his gloves, he peered into the front, then the rear of the car before trying each of the doors in turn, but they were all locked.

Sue Carpenter radioed the request. A few moments later, the operator came back with the number. Grace scribbled it down on his notebook, then immediately dialled it. A few moments later they heard a muted ringtone from inside the rear of the taxi. Grace ended the call, turned to one of the PCs and asked him for his baton, which the young officer handed to him.

'Stand back!' Grace warned, as he swung the baton hard at the driver's door window.

It cracked, with a loud bang, but remained intact. He hit it again, harder, and this time the glass broke. He smashed away some of the jagged edges with the baton, then slipped his arm in, found the handle and tugged it. He pulled the door open, leaned in and released the handbrake.

'Lend a hand,' he said to the officers, and began to push the car forwards.

Slowly, silently, it inched away from the wall. Grace leaned in, looking for an internal boot release. Moments later he found it, and the boot lid popped open.

IN THE TOTAL DARKNESS, Tyler's head hurt. He couldn't see anything, couldn't move his arms or legs. He was frightened and confused and knew this was not a game, that something bad was happening.

They were travelling, he could sense that. Motion. There were strong smells of carpet and plastic, new-car smells. He thought he could detect rubber, too. He must be in the boot of a car, he reckoned. Braking and accelerating. All he could move were his knees. He could bend and flex them just a little. He tried to wedge them against something solid, to get a grip, but moments later he was thrown backwards and felt himself rolling over, until he hit something hard. He tried to shout to the driver, to ask him who he was, where they were going, but he could not move his mouth and his voice sounded all muffled.

After the two police officers had come to their house, his mum had sat down in his bedroom and told him there were bad things happening. Bad people. They had to be careful. They needed to keep a watch for strangers near the house. He must call the police if he saw anyone. Was this one of the bad people driving him now?

At least he knew Friend Mapper would be logging him and his mum would know that. She'd know exactly where he was and she would tell the police. He didn't really need to be afraid. They would find him. He just hoped they would find him soon, because he had an IT class in the afternoon that he did not want to miss. And because he did not like this darkness, and not being able to move, and his arms were hurting, too. But it was going to be all right.

GRACE DASHED ROUND to the rear of the taxi.

The man inside looked terrified and there was a sour reek of urine. Duct tape was wound round his arms, legs and mouth; the same kind of tape with which Evie Preece had been bound. Grace fished out his warrant card and held it up to give the man reassurance.

'Police,' he said. 'Don't worry, you're safe. We'll get you out of there.'

He turned to Branson and to Inspector Sue Carpenter, who had joined them. 'Let's get the tape off his mouth first. Sue, call for a paramedic and a search team. And I want this level of the car park closed, as well as all the stairwells, in case they left by foot.'

'Yes, sir.'

Then he leaned in and, as gently as he could, got his fingertips in the join in the tape. It would have been easier without his gloves, he knew, but he kept them on and finally managed to start peeling it off, mindful that although it would be extremely painful for the man, at the same time he needed to preserve it as best he could for forensic analysis.

As he peeled it away from his mouth, the man shouted out in pain.

'Mike Howard?' Grace asked.

'Yes! Jesus, that hurt,' the man said, then smiled.

'I'm sorry. We're going to lift you out. Are you injured? In pain?'

He shook his head. 'Just get me out.'

Mike Howard was a big, heavy man. With considerable difficulty, they managed to manoeuvre him forward to the edge of the boot. They freed his arms and legs, then they stood him up and walked him round a little, supporting him until the circulation was back in his legs and he was steadier. He was wheezing, so they sat him down on the Skoda's rear bumper.

'Can you tell us what happened?' Grace asked him gently.

'What time is it?'

'Half past one,' Glenn Branson said.

'What day?'

'Friday. Why, how long have you been there?

Mike Howard took several deep breaths. 'I was working nights. I was just heading home, about 1 a.m., and this man hailed me along the seafront. He got in the back and told me to take him to Shoreham Airport. I remember turning into the perimeter road and that's the last thing.'

'The last thing you remember?' Grace asked.

'I woke up being shaken about. I could smell diesel and fumes. I figured I was in the boot of my cab. I was terrified.'

'Can you remember what this guy looked like?'

'He was wearing a baseball cap pulled low. I tried to get a look at his face. You always do in this game when you pick someone up late at night off the street. But I couldn't see it.'

'What about his accent?'

'He didn't say much. Sounded English to me. Do you have any water?'

'I'll get you some. Do you need anything to eat?'

'Sugar. I'm diabetic.'

'An ambulance will be here any minute. They'll have something for you. Will you be all right for a few minutes?'

Mike Howard nodded.

Grace continued his questioning. 'We think the man who did this to you has kidnapped a child and we need to find him urgently. I know you've had a horrendous ordeal, but anything you can tell us, anything at all that you can remember, would be valuable.'

Mike Howard eased himself forwards. 'I'm trying to think. He was short. A short, thin little fellow, like a weasel. Promise me something?'

'What?' Grace asked.

'If you find him, can I get him to pay me what he owes me, then thump him one, really hard, where it hurts?'

For the first time in what felt a long while, Grace smiled. 'You'll have to beat me to it,' he said.

He looked at his watch. Almost two and a half hours since Tyler Chase had been picked up. Why was he brought here? His assumption was that the abductor had a car parked here—with luck, the rental Toyota Yaris—choosing this as a good location to attack and disable the boy, then switch vehicles. Even more ideal with its CCTV cameras out of action. He felt he was starting to recognise the killer's handwriting.

He did a calculation in his head. There were roadworks along the seafront clogging up the traffic, badly. The journey from the school would have been about fifteen to twenty minutes, assuming they came straight here. From the image he was building of the man, Grace was able to make another assumption that he would take the boy somewhere he could film him dying, somewhere dramatic. But where?

He studied his watch again. If he'd brought the boy in here around 11.20 a.m., it was unlikely he would have hung around. He would have left again within a few minutes. Certainly within half an hour.

Grace turned to Glenn Branson and said, 'We're out of here.'

'Where to?'

'I'll tell you in the car.'

TOOTH, KEEPING RIGIDLY to the 30mph speed limit, drove the Toyota west along the main road above Shoreham Harbour. He was looking at the flat water of the basin, down to his left, where Ewan Preece had taken his last drive, and almost didn't notice a roadworks traffic light turning red in front of him.

He braked hard. Behind him in the boot of the car he heard a thud and further back a scream of locked tyres. For an anxious moment, he thought the car behind was going to rear-end him.

Then the sudden wail of a siren gave him a new concern. Moments later, blue lights flashing, a police car tore past from the opposite direction. He kept a careful watch in his mirrors, but it kept on going, either not noticing or not interested in him. Relieved, he drove on for some distance, passing a number of industrial buildings to his left, until he saw his landmark: the low-rise office block of the Shoreham Port Authority building.

He turned right opposite it, and drove a short way up a narrow street, which rapidly became shabbier and went under a railway bridge further along. But before the bridge, he turned off into a messy area that was part industrial estate and part low-rent apartment blocks. He remembered it all well and it seemed unchanged. It was the kind of area where no one would notice you.

He turned right again, into the place he had discovered six years ago. He drove along the side of a shabby apartment block and came into a half-empty parking area at the rear of the building, bounded by a crumbling wall on two sides, a wooden fence on a third and the rear of the apartment block.

He reversed the car in, backing it tight up against the wall, sat and ate the sandwich he had bought earlier at a petrol station, then got out and locked up. With his cap pulled down low and his sunglasses on, he peered up at the grimy windows for any sign of an inquisitive face, but all he saw was laundry flapping from a couple of balconies. Then he pretended to check a rear tyre, listening to make sure his passenger was silent.

He heard a thud. Angrily, he opened the boot and saw the boy's frightened eyes behind his glasses. It didn't matter how tightly he bound him, there was nothing to anchor him to. He wondered if it would be wisest to break his back and paralyse him, but that would mean lifting him out first and he didn't want to take that risk. Instead he said, 'Make another sound and you're dead. Understand what I'm saying?'

The boy nodded, looking even more frightened.

Tooth slammed down the lid.

TYLER WAS TERRIFIED by the man in the black baseball cap and the dark glasses, but he was angry, too. His wrists were hurting from the bindings and he had cramp in his right foot. He listened, hard, could hear footsteps crunching, getting fainter.

He'd felt the car move when the man got out, but it hadn't moved again, which meant he hadn't got back in. He must have gone somewhere.

Tyler tried to work out what time it was, or where he might be. He'd just seen daylight when the boot lid rose up. And the wall of a building, a crummy-looking wall, and a couple of windows: it could have been any-where in the city. But the fresh air that had come in, momentarily, smelled familiar. A tang of salt, mixed with timber and burnt gas and other indus-trial smells. They were close to a harbour, he thought. Almost certainly Shoreham Harbour. He'd been kayaking there with his school.

The daylight wasn't bright, but it didn't feel like it was evening; more just overcast, as if it was going to rain. They would find him soon. His mother would know where he was from Friend Mapper.

Defiantly, he threw himself against the side of the car, kicking out as hard as he could. Then again. And again. He kicked until he had tired himself out. It didn't sound as if anyone had heard him. But surely they would find him soon?

11

Grace, followed by Branson, sprinted up three floors at Brighton's John Street Police Station, hurried along a corridor and went into the CCTV control room, which was manned round the clock.

It was a large space, with three separate workstations, each comprising keyboards, computer terminals, telephones and a bank of CCTV monitors on which there was a kaleidoscope of moving images. Every police CCTV camera in the county could be viewed from there.

Two of the workstations were currently occupied by controllers. One of them turned as they came in and nodded a greeting. His badge gave his name as Jon Pumfrey. Moments later, they were joined in the room by Chief Superintendent Graham Barrington, the Gold Commander.

Barrington, in his mid-forties, was a tall, slim man with short fair hair, and the athletic air of a regular marathon runner.

'Jon,' the chief superintendent said, 'which are the nearest cameras to the Regency Square car park?'

'There's a police one right opposite, boss,' the young man replied, 'but it's hopeless: there's some constant interference with it.'

He tapped the keyboard and a moment later they saw successive waves rippling up and down one of the screens directly in front of him.

'How long's it been like that?' Roy Grace asked suspiciously.

'Months. I keep asking them to do something about it.' He shrugged. 'There are also cameras to the east and west. Which direction do you want?'

'We've just done a quick recce,' Grace said. 'If you exit in a vehicle from the Regency Square car park, you have to turn left on the seafront. I've set some parameters,' he continued. 'What we need to see is the video footage showing all vehicles in motion close to the car park, travelling east or west on King's Road between 11.15 a.m. and 11.45 a.m. today. We're looking particularly for a dark-coloured Toyota Yaris saloon, with a single male driving, either accompanied by a twelve-year-old boy or solo.'

Graham Barrington said, 'All right, I'll leave you to it. Anything you want, just shout.'

Grace thanked him, and the two detectives then stood behind Pumfrey and began to watch intently.

'The Yaris is a popular car, sir,' Pumfrey said. 'Must be thousands on the roads. We're likely to see a few.'

'We'll put markers on the first five we see, to start with,' Grace said. 'If they're turning left, they're heading east, but that might be only for a short distance, before they make a U-turn and head west. Let's check east first.'

Almost as he spoke they saw a dark-coloured Yaris heading east, past the bottom of West Street. The camera was on the south side of the road.

'Freeze that!' Branson said. 'Can you zoom in?'

Jon Pumfrey tapped the keyboard and the camera zoomed in, jerkily but quickly, on the driver's door and window. It was a grainy zoom, but they could see clearly enough that it was two elderly ladies.

'Let's move on,' Grace said.

They watched the images of cars darting by in flickering movements.

Then Grace called out, 'Stop! Go back.'

They watched the tape rewind.

'OK! That one.' They were looking at a dark grey Yaris with what appeared to be a single occupant, a male, driving. The time said 11.38. 'Now zoom in, please.' The image was again grainy, but this time it looked like a male, most of his face obscured by a baseball cap and dark glasses.

'It's not that bright. Why's he wearing dark glasses?' Pumfrey queried.

Grace turned to Branson. 'That was the description by the school teacher—the taxi driver was wearing a baseball cap. And so was the man who rented the car from Avis!' Suddenly he felt his adrenalin pumping. Turning back to Pumfrey, he asked, 'Is that the best image you can get?'

'I can send it for enhancement, but that would take a while.'

'OK, run forward. Can we get the registration?'

Pumfrey inched the car forward frame by frame.

'Golf Victor zero eight Whisky Delta X-ray,' Branson read out, as Grace wrote it down.

'Right. Can you run an ANPR check from here?' he asked Pumfrey.

'Yes, sir.'

They continued watching. Then, to Grace's excitement, the car reappeared, this time travelling west.

'It's gone round the roundabout at the Palace Pier, doing a U-turn!' he said. 'Where's the next camera?'

'Other than the dud one opposite the Regency Square car park, the next is a mile to the west, on Brunswick Lawns.'

'Let's look at that one,' Grace said.

Five minutes later the car appeared, still travelling west.

'Where's the next?' Grace asked.

'That's the last of the city's CCTV cameras in this direction, sir,' Pumfrey said. 'Now, let's see if this vehicle has triggered any ANPR camera since 11.15 a.m.' He turned to a different computer and entered the data. 'Here we are: 11.54 a.m. This is the ANPR camera at the bottom of Boundary Road, Hove, at the junction with the end of the Kingsway.'

Suddenly, a photograph of the front of a dark grey Yaris appeared on the screen, its number plate clearly visible, but the occupant hard to make out through an almost opaque screen. By looking very closely, it was possible to distinguish what might have been someone in a baseball cap and dark glasses, but without any certainty.

'Can't we get a better image of the face?' Branson asked.

'Depends how the light hits the windscreen,' Pumfrey replied. 'These cameras are designed to read number plates, I'm afraid, not faces. I can send it for enhancement.'

'Yes, both of those images, please,' Grace said. 'Is that the only ANPR it's triggered?'

'The only one showing today.'

Grace did a mental calculation: if the driver avoided breaking the law, and with a kidnapped child on board he would not want to risk getting stopped . . . The exit from the car park onto King's Road was a left turn only . . . That meant he would have driven east to the end of King's Road and then gone round the roundabout, by the Palace Pier, and then come back on himself. Allowing for the distance and hold-ups at traffic lights, that would put the car there at the right time from its sighting on King's Road. Excitement was growing inside him.

The car's location was alongside Shoreham Harbour, close to Southwick.

He was certain that the sadist knew this area. A lot of villains perpetrated their crimes in the places they knew, their comfort zones. He made a note of a new line of enquiry: to have Duncan Crocker do a search on all previous violent crimes in this area. But first he called for a check on the car.

The information came back that the owner was Barry Simons, who lived in Worthing, West Sussex, some fifteen miles to the west of Brighton. Grace's excitement waned at this news. That fitted with the car's occupant and position, heading in the direction of where he lived. The only thing that kept him hopeful was the fact that the Yaris appeared to have stopped somewhere in Shoreham or Southwick. He was about to call Gold to ask him to get the helicopter over there and block off the area when his phone rang.

It was Duncan Crocker. 'Roy, we've found a car, a Toyota Yaris, driving on those switched plates taken from the service station at Newport Pagnell—the plates from the young woman's car, the one who was stopped on the M11 near Brentwood. It's just pinged an ANPR camera, heading north from Brighton on the A23.'

IN THE CCTV ROOM, Grace stared at the frontal photograph of a dark grey Toyota Yaris on a familiar stretch of the A23, just north of Brighton. But to his dismay, the windscreen was even more opaque than the car by Shoreham Harbour. He could see nothing at all inside.

Branson immediately informed Gold, then listened intently to his radio.

Grace ordered Jon Pumfrey to put out a high-act, nationwide marker on the car. He did not intend to take any risks.

'What CCTV units do you have on the A23?' he asked the controller.

'The next one is the ANPR on the motorway, at Gatwick.'

Pumfrey pulled up a road map onto one of the monitors, showing the position of the ANPR cameras. There were plenty of opportunities for the suspect to turn off the motorway. But, with luck, the helicopter would have him in sight imminently.

Grace phoned the Incident Room. Nick Nicholl answered. Grace tasked him with finding Simons and establishing for certain that he had been driving his car along Brighton seafront that morning.

From the suspect's current position, it would take him about twenty-five minutes, Grace estimated, to ping that next ANPR camera at Gatwick. The helicopter, which was also fitted with ANPR, would be over the M23 in ninety seconds. One unmarked car was already on the motorway, approximately two miles behind the target, and two more were only minutes away. If they could get unmarked cars in front of and behind the suspect, they could box him in before he realised what was happening.

'I need to get back to Sussex House,' Glenn said.

'Me too.'

'I can patch any images you want through to you in the Incident Room,' Pumfrey said.

Grace thanked him and the two detectives left. As they walked out of the rear of the building into the car park, Grace's phone rang. It was Inspector Sue Carpenter at the Regency Square car park.

'Sir,' she said, 'I don't know if this is significant, but I understand that the Regency Square car park was identified by an application on the missing boy's iPhone.'

'Yes,' Grace replied, his hopes rising. 'An application called Friend Mapper. We're hoping he keeps it on.'

'I'm afraid, sir, one of the search team has found a smashed iPhone in a bin in the car park—close to the taxi.'

As HE CLIMBED into his car, Grace instructed Sue Carpenter to get the phone checked immediately for finger- and footprints, then get it straight to the High-Tech Crime Unit. Getting the contents of the phone analysed was more important to him at this stage than getting forensic evidence from it.

As he drove off, he said to Branson, 'I'm still struggling to get my head round the motive here. Did the perp take this boy as a substitute because his mother was unavailable? Or was taking the boy his plan all along?'

'What's your sense?'

'I think he plans everything. He's not someone who takes chance opportunities. My view is that probably, by going to the States, Carly Chase made seizing the boy a little easier for him.'

Branson nodded and looked at his watch. 'Six hours until she lands.'

'Maybe we'll be able to greet her with good news.'

'I promised I'd get a message to her as soon as we have anything.'

'With a bit of luck, that could be any minute now.'

Grace gave Branson a wistful smile, then glanced at the car clock. It was half past two. He should eat something, he knew, but he didn't want to waste valuable time stopping anywhere. He fished in his jacket pocket and produced a Mars bar in a crumpled wrapper that had been there for days.

'Haven't had any lunch. You hungry?' he said. 'Want to share this?'

'Boy, you know how to give someone a good time,' Branson said, taking it and peeling off the wrapper. He tore the chocolate bar in two and gave the slightly larger portion to Grace.

Grace's phone rang. As he wasn't driving at high speed, he stuck it into the hands-free cradle and answered. Both of them heard the voice of Chief Inspector Trevor Barnes, the newly appointed Silver Commander.

'Roy,' he said, 'we've just stopped the Toyota Yaris on the M23, four miles south of the Crawley interchange.'

Grace, his mouth full of chewy chocolate and toffee, thumped the steering wheel with glee.

'Brilliant!' Branson replied.

'That you, Glenn?' Barnes asked.

'Yeah, we're in the car. What's the situation?'

'Well,' Barnes said, 'I'm not sure that we have the right person.'

'What do you mean?' Grace halted the car at a traffic light.

Barnes read out the licence plate and asked, 'Is that the correct one?'

Grace pulled out his notebook and flipped to the right page. 'Yes. Those are the plates that were taken from a car at Newport Pagnell that we believe our suspect is using.'

'The driver of this Yaris is eighty-four years old and has his wife who is eighty-three with him. It's their car, but it's not their registration number.'

'Not their registration?' Grace echoed.

The lights changed and he drove on.

'The licence plates on the car aren't theirs, Roy. Sounds like someone's nicked their plates and replaced them with different ones.'

'Where's he come from?' Grace asked.

'They've been in Brighton. They enjoy the sea air, apparently. Like to walk along the front between the piers. It's their regular constitutional.'

'Let me guess where they parked. The Regency Square car park?'

'Very good, Roy. Ever thought of going on *Mastermind*?'

'Once, when I had a brain that worked. So, give us their index that's been stolen.'

Branson wrote it down.

Grace drove in silence for some moments, thinking about the killer with grudging admiration. *Whoever you are, you are a smart bastard.*

His phone rang again. It was Nick Nicholl, sounding perplexed.

'Chief, I'm coming back to you on the vehicle owner check you asked me to do, on Barry Simons.'

'Thanks. What do you have, Nick?'

'I've just spoken to him.' The detective constable sounded hesitant. 'You asked me to check if it was him driving his car first east on King's Road, then west past the junction between Kingsway and Boundary Road this morning? Index Golf Victor zero eight Whisky Delta X-ray?'

'Yes.'

'Well, he's a bit baffled, chief. He and his wife are lying on a beach in Limassol in Cyprus at the moment. They've been there nearly two weeks.'

'Could anyone they know be driving this car while they're away?'

'No,' Nicholl said. 'They left it at the long-term car park at Gatwick.'

Grace pulled over to the side of the road and stopped sharply.

'Nick, put a high-act marker on that index. Get on to the Divisional Intelligence Unit. I want to know every ANPR sighting from the day Barry Simons's car arrived at Gatwick to now.'

Grace switched on the car's lights and siren, then turned to Glenn Branson. 'We're taking a ride to Shoreham.'

'Want me to drive?' Branson asked.

Grace shook his head. 'I think I'll be of more help to Tyler Chase alive.'

TOOTH SAT in the Yaris in the parking lot behind the apartment block. The same cars were still there that had been there when he left to do his reconnaissance an hour ago. It was still the middle of the afternoon, and maybe the lot would fill up when people came back from work. But it hadn't filled up last time, six years ago. The windows of the apartment block didn't look like they had been cleaned since then either.

He stared at the text that had come in and which had prompted his early return to the car. It said just one word: CALL.

He removed the SIM card and, as he always did, burned it with his lighter until it was melted. He would throw it away later. Then he took one of the phones he had not yet used from his bag and dialled the number.

Ricky Giordino answered on the first ring. 'Yeah?'

'You texted me to call.'

'What the fuck took you so long, Mr Tooth?'

Tooth did not reply.

'You still there? Hello, Mr Tooth?'

'Yes.'

'Listen to me. We've had another tragedy in our family and that woman, Mrs Chase, she's the cause of it. My sister's dead. I'm your client now, understand me? You're doing this for me now. I want that woman's pain to be so bad. I want pain she's never going to forget, you with me?'

'I'm doing what I can,' Tooth replied.

'Listen up, I didn't pay you a million bucks to do what you *can* do. Understand? I paid you that money to do something different, right? Creative. Give me a big surprise. Blow me away. Show me you got balls!'

'Balls,' Tooth commented.

'Yeah, you heard, balls. You're going to bring those videos to me, right? Soon as you're done?'

'Tomorrow,' Tooth said.

He ended the call, again burned the SIM card, then lit a cigarette. He did not like this man. He didn't do rudeness.

ROY GRACE turned the siren and lights off as they passed Hove Lagoon. The lagoon ended at the eastern extremity of Shoreham Harbour, and from this point onwards the buildings and landscape became mostly industrial and docklands. He slowed as they approached the junction with Boundary Road and pointed up through the windscreen.

'There's the ANPR camera that Barry Simons pinged this morning.'

Then Nick Nicholl radioed through. 'Chief, I've got the information you requested on the Toyota Yaris index Golf Victor zero eight Whisky Delta X-ray. It's rather strange, so I went back an extra two weeks and I now have all sightings for the past month. For the first two weeks it pinged cameras during weekdays that are consistent with a regular morning and evening commute from Worthing to central Brighton and back. Then on Sunday morning, just under two weeks ago, it travelled from Worthing to Gatwick.'

'Consistent with what Simons told you,' Branson said, butting in, 'that they parked it at Gatwick before their flight to Cyprus.'

'Yes,' Nicholl said. 'Now, here's the bit that doesn't make sense. The next sighting was the one this morning, when it pinged the CCTV camera on the seafront at the bottom of West Street, travelling east. There's nothing to show how the car got from Gatwick Airport down to Kingsway.'

'Unless it commenced its journey from the Regency Square car park,'

Grace said thoughtfully. 'Then it would have exited the car park on King's Road and had to make a left turn along the seafront, which would explain why it passed the CCTV camera at the bottom of West Street twice—first going east and then, a few minutes later, west. Followed by the one on Brunswick Lawns, a mile further west, and then this one.'

'You've lost me, sir,' Nicholl said. 'That doesn't explain how the car got from Gatwick Airport to that car park in the first place.'

'It didn't, Nick,' Grace said. 'Our suspect has already demonstrated he is rather cute with number plates. We believe he rented this Toyota from Avis at Gatwick. I'm prepared to put money on Mr and Mrs Simons returning from their Cyprus holiday to find their number plates are missing. What about subsequent sightings since Boundary Road?'

'None, sir.'

Which would indicate, Grace thought, *that either the car is parked up somewhere or the killer has changed number plates yet again.*

He ended the conversation and called Graham Barrington to update him.

'My hunch is that he's in the Shoreham area,' Grace said. 'But we can't rely on that. I think you need to get every dark-coloured Toyota Yaris within a three-hour drive of Brighton stopped and searched.'

'That's already happening.'

'And we need to throw everything we have at Shoreham Harbour and its immediate vicinity.'

'The problem is, Roy, it's a massive area.'

'I know. We also need to search every ship leaving and every plane at Shoreham Airport. We need to check the tides. The harbour has a shallow entrance, so there's a lot of shipping that can't come in or leave for a period of time either side of low water.'

'I'll get that information. Where are you now?'

'At the bottom of Boundary Road with DS Branson—the position of the last sighting of our suspect. I think we should set an initial search parameter of a half-mile radius west of this camera.'

'Harbour and inland?'

'Yes. We need house-to-house, all outbuildings, garages, sheds, industrial estates, ships, boats. We're beyond the range of the Brighton and Hove CCTV network, so we need to focus on commercial premises that have CCTV. A car doesn't disappear into thin air. Someone's seen it.'

'Leave it with me.'

Grace knew that the Gold Commander would leave no stone unturned. He should let Barrington get on with it and return to Sussex House, first to MIR-1 to show support to his team, and then to prepare for this evening's briefing. But he was reluctant to leave the chase.

The killer was in Shoreham somewhere, he was certain of it. If anyone had asked him why, his only answer would have been the lame response, copper's nose.

Grace made a call to the Incident Room and Nick Nicholl answered.

'Nick, I want you to get everyone in MIR-1 to stop doing what they're doing for two minutes and have a hard think about this, right? If you'd abducted a child, where in Shoreham might be a good place to hide him? Somewhere no one goes. Maybe somewhere no one even knows about. This whole city is riddled with secret passages going back to smuggling days. Have a quick brainstorm with the team, OK?'

'Yes, chief, right away.'

'We're dealing with someone cunning. He'll choose a smart place.'

'I'm on to it now.'

Grace thanked him and drove on, turning right at the next opportunity. He drove slowly through a network of streets: a mixture of terraced houses and industrial buildings. Looking for a needle in a haystack, he knew. And remembering, as a mantra, the words that his father, who had been a policeman too, had once told him: *no one ever made a greater mistake than the man who did nothing because he could only do a little.*

CARLY DID NOT HEAR a word from Sussex Police throughout the flight. Every time a member of the cabin crew walked down the aisle in her direction, she hoped it would be with a message. It was now 8.45 p.m., UK time. Tyler had been missing for almost ten hours.

She replayed her decision to go to New York over and over. If she had not gone, she'd have collected Tyler herself from school and he would be safe. He'd be up in his room now, on his computer, or doing something with his fossil collection, or practising his cornet.

Fernanda Revere, who could have stopped all this, was dead.

Having touched down, the plane taxied a short distance then came to a halt. She pulled her bag down, then quickly called her mother to say they had landed, and in the hope that she had some news. But there was none.

A couple of minutes later she followed the passengers in front of her out through the plane's door and onto the bridge. Instantly she saw, waiting for her, the tall figure of Glenn Branson, accompanied by DS Bella Moy.

'Do you have any news?' Carly blurted.

Branson took her bag for her and steered her to one side, away from the crush of emerging passengers.

'I'm afraid not yet,' Bella Moy said. 'Presumably you've heard nothing?'

'I rang all his friends—the parents—before I got on the plane. No one's seen him.'

'One positive thing, Carly,' Branson said, 'is that we are fairly sure that Tyler is still within the Brighton and Hove area. We believe he may be in Shoreham, Southwick or Portslade.'

'We'll keep you constantly updated,' Bella said.

Fifteen minutes later she was in the back of a police car, heading through the airport tunnel. Glenn Branson drove and Bella Moy sat in the front passenger seat. Moy turned to face her.

'We have a number of questions we need to ask you about Tyler. Are you happy to talk in the car or would you rather wait until we get you home?'

'Please, now,' Carly said. 'Anything I can give you that might be helpful.'

'You've already given us the names and addresses of his friends. We're looking to see who he's been in contact with on his computer and iPhone. They're being examined by the High-Tech Crime Unit.'

'His iPhone?' Carly said. 'You have his phone?'

DS Moy's face froze. 'I'm sorry—didn't anyone tell you?'

'Tell me what?' Carly began shivering and perspiring at the same time. She leaned forward. 'Tell me what?' she said again. 'What do you mean?'

'His iPhone was found in that underground car park. The one you alerted us to on his Friend Mapper.'

'Found? How do you mean, *found*?'

Bella Moy hesitated, unsure how much to tell the woman. But she had a right to know the truth.

'There were broken fragments on the ground. Then it was discovered in a waste bin in the car park.'

'No,' Carly said, her voice quavering. 'No. Please, no.'

'He may have dropped it, Carly,' Glenn Branson said, trying to put a positive slant on the situation. 'He might have dropped it while running away. That's our best hope at the moment, that he's hiding somewhere.'

In utter desperation, and shaking with terror, Carly said, 'Please don't tell me you found his phone. Tyler's bright. I thought he was going to keep Friend Mapper on. I thought that would take us to him. I really, really felt that was our best hope.' She began to sob uncontrollably.

BY 9.30 P.M. IT WAS DARK, the wind had risen and rain was falling. Tooth returned to Shoreham in a Toyota Camry that he had rented from Sixt in Boundary Road, using a different ID.

He drove round the side of the apartment block and into the dark parking area at the rear. The space next to the Toyota Yaris was free. He reversed into it, then switched off the engine and lights.

He was in a bad mood. No matter how well you planned things, there was always something you hadn't accounted for. On this particular job, it was tides. It just had not occurred to him. In the rucksack he had bought, lying beside him on the passenger seat, was a tide chart that he'd printed out at an internet café half an hour ago. He'd study it carefully in a few minutes.

Meanwhile, he was anxious to move the boy on. The area was crawling with police and it looked as if a massive search was in progress. A quarter of a mile further up the road there was a roadblock, but the only vehicles they seemed interested in were Toyota Yaris saloons.

Too much heat on those vehicles. Too much danger of his being found. The search line still had a while to go before they reached this locality, he worked out—an hour and a half, maybe two hours. He would make sure they didn't find anything. He climbed out of the car, popped open the boot, then swiftly moved across to the rear of the Yaris.

TYLER HAD HEARD the sound of a car moving close by, then stopping. He was about to start kicking when suddenly there was a sharp, metallic clunk and the boot opened. He felt a blast of fresh, damp air, but could not see any daylight now: just darkness with an orange streetlighting tinge to it.

Then he saw the dazzling beam of a torch and the shadowy shape of a baseball cap and dark glasses beyond. He was truly scared. If he could just speak, maybe the man would get him some water and something to eat.

Suddenly he felt himself being lifted. He was swung through the air, feeling spots of rain on his face, then dropped, painfully, inside another space that smelled similar, but different. Maybe even newer?

There was a thud and he was entombed once more in pitch darkness. He listened for footsteps but instead heard the engine starting up.

The car accelerated away harshly, sending him rolling backwards and cracking his head painfully on something sharp. He let out a muffled cry of pain. Then the car braked sharply and he tumbled forwards a couple of feet.

Whatever he had hit had definitely been sharp. He wormed his way back, as the car accelerated again. He didn't know what it was. He tried to press his gagged mouth up against it and rub, but the car was swaying too much and he was finding it hard to keep steady.

Then he felt the car brake sharply and turn, and keep on turning. He was rolled, helplessly, on his side. There was a massive bump and he cracked his head again on the boot lid, then the car halted, throwing him forwards.

Tooth looked round carefully as he pulled off the side of the road above the harbour, bumping over the kerb and onto the grass, driving far enough away so that the car was almost invisible from the road. He halted beside a small, derelict-looking building directly opposite Shoreham Power Station, across the black water of the harbour.

The little building was constructed in brick, with a tiled roof, and had a rusting metal door with a large, rusted padlock on it. It was the padlock he had put on last time he was there, six years ago. Clearly no one had been in, which was good. Not that anyone had any reason to go in there. The place was condemned, highly dangerous, toxic and in imminent danger of collapsing. A large yellow and black sign on the wall displayed an electricity symbol and the words KEEP OUT—DANGER OF DEATH.

In the distance he could hear a helicopter. It had been flying around, on and off, for most of the afternoon and evening. From his rucksack, with his gloved hands, he pulled out a head-mounted flashlight, strapped it round his baseball cap and picked up the bolt cutters he had acquired earlier in a hardware store. He snapped open the padlock on the door of the brick building and then lifted the boy out of the car. He carried him inside the building and pulled the door closed with an echoing clang.

Now he switched on his flashlight. Directly in front of him was a short, narrow flight of concrete steps going down, between two brick walls. A pair of tiny red eyes appeared momentarily in the darkness at the bottom of the steps, then darted away.

Tooth carried the boy down the steps, brushing past several spider webs. At the bottom was a gridded metal platform, with a handrail, and a whole cluster of rusting pipes. It was as silent as a tomb in there.

On the other side of the handrail was a shaft, with a steel ladder, that dropped 190 feet. Tooth looked at the boy, ignoring the pleading in his eyes, then tilted him over the rail, shining his flashlight beam down, to enable the boy to see the vertical drop. The boy's eyes bulged in terror.

Tooth pulled a length of blue, high-tensile rope from his rucksack and tied it carefully round the boy's ankles. Then he lowered the boy, who was struggling now, and making a whining, yammering sound through the duct tape across his mouth, a short distance down the shaft, and tied the rope round the rail.

'I'll be back in a while, kid,' Tooth said. 'Don't struggle too much. You wouldn't want your ankles coming loose.'

TYLER'S GLASSES were falling up his nose. He was scared that at any moment they would drop into the void below. But worse, he could feel the rope slipping. He was swaying and starting to feel giddy and disorientated.

Something tiny was crawling over his nose. A cold draught blew on his face, the air dank, musty and carrying the fainter, noxious odour of something rotting.

The rope slipped a little more. Was the man going to come back? Where was his phone? In the car? How would anyone find him here without Mapper?

He began to panic, then felt the rope slip further. His glasses fell further, too. He froze, stiffening his legs and feet, pushing them against the bindings to keep them as tight as he could. Suddenly, something touched his right shoulder. He screamed, the sound trapped inside him. Then he realised he had just swung into the side of the shaft.

The walls had looked rough, he realised, in the brief moment he had seen them in the beam of the torch. The edges of the ladder would be rough, or sharp. As gently as he could, he tried to swing himself against the ladder.

Yes! If he could rub the bindings round his arms up and down against the rough edge, maybe he could saw through them.

His glasses moved further up his forehead. The insect was now crawling over his eyelid. The rope slipped further down his ankles.

THE PLACE had worked well for him last week, Tooth reasoned: it was dark, no one overlooked it and there were no cameras. Aside from the power station, there were only timber warehouses, closed and dark for the night, on the far wharf. And the water was deep.

Someone had replaced the padlock on the chain-link fence. He cut through it with his bolt cutters and pushed the gates open. Then he jumped into the Yaris and drove it forward onto the quay, passing the old fork-lift truck that he had used last week. Not that he would need it now.

He got out of the car and took a careful look around. He could hear, in the distance, the clatter of a helicopter again. With the aid of his flashlight, he did a final check on the interior of the vehicle, pulling out the ashtray and throwing the butts and melted SIM cards into the dark, choppy water.

Then he backed the car up, opened all the windows and doors and popped the boot lid. He slid back behind the steering wheel and, keeping the driver's door open, he put the car into gear and accelerated hard at the edge of the quay. At the very last minute, he threw himself sideways and rolled as he hit the hard surface. Beyond him he heard a deep splash.

Tooth scrambled to his feet and saw the car floating, submerged up to its sills, in the choppy water. He was about to snap on his flashlight when he heard an engine. It sounded as if a boat was approaching. He froze.

Bubbles rose all round the car, making a steady *bloop-bloop-bloop* sound. The car was sinking. The engine compartment was almost underwater. The sound of the engine was getting louder.

Sink. Sink, damn you. Sink!

He could see a faint light approaching from the right. Water lapped and bubbled, up to the windshield now. The engine sound was louder. Powerful twin diesels. The roof was going under now. It was sinking. The rear window was disappearing. Now the boot. It was gone.

Moments later, navigation lights on and search lights blazing, a Port Authority launch came into view, with two police officers on the deck.

Tooth ducked down behind the skip. The boat carried on past. For an instant, above the throb of its engines and the thrash of its bow wave, he heard the crackle of a two-way radio. But the sound of the vessel was already fading, its lights getting dimmer again. He breathed out.

TYLER HEARD a loud, metallic clang. Then a sound like footsteps. For an instant his hopes rose. Footsteps getting nearer. Then the smell of cigarette smoke. He heard a familiar voice.

'Enjoying the view, kid?'

Tooth switched on the flashlight, untied the rope from the balcony and began lowering the boy further, carefully paying the rope through his gloved hands. He could feel the boy bumping into the sides, then the rope went slack. Good. The boy had landed on the first of the three rest platforms, spaced at fifty-foot intervals.

With his rucksack on his back and the light on, Tooth began to descend the ladder, using just one hand and taking up the slack of the rope as he went with the other. When he reached the platform, he repeated the procedure, then again, until the boy landed face down on the floor of the shaft. Tooth clambered down the last flight and joined him, then pulled a small lamp from his rucksack, switched it on and set it down.

Ahead was a tunnel that went beneath the harbour. Tooth had discovered it from an archive search during the planning for his previous visit. Before it had been replaced because of its dangerous condition, the tunnel had carried electricity lines from the old power station. The tunnel had been decommissioned at the same time as the new power station had been built, and a new tunnel bored.

The tunnel was lined on both sides with large, asbestos-covered pipes, containing the old cables. The flooring was a rotting wooden walkway, with pools of water along it. But it was something else entirely that Tooth was staring at. A human skull, a short distance along the tunnel, greeted him with its rictus grin. Tooth stared back at it with some satisfaction. The twelve rats he had bought from pet shops around Sussex, then starved for five days, had done a good job: the Estonian merchant navy captain's uniform and his peaked, braided cap had gone, along with all of his flesh and hair. They'd even had a go at his sea boots. Most of his bones had fallen in on each other, or onto the floor, except for one set of arm bones and an intact skeletal hand, which hung from a metal pipe, held in place by a padlocked chain: Tooth hadn't wanted to risk the rats eating through his bindings and allowing the man to escape.

Tooth turned and helped the boy to sit upright, with his back propped against the wall, and a view ahead of him along the tunnel and of the bones and the skull. The boy was blinking and something looked different about him. Then Tooth realised what that was. His glasses were missing. He shone his flashlight around, saw them and replaced them on the boy's face.

The boy stared at him. Then flinched at the skeletal remains, his eyes registering horror and deepening fear as Tooth held the beam on it.

Tooth knelt and ripped the duct tape from the boy's mouth.

'You all right, kid?'

'Not really. Actually, no. I want to go home. I want my mum. I'm so thirsty. Who are you? What do you want?'

'You're very demanding,' Tooth said.

Tyler looked at the skeleton.

'He doesn't look too healthy to me,' Tooth said. 'What do you think?'

'Male, between fifty and sixty years old.'

Tooth frowned. 'You want to tell me how you know that?'

'I study archaeology. Can I have some water, please—and I'm hungry.'

'You're a goddamn smartass, right?'

'I'm just thirsty,' Tyler said. 'Why am I here? Who are you?'

'That guy,' Tooth said, pointing at the skeleton, 'he's been here for six years. No one knows about this place. No one's been here in six years. How would you feel about spending six years down here?'

'I wouldn't feel good about that,' Tyler said.

'I bet you wouldn't. I mean, who would, right?'

Tyler nodded in agreement. This guy seemed a little crazy, he realised. Crazy but maybe OK. Not a lot crazier than some of his teachers.

'What had that man done?'

'He ripped someone off,' Tooth said. 'OK?'

Tyler shrugged. 'OK,' he said, his voice a parched, frightened croak.

'I'll get you sorted, kid. You have to hang on. You and me, we have a big problem. It's to do with the tides, right?'

Tyler stared at him. Then he stared at the remains, shaking. Was this going to be him in six years?

'Tides?' he said.

The man pulled a folded printout from his rucksack, then opened it up.

'You understand these things, kid?'

He held the paper in front of Tyler's face, keeping his flashlight trained on it. The boy looked at it, then shot a glance at the man's wristwatch.

'Big ships can't come into this harbour two hours either side of low tide,' Tooth said. He stared at the boxes, each of which had a time written inside it, below the letters LW or HW. 'Seems like low tide was 11.31 p.m., but I'm not sure I've got that right. That would mean ships start coming in and out again after 1.31 a.m., right?'

'You're not looking at today's date,' Tyler said. 'Today it will be 2.06 a.m. Are you taking me on a boat?'

Tooth did not reply.

12

The phones in MIR-1 had been ringing off the hook ever since the Child Rescue Alert had been triggered, and the abduction of Tyler Chase was headline news. It was coming up to 12.30 a.m. During the nearly fourteen hours since his abduction, just about everyone in the nation who didn't live under a rock knew his name, and many of them had seen his photograph.

The room was as busy now as it was in the middle of the day, and the air was thick with the continuous ringing of landline and mobile phones. Roy Grace sat, jacket off, sleeves rolled up, tie slackened, reading through a list that had been emailed over by Detective Investigator Lanigan of the methods of operation of all known active contract killers. Not wanting to restrict their search to the US, police forces around Europe had also been contacted and their information was starting to come in. But there was nothing matching their man so far. Or his car.

In view of the frequency with which the suspect appeared to go about changing number plates, Grace had sent out requests to every police force in the UK to stop and search every dark-coloured Yaris, regardless of whether it was grey or not. He wanted to eliminate any possible risk of the suspect slipping through the net.

It was possible the boy was already abroad. There were private aircraft and private boats that could easily have slipped the net. But he was fairly certain that the Toyota Yaris belonging to Barry Simons was the one Tyler Chase had been driven in from the Regency Square car park. And if that was the case, Grace did not think he had left the Shoreham area.

Checks had been carried out with the Harbour Master, the Port Authority and the Coast Guard. All vessels that had sailed from Shoreham Harbour that day had been accounted for. No cargo ship had passed through the lock after eight o'clock that evening. A few fishing boats had gone out, but that was all.

Suddenly DS Moy called out, 'Sir, I have a Lynn Sebbage on the phone, from a firm of chartered surveyors called BLB. She's asking to speak to Norman Potting. Said she's tried his mobile but he's not picking up. She says she's been working through the night to look for the information he asked her for, and she thinks she's found it.'

Grace frowned. 'Where is DS Potting?'

'I think he may have gone out to get something to eat, sir.'

'OK, let me speak to the woman.'

He picked up the phone and, moments later, she was put through. 'Detective Superintendent Grace,' he said. 'Can I help you?'

'Yes,' she said. 'I'm a partner in BLB. We had a visit from Detective Sergeant Potting this afternoon, regarding the boy who's been abducted, saying he was looking for places round Shoreham Harbour where someone might be concealed. The port's chief engineer told him that he knew my firm has done a lot of work at the harbour over the past century, particularly in the construction of the original coal-fired power station. He said he thought there was a tunnel bored then that's been disused for decades.'

'What kind of a tunnel?' Grace asked.

'Well, I've been hunting through our archives all night and I think I've found what he was referring to. It's a tunnel that was built for the old power station, about seventy years ago, to carry the electricity cables under the harbour. It was decommissioned when the new power station was built twenty years ago.'

'How would someone other than a harbour worker know about it?'

'Anyone studying the history of the area could find it easily. It's probably on Google if people look hard enough.' She then explained where the access to it was.

A couple of minutes later, just as he hung up, Glenn Branson walked in.

'Want to take a ride? We could both do with a change of scenery.'

'Where to?' Branson asked.

'Somewhere in Brighton you and I have never been before.'

'Thanks for the offer, boss man, but being a tourist at one in the morning doesn't float my boat.'

'Don't worry. We're not going boating—we're going to go underwater.'

'Terrific. This is getting better every second. Scuba-diving?'

'No. Tunnelling.'

'Tunnelling? At this hour? You're not serious?'

Grace stood up. 'Get your coat and a torch.'

'I'm claustrophobic.'

'We can hold hands.'

'WHAT DO YOU THINK the chances are?' Glenn Branson said, as Grace drove along the road, looking for the building Lynn Sebbage had described. A strong wind buffeted the car and big spots of rain spattered the windscreen. 'One in a million? One in a billion that he's in this tunnel?'

'You're not trying to think like the perpetrator,' Grace said.

'Yeah, and that's just as well, 'cause I'd be hanging you on a meat hook and filming you right now if I did.'

Grace smiled. 'I don't think so. You'd be trying to outsmart us. How many times has he changed number plates? Those cameras he left behind, like giving us two fingers. This is a very smart guy.'

'You sound like you admire him.'

'I do admire him—for his professionalism. Everything else about him I loathe beyond words. If he's holed up anywhere with that kid, it's not going to be some garden shed. It's going to be somewhere he knows, that we haven't thought of. So I don't think we're looking at one in a million. I think we're looking at very good odds and we need to eliminate this place.'

'You could have sent a couple of uniforms along,' Branson said grumpily. 'Or Norman Potting.'

'And spoiled our fun?' Grace said, pulling over. 'This looks like it.'

Moments later, in the beam of his torch, Grace saw the broken padlock lying on the ground. He knelt and peered at it closely.

'It's been cut through,' he said.

He pulled the door open and led the way down the concrete steps. At the bottom they stepped onto a metal platform with a handrail. A network of old metal pipes spread out all around them.

Branson sniffed. 'Cigarette smoke,' he said.

Grace peered over the handrail, then shone his torch beam down the vertical shaft.

'Shit,' he said under his breath. It looked a long, long way down. Then he shouted, as loudly as he could, 'POLICE! Is anyone down there?'

His voice echoed. Then he repeated his question again.

Only the echo, falling into silence, came back at them.

The two officers looked at each other.

'Someone's been here,' Glenn Branson said.

'And might still be here,' Grace replied, peering down the shaft again, then looking at the ladder. 'And I'm sodding terrified of heights.'

'Me too,' Branson said.

'Heights and claustrophobia? Anything you're not scared of?' Grace quizzed him with a grin.

'Not much.'

'Shine the torch for me. I can see a rest platform about fifty feet down. I'll wait for you there.'

'What about Health and Safety?' Branson asked.

Grace tapped his chest. 'You're looking at him. You fall, I'll catch you.'

He climbed over the safety rail, decided he was not going to look down, gripped both sides of the rail, found the first rung and slowly, carefully, began to descend. It took them several minutes to get to the bottom.

'That was seriously not fun,' Glenn Branson said, as he flashed his torch around. The beam struck the tunnel.

'Holy shit!' He was staring at the skeletal remains. 'Looks like a new cold case to add to your workload, boss,' he said.

But Grace wasn't looking at the skull and bones. He was looking at a screwed-up ball of paper on the ground. He pulled on a pair of gloves, knelt, picked it up and opened it out. Then he frowned.

'What is it?' Branson said.

Grace held it up. 'A tide chart.'

'How long do you reckon that's been down here?'

'Not long,' Grace replied. 'It's current. This week's: seven days' tides for Shoreham, starting yesterday.'

'Why would someone want a tide chart?'

'The entrance to the harbour is only six feet deep at low tide. There's not enough draught for big ships two hours either side of low water.'

'You think this is connected with Tyler?'

Grace almost failed to spot the tiny object lying beneath a section of rusted piping. He knelt again and picked it up, carefully, between his gloved forefinger and thumb, then held it up.

'I do now, for sure,' he said. 'A Lucky Strike cigarette.' He pressed the burnt end to his cheek. 'You know what? That's still warm.'

Pulling on gloves himself, Glenn Branson took the tide chart and studied it for a moment. Then he checked his watch.

'The harbour mouth opens, if that's what they call it, at 2.06 a.m. That's fifty-six minutes' time. We have to stop any ship from leaving.'

This time, all his fear of heights forgotten, the detective sergeant threw himself up the first rungs of the ladder, with Grace inches behind.

TYLER, UTTERLY TERRIFIED, was whimpering with fear and quaking, yet at the same time did not dare struggle too much. Choppy, ink-black water splashed at him like some wild, angry creature just inches below his feet. Rain lashed down on him. He was hung by his arms, which were agonisingly outstretched as if in a crucifixion.

He had thought he was being thrown into the water but then he had been jerked tight just above it. He tried to cry out, but there was tape over his mouth again and his cries just echoed round and round inside his skull.

He was crying, sobbing, pleading for his mother.

There was a strong stench of seaweed. The blindfold the man had put round his head after he had climbed back up from the tunnel had been taken off only at the last minute before he had been dropped.

Above the sound of the water he heard a helicopter approaching. A dazzling beam of light passed over him, briefly, then darkness again.

Come over here! Come over here! I'm here! Come over here!

Please help me! Please help me. Mum, please help me, please.

IT WASN'T UNTIL they reached the top of the ladder that Grace and Branson were able to get any radio or phone signal. Grace immediately called Trevor Barnes, who was at his desk in Sussex House.

The two detectives then sprinted up the stone steps and out into the fresh wind and rain, sweating profusely, grateful for the cooling air. Above them they heard the clatter of the helicopter swooping low over the harbour basin, its searchlight illuminating a bright pool of choppy water.

Moments later, Barnes radioed back that he'd checked with the Harbour Master and the only vessel scheduled to leave the harbour, via the large lock, was the dredger the *Arco Dee*. It had already left its berth and was heading along the canal towards the lock.

'Trevor, get it boarded and searched while it's in the lock,' he instructed the Silver Commander. For some moments Grace stood still, following the helicopter's beam of light as it crossed Shoreham Power Station. The building had a dog-leg construction, with the first section, which had a flat roof, about sixty feet high, and then the main section about 100 feet high. At the western end was the solitary chimney, rising 200 feet into the sky.

Suddenly he thought he saw something move on the flat roof.

Instantly he radioed the controller. 'Patch me through to Hotel 900.'

Moments later, through a crackling connection, he was speaking to the helicopter spotter. 'Go back round. Light up the power station roof again,' he shouted.

Both detectives waited as the helicopter turned in a wide arc.

The beam struck the chimney first and the ladder that went all the way up it. Then the flat roof of the first section. They could see a figure scurrying across it, then ducking down behind a vent.

'Keep circling,' he instructed. 'There's someone up there!' He turned to Branson. 'I know the quick way there!'

They ran over to the car and jumped in. Grace switched on the blues and twos and raced out into the road.

'Call Silver,' he said. 'Get all available units to the power station.'

A quarter of a mile on he braked hard and swung left, in front of the Port Authority building, then sped down the slip road beside it, until they reached a barrier of tall steel spikes. The sign ahead of them, fixed to the spikes, read: SHOREHAM PORT AUTHORITY. NO UNAUTHORISED ACCESS. PUBLIC ROUTE ACROSS THE LOCKS.

Abandoning the car, they ran along the walkway, which was bounded on each side by a high railing. Grace flashed his torch beam ahead of them. To their right now he could see, brightly illuminated by a bank of floodlights on a tower, the harbour's two locks: a small one for fishing boats and yachts, the other, much larger, for tankers, dredgers and container ships.

A long quay separated the locks, in the middle of which was a substantial building housing the control room. On its wall, beneath the windows, was a vertical traffic light, with three red signals showing.

The gate to the quay had no lock on it, he observed, but his focus was to his left, to the massive superstructure of the power station, partially lit by the helicopter's beam. He ran on, followed by a puffing Branson, stepping over metal slats and then past more red warning lights, to the start of the curved walkway over the main lock gates. A sign cautioned against entering when the red lights were flashing and the siren sounding.

When he reached the join in the middle, between the two halves of the massive wooden lock gates, he turned and looked at the power station. What the hell was he doing up there, if it was the suspect? For sure it would be a terrific vantage point, but for what? Did he have the boy up there with him?

They ran on, round the curve of the other half of the lock gates and onto the quay, then sprinted towards the power station. Ahead, Grace saw a stack of pallets against the tall spikes of the power station's perimeter fence.

'Wait here,' he said to Branson, then scrambled up the pallets.

Having clambered over the top of the spikes, he dropped down ten feet or so to the other side. He landed with a painful jolt and lay there winded. Above, the helicopter clattered, the beam passing momentarily over him, illuminating the steel ladder up the side of the power station superstructure.

He ran to it and began to clamber up, the wind pulling at him as he climbed higher and higher. *This is crazy*, he thought. But he climbed on, gripping each rung tightly, clinging to it, the rain lashing him while the wind pulled at him harder and harder, as if it was on a mission to dislodge him. He clung to the rung, vertigo suddenly hitting him. *Don't let go. Hang on. Remember rule one of ladders. Always keep three limbs on and you can't fall off.*

Finally, he was at the top. He hauled himself over, onto the asphalt roof, and crawled forwards on his knees until he was safely away from the edge. He then stopped and crouched down, trying to get his breath back. He heard the sound of the helicopter and the beam momentarily turned the entire roof, and the wall of the next stage of the superstructure, into daylight.

Then he saw the camera. It was directly in front of him, on a squat metal tripod, the telephoto lens aimed down. He looked beyond it, for a brief instant, for the figure he had seen earlier, but there was no sign of the man. As the helicopter beam moved away, he ran to the camera, found the viewfinder and squinted through it.

Oh, no. Oh, no.

In eerie green night vision, in a tight close-up, he could see Tyler Chase. The boy was suspended across the middle of the lock gates, several feet below the top, his feet inches above the surface of the water. His arms were outstretched, his hands strapped to the left and right gates. A tiny flashing light indicated the camera was running in recording or transmitting mode.

And now, to his horror, he realised what that tide chart was all about.

He tried to raise Glenn on his radio but the channel was busy. Frustrated, he tried again. At the third attempt, with the helicopter right overhead, he heard his colleague's voice.

'Glenn!' he shouted. 'Stop the lock gates from opening! For Christ's sake, stop them! They're going to kill the boy! They're going to tear him in half!'

The din of the helicopter and wind and the rain, which was now pelting down, was deafening.

'Say that again?' Branson said. 'Can't hear you, boss.'

'STOP THE LOCK GATES FROM OPENING!' Grace screamed.

Then a blow on the back of his head sent him crashing to the ground.

He dimly heard a crackle, then a voice from his radio saying, 'Did you say stop the lock gates?'

He tried to stand up, but fell over, sideways. He lay there, feeling like he was going to throw up. Ahead, he saw a figure scramble over the lip of the roof and disappear. In the light beam of the helicopter hovering overhead again, he stared at the camera. In fury he rolled over towards it, into the base of the tripod, and sent it crashing over. He tried to stand again, but his legs gave way. In desperation, he hauled himself onto his hands and knees, looking round for his radio, but it had vanished.

He tried to stand again, but this time the wind blew him over. *No, no, no.* He got up again, virtually oblivious to the splitting pain in his head, and staggered across the roof. He grabbed the top rung of the ladder, then made the mistake of looking down. The whole world spun 360 degrees.

He had to do it. Had to. *Had* to. Gripping the top ladder posts, he swung his legs over the roof. The wind tried to push him over, backwards.

Don't look down.

He thought for an instant of Cleo. Of their unborn child. Of their life ahead. And of how, in the next few moments, he might plunge to his death. Was this worth it? Then he thought of the image of the boy, suspended by his arms from the lock gates. Anything that might save his life was worth it.

Half climbing, half sliding, he descended as fast as he could. Looking ahead all the time, never down. He still had his gloves on, he realised, and they protected his hands for a few seconds until the ladder cut through them, burning into his hands as he slid.

Then his feet hit the bottom and he tumbled over onto his back. He scrambled to his feet. Over to his right he could see the light on the bow of the *Arco Dee* dredger slipping steadily past the end of the power station. He saw red lights on the lock ahead, starting to flash. *No. No. No.*

He ran to the steel fence and realised, to his frustration, that he was trapped in there. It had been OK coming in, over the pallets, but it wasn't so easy to get back again. There was nothing to give him a leg-up now.

'Glenn!' he screamed, having no idea where he might be. 'Glenn!'

'I'm here, boss!' Branson shouted back, from, to Grace's immense relief, the other side of the fence.

'Give me a hand out of here!'

Moments later, Glenn was leaning over the top of the fence. Grace put one, two feet into the chain-links and hoisted himself up. Branson grabbed his outstretched hand and pulled. He scrambled over the top and onto the tarpaulin over the first pallet. As he jumped down on the ground, the front of the dredger was drawing level with them.

'Is anyone at the lock gate?' Grace yelled.

Branson shook his head.

'We have to stop it opening!'

Grace broke into a sprint, with Branson alongside him. As they ran, Grace could hear a cacophony of police sirens approaching. They raced down the quay and reached the entrance to the gate. Red lights were flashing and a klaxon was sounding loudly. As Grace stepped onto the lock walkway, he felt it vibrating. He continued running, the gate juddering harder and harder beneath him. Then he reached the join.

Suddenly the vibration stopped. The gates had paused. He looked down and saw the boy beneath him. The helicopter was right overhead, Tyler clearly illuminated like some grotesque crucifixion figurine, water swirling wildly beneath him. He was about to be torn in half at any second.

Grace clambered over the top of the gate. He could see one end of the rope, tied round a wooden peg just below the top, and he frantically pulled at it.

A wild froth of water was building up beneath him. The gates juddered, the gap widening, inch by inch.

BRANSON RAN ON, over to the far side, the gate juddering more and more. He threw himself over the metal plates, pushed open the unlocked gate and then ran towards the control room. As he did so, he suddenly felt something wrap round his legs and he hurtled, face down, to the ground.

ROY GRACE tugged again at the rope, which was getting tighter by the second. He could hear, above the roar of the helicopter and the wind and the rain and the klaxon, a muffled crying sound. Suddenly, an instant before the gates opened wider, the rope fell free.

The boy dropped down into the water and disappeared with a splash, as the gates parted, one of them swinging steadily away, out of sight to the left.

Grace dived into the mad, thrashing cold water. Bubbles exploded all around him. It was ten times colder than he had imagined. He burst back up to the surface, gulping air. In front of him, towering above him like a skyscraper, he saw the bow of the dredger, less than a couple of hundred yards away. He tried to swim, but the undertow dragged him back down. When he surfaced again, he was choking on vile, oily water. He spat it out, then, despite the weight of his clothes, he swam with all his strength across the width of the lock, to the far side, where he saw a rope hanging straight down into the water from the gate.

He grabbed it and pulled, pulled as hard as he could and, after a few moments, a dead weight surfaced. He cradled the boy's head in his arms, trying to pull the tape free from his mouth. They both went under, then came back up again, Grace coughing and spluttering.

'You're OK! You're OK!' he tried to reassure Tyler.

Then they went under again. They surfaced again. The dredger seemed to have stopped. They were bathed in a pool of light from the helicopter. The boy was thrashing, in wild panic. Grace struggled, kicking with his feet, trying to get a purchase on the weed that was growing on the lock gates, and at the same time hold the boy. He was shivering. He gripped a handful of weed and it held. The boy's head went under. He brought it back up again, then he clung on to the boy and the weed as hard as he could, his hand almost numb with cold.

GLENN BRANSON rolled over and saw a small man running towards the door of the control room. He scrambled to his feet, lunged after him and grabbed him just at he was pulling the door open. The man turned and punched him in the face, then ran off down the dock.

The wrong way, Branson realised, dazed, but not so badly he couldn't think straight. He stumbled after him, then blocked his path as the man tried to zigzag back past him, forcing him close to the edge of the quay. The man tried a feint, to dodge round him, but Branson grabbed him. The man aimed a punch at his face. Branson dodged the blow and swung his leg round in a classic kick-boxing manoeuvre, deadening the man's right leg. As he fell, Branson slammed a punch into the man's left kidney. He hadn't realised they were so close to the edge of the dock. The man plunged backwards, over the edge, and vanished beneath the surface of the maelstrom of water.

The helicopter beam momentarily swept over them. The man had disappeared. Then he heard a voice shouting.

'Hey! Glenn! Where the hell are you? Someone get us out of here! Come on! It's sodding freezing!'

13

It was the first really warm day of the year, with the thermometer in Brighton hitting seventy-five degrees, and the beaches of the city, along with its bars and cafés, were crowded. Roy Grace and Cleo returned home after a short walk, mindful of the instructions of the consultant gynaecologist that Cleo was not to do too much exercise.

Then they sat on the roof terrace of her house, Grace drinking a glass of rosé, and Cleo an elderflower cordial.

'So what happens next with Carly Chase? Your suspect is presumed drowned in Shoreham Harbour, and Tony Revere's mother is dead, right?'

'They're diving and dragging the harbour. But it's pretty murky down there. You can't see anything with underwater lights, so you have to do it all by sonar and feel. And there are some pretty strong currents. A body could get pulled out to sea very quickly.'

'What about Tony Revere's father?'

'I've spoken to Detective Investigator Lanigan in New York. The guy who could be the problem going forward is his wife's brother—the dead boy's uncle, Ricky Giordino. With his father, Sal, locked up in jail for the rest of his life, this guy would have been the one to watch. But Lanigan thinks Ricky will be following his old man to penitentiary very soon: they've got enough on him. We're going to continue with protection on Carly Chase and her family for a while, but I personally don't think the threat is as severe now.'

Cleo placed Roy's hand on her abdomen and said, 'Bump's busy today.'

He could feel their child moving around.

'Probably because you just ate a chocolate ice cream, right? You said he always becomes energetic when you eat chocolate.'

'He?' she said, quizzically.

He grinned. 'You're the one who keeps going on about all these old wives' tales, that if your baby's high up, or sticking out a lot, it's going to be a boy.'

She shrugged. 'We could easily find out.'

'Do you want to?' he asked.

'No. Do you? You didn't last time we discussed it.'

'I will love our child just as much whether it is a boy or a girl. I'll love it because it is our child.'

'Are you sure, Roy? You wouldn't want it to be a boy, so he could be an action man like my hero, Roy Grace? The man who's scared of heights who climbs power stations? The crap swimmer who dives into a harbour and saves a boy's life?'

Grace shrugged. 'I'm a copper. Sometimes in my job you can't make choices based on what you're afraid of or not. The day you do is the day you wake up and know you're in the wrong career.'

'You love it, don't you?'

'I didn't love climbing down that ladder into the tunnel. And I was shit-scared climbing up onto the power station roof. But at least young Tyler's going to be OK. And to see his mother's face when we took her to him at the hospital, where he was being checked over—that was something else. That's why I do this job. I can't think of any other job in the world where you could make a difference like that.'

'I can,' Cleo said, and kissed him on the forehead. 'It doesn't matter what job you did, you'd always make a difference. You're that kind of person. That's why I love you.'

'THE TIME IS 8.30 A.M., Wednesday, May the 12th,' Roy Grace read from his notes to his team in MIR-1. 'This is an update on Operation Violin. To bring you up to speed on the latest regarding the unknown suspect, missing, presumed drowned. One development yesterday was the recovery of a Toyota Yaris car from thirty feet of water at Aldrington Basin, close to the location where Ewan Preece was discovered in the white van. The vehicle bears the last known licence plates of the suspect. It is now undergoing intensive forensic examination.'

Duncan Crocker raised a hand. 'Chief, we haven't heard anything from Ford Prison regarding the death of Warren Tulley. Has there been any progress in that inquiry that could shed light on our suspect?'

Grace turned to Potting. 'Norman, do you have anything for us?'

'I spoke to the West Area Major Crime Branch Team this afternoon, guv, who are investigating. They are preparing to charge their original suspect, Tulley's fellow inmate, Lee Rogan.'

Grace thanked him, then went on, 'We are maintaining protection on Carly Chase and her family for the time being. I'm waiting for intelligence from the US that may help us to decide how long this should go on and in what form.'

This intelligence came sooner than Grace expected. As he left the briefing, his phone beeped, telling him he had a missed call and voicemail. It was from DI Lanigan. As soon as he got to his office, Grace called him back, mindful that it was the middle of the night in New York.

Lanigan answered immediately, seeming wide awake.

'Something strange going on here,' he said. 'Might be significant to you.'

'What's happened?'

'Well, it's not like I'm shedding any tears, you know. I think I told you, Ricky Giordino's the guy we reckon would have hired the guy who's been causing all your problems, right?'

'You did.'

'Well, I thought you should know, Ricky Giordino was found dead in his apartment a couple of hours ago. Pretty gruesome. Sounds like some kind of a hit. You know, wise guys on wise guys kind of thing. Strapped to his bed and, er, well . . . looks like he bled to death. Oh, and there's one other thing, which is why I thought you might be interested: the perp left a video camera running at the scene.'

peter james

How did the idea for *Dead Man's Grip* take shape?
The title came from a member of the Sussex Police Specialist Search Unit, much of whose work involves searches underwater. I was out with the team, and an officer told me about a car they had recovered from an icy river. The driver had drowned trying to get out, and was found with his hands on the top of the door frame, trying to push against the water pressure. He had classic Dead Man's Grip. Underwater, rigor mortis comes on far quicker than on land and, in some cases, it is instant. The grip is so hard they virtually have to break the fingers to release it.

And where did the Mafia element come from?
During the research for another Roy Grace novel, I befriended two NYPD detectives, both of whom had spent time busting the Mafia. After I had told them the plot of *Dead Man's Grip*, they looked at me in astonishment and one said, 'You know that actually happened, don't you?' I did not know. Some twenty years ago, the son of John Gotti, the New York Godfather, was out riding his bike, got hit by a drunk driver and died. Gotti's wife demanded that the driver be tortured and killed. They took me to the street where it happened and showed me the house where Gotti's widow still lives today.

You spend time each month with the Brighton police to keep your research sharp. What is that like?
I spend close to a day a week with the police, mostly in and around Brighton, but overseas, also. I find their world fascinating.

If you were ever to get a consequence-free chance to experience the criminal side of the tracks, what crime would you pick?
When I was at school I used to think about the perfect robbery, which would be tunneling into the Bank of England vaults over a weekend and stealing all the gold. I would definitely choose a crime that physically injured no one and could make me a fortune!

Tell us about real-life Detective Chief Superintendent David Gaylor of Sussex CID, on whom Roy Grace is based.
I was introduced to him years ago, when he was still a young detective. Surrounding his desk were crates full of bulging manila folders. I asked him if he was moving office and

he replied sardonically, 'No, these are my dead friends.' I thought for a moment that I had met a total weirdo, but he explained that, in addition to his homicide investigation work, he worked on cold cases. He told me, 'I am the last chance each of these victims has for justice, the last chance their families have for closure.' In his work he saw the most terrible sights, yet he retained a gentle humanity. It has turned out to be one of the key characteristics of almost every homicide detective I have met. They are calm, kind, very caring people, who often develop a close relationship with the victim's loved ones.

Why is Shoreham Harbour, where the climax of *Dead Man's Grip* takes place, one of your favourite sections of the city?

I fell in love with it when I was a child. I used to cycle there every weekend and roam the quayside. It was a wonderful, mysterious, romantic and sinister place with its own unique smells and characters—and with connections to places all over the world, indicated by flags flying from the ships berthed there. Plus, of course, it has had more than its fair share of murders over the years.

What have been the crowning moments of glory in your career?

The first time I saw my name on the top of the best-seller lists was, quite honestly, among the happiest moments of my life. But I had an even happier one: it was just an amazing feeling when I was awarded an honorary doctorate by the University of Brighton. I suppose, to some extent, given the less-than-spectacular exam results I got at school, I am living proof of Oscar Wilde's maxim that nothing that is worth knowing can be taught.

You've described yourself as a self-confessed, lifelong adrenaline junkie. How has that affected your life?

Well, I used to do ski racing when I was a kid. I was selected to train for the British Olympic ski team when I was fifteen, but my parents thought it would be too disruptive to my education. I got my first car at seventeen and, at eighteen, was banned for three and a half years for racing on a public highway. Two weeks after getting our licences back, the friend I raced with was killed in a crash. I sobered up my road driving after that. Now I race in the Britcar Endurance series on circuits mostly around the UK, such as the Grand Prix circuit at Silverstone. My long-suffering agent would rather I took up a safer sport, such as bowls . . .

Where do you love best, in the whole world, to relax?

The library of my home in Sussex. I go in there followed by the dogs, select a book, close the door, flop down on a sofa and read, surrounded by over a thousand volumes on the shelves—books I have read once, books I have read several times over, like *Brighton Rock*, and books I have promised myself I will read one day. For me, there is no greater joy than reading. As American writer S. J. Corbett said, 'Reading good books gives us a second life.'

One Summer
David Baldacci

When Lizzie's twin sister died as a child, her parents told Lizzie that she had gone to Heaven. Next to the house where they lived was an old lighthouse and Lizzie would go there to search the skies for her twin, with the help of the light. Now, more than twenty-five years since she was last there, Lizzie is making plans to return to her childhood home with her three children. For her husband Jack is dying—and Lizzie knows she may need to find comfort in the skies once again. But then fate deals this family one more mortal blow . . .

1

Jack Armstrong sat up in the secondhand hospital bed that had been wedged into a corner of the den in his home in Cleveland. A father at nineteen, he and his wife, Lizzie, had conceived their second child when he'd been home on leave from the army. Jack had been in the military for five years when the war in the Middle East had started. He'd survived his first tour in Afghanistan and earned a Purple Heart for taking one in the arm. After that he'd weathered several tours of duty in Iraq, one of which included the destruction of his Humvee while he was still inside. That injury had won him his second Purple. And he also had a Bronze Star for rescuing three ambushed grunts from his unit and nearly getting killed in the process. After all that, here he was, dying fast in his cheaply panelled den in Ohio's Rust Belt.

His goal was simple: just hang on until Christmas. He sucked greedily on the oxygen coming from the line in his nose. Before Thanksgiving, he was certain he could last another month. Now Jack was not sure he could make another day. But he would.

I have to.

In high school, the six-foot-two, good-looking Jack had excelled in three sports, quarterbacked the football team, and had his pick of the ladies. But from the first time he'd seen Elizabeth 'Lizzie' O'Toole, it had been all over for him in the falling-in-love department.

His mouth curled into a smile at the memory of seeing her for the first time. Her family had come from South Carolina, and Jack had wondered why the O'Tooles had moved to Cleveland, where there was no ocean, a lot less sun, a lot more snow and ice, and not a palm tree in sight. She'd come into class that first day, tall, with long auburn hair and vibrant green eyes, her face already mature and lovely. They had started going out together in high school and had never been separated since, except for Jack to fight in two wars.

'Jack? Jack, honey?'

Lizzie was crouched down in front of him. In her hand was a syringe. She was still beautiful, though there were dark circles under her eyes and worry lines on her face. The glow had gone from her skin. Jack was the one dying, but in a way, she was, too.

'It's time for your pain meds.'

He nodded, and she shot the drugs into an access line cut right below his collarbone. That way the medicine flowed directly into his bloodstream and started working faster. Fast was good when the pain felt like every nerve in his body was being incinerated.

After she had finished, Lizzie sat and hugged him. The doctors had a long name for what was wrong with him, one that Jack still could not pronounce or even spell. It was rare, they had said: one in a million. When he'd asked about his odds of survival, the docs had looked at each other before one finally answered.

'There's really nothing we can do. I'm sorry.'

'Do the things you've always wanted to do,' another had advised him, 'but never had the chance.'

'I have three kids and a mortgage,' Jack had shot back, reeling from this sudden death sentence. 'I don't have the luxury of filling out some end-of-life wish list.' Then he'd asked, 'How long?' though part of him didn't really want to know.

'You're young and strong. And the disease is in its early stages.'

Jack had survived the Taliban and Al-Qaeda. He could maybe hold on and see his oldest child graduate from college.

'So how long?' he'd asked again.

The doctor had said, 'Six months. Maybe eight if you're lucky.'

Jack did not feel very lucky.

He vividly remembered the morning he started feeling not quite right. It was an ache in his forearm and a stab of pain in his right leg. He was a building contractor, so aches and pains were to be expected. But things soon carried to a new level. His limbs would grow tired from three hours of physical labour as opposed to ten, and his balance began to deteriorate. And one morning he woke up and his lungs were filled with water. Everything had accelerated after that, as though his body had simply given way to whatever was invading it.

His youngest child, Jack Jr, whom everyone called Jackie, toddled in and climbed onto his dad's lap. Jackie's hair was long and black, curled up at the ends. His eyes were the colour of toast. Jackie had been their surprise. Their two other kids were much older.

Jack slowly slid his arm round his two-year-old son. Chubby fingers gripped his forearm, and warm breath touched his skin. It felt like the pierce of needles, but Jack simply gritted his teeth and didn't move his arm because there wouldn't be many more of these embraces. He slowly turned his head and looked out of the window, where the snow was steadily falling. It was truly beautiful.

He took his wife's hand.

'Christmas,' Jack said in a wheezy voice. 'I'll be there.'

'Promise?' said Lizzie, her voice beginning to crack.

'Promise.'

JACK AWOKE, looked round, and didn't know where he was. He could feel nothing; wasn't even sure if he was still breathing.

Am I dead? Is this it?

'Pop-pop,' said Jackie, as he slid next to his father on the bed. Jack stroked his son's soft, thick hair.

Lizzie walked in with more meds and shot them into the access line. An IV drip took care of Jack's nutrition and hydration needs. Solid foods were beyond him now.

'I just dropped the kids off at school,' she told him.

'Mikki?' said Jack.

Lizzie made a face. Their daughter, Michelle, would be turning sixteen next summer, and her rebellious streak had been going strong since she'd become a teenager. She was into playing her guitar, working on her music, and ignoring the books.

'At least she showed up for the math test. I suppose passing it would've been asking too much. On the bright side, she received an A in music theory.'

Jackie got down and ran into the other room. Jack watched him go with a mixture of pride and sorrow. He would never see his son as a man. He would never even see him start kindergarten.

Jack had always been a survivor. A rocky childhood and two wars had not done him in, so he had initially felt confident that despite the doctors' fatal verdict, his disease was beatable. As time went by, however, it had become clear that this battle was not winnable. It had reached a point where making the most of his time left was more important to him than trying to beat his head against an impenetrable wall. Most significantly, he wanted his kids' memories of his final days to be as positive as possible.

Before he'd become sick, Jack had talked to his daughter about making good life choices, about the importance of school. Nothing seemed to make a difference. There was a clear disconnect now between father and daughter. When she'd been a little girl, Mikki had wanted to be around him all the time. Now he rarely saw her. To her, it seemed to Jack, he might as well have been already dead.

'Mikki seems lost around me,' he said slowly.

Lizzie sat next to him, held his hand. 'She's scared and confused, honey. Some of it has to do with her age. Most of it has to do with . . .'

'Me.' Jack couldn't look at her when he made this admission.

'She and I have talked about it. Well, I talked and she didn't say much. She's a smart kid, but she doesn't understand why this is happening. And her defence mechanism is to detach herself.'

'I can understand,' said Jack.

She looked at him. 'Because of your dad?'

He nodded, remembering his father's painful death. He took a pull on the oxygen. 'If I could change things, I would, Lizzie.'

She wrapped her arms round his shoulders and kissed him. 'Jack, this is hard on everyone. But it's hardest on you. You have been so brave; no one could have handled—' She couldn't continue. Lizzie laid her head next to his and wept softly. Jack held her with what little strength he had left.

'I love you, Lizzie. Nothing will ever change that.'

He'd been sleeping in the hospital bed because he couldn't make it up the stairs, even with assistance. He'd fought against that the hardest, because as his life dwindled away, he had desperately wanted to feel Lizzie's warm body against his. It was another piece of his life taken from him, as though he was being dismantled, brick by brick.

After a few minutes, Lizzie composed herself. 'Cory is playing the Grinch in the class play on Christmas Eve, remember?'

Jack nodded. 'I remember.'

'I'll film it for you.'

Cory was the middle child, twelve years old and the ham in the family.

Lizzie smiled, then said, 'I've got a conference call, and then I'll be in the kitchen working, after I give Jackie his breakfast.'

She'd become a telecommuter when Jack had become ill. When she had to go out, a neighbour or Lizzie's parents would stop by to help.

After Lizzie left, Jack sat up, slowly reached under his pillow, and pulled out a calendar and pen. He looked at the dates in December, all of which had now been crossed out, up to December 20.

There was a knock at the door, and Sammy Duvall appeared. He was in his early sixties, with longish salt-and-pepper hair and a trim beard. Sammy was as tall as Jack, but leaner. He was tougher than anyone Jack had ever met. He'd spent twenty years in the military and fought in Vietnam, and done some things after that that he never talked about. A first-rate, self-taught carpenter and handyman, Sammy was the reason Jack had joined the service. After Jack had left the army, he and Sammy had started the contracting business. Lacking a family of his own, Sammy had adopted the Armstrongs.

Sammy looked over all the equipment helping to keep his friend alive. He shook his head slightly, and his mouth twitched. This was as close as stoic Sammy ever came to showing emotion.

'How's work?' Jack asked, and then took a pull of oxygen.

'No worries. Stuff's getting done and the money's coming in.'

Jack knew that Sammy had been completing all the jobs pretty much on his own, and then bringing all the payments to Lizzie. 'Half of that money is yours, Sammy.'

'I got my Uncle Sam pension, and it's more than I need.'

Sammy lived in a converted garage with his enormous Bernese mountain dog, Sam Jr. His needs were simple.

Sammy combed Jack's hair and even gave him a shave. Then the friends talked for a while. The rest of the time they sat in silence. Jack didn't mind; just being with Sammy made him feel better.

After Sammy left, Jack crossed out December 21, even though the day had just begun. He put the calendar and pen away.

And then it happened.

He couldn't breathe. He sat up, convulsing. He could feel his heart racing, his lungs squeezing, as the oxygen left his body.

'Pop-pop?'

Jack looked up to see his son holding the end of the oxygen line that attached to the converter in the next room. An alarm was sounding urgently.

'Jackie!'

A horrified Lizzie had appeared in the doorway, snatched the line from her son's hand, and rushed to reattach it to the converter. Oxygen started to flow into the line, and Jack fell back on the bed, breathing hard, trying to refill his lungs.

Lizzie raced past her youngest son and was by Jack's side in an instant. 'Oh my God, Jack.' Her whole body was trembling.

He held up his hand to show he was OK.

Lizzie whirled round and snapped, 'That was bad, Jackie, *bad.*'

Jackie's face crumbled, and he started to bawl.

She snatched him up and carried him out. The little boy reached his arms out to his father. His look was pleading.

'Pop-pop,' wailed Jackie.

The tears trickled down Jack's face as his son's cries faded away. But then Jack heard Lizzie sobbing.

Sometimes, Jack thought, *living is far harder than dying.*

JACK AWOKE from a nap late the next day to see his daughter opening the front door, guitar case in hand, ready to go out. He motioned to her to come and see him. She closed the door and trudged into his room.

Mikki had auburn hair like her mother's. However, she had dyed it several colours. He had no idea what it would be called now. She was shooting up in height, her legs long and slender, and her face was caught in that time thread that was firmly past the little-girl stage but not yet a woman. Where had the time gone?

'Yeah, Dad?' she said, not looking at him.

In truth, they didn't have much to talk about. Even when he'd been healthy, their lives had taken separate paths. *That was my fault*, he thought. *Not hers.*

'Your A.' He took a long breath, tried to smile.

She smirked. 'Right. Music theory. My only one.'

'Still an A.'

'Thanks for mentioning it.' She looked up, and said awkwardly, 'Look, Dad, I gotta go. People are waiting. We're rehearsing.'

She was in a band, Jack knew. 'OK, be careful.'

She turned to leave, then hesitated. She glanced back but didn't meet his gaze. 'Just so you know, I taped your oxygen line onto the converter so it can't be pulled off again. Jackie didn't know what he was doing. Mom didn't have to give him such a hard time.'

Jack gathered more oxygen and said, 'Thanks.' A part of him wanted her to look at him, and another part of him didn't. He didn't want to see pity in her eyes. 'Mikki?'

'Dad, I really got to go. I'm already late.'

'I hope you have a great . . . day, sweetie.'

He thought he saw her lips quiver for a moment, but then she left. A few moments later, the front door closed behind her.

After dinner that night, Cory, in full costume, performed his Grinch role for his father. Cory was a chunky twelve-year-old, though his long feet and lanky limbs promised height later. His hair was a mop of brown cowlicks, the same look Jack had had at that age.

Lizzie's parents had come over for dinner and had brought Lizzie's grandmother. Cecilia was a stylish lady in her eighties who used a walker. She'd grown up and lived most of her life in South Carolina. She'd come to live with her daughter in Cleveland after her husband died and her health started failing. She was dying, too, only not quite as fast as Jack. This probably would also be her last Christmas, but she had lived a good long life and had apparently made peace with her fate. She was upbeat. Yet every once in a while, Jack would catch her staring at him, and he could sense the sadness she held in her heart for his plight.

After Cory finished his performance, Cecilia leaned down and whispered into Jack's ear, 'It's Christmas. The time of miracles.' This was not the first time she'd said this. Yet for some reason Jack's spirits sparked for a moment.

But then the doctor's pronouncement sobered this feeling.

Six months. Maybe eight if you're lucky.

Later, when everyone was asleep, Jack reached under his pillow and took out his pen. He took out a piece of paper and began to write. It took him at least an hour to write less than one page. Eventually there would be seven of these letters. One for each day of the last week of his life. Each letter began with 'Dear Lizzie' and ended with 'Love, Jack'. In the body of the letter he did his best to convey to his wife all that he felt for her. That though he would no longer be alive, he would always be there for her.

These letters, he'd come to realise, were the most important thing he would ever do in his life. And he laboured to make sure every word was the right one. Finished, he put the letter in an envelope, marked it with a number, and slipped it in the nightstand.

He would write the seventh and last letter on Christmas Eve, after everyone had gone to bed.

2

Jack marked off December 24 on his calendar. He had one letter left to write. After he was gone, Jack hoped the letters would provide some comfort to Lizzie. Actually, writing them had provided some comfort for Jack. It made him focus on what was really important in life.

Jack's mother-in-law, Bonnie, had stayed with him while the rest of the family went to see Cory in the school play. Bonnie had settled down with a book, while Jack was perched in a chair by the window waiting for the van to pull up with Lizzie and the others.

Jack knew how close he was to the end. He had fought as hard as he could. He didn't want to leave his family, but he couldn't live like this either. His mind focused on the last letter he would ever compose. He knew when his pen had finished writing the words he could go peacefully.

He saw the headlights of the van flick across the window. Bonnie went to open the front door, and Jack watched as the kids piled out of the vehicle. Lizzie's dad, Fred, led them up the driveway, carrying Jackie because it was so slick out. Snow was coming down, although it was more ice than snow, making driving treacherous.

His gaze held on Lizzie as she closed the van and then turned, not towards the house, but away from it. Jack hadn't noticed the person approach her. The man came into focus; it was Bill Miller. They'd all gone to school together. Bill had attended Jack and Lizzie's wedding. Bill was single.

Jack saw Bill draw close to his wife. They were so close, Jack couldn't find a sliver of darkness between them. He watched Bill lean in towards Lizzie and his wife rise up on tiptoe. And then Bill staggered back as Lizzie slapped him across the face. He stumbled off into the darkness as she marched towards the house.

A minute later, Lizzie strode into the den, pulling off her scarf. Her face was flushed. 'Time for the presents; then Mom and Dad are going to take off. They'll be back tomorrow, OK, sweetie? It'll be a great day.'

'How's your hand?'

She glanced at him. 'What?'

He pointed to the window. 'Bill's lucky he's still conscious.'

'He was also drunk, or I don't think he would've tried that. Idiot.'

Jack started to say something but then stopped and looked away. Lizzie quickly picked up on this and sat next to him.

'Jack, you don't think that Bill and I—'

He gripped her hand. 'Of course not.' He kissed her cheek.

'So what then? Something's bothering you.'

'You need somebody in your life.'

'I don't want to talk about this.'

'Lizzie, look at me.'

She turned, her eyes glimmering with tears. 'Do we have to talk about this now? It's Christmas Eve.'

'I can't be picky about timing, Lizzie,' he said.

Her face flushed. 'I didn't mean that. I . . . you look better tonight. Maybe . . . the doctors—'

'No, Lizzie. No,' he said firmly. 'That can't happen. We're past that stage, honey.' He sucked on his air, his gaze resolutely on her.

She put a hand to her eyes. 'If I think about things like that, then it means, I don't want to . . . You might . . .'

He held her. 'Things will work out all right. Just take it slow. And be happy.' He made her look at him and managed a grin. 'And for God's sake, don't pick Bill.'

She laughed. And then it turned into a sob as he held her.

When they pulled away a few moments later, Lizzie wiped her nose with a tissue and said, 'I was actually thinking about next summer. And I wanted to talk to you about it.'

Jack's heart was buoyed by the fact that she still sought his opinion. 'What about it?'

'I was thinking I would take the kids to the Palace.'

'The Palace? You haven't been back there since—'

'I know. I just think it's time. It's in bad shape from what I heard. But just for one summer it should be fine.' She reached into her pocket and pulled out a photo. She showed it to Jack. 'Haven't looked at that in years. Do you remember me showing it to you?'

It was a photo of the O'Tooles when the kids were all little.

'That's Tillie next to you. Your twin sister.'

'Mom said she never could tell us apart.'

He said, 'She was five when she died?'

'Almost six. Meningitis. I remember my parents telling me that Tillie had gone to Heaven.' She smiled. 'There's an old lighthouse on the property down there. It was so beautiful.'

'I remember you telling me about it. Your grandmother still owns the Palace, right?'

'Yes. I was going to ask her if it would be all right if we went there this summer. I think leaving the Palace was because of me. I never really told you about this before, and maybe I'd forgotten it myself. But I've been thinking about Tillie lately.' She faltered.

'Lizzie, please tell me.'

She turned to face him. 'When my parents told me my sister had gone to Heaven, I wanted to find her. I didn't really understand that she was dead. I knew that Heaven was in the sky. So I started looking for Heaven to find Tillie. I would go up in the lighthouse. Back then it still worked. And I'd look for Heaven, for Tillie really, with the help of the light.' She paused. 'Never found either one.'

Jack held her. 'It's OK, Lizzie, it's OK,' he said softly.

She wiped her eyes on his shirt. 'It became a sort of obsession, I guess. I don't know why. But every day that went by and I couldn't find her, it hurt. And when I got older, my parents told me that Tillie was dead. It didn't help much.' She paused. 'I can't believe I never told you all this before. But I guess I was a little ashamed.'

His wife's distress was taking a toll on Jack. He breathed deeply before saying, 'You lost your twin. You were just a little kid.'

'By the time we moved to Ohio, I knew I would never find her by looking at the sky. I knew she was gone. And the lighthouse wasn't working any more anyway. It was just . . . silly.'

'It was what you were feeling, Lizzie.'

'I know. So I thought I'd go back there. See the place. Let the kids experience how I grew up.' She looked at him.

'Great idea,' Jack gasped.

She rubbed his shoulder. 'You might enjoy it, too. You could really fix the place up. Even make the lighthouse work again.' It was evident she desperately wanted to believe this could happen.

He attempted a smile. 'Yeah.'

The looks on both their faces were clear despite the hopeful words. Jack would never see the Palace.

LATER THAT NIGHT, Fred helped Jack into a wheelchair and rolled him into the living room, where their little tree stood. It was silver tinsel with blue and red ornaments. Jack usually got a real tree for Christmas, but not this year, of course.

The kids had hot chocolate and snacks. Mikki even played a few carols on her guitar. Cory told his dad about the play, and Lizzie played the DVD for Jack so he could see the performance. Finally his in-laws prepared to leave. The ice was getting worse, and they wanted to get home, they said. Lizzie's father helped Jack into bed.

At the door Lizzie gave them each a hug. Jack heard Bonnie tell her daughter to just hang in there.

'The kids are the most important thing,' said Fred. 'Afterwards, we'll be right here for you.'

Jack heard Lizzie say, 'I was thinking about talking to Cee,' referring to her grandmother Cecilia.

'About what?' Bonnie said quickly, in a wary tone.

'I was thinking of taking the kids to the Palace for the summer break. I wanted to make sure Cee would be OK with that.'

There was silence; then Bonnie said, 'Lizzie, you know—'

'Mom, Tillie's death was a long time ago,' Lizzie said quietly. 'It's different now. It's OK. I'm OK. I have been for a long time, actually.'

'It's never long enough,' her mother shot back.

'Let's not discuss it tonight,' said Lizzie.

After her parents left, Lizzie appeared in the doorway of the den. 'That was a nice Christmas Eve.'

Jack nodded his head, his gaze never leaving her face. 'Don't let her talk you out of going to the Palace, Lizzie. Stick to your guns.'

'My mother can be a little . . .'

'I know. But promise me you'll go?'

She nodded. 'OK, I promise. Do you need anything else?'

Jack looked at the clock and motioned to the access line below his collarbone, where his pain meds were administered.

'Oh my gosh. Your meds. OK.' She started to the small cabinet where she kept his medications, but then stopped. 'I forgot to pick up your prescription today. The play and . . .' She checked her watch. 'They're still open. I'll go get them now.'

'Don't go. I'm OK without the meds.'

'It'll just take a few minutes. I'll be back in no time.'

'Lizzie, you don't have to—'

But she was already gone. The front door slammed. The van started up and raced down the street.

Later Jack woke. He turned to find Mikki dozing in the chair next to his bed. He looked out of the window. There were streams of light whizzing past his house. Then he tried to sit up because he heard sounds on the roof. *Reindeer?* What the hell was going on?

The sounds came again. Only now he realised they weren't on the roof. Someone was pounding on the front door.

'Mom? Dad?' It was Cory. 'There's someone at the door.'

By now Mikki had woken. She looked at her dad. He was staring out at the swirl of lights. He pointed at the front door.

Looking scared, she hurried to the door and opened it. The man was big and dressed in a uniform. He looked uncomfortable.

'Is your dad home?' he asked Mikki. She backed away and pointed towards the den. The police officer stamped the snow off his boots and stepped in. He walked to where Mikki was pointing, saw Jack in the bed with the lines hooked to him, and asked, 'Can he understand? I mean, is he real sick?'

Mikki said, 'He's sick, but he can understand.'

The cop drew next to the bed. Jack lifted himself up on his elbows. He was gasping in his anxiety.

The officer swallowed hard. 'Mr Armstrong?' He paused. 'I'm afraid there's been an accident involving your wife.'

JACK SAT STRAPPED into a wheelchair, staring at his wife's coffin. Mikki and Cory sat next to him. Jackie had been deemed too young to attend his mother's funeral; he was being taken care of by a neighbour.

The weather was cold, the roads still iced and treacherous. They'd been driven to the cemetery in the funeral home sedan. Lizzie's father, Fred, rode up front, while he and the kids were in the back with Bonnie. She had barely uttered a word since learning her youngest daughter had been instantly killed when her van ran a red light and was broadsided by an oncoming snowplough.

The graveside service was mercifully brief.

Jack looked over at Mikki. She'd pinned her hair back and put on a black dress; she sat staring vacantly at the coffin. Cory had not looked at the casket even once.

As a final act, Jack was wheeled up to the coffin. He put his hand on top of it and mumbled a few words. He had played this scene out in his head a hundred times. Only he was in the box and it was Lizzie saying goodbye.

'I'll be with you soon,' he said in a halting voice. As he started to collapse, a strong hand gripped him. 'It's OK, Jack. We'll get you to the car now.' He looked up into the face of Sammy Duvall.

Sammy manoeuvred him to the sedan and put a reassuring hand on Jack's shoulder. 'I'll always be there for you, buddy.'

They were driven home, the absence of Lizzie in their midst a festering wound. Jackie was brought home, and people stopped by with plates of food. An impromptu wake was held. More than once, Jack caught people gazing at him, no doubt thinking, *My God, what now?*

Jack was thinking the same thing.

Two hours later the house was empty except for Jack, the kids and his in-laws. The children instantly disappeared. Minutes later, Jack could hear guitar strumming coming from Mikki's bedroom.

Bonnie and Fred O'Toole looked as disoriented as Jack felt. They had signed on to help their daughter transition with her kids to being a widow and then getting on with her life. Without the buffer that Lizzie had been, Jack could focus now on the fact that his relationship with his in-laws had been largely superficial.

Fred helped Jack get into bed; then he and Bonnie went up to Jack and Lizzie's room. They would be staying until other arrangements were made.

Jack lay in the dark staring at the ceiling. The days after Lizzie had died had been far worse than when he'd received his own death sentence. His life ending he'd accepted. Hers he had not. Could not. Mikki and Cory had barely spoken since the police officer had come with the awful news. Jackie had wandered the house looking for his mother and crying when he couldn't find her.

Jack slid open the drawer of the nightstand and took out the six letters. He obviously had not written one on Christmas Eve. In these pages he had poured out his heart to the person he cherished above all others.

Jack rarely cried. He'd seen fellow soldiers die horribly in the Middle East, watched his father perish from lung cancer, and attended the funeral of his wife. Now, staring at the ceiling, thinking a thousand anguished thoughts, he wept as it finally struck him that Lizzie was really gone.

THE NEXT MORNING, Bonnie took charge. She came to see Jack with Fred in tow. 'This won't be easy, Jack,' she cautioned. She squared her shoulders. 'The children, of course, come first. I've talked to Becky and also to Frances several times.'

Frances and Becky were Lizzie's older sisters, who lived on the West Coast. The only brother, Fred Jr, was on active military duty, stationed in Korea. He had not been able to make it to the funeral.

'Becky can take Jack Jr, and Frances has agreed to take Cory. That just leaves Michelle.' Bonnie had never called her Mikki.

'*Just* Michelle?' said Jack.

Bonnie looked taken aback. When she spoke, her tone was less authoritative. 'This is hard on all of us. You know Fred and I had planned to move to Arizona next year after things were more settled with Lizzie and the kids. We were going this year, but then you got sick. And we stayed on. We tried to do our best, for all of you.'

'We couldn't have carried on without you.'

This remark seemed to please her, and she smiled and gripped his hand. 'Thank you. That means a lot.' She continued. 'We'll take Michelle with us. And because Jack Jr will be in Portland with Becky, and Cory in LA with Frances, they will all at least be on or near the West Coast. I'm sure they'll see each other fairly often. It's really the only workable solution that I can see.'

'When?' Jack asked.

'The Christmas break is almost over, and we think we can get all the kids transitioned in the next month.'

Jack touched his chest. 'And me?'

'Yes, well . . . I was getting to that.' She stood but didn't look at him. 'Hospice. I'll arrange all the details.' Now she looked at him, and Jack had to admit she didn't look happy. 'If we could take care of you, Jack, we would. But we're not young any more, and . . .'

Jack drew a long breath. He said, '*My* kids, *my* decision.'

Bonnie said, 'You can't care for the kids. You can't even take care of yourself. Lizzie did everything. And now she's gone.'

'Still my decision,' he said defiantly. He had no idea where he was going with this, but the words had tumbled from his mouth.

'Who else will take three kids? If we do nothing, they'll go into foster care. They'll probably never see each other again. Is that what you want?'

He sucked in some more air, his resolve weakening along with his energy. 'Why can't I stay here?' he said. Another long inhalation. 'Until the kids leave?'

'Hospice is much cheaper. I'm sorry if that sounds callous, but money is tight. Tough decisions have to be made.'

'So I die alone?'

Fred said, 'Doesn't seem right, Bonnie. Taking the family away like that. After all that's happened.'

Jack shot him an appreciative look.

Bonnie sighed. 'Jack, I'm not trying to be heartless.' She paused. 'But they just lost their mother.' Bonnie paused but didn't continue.

It slowly dawned on Jack what she was getting at.

'And to see me die, too. . .'

Bonnie spread her hands. 'But you're right. You are their father. You tell me what to do, Jack, and I'll do it. We can keep the kids here until . . . until you pass. They can be with you until the end.'

Fred added, 'Anything you want, Jack, we'll take care of it.'

Jack was silent for so long that Bonnie finally rose and said, 'Fine, we can have an in-home nursing service come. Lizzie had some life insurance. We can use those funds to—'

'Take the kids.'

Fred and Bonnie looked at him. Jack said again, 'Take the kids.'

'Are you sure?' asked Bonnie.

He struggled to say, 'As soon as you can.' *It won't be long,* Jack thought. *Not now. Not with Lizzie gone.*

As she turned to leave, Bonnie froze. Mikki and Cory were standing there. Bonnie said, 'I thought you were upstairs.'

'You don't think this concerns us?' Mikki said bluntly.

Bonnie said, 'Michelle, this is hard on all of us. We're just trying to do the best we can under the circumstances.' She paused and added, 'You lost your mother and I lost my daughter.' Bonnie's voice cracked as she added, 'None of this is easy, honey.'

Mikki gazed over at her father. He could feel the anger emanating from his oldest child. 'You're all losers!' yelled Mikki. She turned and rushed from the house, slamming the door behind her.

Bonnie shook her head before looking back at Jack. 'This is a big sacrifice, for all of us.' She left the room, with Fred obediently trailing her. Cory just stood there staring at his dad.

'Cor,' Jack began. But his son turned and ran back upstairs.

A minute went by as Jack lay there, feeling like a turtle toppled on its back. 'Jack?'

When he looked over, Bonnie was standing a few feet from his bed holding something in her hand.

'The police dropped this off yesterday.' She held it up. It was the bag with Jack's prescription meds. 'It was in the van. It was unfortunate that Lizzie had to go back out that night. If she hadn't, she'd obviously be alive today.'

'I told her not to go.'

'But she did. For you,' she replied, tears starting to slide down her cheeks as she hurried from the room.

3

The room was small but clean. That wasn't the problem. Jack had slept for months inside a shack with ten other infantrymen in the middle of a desert. What Jack didn't like in the hospice were the sounds. Folks during their last days of life did not make pleasant noises. Coughs, gagging, painful cries—but mostly it was the moaning. Then there was the squeak of the gurney wheels as the body of someone who had passed was taken away.

Jack reached under his pillow and pulled out the calendar. It was January 11. He crossed the date off. He had been there five days. The average length of stay here, he'd heard, was three weeks. Without Lizzie, it would be three weeks too long.

He again reached under his pillow and pulled out the six letters to Lizzie.

These letters now constituted a weight round his heart: Lizzie would never read them, would never know what he was feeling in his last days of life. At the same time, it was the only thing allowing him to die in peace. He put the letters away and just lay there.

He turned his head when the kids came in. He was surprised to see Cecilia stroll in with her walker. It was hard for her to go out in the cold weather, yet she had done so for Jack.

Jackie immediately climbed up on his dad's lap, while Cory sat on the bed. Arms folded defiantly over her chest, Mikki stood by the door, as far away from everyone as she could be. Her hair was now orange. The colour contrasted with the dark circles under her eyes.

Cory had been saying something that only now Jack focused on. His son said, 'But Dad, you'll be here and we'll be way out there.'

'That's the way *Dad* apparently wants it,' said Mikki sharply.

Jack turned to look at her. Father's and daughter's gazes locked until she finally looked away, with an eye roll tacked on.

Cory moved closer to him. 'Look, I think the best thing we can do, Dad, is stay here with you. It just makes sense.'

Jack said, 'You have to go, Cor.' He didn't look at Mikki when he added, 'You all do.'

'But we won't be together, Dad,' said Cory. 'We'll never see each other.'

Cecilia quietly spoke up. 'I give you my word, Cory, that you will see your brother and sister early and often.'

Mikki came forward, her sullen look replaced with a defiant one. 'OK, but what about Dad? He just stays here alone?'

Jack said, 'I'll be with you. And your mom will, too, in spirit.'

'Mom is dead. She can't be with anyone,' snapped Mikki.

'Mikki,' said Cecilia reproachfully. 'That's not necessary.'

'Well, it's true. We don't need to be lied to. It's bad enough that I have to go and live with *them* in Arizona.'

Cory started to sob quietly. Jack pulled him close.

The visit lasted another half-hour. Cecilia was the last to leave. She rose from her seat by the edge of his bed. 'You'll never be alone, Jack. We all carry each other in our hearts.'

The words were nice, and heartfelt, he knew, but Jack Armstrong had never felt so alone as he did now. He had a question, though. 'Cecilia?'

'Yes, Jack?'

Jack gathered his breath and said, 'Lizzie told me she wanted to take the kids to the Palace next summer.'

'The Palace? After all this time?'

'I know. But maybe . . . maybe the kids could go there sometime?'

Cecilia gripped his hand. 'I'll see to it, Jack. I promise.'

THEY ALL CAME IN to visit Jack for the last time. They would be flying out later that day to their new homes.

Jack was lying in bed. His face and body were gaunt; the machines keeping him comfortable were going full blast. He looked at each of his kids for what he knew would be the final time. He'd already instructed Bonnie to have him cremated. 'No funeral,' he'd told her. 'I'm not putting the kids through that again.'

'I'll call you as soon as I get there, Dad,' said Cory.

'Me, too!' chimed in Jackie.

Jack prepared to do what had to be done. His kids would be gone for ever in a few minutes, and he was determined to make these last moments as memorable and happy as possible.

'Got something for you,' said Jack. He had three boxes. He handed one to Cory and one to Jackie. He held the last one and gazed at Mikki. 'For you.'

'What is it?' she asked, trying to seem disinterested.

'Open them,' said Jack.

Cory and Jackie opened the boxes and looked down at the pieces of metal with the purple ribbons attached.

Mikki's was different.

Fred said, 'That's a Bronze Star. That's for heroism in combat. Your dad was a real hero. The other ones are Purple Hearts for being hurt in battle,' he finished.

Jack said, 'Open the box and think of me. Always be with you that way.'

Even Bonnie seemed genuinely moved by this gesture. But Jack wasn't looking at her. He was watching his daughter. She touched the medal carefully, and her mouth started to tremble. When she looked up and saw her dad watching her, she closed the box and quickly stuck it in her bag.

After they left, Jack lay there. His last ties to his family had been severed. It was over. His hand moved to the call button. It was time now. He had pre-arranged this with the doctor. The machines keeping him alive would be turned off. All he wanted now was to see Lizzie. 'It's time, Lizzie,' he said.

However, his hand moved away from the button when Mikki came back into the room and held up the medal. 'I just wanted to say that . . . that this was pretty cool.'

Father and daughter gazed awkwardly at each other, as though they were two long-lost friends reunited by chance. There was something in her eyes that Jack had not seen for a long time.

'Mikki?' he said, his voice cracking.

She ran across the room and hugged him. Her warm breath burned against his cold neck, warming him, sending packets of energy, of strength, to all corners of his body. He squeezed back, as hard as his wasted body would allow.

She said, 'I love you so much. So much.' Her body shook with the pain, the trauma of a child soon to be orphaned. She stood up. 'Goodbye, Daddy.' She turned and rushed from the room.

'Goodbye, Michelle,' Jack mumbled to the empty room.

JACK LAY FOR HOURS, until day evaporated to night. Something was burning in his chest that he could not identify. His thoughts were focused on his last embrace with his daughter, her unspoken plea for him not to leave her. With the end of his life, with his last breath, the Armstrong children would be without parents. His finger had hovered over the nurse's call button all day, ready to summon the doctor, to let it be over. But he never pushed it.

As the clock ticked, the burn in Jack's chest continued to grow. It wasn't painful; indeed, it warmed his throat, his arms, his legs, his feet, his hands. And still his mind focused only on his daughter.

The nurses came and went. The clock ticked; the air continued to pour into him. At midnight Jack started feeling odd. His lungs were straining, as they had been when Jackie had pulled the line out of the converter at home. *This might be it,* Jack thought.

He took another deep breath, and then another. His lungs were definitely weakening. He could not drive enough oxygen into them to sustain life. He reached up and fiddled with the line in his nose. That's when he realised what the problem was. There was no airflow. He clicked on the bed light. The line had come loose from the wall. He was about to press the call button but decided to see if he could push the line back in himself. That's when it struck him.

How long have I been breathing on my own?

He glanced at the vitals monitor. The alarm hadn't gone off, though it should have. But as he gazed at the oxygen levels, he realised why. His oxygen levels hadn't dropped. *How was that possible?*

He managed to push the line back in and took several breaths. Then he pulled the line out of his nose and breathed on his own for as long as he could. Ten minutes later, when his lungs started to labour, he put the line back in.

Over the next two hours, he kept pulling the line out and breathing on his own until he was up to breathing unaided for fifteen minutes. His lungs normally felt like sacks of wet cement. Now they felt halfway normal.

At 3 a.m. he sat up and did the unthinkable. He released the side rail on the bed and swung round so his feet dangled over the side of the bed. He inched forwards until his toes touched the floor. Straining with effort, little by little, Jack pushed himself up until most of his weight was supported by his legs. He could hold himself up for only a few seconds before collapsing back onto the sheets. Panting with the exertion, pain searing his weakened lungs, he repeated the movement twice more. Every muscle in his body was spasming from the strain, yet as the sweat cooled on his forehead, Jack smiled—for good reason.

He had just stood using his own power for the first time in months.

The next morning, he edged to the side of the bed again. But then his hands slipped and he crumpled to the floor. At first he panicked. Then the same methodical, practical nature that had carried him safely through Iraq and Afghanistan came back to him.

He grabbed the edge of the bed, tightened his grip, and pulled. His emaciated body strained and jerked until he was fully back on the bed. He lay there in quiet triumph, sweat staining his gown.

That night, he half walked and half crawled to the bathroom and looked at himself in the mirror. It was not a pretty sight. He looked eighty-four instead of thirty-four. But as he continued to gaze in the mirror, a familiar voice sounded in his head.

You can do this, Jack.

He looked round, but he was alone.

You can do this, honey.

It was Lizzie. It couldn't be, of course, but it was.

He closed his eyes. 'Can I?' he asked.

Yes, she said. *You have to, Jack. For the children.*

Jack crawled back to his bed and lay there. Had Lizzie really spoken to him? He didn't know. Part of him knew it was impossible. But what was happening to him seemed impossible, too.

The next night, as the clock hit midnight, Jack lifted himself off the bed and slowly walked round the room. He felt stronger, his lungs operating somewhat normally. It was as though his body was healing itself minute by minute. He realised that he was hungry. And he didn't want liquid pouring into a line. He wanted real food. Food that required teeth to consume.

This is a miracle.

TWO WEEKS PASSED, and Jack celebrated the week of his thirty-fifth birthday by gaining four pounds and doing away with the oxygen altogether. Miracle or not, he still had a long way to go. He had to rebuild his strength and put on weight.

Things that Jack, along with most people, had always taken for granted represented small but significant victories in his improbable recovery: holding a fork and using it to put solid food into his mouth; washing his face; using a toilet instead of a bedpan; touching his toes; and breathing on his own.

Jack talked to his kids every chance he got. Jackie was bubbly and mostly incoherent. But Jack could sense that the older kids were wondering what was going on.

Cory said, 'Dad, can't you come live with us?'

'We'll see, buddy. Let's just take it slow.'

With the help of the folks at the hospice, Jack was able to use Skype to see his kids on a laptop. Cory and Jackie were thrilled to see their dad looking better. Mikki was more subdued and cautious, but Jack could tell she was curious. And hopeful.

'Does this mean?' She stopped. 'I mean, will you . . .'

Jack's real fear, even though he did believe he was experiencing a true miracle, was that his recovery might be temporary. He did not want to put his kids through this nightmare again. But that didn't mean he couldn't talk to them. Or see them.

'I don't know, honey. I'm trying to figure that out.'

'Well, keep doing what you're doing,' she replied.

And then she smiled at him.

One time, Bonnie had appeared on the computer screen after Mikki had left the room. She had stared at Jack sitting up in bed. 'What is going on?'

'I'm still here.'

'Your hospice doctor won't talk to me. Privacy laws, he said.'

'I know,' Jack said. 'But I can fill you in. I'm feeling better. Getting stronger. How're things working out with Mikki?'

'Fine. She's settled in, but we need to address *your* situation.'

'I *am* addressing it. Every day.'

And so it had gone, day after day, week after week. Using Skype and the phone and answering all the kids' questions, Jack could see that even Mikki was coming to grips with what was happening. Every time he saw her smile or heard her laugh at some funny remark he made, it seemed to strengthen him even more.

It was on a cold, blustery Monday morning in February that Jack walked down the hall under his own power. He'd gained five more pounds, and his face had filled out. His appetite had returned, and they had stopped giving him pain meds because there was no more pain.

The hospice doctor came to see him at the end of the week. 'I'm not sure what's going on here, but I'm ordering some new blood work and other tests. I don't want you to get your hopes up, though. If this continues, that's terrific. But your disease is a complicated one. And always a fatal one. This might be a false remission.'

'Have others in my condition had a remission?'

The doctor looked taken aback. 'No, not to my knowledge. But I have to tell you that what's happening to you is medically impossible.'

'Medicine is not everything.'

The doctor saw the new muscle and the eyes that burned with intensity. 'Why do you think this is happening to you, Jack?'

Jack reached into his nightstand drawer, pulled out a photo, and passed it to the doctor. It was a photo of Lizzie and the kids. 'Because of them.'

'But I thought your wife passed away.'

Jack shook his head. 'Doesn't matter. When you love someone, you love them forever.'

TWO DAYS LATER, Jack was in his room eating a full meal. The doctor walked in and perched on the edge of the bed.

'OK, I officially believe in miracles. Your blood work came back negative. No trace of the disease. It's like something came along and chased it away. Never seen anything like it.'

Jack saw his kids that night on the computer. He believed he actually made Jackie understand that he was getting better. At least his son's last words had been, 'Daddy's boo-boo's gone.'

Cory had blurted out, 'When are you coming to see me?'

'I hope soon, big guy. I'll let you know. I've still got a way to go. But I'm getting there.'

Mikki's reaction surprised him, and not in a good way.

'Is this some kind of trick?' she asked.

Jack slowly sat up in his chair as he stared at her. 'Trick?'

'When we left you, Dad, you were dying. You said goodbye to all of us. You made me come and live with Gramps and *her*!'

'Honey, it's no trick. I'm getting better.'

She suddenly dissolved into tears. 'Well, then, will you be coming to take us home? Because I hate it here.'

'I'm doing my best, sweetie. With a little more time, I think—'

But Mikki hit a key and the computer screen went black.

I'm coming, Mikki. Dad's coming for you.

A WEEK LATER he weighed over one-sixty and was walking the halls for an hour at a time.

Jack stared at himself in the mirror. He looked more like himself now. He walked slowly to the window and looked outside at a landscape that was still more in the grips of winter than spring, though that season was not too far off.

He went to his nightstand and pulled out the letters. He selected the envelope with the number '1' on it and slid the paper out. The letter was dated December 18 and represented the first one he'd written.

Dear Lizzie,

There are things I want to say to you that I just don't have the breath for any more. That's why I've decided to write these letters. I want you to have them after I'm gone. When I was healthy, you made me happier than any person has a right to be. You gave me three beautiful children, which is a greater gift than I deserved. I tell you this, though you already know it, because sometimes people don't talk about these things enough. I will never understand why I had to be taken from you so soon, but I have accepted it. I loved you from the moment I saw you. The happiest day of my life was when you agreed to share your life with mine. I promised that I would always be there for you. I will never stop loving you. Not even death is powerful enough to overcome my feelings for you. My love for you is stronger than anything.

Love,
Jack

He put the letter back in the envelope and replaced the packet in the drawer. He slipped a photo from the pocket of his robe and looked at it. His family smiled back at him. He thought of all the others in this place who would never leave it alive. He had been spared. *Why me?*

Jack had no ready answer. But he did know one thing. He was not going to waste a second chance at living.

A FEW DAYS LATER, Jack Armstrong was discharged from the hospice and sent to a rehab facility. He rode over in a shuttle van. The driver was an older guy. Jack was his only passenger.

As they drove, Jack stared out in childlike wonder at things he never thought he would experience again. Seeing a bird in flight. A mailman delivering letters. A kid running for the school bus. He promised himself he would never again take anything for granted.

As they pulled up in front of the rehab building, the man said, 'Never brought anybody from that place to this place.'

'I guess not,' said Jack. He held his small duffel bag. Inside were a few clothes, a pair of tennis shoes, and the letters he'd written to Lizzie.

When he got to his room, he looked round at the simple furnishings and single window that had a view of the interior outdoor courtyard, which was covered in snow. Jack sat on the bed after putting his few belongings away.

He looked up when a familiar person walked into the room.

'Sammy? What are you doing here?'

Sammy Duvall was dressed in grey sweats. 'Why the hell do you think I'm here? To get your sorry butt in shape. Look at you.'

'I don't understand. You didn't come by the hospice.'

The mirth left Sammy's eyes, and he sat down next to Jack on the bed. 'I let you down.'

'What are you talking about? You've done everything for me.'

'No, I haven't. I told you at the cemetery that I'd always be there for you, but I wasn't.' Sammy's voice trembled. 'I should've come to see you, boy. But . . . seeing you in that place . . .'

'It's OK, Sammy. I understand.'

'Anyway, I'm here now. And you're gonna wish I wasn't.'

'Why?'

'I'm your drill instructor. Worked a deal with the folks here.'

'How'd you do that?'

'Told 'em you were a special case. And you need special treatment. And if you're OK with it, so are they.'

'I'm definitely OK with it.'

THE WEEKS WENT BY swiftly. And with pain. Much pain.

The sweat streaming off him during one arduous workout, Jack told Sammy, 'I can't do one more damn push-up. I can't!'

'Can't or won't? 'Cause that's all the difference in the world.'

Jack did one more push-up and then another and then a third, until he could no longer feel his arms. Jack had gone on to pump thousands of pounds of weights, run on the treadmill, and jump rope until his knees failed. He cursed at Sammy, who laughed at him and goaded him into doing more and more. On and on it went. But Jack was growing stronger with every rep.

He talked to his kids every day. They knew he was in rehab. They knew he was getting stronger. On one joint Skype session, Jack showed Cory and Jackie his muscles.

'You're ripped, Dad,' said Cory.

'Whipped,' crowed Jackie.

Later that night he saw Mikki. She hadn't agreed to do a Skype session with him in a while.

'You look great, Dad,' she said slowly. 'You really do.'

'You look thin,' he replied.

'Yeah, well, Grandma is watching her weight, which means we all eat like birds.'

'Cheeseburger's on me.'

'When?' she said, quickly.

'Sooner than you think, sweetie. I probably should have come out to see you before now. And I miss you more than anything. But . . . but I want to do this right. When I was in the army and we'd go on patrol, I always analysed everything. Some of the guys liked to wing it. And sometimes in combat you have to do that. But being prepared because you've done your homework is the best way to survive. I hope you understand. I want to do this right. For all of you.'

'I get it, Dad.'

Finally, the day came on a warm spring morning. Jack's bag was packed. Sammy came into the room. 'It's time.'

While his discharge papers were being finalised, Jack sat in a chair outside the rehab office. He looked out of the window, where winter had finally passed and spring had arrived. Crocuses were pushing through the earth. *The world is waking up from a long winter's nap, and so am I.* He opened his duffel bag and pulled out an envelope with the number '2' on it. He slid out the letter.

Dear Lizzie,

Christmas will be here in five days, and I promise I will make it. I've never broken a promise to you, and I never will.

It's hard to say goodbye. Jackie's growing up so fast, and I know he probably won't remember his dad, but I know I will live on in your memories. Tell him his dad loved him. I know he will have a great life.

Cory is a special boy. He has your sensitivity, your compassion. I know what's happening to me is probably affecting him the most of all the kids. He came and got into bed with me last night. He asked if it hurt very much. I told him it didn't. He told me to say hello to God when I saw him. And I promised that I would.

And Mikki. She is the most complicated of all. Not a little girl any more but not yet an adult. She is smart and caring and she loves her brothers. She loves you, though she sometimes doesn't like to show it. My greatest regret is letting her grow away from me. It was my fault, not hers. After I'm gone, please tell her the first time I ever saw her, when I got back from Afghanistan, there was no prouder father who ever lived. Looking down at her tiny face, I felt the purest joy a human could possibly feel. I wanted to protect her and never let anything bad happen to her. Life doesn't work that way, of course. Tell her that her dad was her biggest fan. And that whatever she does, I will always be her biggest fan.

Love,

Jack

AFTER BEING DISCHARGED, Jack rode with Sammy to his house. Along the way, he asked his friend to pass by his old home. Jack was surprised to see his pickup truck in the carport.

Sammy said, 'Went with the house sale, so I heard.'

'Bonnie handled all that. Is that my tool bin in the back?'

'Yep. Guess that went, too.'

Later, Jack drove to his bank. They had kept the account open to pay for expenses. It had a few thousand dollars left in it. He had his wallet, and his credit cards were still valid. Driver's licence was still good. Contractor's licence intact. He drove to his old house and offered the owner $800 for the truck and tools. After some negotiation, he got them for $850. The title was signed over, and he drove off in his old ride the same day.

He called the kids and told them he was out of rehab and getting a place for them all to live in. He next talked to Bonnie and explained things to her.

'That's wonderful, Jack,' she'd said. But her words rang hollow. She asked him what his next step would be.

'Like I said, getting my family back. I'll be coming out there really soon.'

'Do you think that's wise?'

'Bonnie, I'm their father. They belong with me.'

That night he eased his truck down the narrow roads of the cemetery. He walked between the plots until he reached Lizzie's, represented by a simple bronze plate in the grass. There was a metal vase bolted to the plate. Jack placed in it a bunch of fresh flowers he'd brought with him. He sat down on his haunches and read the writing on the plate: ELIZABETH 'LIZZIE' ARMSTRONG, LOVING WIFE, MOTHER, AND DAUGHTER. YOU WILL ALWAYS BE MISSED. YOU WILL ALWAYS BE LOVED.

He traced the letters with his fingers as his eyes filled with tears. 'I'm going to get the kids, Lizzie. I'm going to bring them home, and we're going be a family again.' He choked back a sob and tried to ignore the dull pain in his chest. 'I wish you could be here with me, Lizzie. More than anything I wish that. But you were there for me in the hospital when I needed you. And I promise I will take good care of the children. I will make them proud. And I will raise them right. Just like you did.'

Words failed him, and he lay down in the grass and wept; exhausted, he fell asleep. When he woke he didn't know where he was for a few seconds, before he looked over and saw the grave. Jack walked silently back to his truck and drove off without the one person he needed more than anyone else.

ONE DAY LATER, Jack found a house owned by an elderly couple who had moved to an assisted-living facility. They couldn't sell their home because it needed a lot of repairs. Jack called the realtor and offered his labour for free to fix up the place, in exchange for staying there at no cost. Since the owners weren't making any money off the house anyway, they quickly agreed. It wasn't perfect, but he didn't need perfect. He just needed his kids under the same roof as him. Jack moved his few possessions in the next day and bought some secondhand furniture. Now it was time.

He booked his plane tickets, packed his bag, and left for the airport. He went to collect Mikki from Arizona first. He landed in Phoenix, rented a car, and drove to Tempe. He reached Fred and Bonnie's house but drove past it, parked a little down from the house, and waited.

An hour later a car pulled into the driveway, and Fred and Mikki got out. His heart ached when he saw her. She'd grown even taller. She was wearing a school uniform. Her hair was in a ponytail and had nary a strand of pink or purple in it. She looked utterly miserable.

Taking a deep breath, he climbed out of the car, and walked up the driveway.

'Dad? Dad, is it really you?' Mikki stared at him open-mouthed. When he held out his arms for a hug, she tentatively reached out to him. He stroked her hair and kissed the top of her head. 'It's me, sweetie. It's really me.'

Bonnie and Fred came back out of the house, saw him, and stopped.

'Jack?' said Fred. 'My God.'

Bonnie just stood there, disbelief on her features.

Jack moved towards the house with Mikki. He held out his hand, and Fred shook it. He looked at Bonnie. She still seemed in a daze.

'What is all the commotion?' Cecilia had come into the hall. When she saw Jack through the doorway, she cackled. 'I knew it.' She came forward as fast as she could and gave him a prolonged squeeze. 'I knew it, Jack, honey,' she said again, staring up at him and blinking back tears of joy.

Jack eyed Bonnie. 'The docs gave me a clean bill of health.'

Bonnie just kept shaking her head, but Fred clapped him on the shoulder. 'Jack, we're so happy for you, son.'

Later, when they were alone, Bonnie asked, 'How long will you be staying?'

'From here I'm heading to LA and then on to Portland.'

'To see the kids?'

'No, to take them back with me, Bonnie. I've already told Mikki to start packing her things.'

'But the house was sold. And how will you support them?'

'I'm renting another one, and I've started my business back up.'

'OK, but who will watch them when you're working?'

'Mikki and Cory are in school the whole day. And they're old enough to come home and be OK by themselves for a few hours. Jackie will be in extended day care. And if unexpected things come up, we'll deal with them. Just like every other family does.'

'Michelle has settled into her life here.'

Jack said nothing about how miserable the girl had been. He simply said, 'I don't think she'll mind.'

Bonnie pursed her lips. 'You just expect us to give her back to you, with no notice, no preparation? After all we've done?'

'I've been in constant contact over the last few months. I kept you updated on my progress. Hell, you've *seen* me on the computer getting better. And I told you I would be coming to take the kids back. Soon. So this shouldn't come as a shock to you. And it's not like you're never going to see them again.' He paused, and his tone changed. 'Even though you did leave me by myself.'

'You said it was all right! And we thought you were dying.'

'Bonnie, what else could I tell you under the circumstances? But for the record, dying alone is a real bitch.'

As soon as Jack finished speaking, he regretted it. Bonnie stood, her face red with anger. 'Don't you dare talk to me about dying alone! My Lizzie is lying dead and buried. There was no one with her at the end. No one! Certainly not you.'

Jack eyed her. 'Why don't you just say it, Bonnie. I know you want to.'

'*You* should be dead, not her.' Bonnie seemed stunned by her own words. 'I'm sorry. I didn't mean that.' Her face flushed. 'I'm very sorry.'

'I *would* give my life to have Lizzie back. But I can't. I've got three kids who need me. Nothing takes priority over that. I hope you can understand.'

'What I understand is that you're taking your children from a safe, healthy environment into something totally unknown.'

'I'm their father,' said Jack heatedly.

'You're a single parent. Lizzie isn't here to take care of the kids. I don't think you have any idea what's in store for you.'

Jack started to say something but stopped.

Could she be right?

4

'**M**r Armstrong?'

Jack stared down at the speaker from the ladder he was standing on while repairing some siding.

'I'm Janice Kaplan. I'm a reporter. I'd like to talk to you.'

Jack clambered down the ladder. 'Talk to me about what?'

'Being the miracle man.'

Jack squinted at her. 'Come again?'

'You are the Jack Armstrong who was diagnosed with a terminal illness?'

'Well, yeah, I was. I got better.'

'So, a miracle. At least that's what the doctor I talked to said.'

Jack looked annoyed. 'You talked to my doctor?'

'He's a friend of mine. He mentioned your case in passing. I became interested, did a little digging, and here I am. To do a story on you. People with death sentences rarely get a second chance.'

Jack and the kids had been back four weeks now. With parenting and financial support resting solely on his shoulders, Jack barely had time to eat or sleep. Bonnie had been right in her prediction. He hadn't had any idea what was in store for him. Mikki had really stepped up and had taken the labouring oar, and he had never had greater appreciation for Lizzie. She'd done it all, from school to meals to laundry to shopping to keeping the house clean. Jack had worked hard, but he realised now that he hadn't come close to working as hard as his wife had, because she did all that and worked full-time, too. At midnight he lay in his bed, numb and exhausted, humbled by the knowledge that Lizzie would have still been going strong.

'A story?' Jack shook his head. 'It's really not that special.'

'Don't be modest. I also understand that you turned your life around, built your business back up, got a house and went to retrieve your children, who'd been placed with family after your wife tragically died.'

Jack's annoyance turned to anger. 'You didn't learn all *that* from my doctor. That really is an invasion of privacy.'

'Please don't be upset, Mr Armstrong. I'm a reporter; it's my job to find out these things.' She drew a breath. 'It's strictly a feel-good piece. One man's triumph against the odds, a family reunited. These are hard times. All we hear is bad news. War, crime, people losing their jobs and their homes. This is a story that will make people smile. That's all I'm shooting for. To make people feel good.'

His anger was quickly disappearing. 'So, what exactly do I have to do?'

'Sit down with me and tell your story. I'll do a draft, get back to you, polish it, and then it'll be published in the paper and on our website.'

Jack looked around while he considered her request. 'How about tomorrow after dinner?'

'Great. About eight?'

Jack gave her his address. 'I'll see you then.'

THE STORY RAN and, a few days later, Janice Kaplan called. Jack had just finished cleaning up after dinner.

'The AP picked up my article, Jack.'

'What does that mean?' he asked.

'AP. Associated Press. That means my story about you is running in papers across the country. I just thought I'd give you a heads-up. You're famous now. So be prepared.'

Janice Kaplan's words proved prophetic. Letters came pouring in, including offers to appear on TV and to tell his story to major magazines; one publisher even wanted Jack to write a book. Overwhelmed and just wanting a normal life with his kids, he declined them all. His fifteen minutes of fame couldn't be over soon enough for him. He was no miracle man, he knew, but simply a guy who got lucky.

A WEEK AFTER Kaplan's call, Jack was lying in bed one night when he heard voices downstairs. He crept down the stairs.

'Stop it, Chris!'

Jack took the last three steps in one bound. Mikki was at the door, and a teenage boy had his hands all over her as she struggled against him. It took only two seconds for Jack to lift the young man and hold him against the wall. Jack said, 'What part of *no* don't you get, jerk?' He looked at Mikki. 'What the hell is going on?'

'He just came over to work on some . . . Dad, just let him down.'

Jack snapped, 'Get upstairs.'

She stalked up to her room. Jack turned back to the young man. 'If I ever catch you with one finger on her again, they won't be able to find all the pieces to put you back together, got it?'

The terrified teen merely nodded.

Jack dropped him down and slammed the door behind him. He marched up the stairs and knocked on his daughter's door.

'Leave me alone.'

He opened the door and went in. Mikki was sitting on the floor, her guitar across her lap. 'We need to get a few rules straight around here,' Jack said.

She stared up at him. 'I told you I could handle it.'

'You can't handle everything. That's why there are parents.'

'Oh, is *that* what you're pretending to be?'

Jack looked stunned. 'Pretend? I brought all of you back home so we could be together. Do you think I did that just for the hell of it?'

'I don't have a clue why you did it. And you didn't even ask me if I wanted to come back. You just told me to pack.'

'I thought you hated it out there.'

'Well, I hate it here, too.'

'What do you want from me? I'm doing the best I can.'

'You were gone a long time.'

'I explained that. Remember? I told you that story about being in the army? About taking your time and being prepared for every eventuality.'

'That's crap!'

'What?'

'In case you hadn't figured it out, this isn't the army, Dad. This is *family*.'

'I did all that to make sure we *could* be a family,' he shot back.

'A family? You don't have a clue what to do! Admit it! You're not Mom.'

'I know I'm not, believe me, but I'm trying to make this work. I love you guys.'

'Really? I do most of the cooking and cleaning and the laundry, and looking after Jackie. And Cory's being bullied at school. Did you know that? His grades are going down, even though he's a really smart kid. And Jackie's birthday is in two weeks. Have you planned anything?'

Jack's face grew pale. 'Two weeks?'

'Two weeks, *Dad.* So you might want to try harder.'

When Jack left her room, Cory was standing in his bedroom doorway.

'Cor, are you being bullied at school?'

Cory closed the door, leaving his dad alone in the hall.

JACK AND SAMMY were unloading Jack's truck after a long day at work. Jack nearly dropped a sledgehammer on his foot. Sammy looked over at him.

'You OK? Haven't been yourself the last couple of days.'

Jack slowly picked up the tool and threw it in the back of the truck. 'What do you think Jackie would like for his birthday? It's just round the corner, and I wanted to get him something nice.'

Sammy shrugged. 'Uh, toy gun?'

Jack looked doubtful. 'I don't think Lizzie liked to encourage that. And where can I get a cake and some birthday things?'

'The grocery store up the street has a bakery.'

'How do you know that?'

'It's right across from the beer aisle.'

Jack drove to the store and got some items for Jackie's birthday. He was standing at the checkout aisle when he saw it: his photo on the cover of one of the tabloid magazines. He picked up a copy.

The headline ran: MIRACLE MAN MUDDIED.

What the hell?

Jack read the story. With each word, his anger increased. The writer had twisted everything. He'd made it seem that Jack had forced Lizzie to go out on an icy, treacherous night to get his pain meds. Even worse, the writer had suggested that Jack thought his wife was having an affair with a neighbour. An obviously distraught Lizzie had run a red light and been killed. None of it was true, but now millions of people probably thought he was a monster.

On the drive home, it didn't take him long to figure out what had happened: Bonnie had been the writer's source. But how could she have known? Then it struck him: Lizzie must have called her on the drive over to the pharmacy and told her what she was doing. Maybe she mentioned something about Bill Miller, and Bonnie had misconstrued what Jack's reaction had been, although it would have been pretty difficult to do that. More likely, Bonnie might have just altered what Lizzie had told her to suit her own purposes.

Jack could imagine Bonnie seething. Here he was getting all this adulation and sympathy, and Lizzie was in a grave because of him. At least Bonnie probably believed that. A part of Jack couldn't blame her. But now she had opened a Pandora's box that Jack would find difficult to close. And what worried him the most was what would happen when his kids found out. He wanted to be the first to talk to them about it, especially Mikki.

Unfortunately, he was too late.

Mikki was waiting for him on the front porch with a copy of another gossip paper with a similar headline. She was trembling, and attacked him as soon as he got out of the truck. 'This is all over school. How could you make Mom go out that night? And how could you even think that she would cheat on you?'

Jack exploded. 'That story is full of lies. I never accused your mom of anything. I saw her slap Bill Miller. We had a laugh about it. And I didn't insist she go out that night. In fact, I told her not to.'

'This never would have happened if you hadn't agreed to do that stupid "Miracle Man" story in the first place. That *was* your fault.'

'OK, you're right about that. I wish I hadn't, but—'

Before he could finish, she'd fled inside, slamming the door. He started to go in after her. Staring through the side window at him was Cory. He gave his father a furious scowl and ran off.

JACK ENDED UP taking Cory and Jackie to Chuck E. Cheese's for Jackie's third birthday. Jack wore a baseball cap and glasses so people wouldn't recognise him. While Jackie jumped into mounds of balls along with a zillion other kids, Cory sat slumped in a corner looking like he would rather be attacked by sharks than be there. Jack didn't even know where Mikki was. The only moment in his life worse than then was when the cop told him Lizzie was dead.

Later, after they returned home, Jackie played with the truck that Jack had rushed out to buy him the night before. Cory had escaped into the back yard.

'You like the truck?' Jack asked quietly.

Jackie made truck noises and rolled it across his dad's shoulder.

Carrying his youngest son, Jack walked up the stairs and peered inside Mikki's room. Her clothes were all over the floor. A half-empty jar of Nutella sat on a storage box. Her guitar and keyboard were in one corner. Sheet music was stacked everywhere. There was a microphone on a metal fold-up table that she used as a desk.

Jack put his son down and picked up some of the music. It was blank sheets with pencil notes written in, obviously by his daughter. Jack couldn't read music, but the markings looked complicated.

He took Jackie's hand and walked into the bedroom the boys shared. It was far more cluttered than Mikki's because it was smaller and housed two people. There was a small, built-in shelf crammed with toys and books.

Jack noticed a box of papers on the floor next to Cory's bed. He looked inside. It was printed information about his disease. He saw, in Cory's handwriting, notes on the pages.

'He thought maybe he could find a cure.'

Jack spun round to see Mikki standing there.

She came forward. 'He wanted to save you. Dumb, huh? He's only a kid. But he meant well.'

Jack slowly rose. 'I didn't know.'

'Well, to be fair, you were pretty out of it at the time.' She sat down on one of the beds, while Jackie held out his truck for her to see. 'That's really cool, Jackie.' She hugged her brother. 'Happy birthday, big guy.'

'Big guy,' repeated Jackie with a huge smile.

She glanced at her dad. 'It's a nice gift.'

'Thanks.' He stared at her. 'So where does that leave us?'

'This is not where we say stupid stuff and hug and then bawl our eyes out and everything is OK, cue the dumb music. It's one day at a time. Some days will be good, and some days will suck. Some days I'll look at you and feel mad; some days I'll feel crappy about being mad at you. Some days I'll feel nothing. But you're still my dad.'

'The thing is, *I* was supposed to be gone, not your mom. I'd accepted that. But then your mother was gone. And somehow I got better. It just wasn't supposed to happen that way.'

'But it did happen exactly that way. You *are* here. Mom isn't.'

'So where do we all go from here?'

'You're really asking me?'

'You obviously know a lot more about this family than I do.'

His cellphone rang. He looked at the caller ID. It was Bonnie's number. Now what? Hadn't she done enough damage?

'Hello?' he said, bracing for a fight.

It was Fred. Jack said, 'Fred, is everything OK?'

'Not really, Jack, no. It's Cecilia. She died about two hours ago.'

THOUGH SHE HAD LIVED the last ten years in Ohio with her daughter, except for her short stint in Arizona, Cecilia Pinckney was a Southerner. She'd requested to be buried in Charleston, South Carolina, in the family crypt. So Jack bundled the kids into a pale blue 1964 VW van, which had been lovingly restored by Sammy, and headed south.

A large crowd gathered under a hot sun for the funeral. Bonnie looked older by ten years, shrunken and bowed. As she looked up at him, Jack thought he could see some affection for him underneath the sorrow. 'Thank you for coming,' she said.

'Cecilia was a great lady.'

'Yes, she was.'

'When some time has passed, we need to talk.'

She slowly nodded. 'All right. We probably should.'

After the service, Jack and the kids drove back to the hotel where they were staying, crammed into one room. Jack had just taken off his tie and jacket when the hotel phone rang. He answered, thinking it might be Fred.

'Mr Armstrong, I'm Royce Baxter. I had the pleasure of being Mrs Cecilia Pinckney's attorney for the past twenty years. I was wondering if I could meet with you for a little bit. My office is only a block over from your hotel. It's important, and it won't take long.'

Jack looked round at the kids. Jackie was passed out in a chair, and Mikki and Cory were watching TV.

'Give me the address.'

Five minutes later he was sitting across from Royce Baxter.

'Let me get down to business.' Baxter drew a document out of a file. 'This is Ms Cecilia's last will and testament. She made this change to her will very recently. She told me that even if you never used it, it would always be there for you.'

'What is it, exactly?' Jack said curiously.

'The old Pinckney house on the South Carolina coast, in Channing.'

'The Palace, you mean?'

'That's right. So you know about it?'

'Lizzie told me about it. But I've never been there. Once she moved to Ohio, she never went back.'

'Now, let me warn you that while it's right on the beach, it's not in good condition. But it's in a lovely location. Ms Cecilia told me that you're very good with your hands. I believe she thought you were the perfect person to take care of it.'

'Beach front? I couldn't afford the real estate taxes.'

'There are none. Years ago, Ms Cecilia placed the property into a conservancy so it could never be sold and developed. She and her descendants can use the property but can never sell it. In return, the taxes were waived.'

'But we've got a home in Cleveland. The kids are in school.'

'Ms Cecilia thought that you might have some trepidation. But since most of the summer is still ahead of us, the issue of school does not come into play.'

Jack sat back. 'OK. I see that. But I still don't think—'

Baxter interrupted. 'And Cecilia said that you told her that Lizzie was thinking of taking the kids there this summer.'

'That's right. I thought it was a good idea, but . . .' Jack's voice trailed off. He'd made Lizzie promise him that she would take the kids to the Palace. Now she couldn't.

Baxter fingered the will and studied him. 'Would you like to see it before you make up your mind?'

'Yes, I would,' Jack said, quickly.

LESS THAN TWO HOURS after leaving Royce Baxter's office, Jack and the kids pulled down a sandy drive between overgrown bushes. He surveyed the landscape. There were marshes nearby, and the smell of the salt water was strong, intoxicating.

'Wow!' said Cory, as the old house finally came into view.

Jack pulled the VW to a stop, and they all climbed out. Jack took Jackie's hand as they walked up to the front of the house, which was shaded by two large palmetto trees. It was an elongated, rambling, wood-sided structure, with a broad, covered front porch that ran along three-quarters of the home's face. The siding was faded and weathered but looked strong to Jack's expert eye. Five partially rotted steps carried them up to the front entrance.

Using the key Baxter had given him, he opened the front door.

Inside, the spaces were open and large, with high ceilings. The kitchen was spacious but poorly lighted, and the bathrooms were few in number and small. There was a stone fireplace in the main living area that reached to the ceiling, a big table for dining, and several other rooms, including a laundry room and a library.

The furniture was old but mostly in good shape. The floors were random-width plank, the walls solid plaster. The rear of the house was mostly windows and glass doors. The view out was of the wide breadth of the Atlantic, 200 feet away, the sandy beach less than half that distance. As the kids stared at the view, Jack looked down at the back yard. It was sandy, with dunes covered in vegetation.

They clumped upstairs and looked through the shotgun line of bedrooms, none of them remarkable, but all with views of the ocean.

'What do you think is up there?' This came from Mikki, who was pointing to a set of stairs at the end of the hall.

'Attic, I suppose,' Jack said, as he started to climb. He eased open the door. The room was under the eaves of the house. It was large, with two windows that threw in morning light. There was an old, wrought-iron four-poster, a large wooden desk, a shelf filled with books, and an old trunk set in one corner. A door led to a closet that was empty. Jack stepped cautiously over the floor planks to test their safety.

'Okay,' he said after his inspection was complete. 'Explore.'

Cory made a beeline for the trunk, while Jack led his youngest over to the desk and helped him open drawers. He glanced back at Mikki, who hadn't budged from the doorway.

'You going to look round?'

'Why? You're not thinking about moving here, are you?'

'Maybe.'

Her face flushed with anger. 'I already had to move to Arizona. And all my friends are in Cleveland. My band, everything.'

'I'm just looking around, OK?' But in his mind, Jack was already drawing up plans for repairs and improvements.

In his mind's eye, there was Lizzie seated next to him on his bed, on what would turn out to be her last day of life. *You might enjoy it, too. You could really fix the place up. Even make the lighthouse work again.*

'So Grandma Cee left you this place?' asked Mikki.

Jack broke free from his thoughts. 'Yeah, she did.'

'Well, why don't you sell it? We could certainly use the money.'

'I can't. It's a legal thing. And I wouldn't feel right selling it even if I could.'

Jack glanced over at Cory, who'd nearly tumbled into the large trunk. He came up wearing a top hat, black cloak and a half-mask. 'Moo-ha-ha-ha,' he said, in a dramatically deep voice.

Jack picked up a book and opened it, and his jaw dropped.

'What is it?' asked Cory, who had seen his reaction.

Jack held up the book. There was a bookplate on the inside cover. 'Property of Lizzie O'Toole,' read Jack. 'This was your mother's book. Maybe they all were.' He looked around, excitedly. 'I bet this was your mom's room growing up.'

Now Mikki joined them. 'Mom's room?'

Jack nodded and pointed eagerly to the desktop. 'Look at that.'

Carved into the wood were the initials *EPO*. Mikki looked at her dad questioningly.

He said animatedly, 'Elizabeth Pinckney O'Toole. That was your mom's full name. Pinckney was Grandma Cee's maiden name. She kept her last name after she married.'

'I remember Mom telling me about a beach house she grew up in, but she never said anything else. Do you know much about it?'

'She told me about it. But I've never been here before. She was planning to bring all of you here this summer after I . . . Anyway, that was her plan.'

'Is that why we're here, then? Fulfilling Mom's wishes?'

'Maybe that's part of it.' Jack looked out of the window. 'Hey, guys. Check this out.'

The kids hurried to the window and stared up in awe at the lighthouse that rose into the air out on a rocky point next to the house.

'It's really close to the house,' said Mikki.

Cory asked, 'Do you think it belongs to us, too?'

Jack said, 'I know it does. Your mom told me about it. It was one of her favourite places to go.'

They rushed outside and over to the rocky point. The lighthouse was painted with black and white stripes and was about forty feet tall. Jack tried the door. It was locked, but he peered through the glass in the upper part of the door. He saw a wooden spiral staircase. There were boxes stacked against one wall, and everything was covered in dust.

On the exterior wall of the lighthouse was a weathered sign. He scraped off some of the gunk stuck to it and read, 'Lizzie's Lighthouse'. Jack stepped back and stared up at the tall structure with reverence.

Cory looked at the sign. 'How could this be Mom's lighthouse?'

'Well, it was one of her favourite places, like I said.' Jack gazed round at the property. 'I'm sold.'

'What?' exclaimed Mikki.

'This will be a great place to spend the summer, and spend time together.'

'But Dad,' protested Mikki. 'It's a dump. And my friends—'

'It is *not* a dump. This is where your mother grew up,' he snapped. 'And we're moving here.' He paused and then added in a calmer tone, 'At least for one summer.'

5

Back in Cleveland, they moved out of the rental and parked their few pieces of furniture at Sammy's place, because he'd decided to come with them to South Carolina.

'What am I gonna do by myself all summer?' he'd said when told of the family's plans. 'And Sam Jr expects the kids to be around now. I can get by without you folks, but it's the dog that troubles me.'

Sammy drove the VW, and Jack followed in his pickup truck. They made one stop, to Lizzie's grave. Jack knew it would be hard on everyone, but he didn't want the kids to leave without going there.

They split the trip up into two days, spending the night in adjoining rooms at a motel outside Winston-Salem, North Carolina.

Jack woke up early in the morning and went outside to get some fresh air. He found Mikki already fully dressed and leaning against the VW.

'What's up?' he asked, stretching out his back.

'We just settled back in Cleveland, Dad. And now you're moving us down to South Carolina,' she said in a surly tone.

'Yeah, to the home where your mom grew up.'

'Okay, Dad, but in case you didn't realise it, Mom's not there.'

She turned and walked back to her room.

Jack stared after her, shook his head, and headed off to get ready for the rest of the trip.

They arrived in Channing before lunch. Jack had had the electricity and water turned on at the beach house before they got there. It didn't take them long to unload.

'Man,' said Sammy, dumping his old army duffel bag on the floor and looking round. 'This place is something else.'

'This "something else" needs a lot of work,' said Jack. 'But it's got great bones. I made a list when I was down here before. We'll need materials and a lot of sweat. There's a hardware store the lawyer recommended that's not too far from here.'

Sammy looked at him. 'Fixing it up? You said you couldn't sell it.'

'That's right.'

'So why are you planning to fix it up?'

'Because Lizzie—I mean, because we might be staying down here.'

'Staying down here? For how long?'

Jack didn't answer but pointed out of the window.

Sammy exclaimed, 'Is that a lighthouse? Does it work?'

'It used to. That's Lizzie's lighthouse. It was kind of her place.'

They all spent the next several hours putting things away, cleaning up, and exploring. After that they changed into bathing suits. The kids sprinted towards the water, with Mikki in the lead, Cory second, and Jackie bringing up the rear. Sam Jr stayed back with him. Sammy and Jack carried towels, a cooler full of soft drinks, beach chairs and an umbrella to stick into the sand. They'd found the chairs and umbrella in the lower level of the Palace.

Even though he had never been to the place before, Jack felt like he'd come home. He rose, took off his shoes, and jogged out to the water to be with his kids. After playing in the water for a while, Cory went up to the house and returned with a tattered old football.

'Hey, Dad,' he called out. 'Can you throw with me?'

Jack was tired. However, a memory struck him. It had been a basketball, not a football. In his driveway. His father had driven up after work, and six-year-old Jack was bouncing his new ball. He'd asked his dad to play with him. He wasn't sure if his dad had even answered. All he remembered was the side door closing with a thud.

'You're on, Cor.'

Sammy said, 'OK, big guy, show your old man some moves.'

They threw for more than an hour. Jack hadn't lost his touch. And Cory, after a few dropped balls, started catching everything that came his way. Jackie, and even Mikki, joined them, and Jack ran them through some high school football plays he remembered.

After everyone was sufficiently exhausted, Cory said, 'Thanks, Dad. That was great.'

Jack rubbed his son's head. 'Nice soft pair of hands you got. Wish I had you on my football team in high school.'

Cory beamed and Jackie squealed, 'Me, too?'

Jack snatched Jackie up, held him upside down, and ran to the water. 'You, too.'

Hours later, the sun started to set. The kids were still in the water; Sammy and Jack sat in the tattered beach chairs.

When they were all tired out they headed inside for a late dinner. Jack stayed behind, walking along the beach as the sun dropped into the horizon. The warm waters of the Atlantic washed over his feet. He stared out to sea. It had been a good first day.

THE NEXT DAY, while Sammy stayed with the other kids, Jack and Mikki drove to the hardware store in downtown Channing. Along the way, they reached a stretch of ocean front that was lined with magnificent homes. There was serious money here. If Jack could catch some work from some of these folks, it might really be good.

Mikki said, 'Are those, like, condo buildings?'

'They're mansions. Those places are worth millions each.'

'What a waste. I mean, who needs that much room?' she said derisively.

As they passed one house that was even larger than the others, a teenage girl came out into the cobblestone driveway dressed in a bikini top and tiny shorts with the words HUG 'EM printed on the backside. She was blonde and tanned and had the elegant bone structure of a model. She climbed into a Mercedes convertible about the same time a tall, lean, young man came hustling up the drive. He hopped in the passenger seat, and the car roared off, pulling in front of their pickup and causing Jack to nearly run off the road.

Mikki rolled down the window and yelled, 'Jerks!'

The girl made an obscene gesture.

They reached Channing and climbed out of the truck. Mikki was dressed in knee-length cotton shorts and a black T-shirt. Her skin was pale, and her hair was now partially green and purple. To Jack, his daughter's supply of hair colour seemed endless.

Mikki looked around. 'Pretty old-fashioned place,' she said.

Jack had to admit it was a little like stepping back in time. The streets were wide and clean. A bank, grocery, hardware store, barber's shop with a striped pole, restaurants, an ice-cream parlour, and a sheriff's station with one police cruiser parked in front were all in his line of sight.

Most of the cars parked along the street were late-model luxury sedans or high-dollar convertibles. But then Jack noted dented and dirty pickup trucks and old Fords and Dodges rolling down the street. The people in those vehicles looked more like he did, Jack thought. *Working stiffs*.

They passed a shabby-looking building with an awning out front that read CHANNING PLAY HOUSE. An old man was sweeping the pavement in front of the double-door entrance. He stopped sweeping and greeted them.

'What's the Channing Play House?' Jack asked.

'Back in its day, it was one of the finest regional theatre houses in the low country,' said the man, who introduced himself as Ned Parker. 'We still have the occasional performance, but it's nowhere near what it used to be. Too many video games and big-budget movies.'

Mikki pointed to a sign, which read CHANNING TALENT COMPETITION. 'What's that?'

'Hold it every year in August. Folks compete. Any age and any act. Baton twirling, dancing, fiddling, singing. Lot of fun. It's a hundred-dollar prize and your picture in the *Channing Gazette*.'

They continued on, and Jack and Mikki went on to the hardware store and purchased what they needed. A young man who worked at the store helped Jack load the items.

'Some of this stuff won't fit in my truck,' Jack pointed out.

Before the helper could answer, a stocky man in his seventies with snow-white hair strolled over. He was dressed in khaki pants and a blue polo shirt with the hardware store's name and logo on it.

He said, 'That's no problem: we deliver. Can have it out there today. You're in the Pinckney place, right?'

Jack studied him. 'That's right; how'd you know?'

The man put out his hand and smiled. 'You beat me to it. I was coming out to see you later today and formally introduce myself. I'm Charles Pinckney, Cecilia's "little" brother.' He turned to Mikki and extended his hand. 'And this must be the celebrated Mikki. Cee wrote to me often about you. Let me see, she said you could play a guitar better than anyone she'd ever heard and were as pretty as your mother. I haven't heard you play, but Cee was spot-on with her assessment of your beauty.'

In spite of herself, Mikki blushed. 'Thanks,' she mumbled.

Pinckney looked at the young helper. 'Billy, take the rest of these materials and set it up for delivery.'

'Yes, sir, Mr Pinckney.'

Jack said, 'Now I remember. You were at the funeral, but we didn't get a chance to talk.'

Pinckney nodded. 'I'm the only one left now. Thought for sure Cee would outlive me, even though she was a lot older.'

'There were ten kids? That's what Lizzie told me.'

Pinckney nodded. 'That's right. I was closest with Cee. We talked just about every day. Feel like I lost my best friend.'

'She was a fine lady. Really helped me out.'

'She was one of a kind,' agreed Pinckney. 'Not many ladies of her generation kept their maiden name, but it wasn't a question for her. In fact, she told her husband he could change his surname to Pinckney if he wanted, but she wasn't switching.' He chuckled at the memory.

'Sounds like Cecilia.'

'She thought a lot of you. I suppose that's why she left you the Palace. Wouldn't have left it to just anyone.'

'I appreciate that. But it came as a total shock.'

'Cee actually talked to me about it. I know she wanted you to have it, and I was all for it. Especially after Lizzie died. She loved the place, too; maybe even more than Cee.'

Mikki was listening closely. 'Why do you call it the Palace?'

Pinckney grinned. 'It was our mother's doing. Her mother and father, my grandparents, were quite the Bible-thumpers, but she wasn't. Naming it the Palace made it seem like it was a casino or something. It worked. Her parents never visited there, far as I know,' he said with a smile. Pinckney looked at the materials in Jack's truck. 'So, fixing the place up? Cee said you were good with your hands.'

'If you hear of anyone who needs work done, let me know. I've got a lot of mouths to feed.'

'I'll put the word out. Good luck with the Palace.'

'Thanks,' Jack said. 'It has great bones, just needs some TLC.'

'Don't we all,' said Pinckney. 'Don't we all.'

'FRIENDLY PEOPLE,' remarked Mikki grudgingly as they continued on down the street.

'Southern hospitality, they call it. Hey, how about some lunch?'

'Fine,' she said dully.

As they rounded the corner, the sports car that had almost caused them to wreck earlier flew round the corner. Mikki yelled, 'Hey!'

'Mik,' said her dad, warningly.

But she was already in the street flagging the car down. The girl hit her brakes. 'What the hell do you think you're doing?'

'You cut us up earlier and almost made my dad roll his truck.'

The girl laughed. 'Is your hair naturally that colour or did someone throw up on it?'

The guy in the car grimaced. 'Tiff, knock it off.'

The girl gave Mikki a condescending look and then laughed derisively. 'OK, whatever. Hey, sweetie pie, now why don't you go on off and play somewhere.' She hit the gas, and they sped off.

'Creeps!' Mikki screamed after them. She glared over at her dad. 'So much for Southern hospitality.' Then she saw a sign, and her face brightened. '*That* is the place for lunch.'

Jack looked to where she was pointing. '"Little Bit of Love Bar and Grill"? Why is that the place?'

'Come on, Dad. I have to see if this is what I think it is.'

She hurried inside, and Jack followed. There were twenty retro tables with red vinyl covers and chairs with yellow vinyl covers. The floor was a crazy pattern of black-and-white square tiles. The walls were covered with posters of famous rock-and-roll bands. Behind the bar were acoustic, bass and electric guitars along with costumes actually worn by band members, all behind Plexiglas.

Mikki looked like she'd just discovered gold in a tiny coastal town in South Carolina. 'I knew it.'

Most of the tables were occupied, and the bar was doing a brisk business. A woman about Jack's age headed towards them.

'Two for lunch?' the woman said.

Jack caught himself staring at her. She was tall and slim and had dark hair that curved round her long neck. Her eyes were a light blue and, when she smiled, Jack felt his own mouth tug upwards in response. 'Um, yeah,' he said quickly. 'Thanks.'

They followed her to a table, and she handed them menus. 'Haven't seen you before.'

Jack introduced himself and Mikki.

'I'm Jenna Fontaine,' she said. 'I own this pile of bricks.'

'As soon as I saw the name, I knew,' said Mikki. She and Jenna exchanged smiles. 'Def Leppard, am I right?'

'You know your rock-and-roll lyrics.' When Jack looked puzzled, Jenna said, '"Little Bit of Love" is a Def Leppard song.'

'So you're into music?' said Jack.

'Yes, but not nearly as much as that guy.'

She pointed to a tall, lanky teenager with long black hair who was setting plates of food down at the next table. 'That's Liam, my son. Now, he's the musical madman in the family. When I decided to chuck in the life of a big-city lawyer and move here and open a restaurant, the theme and décor were his idea.'

Mikki eyed Liam and then turned back to her. 'Does he play?'

'Just about any instrument there is. But drums are his speciality.'

Mikki's eyes glittered with excitement for the first time since stepping foot in South Carolina.

'I take it you're into music, too,' said Jenna.

'You could say that,' said Mikki modestly.

'So where y'all staying?'

'My great-grandma left us a house.'

'Wow. That's pretty impressive. Well, enjoy your lunch.'

She walked off, and Jack looked down at the menu. He wasn't really seeing it. Mikki finally touched his hand, and he jumped.

'Dad?'

'Yeah?'

'She's really pretty.'

'Is she? I didn't notice. Let's just get something to eat and get back, OK? I've got a lot of work to do.'

6

It took several days of backbreaking work to thoroughly clean the house, and all the kids pitched in, although Mikki did so grudgingly and with a good deal of complaining. 'Is this how the summer's going to go?' she said as she scrubbed down the kitchen sinks. 'Me being a slave labourer?'

They next attacked the outside, cleaning out flower beds, pruning bushes, clearing away dead plants, and power-washing the decks and the outdoor furniture. The rest of the acreage was beyond their capability—and Jack's wallet.

With much tugging and cursing, Jack and Sammy were finally able to get the door to the lighthouse open. As Jack stepped into the small foyer, he coughed from the dust and looked round.

The rickety steps looked in danger of falling down. He looked through some of the boxes stacked against the wall. There was mostly junk, though he did find a pair of tiny pink sneakers that had the name 'Lizzie' written on the sides in faded marker pen. He held them reverently. He found a few other things of interest and carried them up to his bedroom.

They all trooped down to the beach that afternoon and ate lunch. After the meal was over, Jack looked at Mikki, grinned, and said, 'Let me show you something. Stand up and grab me.'

Mikki looked around, embarrassed. 'Dad, what are you doing?'

'Just grab me.'

'Fine.' She rushed forward and grabbed him, or tried to. The next instant she was face-down on the sand.

She lay there for a second, stunned, then rolled over and scowled up at him. 'Gee, Dad, thanks.'

'Let's do it again, and I'll show you exactly what I did.'

'Why? Is this, like, National Kick Your Daughter's Butt Day and nobody told me?'

Sammy interjected. 'He's showing you some basic self-defence manoeuvres, Mik.'

Mikki looked up at her dad. He said, 'So you can handle yourself in certain situations. Without me helping,' he added.

'Oh,' she said, a look of understanding appearing on her face.

They went through the moves a dozen more times, until Mikki had first her dad, then Sammy, and even Cory lying face-down in the sand.

'Hello!'

They all turned to see Jenna Fontaine holding up a picnic basket. 'I brought you some things from the café.'

Jack came forward. 'There was no need to do that.'

'It's no trouble. I know how it is coming to a new place.' She showed him what was in the basket, and then Jack introduced her to Cory, Sammy and Jackie.

Mikki asked, 'So where do you live, Jenna?'

Jenna pointed to the south. 'About half a mile that way. Our house is the pile of blue shingles with the vibrating roof.'

'Vibrating roof?' said Mikki curiously.

Jenna looked at Jack. 'It's another reason I stopped by. Charles Pinckney said you were a whiz at building things. He was the one who told me you were staying here. What I really need—to stop myself from either killing my son or committing myself to a mental institution—is a soundproof room for his music studio.'

'He has a music studio?' exclaimed Mikki.

'Well, he calls it that. Most of the equipment is secondhand, but he's got a lot of stuff. I don't understand most of what it does, but what I do know is it's killing my ears.' She looked at Jack again. 'Want to come by and give me an estimate?'

Jack said, 'Sure, I'd be glad to.'

'You want to stop by tomorrow evening? Liam will be there, and he can tell you what he needs.'

'It might be a little expensive,' said Jack. 'But we've done soundproofing before. You'll notice a big difference.'

'Saving my hearing and my sanity is worth any price. Say about eight?'

'That'll be fine,' said Jack.

Jenna told them her address, waved, and headed off.

Jack watched her go. When he turned back, he saw Mikki and Sammy staring at him. Jack said nervously, 'Uh, I've got stuff to do.'

He handed the picnic basket to Mikki and trudged to the Palace.

Jack fell asleep that night with the tiny pair of pink sneakers on his chest.

MIKKI HAD INSISTED on coming along with Jack to the Fontaines' house, so Sammy stayed behind to watch the boys.

Jenna met them at the door and ushered them in. The house was old but well maintained, and the interior was surprising. Instead of a typical beach look, it was decorated in a Southwestern style.

'Nice place,' said Jack.

'Thanks. We tried to make it feel like home.'

'Where's that?' asked Mikki as she looked round. 'Arizona? I was just there recently.'

Jenna laughed. 'We came from Virginia. I went to college and law school there. Ended up in D.C., though.'

'You look pretty young to have a teenager,' said Mikki.

'Mik!' her father began crossly, but Jenna laughed.

'I'll take that as a compliment. Truth is, I had Liam while I was in high school.' She pursed her lips but then smiled. 'The best thing that came out of that marriage was Liam.'

'So how did you end up down here?' asked Jack.

'Got tired of the rat race in D.C. I'd made good money and invested it well. We came down to Charleston one summer, took a drive, happened on Channing, and fell in love with it.' She glanced at Jack. 'When I talked to Charles, he told me about his sister leaving you the Palace. It's a great old place. Never been inside, but I've always loved that lighthouse.'

'My wife grew up in that house,' said Jack.

'Charles told me about that, too.' She paused and added, 'And I'm very sorry for your loss.'

'Thanks,' said Jack quietly.

'Well, do you want to see the mad musician's space? It's downstairs.'

'Absolutely,' Mikki replied.

She could see at a glance that it was set up as a recording studio, albeit on a tight budget. A keyboard was against one wall; a guitar sat in a stand in a corner. A banjo and a fiddle hung on hooks on the wall. And yet there were no sheets of music. No songbooks.

'Where's Liam?' Mikki asked.

'He's on his way. What will you be next year, a junior?'

'Yeah.'

'Liam, too.'

Mikki slid over to the guitar. 'Do you think he'd mind?'

'Go for it.'

Mikki strapped the guitar on and started to play.

'Wow,' said Jenna. 'That's really good.'

She started to take off the guitar, but a voice said, 'Play those last two chords again.'

They all turned to see Liam standing in the doorway.

'Liam, I didn't hear you come in,' said his mother. 'Everything OK at the Little Bit?'

'A place for everything, and everything in its place.' He looked at Mikki again. 'So knock those last two chords out.'

Surprised, but pleased at his request, she did so. The sound rocked the room again. He walked over to her and placed her index finger on the guitar neck in a slightly different spot. 'Try that: it'll give the sound more depth,' he said.

She flushed angrily. 'I know how to place my fingers.'

He seemed unfazed by her hostility. 'So let me hear it now.'

'Fine, whatever.' She checked the new position of her index finger and played the chord. The sound was far richer. She looked at him with new respect. 'How did you figure that one out?'

He held up his hand. 'The fingertip has different strength points. Once you understand where they are and place your fingers accordingly, the tightness on the strings is increased. Gives a fuller sound because there's less vibration coming off the neck.'

'You worked that out on your own?'

'Nope. Read about it in *Rolling Stone*. So what's your name?'

'Mikki Armstrong. That's my dad.'

Jack and Liam shook hands.

'Mr Armstrong is here to see if he can save my hearing,' said Jenna.

Jack said, 'Just call me Jack.'

Liam grinned. 'I don't want her going deaf on me. But then again, that might have its advantages.'

Jack surveyed the room and then went round the space knocking on the walls. 'Drywall on two-by-four studs set at standard width.' He reached up and tapped the low ceiling at regular intervals. 'Same here.'

Jenna looked impressed. 'When can you start?'

'Soon as I get materials. I'll work up an estimate.'

Mikki eyed the room. 'Liam, where's your music?'

He tapped his head. 'All up here. I can't read music. I play by ear.' He grinned. 'Want to test me?'

Jenna looked at Jack. 'You want some coffee while our kids talk shop?'

After a pleading look from Mikki, Jack said, 'Sure.'

After they left, Mikki said, 'OK, Mr Play-by-ear, here's your test.' She played a minute-long piece of a song she'd recently composed. She handed him the guitar. 'Go for it.'

He played back her song, note for perfect note.

Mikki exclaimed, 'You're like Mozart!'

Liam picked up his drumsticks. 'Want to score a few sets?'

Mikki strapped the guitar back on. 'I'll try out my new fingertip points.'

JENNA AND JACK were sitting out on her rear deck when the music started up. The deck flooring really did appear to vibrate.

'Now do you see why I need the soundproofing?' she asked. 'Want to carry our coffee down to the beach?'

They strolled along the sand together. It was well after eight but still light outside. An elderly couple was throwing tennis balls to a black lab. As the dog ran, the couple held hands and walked along.

Jenna eyed them and said, 'That's how it's supposed to turn out.'

Jack glanced at her. 'What?'

She pointed at the couple. 'Life. Marriage. Growing old together. Someone to hold hands with.'

Jack watched them. 'You're right.'

'So your wife grew up here?'

'Yeah. And she planned to bring the kids down here this summer. So I thought I'd do it for her. And I wanted to see the place, too.'

'You'd never been here before?'

Jack shook his head. 'My wife had a twin sister who died of meningitis. They lived here for a while longer. But then I guess it just wasn't that . . . um . . . good,' he finished, a bit awkwardly.

'I'm so sorry. So how're the kids dealing with the move and all?'

'They all handle things differently. Mikki is independent like her mom. She and I butt heads a lot. Teenage girls. They need . . . stuff that dads aren't good at.'

'I feel that deficiency with Liam, too, just on the flip side.'

'He looks like he's doing fine. So you're divorced?'

'Long time. Right after Liam was born. My ex moved to Seattle and has nothing to do with him.'

'How'd you manage college and law school with a kid?'

'My parents were a huge help. But sometimes I'd take Liam to class with me. You do what you have to do.'

Jack stopped, picked up a pebble, and threw it into the incoming breakers. 'Yeah, you do.'

Jenna watched him. 'So, are y'all just down here for the summer?'

'That's the plan.' He looked at his watch. 'Look, I'll write up that estimate and get it to you tomorrow.'

'Why don't I just give you a cheque tonight to help cover the materials, and you can get started?'

'You don't want an estimate?' he said in surprise.

'No. I trust you.'

'But you don't know me.'

'I know enough.'

'OK. And thanks for the coffee.' He smiled. 'And the trust.'

Walking back, she said, 'I really am sorry about your wife.'

'Me, too.' Jack glanced back at the old couple still walking slowly hand in hand. 'Me, too.'

MIKKI AWOKE the next morning in her attic bedroom. She stretched, yawned, and sat up. Then she picked up her guitar and started playing a new song she'd been working on, using the new technique Liam had taught her. The fingers of her left hand worked the neck of the instrument, while her right hand did the strumming. She put down the guitar, went to her desk, picked up some blank music sheets and started making notations and jotting down some lyrics. She started singing.

A minute later, someone knocked on her door. Startled, she stopped singing and said, 'Yeah?'

Her father opened the door and came in with a breakfast tray. Bacon, eggs, an English muffin smeared with Nutella, and a glass of milk. He set it down in front of her. Mikki put the guitar aside.

'How'd you know I like Nutella?'

'Did some good old-fashioned reconnaissance.' He pulled a chair up next to the bed. 'Dig in before it gets cold.'

Mikki began to eat. 'Where's everybody else?' she asked.

'Still sleeping. It's early. Did you have fun last night with Liam?'

'Omigod, Dad, he is *so* awesome. That thing he showed me with the fingers? It works. We played some sets together, and he likes the bands I like, and he's funny, and—'

'So is that a yes?'

She grinned sheepishly. 'Yeah.'

Jack slipped something out of his pocket and handed it to her. 'I found this in a box in the lighthouse this morning.'

'The lighthouse? Pretty early to have already been out there.'

'Look at the picture.'

Mikki held it tightly by the edges. 'Is this Mom?'

'Yep. Your mom was about your age in that photo. It was taken down here at the beach. It must've been the summer before she moved to Cleveland.' He paused. 'You see, don't you? That you look just like her.'

Mikki squinted at the image of her mom. 'I do?'

'Absolutely you do. Well, except maybe for the weird hair colour and the goth clothes. Your mom was more into ponytails and pastels.'

'Ha-ha, real funny. And my clothes are not goth, which is, like, so last century anyway.'

'Sorry. Now why don't you finish your breakfast and we can go for a walk on the beach before things get going?'

'Is this part of the "you being a dad" thing?' she asked, bluntly.

'Partly, yeah. And I had a long time to be alone after you guys left, and I hated it. I never want to be alone again.'

As they hit the sand, the sun was coming up and the sky was a sheet of pink. A wind had dispelled most of the night's heat. Gulls swooped and soared over the water.

'It's really different down here,' said Mikki.

'I guess no matter where we'd be right now, it'd be different,' he replied.

'I wake up sometimes and think she's still here.'

Jack stopped walking. 'I wake up every morning expecting to see her. It's only when she's not there that I realise . . . But down here, it's different. I feel . . . I feel closer to her, somehow.'

They threw pebbles into the water, and Mikki found a shell that she pocketed to show her brothers.

'You've got a great voice,' he said. 'I was listening outside the door this morning. Do you want to study music in college?'

'I'm not sure the sort of stuff I want to play would be popular in college curriculums or in the mainstream music industry.'

'What kind is it?'

'Are you asking to be polite, or do you really want to know?'

'Look, do you have to make everything so complicated?'

'OK, OK. It's very alternative: edgy beats, non-traditional mix of instrumentals. No lollipop lyrics. Words that mean something.'

Jack was impressed. 'Sounds like you've given this a lot of thought.'

'It's a big part of my life, Dad; of course I've thought about it.'

'It's nice to have something you're so passionate about.'

'Were you ever passionate about anything?'

'Not until I met your mother. Before your mom came along, I had my sports, but not much else. And my dad was dying.'

'But you still had your mom.'

'Yeah, but we had our issues.'

'What was the issue?'

Jack stopped walking, and Mikki pulled up, too.

'OK, full confessional. It got to the point where I wondered if my mom loved me.'

Mikki looked shocked. 'Why did you think she didn't?'

'Probably because she left when I was seventeen. Right after my dad died. She met some guy and moved to Florida. She kept the house in Cleveland, and I lived there until I married your mom and enlisted. She died when you were still a baby.'

Mikki looked at him. 'You lived there by yourself?'

'Didn't have any other relatives, so yeah. I was over sixteen. I got part-time jobs to pay for expenses. Your mom was my best friend. She helped me through some really tough times.'

When they got back to the Palace, Mikki said, 'Thanks, Dad, for the walk and talk.'

'Hope it's one of many this summer.'

As she ran up the deck steps ahead of her father, Sammy appeared from around the side of the house. 'You got an early start.' He glanced at Mikki as she went into the house. 'A bit of father-and-daughter time?'

'She's an amazing kid, Sammy. Half her life I was carrying a gun for my country. The other half I was driving nails. I've got a lot to learn about her.'

'Probably why I never got married,' said Sammy. 'Too complicated.'

'You ever regret it? No kids, no wife?'

'I didn't, until I started hanging out with you Armstrongs.'

LATER THAT WEEK, before her dad left for work and she had to watch the kids, Mikki pulled on some shorts, tennis shoes and a tank top, stretched her legs, and headed to the beach to run. She was naturally athletic, taking after her dad.

The sun felt great; the views were breathtaking. Her long legs ate up ground at a rapid pace. People were fishing from the shore; kids were playing in the sand; teenagers were bodysurfing.

'What the—' she gasped.

A guy had run right up beside her. 'Hey,' he said, grinning.

Mikki saw that it was the boy from the Mercedes convertible.

'I'm Blake Saunders.' He held out his hand to her as they ran. 'I wanted to apologise for what happened the other day. Tiff can be a real piece of work.'

'Tiff?'

ONE SUMMER | 369

'Tiffany, Tiffany Murdoch. She's pretty spoiled. Her dad was some big-shot investment guy in New York before they moved down here and built the biggest house on the beach.'

'So why do you hang out with her?'

'She can be fun.'

Mikki gave him a scathing look. 'I'm going to finish my run.'

'Mind if I jog along with you?'

'Suit yourself.'

'And your name?'

She hesitated, then said, 'Mikki. Mikki Armstrong.'

They ran on. 'So you just moved down here?' said Blake.

'Yeah, from Cleveland.'

'Wow, Cleveland.'

'Yeah, Cleveland. Got a problem with that?'

'No, I meant that it was cool. Maybe we can hang out sometime? It's nice to meet people who aren't from around here.'

'Well, I plan to run about this time every day.'

'Great. Maybe next time I won't get the evil eye as much.'

Mikki let slip a tiny smile.

'Finally, a crack in the armour,' he kidded.

They finished their run. Blake said, 'See you tomorrow?'

'OK.'

He took off at a full sprint, and she headed to the Palace.

7

At the Channing hardware store, Jack and Sammy loaded up the truck with materials for Jenna Fontaine's house. Charles Pinckney came outside to see them, and Jack introduced him to Sammy.

'Appreciate the referral, Charles,' said Jack.

'Glad to do it. Jenna is a fine person. She runs the most popular restaurant in town, so she can be a great lead for other work.'

'Charles, I had a question,' said Jack. 'I was wondering about the lighthouse. Its history.'

'My father built it along with the house. It was originally listed on the official navigational charts. But it just stopped working.'

'Anybody ever try to get it running again?'

'Why, no. What would be the point? By the time it broke, they didn't use it for a navigational aid any more.'

Jack and Sammy left Pinckney and drove on to Jenna's house. She'd already left for the restaurant, but she'd pinned a note to the front door telling them that the entrance on the lower level was unlocked. They hauled the materials in and, after covering all of Liam's instruments and the furniture with drop cloths, they began to tear out the drywall. The plan was to backfill the wall and ceiling spaces with soundproofing materials and then replace the original drywall with denser material that would also act as a sound block.

Around one o'clock, Jenna came down the steps carrying a large white bag. She held it up. 'I hope you boys haven't eaten yet.'

'You didn't have to do that,' said Jack.

'Well, I'm glad you did. I'm hungry,' exclaimed Sammy.

Jenna smiled and unpacked two turkey and cheese sandwiches, crisps, cookies and sodas on a table against a wall. While she did this, she gazed round the room. 'Boy, you two have been busy.'

Jack nodded. 'It's going better than I thought it would.'

Sammy wiped his hands on a clean rag and examined the food. He bowed formally and said, 'You are a goddess sent from above.'

Jenna laughed. 'It's so nice to meet a real gentleman.'

Jack rinsed off his hands using a bottle of water and a rag and sat down. He looked at Jenna. 'You didn't bring yourself anything?'

'I always eat before the lunch crowd gets in. Place is packed.'

'Looks like you have a gold mine there,' Jack noted.

She sat on a small hassock, crossed her legs, and said, 'We do fine. But the profit margins are small and the hours are long.'

Jack munched on a crisp and said, 'So why do you do it, then?'

Jenna had slipped her heels off and was rubbing her feet. Jack's gaze dipped to her long legs before quickly retreating.

'I'm my own boss. I'm a people person. I admit I get a kick out of walking into the Little Bit and knowing it's mine. And it's something I can leave for Liam—if he wants it, that is.'

'Nice legacy for your kid,' said Sammy.

Jenna smiled. 'I know about Jack, but do you have any children, Sammy?'

'No, ma'am. Uncle Sam was my family. That was enough.'

Jack said, 'Sammy was in the army. 'Nam. Then Delta Force.'

Jenna looked at Sammy in awe. 'That's pretty impressive.'

Sammy wiped his mouth with a napkin. 'Well, Jack won't tell you about himself because he's too modest. So I'll do the honours . . .'

'Sammy,' Jack said in a warning tone, 'that was a long time ago.' He rose. 'We need to get back to work.' He turned away, picked up his tool belt and started cutting out more of the walls.

In a low voice, Sammy said, 'He's a complicated guy.'

Jenna said, 'I'm beginning to see that.'

LATER THAT NIGHT, after the kids were asleep, Jack grabbed a flashlight and headed out to the lighthouse. He walked up the rickety stairs carefully, testing each step before continuing on.

He finally reached the top platform, directly under the access door that led into the space where the light mechanism was located.

His light picked out things in the darkness. Sitting on an old mattress, its back against the wall, was an old doll. Jack reached down and picked it up. The doll's hair was grimy, its face stained with dirt and water. Still, he looked at it as though it were a bar of gold. He'd seen Lizzie holding it in an old photo of her as a child.

Jack felt tears creep to his eyes, and his lungs suddenly couldn't get enough air.

Holding the doll under one arm, he pushed open the door that led to the catwalk that ran around the top exterior of the lighthouse. Jack stared up at the dark sky. Heaven *was* up there somewhere. And so was Tillie, Lizzie's twin. And now Lizzie, too.

Right this minute, his wife seemed so close to him. It couldn't possibly be more than six months since he'd heard her voice and her laugh, felt her skin or watched her smile.

He reached up. His finger covered a star that was probably a trillion light-years away and the size of the sun. *Heaven must be right up there.*

He carefully set the doll down and slipped an envelope from his pocket. It had the number '3' written on the outside. The letter was dated December 20. He already knew what it said. But if Lizzie could not read them, he would do it for her.

Dear Lizzie,

Christmas is four days away, and it's a good time to reflect on life. Your life. This will be hard, but it needs to be said. You have many years ahead of you. Cory and Jackie will be with you for many more years. And even Mikki will benefit. I'm talking about you finding someone else, Lizzie.

I know you won't want to at first, but Lizzie, I cannot allow you to go through the rest of your life alone. It's not fair to you, and it has nothing to do with the love we have for each other. It will not change that at all. Our love will last for ever. But people have the capacity to love many different people. You are a wonderful person, Lizzie, and you can make someone else's life wonderful.

Believe me, Lizzie, if it could be any other way, I would make it so. But you have to deal with life as it comes. And I'm trying my best to do just that. I love you too much to accept anything less than your complete and total happiness.

Love,

Jack

Jack slipped the letter into the envelope and put it back in his pocket. He picked up the doll and stared out over the ocean for a long time. He finally walked back down the stairs and out into the humid night air. He stared up at the lighthouse, then walked back to the house, his heart full of thoughts of what should have been.

MIKKI ROLLED OVER in her bed. Outside she could hear the breakers. She'd grown so accustomed to their presence that she wasn't sure she ever wanted to be without the sound. She sat up and saw it was 6.30 a.m. She liked to take her run early so she could be back before her dad and Sammy left for work.

On her way out, she looked in on both her brothers, who shared a room next to her dad's bedroom. They were both still asleep.

As Mikki passed her dad's room, she could hear him stirring. She rapped on the door. 'Dad, I'm going running. I'll put the coffee on.'

'OK. Thanks,' came his sleepy response.

She put on the coffee and laid out two mugs for her dad and Sammy. She bounced down the steps and passed through the dunes to the flat beach. She did a thorough stretch and started out. About half a mile into her run, Blake joined her. They talked as they ran. All normal subjects that teens gabbed about. She found herself liking him more, in spite of his association with someone like Tiffany Murdoch. He made her laugh.

When he made his goodbyes a few miles later, he said, 'We're having a party on the beach next Saturday night. I wondered if you'd like to come. There's food, a bonfire, and we play some tunes. About the midpoint of our run, near the big yellow house.'

'Sure. Looking forward to it.'

Back at the Palace, Mikki showered and changed her clothes. Her dad had surprised her by making breakfast: pancakes and bacon. 'I help,' announced Jackie.

Before her dad and Sammy left, Mikki ran back up to her closet to get some things to take down to the beach later with the boys. Her bag spilled over, though, and as she started picking things up, she noticed a loose floorboard. When she pressed the board, she saw the edge of a photo. She pulled it out and studied the images. Then went downstairs and showed her dad.

Jack looked at the picture of Lizzie as a young girl. She was surrounded by her family. A much younger Fred and Bonnie. And her siblings.

Mikki pointed to one of the people in the photo. 'That was Mom's twin, right? The one who died?'

'Yes. Her name was Tillie.'

'Is that why they left here? Because it was so sad with her dying and all?'

'I guess that was part of it.' He held out his hand for the photo, but Mikki drew it back.

'Do you mind if I keep this?'

'No, sweetie, I don't mind at all.'

'BONNIE?'

When Jack had opened the door in answer to the knock, his mother-in-law was the last person he had expected to see.

'Can I come in?'

'Of course.' He moved aside. 'When did you get in?'

'A couple of days ago. We're renting a house on the marsh.'

They sat on the couch in the front room.

'I have to say, I was surprised that Mother left the place to you.'

'No more than I was.' Jack hesitated. 'I heard Lizzie tell you she wanted to bring the kids here after I died. That stunned you, didn't it? Her wanting to come back here?'

She looked around, ignoring his question. 'I noticed the new boards on the porch, and the yard looks good.'

'Sammy and I have been doing a little work. Electrical, plumbing, roofing, some landscaping.'

'Probably more than a little.' She stared at him. 'I suppose that's why she left you the place. You could fix it up.'

'I've been thinking about fixing up the lighthouse, too.'

'Please don't do that. Do you know Lizzie became obsessed with it?'

'She told me about it,' said Jack. 'But she was a little kid.'

'No, it lasted for years. She would go up in that lighthouse every night and make us turn on the light and shine it over the sky looking for Tillie.'

'Lizzie said she was looking for Tillie in Heaven.'

'Yes, well, it was very stressful for all of us. And then the light stopped working and she became very depressed. When Fred got the job offer in Cleveland, we jumped at it to get away from here. And to answer your question, I *was* stunned when she told me she was thinking of coming back here.'

'But she was a grown woman with three kids. She wasn't going to be searching the sky for Heaven and her dead sister.'

'Can you be sure of that?'

'Yeah, I can.'

'How?'

'Because I know Lizzie.'

Bonnie looked away but did not appear to be convinced.

Jack decided to change the subject. 'You and Fred are welcome to use the place anytime you want.'

'That's very nice of you, but I really couldn't. It took everything I had just to come here today.' Bonnie went over to the window and gazed up at the lighthouse, and then shuddered. 'I can't believe the thing is still standing.' She sat down. 'I'd like to see the kids while Fred and I are here.'

'Of course. Anytime you want.' Jack started to say something else but then caught himself.

However, Bonnie seemed to sense his conflict. 'What is it?'

'The tabloid story about the Miracle Man?' he said.

'It was disgusting. If I could have found that damned reporter, I would have strangled him.'

Jack looked confused. 'If you could have found him?'

She stared at him, and then what he was thinking apparently dawned on her. 'Do you really think I would have spoken to a trashy gossip paper about my own daughter?'

'But the things in the story. Who else would have known about them?'

'I don't know. But I can assure you it wasn't me.'

'And her going back out that night for the meds? You brought me the bag of pills. You seemed really angry about it.'

Bonnie looked embarrassed. 'I *was* angry about it. But I knew it wasn't your doing. I called Lizzie thinking she was home. She was at the pharmacy. She told me you hadn't wanted her to go out. I only acted that way towards you because . . . well, I'd just buried my daughter, and I was hardly thinking clearly. I'm sorry.'

'OK, I completely understand that.'

'I care about the children. I want the best for them.'

'I know. So do I.'

She drew a long breath. 'Jack, this is hard, but hear me out.'

OK, here it comes, thought Jack. *The real reason she's here.*

'I've spoken with numerous doctors since your recovery.'

'Why would you do that?' he said sharply.

'Because the children are only one parent from becoming orphans.'

'I'm alive, Bonnie, in case you hadn't noticed.'

'Every doctor I talked to said it's not possible. The disease you have is fatal, without exception. That's what they said.'

'Had. I *had* the disease. I don't have it any longer.'

'Which these doctors said was also impossible. It may go dormant, but it always comes back. Those three children have been through so much. You on your deathbed. Lizzie dying. Having to be uprooted. What if you get sick again? And you die? Do you have any idea what it will do to them? They're only children; it will destroy them.'

'What do you want me to do? Give them back to you? Go crawl off in a corner and wait and see if I get sick again?'

'No, but you could come and live with us in Arizona. You and the kids. That way if something does happen to you, we'll be there to help you, and the kids will be used to living with us.'

Jack looked at her askance. 'Are you telling me that you're willing to take me and all three kids?'

'Yes. Mother left me quite a bit of money. We're in a position to purchase a larger house and support all of you.'

'I can support my own family,' he said.

'I didn't mean it that way. I'm just looking to help you.'

'I appreciate that.'

'So you won't consider my offer?'

'No, I'm afraid not.'

Bonnie stood. 'Well, I guess that's that. Can I go and see the children now?'

'Absolutely. I want you involved in the kids' lives.'

'I want that, too.'

8

On Sunday, Jack piled all the kids into the VW and drove into Channing. He'd been working hard at Jenna's house and a few other jobs, and the kids needed a break from the Palace. Jack had got hold of Ned Parker, and he'd agreed to give the family a tour of the Channing Play House.

Parker showed Cory how to manipulate the house lights, lift and lower scenery, move equipment on stage dollies, and work the trapdoor in the middle of the stage that would allow people to seem to vanish. Jackie, in particular, thought that was very cool.

They left the theatre and walked along, looking at various restaurants. Someone called out to Jack from across the street. He saw Charles Pinckney hurrying over to them.

'Taking the Sabbath off to enjoy the pleasures of Channing?'

Jack nodded. 'Get away from the house for a bit. See the town.'

'You hungry?'

Jack said, 'We're deciding where to go.'

Charles's eyes twinkled. 'Then there's only one real option.'

'A Little Bit of Love,' said Mikki immediately.

Jack said, 'We've already been there. How about another place? There're three right here on this block.'

'But Jackie and Cory haven't seen it.' Mikki turned to her brothers. 'It's full of musical stuff; it's so cool.'

'Cool,' chimed in Jackie.

She smiled. 'You want a bit of love, Jackie, huh?'

He jumped up and down. 'Bit-a-love! Bit-a-love!'

'Jenna does the best Sunday brunch in town, actually,' advised Charles. 'I was just heading there myself.'

'OK,' Jack said in a resigned tone.

Jenna smiled when she saw them come in. The place was crowded, but she said, 'I've got a nice window table. Follow me.' She seated them, handed out menus, and took their drink orders.

After Jenna left, Jack turned to Charles. 'Bonnie came by.'

'She told me she was going to.'

'Did she tell you what about?'

'Yes. I saw her afterwards. She told me what you said. And I told her I agreed with you. I don't think that's what she wanted to hear.'

Mikki said, 'What didn't she want to hear?'

'Another time, Mik,' said her father, shooting a glance at the boys. Then he added, 'Did you have a good time with her?'

'She was more laid back than in Arizona,' Mikki replied. 'There, she was like a control freak. Drove me nuts.'

Jack turned back to Charles. 'I checked out the lighthouse the other night.'

'Did you? It really was something in its day.'

'I bet it was,' said Jack. 'I bet it was.'

AFTER LUNCH, they were walking back to the van when Charles pointed across the street and said, 'Speak of the devil.'

Bonnie and Fred were just entering a gift shop. Mikki walked up beside Jack and said in a low voice, 'OK, Dad, what is going on with Grandma? Why is she really here?'

'She just came by to make an offer.' Mikki waited expectantly. 'For us all to go and live with her in Arizona.'

'No way. You're not thinking of doing that, are you?'

'No, I'm not.'

She was about to say something else when they heard, 'Hey, Miracle Man!'

Jack jerked round to see where the voice had come from. He saw two large men sitting in the cab of a pickup truck. One man stuck his head out of the truck. 'I need me a miracle.' He waved a five-dollar bill. 'I'll pay good money for it.' Both men laughed. They got out of the truck and leaned against it.

Cory said fearfully, 'Dad?'

'It's OK, son. We'll just keep on walking.'

One of them said, 'Hey, you too good to stop for us poor folk?'

Jack said to the kids, 'We'll go on down to the beach when we get back, and—'

'Hey, was it true your slutty wife was cheating on you?'

Jack moved quickly. When he rushed at them, the first man threw a punch. Jack ducked it, grabbed the man's hand, swung him round, and slammed him into the truck. The second man cannoned into Jack's back, propelling him face-first into a lamppost. Jack spun out of the man's grasp, laid a fist into his diaphragm and then kicked his legs out from under him, sending him down to the pavement, where he stayed, groaning.

Jack was bent over, his breaths coming in gasps, blood pouring down his face from where he'd hit the post. As he looked round, it seemed like the entire town of Channing was staring back at him. He saw Jenna and Liam staring at him from the door to the Little Bit, and saw Bonnie and Fred gawping at him in shock from the entrance to the gift shop.

'Daddy!'

Jack looked over his shoulder. Jackie was standing on the sidewalk bawling. Cory stood there looking in amazement at his dad, while Mikki glowered contemptuously at the two men lying on the pavement. 'Idiots,' she said.

Jack quickly piled his kids into the VW and drove off.

JACK SAT AT THE KITCHEN TABLE with ice wrapped in a paper towel and held over his left cheek. When someone knocked on the door, he half expected it to be the police.

'Old man and wady,' squealed Jackie after he opened the door.

Jenna and Charles strode in. She was carrying a small bag and sat down next to Jack. She started pulling things out: sterilised wipes, Band-Aids, an ice pack and antibiotic cream.

'What are you two doing here?' asked Jack.

Jenna cleaned up the cuts, applied ointment, and covered it all with a large Band-Aid. 'Those two idiots,' said Jenna. 'Going off like that. Probably drunk.'

'You know them?' asked Jack.

'They come into the bar every once in a while.' She closed her bag. 'OK, you should be good to go.' She gazed steadily at Jack. 'Looks like you didn't forget your army training. Those weren't small guys, and you put 'em down fast.'

Jack grimaced. 'It was stupid. Never should've happened.'

The door opened, and Sammy walked in. When he saw Jack, he exclaimed, 'What the hell happened? You fall off a ladder?'

Jackie yelled, 'Daddy pighting.'

'Fighting? Who with?' demanded Sammy.

Mikki and Cory both started telling Sammy what had happened. The older man's features darkened as he listened.

'Uh-oh,' said Jackie. He was peering out of the window into the front yard. *'Cop dude,'* he said, in a very un-Jackie-like whisper.

'Great,' said Jack stiffly, as he rose to answer the door.

The sheriff identified himself as Nathan Tammie. He was a big man with a serious face and dark, curly hair. He took Jack's statement and scratched his chin. 'That pretty much matches up with what other people said happened. But you *did* go after them.'

'He was provoked. They were saying nasty things about our mom,' exclaimed Mikki. 'What did you expect him to do?'

Jenna said, 'Sheriff, Charles and I saw the whole thing. It's exactly as Mikki said. He was provoked.'

'I'm not saying I wouldn't have done the same thing, Jenna, but I also can't let things like this happen in town without consequences. I've already told those two boys to back off. And I expect you to hold on to your temper, Mr Armstrong. If something happens again, you come tell me, and I'll handle it. 'Cause if there's a next time, people are gonna end up in jail.'

'I understand.'

The sheriff left. Charles said, 'He's a good man, but he means what he says.' He looked at Jenna. 'I can drive you back to town.'

'Can you give me a minute, Charles?'

Sammy had gone into another room, and the kids had disappeared.

Jenna said to Jack, 'Miracle Man?'

Jack stared at her. 'It's a long story.'

'I'm a good listener.'

'Maybe we can talk about it. Just not right now.'

'Well, you need anything else, just let me know.' She rose to go.

'Jenna? Thanks for coming over. Means a lot.'

She smiled. 'Next time, I hope I don't have to bring my first-aid kit.'

THE SOUND WOKE all of them. Lights burst on. Jack and Sammy made sure the kids were OK before checking the rest of the house.

'Sounded like a bomb,' said Sammy. 'Or a building collapsed.'

Jack looked at him quizzically and then said, 'Oh, damn!'

He ran outside, Sammy racing after him.

Jack sprinted over the rocks. He ripped open the door of the lighthouse and stopped. The stairs had collapsed. He shone his light upwards. Forty vertical feet of wood had tumbled down.

Jack swallowed. Now he couldn't get to the top. He turned to Sammy. 'I need to rebuild the stairs. We can get the materials tomorrow.'

'But we still have to finish some other jobs. And Charles has got some more referrals for us. Lady named Anne Bethune has a big house on the beach. She wants a porch enclosed and some other stuff done. Good money.'

'I *have* to do it, Sammy.'

'Gonna be expensive.'

'Take it out of my share. And I don't expect you to help.'

Sammy frowned. 'Since when do we have shares and not help each other?'

'But this is different, Sammy. I can't expect you to do this, too.'

Sammy looked at the hand-painted sign next to the door and said quietly, 'We'll do the paying stuff during the day and this after hours. OK?'

'OK,' said Jack. As Sammy turned to go back in the house, he added, 'Thanks, Sammy.'

He turned around. 'Never been married, Jack. But I understand losing somebody. Especially someone like Lizzie.'

'WHAT'S ALL THIS FOR?' Charles asked as Jack and Sammy finished loading the truck the next morning.

'Stairs in the lighthouse fell down,' said Jack. 'No one was hurt.' He finished strapping everything down before he pulled out a sheet of paper. 'I found a blueprint on the lighting system. I'd appreciate it if you could see if these pieces of equipment could be ordered.'

Charles glanced at the list. 'Might take some time. And it won't be cheap.'

Jack climbed into the truck. 'Thanks.'

Sammy gave Charles a helpless look and got in the truck.

As they were driving out of town, Sammy said, 'Isn't that Bonnie?'

Jack looked to where he was pointing. It was indeed Bonnie. And she was sitting in a car with a younger man dressed in a suit.

'Who's the guy?' asked Sammy.

'Never seen him before.'

They unloaded the materials at the Palace. Then Sammy drove off to meet Anne Bethune while Jack continued on to Jenna's.

Jenna met him at the door, still dressed in a robe and slippers.

'Sorry about my appearance. The restaurant business isn't nine to five: it's more like ten in the morning to midnight. You want some coffee?'

'OK, thanks.'

She poured him a cup and brought it down to him in the music room. She watched him hanging new drywall.

'Our kids have really hit it off playing music together. First time I've seen Liam really take an interest in anyone down here.'

'He seems like a fine young man. And Mikki's mood is a lot better. That's worth its weight in gold.' He put down his tools and took a sip of coffee. 'Mind if I ask you a personal question?'

'Shoot.'

'Ever think about getting married again?'

'I've thought about it, sure.'

'I mean, you've been divorced a while. You're young, well-off, smart and educated. And . . . really pretty.'

She put her cup down and sat. 'There have been some men interested in a permanent relationship with me. But they weren't the right ones. And I'm a woman who's willing to wait for the real Mr Right. Especially considering how *wrong* I got it the first time.'

'Lizzie and I met in high school. We would've celebrated our seventeenth wedding anniversary this year.'

'Sounds like you found Mrs Right on your first try.'

'I did,' he said frankly.

'I suppose that makes the loss that much harder.'

'It does. But I've got our kids to raise. And I have to do it right. For Lizzie.'

'And you, Jack. You're part of the equation, too.'

'And me,' he said. 'And I hope you find Mr Right.'

'Me, too,' said Jenna wistfully, as she stared at him.

SAMMY TURNED TO JACK and said, 'It's time to knock off. It's past midnight.'

'You go on. I'm just going to finish up a few things.'

After working most of the last three days at Anne Bethune's, Sammy and

Jack had eaten a hasty dinner and worked another four hours on the lighthouse. They had cleared out all the wood from the collapsed stairs and assembled the scaffolding up to the top platform, which also needed repair. Fresh lumber delivered from Charles Pinckney's hardware store was neatly stacked outside.

'Jack, you've put in sixteen hours today. You need to rest.'

'I will, Sammy. Just another thirty minutes.'

Sammy shook his head, dropped his tool belt, stretched his aching back, and walked slowly back to the Palace.

Jack tightened some of the scaffolding supports and then climbed up to the top and stepped out onto the catwalk. He was trying to imagine what Lizzie the little girl would have thought of the view from up there.

He stared out at the dark ocean and let the breeze wash over his face. As he eyed the sky, he looked to his right and was surprised to see someone walking along the beach. As the person drew closer, Jack could see that it was Jenna. He looked at his watch. It was nearly one in the morning. What was she doing out there?

She looked up, and under the arc of moonlight she saw him. She waved and started toward the rocks, calling up to him, 'Working late?'

He said, 'Just finishing up. Surprised to see you out.'

'I take a walk on the beach after closing Little Bit. Helps to relax me.' She gazed at the lighthouse. 'Heard you were fixing it up.'

'Trying.' He added, 'Guess it seems pretty crazy.'

'I think it's a good idea,' she said, surprising him. 'By the way, you did a great job on the soundproofing. It's raised the quality of my life a thousand per cent. And I won't have to kill my only child.'

'I'm glad I could help.'

'Well, I guess I'd better head back.'

Jack looked down the dark beach. 'Do you want me to walk back with you? It's pretty dark out there.'

'I'll be fine. You look like you have some thinking to do, still.'

Before he could say anything, she'd turned and walked off. He slowly climbed back down the scaffolding. When he touched bottom, he passed through the doorway and turned to look at the hand-painted sign.

'I'm going to get it working,' he said. 'Lizzie, I promise that this light will work again. And then you can look down from Heaven and see it.'

And maybe see me.

9

'Oh, great,' said Mikki. It was Saturday night, and she was at the beach party Blake Saunders had invited her to. There were lots of people already there, and one of them was Tiffany Murdoch, holding court by the large bonfire. There were quite a few young men in football jerseys and girls in short shorts, tight skirts and tighter tops. A catering truck was parked on the road near the beach.

Blake spotted her and strolled over. 'Hey, glad you could make it.'

'Never been to a beach party that was catered before,' she said.

'I know. But Tiffany's dad is a big football fan, and he pays for the party every year.'

'Well, look who we have here.'

Inwardly groaning, Mikki closed her eyes and then opened them. Things were about to get worse.

Tiffany stood in front of her, swaying slightly, plastic cup filled with beer in hand. She had on a bikini bottom with a cut-off jersey that barely covered her chest. 'What's your name again?'

Between gritted teeth she said, 'Mikki.'

'Oh, like Mickey Mouse.' Tiffany giggled and looked around. 'Mickey Mouse, people.'

A nervous-looking Blake put his arm round Tiffany's bare waist. 'Hey, Tiff, let's go get something to eat.'

'Not hungry,' Tiffany said with a pout.

Mikki looked at the beer and then eyed Tiffany's red convertible. 'Hope you're not the designated driver.'

'I can be anything I want,' Tiffany replied.

Blake pulled on her arm. 'Come on, Tiff, let's get some food. You don't want to piss off your dad again, remember?'

'Shut up!' snapped Tiffany. She looked at Mikki. 'I hear you and Blake have been running together on the beach.'

'Yeah, so?'

'I didn't think he liked hanging out with freaks.'

'OK, I'm leaving now.' Mikki turned to walk away.

'Hey, I'm talking to you.' Tiffany grabbed Mikki hard by her shoulder.

Mikki's arms and legs seemed to move of their own accord. Her hand clamped like a vice on the girl's wrist. She spun the arm behind Tiffany's back, jerked upward, angled one of her feet in front of Tiffany's legs, and gave a hard shove from behind. The next moment, Tiffany was lying face down in the sand.

Blake looked at her in amazement. 'How'd you do that?'

Mikki looked down at her hands. 'My . . . my dad taught me.'

They looked down at Tiffany, who was spitting out sand and crying. Other people were walking towards them.

'I'm outta here,' said a panicked Mikki. She turned and raced off. Hurrying down the beach, she collided with someone. 'Liam? What are you doing here?' she asked.

'Walking. What about you?' He looked over her shoulder in the direction of the party Mikki had just left. 'Tiffany's party? Don't tell me you've gone over to the dark side?' he said with a grin.

'It was stupid,' admitted Mikki.

'Well, I'll show you a much better party.'

He started to walk off, and Mikki hurried after him.

The sounds and the lights reached them about a quarter of a mile down the beach. As they drew closer, the scene became clearer. The bonfire was full and the flames high. Mikki could hear a guitar strumming and sticks popping on a drum pad. Laughter and whoops amid the crash of waves.

'Hey, Liam,' said one guy as he approached them. 'Everyone was hoping you'd make it.' He handed them each a long stick. 'Dogs are cooking.' They joined the crowd. Everyone greeted Liam with high fives, chest bumps and knuckle smacks.

'Pretty popular guy,' Mikki remarked.

'Nah, the guys think my mom is hot, and the girls want jobs at the Little Bit. They're just looking to use me.'

Mikki laughed.

Liam eyed the two guys playing the guitar and the drum pad. He looked at Mikki. 'Want to really get this party cooking?'

She instantly got his meaning. 'Oh, let's *so* do it.'

They played while the crowd whooped and cheered. Mikki sang parts of a song she was working on that the crowd really got into. Then she grabbed the drumsticks and showed herself to be nearly as adept at drums as she was at guitar. Even Liam looked at her in amazement. She explained, 'When I formed my band, I learned every instrument. I'm sort of a control freak.'

Later, they roasted some hot dogs. When someone started playing tunes on a portable CD player, Liam said, 'You want to do some sand dancing?'

'What's that?'

'Uh, it's really complicated. It's dancing in the sand in your bare feet.'

She smiled. 'I think I can manage that.'

He put both arms round her waist, and she put her hands on his shoulders. They danced slowly over the beach.

As the music played on, they grew closer.

'This is really nice, Liam.'

'Yeah, it is.'

She cupped his chin with her hand, kissed him, and then stepped back. 'I had a great time. Thanks for bringing me.'

'You need a ride home?' he asked.

'I actually rode a bike I found at the house. Left it up on the street. It's not that far.'

'I've got a bike, too. I'll ride with you. It's on my way.'

'You don't have to do that.'

'I know. I want to.' He paused, looking embarrassed. 'I mean . . .'

'I know what you mean,' she said softly.

He saw her safely to her house, waved, and cycled off.

When she walked in, her dad called out from the front room. 'So?' he said. 'Have fun?'

'Yeah, just at a different party.' She told him about the evening.

'Sounds like you made the right choice.'

She sat down next to him. 'So how's the lighthouse coming? You've really been spending a lot of time on it.'

He looked at her. 'I know it must seem strange.'

'Dad, it doesn't seem strange. OK, maybe a little,' she amended with a smile. 'It's just that you said we came down here so you could spend more time with us. But you and Sammy work all the time, and I'm stuck watching Cory and Jackie.'

Jack's head dropped. 'It's complicated, Mikki.'

Mikki rose. In a disappointed tone she said, 'Yeah, I guess it is.'

'I'll try to get better. Maybe we can do something next weekend?'

She brightened. 'Like what?'

Jack said lamely, 'Um, I haven't thought of it yet.'

Her face fell. 'Right. Sure. Goodnight.' She headed upstairs.

Neither one of them noticed Sammy standing at his bedroom door listening to their exchange. The former Delta Force member went into his room, picked up his cellphone, and made a call.

'I'M HUNGRY, Jack, so let's go.'

They were parked on the street in Channing. Sammy was eyeing Jenna's restaurant, but Jack didn't seem to want to budge.

'It's not like this is the only place to eat in town, Sammy.'

Sammy snapped, 'She's just a nice lady who's trying to be friends with you, and you won't give her the time of day because you feel guilty about Lizzie. I'm going to eat. Stay here if you want.' Sammy slammed the truck door behind him and went inside A Little Bit of Love.

Jack sat there brooding. Finally, he followed Sammy inside. His friend was tucked in a corner, studying his menu. Jack wandered over and sat down across from Sammy, who handed him a menu. 'Figured your empty belly would bring you to your senses.'

Jack took the menu, glanced at it, and then dropped it on the table. 'I don't know what you expect from me.'

'OK, let's hash this out. When's the last time you played with Jackie? Or Cory? Or said two words to Mikki?'

'I talked to Mikki about stuff just last night.'

'I know you did because I was there listening. But what exactly has changed? You work all day, and then you work on that damn lighthouse all night. It's not healthy, Jack. You half killed yourself clawing your way back from a death sentence. And for what? To be miserable the rest of your life? You got kids, Jack. They need you.'

'I know I haven't exactly been the perfect father. My daughter has already reminded me of that.'

'She does that because she cares about you. And, hell, she's damn near sixteen. She probably wants to spend her time doing something other than watching her two kid brothers all day.'

'She went to a party on the beach. Plays music with Liam.'

'OK, fine, excuse me for giving a damn.'

Jack's anger evaporated with this last comment. 'You're right. It's not enough to support my kids. I have to be there for them.'

Sammy looked relieved. 'Well, hallelujah.'

But Jack wasn't listening to him any more. He was thinking about something else Sammy had said. *She's damn near sixteen.*

The date popped into Jack's head. Her birthday. Coming up fast. And it was a big one.

'You guys ready to order?'

Jack looked up to see a waitress standing next to their table.

'I'll take care of these two, Sally,' said a voice. Jenna walked up. 'They could be trouble,' she added with a coy smile.

Sammy looked at her and grinned. 'So tell me the specials.'

'How about our famous pork barbecue sandwich with fried onion rings?'

'Sounds good.' Sammy stared at Jack. 'Make it two. Put a smiley face on his: might improve the man's mood.' He winked.

Jenna said, 'Well, I wanted to talk to you about something anyway, Jack. Let me put your order in, and I'll be right back.'

She walked off and returned a minute later, drawing up a chair.

'I'll get to the point. Your daughter would like to waitress here. And I want to hire her.'

'What?' said Jack. 'She didn't tell me about it.'

Sammy said testily, 'She wanted to, but it's not like you've been around.'

Jack ignored this and looked at Jenna. 'Waitress?'

'It's an honest profession, and I pay a fair wage.'

Jack glanced at Sammy. 'I'll have to get someone to watch the boys.'

Jenna said, 'I actually thought of that. The lady you're doing work for, Anne Bethune? She runs a summer camp at her place. It's right on the beach. The boys could go there.'

Sammy said, 'I've gotten to know Anne, and I saw how the camp was set up. They'll love it.' Sammy added, 'And this way, Mikki can work here during the day. Earn some money, get out of the house. Have a life.'

'How much does it cost?'

'Now, that's the interesting thing,' said Sammy. 'I'm doing some extra work for her on the side, and Anne agreed to let the boys go there in exchange for it.'

'Sammy, you didn't have to do that.'

'Like hell I didn't. They need to have some fun, too.'

Jack looked between Jenna and Sammy. 'Why do I sense this was all planned out?'

Sammy snapped, 'You got a good reason not to do it?'

Jack locked gazes with Sammy for a long moment before finally looking away. 'OK, fine.'

Sammy slapped the table. 'That wasn't too hard, was it? Jenna, can you add two beers to our order? I feel the need to celebrate.'

Jenna went off to do this while Jack pretended to go to the restroom. Instead, he followed Jenna. 'I need to ask you something.'

She looked at him in surprise. 'Look, Jack, I know it seemed like we ganged up on you about camp and Mikki working here, but—'

He smiled. 'I actually really appreciate what you're doing.'

'Thank Sammy. It was his idea. You've got a good friend in that man.'

'You're right. I do. And a good friend in you, too.'

This comment seemed to catch Jenna off-guard. She looked away, flustered, but then she quickly looked back at him. 'So what did you want to ask me?'

'I don't want to do it now. What time would be good later?'

'I can get away from here around nine.'

'I can pick you up here. Drive you home.'

'That's fine.'

'I'll see you then.'

JACK WAS WAITING OUTSIDE the restaurant when Jenna came out promptly at nine. She climbed into the VW van, and he pulled off.

She rolled down the window and breathed in the crisp evening air. 'In college, a guy I dated had a Harley. One time, when Liam was staying with my mom, we rode it all over the Blue Ridge Parkway. It was so much fun.'

'Were you away from Liam a lot back then?'

She rolled the window back up. 'Hardly ever, actually. I went to college close to home so I could stay there. My mom would often watch Liam for me when I was at class or working.'

'Working?'

'Only way to pay for school. I knew I wanted to go to college and then law school. And then work at a big firm in a big city.'

'Sounds like you had it all mapped out.'

'Well, I didn't have Liam mapped out. He just happened.' Her features grew solemn. 'But I don't know what I'd do without him in my life. He's a great kid. And he and Mikki really seem to have hit it off. When I told him she was going to be working at the Little Bit, he was really psyched.'

'Well, that's actually the reason I wanted to talk to you. About Liam.' Jack told her his plan.

She was nodding and smiling as they pulled up to her house. 'OK, that sounds terrific. Liam's not here yet. Would you like to come in for some tea or coffee, or something stronger?'

They sat out on the rear deck sipping glasses of chardonnay. After going over the details of Jack's plan in more depth, Jenna said, 'How's the lighthouse coming?'

He put down his glass. 'Good. Stairs are coming along, and Charles found the parts to repair the light.'

'I bet it'll be something to see it fired up again.'

'Yeah, I think it will,' Jack said absently. He drained the rest of his glass. 'I'd better get going.' He rose.

'Jack? Let me know when you get the lighthouse working. I'd really love to see it.'

Taken aback by her obvious sincerity, he said, 'I will, Jenna.'

10

The next morning, at the breakfast table, Mikki said, 'I'm going into town today.'

'Why?'

'Just an errand to run. Liam's going with me. I won't be long. Sammy said he'd watch Jackie.'

'When do you start working at the restaurant?'

'Tomorrow. That's when Cory and Jackie start camp.'

'You know, you could have come to me with all that.'

She put a hand on her hip and said, 'Could I have, Dad?'

He looked away. 'So how are you getting to town? Want a lift?'

'Liam's picking me up.'

'Look, Mikki, I want you to be able to talk to me about stuff. If we can't do that, then we've got no shot at this father-daughter thing.'

'You really mean that?'

'Yeah, I do.'

'Well, it would be a nice start if you didn't work all day and then go to the lighthouse all night.'

'But I've almost got it finished.'

'OK, Dad, whatever. We can talk when you're done with it.'

MIKKI WALKED OUT to the street, where Liam was waiting.

They arrived in downtown Channing and parked in front of the Play House. There were a number of cars sitting at the kerb, including Tiffany's red convertible. The marquee read CHANNING TALENT COMPETITION APPLICATIONS TODAY.

They walked inside the lobby and joined a line of people standing in front of a long table, behind which sat a number of ladies with hair styled to the max. One of them, an attractive blonde woman in a close-fitting dress, seemed to be in charge.

'Let me guess,' Mikki whispered to Liam as she pointed at the woman. 'Tiffany's mom?'

Liam nodded. 'I heard she was even worse than her daughter.'

When Liam and Mikki reached the table, Chelsea Murdoch looked up at them. 'Yes?'

'We'd like to enter the competition,' said Mikki politely.

Murdoch glanced at Liam. 'Liam Fontaine, right?' she said. Then her gaze swivelled to Mikki. 'And you are?'

'Michelle Armstrong. We're down here from Cleveland for the summer.'

The woman looked amused. 'Cleveland?'

'Why, yes, it's the largest city in Ohio. Did you know that?' Mikki asked, innocently.

'No, I never saw a good reason to find out,' Mrs Murdoch replied. She pushed a piece of paper towards them. 'Fill this out. And there's a ten-dollar processing fee. What are you going to do for your act?'

'Music,' said Mikki. 'Drums, keyboard and guitar.'

Chelsea Murdoch looked at her coolly. 'Pretty ambitious.'

Mikki replied sweetly, 'I'm sure the competition is pretty tough.'

'It is. In fact, one young lady has won it three years in a row and is looking to make it four. Just put the form in the box over there and give your money to the lady in the blue dress.'

'Great. Thanks for all your help, Mrs Murdoch,' Mikki said in her most polite schoolgirl voice. She filled out the form and gave it and their entry fee to the woman in the blue dress.

'OK, step one is done,' Liam said.

'And here comes step two.'

Tiffany and some of her friends had just walked into the theatre. When Mikki nodded at them, Tiffany blanked her.

'Hey, Tiff.'

'Hi,' she said coolly.

'I just wanted to thank you for making me feel so welcome at your party.'

'Uh, OK.'

Mikki smiled pleasantly. 'Just so we're straight, we're going to kick your ass in the talent competition.'

Tiffany blinked. 'You think you're so tough?'

'I'm from Cleveland. It's a requirement.'

'SO WHAT'S THE CONSPIRACY?' Jenna had come into the kitchen at the Little Bit to find Liam and Mikki using their break to huddle in one corner.

'Nothing, Mom,' Liam said, a little too innocently.

'Son, you forget I was a lawyer. My lie detector is well oiled.'

He glanced at Mikki. 'You want to tell her?'

Mikki said, 'We entered the talent competition as a musical act.'

'Well, that's great. Why keep it a secret?'

Liam answered, 'We'll be going up against Tiffany, and her family is an important player in town. If we beat her out of winning for the fourth year in a row, the Murdochs might mess with you.'

'They can try, but I don't think it'll do much good. The Little Bit is here to stay. But does your dad know you're entering?'

'Not yet.' Mikki gazed at her. 'Would you mind telling him? It might be better coming from another parent. And we've already entered. I can't pull out now.'

Jenna thought about this. 'OK, I'll talk to him.' She checked her watch and smiled. 'Break time's over.'

Mikki gave her a quick hug. 'Thanks. You're a lifesaver.'

AT A LITTLE PAST MIDNIGHT, Jack stood on the catwalk of the lighthouse, staring out at a clear sky. After his conversation with Mikki, he had tried to not come out here, but here he was.

He'd worked all day with Sammy on Anne Bethune's project, which had also given him time to see her camp. He had to admit that Jackie and Cory were having a wonderful time. It was exactly the sort of experience Jack had hoped for them when they came for the summer. However, Jack was trying not to focus on the fact that he wasn't an integral part of that experience.

If I can just finish the lighthouse.

He took a letter from his shirt pocket. The envelope had the number '4' written on it. The letter was dated December 21. He leaned against the railing and read it.

> *Dear Lizzie,*
>
> *Christmas is almost here, and I promise I will make it. It will be a great day. Seeing the kids' faces when they open their presents will be better for me than all the medications in the world. I know this has been hard on everyone. But I know your mom and dad have been a tremendous help to you. Sometimes I feel your mom thinks you might have married someone better suited to you, more successful. But I know deep down that she cares about me, and I know she loves you and the kids with all her heart. I hope that one day she will feel that I was a good father who tried to do the right thing. And that maybe I was worthy of you.*
>
> *Love,*
> *Jack*

'Am I interrupting something?'

Jack turned to see Jenna standing there on the catwalk, a bottle of wine and two glasses in hand. He thrust the letter into his jeans pocket. 'What are you doing here?' he said, a little harshly.

She took a step back. 'I'm sorry if I snuck up on you.'

'No, it's OK. I'm sorry. I just wasn't expecting anyone.'

She smiled. 'I wonder why? It's after midnight and you're standing on your own property at the top of a lighthouse.'

His anger faded. He eyed the wine. 'Coming from a party?'

She looked round and set the glasses on an old crate, then uncorked the wine. She poured some out, handed him a glass and told him about Liam and Mikki entering the talent competition.

'Hey, that's great. I bet they have a good chance to win. But why didn't Mikki just come and tell me?'

'I'm not sure. You should ask her.'

Jack nodded. 'I know I've got my priorities screwed up.'

'Well, realising the problem is the first step to fixing it. And you're good at fixing things.'

'Yeah, well, lighthouses are easier than relationships.'

'I would imagine anything is easier than that. But that doesn't mean you can ignore it.'

'I'm starting to see that.'

Jenna paused, then asked, 'Why is the lighthouse so important to you?'

He put his wineglass down. 'This feels like the place I can be closest to her,' Jack said slowly. '"The Miracle Man." I wasn't supposed to be here. I mean living. I was just hanging on 'til Christmas, for the kids. For Lizzie.' He paused. 'I spent half our marriage in the army, most of it away from home. I was crazy in love with my wife. I always saw Lizzie and me as one person. That's how lucky I was.'

Jenna said quietly, 'You were truly blessed.'

'The last night we were together, she told me she wanted to come back here for the summer. I could tell she wanted to believe that I would be alive to come with her. She even talked about me fixing up the place. This lighthouse. I never thought I'd have the chance.'

'So you're fulfilling Lizzie's last wish?'

'I guess. Because she never got the chance to come back.'

Jenna said, 'And then you got better?'

He glanced at her. 'But do you know why I got better? Because Lizzie was right there with me. She wouldn't let me die.'

'Why are you telling me all this?'

'You seemed like someone who would understand.'

A gentle rain began to fall. Jenna put down her glass, gripped Jack's shoulders, turned him to her, and put her arms round him.

'I do understand, Jack. I really do.'

'JENNA, YOU REALLY don't have to do this,' said Mikki.

They were at a women's clothing store in downtown Channing during a break from the restaurant. 'It's no big deal. I mean, it's only dinner out with my family.'

'But it's your sixteenth birthday.'

They'd selected five or six outfits, and Mikki was trying them on. After

Mikki decided on a dark sleeveless dress, Jenna helped her pick out shoes, a purse and other accessories.

Mikki was looking at all the items and mentally calculating the prices. 'Uh, I'm going to have to put some of these things back. I don't have enough money.'

'Sure you do: I just gave you an advance on your salary.'

'What?'

'I do it with all my new employees, or at least the ones turning sixteen who want something new to wear.'

Mikki laughed. 'Are you sure?'

'Absolutely. Seriously, you're a really good waitress and a hard worker. That should be rewarded.'

After they left the shop, Jenna said, 'How about an ice cream? I've got something I want to talk to you about.'

They sat outside the ice-cream parlour with their cones. 'I spoke with your dad about the talent competition, and he's fine with you entering.'

'Wow, that's great.'

Jenna licked her cone and, choosing her words, said, 'The lighthouse?'

Mikki sighed. 'What about it?'

'Have you ever been out there with him?'

'No.' Mikki swallowed.

'You resent it?'

'Look, if he chooses to be out there instead of with his family, who am I to rock the boat?'

'You know that was your mom's lighthouse?'

Mikki scowled. 'Yeah, my mom when she was a little girl.'

'So you think it's odd he seems so . . .'

'Obsessed? Yeah, a little. What would you think?'

'Difficult to say. It's the hardest thing in the world to put yourself in someone else's place; to try to really feel what they feel, figure out why they do the things they do. Especially when it's easier to stick a label on something. Or someone.'

'And the lighthouse?'

'Lizzie loved it at some point in her life. It was important to her. She wanted to see it work again. That's good enough for your father. He'll work himself to the bone to try and fix it.'

'For her?'

'Your dad isn't crazy. He knows she's gone, Mikki. He's doing this for her memory. At least partly. This is all part of the healing process. Everyone does it differently. This is your father's way.'

'So what do you think I should do?'

'At some point, find the courage to talk to him.'

'About what?'

'I think you'll figure it out.'

Mikki put her hand on Jenna's arm. 'Thanks for the ice cream. And for the advice.'

'You're very welcome to both, sweetie.'

11

On Saturday night, Jenna helped Mikki get dressed in her new clothes and did her hair. She pinned most of it back but let a few strands trickle down Mikki's long, slender neck.

Cory and Jackie were sitting on the couch together watching TV. They both stared wide-eyed at their sister when she came down the stairs followed by a proud-looking Jenna.

'Mikki bootiful,' said Jackie.

Cory didn't say anything; he just kept staring, as if it was the first time he'd realised his sister was a girl.

Sammy came out of the kitchen, saw her, and said, 'Wow. OK, people, heartbreaker coming through, make room. Make room.'

Mikki blushed deeply and said, 'Sammy, knock it off!'

Jack walked in from the kitchen and froze. 'You look terrific.'

'Jenna helped me.'

Jack flashed Jenna an appreciative look. 'Good thing. I'm not all that great with hair and make-up.'

'So where are we going?' asked Mikki.

'Like I said, dinner with the family to celebrate your sweet sixteen.'

She looked at Cory and Jackie watching cartoons and munching on cheese curls. Jackie's face and hands were totally orange. Cory let out a loud belch. 'Great,' she said, trying to sound enthusiastic.

Sammy looked at Jack. 'Hold on a sec. You said we had to finish that job tonight. Remember?'

'Oh, damn, that's right. What was I thinking?'

Mikki scowled. 'Tonight? Dad, it's my *sixteenth* birthday.'

'I know, sweetie, I know. Thank goodness I had a back-up plan.'

He opened the front door, and Mikki gasped. Liam was standing there dressed in pressed chinos and a white, button-down shirt. In his hand was a bouquet of flowers.

Mikki looked from him to her dad. 'Uh, what is going on?'

Jack grinned. 'Like you really wanted to go out on your sixteenth birthday with your old man and two little brothers?'

'That would've been fine,' she said, trying to keep a straight face.

Liam handed the bouquet to Mikki. 'You really look great.'

'Pretty slick yourself.' She eyed her dad. 'So what's the plan?'

'Like I said, dinner. For two. Reservations have been made. Not the Little Bit. At the fancy restaurant in town.'

'Wow, I can't believe this is happening. I feel like Cinderella.'

Jack put his arm round his daughter. 'Nice to know I can still surprise you. Happy birthday, baby.'

JACK LAY ON HIS BACK in the room of the lighthouse that contained the lighting machinery. He was not making much progress. He'd followed the blueprint detailing the electrical and operational guts of the machinery to the letter, but still something was off.

'Dad?'

He pulled himself out from the confined space and looked over at the opening to the area below. Mikki, her hair plastered back on her head, was staring back up at him.

'Mik, are you OK?' He sat up. 'You're wet.'

'I'm fine. It's raining.'

He looked out of the window. 'I guess I came out before it started.'

'Can I come up?'

He gave her a hand and pulled her up. As she drew closer, he said, 'It looks like you've been crying. Liam didn't—'

'No, Dad. It has nothing to do with him. Liam was great. We had an awesome date. I . . . I really like him. A lot.'

Jack relaxed. 'OK, but then why . . .'

Mikki took her dad's hand and drew him over to a narrow ledge that ran the length of the room under the window. They sat.

'We need to talk.'

'What about?' he said warily.

'What happened with Mom, you, me. Everything, basically.' She paused. 'Jenna talked to me about some things.'

'What things?' Jack said abruptly.

'Like how you've basically been through hell, and we all need to cut you some slack. And that everybody grieves in their own way.'

'Oh.' Jack looked over at the lighting apparatus and then back at her. 'I'm trying to get through this, Mikki; I really am. It's just not easy. Some days I feel OK; some days I feel completely lost.'

Mikki's face crumpled. 'Dad, I was so scared when you were sick. I didn't know how to handle it. So I thought if I ran away from it, I wouldn't have to deal with it. It was selfish. I'm so sorry.'

He put his arm round her shoulders and let her cry. When she was done, he straightened up and said, 'Mikki, you are one smart kid, but you're also only sixteen. You're not supposed to have all the answers. I'm thirty-five and I don't have all the answers.' He stroked her hair. 'Let me tell you something. When my dad was dying, I did pretty much the same thing. This was a big, strong guy I'd always looked up to. And now he was all weak and helpless. And I didn't want to remember my dad like that. So I pushed everything inside and tuned everyone out. Even him. I was a coward. Maybe that's why I went into the military. To prove that I actually had some courage.'

She looked at him with wide, dry eyes. 'You did, honest?'

'Yeah.'

'Life really sucks sometimes.'

'Yeah, sometimes it really does. But then sometimes it's wonderful and you forget all about the bad stuff.'

She looked down, nervously twisting her fingers.

'Mik, is there something else you need to tell me?'

'Will you promise not to get mad?'

Jack sighed. 'You can tell me anything.'

She faced him. 'I was the one who talked to that gossip paper.'

Jack gaped at her. 'You?'

'I know, it was so stupid. And it got completely out of hand. Most of the junk he wrote he just made up.'

'But why would you talk to a tabloid?'

'I . . . I don't know why I did it. I was confused and angry. And I know you probably hate me. And I don't blame you. I hate myself for doing it.' All of this came out in a rush.

Jack put his arm back round her. 'It doesn't matter any more. You messed up. And you admitted to it. That took a lot of courage.'

'I'm just really, really sorry, Dad. Now that my head's on right about things, it just seems so stupid what I did.'

'I don't think either of us was thinking too clearly for a while.'

'Will you ever be able to forgive me? To trust me again?'

He touched her cheek. 'I do, on both counts.'

'Why?'

'Something called unconditional love, honey.'

JENNA LOOKED UP FROM the counter at the Little Bit to see Jack standing there. She smiled. 'I heard the kids had a fabulous time.'

'Yeah, Mikki's still gushing about it. Look, I was wondering if you had time tonight for some dinner?'

'Sure. What did you have in mind? Not here. Even I get sick of the menu. Hey, I can cook for you.'

'I don't want you to have to do that.'

'I love to cook. But you'll have to be my sous chef.'

'What does that mean?'

'Slicing and dicing mostly. Say around seven thirty?'

'OK, great.'

WHEN JACK GOT TO Jenna's house that night, music was on, wine was poured, and scented candles were lit.

'Don't be freaked out by any of this,' she said as she ushered him in. 'I just like to be comfortable.' She eyed him. 'You look nice.'

He looked down at his new pair of jeans, his pressed white shirt and a pair of pristine loafers that were pinching his feet. Then he looked at her. She had on a yellow sundress and was barefoot.

'Not as nice as you,' he replied. 'And can I go barefoot, too? These shoes are killing me.'

She smiled. 'Go for it.' She led him into the kitchen and pointed to a cutting board and a pile of vegetables. 'Your work awaits.'

Jack chopped and sliced while Jenna moved round the kitchen preparing the rest of the meal.

'So you like to cook?'

'Yep. It was one of those zigzags that life takes. When Liam was older, I took culinary classes. Then when I was thinking about changing careers, running a restaurant seemed a nice fit. The Little Bit's menu is limited, but I've made every dish on it.' She slid a pan of chicken into the oven. 'At home is where I get to impress people.'

'I'm looking forward to being impressed, then.'

An hour later they sat down to eat. After a few bites, Jack raised his glass of wine in tribute to her skills in the kitchen. 'This is great.'

They walked on the beach after cake and coffee.

'Mikki said you and she talked,' Jack began.

'She's a really smart kid. She gets it, Jack. She really does.'

'We talked after she came back from her date. She said you had basically told her to see things from my perspective.'

'I thought that was important.'

'I can understand why she was upset.' He stopped and kicked at the wet sand. 'After I got the kids back, I fell into my old routine. And Mikki jumped on that.'

'On what?'

'That I didn't have a clue how to run a family.'

'Who does? We all just wing it. You really put a lot of pressure on yourself. Bet you did that in the army, too.'

'Only way you survive. You have a mission, you prep it, and you execute that prep. Same with building stuff. You have a plan, you get your materials, and you build it according to the plans.'

'OK, but did every mission and building project go according to plan?'

'Well, no. They never do. You improvise.'

'I think you just defined parenting in a nutshell.'

'You really believe that?'

'*Believe* isn't a strong enough word. I basically *live* that.'

'Does it get easier?'

'Truthfully, some parts of it do, only to be replaced by other parts that are actually harder.' Jenna gripped his shoulder. 'Time, Jack. Time. And little steps. You nearly died. You lost the woman you love. You've moved to a different town. That's a lot.'

'Thanks, Jenna. I needed to hear all this.'

'Always ready to give advice, even if most of it is wrong.'

'I think most of it is right, at least for me.'

She slowly pulled her hand away. 'Things get complicated, Jack, awfully fast. I'm a big believer in taking your time.'

'I think I'm beginning to see that. Thanks for dinner.'

She pecked him on the cheek. 'Thanks for asking. I think you just wanted some assurance, maybe some comfort.'

'But those are big deals for me. I don't go to people with things like that. I'm more of a loner. When Lizzie was alive, I'd go to her. There was nothing we couldn't talk about.'

Heading back to the house, Jenna asked, 'How's the lighthouse coming?'

'Not great,' he admitted. 'I guess I'll die trying to get it to work again.'

A WEEK LATER, Jack turned the wrench one more time, spun the operating dial to the appropriate setting, and stepped back. It had been a week since he'd had dinner with Jenna. And every night he'd been out there working until the wee hours of the morning on the lighthouse. Three times he thought he had it right. Three times he turned out to be wrong. And his anger and frustration had grown with each disappointment.

'Come on,' he said. 'There is no good reason you won't work.'

He stood back and reached for the switch that powered the system. He counted to three, took a breath, and hit the switch.

Nothing happened.

Something seemed to snap in Jack's head. All the misery, all the frustration, all the loss bottled up inside him was suddenly released. He grabbed his wrench and threw it at the machinery. It struck the wall and ricocheted off. Then he ran down the steps, grabbed a crate, carried it out to the rocks, and hurled it as far as he could. Its contents exploded over the wet rocks. He ran down to the beach, yelling and cursing, spinning around uncontrollably, before he dropped onto the sand and sat there, rocking back and forth, face in his hands, tears trickling between his clenched fingers.

'I'm sorry, Lizzie. I really tried. I just can't make it *work*. I can't make it work,' he said again in a quieter voice. 'I can't accept you're gone. I can't! You should be here, not me. Not me!'

His breathing slowed. His mind cleared. The longer he sat there, the greater his calm grew. He looked out to the darkened ocean, seeing the pinpoints of light of far-off ships. They were like earthbound stars. So close but so far away.

He looked skyward towards Lizzie's little patch of Heaven . . . somewhere. He'd never found it.

Now he could fully realise how a little girl could become obsessed over a lighthouse. He was a grown man, and it had happened to him. The mind, it seemed, was a vastly unpredictable thing.

'Dad?'

Jack turned to see Mikki standing behind him. She was in pyjama bottoms and a T-shirt, with a scared look on her face.

'Are you OK?' she said breathlessly. 'I heard you yelling.'

He drew a long breath. 'I'm just trying to understand things that I don't think there's any way to understand.'

'OK,' she said, in a halting voice.

He looked back at the Palace. 'I moved us here for a really selfish reason. I wanted to be close to your mom again. She grew up here. Place was filled with stuff that belonged to her.'

'I can understand that. I didn't want to come here at first. But now I'm glad I did. I look at that photo of Mom you gave me every day. It makes me cry, but it also feels so good.'

He pointed to the lighthouse. 'Do you want to know why I've been busting my butt trying to get that damn thing to work?'

She sat down next to him. 'Because Mom loved it?' she said cautiously. 'And she wanted you to repair it?'

'At first I thought that. But it just occurred to me when I saw you standing there. It was like a fog lifted from my brain.' He paused. 'I realised I just wanted to fix something, anything. I wanted to go down a list, do what I was supposed to do, and the end result would be, presto, it works. Then everything would be OK again.'

'But it didn't happen?'

'No, it didn't. And you know why?'

Mikki shook her head.

'Because life doesn't work that way. You can do everything perfectly. Fulfill every expectation that other people may have. And you still won't get the results you think you deserve. Life is crazy and maddening and often makes no sense.' Jack grew silent.

Mikki leaned against him and gripped his hand. 'We're here for you, Dad. I'm here for you.'

He smiled. And with that smile her look of fear was finally vanquished. 'I know you are, baby.' He hugged her.

She shivered. He put his arm around her. 'Let's go in.'

AFTER JACK GOT BACK to his room, he dropped onto the bed, but he didn't go to sleep. He had been given a miracle. He had already squandered large parts of it. That was going to stop. Now.

He opened his nightstand and pulled out the stack of letters. He selected the envelope with the number '5' on it and slid out the letter. What he'd just told Mikki he firmly believed. He had just forgotten or, more likely, ignored them in his quest for the impossible. He began to read.

> *Dear Lizzie,*
>
> *As I've watched things from my bed, I have a confession to make. And an apology. I haven't been a very good husband or father. Half our marriage I was fighting a war, and the other half I was working too hard. When I see the kids coming and going, I realise how much I missed. Mikki is already grown up. Cory is complex and quiet. Even Jackie has his own personality. And I missed most of it. My greatest regret in life will be leaving you long before I should. My second greatest regret is not being more involved in my children's lives. They say Christmas is the season of second chances. My hope is to make these last few days my second chance to do the right thing for the people that I love the most.*
>
> *Love,*
> *Jack*

Jack folded the letter and put it away. These letters, when he was writing them, represented the outpouring of his heart. But, in the end, they were only letters. Lizzie would have read them, and perhaps they would have made her feel better, but they were still just words. Now was the time for action. He knew what he had to do.

Be a father for my children. Repair that part of my life.

Jack slept through the night for the first time in a long time.

BEGINNING THE NEXT DAY, Jack literally hung up his tool belt for the rest of the summer. Instead of going to work, he drove Jackie and Cory to camp. And he didn't just drop them off and leave. He stayed. He sat and drew pictures and built intricate Lego structures with Jackie, and then, laughing, helped his son knock them down. He instructed Jackie on how to tie his shoes and cut up his food. He helped construct the sets for a play that Cory was going to be in. He also helped his oldest son with his lines.

After camp they would go to the beach, swim, build sand castles, and throw the ball or the Frisbee. Jack got some kites and taught the boys how to make them do loops and twisters. They found some fishing tackle under the deck at the Palace and did some surf fishing. They never caught anything but had great fun.

Jenna and Liam came by regularly. Sometimes, Liam and Mikki would practise for the talent competition. Since the Palace wasn't soundproofed, the pair would go up to the top of the lighthouse. That high up, their powerful sound was dissipated.

At least the lighthouse is good for something, thought Jack.

He and Mikki took walks on the beach, talking about Lizzie and high school and boys and music and what she wanted to do with her life.

Mikki continued to waitress at the Little Bit. Jack and Sammy dropped in to eat frequently. Charles Pinckney visited them at the Palace. He would tell them stories of the past, of when Lizzie was a little girl about Jackie's age.

Jack and Jenna would take walks on the beach and talk. They laughed a lot and occasionally drew close, and arms and fingers touched and grazed, but that was all. They were friends.

The summer was finally going as Jack had hoped it would.

'WE'RE ON NEXT TO LAST,' said Mikki, coming backstage at the Play House.

Liam looked at her. 'Who's last?'

Mikki made a face. 'Who do you think? Ms Reigning Champion. That way her performance is the clearest in the judges' minds.'

Liam shrugged. 'I don't think it'll matter. I've seen the judges. They're all cronies of her mom's.'

'Keep the faith. We've got a terrific act.'

When Mikki turned round Tiffany was standing there, wearing a short, white robe.

Mikki eyed her. 'Saving the debut of the skimpy for the crowd?'

'My daddy always said you don't give it away for free, sweetie.' Tiffany looked Mikki up and down. 'But then if you don't have anything somebody wants, I guess you *have* to give it away.'

Mikki smirked. 'Wow, that's really deep. So, do you do flaming batons?'

Tiffany looked at her as if she was insane. 'No. Why would I? That stuff is dangerous.'

'Well, to beat us you're going to have to get out of your comfort zone. 'Cause the level of competition just got stepped up big-time, *sweetie*.'

There were twenty-one acts, mostly younger people, but there was an older barbershop quartet that was pretty good. Mikki watched from the side of the stage, mentally calculating where the serious competition was. Liam stayed backstage chilling and idly tapping his sticks together. She came back to him and strapped on her guitar.

'It's showtime, big guy.'

Liam smiled. 'Let's rock this sleepy little town.'

'Oh, yeah,' said Mikki.

AT FIRST THE BEAT was mellow. Still, the crowd whooped and clapped. Sensing the rising energy, Mikki gave Liam the cue they'd practised. She cranked her amp and stomped on her wah-wah pedal, and her hand started flying across the face of the Fender guitar. They went right into a classic Queen roof blaster, with Liam moving so fast he appeared to be two people, alternating between drums and keyboard. The crowd was on its feet singing the lyrics.

Mikki knew that once you had the crowd right where you wanted them and they thought you'd already given everything that was in your tank, you did something special. You gave them more.

She unplugged her amp, pulled off her guitar, and pitched it across the stage. At the same moment, Liam tossed his sticks in the other direction. She snagged the sticks, he caught the Fender, and they exchanged positions. Liam plugged in the amp and became the guitarist. Mikki perched on the stool and hammered away at the full array of the drum set.

The finale was a dual one, with a solo each. Mikki rocked the house with a six-minute broadside, and Liam performed a guitar solo. He held the last chord for a full minute, the amp-powered beat shaking the Play House.

There was silence as the crowd caught its collective breath, and then the applause and cheers came in waves. Mikki held hands with Liam and took bow after bow.

As they went backstage, the other performers rushed up to congratulate them. Tiffany passed by them, not saying a word. She loosened her robe and let it fall off. The outfit underneath did not leave much, if anything, to the imagination.

Other than stumbling twice and nearly dropping her baton, she did OK. The applause was polite except for the section led by her mother.

A few minutes later, all the contestants were called to the stage. Mikki found her dad in the crowd and gave a thumbs-up. Jack gave her two thumbs-up back.

The head judge stood and cleared her throat. 'We have reached our decisions. But first I would like to thank all the contestants for their fine performances. Now, in third place, Judy Ringer for her sterling dance performance. In second place, we have Dickie Dean and his Barbershop Four. And now for the first-place champion.' The judge cleared her throat one more time. 'For the fourth year in a row, Tiffany Murdoch and her fabulous baton routine.'

Tiffany stepped forward, all smiles, and whisked over to get her trophy, $100 cheque, and flowers, while her mother beamed. Trophy and flowers in hand, Tiffany strode to the microphone. 'I'm truly overwhelmed. Four years in a row. Who would have thought it possible? Now I'd like to thank the judges and—'

'That's a load of crap,' bellowed a voice. 'This sucks!'

All heads turned to see Cory standing up on his seat and pointing an accusing finger at the head judge.

'This sucks!' repeated Jackie.

'Cor,' snapped Jack. 'Get down and be quiet.'

But Jenna put a hand on his arm. 'No. You know what? They're right.' She stood and yelled, 'This stinks.'

Jack shrugged, stood, and called out, 'Are you telling me that Mikki and Liam didn't even make the top three?'

The head judge and Chelsea Murdoch scowled at them.

Another voice came from further back in the theatre. Mikki craned her neck to see. It was Blake.

'Recount,' demanded Blake.

'Recount! Recount!' chanted the crowd. Tiffany stood in the centre of the stage trying to pretend she was oblivious to all of the criticism.

Then the crowd started chanting, 'Encore! Encore!'

Mikki looked over at Liam. He said, 'What the heck, Mikki, let's give 'em the Purple.'

A moment later, the heart-pumping sound of 'Smoke on the Water' by Deep Purple roared across the theatre.

Later, on the drive home, Mikki and Liam sat in the back of the VW bus. The two teens glowed.

Liam said, 'This is, like, the greatest day of my life. I mean, I've *never* felt this good about losing before.'

Jack looked in the rearview mirror at his daughter. 'So what happened to alternative edgy beats with a non-traditional mix of instrumentals?'

She grinned. 'Wow—you *were* listening. I'm impressed. Anyway, sometimes you just can't beat good old rock and roll, Dad.'

12

'Hey!' Jack yelled.

He and Sammy had just come out of the grocery store when Jack saw a guy grab his tool belt out of the truck and run off. Jack and Sammy raced after him. The guy ducked down a side street. Jack turned the corner and accelerated, Sammy right behind him. The side street turned into an alley. Then they left the alley and entered a wider space. But it was a dead end: a blank brick wall faced them. They pulled up, puffing.

Jack realised what was going on about the same time Sammy did.

'Trap,' Jack said.

'And we just ran into it like a couple of knuckleheads.'

They looked behind them as five large men holding baseball bats came out of hiding from behind a dumpster. Jack could see that the man in the lead was the same one he'd thrown into the side of the pickup truck shortly after they'd arrived in Channing.

The men moved forward as Jack and Sammy fell back until they were against the brick wall. Jack slipped off his belt, coiled it partially round his hand, and stood ready. Sammy rolled up the sleeves of his shirt and assumed a defensive stance. He beckoned them on with a wave of his hand.

The biggest man ran forward and raised his bat. Jack whipped his belt, and the metal tip caught the man on the arm, cutting it open. He screamed and dropped the bat. Sammy drilled a foot into his gut, sending him to his knees, then crushed the man's jaw with a sledgehammer right. 'One down, four to go. Who's next?'

Two more men, including the one whom Jack had dealt with before, yelled and ran forward. Jack grabbed one man's bat, pivoted his hips, and pulled hard. The man sailed past him and hit the wall, bouncing off. Groggy, he rose in time to be put back down by Jack's fist slamming into his face.

The other guy had his feet kicked out from under him by Sammy. He ripped the bat out of the guy's hands and bopped him on the head with it, knocking him out. When Jack and Sammy looked up, the other two men had disappeared.

'OK, that was fun,' said Sammy.

His smile vanished when Sheriff Tammie hustled into the alley with a deputy in tow. Tammie took one look at the men lying on the ground and Jack and Sammy holding bats and pulled his gun.

'Put those bats down now. You're both under arrest.'

'They attacked us!' exclaimed Jack as he and Sammy dropped the bats.

'Then how come they're knocked out and you two had the bats?'

Jack pointed at one of the men on the ground. 'Look, he's the same one I fought with before. He and a bunch of his guys came after us to settle the score. We were just defending ourselves.'

'That's for a court to decide.'

'You're charging us?' said Jack. 'What about the other guys?'

'Their butts are going to jail, too.'

Jack and Sammy were cuffed, loaded into the sheriff's cruiser, and transported to the jail. Jack slumped down on a bench at the back of the cell, but Sammy said, 'Hey, we get a lawyer, right?'

The sheriff let Jack make a call.

Jack said, 'Jenna, it's Jack. Uh, I'm in a little bit of trouble.'

Ten minutes later, Jenna and Charles Pinckney hurried into the sheriff's office and were escorted back to see the prisoners.

'My God, Jack, what happened?' she asked.

He explained everything that had happened in the alleyway.

'I talked the sheriff into releasing you on your own recognisance,' she said. 'But it looks like the men are pressing charges.'

'Isn't it our word against theirs?' said Sammy.

'Still have to go to court.'

'But we didn't do anything wrong.'

'I'm sorry, Jack,' said Jenna. 'I'm doing the best I can.'

His anger faded. 'I know. And I appreciate you getting down here so fast. Didn't know anyone else to call.'

'Well, for now, you're free to go. I'll get the sheriff.'

TWO DAYS LATER, a man knocked on the door of the Palace. Jack answered it.

'Jack Armstrong?'

'Yeah. Who are you?'

The man quickly stuffed some papers into Jack's hand. 'Consider yourself served.'

The man walked off as Sammy joined Jack at the door. 'What is it? Served with what? Those jerks from the alley really suing us?'

Jack read quickly through the legal documents. When he looked up, his eyes held both anger and fear.

'No. Bonnie is suing for custody of the kids.'

'I CAN'T BELIEVE Grandma is doing this,' said Mikki. 'Why would she?'

The Armstrongs were arrayed on the couch and floor at the Palace. Sammy was there, as were Liam and Jenna. Jack had shown Jenna the documents.

'I don't know,' said Jack, though he actually had a pretty good idea.

Jenna looked up from the papers. 'She's requested an expedited hearing to get temporary custody pending a full hearing. In non-legalese, that means she wants to get in front of a judge fast to get the kids now and then worry about the rest later.'

'She can do that?' said Sammy.

'The courthouse is open to everyone. But she has to prove her case. It's difficult to have children taken away from a parent.'

Jack asked, 'Exactly when and where is this going to happen?'

'In two days. In family court in Charleston.'

'But we live in Ohio.'

'But you have property in South Carolina, and you're living here now, if only for the summer. However, I can argue that the South Carolina court lacks jurisdiction.'

'*You* can argue?' said Jack.

'Do you have anyone else in mind to represent you? I've got a licence to practise in South Carolina, and I've kept everything current. But we don't have much time to prepare.'

'Jenna, you've got a business to run.'

Liam said, 'I can do that. It'll be fine.'

Jenna smiled. 'See?'

Mikki said, 'What exactly is she saying that would make a court take us from Dad?'

Jenna looked at Jack questioningly. He nodded. 'You can tell them.'

'Basically that your father is unfit to be your guardian. That he's a danger to himself and others.'

'That's stupid,' said Cory, jumping to his feet.

'Yeah, stupid,' said Jackie.

'Does she have any proof of that?' Mikki asked heatedly.

'She'll be able to show any proof she has at the hearing,' Jenna explained. She looked at Jack again. 'And we have to show proof that you are fit. You can testify. So can Mikki and Cory. Jackie's too young. I can get Charles to be a character witness. And Sammy. I can't imagine she'll be able to show the level of proof required to take children away from their surviving parent.'

Later, as Jack walked Jenna out to her car, she said, 'Jack, there is one thing I didn't want to say in front of the kids.'

'What?'

'I don't think the timing on Bonnie's action is a coincidence. I think it's tied to your arrest for assault. She could've easily found out. And I can guarantee they'll use that to prove their case.'

'But I'm innocent.'

'Doesn't matter. It's all perception. And if they can convince the judge you're violent? Not good. So if there's anything to tell me about this, now would be a good time: why do you think your mother-in-law is doing this?'

'She blames me for Lizzie's death. She came here pretending to want to reconcile, but I turned down her offer of moving in with her in Arizona. And she only came by *once* to see the kids this summer. Some grandparent she is.'

'Uh, that's actually not right, Dad.'

They turned to see Mikki standing behind them.

'Grandma came by, like, six times while you were out working.'

'You never told me that.'

'She asked us not to. Said you might get mad.'

'I told her to come and visit. I wouldn't have got mad.'

'Well, that's not what she said.'

Jenna looked at her. 'What did you talk about? Did she ever ask about your dad?'

'Yeah.' Mikki started to tear up. 'It was when Dad was working so hard and he was out in the lighthouse all the time.'

Jack said gently, 'It's OK, sweetie; I understand. Tell us what you told her.'

Mikki calmed. 'She asked what your mood was, if you were doing anything strange. If you didn't seem to be feeling well.'

'And you told her about the lighthouse and . . . things?'

Mikki nodded, a miserable expression on her face. 'I'm sorry, Daddy. I didn't know she was going to sue you.'

'It's not your fault. It'll be OK.'

'Are you sure?'

'Absolutely.' He looked at Jenna. 'I've got a great lawyer.'

Mikki went back in the house, and Jack looked at Jenna. 'I lost the kids once. I can't lose them again.'

She put her hand over his. 'Listen to me, Jack. You're not going to lose them, OK? Now, I've got to go. Lots of stuff to prepare.'

She drove off, leaving Jack looking at the ground and wondering if his second chance was coming to a premature end.

THE KIDS WERE SCRUBBED and in their best clothes. Jack and Sammy had bought jackets and smart trousers for the courtroom appearance. Liam had taken time off work to join them for moral support.

The courtroom was small, and Jack felt claustrophobic as he stepped inside. The judge was not on the bench yet, but the bailiff was standing ready. Bonnie's lawyer was already seated at his table. Jack jerked when he saw Bonnie and Fred sitting behind him. Fred was studying his hands, while Bonnie was in a discussion with her lawyer and another man.

Jack suddenly remembered where he'd seen the other man before. In a car with Bonnie parked on the streets of Channing.

Jenna walked over and spoke to the bailiff before approaching Bonnie's lawyer. They went off to speak in private, while Bonnie stayed talking to the other man, who was showing her something on a laptop.

Jack watched as Bonnie's lawyer handed Jenna a packet of documents. She frowned and asked him something, but he shook his head. She whipped round, marched over to Jack, and sat down.

At that moment, Sammy walked in with Charles Pinckney. Pinckney greeted Jack, Jenna and the kids. Then he eyed Bonnie. He surprised Jack by walking over to her. 'Hello, Bonnie.'

She nodded curtly. 'Charles.'

'Let's just be thankful Lizzie and Cee aren't alive to see this god-awful spectacle,' he said in a tight voice.

Bonnie looked as though she had been slapped. But Charles had already turned away.

Jenna held up the stack of documents and whispered, 'Opposing counsel just gave me these documents. I asked if he would not contest an extension on the hearing date, but he refused.'

'What's in those documents?' Jack asked.

'I've glanced at a few pages. Your mother-in-law apparently has had a private detective follow you this summer.' She pointed to the other man holding the laptop. 'That guy.'

'What?' said a shocked Jack. 'What's he got on the laptop?'

'Apparently some video they intend to show the judge.'

'I didn't think they could do stuff like this,' said Sammy. 'Surprise the other side with crap.'

'Normally they can't. But this is family court. Everything is supposed to be done with the best interests of the children in mind. That sometimes trumps official procedures. And they're alleging that the children are in an unsafe and dangerous environment.'

The bailiff announced the entrance of the judge. He turned out to be a balding man with thick spectacles named Leroy Grubbs.

They rose on his entrance and then took their seats. The case was called. Jenna asked the court for an extension, citing the late delivery of crucial documents. This was denied by Grubbs almost before Jenna finished speaking.

Bonnie's lawyer, Bob Paterson, made his opening statement.

'Fine. Call your witnesses,' said Grubbs.

The lawyer said, 'Bonnie O'Toole.'

BONNIE WAS SWORN IN and sat down in the witness box.

'You're the children's grandmother?' asked Paterson.

'Yes.'

'Can you lead us through the series of events leading up to your filing this legal action?'

Bonnie spoke about Jack's illness, her daughter's death, Jack being in the hospice, the children living with relatives, and Jack's recovery and his taking the children back. She described her offer to have them live with her because of her concerns, after consulting with doctors, that Jack's illness would come back with fatal results.

'And what was Mr Armstrong's response to your offer?'

'He categorically refused it.'

'And what specific event prompted you to have your son-in-law put under surveillance?'

'I saw Jack beating up two men in broad daylight while his children were with him. It was awful. It was like Jack had lost his mind. I don't know if it was a symptom of the disease coming back or not, but I was terrified, and I could tell the children were, too.'

The lawyer finished with Bonnie, and Jenna rose.

'Mrs O'Toole, do you love your grandchildren?'

'Of course I do.'

'And yet you seek to separate them from their father?'

'For their own good.'

'And not to punish Mr Armstrong? You don't blame him for your daughter's death?'

'I've never blamed him. I told him that I knew it was an accident.'

'But did you really believe that? Didn't you tell Mr Armstrong that you thought he should be dead and not your daughter?'

Bonnie pursed her lips. 'I've tried to move past that.'

'But you still harbour resentment towards him? And that is partly the reason you're filing for custody: for revenge?'

'Objection,' Paterson cut in sharply. 'The witness has said she harbours no resentment.'

'Withdrawn,' said Jenna. 'No more questions.'

'Next witness,' said Grubbs.

Jack was surprised to see Sheriff Nathan Tammie amble into the courtroom, not looking too happy about being there. He was sworn in, and Paterson took him through his paces as a witness.

'So you warned Mr Armstrong on the occasion of the first assault he was involved in?'

'Yes, although apparently Mr Armstrong was provoked.'

'And there was a second, more recent, assault involving Mr Armstrong. Can you tell us the circumstances?'

Tammie glanced at Jack and explained the altercation in the alley.

'So, to sum up, Mr Armstrong and Mr Duvall were holding baseball bats in an alley, and three unconscious men were lying at their feet? So you arrested Mr Armstrong and Mr Duvall?'

'Yes. But I arrested the other guys, too.'

'But Mr Armstrong will be going to court on these charges?'

'Yes.'

'Could he receive prison time?'

'I really doubt that—'

'Could he?'

'Well, yes.'

'No further questions.'

Jenna rose. 'Sheriff Tammie, why didn't you charge Mr Armstrong on the first altercation?'

'From the witness statements, it was clear that he was provoked.'

'Provoked how?'

Tammie took out his notebook. 'Witnesses said that one of the guys had yelled something about him being the Miracle Man, and they were willing to pay him five dollars to perform a miracle. And he said other stuff, trying to get Mr Armstrong's goat, I guess.'

'All directed at Mr Armstrong personally?'

'Yes.'

'Did Mr Armstrong attack at that point?'

'No. He just kept walking along with his kids. Then the guy said, "Hey, Miracle, was it true your slutty wife was cheating on you? That why you came back from the dead?"'

Jenna turned to look at Bonnie in time to see her glance sharply at Jack.

'And is that when Mr Armstrong went after them? Because they insulted his deceased wife?'

'Yes.'

'So he exercised restraint when the insults were only directed to him?'

'More restraint than I would have exercised if it'd been me.'

'And the alleged second assault? Is it true that one of the men engaged in this assault was also involved in the first altercation?'

'Yes.'

'So it could have been that these men attacked Mr Armstrong in that alley and he was merely defending himself?'

'Objection,' said Paterson. 'Calls for a conclusion that the witness is not qualified to give.'

'Sustained,' said Grubbs.

Jenna said, 'No further questions.'

Paterson said, 'I call Michelle Armstrong to the stand.'

As Mikki rose and moved forward, she stopped next to her dad. He gave her a reassuring smile. 'Just tell the truth, sweetie.'

'MS ARMSTRONG?' said Paterson politely. 'You had a number of conversations with your grandmother this summer, didn't you?'

Mikki took a deep breath. 'Yes, I spoke with Grandma.'

'And what did you tell her about your father's . . . um . . . actions during the summer? With regards to the lighthouse, for instance.'

'Lighthouse?' said the judge.

Paterson spoke up. 'It was apparently Mr Armstrong's deceased wife's favourite place as a child, and he was spending most of the nights there.'

Jenna rose. 'Objection. Mr. Paterson has not been sworn in as a witness, Your Honour, and has no personal knowledge of the situation.'

'All right,' said Grubbs. 'Sustained.'

Paterson turned back to Mikki. 'Your statements about the lighthouse? Can you tell the court please?'

Mikki fidgeted. 'I just told her that Dad was working on the lighthouse, that's all. It was no big deal.'

'Would he work out there late at night, leaving you and your younger brothers alone in the house?'

'Sometimes, but nothing happened.'

'On the contrary, did you not tell your grandmother on at least three occasions that your younger brother, Jack Jr, got out of bed, and once fell down the stairs?'

Jack looked shocked. He stared at Mikki. She swallowed hard. 'But he was OK. Just a bruise on his back.'

'And on another occasion Jack Jr wandered out of the house and you couldn't find him for at least an hour?'

Jack slumped back in his chair, totally flummoxed.

'Yes. But he was OK.'

'And did you tell your father about these incidents?'

'No.'

'Why not?'

'I . . . I didn't want him to get upset.'

'Does he get upset often?'

'Well—I mean, no; no, he doesn't.'

'Did you also tell your grandmother that your dad was obsessed with the house and the lighthouse because your deceased mother loved it so much there and he was trying to reconnect with her?'

'I was mad at him; that's why I said those things.'

'So they weren't true? Remember you are under oath.'

Mikki flushed a deep red, and tears trickled from her eyes.

Jenna rose. 'Your Honour, counsel is badgering. I request a recess so the witness can compose herself.'

Grubbs looked at Mikki. 'Are you all right?'

Mikki drew in a deep breath, wiped her eyes, and nodded.

'Proceed.'

Paterson continued. 'And did you also tell your grandmother that your father had no clue how to run a family and didn't seem to care about you and your brothers?'

Jack looked down.

Mikki teared up again. 'That was before he changed. I mean, he was like that before. No, I mean, not bad. He did love us. I mean he *does* love us. He takes great care of us.'

'But didn't you also tell your grandmother that you were worried about your dad's mental state?'

Mikki said, 'No, I don't remember saying that.'

'So you've never seen him acting irrationally or in a fit of rage?'

'No.'

Paterson turned to the man sitting next to Bonnie. 'Mr Drake, if you would?' The man rose and wheeled forward a TV on a rolling stand and slid a DVD into a player underneath the TV.

Paterson said to the judge, 'Your Honour, Mr Drake is a licensed private investigator hired by Mrs O'Toole. The video you're about to see represents one of the results of his surveillance.'

The TV screen came to life, and they all watched as Jack came running out of the lighthouse carrying the crate. He smashed it on the rocks and then raced down to the beach, twisting and turning in what looked unmistakably like a fit of insane rage. Then the screen showed him dropping to the sand as he wept. The next image was of Mikki creeping up to her father.

The DVD was stopped, and Paterson turned back to Mikki.

'You obviously saw your father that night?'

Mikki nodded. 'He was upset, but he got better.'

'So in your mind he was . . . sick?'

'No, that's not what I meant.' She stood. 'You're putting words in my mouth,' she cried out.

Grubbs said, 'Young lady, I understand that this is very stressful, but please try to keep your emotions under control.'

Mikki sniffled and settled back in her chair.

'If your father were to fall ill again, who would take care of the family?'

'I would.'

Paterson smiled. 'You're not of legal age to live alone with your brothers.'

Mikki looked furious. 'And Sammy. He's my dad's best friend.'

'Ah, Mr Duvall.' Paterson glanced at his notes. 'Did you know that after he returned from Vietnam, Mr Duvall underwent psychiatric counselling and that he also received two drunk-driving citations?'

Sammy erupted from his chair. 'My whole damn unit was ordered to undergo that counselling because we'd done two tours in 'Nam and seen atrocities you never will, slick. And those DUIs were over thirty years ago. Never had a damn one since.'

The judge smashed his gavel down. 'Another outburst like that, sir, and you will be removed from this courtroom.'

Paterson turned to Mikki. 'So, Mr Duvall will look after you?'

'Yes,' Mikki said stubbornly.

'Now, Ms Armstrong, can you tell us what you think your mother's death did to your father?'

Jenna jumped to her feet. 'Relevance?'

'We're trying to determine the conditions of the environment, Your Honour. State of mind of the surviving parent is highly relevant.'

'Go ahead. Ms Armstrong, please answer the question.'

'He was devastated. We all were.'

'Is he still devastated?'

'What do you mean?'

'Your father has been involved in two fights and been arrested for an assault for which he could go to prison. You saw the video of him throwing things and jumping around in a state of fury. You've given testimony that he neglected his children to work on a lighthouse. Do you believe those to be the acts of a rational person?'

'Look, I know what you're trying to do, but my dad is not crazy, OK? He's not.'

'But you're not qualified to make that judgment, are you?'

Mikki stood again, tears streaming down her face. 'My dad is not crazy. He loves us. He is a great dad.'

Paterson gave her a weak smile. 'I'm sure you love your dad. And you'd say anything to protect him.'

'Yes, I would. I . . .' Mikki realised her mistake too late.

'No further questions.'

Mikki looked at her dad. 'I'm sorry, Dad. I'm really sorry.'

Jack said quietly, 'It's OK, sweetie.' When Jenna rose to question Mikki, Jack put a hand on her arm and shook his head. 'No, Jenna, she's been through enough.'

Jenna turned to the judge. 'No questions,' she said reluctantly.

Grubbs looked at Paterson. 'Any more witnesses?'

'Just one, Your Honour, before we rest. We call Jack Armstrong.'

JACK WAS SWORN IN and settled into the witness box.

Paterson approached. 'Mr Armstrong, did you know that your illness can cause severe depression and even mental instability?'

'I don't have an illness. I was given a clean bill of health.'

Paterson picked up some documents and handed them to the bailiff. 'These are opinions from three doctors, all world-class physicians, who state categorically that there is no cure for your illness and that it is fatal one hundred per cent of the time.'

'Then they'll have to change that to ninety-nine point nine per cent, won't they?'

'Do you blame yourself for your wife's death, Mr Armstrong?'

'A person will always blame themselves, even if they could do nothing to prevent it. It's just the way we are.'

'So is that a yes?'

'Yes.'

'That must be emotionally devastating.'

'It's not easy.'

'Talk to me about your obsession with the lighthouse.'

Jenna said, 'Objection. Drawing a conclusion.'

'Sustained.'

'Tell us about your reasons for working so long and hard on the lighthouse, Mr Armstrong.'

Jack furrowed his brow and hunched forward. 'It's complicated.'

'Do your best,' said Paterson politely.

'It was Lizzie's special place,' Jack said, simply. 'That's where'd she go when she was a kid. I found some of her things there—a doll, a sign she'd made that said "Lizzie's Lighthouse". And when she was alive she said she wanted to come back to the Palace. I guess me going there and fixing it up was a way to show respect for her wishes.'

'All right. What else?'

Jack smiled. 'Lizzie thought she could see Heaven from the top of the lighthouse when she was a little girl.'

'But you're an adult. So you didn't believe that, or did you?'

Jack hesitated. Jenna glanced at the judge and saw his eyebrows rise higher the longer Jack waited to answer.

'No, I didn't. But . . .' Jack shook his head and stopped talking.

The lawyer let this silence linger as he and the judge exchanged a glance.

'So you wanted to fix up the place?'

'Yes. The stairs to the lighthouse fell in, and I wanted to repair them. And the light, too.'

'Fix the light? It's my understanding that the lighthouse in question is no longer registered as a navigational aid.'

'It's not. But it stopped working while Lizzie was still there. So I decided to try and repair it.'

'So let me get this straight. You neglected your family so that you could repair a lighthouse, solely because your wife as a child thought she could see Heaven from there? Let me ask the question again: did *you* think you could see Heaven from there?'

'No, I didn't,' said Jack firmly.

'We have one more video to show, Your Honour.'

The image appeared on the TV of Jack standing on the catwalk around the lighthouse reading one of his letters to Lizzie.

'Could you tell us what you're doing there, Mr Armstrong?'

'None of your business,' snapped Jack.

Jenna stood. 'Your Honour, relevance?'

'Again, state of mind,' replied Paterson.

'Answer the question,' instructed the judge.

'It's a letter,' said Jack. 'To my wife.'

'But your wife is deceased.'

'I wrote the letters to her before she . . . before she died. I wrote them when I was sick. I wanted her to have them after I was gone.'

'But she can't read them now. So why were you reading them? In the middle of the night on top of a lighthouse while small children are alone in the house.'

'Argumentative,' snapped Jenna.

'Sustained,' said Grubbs.

'I know you're trying to make it look like I'm nuts. But I'm not. And I'm not unfit to care for my children.' He looked at Bonnie, his eyes burning into hers. 'You know how much I loved Lizzie.'

Paterson said, 'Mr Armstrong, you're not allowed to do that.'

Jack sat there for a few seconds. The walls of the courtroom seemed to be closing in on him, cutting off his oxygen. Suddenly he stood. 'I would've gladly given my life so that she could have lived. You know that,' Jack cried out to his mother-in-law. 'No one feels worse than I do about what happened. It is a living hell for me every day. I lost the only woman I have ever loved. The best friend I will ever have!' Tears were sliding down Jack's face.

The judge barked, 'Bailiff!'

Jack said, 'The best things that Lizzie and I ever created were our kids. *Our* kids. So how dare you try to take away the only parent they have left just because you're mad at me? How *dare* you?'

The bailiff forcibly removed Jack from the courtroom while Bonnie looked on, obviously shocked by his outburst.

Paterson said, 'Nothing further, Your Honour.'

The judge looked at Jenna. 'Do you have anything to add?'

Jenna looked at the distraught kids. 'No, Your Honour.'

'I'll render my judgment on the motion this afternoon.'

Jack was released from the bailiff's custody a few minutes later. They drove back in silence to Channing and waited in a small room at the back of the Little Bit. They all jumped when Jenna's cellphone buzzed. She answered the call and listened, and her expression told Jack all he needed to know.

'The judge granted the motion for temporary custody,' she said.

And it's my fault, thought Jack. *I've lost my family. Again.*

13

Jack sat on his bed at the Palace holding the sixth letter in his hand. He hadn't read it yet. He was thinking about other things.

Bonnie and representatives from Social Services were coming that evening to take the kids away, perhaps for ever. He looked down at the letter, balled it up, and threw it down on the bed next to the others. As he looked out of the window, two cars pulled into the driveway of the Palace. Though it was only seven in the evening, the sky was as dark as midnight. A tropical storm was just off the coast, and the wind was beginning to slam. That was the major reason they were coming tonight: to move the kids further inland. Jack had put up no fight, because he wanted his kids to be safe.

As Jack went downstairs, he stared at the three packed bags standing next to the front door. Then he looked over at the kids. Cory and Mikki were on the couch crying, and Jackie, not understanding what was going on, was crying, too. Liam simply stood by, not knowing what to do.

Jack went over to his kids and started whispering to them. 'It's going to be OK, I promise. This is only temporary.'

Jenna answered the door. Bonnie, Fred and the Social Services people stood there with umbrellas in hand.

Jack's gaze was on Bonnie. 'Do we have to do it this way?'

'I'm only thinking of the children, Jack.'

'Are you sure about that?'

Sammy, Liam, Jackie and Cory had joined them on the porch.

Cory said, 'Please don't do this. We want to stay with Dad.'

One of the Social Services people, a woman, stepped in and said, 'This is not the time or place to discuss this. The judge has ruled.'

Jack looked at his two kids. 'OK, guys, you're going to be back here faster than you can say Jack Rabbit.'

Cory nodded, but the tears still slid down his face. Jack hugged both of them. 'It's going to be OK,' he said. 'We're a family. We'll always be a family, right?' They nodded. 'Liam, go and get Mikki. They need to get on the road before the storm gets any worse.'

Sammy and Jack carried the bags out to the car, but when Jack looked back up at the porch, he knew something was wrong. Liam was standing there, his face pale and his expression wild.

'What is it?' said Jack as he ran up to Liam.

'I can't find Mikki.'

Jack and the others raced into the house. It took only five minutes to search the place. His daughter was gone.

A QUARTER OF A MILE down the beach, Mikki was stumbling along, crying hard. The wind and rain battered her, but she kept going. She didn't see the palmetto tree toppling until it was almost too late. At the last instant, she lunged out of the way, but dodging the tree carried her too close to the water-line. She didn't have time to scream before a huge wave swept her away.

JACK STARED OUT at the darkened sky from the front room of the Palace. The rain was coming down even harder. Liam had quickly driven home to see if Mikki had gone there, but he'd called to say she wasn't at his house.

Bonnie said, 'Jack, what do we do?' Her voice was hysterical.

Jack turned to her and said, 'The first thing we do is not panic.'

One of the Social Services personnel said, 'We should call the police.'

Jack shook his head. 'There's only Tammie and one deputy, and they'll be preoccupied with the storm. We have to start searching the area. We need to split up. Search by street and also the beach.' He pointed to Fred. 'Fred, you and Bonnie drive west in your car. Go slow, look for Mikki that way.' He turned to the pair from Social Services. 'You go east in your car and do the same thing. Let's exchange cellphone numbers. Whoever finds her calls the others. Sammy and I will take opposite directions on the beach.' He turned to Cory. 'Cor, can you be a real big guy for me and stay here with Jackie? Go to the lower level and stay away from the windows.'

Cory shot a terrified look at his dad. 'Mikki's coming back, right?'

'She absolutely is. I bet she shows up here any minute. And we need someone to be here when she does, OK?'

'OK, Dad.'

JACK HEADED RIGHT on the beach while Sammy went left. Most of the sand was underwater. Jack swung his flashlight in wide arcs, but it barely penetrated the darkness. It finally caught on one object, and when Jack saw what it was, his heart thudded in his chest.

It was Mikki's sneaker, floating in a pool of shallow water. He looked in all directions but could see nothing. He called her name, but the only thing he heard in response was the scream of the wind.

He turned and jogged back, his gaze toggling between land and sea. He had to bend forward to keep from being blown back by the wind. Every ten seconds he screamed out her name. Near the Palace he met Sammy, who reported similar failure. Jack showed him the sneaker.

'That is not good, Jack,' said Sammy.

'We're running out of time. The storm is just about to really hit.'

'What do you want to do?'

'We need to be able to see a big swath of land and water.'

'No way you can get a chopper with a searchlight up in these conditions.'

At this remark, Jack started and looked up at the lighthouse. He turned and ran towards it, Sammy on his heels. He burst through the door and took the steps two at a time. He reached the top and hoisted himself through the access door. Sammy poked his head through a few seconds later, breathing hard.

'Jack, this damn thing doesn't work.'

'It's going to work tonight!' Jack shouted back at him. He ripped open his toolbox, snatched some wrenches, and grabbed the blueprint. While Sammy held the paper, Jack worked on a section of the mechanism.

Sammy said, 'But we need a searchlight, not something that's—'

'There's a manual feature,' Jack snapped. He checked the wiring and hit the power switch. 'Damn it!' He flung his wrench and peered out into the darkness, where his little girl was . . . somewhere.

No. I will not lose my daughter.

A burst of lightning was followed by a boom of thunder as the storm reached its peak. Footsteps came from below, and first Jenna's and then Liam's faces appeared. They were both soaked.

'We've been searching the street and beach, but there's no sign of Mikki,' Jenna said.

Sammy said, 'Bonnie called. And so did the others. They found nothing either.' He held up Mikki's shoe. Jenna and Liam paled.

Jack remained frozen against the glass, staring out into the darkness. The electricity to the lighthouse flickered, went out, and then sputtered back on. He was still staring at the darkness when he saw it. At first he thought it was another bolt of lightning lancing into the water, but there was no boom of thunder following it. Yet it had been a jagged edge of current:

he'd seen it. Jack suddenly realised that in that second of darkness, what he'd seen had been reflected in the glass, only to become invisible when the lights were restored.

He leaped towards the machinery. 'Turn the light off, Sammy,' he yelled.

Sammy hit the switch, plunging them all into darkness.

Jack, his chest heaving with dread because he knew this was his last chance, stared at the machinery with an intensity he didn't know he had. There was nothing else in the world; only him and this metal beast that had confounded him all summer. And if he couldn't figure it out right now, his daughter was lost to him.

'Turn the lights back on.'

Sammy hit the switch.

And Jack saw the beautiful arc of electrical current nearly buried between two pieces of metal in a gap so narrow he didn't even know it was there. *That* was what had been reflected in the window.

He dropped to his knees, scuttled forwards, and hit the gap with his flashlight. Two wires were revealed, less than a centimeter apart, but not touching.

'Sammy, get me electrical tape and a wire nut and then turn the main power off.'

Sammy grabbed the tape from the box, tossed the roll and red wire nut to Jack, and then turned off the power. While Jenna held the flashlight for him, Jack slid his hands into the gap, pieced the two wires together using the wire nut, and then wound tape around it.

Jack stood and called out, 'Turn the power back on, and then hit the switch. Everyone look away from the light.'

Sammy turned on the power and flicked the switch. At first nothing happened. Then, as if awakening from years of sleep, the light began to come on, building in energy until, with a burst of power, it came fully to life. The powerful beam illuminated the beach and ocean as it started to whirl around the top of the lighthouse.

Jack raced round to the back of the equipment, hit a button, and grabbed a slide lever. The light stopped swirling across the landscape and became a focused beam that he could manoeuvre.

'Sammy, take control of this. Start from the north and move it slowly southward in three-second stages.'

While Sammy guided the light, Liam, Jack, and Jenna stayed glued to the window, looking at the suddenly lightened nightscape.

Jenna spotted her first. 'There! There!'

'Steady on the beam, Sammy,' Jack screamed. 'Hold right there.'

He threw himself through the opening and took the steps three at a time. He nearly flattened Bonnie, who was coming up the stairs.

The light had revealed Mikki's location. She was in deep water, clinging to a piece of driftwood as ten-foot-high waves pounded her. She might have only a few minutes left to live.

Then so do I, thought Jack.

JACK ARMSTRONG ran that night like he had never run before. Not on the football field and not even on the battlefield when his very life depended on sheer speed. He high-stepped through four-foot waves that were nearly up to the rocks the lighthouse was perched on. A towering breaker ripped out of the darkness and knocked him down. He struck his head on a piece of timber thrown up on the sand by the storm. Dazed, he struggled to his feet and kept slogging on. He saw the light, a pinpoint beam. But he couldn't see Mikki. Frantic, he ran towards the illumination.

'Mikki! Mikki!'

Another wave crushed him. He got back up, vomiting salt water driven deeply down his throat. He ran on, fighting rain driven so hard by the wind that it felt like the sting of a million wasps.

'Mikki!'

'Daddy!'

It was faint, but Jack saw the light shift to the left. And then he saw it: a head bobbing in deep water. Mikki was being pulled inexorably out to sea.

Jack ran headlong towards the brunt of the storm. An incoming wave rose up far taller than he was, but he avoided most of its energy by diving under it. He emerged in water over his head. The normal riptide was multiplied tenfold by the power of the storm, but Jack fought through it, going under and coming up yelling, 'Mikki.' Each time she called back, and Jack swam with all his might towards the sound of her voice.

'Mikki!'

This time there was no answer.

'Michelle!'

A second later he heard a faint 'Daddy.'

Jack redoubled his efforts. She was getting weak. It was a miracle she was still alive. If that piece of driftwood got ripped from her, it would all be over. And then he saw her. The sturdy beam of light was tethered to the teenager like a golden string.

Jack swam as hard as he could, fighting through wave after wave. Yet he realised that she was moving further from him. It was the storm, the riptide, the wind, everything. He swam harder. But now he was fifty feet away instead of forty. Jack looked to the shore, then at the angry sky. He was being pulled out now. And he wasn't sure he had the strength to get back in.

I'm not going back without her.

Jack trod water, looking in all directions as the storm bore down with all its weight on the South Carolina coast.

He shook with anger and fear and . . . loss.

I'm sorry, Lizzie. I'm so sorry.

What if I just stop swimming? What if I just stop?

He would sink to the bottom. He looked at the shore. He could see flashlights. His family—what was left of it—was there. Bonnie would raise the boys. He and Mikki would go to join Lizzie.

'Daddy!'

Jack turned in the water. Mikki was barely twenty feet from him. This time, the movement of the water had carried him towards her.

Finding a reserve of strength he didn't think he had, Jack exploded through the water. A yard. A foot. Six inches.

'Daddy!' She reached out to him.

'Mikki!' He lunged, his hand closed like a vice round her wrist, and he pulled his daughter to him.

She hugged him. 'I'm sorry, Daddy. I'm so sorry.'

'It's OK, baby. I've got you. Just lie on your back.'

Now all I've got to do is get us back, thought Jack.

The problem was that when Jack tried to ride a wave in, the undertow snatched him back before he could gain traction on the shore. Then a huge wave forced them both underwater, before Jack brought them back, coughing and half-strangled.

'Jack!'

He looked towards the beach. Liam and Sammy were standing there with a long coil of rope, screaming at him. Tied to the end of the rope was a red buoy. He nodded to show he understood. Sammy wound up and tossed the rope. It fell far short. Sammy pulled it back and tried again. Closer, but still not close enough.

'Sammy,' he screamed. 'Wait until the waves push us towards the beach, and then toss it.'

Sammy nodded, timed it, and threw the rope. Just a few feet short. Jack lunged for the buoy and snagged it. But a monster wave crashed down on them, and Mikki was ripped from him. He felt her sliding past him. He shot his hand out and grabbed his daughter's hair an instant before she was past him and gone for ever.

Sammy and Liam pulled with all their strength on the rope. Slowly, father and daughter were pulled to shore.

As soon as he hit solid earth, Jack carried Mikki away from the pounding waves. She was completely limp, her eyes closed.

As Jack bent down, he could see that Mikki was not breathing. He immediately began to perform mouth-to-mouth resuscitation. Sammy called 911 while Jack continued to work on his daughter.

A minute later, Jack sat up. He looked down at Mikki. She wasn't moving; her skin was turning blue. His daughter was dead.

A crack of lightning pierced the night sky, and Jack looked up, perhaps to that solitary spot his wife had tried to find all those years ago. With a sob he screamed, 'Help me, Lizzie, help me. Please.'

He looked down. No more miracles left. He'd used the only one he would ever have on himself.

Suddenly Jack felt a force at the back of his neck. At first he thought that Sammy was trying to pull him away. But the force was *pushing* him back to Mikki. Jack took an enormous breath, put his mouth over Mikki's, and blew with all the strength he had left.

As the air fell from him and into Mikki, everything for Jack stopped, and the storm was gone. It was as he had envisioned dying to be: quiet, peaceful, isolated, alone. Jack felt himself drifting away. Lizzie and now Mikki were gone. He no longer wanted to live. It didn't matter any more.

The water hitting him in his face brought him back. He was once more in the present. It was still raining. But that was not what had struck him. He looked down as Mikki gave another shudder and coughed up the water that had been buried deeply in her lungs.

Her eyes opened, fluttered, opened again. Her pupils focused, and she saw her dad hovering above her. Mikki put out her arms.

'Daddy?' she said in a tiny voice.

Jack sank down and held her. 'I'm here, baby. I'm here.'

THE AMBULANCE TOOK Mikki and Jack to the hospital to be checked out. Sammy followed in his van with Liam, while Jenna stayed with the boys at the Palace. Jenna had made hot tea for Bonnie, who had watched Jack's heroic rescue of his daughter from the top of the lighthouse. Now she just sat small and stooped on the edge of the couch. When Sammy called from the hospital and told them they would be home shortly and that everyone was OK, Jenna had finally broken down and wept.

Afterwards, she had ventured into Jack's room. As her gaze swept the space, it settled on the letters, which were still lying on the bed. She went over, sat down, picked them up and started reading.

She emerged ten minutes later. When Bonnie looked up, Jenna said, 'I think you need to read these, Mrs O'Toole.'

Bonnie looked confused, but she accepted the letters from Jenna, slipped on her reading glasses, and unfolded the first one.

THE STORM, its fury rapidly spent after hitting land, had largely passed by the time they returned from the hospital the next morning. An exhausted Mikki was laid in her bed with Cory and Liam watching over her.

Jack told everyone that Mikki had suffered no permanent damage and would be as good as new. Then he went outside and up to the top of the lighthouse. He bent down and saw the wires he had spliced the night before. It was a miracle that he had finally spotted the trouble that had befuddled him for so long. Yet a miracle, realised Jack, was somehow what he had been counting on.

He leaned against the wall of glass and stared out. He turned when he heard her. Bonnie appeared at the opening for the room. He helped her through, and they stood looking at each other.

'Thank God for what you did last night, Jack.'

Jack turned and looked back out of the window. 'It was Lizzie.'

'What?' Bonnie moved closer to him.

Jack said, 'I'd given up. Mikki was dead. I didn't have any breath left. And I asked Lizzie to help me. I looked up to the sky and I asked Lizzie to help me.' A sob broke from his throat. 'And she did. She saved Mikki, not me.'

Bonnie nodded slowly. 'It was both of you, Jack. You and Lizzie. Two people meant for each other if ever there was.'

He stared at her, surprised by the woman's blunt words.

From her pocket she drew out the letters. 'These belong to you.' She handed them to him and reached out and touched his face. 'Sometimes people can't see what's right in front of them, Jack. It's strange how often that happens. And how often it hurts the people we're supposed to love.' She paused. 'I do love you, son. And one thing I know for certain is that you loved my daughter. And she loved you. That should have been enough for me. And now, it is.'

They exchanged a hug, and she turned to go.

'Bonnie?'

She looked back.

'The kids?' he said in a small voice.

'They're right where they should be, Jack. With their father.'

WHEN MIKKI opened her eyes, the first thing she saw was her dad. Right after that she saw Liam peering over Jack's shoulder.

'I'm really OK, guys,' she said, a little groggily.

Jack smiled and looked at Liam. 'Give us a minute, will you?'

Liam nodded, flashed Mikki a reassuring grin, and left the room.

Jack gripped her hand, and she squeezed back. Mikki said, 'Sorry for all the excitement I caused. It was really dumb.'

'Yes, it was, but we were all under a lot of pressure.'

'So the lighthouse finally worked?'

He let out a long breath. 'Yeah. If it hadn't . . .' His voice trailed off, and father and daughter started to weep together, each clutching the other, their bodies shaking.

'I can't believe how close I came to losing you, sweetie.'

'I know, Dad, I know,' she said in a hushed voice.

They finally drew apart.

'So what now? We still go with Grandma?'

'No, you're staying right here with me.'

Mikki screamed with joy and hugged him again. 'Does Liam know?' she said excitedly.

'No, I thought I'd leave that to you.' He rose. 'I'll go and get him.'

As he turned to leave, she said, 'Dad?'

'Yeah?'

'No matter what happens in my life, you'll always be my hero.'

He bent down and touched her cheek. 'Thanks . . . Michelle.'

Later, as he stood by the doorway watching the two teens excitedly talking and hugging, Jack first smiled, then teared up, and then smiled again. She was clearly not a little girl any more. And he could easily see how fast her life, and his, would change in the next few years.

LATER, AS JACK WALKED along the beach, a voice called out, 'I'm going to miss you Armstrongs when you go back to Ohio.'

He turned to see Jenna walking towards him. 'No, you won't,' said Jack, 'because we're staying right here.'

She drew next to him. 'Are you sure?'

He smiled. 'No, but we're still staying.'

She slipped an arm around him. 'I'm glad things have worked out.'

'I couldn't have done it without you.'

'You're way too generous with your praise.'

'Seriously, Jenna, you helped in a lot of ways. A lot.'

'So what are we going to do about the budding romance?'

'What?' he said, in a startled voice.

'Between our kids.'

'Oh.'

She laughed, and he grinned sheepishly.

'I think we take it one day at a time.' He looked directly at her. 'Does that sound OK, Jenna?'

'That sounds very OK, Jack.'

Epilogue

A little over two years later, Jack sat on the beach in almost the exact spot he and Mikki had occupied the night he'd realised he had so much to live for. The house was quieter now. Mikki and Liam had just left for college. She'd aced her last two years in high school and gone out to Berkeley on a scholarship. Liam the drummer had cut off his hair and was at West Point. Though they were a continent apart, the two remained the best of friends.

Cory was working part-time at the Play House and learning the ropes of theatre management from Ned Parker, while young Jackie had started talking full blast one morning about a year ago and had not stopped since.

Jack got up and made his way to the top of the lighthouse.

He hadn't been up there since the morning after almost losing Mikki. He stepped out onto the catwalk and looked towards the sea. His eyes gravitated to the spot where father and daughter had fought so hard for their lives. Then he looked away and up to a clear, blue summer sky.

Lizzie's lighthouse. It worked when I needed it to.

Jack had two very important things to do that day. And the first one was waiting for him down the beach. He left the lighthouse and set off. As he drew closer, Jack realised he had just travelled over a half mile by beach and a lifetime by every other measure.

She was waiting for him by prearrangement. He slipped his arms round Jenna and kissed her. Then he knelt down and asked a woman he loved if she would do him the honour of becoming his wife.

Jenna cried a little, and allowed him to slip the ring over her shaky finger. After that they held each other for a long time, as a gentle breeze rippled across them.

'Sammy's going to be the best man,' Jack said.

'And Liam will be giving me away,' Jenna replied. 'I love you, Jack.'

'I love you, too, Jenna.'

They kissed again and sat for a while, discussing plans. Then Jack walked back to the Palace. The distance seemed a lot longer going back. There was a reason for this.

The first trek had been to create a bridge for his future. This trip involved him making a painful separation from the past.

He reached the beach in front of his house and sat down in the sand. He pulled out a photo of Lizzie and held it in front of him. It was still nearly impossible for him to believe that she had been gone nearly three years. It just couldn't be. But it was.

He traced the curve of her smile with his finger while he stared into her beautiful green eyes. While Jack had just asked another woman to marry him, and this seemed right in so many ways, he knew that a significant part of him would always love Lizzie.

You should respect the past. But you can't live there.

And now he had something else to finish. Something very important.

From his coat pocket he pulled out a piece of paper and a pen. Jack Armstrong touched the pen to the paper and began to write.

Dear Lizzie,
    A lot has happened that I need to tell you about.

An hour later he finished the letter with, as always,

    Love,
    Jack

He sat there for a while, then he folded the letter and placed it in an envelope marked with a '7'. He put the envelope and the photo of Lizzie in his pocket and walked towards the house.

When he reached the grass, he turned and looked upwards. His mouth eased into a smile when he realised what he was looking at. Today, he'd finally found it, after all this time searching.

Right there was the little piece of the sky that contained Heaven. He somehow knew this for certain. Ironically, like so many complexities in life, the answer had been right in front of him the whole time.

'Pop-pop!'

He turned to see Jackie flying towards him. The boy gave a leap, and Jack caught him in midair.

'Hey, buddy.'

'What are you doing?'

Jack turned so they were both looking out towards the ocean. He pointed to the sky. 'Mommy's up there watching us, Jackie.'

Jackie looked awestruck. 'Mommy?' Jack nodded. Jackie waved to the sky. 'Hi, Mom.' He blew her a kiss.

Then Jack carried his son towards the house. Right before he got there, he slowly looked back at that little patch of blue sky.

Goodbye, Lizzie.

For now.

david **baldacci**

Profile

Born:
August 5, 1960,
Richmond, USA.

Family:
Wife, Michelle; teenage
son and daughter.

Education:
BA from Virginia
Commonwealth University;
Law degree from

University of Virginia.

First Profession:
Attorney.

Most Exciting Moment:
Births of his children.

Favourite Drink:
Full-bodied Italian red
wine.

Website:
DavidBaldacci.com

David Baldacci got the writing bug at a very young age. 'My mom gave me notebooks that I would fill and I got the fever. Books fuelled the fever. They were everything to me,' the prolific author says.

Although Baldacci always wanted to be a writer, for practical purposes he went on to get a law degree after receiving his BA in political science. 'I had a wife and child; the starving artist route didn't work for me,' he says. 'I thought I could be a good lawyer. I liked to write and I loved to do research.'

While practising as both a trial and corporate attorney for over nine years in Washington, DC, he continued to write whenever he could. He followed the advice to 'write about what you know' and penned legal thrillers. And all his hard work paid off. His first novel, *Absolute Power*, published in 1996, was an immediate hit and was turned into a movie starring Clint Eastwood. The success of both enabled him to quit his day job and devote himself to writing full time.

Like *Absolute Power*, most of Baldacci's novels take place in Washington, DC, and are filled with political intrigue. He has now published over twenty best sellers and these days he often publishes two books a year. 'If I'm not writing, I'm not comfortable. I do what I love to do for a living. I just love to write.'

David Baldacci likes nothing better than to challenge himself and push himself beyond his comfort zone in his writing. To do this he immerses himself in research and has an office both at home and outside the home. 'With that said, I have no set schedule or particular word count that I strive for each day. I can write as easily during the day as the middle of the night. I think about what I'm going to write for a long time before I sit down and actually do it. Then I tend to write in bursts. Research/write/think/research/write.'

So what made him change genres and write *One Summer*, an emotional family drama that departs wildly from his standard fare? As the author tells it, 'I was saving seats in church for my son's confirmation and, as I sat there, I started thinking about my life. My dad had passed away, my mom was ill, and my daughter was getting ready to go off to college. The story came to me in one breathtaking mind rush, unfolding like frames of film in my head. I then spent the next three or four months writing it.'

One Summer is a story of love, tragedy, second chances, fear and uncertainty, and the story was so important to Baldacci that he put everything aside to write it, the words pouring out of him so fast it felt like someone else was telling him what to write. 'And I guess if I had never gone to church, I never would have written it.'

For David Baldacci, *One Summer* is good old-fashioned American storytelling, but as a thriller writer, predominantly, he wanted to give the novel a twist. So when the story opens, the reader is lead to believe that Jack Armstrong is about to die, but the author stands this premise on its head and it is Jack who becomes the surviving character, rather than his wife Lizzie. 'I wanted to explore how much harder it is for Jack to live than for him to die. How his brush with death has changed him and his relationship with his kids. That's the premise and I wrote the story exploring how Jack responds to this.'

When Baldacci was once asked why he had not published this very different novel under a pseudonym, he laughed and replied that he only writes under a pseudonym in Italy. The reason being, 'in Italy it is believed that writers with Italian names can't write!'

Baldacci believes so strongly in the power of storytelling and literacy that he and his wife established the Wish You Well Foundation in 2002. With a mission of 'supporting family literacy in the United States by fostering and promoting the development and expansion of new and existing literacy and educational programmes', the foundation funds both individual literacy projects and existing organisations that share its mission.

The author has created a way to get his readers involved in the cause, too. In a joint effort of Wish You Well and Feeding America, the Feeding Body & Mind programme was created. At David Baldacci's, and at some other authors' book signings, fans can donate gently used books, which are then distributed to recipients of Feeding America's food assistance programme, thus feeding body and mind.

As Baldacci says, 'The ability to read is the foundation for everyday life. Indeed, virtually none of the major issues we face as a nation today can be successfully overcome until we eradicate illiteracy.'

GAMBLE

FELIX FRANCIS

Former jockey Nick Foxton can no longer ride, but he still loves the races. Standing among the Grand National spectators at Aintree, he's stunned when his work colleague, Herb Kovak, is gunned down right next to him. The gunman disappears into the crowd, leaving Nick wondering how well he knew his friend and just why anyone would have cause to murder him . . .

1

I was standing right next to Herb Kovak when he was murdered. Executed would have been a better word. Shot three times from close range, twice in the heart and once in the face, he was almost certainly dead before he hit the ground, and definitely before the gunman had turned away and disappeared into the Grand National race-day crowd.

The shooting had happened so fast that neither Herb nor I, nor anyone else for that matter, would have had a chance to prevent it. In fact, I hadn't realised what was actually going on until it was over, and Herb was already dead at my feet. I wondered if Herb himself had had the time to comprehend that his life was in danger before the bullets tore into his body to end it.

Probably not, and I found that strangely comforting.

I had liked Herb.

But someone else clearly hadn't.

THE MURDER OF Herb Kovak changed everyone's day, not just his. The police took over the situation with their usual insensitive efficiency, cancelling one of the world's major sporting events with just half an hour's notice and requiring the more than sixty thousand frustrated spectators to wait patiently in line for several hours to give their names and addresses.

'But you must have seen his face!'

I was sitting at a table opposite an exasperated police detective inspector in one of the restaurants that had been cleared of its usual clientele and set up as an emergency incident room.

'I've already told you,' I said. 'I wasn't looking at the man's face.'

I thought back once again to those few fatal seconds and all I could remember clearly was the gun. 'The gun was black. With a silencer.'

It didn't sound very helpful. Even I could tell that.

'Mr . . . er—' the detective consulted the notebook on the table—'Foxton. Is there nothing else you can tell us about the murderer?'

'I'm sorry,' I said, shaking my head. 'It happened so quickly.'

He changed his line of questioning. 'How well did you know Mr Kovak?'

'We work together. Have done for the past five years or so. I'd say we are work friends.' I paused. 'At least, we were.'

It was difficult to believe that he was dead.

'What line of work?'

'Financial services,' I said. 'We're independent financial advisers.'

I could almost see the detective's eyes glaze over with boredom.

'It may not be as exciting as riding in the Grand National,' I said, 'but it's not that bad.'

He looked up at my face. 'And have you ridden in the Grand National?' His voice was full of sarcasm, and he was smiling.

'As a matter of fact, I have,' I said. 'Twice.'

The smile faded. 'Oh,' he said.

Oh, indeed, I thought. 'And I won it the second time.'

He looked down again at his notes. 'Foxton,' he said. 'Not Foxy Foxton?'

'Yes,' I said, although I had long given up 'Foxy', preferring my real name of Nicholas, which was more suited to a serious life in the City.

'Well, well,' said the policeman. 'Not riding today then?'

'No,' I said. 'Not for a long time.'

Had it really been eight years, I thought, since I had last ridden in a race? In some ways it felt like only yesterday.

'So now you're a financial adviser? Bit of a comedown, wouldn't you say?'

I thought about replying that I believed it was better than being a policeman but decided, in the end, that silence was probably the best policy. Anyway, I tended to agree with him. My whole life had been a bit of a comedown since those heady days of hurling myself over Aintree fences with half a ton of horseflesh between my legs.

'Which firm?' he asked.

'Lyall and Black. Our offices are in Lombard Street, in London.'

He wrote it down. 'Can you think of any reason why anyone would want Mr Kovak dead?'

It was the question I had been asking myself over and over again for the past two hours. 'No,' I said. 'Everyone liked Herb. He was always smiling and happy. He was the life and soul of any party.'

'How long did you say you've known him?' asked the detective.

'Five years. We joined the firm at the same time.'

'I understand he was an American citizen.'

'Yes,' I said. 'He came from Louisville, in Kentucky.'

'Was he married?'

'No.'

'Girlfriend?'

'None that I knew of. But what difference would it make anyway?'

'Lots of murders have a sexual motive,' said the detective. 'Until we know differently, we have to explore every avenue.'

IT WAS NEARLY DARK before I was allowed to leave the racecourse. I sat for some while in the car before setting off, going over in my mind the events of the day. I had picked Herb up from his flat at Seymour Way in Hendon soon after eight in the morning and we had set off to Liverpool in great good humour. It was Herb's first trip to see the Grand National and he was excited by the prospect.

He had grown up in the shadow of the iconic twin spires of Churchill Downs racetrack, the venue of the Kentucky Derby and spiritual home of American Thoroughbred racing, but he had always claimed that gambling on the horses had ruined his childhood.

I had asked him to come to the races with me before but he had always declined, saying that the memories were still too painful. However, there had been no sign of that today as we had motored north on the motorway chatting amicably about our work and our lives.

He and I had got on fairly well over the past five years but on a strictly colleague-to-colleague level. Today had been the first day of a promising deeper friendship. It had also been the last. I still had no idea why anyone would want him dead.

MY JOURNEY HOME to Finchley, north London, seemed never-ending. There was an accident on the M6 with a five-mile tailback. It said so on the radio, sandwiched between news bulletins about the murder of Herb and the cancellation of the Grand National. Not that they mentioned Herb by name. The police would withhold his identity until his next of kin had been informed.

But who were his next of kin? Thankfully, that wasn't my problem.

I was usually an impatient driver, a case of 'once a racer, always a racer'. It made little difference if my steed had four legs or four wheels: if I saw a gap I'd take it. It was the way I'd ridden during my all-too-short four years as a jockey. But that evening, I didn't have the energy to get irritated by the queues of near-stationary cars. Instead I stopped at one of the service areas and called home.

Claudia, my girlfriend, answered at the second ring.

'Hello, it's me,' I said, 'I'm on my way home. Have you seen the news?'

'No. Why?'

I knew she wouldn't have. Claudia was an artist and she had planned to spend the day painting in what she called her studio but what was actually the guest bedroom of the house we shared. Once she closed the door and set to work on a canvas it would take an earthquake to penetrate her bubble.

'The National was cancelled,' I said. 'Someone was murdered.'

'How inconvenient of them.' There was laughter in her voice.

'It was Herb,' I said.

'Herb?' she asked. The laughter had gone. 'Oh my God! How?'

'Watch the news.'

'But, Nick,' she said, concerned. 'I mean—are you OK?'

'I'm fine. I'll be home as soon as I can.'

Next I tried to call my boss, Herb's boss, to warn him of the coming disruption to business, as I was sure there would be, but there was no answer. I decided against leaving a message. Somehow voicemail didn't seem the right medium for bad news.

I set off again and spent the remainder of the journey wondering why anyone should want to kill Herb. How did the murderer know Herb would be at Aintree today? Had we been followed from London? Had Herb been the real target or had it been a case of mistaken identity? And why would anyone commit murder with sixty thousand potential witnesses in attendance when surely it would be safer to lure their victim alone into some dark, quiet alley?

I'd said as much to the detective inspector but he hadn't thought it particularly unusual. 'Sometimes it is easier for an assailant to get away if there is a big crowd to hide in,' he'd said.

'But it must make it more likely that he would be recognised?'

'You'd be surprised,' he'd said. 'More witnesses often mean more confusion. They all see things differently.'

'But how about CCTV?' I'd asked him.

'The spot behind the grandstand where Mr Kovak was shot is not in view of any of the racecourse security cameras.'

The assassin had known what he was doing.

Every line of thought came back to the same question. Why would anyone want to kill Herb Kovak? Some of our clients could get pretty cross when an investment that had been recommended to them went down in value rather than up, but to the point of murder? Surely not.

People like Herb and me didn't live in a world of contract killers and hit men. We existed in an environment of figures and computers, profits and returns, not of guns and bullets and violent death.

The more I thought about it the more convinced I became that the killer must have shot the wrong man.

I WAS HUNGRY and weary by the time I pulled the Mercedes into the parking area in front of my house in Lichfield Grove, Finchley. Claudia came out. 'I watched the news,' she said. 'I can't believe it.'

Neither could I. It all seemed so unreal. 'I was standing right next to him,' I said. 'One moment he was alive and laughing about which horse we should bet on and the next second he was dead.'

'Awful.' She stroked my arm. 'Do they know who did it?'

'Not that they told me,' I said. 'What did it say on the news?'

'Not much,' Claudia said. 'Just a couple of experts disagreeing with each other about whether it was terrorism or organised crime.'

'It was an assassination,' I said firmly. 'Plain and simple.'

'But who would want to assassinate Herb Kovak?' Claudia said. 'I only met him twice but he seemed such a gentle soul.'

'I agree,' I said. 'It must have been a case of mistaken identity. Perhaps that's also why the police haven't yet revealed who was shot. They don't want to let the killer know he hit the wrong man.'

I walked round to the back of the car and opened the boot. It had been a warm spring day when we had arrived at Aintree and we had left our overcoats in the car. I looked down at them both lying in the boot, Herb's dark blue one on top of my own brown.

'Oh God,' I said out loud. 'What shall I do with that?'

'Leave it there,' said Claudia, slamming the boot shut. She took me by the arm. 'Come on, Nick. You need a stiff drink, then bed.'

I DIDN'T FEEL much better in the morning, but that might have had something to do with the drinks I'd consumed. I'd never been much of a drinker, not least because I'd needed to keep my weight down when I'd been a jockey. I'd left school with three top grades at A level and, much to the dismay of my parents, had forgone the offered place at the LSE, the London School of Economics, for a life in the saddle. So when young men going up to university were learning how to pour large amounts of alcohol down their throats, I'd been sitting in a sauna trying to shed an extra pound or two.

However, the previous evening I had dug out the half bottle of whisky left over from Christmas and polished it off before climbing the stairs to bed. But the spirit didn't take away the demons in my head and I had spent much of the night awake, unable to remove the mental image of Herb growing cold on a marble slab in some Liverpool mortuary.

The weather on Sunday morning was as miserable as me, with a string of April showers blowing in on a bracing northerly breeze.

At about ten, during a break in the rain, I went out for a Sunday paper, nipping up to the newsagent's on Regent's Park Road.

'A very good morning to you, Mr Foxton,' said the shop owner.

'Morning, Mr Patel. But I'm not sure what's good about it.'

Mr Patel smiled at me and said nothing. We may have lived in the same place but we did so with different cultures.

All the front pages had the same story: DEATH AT THE RACES read one headline, MURDER AT THE NATIONAL read another.

There appeared to be far greater coverage about the aggravation and inconvenience suffered by the crowd rather than any sympathy for poor Herb. One paper even suggested the murder was drug related and implied that everyone was better off with the victim dead. I bought a copy of the *Sunday Times* for no better reason than its headline—POLICE HUNT RACE-DAY ASSASSIN—was the least sensational.

'Thank you, sir,' said Mr Patel, giving me my change.

I tucked the paper under my arm and retraced my tracks home.

Lichfield Grove was a typical London suburban street of semidetached houses with bay windows and small front gardens. I had lived here now for eight years yet hardly knew my neighbours. I knew Mr Patel the newsagent better than those I lived right next to. At least it made a change from the rural village life I had experienced before, where everyone knew every other person's business, and where nothing could be kept a secret for long.

My racing friends had thought that Finchley was a strange choice but I had needed a clean break from my former life. A clean break—that was a joke. It had been a clean break that had forced me to stop race riding just as I was beginning to make my mark. The clean break was to my second cervical vertebra. I had broken my neck.

I suppose I should be thankful that the break hadn't killed or paralysed me. The fact that I was now walking down Lichfield Grove at all was due to the prompt care of the paramedics at Cheltenham racecourse that fateful day. They had taken great pains to immobilise my neck and spine before I was lifted from the turf. It had been a silly fall, and I had to admit to a degree of carelessness on my part.

The last race on the Wednesday of the Cheltenham Festival was what was known as 'the Bumper'—a National Hunt flat race. No jumps, no hurdles, just two miles of undulating green grass between start and finish.

That Wednesday, just over eight years ago, I had been riding a horse the *Racing Post* had kindly called 'an outsider'. The horse had just one speed—moderate—and no turn of foot to take it past others up the final climb to victory. My only chance was to go off fast from the start and try to run the 'finish' out of the others.

The plan worked quite well, up to a point.

At about halfway, my mount and I were going reasonably well as we swung left-handed and down the hill. But the sound of the pursuers was getting ever louder in my ears, and six or seven of them swept past us like Ferraris overtaking a steamroller as we turned into the straight. The race was lost, and it was no great surprise to me, or to the few still watching from the grandstands.

Perhaps the horse beneath sensed a subtle change in me—a change from expectation and excitement to resignation and disappointment. Perhaps the horse was no longer concentrating on the task in hand in the same way that his jockey's mind was wandering to the following day's races. Whatever the cause, one moment he was galloping along serenely, and the next he had stumbled and gone down as if shot.

I had seen the television replay. I'd had no chance.

The fall had catapulted me over the horse, headfirst into the ground. I woke up two days later in the spinal injuries department of a Bristol hospital with a humdinger of a headache and a metal contraption called a halo brace literally screwed into my skull.

Three months later, with the brace removed, I set about regaining my fitness and place in the saddle only for my hopes to be dashed by the horse-racing authority's medical board who decided that I was permanently unfit to return to racing. 'Too risky,' they had said. 'Another fall could prove fatal.' I had argued that all jockeys risk their lives every time they climb aboard half a ton of horse and gallop at thirty miles per hour over five-foot fences. But it was all to no avail. 'Sorry,' they said. 'Our decision is final.'

From being the new kid on the block, the youngest winner of the Grand National since Bruce Hobbs in 1938, I was suddenly a twenty-one-year-old ex-jockey with nothing to fall back on.

'You will need an education for when your riding days are over,' my father had once said in a last futile attempt to make me take up my place at university instead of going racing when I was eighteen.

'Then I'll get my education when I need it,' I'd replied.

And so I had, applying again and being accepted by the LSE to read for a combined degree in government and economics. And hence I had come to live in Finchley, putting down a deposit on the house from the earnings of my last successful season in the saddle.

But it hadn't been an easy change.

I had become used to the adrenalin-fuelled excitement of riding horses at speed over obstacles when winning was the thing. I loved it. It was like a drug, and I was addicted. In those first few months I tried hard to put on a brave face, busying myself with buying the house and getting ready for my studies, telling everyone that I was fine, but inside I was sick, shaking and near suicidal.

ANOTHER SHOWER was about to fall out of the darkening sky as I hurried along the road to my house with the newspaper.

In keeping with many of my neighbours, I had converted my small front lawn into a parking space, now occupied by my Mercedes SLK sports car. I opened the boot and looked at the two coats lying there. I picked them up, slammed the boot shut, and hurried inside as the first large drops of rain began to wet my hair.

I hung my coat on one of the hooks behind the front door. I hung Herb's next to mine. I am not quite sure why I went through the pockets. Maybe I thought I'd find his flat key. There was no key, but there was a folded-over piece of paper deep in the left-hand pocket.

I flattened it out on the wall and stood there in disbelief reading the stark message written in black ballpoint capital letters:

YOU SHOULD HAVE DONE WHAT YOU WERE TOLD. YOU MAY SAY YOU
REGRET IT, BUT YOU WON'T BE REGRETTING IT FOR LONG.

Did that mean Herb had been the real target? Had the assassin actually shot the right man? And if so, why?

I SPENT MUCH of Sunday reading and rereading the message, trying to work out whether it actually was a prediction of murder or just an innocent communication with no relevance to the events at the Grand National the previous afternoon.

I dug out the business card I'd been given at Aintree by the detective: Inspector Paul Matthews, Merseyside Police. I tried the number, but he wasn't available. I left a message asking him to call me back. I wondered what it was that Herb should have done, what he had been told to do. And to whom had he expressed regret?

I read about the murder in the *Sunday Times*. I thought again about calling our boss, but he would find out soon enough that the victim had been his senior assistant. Why spoil his Sunday?

The *Times* correspondent speculated that the name of the victim was being withheld because he was a well-known criminal and the police didn't want potential witnesses not to bother coming forward.

'That's rubbish,' I said out loud.

I was sitting in our kitchen while Claudia was baking a cake, her long black hair tied back in a ponytail.

'They're suggesting that Herb was a criminal,' I said.

'And was he?' Claudia asked, turning round.

'Of course not,' I said firmly.

'How do you know?' she asked.

'I just do,' I said. 'I worked at the next desk to him for the past five years. Don't you think I'd have noticed if he was a criminal?'

'Not necessarily,' Claudia said. 'Do you think those who worked next to Bernie Madoff realised he was a crook?'

She was right. She usually was.

I had met Claudia during my second year at the LSE. It was strictly business. I was finding student life expensive, and Claudia was in need of digs close to the art college where she was studying. We made a deal. She would move into the guest bedroom in my house as a lodger and pay a contribution towards the mortgage.

By the end of the month she had moved into my bedroom as full-time girlfriend, while she still went on renting the guest bedroom as her studio.

The arrangement still existed although, since our student days, the rent she paid had decreased steadily to nothing as my earnings had risen and hers had remained stubbornly static at zero.

'Making your mark as an artist is not about commercial sales,' she said. 'It's all to do with creativity.'

And creative she was. Sometimes I just wished that others would appreciate her creations enough to write out a cheque. But the main problem was that she didn't actually want to part with any of them so she didn't even try to sell them. It was as if she painted them for her own benefit. And they were definitely an acquired taste—dark and foreboding, full of surreal images of pain and distress.

For a long while I had worried about her state of mind, but it was as if Claudia placed all her dark thoughts into her paintings, leaving her to exist outside of her work in a world of brightness and colour.

'But it says here,' I said to Claudia, 'that the murder had all the characteristics of a gangland killing. Now surely I would have known if Herb had been involved in that sort of thing.'

'I bet my friends have all sorts of skeletons in their cupboards.'

'You're a cynic,' I said, but she did have some strange friends.

'A realist,' she replied. 'It saves being disappointed. If I believe the worst of people then I'm not disappointed when it turns out to be accurate.'

'And do you believe the worst of me?'

'Don't be silly,' she said, coming over and stroking my hair with flour-covered hands. 'I know the worst of you.'

'And are you disappointed?'

'Always.' She laughed.

But I began to wonder if it was true.

I ARRIVED at the offices of Lyall & Black on the fourth floor of 64 Lombard Street at 8.15 a.m. on Monday morning to find both senior partners, Patrick Lyall and Gregory Black, in the client waiting area leaning on the chest-high reception desk.

'Hi, Nicholas,' said Patrick as I entered. 'The police are here.'

'So I see,' I said. 'Is it to do with Herb?'

They nodded. 'They won't let us into our offices,' Patrick said.

'Have they said what they are looking for exactly?' I asked.

'No,' Gregory said sharply. 'I presume they are hoping to find some clues. But I'm not happy about it. There may be confidential client material on his desk that I wouldn't want them to see.'

I thought it was unlikely the police would accept that anything was confidential if it could have a bearing on unmasking a murderer.

'When did you find out he was dead?' I asked. Herb's name had finally been included in the late news on Sunday evening.

'Yesterday afternoon,' said Patrick. 'I received a call from the police asking to meet us here this morning. How about you?'

'I did try to call you on Saturday but there was no reply,' I said. 'I was actually with Herb when he was shot. I was standing right next to him.'

'How awful,' Patrick said. 'Did you see who killed him?'

'Well, sort of,' I said. 'But I was looking mostly at his gun.'

'I just don't understand it.' Patrick shook his head. 'Why would anyone want to kill Herb Kovak?'

'Dreadful business,' said Gregory, also shaking his head. 'Not good for the firm. Not good at all.'

It wasn't too hot for Herb either, I thought, but decided not to say so. Lyall & Black, although small, had risen to be a significant player in the financial services industry. Patrick Lyall and Gregory Black took an innovative approach to investment, recommending opportunities that traditional advisers might classify as too risky, such as financing films or plays, or buying shares in foreign property portfolios. Returns could be vast, but so were the chances of losing everything.

It was the attitude that had first attracted me to them. Kicking a horse to ask it to lengthen its stride, to make it right for a jump, was also an extreme-risk strategy that could so easily result in a crashing fall. A safer approach might be to take a pull, to ask the animal to shorten and to put in an extra stride. It may have been safer, but it was slower. A great deal better in my mind to crash to the turf trying to win than to be satisfied with second place.

'How much longer are they going to keep us waiting?' Gregory Black demanded. 'Don't they realise we have work to do?'

No one answered.

One by one the other staff had turned up and the client waiting area was now full. The receptionists were in tears. Herb had been popular, not least because he'd loved being the American abroad, turning up on the Fourth of July with gifts of candy and apple pie, and drawling 'yee-haw' like a cowboy when he'd lassoed a new client. Herb had been fun, and office life was going to be a lot less cheerful for his passing.

Finally, around nine thirty, a middle-aged man in an ill-fitting grey suit came into the reception area and addressed the waiting faces. 'I am Detective Chief Inspector Tomlinson of the Merseyside police,' he began. 'Sorry for the inconvenience but my colleagues and I are investigating the murder of Herbert Kovak. We will be here for some time, and I must ask you to remain here as I will want to speak to all of you individually.'

Gregory Black didn't look pleased. 'Can't we work in our offices while we wait?'

'I'm afraid that won't be possible,' replied the policeman. 'I do not want any of you having any access to your computers.'

'But that's outrageous.' Gregory was building up a head of steam. 'Are you accusing one of us of having something to do with Mr Kovak's death?'

'I'm not accusing anyone,' Chief Inspector Tomlinson replied. 'I just need to cover every avenue. If evidence exists on Mr Kovak's computer then I am sure you will all understand that it has to be free from contamination due to any of you accessing the files through the company server.'

Gregory was hardly placated. 'But all our files are remotely saved and can be viewed directly as they were at any time.'

'Mr Black,' the policeman said. 'You are wasting my time. The sooner I get to work, the sooner you will get into your office.'

Gregory Black muttered something under his breath and turned away.

But Gregory was right, the restriction on our computers was ridiculous. Our system allowed for remote access so that certain members of the firm could access the company files when away from the office. If any of us had wanted to 'contaminate' the files since Herb's death, we'd had most of the weekend to do so.

'Can we go out for a coffee?' asked Jessica Winter, the firm's compliance officer.

'Yes,' said the inspector, 'but not all of you at once. I will be starting the interviews soon. And if you do go, please be back by ten o'clock.'

Jessica stood up and made for the door. Half a dozen more made a move in the same direction, including me. Clearly none of us relished being confined in close proximity to Gregory Black for the next half an hour.

I HAD TO WAIT until after eleven before I was interviewed.

'Now then, Mr Foxton,' said Chief Inspector Tomlinson while studying his papers, 'I understand you were at Aintree races on Saturday afternoon and were interviewed by one of my colleagues.'

'Yes,' I replied. 'By Detective Inspector Matthews.'

He nodded. 'Have you anything to add?'

'Yes,' I said. 'I tried to call Inspector Matthews yesterday. I left a message for him to call me back, but he didn't. It was about this.'

I removed from my pocket the folded piece of paper I had found in Herb's coat and spread it out on the desk. I knew the words now by heart: YOU SHOULD HAVE DONE WHAT YOU WERE TOLD. YOU MAY SAY YOU REGRET IT, BUT YOU WON'T BE REGRETTING IT FOR LONG.

After a moment, he looked up at me. 'Where did you find this?'

'In Mr Kovak's coat pocket. He'd left his coat in my car when we arrived at the races. I only found it yesterday.'

The chief inspector studied the paper without touching it.

'Did you not think this might be evidence? Handling it may jeopardise the chances of recovering any forensics.'

'It was in his coat pocket,' I said in my defence. 'I didn't know what it was until I'd opened it up and by then it was too late.'

He studied it once more. 'And what do you think it means?'

'I've no idea,' I said. 'But I think it might be a warning. It's clearly not a threat or it would say "*do as you are told or else*" and not "*you should have done what you were told*".'

'OK,' the policeman said, 'but that doesn't make it a warning.'

'Think about it. If you wanted to kill someone you'd hardly ring them up and tell them, would you? It would put them on their guard. Surely you would just do it, unannounced.'

'You really have thought about it,' he said.

'Yes,' I said, 'a lot. And I was there when Herb was killed. There was no "*you should have done so-and-so*" from the killer before he fired. Quite the reverse. He shot so quickly and without preamble that I reckon Herb was dead before he even knew what was happening. And that is not in keeping with this note.' I paused. 'So I think this might have been a warning from someone else, not from the killer. In fact, I believe that it's almost more than a warning, it's an apology.'

The chief inspector looked up at me for a few seconds. 'Mr Foxton,' he said finally. 'This isn't a television drama, you know. In real life people don't apologise for murdering someone before the event.'

'So you're saying I'm wrong.'

'No,' he said slowly, 'I'm not saying that. But I'm not saying you're right either. I'll keep an open mind on the matter.'

It sounded to me very much like he thought I was wrong. He stood up and went to the door and presently another officer came in and removed the piece of paper, placing it into a plastic bag with some tweezers.

'Now,' said the chief inspector as the door closed. 'You and Mr Kovak worked together. What did he do exactly?'

'The same as me. He worked for Patrick Lyall, monitoring investments of Mr Lyall's clients, but he also had clients of his own.'

'Could you describe what you do here, and what this firm does?'

I thought about how to explain it so DCI Tomlinson would understand. 'We manage other people's money,' I said. 'We advise clients where they should invest and then, if they agree, we invest their money and monitor the performance of the investments.'

He wrote some notes. 'How many clients does the firm have?'

'It's not that simple,' I said. 'The advisers are all individuals and it's they who have the clients. There are six registered IFAs, at least there were before Herb got killed.'

'IFAs?'

'Independent financial advisers.'

'You are one of those?' he asked. 'You have clients of your own?'

'Yes,' I said. 'I have about fifty clients but I spend about half my time looking after Patrick's clients.'

'And how many clients does Mr Lyall have?'

'About six hundred,' I said.

'Could Mr Kovak have been stealing from his clients?'

'Impossible,' I replied, but I couldn't help thinking about what Claudia had said about not knowing if someone was a crook. 'Everything we do is subject to spot-check inspections by regulators, and we have a compliance officer in the firm whose job is to scrutinise the transactions to ensure they are done according to the rules. If Herb had been stealing from his clients the compliance officer would have seen it, not to mention the regulator.'

He looked at the staff list. 'Which is the compliance officer?'

'Jessica Winter,' I said. 'The woman who asked you earlier if we could go out for coffee.'

He nodded. 'How well did Mr Kovak know Miss Winter?'

I laughed. 'If you're suggesting Herb Kovak and Jessica Winter conspired to steal from his clients, forget it. Herb thought our compliance officer was an arrogant prig, and she didn't like Herb.'

'Maybe that was just a front,' said the detective, writing a note.

'My, you do have a suspicious mind,' I said.

'Yes,' he said. 'And it's surprising how often I'm right.'

Could he be right? Could Herb and Jessica have been fooling the rest of us all the time? Could anyone else at the firm be involved?

I returned to the reception area after my interview and joined the other members of the firm.

'What did they ask you?' Jessica said.

'Not much,' I said, trying not to let her see in my face the questions the chief inspector had triggered in my mind. 'They just want to know what Herb did here, and why anyone would want to kill him.'

'Surely he wasn't killed because of his work.' Jessica looked shocked. 'I thought it must be to do with his private life.'

'I don't think they have the slightest idea why he was killed,' said Patrick Lyall. 'That's why they're asking about everything.'

There was a slight commotion outside in the lobby as someone not on the company staff list tried to gain access. I could see through the glass door that it was Andrew Mellor, the company solicitor. Lyall & Black was too small to have a full-time lawyer, so we used Andrew who worked in a legal practice round the corner.

Patrick saw him as well and went over to the door.

'Sorry, Andrew,' said Patrick. 'It's all a bit of a nightmare here.'

'Yes, so I can see.' Andrew Mellor looked around. 'I'm so sorry to hear about Herb Kovak. Unbelievable business.'

'And bloody inconvenient too,' interjected Gregory.

'I need to talk to Nicholas,' said the lawyer. He held his arm out towards the door. 'Do you mind?' he said to me.

I went out to the lobby with Andrew. 'I have something to give you,' he said as he pulled an envelope out of his jacket pocket and held it out to me. 'Herb Kovak's last will and testament. He named you as his executor.'

'Me?' I said, somewhat taken aback.

'Yes,' Andrew said. 'You're also the sole beneficiary of his estate.'

I was astonished. 'Has he no family? Why would he leave it to me?'

'I've no idea,' Andrew said. 'Perhaps he liked you.'

Little did I realise at the time how Herb Kovak's legacy would turn out to be a poisoned chalice.

2

On Tuesday I went to the races, Cheltenham races to be precise. But this was no pleasure outing: it was work.

Racing can be a funny business, especially among the jockeys. Competition is intense. But there exists a camaraderie among those who risk their lives five or six times an afternoon for the entertainment of others. And they look after their own.

So it was with me. My erstwhile opponents who, during my riding days, would have happily seen me dumped onto the turf if it meant that they could win a race, were the first to express their support when I'd been injured. When I had been forced to retire at the ripe old age of twenty-one it had been my fellow jocks who had clamoured to become my first clients when I'd qualified as an IFA.

Since then I had acquired a bit of a reputation as horse racing's very own financial adviser. Nearly all my clients had some connection with racing and I had a near monopoly within the jockeys' changing room that I believed had much to do with a shared view of risk and reward.

So I now regularly spent a couple of days a week at one racecourse or another, all with Patrick and Gregory's blessing, making appointments to see clients before or after the racing.

This April meeting in Cheltenham was competitive, with two of the top jockeys still vying to be crowned as champion for the current season, which concluded at the end of the month. Both were my clients and I had arranged to meet one of them, Billy Searle, after racing.

I had also discovered that being seen regularly at the races was the best way to recruit new clients, which was why I was currently standing on the terrace in front of the weighing room in the midday sunshine more than ninety minutes before the first race.

'Hi, Foxy. Penny for your thoughts?'

Martin Gifford was a large, jovial, middle-ranking racehorse trainer who joked that he had never made it as a jockey due to his large feet. The fact that he had a waist measurement that a sumo wrestler would have been proud of seemed to have passed him by.

'Bloody rum business, that Aintree was,' Martin said. 'Fancy postponing the Grand National just because some bastard got themselves killed.'

He had obviously been reading the papers. 'The person murdered was a friend of mine,' I said. 'I was standing next to him when he was shot.'

'Bloody hell!' shouted Martin. 'Sorry. Trust me to jump in with both feet.'

Trust him, indeed. 'It's OK,' I said. 'Forget it.'

I was cross with myself for mentioning it. Martin Gifford was a five-star gossip. Telling him that the murder victim had been a friend of mine was akin to placing a full-page ad in the *Racing Post* to advertise the fact, except quicker. Everyone at Cheltenham would know by the end of the afternoon.

'Any runners today?' I asked, trying to change the subject.

'Fallen Leaf in the first. Yellow Digger in the three-mile chase.'

'Good luck,' I said.

'Yeah. We'll need it,' he said. 'Fallen Leaf probably wouldn't win if he started now, and Yellow Digger has no chance.' He paused. 'So who was this friend of yours who got killed?'

'Just a work colleague,' I said, trying to sound indifferent.

'What was his name?'

Should I tell him? I wondered. Why not, it had been in all of yesterday's papers. 'Herbert Kovak.'

'And why was he killed?' Martin demanded.

'I've no idea,' I said. 'As I told you, he was only a work colleague.'

'Come on, Foxy,' Martin implored. 'You must have some inkling. You're holding something back. You can tell me.'

'Honestly, Martin,' I said. 'I have no idea about why he was killed or who did it. And if I did, I'd be telling the police, not you.'

Martin shrugged his shoulders as if to imply he didn't believe me.

I was saved from further inquisition by another trainer, Jan Setter, who was everything Martin Gifford wasn't—slim, attractive and fun. She grabbed my arm and turned me away from Martin. 'Hello, lover boy,' she said.

We'd met more than ten years ago. I had been an eighteen-year-old just starting out and she was an established trainer for whom I was riding. Now she was a mid- to late-forties divorcée, and her stables in Lambourn were full with about seventy horses in training. Jan had been one of my clients now for three years. And she was a terrible flirt.

'How was the preview?' I asked. At my suggestion, Jan had invested a considerable sum in a new West End musical.

'Fabulous,' she said. 'I took my daughter and we had a wonderful time. I am sure the reviews will be fabulous.' She laughed again. 'But I'll blame my financial adviser if they aren't and I lose it all.'

But it wasn't a laughing matter. Investing in the theatre had always been a high-risk business, not that investing in anything was certain. It was always a gamble. I had known some seemingly gold-plated investments go belly up almost without warning.

Could such a calamitous loss have resulted in Herb's murder?

I couldn't believe it was possible. Patrick Lyall held regular meetings when investment plans for our clients were discussed. None of our client money could be invested without the approval of either Patrick or Gregory. Our risks were well spread, and no individuals ever lost their shirt. Certainly not enough, I thought, to murder their adviser.

'Come and stay and ride out for me one Saturday,' said Jan, bringing my daydreaming back to the present. 'You'd enjoy it.'

I would enjoy it. But I hadn't sat on a horse in eight years. I recalled the specialist telling me, 'You are lucky to be alive. Quite apart from the main fracture, many of the interlocking bone protrusions that help hold the two vertebrae together have been broken away. With that neck, I wouldn't ride a bike, let alone a horse.' He'd smiled. 'And, whatever you do, don't get into a fight.'

For weeks afterwards I had hardly turned my head at all. I remember being terrified to sneeze in case my head fell off.

'I'd love to come and watch your horses work,' I said to Jan, returning once again to the present. 'But I'm afraid I can't ride one.'

She looked disappointed. 'I thought you'd love it.'

'I would,' I said. 'But it's too much of a risk with my neck.'

'What a bloody shame,' she said.

Bloody shame was right. I longed to ride again. Each day I chatted amicably to my clients as they wore their racing silks and I positively ached to
be one of them again.

I shook my head, albeit only slightly, and put self-pity out of my mind. I
had much to be thankful for and I should be happy to be twenty-nine years
old, alive, employed and financially secure.

But, oh, how I wanted still to be a jockey.

I WATCHED the first race from the grandstand. Even though Cheltenham had
been the scene of my last, ill-fated ride, I held no grudge towards the place.

Cheltenham had been the first racecourse I had ever known. I had grown
up in Prestbury village, next to the course, and I'd ridden my bicycle past it
every morning on my way to school. Each March, as the Cheltenham Festival
approached, the excitement had been the inspiration for me, first to ride a
horse, then to pester a local trainer for holiday jobs, and finally to give up a
future of academia for the perilous existence of a professional jockey.

Away to my left, at the far end of the straight, the fifteen horses for the
first race were called into line by the starter. 'They're off,' sounded the
public-address system, and they were running, two miles of fast-paced
hurdle racing. The horses swept up the straight towards us, then turned to
start another complete circuit of the course. Three horses jumped the final
hurdle side by side, and a flurry of jockeys' legs, arms and whips encour-
aged their mounts up the hill to the finish. 'First, number three, Fallen
Leaf,' sounded the public-address system.

Mark Vickers, the other jockey in the race to be champion, had just
extended his lead over Billy Searle from one to two.

And Martin Gifford, the gossip, had trained the winner in spite of his
expressed lack of faith in its ability. I wondered if he had simply been trying
to keep his horse's starting price high by recommending that other people
should not bet on it. I looked at my racecard and decided to invest a small
sum on Yellow Digger in the third race, the other runner Martin had told me
would have no chance. I turned to go back to the weighing room.

'Hello, Nicholas.'

'Hello, Mr Roberts,' I said in surprise. 'I didn't realise you were a
racing man.'

'Oh, yes,' he said. 'My brother and I have horses in training. I often used
to watch you ride. You were a good jockey.'

'Thank you,' I said.

Mr Roberts or, to use his proper title, Colonel The Honourable Jolyon Westrop Roberts MC OBE, younger son of the Earl of Balscott, was a client. To be precise, he was a client of Gregory Black, but I had met him fairly frequently in the offices at Lombard Street.

'Are you on your day off?' he asked.

'No,' I replied, 'I'm seeing a client after racing, you know, the jockey Billy Searle.'

He nodded. 'I don't suppose . . .' He paused. 'No, it doesn't matter.'

'Can I help you in some way?' I asked.

'No, it's all right,' he said. 'It's fine. I'm sure it's fine.'

'What is fine?' I asked. 'Is it something to do with the firm?'

'No, it's nothing,' he said. 'Forget I even mentioned it.'

I stood there on the grandstand steps for a few seconds. 'Right then,' I said. 'No doubt I'll see you sometime in the office. Bye now.'

'Yes,' he replied. 'Right. Goodbye.'

I walked away leaving him looking out across the course as if in deep thought. I wondered what that had all been about.

MARK VICKERS won twice more during the afternoon, including the race on Yellow Digger, giving him a four-winner lead over Billy Searle in the championship race, and me a tidy payout from the Tote.

Billy Searle was not happy when he emerged from the weighing room for our meeting. 'Bloody Vickers,' he said to me. 'Did you see the way he won the first? Beat the poor animal half to death with his whip. Steward should have banned him for excessive use.'

I decided not to say that I actually thought that Mark Vickers had ridden a textbook finish to win by a head. 'There's still plenty of time left for you to catch him,' I said, but I knew there wasn't, and Mark Vickers was bang in form while Billy wasn't.

'It's my bloody turn. I've been waiting all these years to get my chance and now, with Frank injured, I'm going to lose out to some young upstart.'

Life could be hard. Billy Searle was four years older than me and he'd been runner-up in the championship for the past eight years. Every time he'd been beaten by the same man, the jump jockey recognised by all as the best in the business, Frank Miller. But Frank had broken his leg in a fall and had been out of action now for four months. This year, it would be someone else's turn to be champion jockey, but, after today's triple for Mark Vickers, it seemed likely that it wouldn't be Billy. And time was no longer on Billy's side. Thirty-three is getting on for a jump jockey.

It was obvious that Billy was in no mood to discuss finances even though it had been he, not me, who had called the previous afternoon asking for this urgent meeting. But I'd come all the way from London to talk to him, and I didn't want it to be a wasted journey.

'What was it that you wished to discuss?' I asked him.

'I want all my money back,' he said suddenly.

'What do you mean, back?' I asked.

'I want all my money back from Lyall and Black.'

'But your money is not with Lyall and Black,' I said. 'It's in the investments that we bought for you. You still own them.'

'Well, I want it back anyway,' he said.

'Why?' I asked.

'I just do,' he said crossly. 'It's my money and I want it back.'

'OK. OK, Billy,' I said, trying to calm him down. 'Of course you can have the money back, but it's not that simple. I will need to sell the shares and bonds you have. I can do that tomorrow.'

'Fine,' he said.

'But, Billy,' I said, 'some of your investments were bought with long-term growth in mind. If I have to sell them tomorrow, you are likely to sustain a loss.'

'I don't care,' he said. 'I need the money now.'

'Billy,' I said, 'are you in some sort of trouble?'

'No, of course not,' he said.

Billy Searle's investment portfolio was rather smaller than one might imagine after so many years at the top of his profession, but he had always been a spender rather than a saver. However, he had a nest egg of around a hundred and fifty thousand, more than he would prudently need just for a new car or a foreign holiday.

'OK, Billy,' I said. 'I'll get on with liquidating everything tomorrow. But it'll take a few days for you to get the cash.'

'Can't I have it tomorrow? I need it tomorrow.'

'Billy, that simply isn't possible. I need to sell the shares and bonds, have the funds transferred into the company's client account, then transfer it to your own. Today's Tuesday. You might have it by Friday.'

Billy went pale. 'You don't understand. I owe some guy and I need a hundred thousand by tomorrow night.'

'Why?' I asked him. 'Why do you owe so much?'

'I can't tell you.' He almost screamed the words and the heads of a few racegoers turned our way. 'But I need it tomorrow.'

'I cannot help you,' I said quietly. 'I think I'd better go now. I'll try to get the cash into your account by Friday.'

He was almost in a trance. 'I hope I'm still alive by Friday.'

I SAT in my car in the members' car park and thought through my conversation with Billy Searle. I wondered what I should do.

As he had said, it was his money and he could do what he liked with it. Except he'd also told me he owed some guy about a hundred thousand, and had implied that his life would be in danger if he didn't repay it by the following evening. I would normally dismiss such a threat as melodramatic nonsense but, after the events at Aintree the previous Saturday, I wasn't so sure.

Should I tell someone? But who? The police would want evidence, and I had none. I didn't want to get Billy into trouble. Jockeys who owe money would always be suspected of involvement with bookmakers. But perhaps Billy's need for cash was legitimate. I decided to do nothing until I discussed it with Patrick. It was past six o'clock and the office would be closed. I'd speak to him in the morning. Nothing could be done now anyway, the London markets were closed for the day.

Instead, I went to stay with my mother.

'HELLO, DARLING,' she said, opening her front door. 'You're too thin.'

It was her usual greeting and one that was due to her long-standing pathological fear that I was anorexic. It had all started when I'd been a fifteen-year-old who had been desperate to be a jockey. I'd begun starving myself to keep my weight down. Now she sent food parcels to Claudia with instructions to feed me more protein, or more carbohydrate, or just more.

'Hello, Mum,' I said, ignoring her comment and giving her a kiss.

She still lived near Cheltenham but not in the big house in which I had grown up. That had to be sold during my parents' divorce. My mother's current home was a small whitewashed cottage, hidden down a rutted lane on the edge of a village just north of the racecourse, with two double bedrooms and a bathroom upstairs, and a single open-plan kitchen/diner/lounge downstairs, the levels connected by a narrow, twisting, boxed-in staircase in the corner, with a lever-latched door at the bottom.

'I've bought you some fillet steak for dinner,' she said. 'And I've made some profiteroles for pudding.'

'Lovely,' I said. And I meant it. I hadn't eaten anything all day in preparation for a high-calorie encounter with her cooking and, by now, I was really hungry. I went up to the guest bedroom and changed out of my suit and into jeans and a sweatshirt. I tossed my mobile onto the bed. As always, the closeness to Cleeve Hill, and the phone-signal shadow it produced, rendered the thing useless.

When I came down my mother was standing by the stove with saucepans already steaming on the hob. 'Help yourself to a glass of wine.'

I poured a glass of Merlot from the open bottle.

'How is Claudia?' my mother asked.

'Fine, thank you,' I said. 'She sends her love.'

'She should have come with you.'

Yes, I thought, she should have. There had been a time when we couldn't bear to be apart even for a single night, but now that longing had seemingly evaporated. Perhaps that happens after six years.

'High time you made an honest woman out of her,' my mother said. 'Time you were married and raising children.'

Was it? I'd always believed that someday I would marry and have a family. A few years ago I'd even discussed the prospect with Claudia, but she had dismissed the notion, saying that marriage was for boring people, and that children were troublesome and not for artists like her. I wondered if she still felt the same way.

'But you and Dad are hardly a great advertisement for marriage,' I said, possibly unwisely.

'Nonsense,' she said. 'We were married for thirty years and brought you into the world. I would call that a success.'

'But you got divorced,' I said. 'And you fought all the time.'

'Well, maybe we did,' she said. 'But it was still a success. And I don't regret it for a second because otherwise you wouldn't exist.'

What could I say? Nothing. So I didn't.

She turned to face me. 'And now I want some grandchildren.'

Ah, I thought. There had to be a reason somewhere.

And I was an only child.

WE SAT AT the kitchen table for dinner and I ate myself to a complete stand-still. 'Another profiterole?' she asked.

'Mum,' I said. 'I'm stuffed. I couldn't eat another thing.'

She looked disappointed, but I had eaten far more than I would have normally. I had tried to please her, but enough was enough.

'Are you going to the races tomorrow?' she asked.

The April meeting at Cheltenham ran for two days.

'Yes,' I said. 'But I have some work to do here in the morning. I have my computer with me. Can I use your phone and your broadband connection?'

'Of course,' she said. 'I'll get you some lunch before you go.'

The thought of yet more food was almost unbearable. 'No, thanks, Mum,' I said. 'I'm meeting a client there for lunch.'

She looked at me as if to say she knew I'd just lied to her.

She was right.

'I DON'T LIKE IT but we have to do as he asks,' said Patrick when I called him at eight in the morning using my mother's phone. 'I'll get Diana on it.' Diana was another of his assistants. 'Are you at Cheltenham again today?'

'Yes,' I said. 'But I'll probably just stay for the first three races.'

'Try to have another word with Billy. Get him to see sense.'

'I'll try,' I said. 'But he seemed determined. Scared even.'

'Sounds a bit fishy to me,' Patrick said. 'But we are required by the regulator to do as our clients instruct. We can't go off to the authorities every time they instruct us to do something we don't think is sensible.'

'But we have a duty to report anything we believe to be illegal.'

'Do you have any evidence that he wants to do something illegal with the funds?'

'No.' I paused. 'But Billy told me he owed some guy a hundred grand. I wonder if he's got mixed up with a bookmaker.'

'Betting is not illegal,' Patrick said.

'Maybe not,' I agreed, 'but it is against the rules of racing for a professional jockey to bet.'

'That's not our problem,' he said. 'And for God's sake, try to be discreet. We also have a duty to keep his affairs confidential.'

'OK, I will. I'll see you in the office tomorrow.'

'Right,' said Patrick. 'Oh, yes. Another thing. That policeman called yesterday asking for you.'

'He didn't call my mobile, although the damn thing doesn't work here. My mother lives in a mobile-phone-signal hole.'

'No, well, that wouldn't have mattered anyway because it seems he was rather rude to Mrs McDowd so she refused to give him your number. She told him you were unavailable.'

I laughed. Good old Mrs McDowd, one of our fearless office receptionists.

'What did he want?' I asked.

'Seems they want you to attend at Herb's flat. Something about being his executor.' He gave me the policeman's number and I stored it in my phone. 'Call him. I don't want Mrs McDowd arrested for obstructing the police.'

'OK,' I said. I disconnected from Patrick and called Detective Chief Inspector Tomlinson.

'Ah, Mr Foxton,' he said. 'How are you feeling?'

'I'm fine,' I replied, wondering why he would ask.

'Is your toe OK?' he asked.

'Sorry?'

'Your toe. Your receptionist told me about your operation.'

'Oh, that,' I said, trying to suppress a laugh. 'My toe is fine, thank you. How can I help?'

'Was Mr Kovak in personal financial difficulties?' he asked.

'Not that I am aware of,' I said. 'Why do you ask?'

'Mr Foxton, are you well enough to come to Mr Kovak's home? There are a few things I would like to discuss with you, and I also need you, as his executor, to agree to the removal of certain items from his flat to assist with our enquiries. I can send a car if that helps.'

I thought about my planned day at Cheltenham. 'Tomorrow would be better.'

'How about eight a.m.?' he said. 'Do you need me to send a car?'

Why not, I thought. 'Yes, that would be great.'

I'd have to develop a limp.

BILLY SEARLE was in no mood to explain why he suddenly needed his money.

'Just put the bloody cash in my bank account,' he shouted.

We were standing on the terrace in front of the weighing room and heads were turning our way.

'And what are you doing here anyway? You should be at your desk getting my bloody cash together.'

So much for keeping things discreet. The racing journalists were moving ever closer.

I leaned forward and spoke into his ear. 'You clearly need someone's help and I'm on your side.' I paused. 'Call me when you've calmed down. The money will be in your bank by Friday.'

'I told you I need a hundred grand by tonight.'

We were now the centre of attention for the Cheltenham crowd. 'Sorry,' I said, trying to maintain some dignity. 'That's impossible. It will be there by Friday, maybe Thursday if you're lucky.'

'Thursday's too late,' he screamed. 'I'll be dead by Thursday.'

There was no point in arguing so I walked away, conscious of the hacks scribbling in their notebooks.

'Why are you trying to murder me?' Billy shouted after me.

I ignored him and continued over to the pre-parade ring where I called the office to check how the liquidation of Billy's assets was progressing.

Mrs McDowd answered the telephone.

'What on earth did you say to that policeman?' I asked her.

'I told him you were having an ingrowing toenail removed.'

'Why?'

'Because he was rude to me,' she said with indignation. 'Spoke to me as if I was the office cleaner, so I told him you couldn't be reached. He wanted to know why you couldn't be reached, so I told him you were having an operation. Seemed like a good idea at the time, but the damn man was persistent, I'll give him that. Demanded to know what you were having done so I told him it was an ingrowing toenail.'

'Mrs McDowd, if I ever need someone to make up an alibi, I promise I'll call you,' I said, never thinking for a second that I would need an alibi much sooner than I realised. 'Can I speak to Miss Diana, please?'

She put me through.

The sale of Billy Searle's assets was progressing smoothly, albeit with a loss on some recent purchases. I thanked Diana and disconnected.

COLONEL THE HONOURABLE Jolyon Westrop Roberts MC OBE, younger son of the Earl of Balscott, was waiting for me in the same place on the grandstand where I had met him the previous day. 'Ah, Nicholas,' he said as I made my way up to watch the first race. 'I was hoping you might be here again today.'

'Hello, sir,' I said. 'How can I help?'

'Well,' he said with a slight laugh. 'I hope you can help. But there may be nothing to help about. If you know what I mean?'

'No,' I said. 'I don't know, as you haven't told me anything.'

He laughed again, nervously. 'I'm probably wasting your time. And I wouldn't want to get anyone into trouble.'

'Sir,' I said with some determination. 'What is it that is worrying you?'

He stood for a few seconds in silence looking out to the racecourse. 'Gregory,' he said finally. 'I'm worried about Gregory.'

'What about Gregory?' I asked. We all worried about Gregory. He ate too much and didn't exercise, other than walk to the end of Lombard Street for a substantial lunch five days a week. 'Are you worried about his health?'

'His health?' Mr Roberts repeated. 'Why would I worry about Gregory Black's health? I'm worried about his judgment.'

My planned early departure from Cheltenham was put on hold as I steered Mr Roberts into a corner of the seafood bar. When a client, especially one with as large an investment portfolio as the younger son of the Earl of Balscott, questions the judgment of a senior partner, it is no time to hurry away home.

'Now, sir,' I said when we were each settled with a plate of prawns. 'In what way do you question Gregory Black's judgment?'

'It's probably nothing,' he said.

'Why don't you let me be the judge of that.'

'Yes,' he said slowly. 'I think you might be a good judge. You always were on a horse. Bloody shame you got injured.'

Yes, I thought, a bloody shame. 'Tell me about Gregory Black,' I said. 'I promise you that I will treat what you say in strictest confidence.'

I *hoped* I could treat what he told me in confidence. Independent financial advisers were governed by the financial regulator. I would not be able to suppress information of wrongdoing solely because it would embarrass another IFA, even if he were my boss.

'Is it about one of your investments?' I asked. 'Do you disapprove of something Gregory has asked you to do?'

He absent-mindedly ate some of his prawns. 'He may be mistaken,' he said finally.

'Who might be mistaken? Gregory Black?'

'No,' he said. 'My nephew, Benjamin. He visited the site and he tells me there are no houses, no factory and no building work being done. He said it was just waste ground with pollutants sitting in stagnant pools.'

'I'm sorry. What has this to do with Gregory Black?'

'He advised me to invest in the project.'

'What project?' I asked.

'A Bulgarian property development project,' he said. 'Houses, shops and a new factory making low-energy light bulbs.'

I vaguely remembered the project being discussed at one of Patrick's meetings. 'Are you sure it's on the same site that your nephew visited?'

'He says there is no mistake. The site where there should be a factory and new homes and shops is nothing but an industrial wasteland.'

'How much have you invested in the scheme?' I asked him.

'The family trust has invested about five million. The factory is named the Lord Balscott Lighting Factory. I've seen pictures. The project is a social experiment for one of the most deprived areas of the European Union. A lot of EU money has gone into it.'

'Do these pictures show a factory and new homes?'

'Yes they do,' he said. 'Gregory Black showed them to me. But what am I to believe, the photos or my only nephew?'

'There must be an explanation. Why don't you ask Gregory?'

'I've already approached him and he just told me not to be so silly, of course the factory has been built. But Benjamin is adamant. He says that no Balscott lighting factory exists anywhere in Bulgaria.'

'So what do you want me to do?' I asked him.

'Find out the truth.'

'But why me?' I asked. 'If you think there is a fraud being perpetrated then you should go to the police, or to the financial services regulators.'

He sat and looked at me for a moment. 'I trust you,' he said, and smiled. 'And it was me who persuaded my brother, Viscount Shenington, that the family trust should invest in something that appeared so worth while. I just need to know what is going on.'

'Sir,' I said. 'I am under an obligation to report it if I find that there is a fraud, or even if there is misrepresentation in advertising an investment.'

'Mmm, I see,' he said, stroking his chin. 'My brother and I are most concerned that the good name of the Roberts family should not be dragged through the courts. He is in favour of simply writing off the investment and saying nothing. However . . .' He stopped.

'You feel responsible?' I asked.

'Exactly,' he said. 'But I would prefer it if you could be very discreet. If this *is* a scam, well, to be honest, I would rather not have everybody know that I've been a fool.'

'But I will have to talk to Gregory about it,' I said.

'Can you not have a look at things first without telling anybody? I'm sure that someone with your keen nose for a good investment will be able to spot a rotten egg pretty quickly if there's one to find.'

I laughed. 'My nose isn't that keen.'

'I think it is,' Jolyon Roberts replied. 'I have a friend who's forever telling me about the money you've made for her in films and theatre.'

'I've just been lucky,' I said.

'Yes,' he said, smiling. 'You and Arnold Palmer.'

I looked at him quizzically. 'What about him?' I asked.

'When a reporter asked Palmer why he was so lucky in golf, he replied, "It's a funny thing, the harder I practise the luckier I get."'

But my luck was about to run out.

3

True to his word, Detective Chief Inspector Tomlinson sent a car to collect me from home on Thursday morning, and he was waiting at Herb Kovak's flat when I arrived at 8 a.m. sharp.

'Ah, good morning, Mr Foxton,' he said, opening the front door and offering his hand. 'And how is your toe today?'

'It's fine,' I said honestly. 'It doesn't hurt at all.'

'Nasty things, ingrowing toenails,' he said. 'Had one myself years ago. Hurt like hell.'

'Luckily, I'm a quick healer,' I said. 'Now, how can I help?'

He stepped to the side and I walked past him and into the hallway of Herb's flat.

'Are you certain Mr Kovak was not in personal financial difficulties?' the chief inspector asked while closing the front door.

'No, I'm not certain, but I have no reason to think he was.'

He waved a stack of papers towards me.

'What are they?' I asked.

'Credit-card statements,' said the chief inspector. 'Mr Kovak appears to have had more than twenty credit cards and, according to these statements, owed nearly a hundred thousand pounds.'

I could hardly believe it. Not only because Herb was in so much debt, but because his debt was on credit cards. If anyone knew how expensive it was to borrow on plastic, a financial adviser would.

And yet he'd always had plenty of money. He was always wearing new clothes, and dining out was the norm. It didn't make sense.

'Can I have a closer look at those?' I asked the chief inspector.

He handed them over and I skimmed through the statements. The outstanding balance on each was very large, but that did not show the full picture. 'There are no interest payments from previous months. All the charges on these statements are new.'

I looked to see what Herb had spent a hundred thousand pounds on in a month and was shocked again. There were no purchases, as such, just payments to and from Internet gambling sites. Masses of them. Quite a few of the sites had paid money back to the accounts, but most showed a deficit. Overall, Herb had been a loser not a winner, to the tune of nearly a hundred thousand pounds a month.

All the statements showed that the previous month's balances had been settled in full by the due date. Where had he obtained that sort of money?

As Claudia had said, you never really knew what your friends were up to. Could this online gambling be the reason that Herb was killed?

'There are some other things I would like you to have a look at,' said the chief inspector. 'You may be able to help me understand them.'

He walked down the hallway, turning left through a door. I followed him into Herb's living room. On the far side was a desk with a laptop computer, a printer and three piles of papers in metal baskets.

'We need your permission, as Mr Kovak's executor, to remove certain items that we believe may help with our enquiries. These, for example. But we would like your opinion on them first.'

He handed me two sheets of paper covered on both sides by handwritten lists with columns of what appeared to be dates with amounts of money alongside, together with a further column of capital letters. 'Could they have something to do with Mr Kovak's work?'

I studied the lists briefly. 'I doubt it. They are handwritten and we do everything on computer. These could be amounts of money.' I pointed at the centre two columns. 'And these look like dates.'

'Yes,' he said. 'I worked that much out.'

'Do they correspond to the amounts on the credit-card statements?'

'No. I looked at that. None of the figures are the same.'

'Could that fourth column be people's initials?'

'It might be. Do you recognise any of them? For example, do they match any of your work colleagues?'

I scanned through the list. 'Not that I can see.'

'Right,' he said, as if making a decision. 'With your permission we will take these papers away, together with the credit-card statements, Mr Kovak's laptop computer, and these other things.'

The chief inspector waved a hand towards a box on a side table near the door. I went over and looked in. The box contained various bits and pieces including Herb's American passport, an address book, a desk diary and a folder full of bank statements.

'Fine,' I said. 'Can I make copies of that credit-card stuff? I do know that one of the first tasks for executors is to close the bank accounts and pay the debts of the deceased but goodness knows where I will get a hundred thousand to do that. Do you mind if I look at his bank statements?'

'Not at all,' he said. 'They will be yours anyway.'

I pulled the folder out of the box and looked at the most recent statements. The balance didn't run to anything like a hundred thousand. I unclipped the last statement from the folder and made a photocopy using the printer/copier on the desk. I then photocopied the credit-card statements, and the two sheets of handwritten figures, before handing them all back to the policeman.

"Thank you,' he said. 'I just need your signature on this form to give us permission to remove these items, and I have a receipt for them to give you.'

He handed me the form, which I signed, and the receipt, which I put in my pocket.

'Have you searched everywhere?' I asked.

'Not a proper forensic search,' he said. 'But we had a reasonable look around.'

'How did you get in?' I asked.

'The key was in Mr Kovak's trouser pocket.'

I thought again about Herb lying in some Liverpool morgue. 'How about his funeral?' I asked. 'I suppose it's my job to organise it.'

'Not before the coroner has released the body,' he said.

'And when will that be?' I asked.

'Not for a few weeks. He hasn't been formally identified yet.'

'But I told you who he was.'

'Yes, I know that. But you are not his next of kin and, to be fair, you have only known him for five years. He could have told you that he was Herbert Kovak while not actually being so.'

'You're showing that suspicious mind of yours again.'

He smiled. 'We are still trying to trace his next of kin.'

'He lived in New York before he came to England,' I said. 'But he was brought up in Kentucky. At least, that is what he said.'

Did I now doubt it?

'Yes,' said the chief inspector. 'We have been in touch with our counterparts in New York and Kentucky but, so far, they have been unable to contact any members of his family. It would appear that his parents are deceased. In the meantime, if you think of anything else that might help us with our enquiries please call me.' He dug in his inside pocket for a card. 'Use the mobile number.'

I put the card in my wallet and Chief Inspector Tomlinson collected the box of evidence. 'Can I offer you a lift home?' he asked.

'No, thank you. I think I'll look around here first. I can catch the bus.'

'Don't overdo it with that toe,' he said.

'I'll be careful,' I said with an inward smile. I would, in fact, be going into the office and not home when I left here. 'How do I lock up?'

'Ah, yes,' he said, digging into a pocket. 'I had another key cut.'

I took the offered key. 'You'll let me know when I can start making funeral arrangements?'

'The Liverpool coroner will be in contact with you in due course,' he said. Then he departed, carrying his box under his arm.

I sat for a while at Herb's desk looking again at the credit-card statements. There were between twenty and thirty Internet gambling websites on each statement.

In total there were twenty-two credit cards and 512 entries on the statements. The total owed was £94,626.52. Some of the entries were credits but, overall, the average loss per entry was £185. I checked the actual amounts against the handwritten lists but, as the chief inspector had said, not one of them matched.

It wasn't so much the amount of money that amazed me, even though it did, it was the number of different entries.

I went on studying the credit-card statements. I spotted that there was something else slightly odd about them.

They didn't all have the same name or the same address at the top.

Some of them had this flat's address and others the Lyall & Black office's address in Lombard Street. Nothing too unusual about that. But the names on them also varied. Not very much, but enough for me to notice.

I looked through them again, carefully making two piles on the desk, one for each address.

There were eleven statements in each pile and eleven slight variations in Herb's name: Herb Kovak, Mr Herb E. Kovak, Herbert Kovak Esq., Mr H. Kovak, Herbert E. Kovak, Mr H. E. Kovak, H. E. Kovak Jr, H. Edward Kovak, Bert Kovak Jr, Herbert Edward Kovak and Mr Bert E. Kovak.

No two statements had the exact same name. Now, why did I think that was suspicious?

I heard the key turn in the door and thought that DCI Tomlinson must have forgotten something. I was wrong.

I went out into the hallway to find an attractive blonde-haired woman struggling through the front door with a suitcase. She saw me and stopped. 'Who are you?' she demanded in an American accent.

'Nicholas Foxton,' I said. 'And you?'

'Sherri Kovak,' she said. 'Where's my brother?'

There was no easy way to tell Sherri that her brother was dead, but it was the nature of his death she found most distressing. She sat in an armchair and wept while I made her a cup of tea. She had arrived on an overnight flight from Chicago, and had been surprised, and rather annoyed, that Herb had not been at the airport to meet her as he had promised, but she had eventually made her way to Hendon by train and taxi.

'But how did you have a key to get in?' I asked her.

'Herb gave me one when I was here last year.'

Herb hadn't mentioned to me last year that his sister was visiting, or even that he had a sister in the first place. But why would he have? We had been work colleagues rather than close friends. He also hadn't mentioned that he was a compulsive online gambler.

I wondered if I ought to inform DCI Tomlinson that Herb Kovak's next of kin had turned up. Probably, but then he'd be back round here with a list of awkward questions when it was clear to me that she needed a good sleep. I'd call the chief inspector later.

I found some fresh bed linen and made up the bed in the smaller of the two bedrooms. I then guided the still-crying Miss Kovak from the living room to the bed. 'You sleep for a bit,' I said, covering her with a blanket. 'I'll still be here when you wake.'

'But who are you?' she asked between sobs.

'A friend of your brother's,' I said. 'We worked together.' I decided not to mention to her, just yet, that her brother had left his estate to me and not to her. I left her there and went back to Herb's desk and the credit-card statements. It was gone nine o'clock and I called the office number on my mobile. Mrs McDowd answered.

'It's the man with the ingrowing toenail calling in sick,' I said.

'Shirker,' she announced with a laugh.

'No, really,' I said. 'I won't be in the office this morning. Please tell Mr Patrick that something has come up and that I'll see him later today,' I said.

'Right, I will,' she said. 'It's a good job you're not here now anyway. Mr Gregory is angry fit to bust. Claims you've brought the whole firm into disrepute. He wants your head on a stick.'

'But why?' I asked, rather worried. 'What have I done?'

'Read the front page of the *Racing Post*.'

I went along the hall to check on Sherri Kovak. She was sound asleep. Best thing for her, I thought. I slipped out of the front door and walked towards Hendon Central in search of a newsagent. Even before I picked up the paper I could see the bold headline:

FOXY FOXTON AND BILLY SEARLE IN £100,000 GAMBLE?

I bought the paper and read it in the shop. There were photographs of Billy and me. The article was as damning as the headline:

Leading National Hunt jockey Billy Searle was in a heated argument at Cheltenham races yesterday with former jockey Nick (Foxy) Foxton. The topic of their exchange? Money.

The amount was £100,000, with Searle demanding instant payment of this amount, which he claimed he was owed by Foxton.

Searle was heard to ask why he, Foxton, wanted to murder Searle.
Trainer Martin Gifford stated that Herbert Kovak, the man
murdered last Saturday at the Grand National, was Foxton's best
friend and a fellow stock market speculator who had also worked for
Lyall & Black.

The article didn't actually accuse Billy Searle or me of any wrongdoing, but implied there was a criminal conspiracy between us, which had something to do with the death of Herb Kovak.

No wonder Gregory Black was steaming round the office. Bugger, I thought. What should I do now?

I called Patrick on his mobile.

'Hello, Nicholas,' said Patrick. 'I told you to be discreet. Gregory's after your blood. I'd keep your head down if I were you.'

'I will,' I said. 'But it's all a pack of lies.'

'I told Gregory not to believe what he reads but he says you shouldn't have been having a public argument with a client in the first place.'

'It wasn't an argument,' I claimed in my defence. 'Billy Searle just started shouting and swearing at me for no reason.'

'Don't worry,' Patrick said. 'It'll blow over in a couple of days.'

I wish he'd been right.

I WALKED BACK to Herb's flat. What a bloody mess. I could imagine that Billy Searle wasn't too happy about it either. I thought the last thing he'd want would be the racing authorities asking him questions about why he needed £100,000 so urgently.

I let myself in through Herb's front door and went to check on Sherri. She was still sound asleep. I went back to the living room where I sat at Herb's desk wishing I'd brought my laptop computer with me. It was lying on the kitchen table in Finchley and I was tempted to go home to fetch it. Instead I called Claudia.

'Hi, it's me,' I said when she answered. 'Could you bring my computer over to Herb's flat? His sister has turned up and she didn't know he was dead. I don't feel I can leave her. I'll stay and work here, but I do need my laptop.' I didn't mention the unwelcome coverage in the *Racing Post*.

'OK,' Claudia said in a slightly irritated tone.

'It's not very far,' I said encouragingly. 'Use the car. You won't need to park or anything, just drop it off.'

'OK,' she said again, lacking enthusiasm. 'But I was just going out.'

Bloody hell, it wasn't much to ask. 'Where are you going?'

'Oh, nowhere,' she said. 'Just to have coffee with a friend.'

'Please, Claudia,' I said. 'I need it so I can do my job.'

'OK,' she said once more, resigned. 'Where is the flat?'

I gave her the address and she promised she would bring the computer right over. While I waited I went through the papers on Herb's desk. There was the usual clutter of utility bills and debit-card receipts, financial services magazines and insurance documents. Nothing gave a clue as to who would want Herb dead, or how he came to gamble away nearly a hundred thousand pounds a month on the Internet.

Invoices from a travel agent showed that Herb had bought two first-class round-trip tickets across the Atlantic at £8,000 each, for a planned, but not yet taken, trip in May. There was no way he could have financed those out of his income from Lyall & Black, even without the online gambling debts he had run up. I wondered if he had inherited a large sum from his parents. I thought it unlikely as he had always claimed that his father had gambled away most of his family's money.

I looked at my watch. I had called Claudia nearly half an hour ago and the journey should have taken her only ten minutes. I went to the door to see if she was outside but there was no sign of her.

I waited in the doorway with slightly increasing irritation. Once, I would have been so excited by the prospect of seeing her, I wouldn't have minded if she had been half a day late arriving. Now, and not for the first time, I wondered if our relationship had run its course.

She finally arrived some thirty-five minutes after I had called. She stopped in the middle of the road and put down the passenger window. I leaned through it and picked up my computer from the seat.

'Thanks,' I said. 'See you later.'

'OK,' she said, and drove off quickly.

I stood in the road waving but she didn't wave back. I sighed. Claudia still excited me, and the sex was good, albeit rarer than it once had been. In fact, sex had been non-existent over the last couple of weeks with Claudia always making some excuse. What had gone wrong? Why was she not so loving towards me? I wondered if she was seeing someone else.

Miserably, I went back into Herb's flat and sat down again at his desk but I couldn't concentrate.

Instead, I logged on to the Internet and checked my office emails, many of which were junk from various finance firms offering rates of return that were well above the norm for the market. Nestled among the junk were two work emails, one from Diana confirming the sales of all Billy Searle's assets, and the other from Jessica Winter advising me to wear a bulletproof vest if I was planning on coming into the office. I thought it a particularly insensitive comment considering what had happened to Herb only five days previously.

I looked again at all the junk mail. If a promised return appeared to be too good to be true, then it probably was just that, too good to be true. I thought back to my conversation with Jolyon Roberts at Cheltenham. Had the promised return on the Bulgarian project been too good to be true? Not as far as I could remember. The main concerns had been the distance away and the potential difficulty in acquiring accurate information on the progress of the project. In fact, just the problem that Mr Roberts believed to be the issue.

I started to type 'Roberts' into the company client index but thought better of it. The office software system kept a visible record of all files accessed, so any of us could see who had been looking at each file. Whenever any of us opened a file it clearly showed, in the top right-hand corner of the computer screen, a list of the five people in the firm who had accessed the file most recently, together with the date and time of their access.

As one of the IFAs, I had authority to look at any of the company files, but I might have had difficulty explaining to Gregory why I had accessed those of one of his clients without his knowledge, especially now.

I told myself that I should go straight to Gregory and Patrick, and probably to Jessica Winter as well, and tell them about my conversation with Jolyon Roberts. But did I want to go and effectively accuse Gregory of misleading a client, and today of all days?

Then I really would need that bulletproof vest.

But was I following regulations not to immediately mention to my superiors, and to the compliance officer, that a client of the firm was questioning the judgment of one of the senior partners? Probably not.

And I would mention it to them, I thought, just as soon as Gregory had calmed down a bit. In the meantime, I would do a bit of discreet investigating just as Jolyon Roberts had asked.

I decided that I'd try to have a look through the paper records at the office. Transactions happened electronically but the deals were still backed up with physical paperwork. The office was stacked with boxes of transaction reports, and somewhere among them would be the Roberts Family Trust paperwork for their investment in the Lord Balscott Lighting Factory.

I sat back in the chair and thought about Claudia. I wished I had told her about the article in the *Racing Post* when she had brought over my computer. I tried her mobile but it went straight to voicemail without ringing. I left a message. 'Darling,' I said. 'Could you please give me a call? Love you.' I hung up. I wondered what Claudia could be doing, and with whom, which required her to have her phone switched off. Perhaps I didn't want to know.

As Herb's executor, I emailed his bank informing them that Mr Kovak was deceased, and asking if they could please send me details of his accounts. Somewhat surprisingly I received a reply almost immediately thanking me for the sad news and advising me that they would need various pieces of documentation before they could release the information, including the death certificate, a copy of the will and an order for probate.

How long would it take to get that lot? I wondered.

I heard Sherri go along the corridor to the bathroom.

I took the front cover sheet off the *Racing Post* and folded it up, as if not being able to see the damning words would in some way limit their damage to my career. I put the offending piece in my pocket and went to throw the rest of it into the waste bin under Herb's desk. The bin had some things in it already and, I thought, as I've looked everywhere else, why not there?

I poured the contents of the bin out onto the desk.

Among the opened envelopes, the empty Starbucks coffee cups and the screwed-up tissues were lots of little pieces of paper about an inch square. I put the envelopes, cups and tissues back in the bin, leaving a pile of the paper squares on the desk. It was fairly obvious that they were the torn-up remains of a larger piece so I set about trying to put them back together. It was a bit like doing a jigsaw puzzle.

I fairly quickly established that the pieces had not been from one larger piece but three. I slowly built up the originals in front of me. They were each about six inches by four, printed forms with words written on them in pen. I stuck the bits together with sticky tape.

'What are you doing?' Sherri asked from the doorway.

She made me jump. 'Nothing much,' I said, swivelling the desk chair round to face her. 'How are you feeling?'

'Dreadful,' she said, coming into the room and flopping down into the deep armchair. 'I can't believe it.'

'I'll get you some more tea,' I said, standing up.

'Lovely,' she said with a forced smile. 'Thank you.'

I went through to the kitchen and boiled the kettle. I made myself a cup as well and took them back to the living room.

Sherri was sitting at the desk looking at the pieces of paper. I gave her one of the cups and sat down on the arm of the big armchair. 'Do you know what they are?' I asked.

'Of course,' she said. 'They're MoneyHome payment slips.' She sipped her tea. 'One for eight thousand, and two for five.'

'Pounds?' I asked.

She looked at them. 'Dollars. Converted into pounds.'

'How do you know?' I asked.

She looked at me. 'I use MoneyHome all the time. It's a bit like Western Union only cheaper. They have agents all over the world. Herb sent me the money for my air fare via MoneyHome.'

'Are any of these slips from that?'

'No,' she said with certainty, 'these are the slips you get when you collect money, not when you send it.'

'So Herb collected eighteen thousand dollars' worth of pounds from MoneyHome?'

'Yes,' she said.

'When?' I asked.

She looked at the reconstructed slips. 'Last week. Eight thousand on Monday, and five each on Tuesday and Friday. They don't say who sent the money. What's all this about anyway?'

'I don't know,' I said. 'I just found those torn-up sheets in the waste bin.'

She sat drinking her tea, looking at me over the rim of the cup.

'Why are you here?' she asked.

'I was a friend of Herb's, and a work colleague,' I said, giving her one of the business cards from my wallet. 'He made me the executor of his will.' I decided again not to mention that he had also made me the sole beneficiary.

'I didn't know he even had a will,' Sherri said.

'He made it five years ago when he arrived at Lyall and Black,' I said. 'Everyone in the firm has to have a will. The senior partners are always saying that we can hardly advise our clients to plan ahead if we aren't prepared to do the same. But I have no idea why Herb chose to put me in his. He'd only just landed in the country and perhaps he didn't know anyone else. But he should still have named you as his executor, even if you were in the United States.'

'Herb and I weren't exactly talking to each other five years ago.' She sighed. 'We had a flaming row over our parents.'

'What about them?' I asked.

She looked at me as if deciding whether to tell me.

'Our mom and dad were, shall we say, an unusual couple. Dad had made a living, if you can call it that, as a bookie around Churchill Downs. He was supposed to be a groom but he didn't do much looking after the horses. He spent his time taking bets from the other grooms, and some of the trainers and owners, too. Sometimes he won, but mostly he lost. Mom, meanwhile, had worked as a cocktail waitress in one of the swanky tourist hotels in downtown Louisville. At least that's what she told people.'

She paused, and I waited in silence. She'd say if she wanted to.

'She'd been a prostitute.' Sherri was crying again.

'You don't have to tell me,' I said.

She looked at me with tear-filled eyes. 'I've got to tell someone,' she gulped. 'I've bottled it all up for far too long.'

Between bouts of tears she told me the sorry saga of her and Herb's upbringing. It amazed me that I had sat next to Herb for all those years without realising the hurdles he'd had to overcome to be a financial adviser.

Herb and Sherri's father had been an abusive drinker who treated his children as unpaid slave labour. Both of them had excelled at school but he insisted that they drop out aged sixteen to work, Herb as a groom in the Churchill Downs stables, and Sherri as a chambermaid in one of the hotels where her mother had plied her trade.

Herb had rebelled and run away to Lexington where he had secretly applied for, and won, a scholarship to a private high school. But he'd had no accommodation, so he'd slept on the streets. One of the trustees of the school had found him there and offered him a bed. The trustee had been in financial services and hence Herb's career had been decided.

He'd stayed in Lexington after high school to attend the University of Kentucky, before landing the top graduate job at J. P. Morgan in New York. He later moved to London and Lyall & Black.

Sherri, meanwhile, had been good at her job, and bright with it, and she had been spotted by the management of the hotel for further training. That was ultimately how she came to be in Chicago, where she was currently assistant housekeeper in a big hotel of the same chain.

I didn't see how all this information was going to be of any use to me, but I sat quietly and listened as she unburdened her emotions.

'How come you and Herb fell out?' I asked finally.

'He refused to come home from New York for the funeral when Dad died. I said he should be there to support Mom, but he refused and he said he wouldn't come to her funeral either if she dropped down dead tomorrow. Those were his exact words. And Mom heard him say them because she and I were in my car and the call was on speakerphone.' She paused and more tears ran down her cheeks. 'I still think it's the reason why she did it.'

'Did what?' I asked.

'Swallowed a whole tub of Tylenol Extra. A hundred tablets.'

'Dead?' I asked.

She nodded. 'That night.' She sat up straight and breathed in deeply through her nose. 'I accused Herb of killing her, and that's when I told him I never wanted to see or hear from him again.'

'How long has it been since your parents died?'

She thought for a moment. 'It'll be seven years in June.'

'When did you change your mind?'

'I didn't. It was he who contacted me, about two years ago.' She sighed again. 'He wrote to me and we arranged to meet in New York. Then last summer, he invited me here to stay with him for a holiday. It was great.' She smiled. 'Just like old times.'

The smile faded and the tears began again. 'I just can't believe he's dead.'

Neither could I.

I ARRIVED at the office at twenty past one, when Gregory should be just sitting down to his substantial lunch at the far end of Lombard Street. I put my head through the glass entrance doors. 'Has Mr Gregory gone to lunch?' I whispered to Mrs McDowd who was sitting at the reception desk.

'Ten minutes ago,' she whispered back.

'And Mr Patrick?' I asked.

'Went with him,' she replied. 'Both gone for an hour at least.'

I relaxed and smiled at her. 'Maybe I'll just stay for an hour.'

'Very wise,' she said with a grin from ear to ear.

I walked past the reception desk and down the corridor. As I passed by, I glanced through the open door of the compliance office, but Jessica Winter was not at her desk.

I went on and into my office, not that I had it to myself. There were four cubicles crammed into the small room, one of which was mine. Herb had been next to me, both of us close to the window, while Diana and Rory, Patrick's other assistants, occupied the two cubicles nearer the door.

Diana was out to lunch, while Rory was sitting at his desk. 'The invisible man returns,' said Rory. 'Gregory's been looking for you. You're in trouble.' He sounded as if he was rather pleased about it.

'You haven't seen me, all right!' I said.

'Don't involve me in your sordid little affairs,' he said rather haughtily. 'I'm not putting my career at risk for you.'

Rory could be a real pain sometimes.

'Rory,' I said. 'When, and if, you ever qualify to be an IFA, you can then start talking about your career. Until then, shut up!'

Rory had failed his exams twice. He sensibly kept quiet.

I took off my suit jacket and hung it on the back of my chair. Then I sat down at Herb's desk and pulled open the top drawer.

There were two more MoneyHome payment slips lurking in the drawer and, this time, not torn up into squares. There was also another sheet with handwritten lists on both sides, like the one DCI Tomlinson had shown me in Herb's flat. I folded them and put them in my pocket.

Apart from that, the desk was almost too clean. Some of the staff personalised their notice boards with family pictures, but there were no items pinned to Herb's, not even a picture of Sherri. There was only the mandatory company telephone directory and a small key, pinned to the board with a drawing pin. I looked at it closely but left it where it was. A key without a lock wasn't much use.

I walked along the corridor and put my head right into the lion's den. Gregory, as a senior partner, did qualify for an office of his own. I sat down in his chair and looked at his computer screen. As I had hoped, he hadn't bothered to log out from his session when he went to lunch. Most of us didn't.

I typed 'Roberts Family Trust' into Gregory's computer and it instantly produced the details of the file on his screen with the date of the original investment prominently displayed at the top. The access list in the top right-hand corner showed me that Gregory himself had looked at the file only that morning, at 10.22. I hoped he wouldn't notice that his computer had accessed it again at 1.46 p.m.

However, it was one of the other names on the recent-enquiry list I found most interesting. The list showed that Herb Kovak had accessed the file just ten days previously. Now why had Herb looked at one of Gregory's client files? It would have been most improper, just as it was for me to be looking at it now. Perhaps Herb had also had suspicions about the Bulgarian investment.

I would have loved to print out the whole file but, unfortunately, the office server used a central printing system and it recorded who had asked for what to be printed. How could I explain away an apparent request from Gregory when he was out to lunch?

I looked at my watch. It was ten to two. I should be safe for another twenty minutes.

I flipped through the pages of the file trying to find the names of the Bulgarian agents involved in the project, but the relevant documents were all in Cyrillic script. I copied a telephone number onto the back of one of Herb's MoneyHome payment slips. It began +359, which was the international code for Bulgaria.

I opened Gregory's email in-box and did a search for 'Bulgarian'. There were six emails, all from September two years ago, all from the same source. I copied down the email address of the sender, uri_joram@ec.europa.eu, and also that of the recipient, dimitar.petrov@bsnet.co.bg. Gregory had been copied into the correspondence but there was no sign of any replies. I took a chance and forwarded the emails to my private email address, then I deleted the forwarded record from Gregory's 'sent' folder.

I closed Gregory's in-box and the Roberts Family Trust file. I slipped out into the corridor and no one shouted a challenge or questioned what I had been doing in Gregory's office.

The corridor outside was lined with cardboard document boxes holding the paper transaction reports. I searched for the box containing those for the date at the top of the computer file.

Mrs McDowd was very methodical in her filing. All the boxes were clearly in chronological order. I lifted the box for the correct date and dug through the papers until I found the correct transaction report and associated paperwork. I pulled them out, folded them, and stuffed them in my trouser pocket, before putting the box carefully back in the same place I'd found it.

I glanced at my watch once more, twenty past two. I went back into my office to collect my jacket.

'Leaving already?' said Rory. 'What shall I tell Gregory?'

I ignored him. As I walked down the corridor towards the reception area

I realised that I'd left it too late. I could hear Gregory and Patrick talking. I would just have to face the music.

'There you are, Foxton,' Gregory announced at high volume.

I was so mesmerised by Gregory that I hardly took any notice of a man standing next to Patrick. The man suddenly stepped right in front of me.

'Nicholas Foxton,' the man said. 'I arrest you on suspicion of the attempted murder of William Peter Searle.'

4

I spent the afternoon waiting in an eight-by-six-feet holding cell at Paddington Green police station not quite knowing what to think.

The man in the office had identified himself as a detective chief inspector from the Metropolitan Police. I'd missed his name. I hadn't been listening. I'd just stood there with my mouth open in surprise as a uniformed policeman had applied handcuffs to my wrists and then led me down in the lift to a police car.

William Peter Searle, the chief inspector had said when I was arrested. That had to be Billy Searle.

So, Billy had been right about one thing. Thursday had been too late.

I suppose I couldn't really blame the police for arresting me. Hundreds of witnesses had heard Billy shouting the previous afternoon at Cheltenham: 'Why are you trying to murder me?'

I hadn't been trying to murder him, but I hadn't taken him seriously either. But to whom could Billy have owed so much money? Clearly, someone who was prepared to try to kill him for non-payment by the Wednesday-night deadline.

First Herb Kovak, now Billy Searle. Could the two be connected?

Thursday afternoon dragged on into evening. For the umpteenth time I looked at my wrist to check the time and, for the umpteenth time, saw no watch. It had been removed when I was 'checked in' by the custody sergeant, along with my tie, belt, shoelaces and the contents of my pockets, including Herb's MoneyHome payment slips and the transaction report from the box outside Gregory's office.

The detective chief inspector finally opened the cell door long after the barred window had turned from daylight to night-black.

'Mr Foxton,' he said. 'You are free to go. We will not be charging you.' He paused. 'And I'm sorry for any inconvenience.'

'Sorry!' I said. 'Sorry! I should bloody well think you're sorry.'

'Mr Foxton,' the chief inspector replied, somewhat affronted. 'You have been treated exactly in accordance with regulations.'

'So why was I arrested?' I demanded.

'We had reason to believe you were responsible for the attempted murder of the jockey, William Searle.'

'So what's happened that now makes you so sure I'm not responsible?'

'You have an alibi.'

'Where was this attack?' I asked. 'And when?'

The chief inspector looked uncomfortable, as if he didn't like answering questions. 'Mr Searle was deliberately knocked off his bicycle on the road outside his home in the village of Baydon in Wiltshire at exactly five minutes past seven this morning. He is in a critical condition at the Great Western Hospital in Swindon.'

'And how are you so sure I was somewhere else at exactly five minutes past seven this morning?' I asked.

'Because you were at 45 Seymour Way in Hendon fifty-five minutes later,' he said. 'You were interviewed at that address by Detective Chief Inspector Tomlinson of Merseyside police. There is no way you could have travelled the seventy-two miles from Baydon to Hendon in fifty-five minutes, especially during rush hour.'

'So I am now free to go?' I said.

'Yes,' he said. He waved a hand towards the doorway.

The custody sergeant sneered at me as he returned my watch and mobile phone, my tie, belt and shoelaces, and the contents of my pockets. He pointed at one of the doors, pushed a button on his desk, and the lock on the heavy steel door buzzed. I pulled it open and walked out to the reception area.

Claudia was waiting, sitting on an upright chair. She jumped up, rushed over, and hugged me tight. 'Oh, Nick,' she sobbed, 'I've been so frightened.'

'Come on,' I said, hugging her back. 'Let's go home.'

We walked out into the night, hand in hand, and hailed a passing black cab. 'I didn't think you'd be here,' I said to Claudia.

'Why ever not? I've been here ever since Rosemary called.'

'Rosemary?' I asked.

'You know,' she said. 'Rosemary McDowd. She's a dear.'

I had worked at Lyall & Black for five years and, for all that time, I'd had no idea that Mrs McDowd's name was Rosemary.

'She called me on my mobile.'

'And how did she have that number?'

'Oh, we speak quite often.'

'What about?' I asked.

'Oh, nothing,' she said evasively.

'No. Come on,' I said. 'Tell me.'

Claudia sighed. 'I sometimes call her to find out what sort of mood you're in when you leave the office.'

More likely, I thought suspiciously, to check that I was actually in the office, or to know when I'd left it.

'So what did Mrs McDowd tell you today?' I asked.

'She told me you'd been arrested for attempted murder.'

I nodded. 'Billy Searle was attacked this morning. He was a top jump jockey, and also a client of mine.'

'What the hell's going on?' Claudia said.

That's what I wanted to know.

IT WAS ELEVEN O'CLOCK by the time I'd been released, and I asked the taxi driver to go to the kiosk on the Edgware Road where they received early editions of the daily newspapers. Claudia stayed in the cab as I went and bought a copy of the *Racing Post*. If its previous day's front-page headline had been vague, this one pulled no punches:

BILLY SEARLE ATTACKED. FOXTON ARRESTED FOR ATTEMPTED MURDER

Gregory was going to have a field-day in the morning. Who would trust a financial adviser who was on the front page of a national newspaper, having been arrested for attempted murder?

I climbed back into the cab with the paper.

'It's so unfair,' Claudia said, reading the headline. 'How can the police give out your name when you haven't even been charged?'

I suspected that the information had not come from the police. My money would be on Rory to be the office mole, although what he hoped to gain by it was anyone's idea.

I switched on the television before I went to bed and watched the news on one of the twenty-four-hour channels. They had a report live from Baydon.

'Jockey Billy Searle was leaving his home to ride his bicycle to Lambourn when a car accelerated into the bicycle, knocking Searle to the ground, before being driven away at speed,' said the reporter. 'Searle was taken to hospital in Swindon where he is in a critical condition with head and leg injuries. Ex-jockey Nicholas Foxton was arrested in connection with the attack but he has since been released without charge.'

'Well at least they said you'd been released,' said Claudia.

'I'd rather they hadn't mentioned my name at all,' I said. 'You watch. Most people will already have me tried and convicted in their minds. Being released will make no difference.'

Claudia and I went upstairs to bed but I couldn't sleep. I lay awake in the darkness going over and over everything in my head.

Last Saturday morning my life had been settled and predictable, even if it was a little boring. But in the last six days I had witnessed one murder and been arrested for attempting another; I'd begun to doubt my relationship with Claudia, even suspecting that she might be having an affair; and I'd gone behind the back of my superior at work to try to determine if he was complicit in a multi-million-pound fraud. Not to mention becoming the executor and beneficiary of someone that I hardly knew.

I lay awake in the dark wondering what I should do next, and also if I would still have a job to go to in the morning.

I WOKE AFTER a restless night, the space in the bed next to me already empty and cold. I rolled over and looked at the bedside clock. It was gone eight o'clock. I was usually on the tube by now.

The phone rang. Claudia answered it downstairs, then came into the room. 'It's your mother,' she said.

I picked up the phone. 'Hello, Mum,' I said.

'Darling,' she said. 'What's going on? You're in all the papers and on the TV.' She sounded very upset, as if she was in tears.

'It's all right, Mum,' I said. 'I didn't do anything and the police know it. I promise you, all is fine.'

It took me five minutes to calm my mother down. I knew when I'd managed it because she told me to have a good breakfast. Eventually I put the phone down and laid my head back on the pillow.

'Aren't you going to the office today?' Claudia asked, coming back into the bedroom carrying two cups of steaming coffee.

It was an innocent enough question, so why did I wonder if she was checking on my movements in order to plan her own?

'I don't know,' I said, taking one of the cups. 'What plans do you have?'

'Nothing much,' she said. 'I might go shopping later. I need a new dress for the show next week.'

'Oh,' I said. 'I'd forgotten about that.'

Claudia and I had accepted an invitation from Jan Setter to join her at the opening night of a West End musical. Now the thought of attending the star-studded event with all the associated press coverage did not fill me with joy.

'Right,' I said with determination. 'It's time to show a defiant face to the world. I'm going to get up and go in to work and bugger what anyone thinks. I'm innocent and I'm going to act like it.'

'That's my boy,' said Claudia. 'Bugger the lot of them.'

She lay down on the bed and snuggled up to me, slipping her hand down under the sheets. 'But do you have to go immediately?'

Now I was really confused. 'Hmm, let me think,' I said, laughing. 'Work or sex? Sex or work? Such difficult decisions.'

I DIDN'T GO to the office until after lunch. I went to Hendon on the way, to check on Sherri, and to collect my laptop that I'd left on Herb's desk. 'What have you been up to?' I asked her.

'I've started going through Herb's things in his bedroom.'

'Did you find anything of interest?' I asked as I followed her down the corridor to the bedroom.

'Only this,' she replied, picking up something from the bed. 'It was at the back of his wardrobe, hanging on a hook behind his coats.'

She handed me a small blue plastic box with a clip-on lid. Inside, neatly held together by a rubber band, were twenty-two credit cards. I rolled off the band and shuffled through them. They matched the statements, right down to the variations in Herb's name.

'Why would anyone have so many credit cards?' Sherri asked. 'And why would they be hidden in his wardrobe? They all look brand new to me.'

And to me. Herb hadn't even bothered signing them on the back. These cards had been obtained solely for use on the Internet.

Underneath the cards were four pieces of folded-up paper similar to the ones that Chief Inspector Tomlinson had shown me the previous morning. I looked at the lists of numbers and letters. The first columns on each side were definitely dates.

Sherri was sitting on the floor busily looking through a chest of drawers. I went out of the bedroom, along the corridor and into the living room. The handwritten lists I had photocopied yesterday were still on the desk next to my computer along with the photocopied bank and credit-card statements.

I took them back to the bedroom.

On the lists, the second and third columns looked like amounts of money. The fourth column was a list of capital letters, possibly initials. I counted them. There were ninety-seven sets of letters.

'What are you looking at?' Sherri said.

'I don't know,' I replied. 'Lists of numbers and letters. Have a look.' I handed her the sheets. 'Do you recognise any of the initials?'

She shook her head.

'Did you know that Herb liked to gamble?' I asked.

She looked at me. 'Of course,' she said. 'Herb had always been one for an occasional flutter on the horses. Just like his father.'

'Did you know how much he gambled?' I asked.

'Never very much,' she said. 'He would never have staked more than he could afford to lose. What are you getting at?'

'Herb gambled on the Internet,' I said. 'And he lost. He lost big time.'

'I don't believe it,' Sherri said. 'How do you know?'

I held out photocopies of the credit-card statements to her. 'Herb lost more than ninety thousand pounds last month. The same the month before.'

'He can't have,' she said. 'Herb didn't have that sort of money.'

'Look for yourself,' I said, handing her the statements.

She looked at them. 'That's why he was killed?' she asked.

'I don't know,' I said. But I thought it quite likely.

'I wish he'd never come to England,' Sherri said sadly. 'Herb wouldn't have been able to gamble like that at home. Internet gambling is illegal in most of the United States.'

So it was. I remembered reading about the head of an Internet gambling website who'd been arrested when he'd arrived at a US airport and charged with racketeering, for allowing Americans to gamble on his website, even though it was based in England. It had been about accepting credit-card accounts with US addresses.

I looked again at the lists of dates, amounts of money and initials. Only last week, according to the payment slips I'd found in his waste bin, Herb had received three large amounts of cash, two equivalent to $5,000 and one to $8,000.

Suddenly all of it made complete sense to me.

It hadn't been Herb who had lost over ninety thousand pounds last month, it had been the people whose initials were on Herb's lists, the ninety-seven people responsible for the 512 entries on the credit-card statements. And I'd like to bet they were all Americans. If I was right, Herb had been running a system to provide Americans with UK accounts in order for them to play on Internet betting sites.

But why would that have got him murdered?

To say my arrival at the offices of Lyall & Black about an hour after lunch caused a bit of a stir would be an understatement.

'Get out of these offices,' Gregory shouted at me almost as soon as I walked through the door. 'You are a disgrace to this firm.'

I had made the mistake of not sneaking in while he was at lunch.

Mrs McDowd looked frightened. I probably did as well.

'Gregory,' I tried to say, but he advanced towards me. He grabbed me by the sleeve and dragged me towards the door.

He was surprisingly strong and fit for someone whose only workout was the walk to and from the restaurant on the corner.

'Leave me alone,' I shouted at him. But he took no notice.

'Gregory. Stop it!' Patrick's deep voice reverberated round the reception area. Gregory stopped pulling and let go of my sleeve.

'I will not have this man in these offices,' Gregory said. 'He has brought the firm of Lyall and Black into disrepute.'

'Let us discuss this in your office,' Patrick said calmly. 'Nicholas, best to go home. I'll call you later.'

I waited while Gregory moved off down the corridor.

'You had better go,' said Mrs McDowd firmly. 'I don't want you upsetting Mr Gregory any more. His heart can't take it.'

I looked at her. Mrs McDowd, who knew everything about everyone in the firm. She probably knew Gregory's blood pressure.

'Tell me, Mrs McDowd, do you think Herb gambled much?'

'You mean on the stock market?' she asked.

'On the horses.'

'Oh, no,' she said. 'Mr Herb didn't bet on the horses. Too risky, he said. Better to bet on a certainty, that's what he always told me.'

Death was a certainty.

I DID GO HOME but not immediately. Before I left Hendon I had looked up the locations of MoneyHome agents near to Lombard Street. The nearest one was just round the corner.

I had expected the agency to be like a bank or a money exchange but this one was right at the back of a convenience store.

'This didn't come from here,' said the lady sitting behind a glass screen. 'It hasn't got our stamp on it.'

'Can you tell me where it did come from?' I asked.

'Sorry. I don't recognise the stamp. But I know it's not ours.'

'Can you tell who sent the money?' I asked.

'No,' she said.

'What do you need to produce in the way of identification to collect money from a MoneyHome transfer?'

'The recipient's name and the MTCN.' She pointed at the payment slip. 'The Money Transfer Control Number.'

'That's all you need?' I said. 'No passport or driving licence?'

'Not unless it's been specially requested by the sender,' she said.

'So, in fact,' I said, 'you have no way of knowing who has sent the money, or who has collected it?'

'The recipient's name is on the slip.'

The recipient's name on the slip I had shown her was Butch Cassidy. The names on the others were Billy Kid, Wyatt Earp, Jessie James and Bill Cody.

'That isn't his real name,' I said.

'No,' she said. 'But it's not our business who they really are.'

'Are your transfers always in cash?' I asked.

'Yeah, of course,' she said. 'That's what we do. Cash transfers. Lots of the immigrant workers round here send cash home.'

Herb had set up a system that would be impossible to unravel. It was clear that he'd received cash from multiple sources, money he must have then used to pay the balances on the twenty-two credit cards. Herb had collected $18,000 only the previous week, $5,000 of it just the day before his death. Some of that cash must still be hidden somewhere.

My problem was that while I had the statements showing the £94,000 outstanding, and as his executor and beneficiary I was liable for the debt, I hadn't yet found the stash of cash to pay it.

CLAUDIA WASN'T AT HOME when I arrived back at three thirty. I tried her mobile but it went straight to voicemail.

I went up to her studio wondering what had gone wrong with our relationship. I didn't understand it. The sex that morning had been as good as ever but Claudia had been uncharacteristically quiet, as if her mind had been elsewhere.

Claudia and I had been together for six years. I was twenty-nine, she was three years my junior. Apart from my concern about her weird paintings, I found the set-up comfortable and fulfilling. I was happy as things were. Did Claudia want something more? Had she tired of me? Perhaps there was someone else lined up to take my place.

The house phone rang and I went in to our bedroom to answer it, hoping it would be Claudia. It was Patrick.

'I'm sorry for Gregory's outburst,' he said. 'He's calmed down. He was just upset by what had been written in the papers.'

Not as upset as me, I thought.

'So can I come back into the office?' I asked.

'Not today,' he said rather too quickly. 'Maybe on Monday, or later next week. Let the dust settle for a few days.'

'I'll work from home then,' I said, 'using the remote access facility.'

'Right,' Patrick said slowly. 'But I agreed with Gregory that you would not be representing the firm for the immediate future.'

'Are you telling me I'm fired?'

'No, of course not,' he said. 'Just that it might be better for you to take some paid holiday until the police sort out who really did try to murder Billy Searle. I'll call you next week. In the meantime I must ask you not to use the remote access facility, and not to contact anyone at the firm.' He disconnected without saying goodbye.

I sat on the bed feeling more miserable than I had since the day I had been told I couldn't ride again. But I decided that feeling sorry for myself wasn't going to achieve anything, so I went downstairs and sat at the kitchen table with my laptop.

I looked at the six emails I had forwarded to my in-box from Gregory's, concerning the Bulgarian property development. They were all from the same man, Uri Joram, and the first two were about grants available to disadvantaged parts of the European Union for industrial development. EU money would only be forthcoming if there was private investment in the project on the basis that two euros would be granted for each euro invested privately. Jolyon Roberts had told me that his family trust had invested £5 million, so that could have attracted a further ten million from the EU. But that was not all, not by a long way.

The remaining emails were about funding for the homes to be constructed close to the factory to house the workers. This was to come from the EU Social Housing Fund, and required no similar two-for-one arrangement. It appeared that the new factory alone was sufficient to trigger the 100 per cent grant for housing, which was in the region of eighty million euros.

If, as Jolyon Roberts's nephew had implied, no houses and no factory had been built in Bulgaria, then someone had very likely pocketed nearly a hundred million euros, most of it public money.

I looked at the email addresses. The emails had been sent by uri_joram@ec.europa.eu to dimitar.petrov@bsnet.co.bg, with Gregory Black being copied in. The ec.europa.eu domain indicated that Uri Joram worked in the European Commission, probably in Brussels, and I could deduce that Mr Petrov must be in Bulgaria from the extension .bg.

It wasn't a huge help.

It may very well have been a simple mistake made by Mr Roberts's nephew. He might have gone to the wrong place in Bulgaria. Surely there would have been checks made by European Union officials running the EU Social Housing Fund to confirm that their eighty million euros had been spent properly on bricks and mortar.

I decided that, having been asked by Jolyon Roberts to look into it, I couldn't just do nothing. So I sent a short email to Dimitar Petrov asking him to send me the names and addresses of the directors of the Lord Balscott Lighting Factory, if he had them.

By the time I realised that sending the email was possibly not such a good idea if Mr Petrov was one of those involved in the potential hundred-million-euro fraud, it was well on its way.

I closed my computer and made myself a cup of tea.

I noticed that Claudia had left her latest mobile phone bill lying on the worktop next to the kettle. I couldn't resist the temptation to look at it. I looked for numbers I didn't recognise. There was one, with calls almost every day for the past two weeks.

Claudia arrived home at five thirty and I resisted the temptation to ask her where she had been.

'Why aren't you at the office?' she asked.

'Patrick sent me home,' I said. 'Gregory says I've brought the company into disrepute. Patrick thinks it would be best for me to have some time off.'

'But that's ridiculous,' she said. 'The police let you go. You have a cast-iron alibi.'

'I know that, and you know that,' I replied crossly. 'But you know what most people are like, they believe what they read.'

'Those bloody newspapers,' she said.

'Patrick says it will all blow over in a few days,' I said. 'So did you get your dress?'

'What dress?' she said.

'Come on, darling,' I said, slightly irritated. 'You know. The one you were going to buy for the opening night on Wednesday.'

'Oh, that,' she said, clearly distracted. 'Perhaps I'll go tomorrow. Something came up this afternoon.'

I didn't like to think what, so I didn't ask.

'How long did Patrick say you had to stay away from the office?' Claudia asked into the silence.

'Maybe a week,' I said, wondering if she was asking for reasons other than worries over my reputation and career. 'Perhaps I'll go to the races.'

'Great idea. Give your mind a rest from all those figures.'

Perhaps it was time to start looking at figures of a different kind.

5

On Saturday afternoon I put on my thick skin and went to Sandown Park races on the train from Waterloo.

'Bloody hell,' said Jan Setter. 'I didn't expect to see you here. I thought you'd been sent to the Tower.'

'Not quite,' I said. I was standing on the grass close to the parade ring.

'Did you do it?' Jan asked in all seriousness.

'No, of course I didn't,' I said. 'The police wouldn't have let me go if they still thought I'd tried to kill Billy. I have an alibi.'

'Then why were you arrested?'

I sighed. People, even good friends, really did believe what they read in the papers. 'Someone told the police that Billy had shouted at me at Cheltenham demanding to know why I was going to murder him. They put two and two together and made five. That's all. They got it wrong.'

'So why did Billy shout at you?'

'It was to do with his investments,' I said. 'It's confidential. You wouldn't want me telling everyone about your investments, would you?'

'No,' she agreed.

Mind you, I thought, there was a limit to confidentiality.

I had spent time with the Wiltshire police earlier, going over all the events of Tuesday and Wednesday at Cheltenham races with particular reference to Billy Searle's investments. I'd told them that Billy had about a hundred and fifty thousand invested through me and he told me on Tuesday that he urgently wanted all his money out in cash.

'Why do you think Mr Searle needed such a large sum so quickly?' one of the policemen had asked.

'He told me he owed some guy a hundred thousand and he needed to pay it back by Wednesday night, or else.'

'Did he give you any indication who this guy was?'

'None, but he was clearly terrified. Why don't you ask Billy?'

'Mr Searle is still in a critical condition,' he had replied.

Eventually, the policemen had been satisfied that I had nothing else to tell them and had gone away. As soon as they'd gone, I rushed out, just making it to Sandown in time for the first race. I'd had to endure a few stares, but, even so, it felt good to be in a familiar environment.

'Do you have any runners today?' I asked Jan.

'One in the big chase,' she said. 'Ed's Charger. Not much chance but the owner insisted.'

Jan went into the weighing room to find the jockey who was riding her horse, while I leaned on the rail of the paddock and looked up Ed's Charger in the racecard. I noticed it was to be ridden by Mark Vickers, my client, and now, with Billy Searle out of the running, the champion jockey in waiting.

Billy's attempted murder had certainly been convenient for Mark's championship ambitions but I didn't really believe that the attack in Baydon had been arranged for that purpose.

'Hi, Foxy. Penny for your thoughts?' said a voice behind me, and I groaned inwardly. Martin Gifford was the last person I wanted to see.

I turned round and forced a smile at him. 'Just working on my next murder,' I said. 'Do you fancy being the victim?'

Martin looked really worried for a fraction of a second before he realised I was joking. 'Very funny,' he said.

'Why did you tell the *Post* that Herb Kovak was my best friend when I specifically told you he was only a work colleague?'

'I only told them what I believed to be true,' he said.

'Bastard,' I said. 'You made it all up, and you know it.'

'Now, come on, Foxy,' he said. 'You weren't being honest with me.'

'Bollocks,' I said forcefully. 'What makes you think you have a right to know everything? You're the most indiscreet man on a racecourse. You couldn't keep a secret if your life depended on it.'

'Well, if that's what you think,' he said haughtily, 'you can bugger off.' He turned and walked away with his nose held high.

My real reason for coming to Sandown had been to see Jolyon Roberts. According to the morning paper, one of the horses running in the third race was owned by Viscount Shenington, and I hoped it was one of those he co-owned with his brother.

I went down to the parade ring before the third race and, sure enough, Jolyon Roberts was there, standing on the grass in the centre with three other men and two ladies. I manoeuvred myself next to the gap in the rails through which the Roberts party would eventually need to pass, and waited. He saw me when he was about five strides away and looked me square in the eye.

He stepped to the side to allow the others in his party to pass through the exit first. 'Chasers Bar after the sixth,' he said quietly but distinctly as he went through the gap, not breaking step. I stood still and watched as he caught up with one of the ladies and took her arm. He didn't look back at me. His message had been crystal clear—'Don't stop me now, I'll speak with you later, in private.'

I was in the Chasers Bar ahead of him, with two glasses of wine in front of me, one red and one white. Jolyon Roberts appeared, stopped briefly to look around, then strode over and sat down opposite me.

'Drink?' I asked, indicating the wine.

'No, thank you. I don't. Never have. Now, tell me what you've found.'

'Nothing much, I'm afraid,' I said, taking a sip of white wine. 'Except that, if it is a fraud, it's a much bigger fraud than either of us thought.'

'In what way?' he asked.

'The factory would seem to be the key to a bigger enterprise,' I said. 'The factory was to have cost about twenty million euros with your family trust putting in just over six million and getting European Union funding at the rate of two euros for one of yours.'

'That's right,' he said. 'It was about five million pounds.'

'Yes,' I said. 'But it was the funding of the factory that triggered the grant for the housing project. And that was a whopping eighty million euros, without the need for any further private finance. So it was your investment that was the key to it all.' I paused. 'How did you hear about the investment opportunity in the first place?'

'I can't really remember,' he said. 'But it must have been through Gregory Black. The important thing is whether the factory exists. That's what I'm most concerned about.'

'I haven't yet managed to find that out. Is there any chance I could speak with your nephew? I'd just like to ask him where he went and what he saw, or not as the case may be.'

'He's up at Oxford,' he said. 'At Keble. Reading PPE. Thinks he wants to change the world. Bit full of himself, if you ask me.'

PPE was politics, philosophy and economics. PPE at Oxford was often seen as the first step on the political ladder. If Jolyon Roberts's nephew wanted to change the world he was starting at the right place.

'Do you have a telephone number for him?' I asked.

Jolyon Roberts seemed rather hesitant. 'Look,' he said. 'I'd much rather he wasn't involved.'

'But, sir,' I said. 'He is involved. You told me he was the one who started your concerns in the first place by visiting Bulgaria.'

'Yes, but my brother, his father, has told him to forget it.'

'Does your brother have any idea you have spoken to me?'

'Good God, no,' replied Mr Roberts. 'He'd be furious.'

'Sir,' I said formally. 'I think it might be best if I left you to sort out any further questions you might have with Gregory himself. I have rather gone out on a limb here to find out the small amount I have but I think it's time to stop. The Roberts Family Trust is our client in this matter and your brother is the senior trustee. I really should not act behind his back.' Nor behind Gregory's, I thought.

'No,' he said. 'Quite right. I can see that.' He paused. 'Sorry. I'll give Gregory Black a call about it on Monday. I'll trouble you no further.' He stood up, nodded at me and walked out of the bar.

I sat there for a while longer and transferred my allegiance from white wine to red. Had I done the right thing? Definitely. I was a financial adviser, not a fraud investigator. But what if there really was a hundred-million-euro fraud going on? Had I not a responsibility to report it? But to whom? Perhaps I should send an email to Uri Joram at the European Commission.

I finished the red wine and decided it was time to head home.

Going home to Claudia had always filled me with excitement, raising the pulse a fraction. But now, I was hesitant, even frightened of what I might find, of what I might hear, of what I might see.

CLAUDIA WAS AT HOME when I arrived back, and she'd been crying. She tried to hide it from me but I could always tell.

'You could have phoned me,' she said crossly as I walked into the kitchen. 'You should know better than to sneak up on a girl.'

I'd hardly sneaked up, I thought. This was my home and I was arriving back from the races at six thirty on a Saturday evening.

'What's the matter?' I said, putting an arm round her shoulders.

'Nothing,' she said, shrugging me off. 'Just my back hurts. I'm going up to have a bath.'

She walked briskly out of the kitchen, leaving me standing there alone. She had complained of backache a lot recently. Probably from too much lying on it, I thought somewhat ungraciously.

I mixed myself a gin and tonic. Not really a great idea after two glasses of wine at Sandown, but who cares: I wasn't trying to make a riding weight for the next day's racing, more's the pity.

I could hear her bath running upstairs and, quite suddenly, I was cross. Did she think I was a fool? Something was definitely not right in this household. I walked through into the sitting room and flicked on the television but I didn't watch it. Instead I sat in an armchair feeling miserable, and drank my gin.

In due course, Claudia came downstairs and went into the kitchen.

I sat in the armchair going over and over in my head what I needed to say to Claudia. Doing nothing was no longer an option.

If our relationship was dead, so be it. Anything was better than remaining in this state of limbo with my imagination running wild. I loved Claudia, I was sure of it. But here I was, angry and hurt, accusing her in my mind of deceiving me. It was time for the truth.

When I walked into the kitchen she was crying. She was sitting at the kitchen table in her blue towelling dressing gown. She didn't look up as I went in. I went over to the worktop beside the fridge and poured myself another gin and tonic. I was going to need it.

'Darling, what's the matter?' I said, without turning round. Perhaps it would be easier for her to talk if she couldn't see my face.

'Oh, Nick,' she said, her voice quivering slightly. 'There's something I have to tell you.' She gulped. 'And you're not going to like it.'

I turned round to face her. Maybe I didn't want to make it too easy for her after all.

She looked up at me. 'I'm so sorry,' she said. 'I've got cancer.'

'What?'

'Cancer,' she repeated. 'I've got ovarian cancer. I've sort of known for two weeks, but I found out for certain on Thursday.'

How could I have been so wrong? And so stupid?

'So why didn't you tell me?' I asked.

'I was going to, but to start with you were so busy at work. Then there was all that Herb Kovak business. Then on Thursday, when I left the hospital after the doctor confirmed everything, I was sort of numb.' She paused and wiped a tear from her cheek with the sleeve of her dressing gown. 'Rosemary called to tell me you'd been arrested. It was all dreadful. I couldn't tell you that night.'

'You silly gorgeous girl,' I said. 'Nothing is more important to me than you.' I went round behind her and put my hands on her shoulders and rubbed them. 'So what do we do now?' I asked.

'I've got to have an operation on Tuesday.'

Suddenly this was very real, and very urgent. 'What are they going to do?'

'Remove my left ovary,' she said. 'They might have to remove them both. Then I'll never be able to have a baby. And I know how much you want to have children.' The tears flowed freely again.

'Now, now,' I said, stroking her back. 'Your health is far more important than any future children. You said children were troublesome anyway.'

'I've been desperate,' she said. 'I thought you'd be so cross.'

'The only thing I'm cross about is that you didn't tell me straight away.'

'My doctor has been wonderful,' she said. 'He gave me the name of a cancer counsellor.' She produced a business card from the pocket of her dressing gown. 'I've called so many times I know her number by heart.'

I looked at the card. The number was the much-called one from her mobile phone bill. How, I asked myself again, could I have got things so wrong? 'Tell me,' I said. 'What did the doctor say?'

'I first went to my GP because I didn't feel very well. He asked me if I had any back pain, and I said yes, so he sent me to see a cancer specialist who did some tests and they came back positive. I have a tumour in the left ovary, called a germ cell tumour.'

'Is it malignant?' I asked, dreading the answer.

'Yes,' she said. 'But it's small. The oncologist is hopeful that it hasn't spread. But he will find out for sure about that on Tuesday.'

'Where are you having the op?' I asked.

'University College Hospital,' she said. 'It's where I've been, seeing the oncologist and having tests, all week. I was there most of the day today having MRI scans so they know where the cancer is and how big.'

'What can I do to help?' I asked.

'Just be here.' She smiled. 'I love you so much.'

'I love you so much more,' I said, kissing the top of her head.

I LAY AWAKE trying to get my head round this new problem. I had feared so much losing her to another man that the news of the cancer had almost been a relief. But this was now a much more serious battle, with the unthinkable outcome of losing her altogether if the fight was lost.

Claudia had gone to sleep around ten o'clock and I had spent the next couple of hours at my computer researching ovarian cancer on the Internet. Ovarian cancer five-year survival rates were only about 50 per cent. However, if the cancer hadn't spread, the survival rate was nearly 92 per cent.

I could hear Claudia's rhythmic breathing on the pillow next to me. Funny, I thought, how it often takes a crisis to reveal one's true feelings.

SUNDAY MORNING dawned bright and sunny, both in terms of the weather and my disposition. The coming battle against the cancer, while not easy, somehow seemed manageable. Especially as Claudia and I would both be fighting on the same side.

I got up quietly, leaving her sleeping, and went downstairs to the kitchen, and my computer. I pulled up the emails from Uri Joram and read them again. I wondered what I should do about them.

A hundred million euros was a lot of money but it was a drop in the ocean compared to the European Union total budget. I decided that it wasn't my fight. Claudia and I now had more pressing things on our minds. If Jolyon Roberts needed to ask further questions about his investments, he'd have to speak to Gregory.

I, meanwhile, turned to other matters, in particular, the copies of the statements from Herb's twenty-two credit cards. I sorted them into date order and noticed that four of them were due for payment in the coming week. It might take months before probate was granted and I was able to pay off the debts from other assets in Herb's estate. I had to find the cash.

The $18,000 he collected from the MoneyHome agents the week of his death would pay off the four most urgent ones.

And that would not be all. The ninety-seven individuals using Herb's accounts for their Internet gambling and casino playing probably didn't know Herb was dead. If their past form was anything to go by, they would be racking up further charges.

I decided that the first thing I had to do was to cancel the cards so that no more charges could be made on them. Each of the statements had a phone number and I set about calling them. As soon as I said that Mr Kovak was dead, they all required me to contact them in writing enclosing an original death certificate.

'Fine,' I said to one man, making a mental note to ask the police chief inspector for twenty-two originals of Herb's death certificate.

I just had to find that cash.

Claudia came downstairs in her blue dressing gown.

'What are you doing?' she asked.

'Nothing for you to worry about,' I said, closing the lid of my laptop.

'Look here,' she said, putting on a stern face, 'I told you my troubles so now you have to tell me yours.'

'It's just something to do with Herb Kovak. In his will he appointed me as his executor.'

'And what does that mean exactly?' she asked.

'It means,' I said, 'that I have to sort out all his bloody affairs when I should be looking after you.'

'Quite right,' she said, coming over and sitting on my lap. She put her arms round my neck. 'Naughty boy.'

I smiled. Life was back to normal—or almost.

DURING THE AFTERNOON I called Detective Chief Inspector Tomlinson on the mobile number he had given me.

'Hello, yes,' he said. 'How can I help you?'

'This is Nicholas Foxton. I think it's me who's going to help you,' I said. 'Herb Kovak's sister has turned up.'

'Really,' he said. 'When?'

'Well, actually, on Thursday morning not long after you'd left his flat. But so much has been happening since then I forgot to tell you.'

'Yes,' he said. 'I did hear that you've been kept rather busy.'

'Yes,' I agreed. 'Thank you for giving me an alibi.'

'Don't thank me,' he said. 'I simply told them there was no way, short of using a helicopter, that anyone could travel the seventy-two miles from Baydon to Hendon in fifty-five minutes.'

'I have some other information for you,' I said. 'I think I may have solved the riddle of the credit cards.'

'Go on,' he said.

'I think that Herb Kovak was allowing other people to use his credit-card accounts to gamble on the Internet, probably fellow Americans because it's illegal to gamble in most states over there.'

'What evidence do you have?' he asked.

'Not much,' I said. 'But I think I'm right. There are five hundred and twelve entries on those statements. But there aren't five hundred and twelve different individuals because many of them bet or play on more than one Internet site.'

'Do you have any idea who these people are?'

'No. But we have ninety-seven sets of initials on the sheets you showed me. I think they refer to ninety-seven different people.'

'So you're saying that you think ninety-seven people, who all live somewhere in the United States, were using Herb Kovak's credit-card accounts to bet on the Internet.'

'Yes,' I said. 'I found some MoneyHome receipts that show Herb collected large amounts of cash the week before he died. I believe that cash was to pay off some of the credit-card debts.'

'And this has something to do with why he was killed?'

'Not necessarily,' I said. 'I have no idea why he was killed. I thought that was your job.'

He didn't rise to my bait. There was just silence from his end.

'I've been trying to cancel the credit cards, but they all need an original death certificate. Can you get me some?'

'No death certificate has been issued as yet,' he said. 'But as executor, you can apply for probate before the death certificate is issued. The coroner will issue a letter. I'll arrange it.'

'Thank you.'

'So where can I find Mr Kovak's sister?' he asked.

'Sherri. At his flat, I think. She was there on Friday afternoon.'

'Good. She can make an official identification.'

'Have you any leads at all?' I said. 'How about the note I found in Herb's coat pocket?'

'Nothing to go on,' he said. 'The paper was just common photocopying paper, and the only fingerprints were either yours or Mr Kovak's.'

'So where do you go from here?'

'I think I had better take another look at those lists,' he said. 'And I want to see those MoneyHome receipts.'

'I have two receipts here but the three from last week are at Herb's flat.'

'I may need to go and see Mr Kovak's sister. I'll call you back later when I know my movements.'

CLAUDIA AND I went out to dinner and managed to spend the whole meal talking without once mentioning the 'c' word.

'My mother sent her love,' I said.

'Oh, thanks,' Claudia replied. 'How is she?'

I wanted to say she was in need of grandchildren, but I didn't. My mother would have to take her chances on Tuesday with the surgeon's knife, like the rest of us.

'Fine,' I said. 'She loves her cottage.'

'Perhaps we can go and see her together,' Claudia said. 'After.'

After the operation, she meant.

'I'd better call Jan Setter in the morning and tell her we won't be able to make the opening night on Wednesday.'

'You can go on your own,' Claudia said. 'You'll enjoy it.'

'No,' I said. 'I'll tell her that neither of us will be there.'

Claudia smiled at me. I knew it was what she really wanted.

'It saved me buying a new dress anyway.'

We laughed.

That was the closest we came all evening to discussing her operation and, presently, I paid the bill and took my girl home to bed.

6

At 9 a.m. sharp on Monday morning I called Patrick in the office. 'Am I forgiven yet?' I asked him.

'Gregory's not here,' he replied. 'He isn't back until tomorrow or Wednesday. I think it best if you stay away a while longer.'

I wasn't going to argue. Not having to be in the office over the next couple of days suited me very well. 'Can I use the remote access facility?' I asked. 'Just to check that I'm not missing something that should be done today.'

'Of course,' Patrick replied.

Things had clearly mellowed over the weekend.

'So shall I plan on being in again on Wednesday?' I asked.

'Thursday might be better,' Patrick said, seemingly a little undecided. 'I'll speak to Gregory over lunch on Wednesday.'

'Thursday it is, then,' I said. 'Unless I hear from you sooner.'

DCI TOMLINSON had called on Sunday evening to ask if I could meet him at Herb Kovak's flat at eleven the following morning. Yes, I'd said, I could. In the end both Claudia and I went over to Hendon together in the Mercedes because she didn't want to be left alone, and I was delighted to have her with me.

The policeman was there ahead of us, and he had been interviewing poor Sherri Kovak, who had clearly been distressed by the experience. Claudia put her arm round Sherri's shoulders, even before they were introduced, taking her off into the kitchen.

'Thank you for coming,' the chief inspector said. 'I seem to have upset

Miss Kovak. I told her that I needed her to come back with me to Liverpool to carry out a formal identification of the body.'

I nodded. 'I feared you might. You would think it wouldn't be necessary to put people through such emotional trauma.' Especially, I thought, as one of the bullets had entered through his face.

'I'm afraid the law takes little notice of people's feelings. Now,' he said, getting down to business, 'where are these MoneyHome receipts?'

The chief inspector and I went into the living room. I spread out the squares on Herb's desk. 'I found them torn up in the waste bin,' I said. 'I stuck them together. There are three payment slips, one for eight thousand dollars and two for five thousand each.'

'And you say that Mr Kovak collected this money the week before he was killed. Do you know who sent him the money?'

'No,' I replied. 'MoneyHome only require the recipient's name and something called the Money Transfer Control Number in order to pay out. The agent doesn't know the sender's name.'

'And the name used by Mr Kovak when he collected the money?' he asked.

I added the two payment slips from my pocket to the ones on the desk. 'Butch Cassidy, Billy Kid, Wyatt Earp, Jessie James and Bill Cody. It's not very difficult to spot they're false.'

I could see from his expression that the chief inspector immediately cast Herb as one of his villains.

'He wasn't a crook,' I said. 'He was just allowing his fellow Americans to do what we in England can do every day.'

'Gambling is a mug's game,' he said.

'That's as may be,' I said, 'but it's legal, taxed and, without it, there probably wouldn't be any horse racing.'

The policeman pursed his lips. 'Mr Kovak was still breaking the law. He was aiding and abetting others,' he said with certainty.

I wasn't going to argue with him. I was pretty certain myself that Herb would have faced racketeering charges in the United States if they had known what he was up to.

I also showed the chief inspector the unsigned credit cards, but he seemed far more interested in the MoneyHome payment slips.

'So where do we go from here?' I asked.

'I will try to get MoneyHome to divulge which of their offices the money was sent from. The transfer number should be enought to do that. Then we will have to try to find out whose initials are on the papers.'

'You think this must have something to do with Herb's murder?' I asked.

'Don't you?' he said. 'We've no other leads. Perhaps Mr Kovak was blackmailing one of his clients, threatening to tell the US authorities about their illegal gambling. So they killed him.'

'There goes that suspicious mind of yours again.'

'Suspicion is all we have at the moment,' he said seriously.

There was a heavy knock at the front door.

'That will be my sergeant,' the chief inspector said. 'He's come to drive Miss Kovak and me to Liverpool.'

I ORDERED A TAXI to take us to the hospital that evening. 'Why do you need to go in the night before?' I asked Claudia as we made our way down the Finchley Road.

'Something about wanting to monitor me overnight.'

'What time is the op?' I asked.

'The surgeon said it would be first thing, just as soon as he's finished his early-morning rounds.'

'At least we won't have to wait all day,' I said.

'I know,' she said. 'But I'm frightened.'

So was I. But now was not the time to show it. 'They've found it early,' I said reassuringly. 'You're going to be just fine. You'll see.'

But it was a difficult evening, and night, for both of us.

Claudia was checked into the hospital with brisk efficiency. I kept having to wait in the corridor outside her room as nurses and technicians came to perform some action or another. Swabs were taken, blood was drawn, urine was tested.

After a couple of hours they finally left us in peace. I dimmed the lights, sat on a chair by her bed and held her hand.

'You ought to go home,' Claudia said. 'I'll be fine.'

'I'm not going anywhere,' I said.

Claudia laid her head back on the pillow. 'Good,' she said.

'You get some sleep now, my love,' I said to her. 'You'll need all the strength you can get for tomorrow.'

In time, I could tell from her breathing that she was asleep. I settled down into the chair and closed my eyes. No one told me to go home, so I didn't, although I had to admit, it was not the best night's sleep I'd ever had.

Breakfast wasn't offered, there being a large NIL BY MOUTH sign hanging on a hook by the door, so I went down to the lobby at 6 a.m. in search of a coffee, while the patient had a shower.

At eight thirty Mr Tomic, the surgeon, arrived, wearing a light blue scrub tunic and trousers. He had a permanent marker, and drew a big black arrow on the left side of Claudia below her bellybutton.

'Don't want to take out the wrong one now, do we?' he said.

'What exactly are you going to do?' I asked.

'I will make two small incisions here and here.' He pointed to each side of Claudia's lower abdomen. 'I will then use a laparoscope to have a good look at all your bits, and then I'll remove the left ovary completely. I also plan to take a biopsy of the right ovary. Then I will sew everything up and Claudia will be back here before you know it. About two hours in total.'

'And if the right ovary's not clear?' Claudia asked.

'If I can tell that straight away just by looking,' the surgeon said, 'then I'll have to remove that ovary as well, otherwise the biopsy will be sent to the lab.'

'Can't you just remove the tumour?' I asked. 'Do you have to take the whole ovary?'

'The tumour will probably have taken over most of the ovary and it is the only way of ensuring it doesn't return.'

'If the second ovary is clear does that mean it will remain so?' I asked.

'Let's cross one bridge at a time,' he said. 'We'll discuss the future after the operation.'

I took that to mean 'no', it probably wouldn't remain clear. My mother's wish for grandchildren was not looking too promising.

'OK,' said the surgeon. 'I'll see you in theatre in about twenty minutes. Wait here, they'll come for you.'

The next twenty minutes were intolerable. Every time someone walked down the corridor outside, we both jumped. Claudia held onto my hand as if her life depended on it.

'It'll be all right,' I said. 'You heard what he said, you'll be back in here before you know it.'

'Oh, Nick,' she said miserably, 'if I come out of this with only a tiny piece of an ovary left, let's use it to have kids.'

'OK,' I said. 'You're on.'

'Marry me first?' she asked.

'You bet,' I said.

It was an unusual proposal, but we were in an unusual situation.

At nine fifteen, a porter arrived wearing blue scrubs.

'Please be careful with my fiancée,' I said to him as he wheeled her out of the room. 'She's very precious to me.'

I went with her to the lift, however the porter said that I couldn't go any further. I looked at Claudia's frightened face until the closing doors cut off our line of sight, and she was gone.

I went back into her room and sat down on the chair.

Never before had I felt so desperate, so helpless, and alone.

In truth, it was not a great start to an engagement.

CLAUDIA DIDN'T COME BACK for three hours, by which time I was almost crawling up the walls with worry. Sitting in that hospital room was far worse than spending three times as long in a cell at Paddington Green police station. By the time I finally heard her being wheeled back along the corridor, I had convinced myself that the whole thing had gone wrong and Claudia had died on the operating table.

But she wasn't dead, she was just cold, and shivering uncontrollably. She was sore from the surgery and feeling nauseous from the anaesthetic. And she couldn't stop the shivering.

'It's quite normal,' said a nurse. 'She'll be fine soon.'

'Can she please have another blanket?' I asked.

Reluctantly she agreed and, in time, the shivering did abate and Claudia relaxed and, eventually, she went to sleep.

MR TOMIC CAME to see us at about two o'clock.

'I have some good news and some not quite such good news,' he said. 'Firstly, the good news is that I removed only one ovary and the other one looked perfectly fine, although I took a piece for a biopsy and it's currently being assessed in the path lab.'

'And the not so good news?' I asked.

'The tumour was not quite fully contained in the ovary, and it had erupted on the surface. It means there is every likelihood that there will be some cancer cells present in the fluid within the abdominal cavity. We will know for sure when the lab tests are complete.'

'And?' I said.

'In order to be sure we've killed off the cancer completely, I think a course or two of chemo will probably be needed.'

'Chemotherapy?' I said.

'I'm afraid so,' he replied. 'Just to be sure.'

'Does that mean I'll lose my hair?' Claudia asked.

'It might,' he said. I took that to mean yes, she would lose her hair. 'But even so, it will grow back.'

Claudia's long, flowing, jet-black hair was her pride and joy.

'Does the chemo start straight away?' I asked.

'Within a few weeks,' he said. 'We'll give Claudia time to recover from the surgery first.'

'Will it affect the other ovary?' I asked. 'I read on the Internet that some cancer drugs make women infertile.'

'The drugs are powerful,' he said. 'Am I to assume that preserving fertility is a priority?'

'Yes,' said Claudia unequivocally.

'Then we will just have to be very careful,' he said. 'Won't we?'

At three thirty in the afternoon I left Claudia resting in the hospital while I went home to change and have a shower.

'I won't be long,' I told her. 'Is there anything I can get you?'

'A new body,' she said miserably.

'I love the one you have,' I said, and she forced a smile.

The doctor had told us that she would have to stay in hospital for another night but she should be able to go home the following day.

The sun was shining as I walked down Lichfield Grove towards home. I could see that there was a man standing outside my house with his finger on the doorbell. I was about to call out to him when he turned his head slightly, as if looking over his shoulder.

In spite of telling the police that I hadn't seen Herb's killer, I knew him instantly. And here he was standing outside my front door. I didn't think he was visiting to enquire after my health.

My heartbeat jumped to stratospheric proportions and I stifled the shout that was rising in my throat. I started to turn away from him but not before our eyes had made contact, and I had glimpsed the long black shape in his right hand: his gun, complete with silencer.

I turned and ran as fast as I could back up Lichfield Grove towards Regent's Park Road.

Lichfield Grove was sleepy and deserted at four o'clock in the afternoon, and safety, I thought, would be where there were lots of people. Surely he wouldn't kill me with witnesses, but he had killed Herb with over sixty thousand of them.

I chanced a glance back, having to turn my upper body due to the restricted movement in my neck. It was a mistake.

The gunman was behind me, running hard and lifting his right arm to aim. I heard a bullet whiz past me on my left.

I ran harder. I thought I heard another bullet fly past me and zing off the pavement ahead as a ricochet, but I wasn't stopping to check.

I made it unharmed to Regent's Park Road and went left round the corner. Without breaking stride I went straight into Mr Patel's newsagent's, pushed past the startled owner and crouched down under his counter, gasping for air.

'Mr Patel,' I said. 'I am being chased. Please call the police.'

I didn't know why, but he didn't become angry or question why I had invaded his space. He simply stood quietly and looked down at me, as if in slight surprise at the strange behaviour of the English.

'Mr Patel,' I said again with urgency, still breathing hard. 'I am being chased by a very dangerous man. Please do not look down at me or he will know that I am here. Please call the police.'

I remembered that I had my mobile in my pocket. As I dialled 999 I heard the shop door being opened, the little bell ringing once.

I held my breath. I could feel my heart going thump, thump.

'Emergency, which service?' said a voice from my phone.

I stuffed the phone into my armpit, hoping that the newcomer into the shop hadn't heard it.

'Yes?' said Mr Patel. 'Can I help you, sir?'

The newcomer made no reply and I went on holding my breath, my chest feeling like it was going to burst.

'Can I help you, sir?' Mr Patel said again but more loudly.

Again there was no reply. All I could hear were faint footsteps.

I had to breathe so I let the air out as quietly as I could, and took another deep breath in. I wished I could see what was happening in the shop. After a few seconds I heard the door close, ringing the bell once again, but was the gunman on the inside or the outside?

Mr Patel stood stock-still above me giving me no indication either way. Finally, he said, 'He has gone outside.'

'What's he doing?' I asked.

'He is standing and looking around,' Mr Patel said.

I remembered the phone under my arm. The operator had obviously got fed up waiting and had hung up. I dialled 999 again.

'Emergency, which service?' said a voice again.

'Police,' I said.

'Police incident room, go ahead,' said another voice.

'There's an armed gunman on Regent's Park Road in Finchley, near the corner of Lichfield Grove,' I said. 'Please hurry.'

'Your name, sir?' said the voice.

'Foxton,' I said. 'Mr Patel, what is the man doing now?'

'It's all right, Mr Foxton. He is gone. I cannot see him any more.'

It didn't mean he wasn't there, so I remained sitting on the floor behind the counter, until the police arrived. Finally, after forty-five minutes, two heavily armed officers appeared at the shop door. Mr Patel let them in.

I stood up from my hiding place. 'What took you so long?'

'We had to seal off the area,' he said. 'Standard practice when there's a report of a gunman. Now, sir, do you have a description of this man?' His tone suggested that he didn't believe that a gunman had been stalking the streets of Finchley on a Tuesday afternoon in April.

'I think I may have better than that,' I said. 'Mr Patel, does your closed-circuit TV system have a recorder?' I had passed some of my time waiting for the police by looking up at the small white video camera situated above the racks of cigarettes.

'Of course,' Mr Patel replied.

'Then, officer,' I said, 'please would you kindly inform Detective Chief Inspector Tomlinson of the Merseyside police that we have the murderer of Herb Kovak caught on video.'

But how had he known where to find me? And why?

IN THE END, it was me who rang Chief Inspector Tomlinson, but not before the Armed Response Team had completed a full debrief of the events in Finchley.

'So you say you saw a man standing outside your door?' asked the armed response team superintendent as we stood in Mr Patel's shop.

'Yes,' I said. 'He was ringing the doorbell.'

'And he had a gun?'

'Yes,' I said again, 'with a silencer. He shot at me as I ran up Lichfield Grove. The bullets whizzed past my head.'

A team was dispatched to search and, in due course, one of them returned with two brass empty cases in a plastic bag.

'You will have to come to the police station,' said the superintendent. 'To give a statement.'

'Can't I do it here?' I asked.

'I need to reopen my shop,' said Mr Patel anxiously.

'At my house then?' I asked. 'I need to get back to the hospital. My girl-friend had an operation this morning.'

Reluctantly the superintendent agreed to do it at my house, and we walked down Lichfield Grove together. The road had been closed to traffic and about a dozen police officers were moving up the road in line abreast, crawling on all fours.

'Looking for the bullets,' the superintendent informed me. 'Don't touch the door,' he said as we arrived at my house.

I carefully opened the door with my key and we went into the kitchen.

'Now, Mr Foxton,' the superintendent said formally, 'tell me why a gunman would come calling at your front door.'

'I'm sure he was here to kill me,' I said.

'That's very dramatic. Why?'

Why, indeed, when he could have done it at Aintree at the same time as he killed Herb. What had changed in the intervening ten days that meant I needed to be killed now?

I told the superintendent all about the murder at the Grand National and it was then that I again suggested calling DCI Tomlinson.

'My goodness, Mr Foxton,' the chief inspector said with a laugh. 'You seem to be making a habit of being interviewed by the police.'

'I can assure you it's a habit I intend to give up immediately,' I said.

The two policemen then spoke together and it was frustrating for me listening to only half of the conversation. Mostly they spoke about Mr Patel's videotape. The superintendent and I had watched it on the small screen in the storeroom behind the shop. Just seeing the grainy image of the man as he had come through the shop door made the hairs on the back of my neck stand upright.

'Chief Inspector Tomlinson would like another word,' the superintendent said to me finally, handing over the phone.

'Yes,' I said.

'Can you think of any reason why someone would want you killed?'

'No, I can't,' I said. 'And, if they did, why wait until now? Why not do it at Aintree at the same time as killing Herb? Something must have changed since then.'

'But what?' he said. 'Have you been trying to find out whose initials are on those sheets?'

'No, I haven't. I did go into a MoneyHome agency and ask about the payslips, but that was last Friday.'

'Leave the investigating to the professionals, Mr Foxton,' said the chief inspector somewhat formally.

'But if I hadn't,' I said, 'then you wouldn't know it was other Americans who were gambling using Mr Kovak's credit cards.'

'We still don't know that for certain,' he said.

'So how are you going to catch this guy, before he kills me?'

'Superintendent Yering will issue an alert to all stations, with the man's image from the tape. We will approach the TV stations to run the video in their news broadcasts. And perhaps we'll get a fingerprint from your doorbell. Be patient, Mr Foxton. The video should bear dividends when it's shown on the news.'

It didn't sound sufficiently proactive to me. I asked Superintendent Yering to provide me with some police protection.

'I'm sorry,' he said. 'We don't have the manpower.'

'What am I to do?' I asked. 'Just sit here and wait to be killed?'

'Perhaps it wouldn't be sensible to stay here,' he conceded. 'Have you anywhere else to go to?'

My home and my office were now off limits. Where else?

'I'm going to go back to the hospital to see my girlfriend,' I said.

Some of the armed response team waited in my house while I had a shower and changed clothes. I threw some things into a suitcase, including my computer, and set off for the hospital in the back of one of their vans. I insisted that the driver go right round the big roundabout at Swiss Cottage to make sure we were not being followed.

We weren't, of course. What sort of killer would follow a van full of heavily armed police? But what sort of killer would gun a man down with sixty thousand witnesses close to hand? Or try to kill someone on their own front doorstep?

I couldn't help but think of Jill Dando, the British TV personality, gunned down in exactly that way in a Fulham street.

And her killer had never been identified.

CLAUDIA WAS STILL RESTING when I made it back to her room in the hospital. I had made it unmolested from the police van outside the main door to her room, but not without a nervous glance at every person I met on the way. I closed the door to Claudia's room but, of course, there was no lock on the inside. It made me feel very uneasy.

I thought it unlikely that the gunman would give up just because he'd lost me once. Maybe I might be killed even if I had a bodyguard, but at least it would make me feel a little safer.

I couldn't hide for ever. But what was the alternative?

My main objective had to be to find out who was trying to have me killed and stop them, or at least remove the need, as they saw it, for my life to be terminated. Why exactly would anyone want me dead? I must know something, or have something, that someone didn't want me to tell or show to somebody else.

So what was it that I had, or knew?

The police already had the credit-card statements and the MoneyHome payment slips so it couldn't be them. Was there something else I had inherited from Herb that was so incriminating that murder was the only answer?

Claudia groaned a little and woke up.

'Hello, my darling,' I said. 'How are you feeling?'

'Bloody awful,' she said. 'And really thirsty.'

I poured some water from the jug on her bedside cabinet into a plastic glass and held it out to her.

'Can you help me sit up?' she asked. 'I'm so uncomfortable.'

I did as she asked, but it didn't really improve matters. 'Let's get you some painkillers,' I said and pushed the nurse call bell.

They gave her an injection of morphine that deadened the pain but also sent Claudia back to sleep. It was probably the best thing for her. I put on the television to watch the news, but I kept the sound down to a minimum so as not to disturb the patient.

The gunman in a London newsagent's was the lead story, including the whole video clip of Herb's killer coming into the shop, looking around, then leaving again. They even showed a blown-up still of the man's face as he had glanced directly up at the camera.

Just looking at his image made me nervous once more.

While Claudia went on sleeping, I tried to work out where I could spend the night. I wasn't going back to Finchley, that was for sure, but a second night sitting upright in the chair in Claudia's hospital room wasn't a very attractive proposition either. So, instead, I used my phone to find a cheap hotel room near the hospital.

One of the nurses came into Claudia's room to take her vital signs and to settle her for the night. I took it as my cue to leave.

'Night-night, my darling,' I said. 'I'll be back in the morning.'

She laid her head back on the pillow, looking very vulnerable. We had to beat this impostor within her body, this cancer that would eat away at our happiness. If chemotherapy was what was needed, so be it. Short-term discomfort for long-term gain, that was what we had to think, to believe.

I left the hospital by the main door, but not before I had stood for a while behind a pillar watching the road, checking for anyone lurking in wait for me with a silenced pistol.

I checked into the hotel using a false name, locked my bedroom door, then propped a chair under the door handle for good measure.

I removed my computer from my bag and logged on to the Internet to check my emails.

Among the usual messages, there was one from Patrick to all Lyall & Black employees expressing his disquiet over recent happenings, and urging everyone to refrain from making any comments that may place the firm in a bad light.

I assumed the recent happenings included my arrest, and it made me wonder how Billy Searle was faring and whether the police had made any progress in finding his attacker. Claudia's cancer operation, coupled with the minor matter of finding an assassin on my doorstep, had kept my mind somewhat occupied elsewhere.

I went to the *Racing Post* website. Billy was reported to be making steady progress. There was nothing in the report about his attacker. I, meanwhile, wondered if Billy was getting police protection.

I lay awake half the night listening for someone climbing the drainpipe outside my window with gun in hand, and murder in mind. I also spent time thinking about the note I had found in Herb's coat pocket. I knew the words of it by heart.

> YOU SHOULD HAVE DONE WHAT YOU WERE TOLD. YOU MAY SAY YOU
> REGRET IT, BUT YOU WON'T BE REGRETTING IT FOR LONG.

I had told DCI Tomlinson that I thought it hadn't been so much a warning as an apology, even though he'd pooh-poohed the idea.

However, it did mean one thing for certain: Herb had known his killer, or at least he knew someone who knew he was going to die.

What had Herb been told to do that he hadn't done? Was it something to do with the gambling, or was there something else?

And to whom had Herb expressed regret? And why had he regretted it? Because it had been wrong, or because it had placed him in danger? Still so many questions and still so few answers.

'Leave the investigating to the professionals,' the chief inspector had said to me. But how long would they take? And would I still be alive by then? Maybe it was time for me to start poking a few hornets' nests, and hope not to get stung.

I WENT INTO the hospital at seven thirty on Wednesday morning. Claudia was much improved, sitting up in bed eating breakfast.

'You look well enough to run a marathon,' I said, smiling. 'I'm sure they'll chuck you out just as soon as Mr Tomic's seen you.'

'The nurse says he's usually here by eight.'

As if on cue, Mr Tomic swept into the room. 'Good morning, Claudia,' he said, and he nodded at me. 'How are you feeling?'

'Much better,' Claudia replied. 'But I'm rather sore.'

'That's normal. Do you think you are up to getting up?'

'I have been,' she said almost in triumph. 'I went to the loo last night and again this morning.'

'Good,' he said. 'Then I think you can go home today. I'll see you in ten days to check on everything and take out the stitches. Until then, take it easy.'

'Great,' I said. 'She will. I'll see to that.'

'And,' he went on, 'we've had the first results from the tests.'

'Yes?' Claudia said. 'You can tell me.'

'The right ovary seems clear but, as I feared, there were some cancer cells in the peritoneal fluid. Not many, but enough.'

We were all silent for a moment. 'Chemotherapy?' Claudia said.

'I'm afraid so,' said Mr Tomic. 'But maybe just one course. Two at most. I'm sorry, but it's the best way forward.'

He left us digesting that not-so-tasty morsel. 'Let's look on the bright side, my darling,' I said finally. 'The right ovary is clear.'

'That's true,' Claudia replied, trying to be a little enthusiastic.

'So we might still have kids,' I said.

'If the chemo doesn't make me infertile,' she replied gloomily.

Even the thought of being discharged from hospital didn't cheer her up much, especially when I told her we weren't going home but to my mother's house in Gloucestershire. There was no way I was going home, and neither was she. It was far too risky.

'Nick, you've got to be kidding?' were her exact words.

'Nope,' I said.

'But I want to go home,' Claudia whined. 'I want my own bed.'

'How would I look after you there when I have to go to work?'

'And how,' she asked drily, 'are you going to go to work from Cheltenham?' She paused. 'Please, let's just go home.'

Now, what could I say? I could hardly tell her I was worried we might get murdered on our own doorstep. But returning to Lichfield Grove was completely out of the question.

'My mother is so looking forward to it,' I said. 'And you yourself said it would be nice to go down to see her after the operation.'

'Yes,' she replied, 'but I didn't mean straight from the hospital. And what about my things?'

'You've got many of them here with you, and I collected a few more yesterday from home,' I said.

So we went to my mother's, but not before I'd received another tongue-lashing over my extravagance in hiring a car for the trip.

'And what's wrong with our Mercedes?' Claudia had asked.

'I thought you'd rather have a bit more space after your op,' I said. 'The SLK is so cramped for the passenger.'

And rather conspicuous, I thought.

At the car rental centre I had opted for a bog-standard, four-door, blue saloon with not so much as a 'go-faster' stripe down the side. I wanted to blend into the background, not stand out from it.

I'd told Claudia that my mother was looking forward to having us to stay, and she was, but only after I had talked her out of going to her regular Wednesday afternoon whist drive in the village.

'Mum,' I'd said on the telephone, having woken her at ten to seven in the morning, 'I just need to get us away for a few days.'

'Oh, all right,' she'd said. 'But I'll have to go shopping for some food. And I really don't like letting down the other players.'

'They'll understand,' I'd said. 'Just tell them your son is coming and bringing his fiancée home for the first time.'

She hadn't been able to speak for a few moments. 'Oh, darling,' she'd said eventually. 'Is it really true or are you just saying that?'

'It's really true,' I'd replied.

Hence, when we drove down the lane to her cottage, my mother was already outside to welcome us, almost unable to speak with joy. She hugged Claudia like she'd never done so before.

'What did you say to her?' Claudia asked me as we went inside.

'I told her we were engaged,' I said. 'We are, aren't we?'

'Yes,' she said, smiling. 'Of course we are. But what else did you tell her? You know, about the cancer?'

'Nothing,' I said. 'I'll leave that for you to decide.'

'I think not,' she said. 'Not yet.'

'Fine,' I replied.

We went into the open-plan kitchen/diner/lounge and Claudia sat down gingerly on a chair.

'What's the matter, my dear?' my mother asked with concern. 'You look like you're in pain.'

'I am,' Claudia said. 'I've just had an operation. A hernia.'

'My dear,' said my mother, 'come and put your feet up on the sofa.'

She soon had Claudia propped up on the sofa with multiple pillows. 'There,' she said. 'How about a nice cup of tea?'

'That would be lovely,' Claudia said, and she winked at me.

I took our things upstairs to the guest bedroom, negotiating the narrow, twisting staircase with our bags. I sat on the bed and called the office using my mother's cordless phone. Gregory should have returned from his long weekend away by now and, with luck, Patrick would have convinced him over lunch to let me back into the offices.

Mrs McDowd answered. 'Lyall and Black,' she said crisply.

'Hello, Mrs McDowd,' I said. 'Mr Nicholas here.'

'Mr Patrick said you might ring,' she said curtly. She was being neither friendly nor hostile towards me.

'Are Mr Patrick and Mr Gregory back from lunch yet?' I asked.

'They didn't go to lunch,' she said. 'They've gone to a funeral.'

'That was rather sudden,' I said. 'Whose funeral is it?'

'A client of Mr Gregory's,' she said. 'Colonel Jolyon Roberts.'

7

'What?' I said. 'What did you say?'

'Colonel Jolyon Roberts,' Mrs McDowd said again. 'Mr Patrick and Mr Gregory have gone to his funeral.'

'But when did he die?' I asked. I'd been talking to him only on Saturday at Sandown races.

'Seems he was found dead early yesterday morning,' she said. 'Heart attack, apparently. Very sudden.'

'The funeral is sudden too,' I said, 'if he only died yesterday.'

'Jewish,' she said by way of explanation. 'Quick burial is part of their culture, and usually within twenty-four hours.'

She was a mine of information, Mrs McDowd. And I'd never realised that Jolyon Roberts had been Jewish. But why would I?

'Are you sure it was a heart attack?' I asked her.

Never mind the chief inspector's suspicious mind, I thought, mine was now in overdrive.

'That's what I heard from Mr Gregory,' said Mrs McDowd. 'He was quite shocked by it. Seems he'd only been talking to Colonel Roberts on Monday afternoon.'

'I thought Mr Gregory was away for a long weekend.'

'He was meant to be,' she said. 'But he came back on Monday. Something urgent cropped up.'

'OK,' I said, 'I'll call Mr Patrick on his mobile.'

'The funeral service is at three,' she said.

I looked at my watch. It was well past two thirty.

'I won't call him until afterwards,' I said.

I disconnected and sat on the bed for a while, thinking.

Herb Kovak had accessed the Roberts Family Trust file, and the Bulgarian investment details, and, within a week of doing so, he'd been murdered. I'd sent an innocent-looking email to a man in Bulgaria about the same development and, four days later, someone turned up on my doorstep trying to kill me.

And now, Jolyon Roberts, with his questions and doubts about the whole Bulgarian project, conveniently dies of a heart attack the day after speaking to Gregory about it, as I had told him he should.

Was I going crazy, or was a pattern beginning to appear?

A hundred million euros of EU money was a lot of cash. Was it enough to murder for? Was it enough to murder three times for?

I decided to call Detective Chief Inspector Tomlinson, if only to try to get some more information about the death of Jolyon Roberts.

'Are you suggesting that this Colonel Roberts was murdered?' he asked in a sceptical tone.

Suddenly the whole idea appeared less plausible. 'I don't know. But I'd love to hear what the pathologist said.'

'Assuming there was an autopsy.'

'Surely there would be,' I said. 'I thought all sudden deaths were subject to post-mortems.'

'But why do you believe he was murdered?'

'Murder is pretty uncommon, right?' I said. 'For us non-homicide detectives, it's a pretty rare thing to know a murder victim. Wouldn't you agree?'

'OK, I agree. Murder is uncommon.'

'Well,' I said, 'if I'm right and Colonel Roberts was murdered, then I've known two murder victims, and I nearly became the third.' I paused. 'So, I looked to see what connection Herb Kovak had with Colonel Roberts, and also with myself.'

'Yes?' he said with greater eagerness.

'Lyall and Black for one thing,' I said. 'Herb Kovak and I worked for the firm and Colonel Roberts was a client, although not a client that Herb, nor I, would usually have contacted. But Herb accessed the Roberts file just five days before he died, looking at the details of a Bulgarian investment that the Roberts Family Trust had made. I saw the record of him having done so on a company computer.'

'And what is significant about that?' the detective asked.

'Colonel Roberts approached me just a week ago over his concerns about that very same investment. He was worried that the factory he had invested in hadn't actually been built, but he didn't want a full enquiry as he was worried he'd been duped and didn't want the whole world to know. So he asked me to quietly have a look and check that all was well with the investment.'

'And did you?' he asked.

'I did a little bit of digging, but I told him on Saturday that I couldn't go searching behind the backs of others at the firm and he should speak to his investment manager about it.'

'Who is?' he asked.

'Gregory Black,' I said. 'Colonel Roberts spoke to him on Monday, only the day before he died.'

'Are you telling me you suspect Gregory Black of killing him?'

'No, of course not,' I said. 'Gregory Black may have an explosive temper but he's hardly a murderer.'

Or was he? Could I really tell what went on in his head?

'But that's not all,' I said. 'I sent an email to someone in Bulgaria last Friday, and a would-be assassin turned up at my door on Tuesday afternoon.'

'OK,' he said. 'I'll try to find out if there was an autopsy carried out on Colonel Roberts. I'll call you if I get anything.'

'I'm not at home. And my mobile doesn't work where I am.'

'And where is that?'

'I'm in a village called Woodmancote,' I said. 'It's near Cheltenham racecourse. It's where my mother lives.' I gave him my mother's telephone number.

'Cheltenham is a long way from your office,' he said.

'I know. I ran away. Superintendent Yering was unable to provide me with protection and I felt vulnerable, so I didn't go home.'

'I can't say I really blame you,' he said.

'So how about you giving me a bodyguard?' I asked. 'Preferably one bristling with guns, and with evil intent towards assassins.'

'I'll see what I can do,' he said. 'Especially if it does turn out that Colonel Roberts was murdered.'

'And another thing,' I said. 'Can you find out whether Billy Searle has talked to the Wiltshire police? And what he's told them.'

'Do you think he has something to do with all this as well?'

'No, I don't,' I said. 'I happen to know where Billy's money was invested because I did it, and it was nowhere near Bulgaria. I'm just interested to know what he's told the police. After all, I was arrested on suspicion of trying to kill him.'

'OK, OK,' he said. 'I'll try.'

WHEN I WENT DOWNSTAIRS, my mother and Claudia were in full flow with wedding plans. 'Would you like some late lunch?' my mother asked me. 'I've a shepherd's pie in the oven.'

'Mum,' I said, 'it's gone three o'clock.'

'So? I thought you might be hungry when you arrived.'

Surprisingly, I was, and I could tell from Claudia's eager look that she was too. Consequently the three of us sat down to a very late lunch of shepherd's pie and broccoli, with my mother insisting that I have a second helping.

I CALLED PATRICK on his mobile at twenty to six, late enough for the funeral to be over. Claudia was upstairs having a rest and my mother was preparing chicken casserole for dinner. I sat in the lounge area, facing her, but at the furthest point of the room.

'Ah, yes. Nicholas,' Patrick said. 'Mrs McDowd told me you'd called. Sorry I wasn't able to speak to you earlier.'

'And I am sorry to hear about Colonel Roberts,' I said.

'Yes, what a dreadful thing. He was only sixty-two.'

'Have you spoken to Gregory?' I asked, getting to the point.

'Yes, I have,' he said. 'He is still very angry with you.'

'But, why?' I asked.

'Why do you think?' he said crossly. 'For getting arrested and being splashed all over the papers and the television. He believes you brought the firm into disrepute.'

'But his anger is misplaced. It wasn't my fault I was arrested, the police jumped to an incorrect conclusion.'

'Yes,' he said. 'But you did give them reason to draw it.'

'I did not,' I said. 'It was that idiot Billy Searle who shouted out about murder. I did absolutely nothing wrong.'

'Gregory still thinks you must have had something to do with it.'

'Well, in that case, Gregory is more of an idiot than I thought.' My raised voice caused my mother to look at me from across the room. I paused, then spoke more quietly. 'Am I being fired?'

He did not reply, and I stayed silent. I could hear his breathing.

'You had better come in to the office tomorrow,' he said at last. 'I will tell Gregory to hold his tongue.'

'Thank you,' I said. 'But Claudia is not well and I'll probably work from home. I hope to see you on Friday.'

'Right,' he said, sounding relieved that he had another day to dampen the erupting Gregory volcano. 'I'll see you on Friday.'

He hung up and I sat for a while wondering about my future.

'What was all that about?' my mother asked with concern.

'Just a little problem at work,' I said. 'Nothing to worry about.'

But I did worry. I had enjoyed working for Lyall & Black. But what sort of future did I have in a firm where one of the senior partners believed me to be involved in an attempted murder and, at the same time, I wondered if he had been involved in a successful one?

THE THREE OF US sat at my mother's dining table for dinner, and I ate too much. Claudia and I went up to bed around ten o'clock.

'You are such a clever thing, insisting we came here,' Claudia said as we snuggled together under the duvet. 'If we'd gone home I would have felt pressured to cook or clean. Here I can relax, my phone doesn't even ring, and your mother is such a dear.'

I smiled in the darkness. Now that was a turnaround.

'But we can't stay here very long,' I said seriously.

'Why not?' she asked.

'Because, if she goes on feeding me as she's done today, I'll end up with a waistline like Homer Simpson.'

We giggled uncontrollably.

Since we'd left the hospital that morning, neither of us had mentioned anything about the cancer, or the upcoming chemo treatments. It was as if we had left all our troubles behind us in London.

But they were about to come looking for us.

I DREAMT that I was riding in a race. I was racing against Gregory. He was smiling, and aiming a gun with a silencer at my head.

I woke up with a jerk, breathing fast, ready to run.

I lay there listening to Claudia's rhythmic breathing beside me.

Did I really think Gregory Black was involved in fraud and murder? I didn't know, but I was interested to hear the results of the post-mortem on Jolyon Roberts, if there had been one.

I drifted back to sleep but only fitfully, waking often to listen for sounds that shouldn't have been there. I was wide awake long before the sun lit up the bedroom window soon after six o'clock. I got up quietly, padded down-stairs with my computer and logged on to the Internet. I had forty-three unread emails, including one from Jan Setter telling me how fantastic the first night of the West End musical had been and how crazy I was to have missed it.

I emailed back to her and said how pleased I was she had enjoyed it and how I hoped it would make her lots of money.

It took me over two hours just to answer my outstanding emails by which time I could hear movement above and, presently, my mother came down-stairs in her dressing gown. 'Hello, dear,' she said. 'What would you like for breakfast? I have bacon and eggs, and some wonderful sausages.'

'Just a coffee and a slice of toast would be lovely,' I said.

It was like King Canute trying to hold back the tide.

'Don't be ridiculous,' she said, already placing a frying pan on the stove. 'You've got to have a proper breakfast. What sort of mother would I be if I didn't feed you?'

I sighed. I took Claudia a cup of tea while the sausages and bacon were siz-zling in the pan. 'Morning gorgeous,' I said. 'How are you feeling today?'

'Still a bit sore,' she said, sitting up. 'But better than yesterday.'

'Good,' I said. 'Time to get up. Delia Smith is cooking breakfast.'

'Mmm, I can smell it,' she said, laughing. 'Now don't you expect that every morning when we're married.'

'What?' I said in mock horror. 'No cooked breakfasts! The wedding's off!'

'We haven't even fixed a date for it yet,' she said.

'Before or after the hair loss?' I asked seriously.

She thought for a moment. 'After it grows back. Give me time to get used to this engagement business first.'

'After it is then,' I said. I leaned down and kissed her. 'Don't be long or the sausages will get cold.'

My mother hadn't lied, the sausages were excellent, and there was a mountain of bacon and scrambled eggs. I felt totally bloated by the time I sat down again at my computer to check through my client files using the firm's remote access facility.

Claudia, meanwhile, had managed to extract herself from bed, coming down to join us in a dressing gown, but she ate just a small bowl of muesli. And grinned at me as she did so. It really wasn't fair.

I spent the morning briefly looking through all the files for my fifty or so personal clients, ensuring that I hadn't missed reinvesting the proceeds of maturing bonds or suchlike.

I used my mother's phone to check on my voicemail. There was one new message from Sherri, asking me to call her at Herb's flat.

'Hi,' I said when she answered. 'Is everything all right?'

'Monday in Liverpool was a bit of an ordeal,' she replied. 'It's over, anyway. I'm going home tomorrow morning. I'm on a flight at ten forty-five to Chicago. I just called to say goodbye.'

'Thanks,' I said. 'I'm glad you did.'

'A few letters arrived for Herb and I had a phone call from his gym, about Herb not paying them and they want his locker back. Somewhere called the Slim Fit Gym.' She read out the telephone number and I jotted it down on the back of the rental car agreement.

'Leave the letters on the desk,' I said. 'I'll deal with them, and I'll call the gym. You look after yourself. Have a safe trip home. I'll let you know about the funeral and such when I know.'

I called the Slim Fit Gym.

'Mr Kovak's direct debit has been cancelled,' the person said. 'So we want his locker back.'

'He died,' I said. 'So take it back.'

'There's a padlock on it. We need Mr Kovak's key.'

I remembered the key pinned to the board above Herb's desk.

'OK,' I said. 'I'll bring the key in next week.'

I disconnected and leaned back in the chair, stretching.

The phone rang. 'Hello,' I said.

'It was definitely a heart attack,' said Chief Inspector Tomlinson down the line. 'While he was swimming in his own pool. Then he drowned as a result. A full post-mortem was carried out on Tuesday afternoon. Seems Colonel Roberts had a history of heart problems.'

'Oh,' I said. 'Such are the perils of early-morning swimming.'

'It was late-night swimming apparently, and on his own. And he'd been drinking. Stupid fool. His blood alcohol level was more than twice that for drink-driving.'

'Hold on a minute,' I said, suddenly remembering something from our meeting in the Chasers Bar at Sandown races. 'Colonel Roberts told me, categorically, that he didn't drink alcohol. And he never had.'

'I'll get back to you,' said Chief Inspector Tomlinson suddenly. 'I need to call in a few favours.'

He hung up and I was cross I hadn't asked him about Billy Searle. But it would wait.

The phone rang again. 'Hello,' I said. 'Did you forget something?'

'Sorry?' said a female voice. 'Is that you Mr Nicholas?'

'Mrs McDowd,' I said. 'How lovely to hear from you.'

'I have a message from Mr Patrick,' she said.

'How did you get this number?' I asked.

'He wants you to—' she started but I interrupted her.

'Mrs McDowd,' I said again. 'How did you get this number?'

'It was on caller-ID when you called in this morning,' she said.

That was careless, I thought, for someone meant to be in hiding.

'Anyway,' she said. 'I know that number. You're staying with your mother. How is she?'

Bloody Mrs McDowd, I thought. How does she know so much? 'She's fine, thank you,' I said. 'What does Mr Patrick want?'

'He wants you to call him in the morning before you come into the office, to arrange a meeting between you and Mr Gregory.'

'Did he say what the meeting was about?' I asked.

'No,' she said, but I bet she knew. Mrs McDowd knew everything.

'Please tell Mr Patrick that I won't be in the office very early.'

'I've told him that,' she said. 'With you being down in Gloucestershire.'

Who else had she told? I wondered. Had she told Mr Gregory?

I spent the afternoon catching up on the markets. The trick to winning in the financial game was to invest in things about to go up in value, while selling those about to go down. A bit like gambling. Money went round and round but it did not always end up with the same people.

Then there were the fraudsters, those who tried to load the odds in their favour through insider dealing. They're the ones who think they can beat the system, and many of them do, because betting on a certainty is like having a licence to print money.

Herb Kovak had said to Mrs McDowd that he liked to bet on certainties. She'd told me.

CHIEF INSPECTOR TOMLINSON called back at five o'clock.

'He'd definitely been drinking,' he said. 'I've seen the full autopsy report. There's no mistake. They tested both his blood and the aqueous humour in his eye. The stomach contained whisky residue.'

'How easy is it to force someone to drink whisky?' I asked.

'My, my,' he said. 'Now who has the suspicious mind?'

'It's just too convenient,' I said.

'But how could you give someone a heart attack?' he asked.

'Hold his drunken head under the surface of his own swimming pool,' I said. 'Either he drowns straight away or, as he has a history of heart problems, he has a heart attack and then drowns.'

'But why the alcohol?' he asked.

'To add confusion,' I said. 'When you knew he'd been drinking, you instinctively believed he had been a stupid fool, and you probably thought he half deserved to die for it.'

'True,' he said. 'But you are speculating. There's no evidence of foul play.'

'No,' I agreed, 'and what there was has conveniently been buried in Golders Green cemetery.'

He laughed. 'Story of my life.'

'What about Billy Searle?' I asked. 'What did you find out?'

'He's awake,' he said, 'but he refuses to say if he knew the person who knocked him off his bike. Says it was an accident.'

I wasn't surprised. If it was a bookmaker, and Billy was involved in some betting scandal, he was hardly likely to admit it. It would be tantamount to handing in his jockey's licence for good.

'Well, thanks for finding out. Any news on the gunman? Did you get any response from the video?'

'Too much,' he said. 'We're sifting through it all.'

'So how about that bodyguard?' I asked. 'I can't stay here for long, but I don't fancy going home with our friend still out there.'

'I'll talk to my super,' he said.

'Thanks,' I said. 'And please make it soon.'

We disconnected and I looked at my watch. It was just after five. I leaned back in the chair and pushed the 'get mail' button for a final check on my emails. One arrived from Gregory Black.

I sat forward quickly and opened it.

'Nicholas,' he had written, 'Patrick has asked me to apologise for my outburst of last week. So I am sorry. I can also assure you there will be no repetition of my actions when you return to this office after your stay with your mother. Yours, Gregory Black.'

Wow, I thought. I could imagine Gregory absolutely hating having to write that email with Patrick standing over him. He would resent it for ever. It wouldn't make my future at the firm any easier. I also didn't like the fact that Gregory knew I was staying with my mother.

Mrs McDowd not only wanted to know everything, she liked everyone to know she knew it, by spreading the information. The whole office would now be aware that I was in Gloucestershire.

AT ABOUT SEVEN THIRTY my mother insisted I open a bottle of champagne to properly celebrate Claudia's and my engagement.

'I put one in the fridge last night,' she said. 'So it should be cold.'

And it was.

I retrieved the bottle and poured three glasses of the golden bubbly liquid, then we each, in turn, made a toast.

'To a long and happy marriage to my Claudia,' I said, and we drank.

'To long life and good health,' Claudia said, looking at me, and we drank again.

'To grandchildren,' my mother said, and we all drank once more.

Claudia and I held hands. We knew without saying what we were each thinking. Oh yes, please, to all three of the above. But, with cancer, it was all so scary and unpredictable.

Claudia laid the dining table as my mother busied herself with saucepans of potatoes and carrots, and the lamb roasted away gently in the oven. I, meanwhile, poured us all more champagne and let them get on with it, leaning up against the worktop and enjoying the last of the evening sunshine as it shone brightly through the west-facing kitchen window.

'Bugger,' my mother said.

'What's wrong?' I asked.

'The cooker's gone off,' she said. She tried a light switch. Nothing happened. 'Bloody electric company. I'll call them straight away.' She rummaged in a drawer for a card, then picked up the phone.

'That's funny,' she said. 'The phone's dead too.'

There was a heavy knock on the front door.

'I'll get it,' said Claudia, turning away.

The power was off, the telephone was dead, there was a knock on the door, and the hairs on the back of my neck suddenly stood up.

'Don't touch it,' I shouted at Claudia. 'Get away from the door.'

I was already halfway towards her when the knock was repeated. I grabbed her just as she was reaching for the handle.

'What on earth are you doing?' she said loudly.

'Keep your voice down,' I hissed at her.

'Why?' she said, but much quieter. She read the fear in my face.

'Please. Go over to the kitchen area.' I looked over at my mother who was staring at us, holding the useless telephone in her hand.

The urgency of my voice finally got through to Claudia and she went over to join my mother. They suddenly looked frightened.

I went into the cloakroom next to the front door and peaked through a gap in the curtains at the person standing outside. He had on a grey anorak and a dark blue baseball cap. There was no doubt it was the same man I had last seen in the grainy video from Mr Patel's newsagent's, the same man who had gunned down Herb Kovak at Aintree, and the same man who had shot at me in Lichfield Grove.

I went back into the big room. The front door was locked. It was quite strong, but was it strong enough?

I went quickly across to the kitchen and locked the back door as well, turning the key slowly to keep the noise to a minimum, and sliding across the bolt at the top.

We heard the man rattle the front door.

'Who is it?' whispered my mother.

I had to tell them. 'A dangerous man,' I whispered. 'He's trying to kill me. It's the man who killed Herb Kovak at Liverpool races.'

They both looked more frightened than ever. And I was, too.

'Call the police,' Claudia said, then she remembered. 'Oh my God, he's cut the phone line.'

And the electricity. And our mobiles didn't have any signal here.

We were on our own.

'Upstairs,' I said quietly. 'Both of you. Lock yourselves in the bathroom, sit on the floor, and don't come out until I tell you to.'

Claudia hesitated a moment, but then she nodded and took my mother by the hand. They started to go but then turned back. 'But what are you going to do?' Claudia asked.

'Try to keep him out,' I said. 'Now go on, go!'

They disappeared up the boxed-in staircase and I heard the bathroom door being shut and locked above me. I heard the back door being tried and I ducked away from it.

The last of the sun's orange rays disappeared from the kitchen window. It began to get dark indoors with no electric lights to brighten the gathering gloom. I looked around in desperation for something to use as a weapon. An umbrella stood in a large china pot near the front door, one of those big golf umbrellas with a heavy wooden handle. It wasn't much but it was all there was.

I had one advantage over my assailant in so far as I could see him more easily than he could see me. I watched him through the windows as he went right round the house. At one point he came close to the kitchen window, cupping his hands round his face and up against the glass in order to peer in. I was standing to the side of the window in a corner, where he would have no chance to spot me.

Perhaps he would go away, I thought.

He didn't.

The sound of breaking glass put paid to any hope I may have had that this was going to end simply and without violence.

My mother's windows were a version of the old leaded lights, small panes of glass held together by a lattice framework of metal strips. The gunman had broken one of the panes, enough for him to put his gloved hand through the opening and unlatch the whole thing. I watched the window swing open.

Where could I hide? Nowhere. In any case, hiding would give the advantage to the gunman who could take his time finding me, and then I would get a couple of bullets in my heart and another in my face, just as poor Herb had.

So, if I wasn't going to hide, the only other option was to attack.

He started to climb through the window, his gun with its long black silencer entering first.

I stood just to the side of the window and raised the umbrella, holding it by the pointed end so that I could swing the heavy wooden handle. I brought the handle down hard onto the gun.

The gun went off, the bullet ricocheting off the granite worktop below the window with a loud zing before burying itself in the wall opposite. But the blow had also knocked the gun from the man's grasp. It clattered to the floor, sliding across the stone quarry tiles and out of sight under my mother's fridge.

'*Kapole!*' the man said explosively. '*Ebi se!*'

I didn't know what he meant, and it didn't stop him coming through the window. I raised the umbrella for another strike but he grabbed it and tore it from my grasp, tossing it aside as he stepped through the open window, crouching on the worktop.

I rushed at him but he was ready, pushing me aside with ease so that I stumbled across the kitchen towards the sink. I turned quickly but he had already jumped down to the floor. I watched him as he looked around and then withdrew a large carving knife from a wooden block next to my mother's stove. Now why hadn't I thought of that?

I moved quickly to my right, putting the dining table between him and me. If he couldn't reach me, he couldn't stab me either.

There followed a sort of ballet with him moving one way or the other, and me mirroring him, always keeping the table between us. We ran round the table. He pulled out chairs to try to slow me down, but I was quick. I may not have been as fit as I was as a jockey but I was still no slouch in the running department. It had fared me well in Lichfield Grove and was doing so again here.

He changed his tactics, using one of the chairs to climb up onto the table, and then he came straight at me across it. I turned and ran for the stairs, pulling open the door, and bounding up the steps two at a time. I could hear him behind me and he was gaining.

Where could I go? Panic rose in my throat. I didn't want to die.

I turned to face him, at least I would see it coming and I'd be able to make some effort to get away from the thrust of the knife.

He stood at the top of the stairs with me in front of him. He advanced a step and I retreated, my back up against the wall. He came a step closer and I readied myself for his strike.

Claudia stepped out of the bathroom, just down the corridor to his right. 'Leave him alone,' she shouted.

He turned towards the noise and I leapt at him, wrapping my right arm round his neck with my forearm across his throat while I tried to gouge his eyes out with the fingers of my left hand. I squeezed his neck with all my strength. But it was not enough.

The man was taller and stronger than I and he began to turn himself round to face me. With my arms held up round his head, my abdomen would be defenceless to a thrust of the knife.

What had that spinal specialist told me? 'Whatever you do, don't get into a fight.' He'd said nothing about falling down stairs.

I hung on to the man's neck as if my life depended on it, then I dived headfirst down the narrow boxed-in stairway, taking the man with me. It was a crazy thing to do. But it was my only chance.

I twisted as we fell so that I landed on top of the man, his head taking the full force of the heavy contact with the wall where the stairway turned ninety degrees halfway down. We slithered on to the bottom of the wooden stairs, coming to a halt still locked together by my right arm. We were lying partially through the doorway, our legs on the stairs, our heads stuck out into the room below.

Even for me on top, and using the man's body to break my fall, the first impact with the wall had been enough to drive the air from my lungs, but at least my head hadn't fallen off with it.

I pulled my arm from under his neck and jumped to my feet ready to continue the fight, but there was no need. The man lay limply, face down, where he'd come to rest.

I went quickly to retrieve the gun from beneath the fridge. If the man moved so much as an eyebrow, I thought, I'd shoot him.

I stood over him for what felt like a very long time, pointing the gun at his head and watching for any movement. But the man didn't move. Not even to breathe. Nevertheless, I still didn't trust him not to jump up and kill me, so I kept the gun pointing at him all the time.

'Claudia,' I shouted. 'Claudia, I need your help.'

I heard footsteps on the floorboards above my head.

'Has he gone?' Claudia asked from the top of the stairs.

'I think he might be dead,' I said. 'But I'm taking no chances, and it's getting so dark I can hardly see him.'

'I've got a torch by my bed,' my mother said.

I heard her walk along the corridor to her room, then she came back shining the torch brightly down the stairwell.

'Oh my God!' Claudia said, looking down.

In the torchlight we saw that the man's head was lying almost flat against his right shoulder. His neck was broken, just as mine had once been. But, on this occasion, there had been no paramedics to apply an immobilising collar, no one to save his life as there had been for me at Cheltenham racecourse all those years ago.

This man's neck had bumped down to the bottom of a wooden stairway, all the time being wrenched to one side by my arm.

And it had killed him.

8

'What do we do now?' Claudia said, from the top of the stairs.

'Call the police,' I said from the bottom.

'How?'

'I'll take the car and find somewhere with a signal,' I said.

But there was no way Claudia and my mother were allowing me to go off in the car, leaving them alone in the house with the gunman. Dead or not, they were still very frightened of him.

'Pack up our things,' I said to Claudia. 'Mum, pack enough for a few days. We're going somewhere else.'

They both quickly went together to pack, taking the torch with them, and leaving me in the dark. I was shaking, perhaps from fear, or relief, or maybe it was a reaction to the realisation that I had killed a man. Probably a bit of all three.

The shaking continued for several minutes and I became totally exhausted by it. I wanted to sit down, and I felt slightly sick.

'We're packed,' Claudia said from upstairs. She handed down our bags and my mother's suitcase. I guided each of them down, making sure they stepped only on the wood and not on the man.

The three of us went out to the car, loaded the stuff, and drove away, leaving the dead man alone in the dark house.

I drove into Cheltenham and called Chief Inspector Tomlinson on his mobile. 'The man who killed Herb Kovak,' I said, 'is lying dead at the bottom of my mother's stairway. We fell down the stairs together. He was trying to stab me with a knife at the time.'

'What happened to his gun?' he asked.

'He lost it under the fridge,' I said.

'Hmm,' he said. 'And have you told the local constabulary?'

'No,' I said. 'I thought you could do that. And you can also tell them he was a foreigner. He said things I didn't understand.'

'And where are you now?' he asked.

'In Cheltenham,' I said. 'The gunman cut the power and the telephone wires. I've had to leave to make a call on my mobile. There's no signal at the cottage.'

'Is anyone still at the cottage?'

'Only the dead man,' I said. 'I have Claudia and my mother with me in the car.'

'So are you going back there now?' he asked.

'No,' I said firmly. 'Whoever sent this man could send another.'

'So where are you going?' he asked.

'I don't know yet,' I said. 'I'll call you when I do.'

'I'll call the Gloucestershire police but they'll definitely want to talk to you. They may even want you back at the cottage.'

'Tell them I'll call them there in two hours,' I said.

'But you said the line had been cut.'

'Then get it fixed,' I said. 'I left the back door unlocked so they won't have to break the front door down to get in.'

'OK, I'll tell them.' he said. 'Is the gun still under the fridge?'

'No,' I said. 'I retrieved it.'

'So where is it now?'

I had so wanted to bring it with me, to give myself the armed protection that I'd been denied by the police.

'It's outside the front door,' I said. 'In a bush.'

'Right,' he said, sounding slightly relieved. 'I'll tell the Gloucestershire force that too. Save them hunting for it, and you.'

'Good,' I said.

I hung up, and switched off my phone. I would call the police on *my* terms, and I also didn't want anyone being able to track my movements from the phone signal.

'Do you really think we're still in danger?' Claudia asked.

'I don't know,' I said, 'but I'm not taking any chances.'

'Who knew we were there?' she asked.

'Everyone at the office, I expect,' I said. 'Mrs McDowd definitely knew, and she'd have told everyone else.'

I made one more stop in Cheltenham, at a public phone box. I didn't want to use my mobile for fear that someone could trace who I was calling. We were going where no one would find us.

It was my mother who finally asked the big question. 'Why was that man trying to kill you?' she said calmly from the back seat.

'I'm not sure, but it may be because I am a witness to him killing a man at Aintree races,' I said. 'It wasn't the first time he'd tried. He was waiting outside our house in Lichfield Grove when I got there on Tuesday afternoon. Luckily, I could run faster than him.'

'Is that why we came to Woodmancote?' Claudia asked. 'Instead of going home?'

'It is,' I said. 'But I didn't realise that Woodmancote wasn't safe either. I won't make that mistake again.'

'But what about the police?' my mother asked. 'Surely we must go to the police. They will look after us.'

But how much did I trust the police? They hadn't given me any protection when I'd asked for it, and that omission had almost cost us our lives. No, I thought, I'd trust my own instincts.

'I have been to the police,' I said, driving on through the darkness. 'But it will be *me* who will look after you.'

And I would also find out who was trying to have me killed, and why.

'WELL, LOVER BOY,' Jan Setter said. 'When I asked you to come and stay, I didn't exactly mean you to bring your girlfriend and your mother with you!'

We laughed.

We were sitting at her kitchen table in Lambourn drinking coffee, my girlfriend and mother having been safely tucked up in two of Jan's many spare bedrooms.

'I didn't know where else to go,' I said.

All I had said to her on the phone from Cheltenham had been that I was desperate and could she put us up for a night or two. She had simply said 'Come' and asked no questions, not until after my traumatised mother and fiancée had been safely ushered up to bed.

In all the years I had known Jan, both as her former jockey and as her financial adviser, I had never known her to be flustered or panicked by anything. She was the steady head I needed in this crisis.

'Someone is trying to kill me,' I said. 'Tonight a man came to my mother's cottage. He had a gun. We are extremely fortunate to be alive. The same man has now tried to kill me twice.'

'Let's hope it isn't third time lucky.'

'He won't get a third time. He's dead. He is lying on the floor of my mother's sitting room with his neck broken.'

'Have you called the police?'

'Yes,' I said. 'But I need to call them again.' I looked at my watch. It had been at least two hours since I'd spoken to Chief Inspector Tomlinson. But they could wait a little longer.

'So why come here?'

'I need somewhere to hide where no one can find me.'

'If the man's dead, why do you still need to hide?' she asked.

'Because he was a hired killer and I am worried that whoever hired him will simply hire another. I think it's all to do with stealing a hundred million euros from the European Union. I may have asked the wrong questions, and somebody believes I need to be permanently removed before I ask more questions and bring the whole scheme tumbling down.'

'So what are you going to do?' she said.

'Ask the questions quickly,' I said. 'Then keep my head down.'

SOMEONE ANSWERED after just one ring when I called my mother's cottage. I was sitting in Jan's office and using her mobile phone, and I had carefully dialled 141 first to withhold the number from caller-ID.

'Nicholas Foxton?' came a man's voice.

'It is,' I said. 'To whom am I talking?'

'Detective Chief Inspector Flight,' he said. 'Gloucestershire police. Where are you, Mr Foxton?'

'Somewhere safe. Who was the man who tried to kill me?'

'Mr Foxton,' he said. 'I need you to come to the police station to be interviewed. Tonight.'

'I suggest you speak to DCI Tomlinson from Merseyside police. And Superintendent Yering from the Metropolitan Police.'

'Mr Foxton,' he said. 'You are in danger of obstructing the police in the course of their duties. Now, please, tell me where you are.'

'No,' I said. 'Did you watch the television news on Tuesday? The dead man in my mother's cottage is the same man as in the video. And I think he was foreign.'

'Mr Foxton.' Detective Chief Inspector Flight was getting quite worked up. 'I must insist you tell me where you are.'

'And I must insist you speak to DCI Tomlinson or Superintendent Yering.' I hung up. I was not going to any police station to be interviewed tonight, or any other night if I could help it. People could get shot at police stations. Ask Lee Harvey Oswald.

I HEARD JAN leave the house in the morning to supervise the exercising of her horses on the gallops. She had asked if I wanted to accompany her up onto the downs, but I had declined. I didn't want anyone to recognise me and hence know where I was staying.

I got up as quietly as I could but Claudia was already awake. 'I was so frightened last night,' she said. 'Can we go home now?'

'I have to do a few things before we can go home,' I said.

'I think we should go to the police,' she said.

'I spoke to them last night after you went to bed.'

'So what is it that you have to do?' she asked.

'First, I have to go to Oxford, to see a young man at the university,' I said. 'I want to ask him some questions about a factory, or rather, the lack of a factory.' I started to dress. 'You stay here with Jan and my mother. You'll be quite safe here.'

I STOPPED on the outskirts of Oxford and turned on my mobile to call Detective Chief Inspector Tomlinson. 'DCI Flight is not happy with you,' he said. 'He's applied for a warrant for your arrest.'

'But that's ridiculous,' I said.

'Maybe it is,' he agreed, 'but he's really pissed off. I do think it might be better if you go and see him.'

'Not if he's going to arrest me.' I didn't relish spending another day in a police cell. 'Anyway,' I said. 'I have things to do first.'

'Not investigating again, are you?' said the professional detective. 'I've told you to leave that to the police.'

'But it is me, not you, that believes Colonel Jolyon Roberts was murdered. The police see no crime, so there is no investigation.'

'So what do you want me to do?' he asked.

'Speak to Flight,' I said. 'Get him off my back.'

'I'll try,' he said. 'But you ought to at least talk to him.'

'Get me his number,' I said. 'Then I'll call him.'

'How can I contact you?' he asked.

'Leave a message on this phone,' I said. 'And can you find out if the dead man in my mother's cottage was Bulgarian?'

I thought about also asking him to get the fraud squad to initiate an investigation into the Balscott factory project but, as I knew from experience, fraud investigations into foreign investments involved months of paperwork. Add to that the complexities of the European Union grants system, and it would take years. And I'd be dead and buried long before that.

I disconnected from DCI Tomlinson but the phone rang again in my hand almost immediately. I had two new voicemail messages.

One of them was from DCI Flight and he didn't sound happy. I ignored it. The other was from Patrick Lyall who also wasn't pleased with me, in particular because I had left a message on his mobile saying that I wouldn't be coming into the office today.

'Nicholas,' Patrick's voice said, 'I am sorry that you have decided not to be in the office once again. I think we need to have a talk about your commitment to the firm. I will be writing to you today, formally warning you as to your future conduct. Please would you call me and tell me where to have the letter delivered.'

I ignored him too.

Did I, in fact, have any future in the firm? And did I really care?

KEBLE COLLEGE was near Oxford University's Museum of Natural History. I parked in Museum Road and walked back to the college.

'I've come to see a student, Benjamin Roberts,' I said to the man in a smart blue jersey who intercepted me in the entrance archway. 'Tell him I'm from the Balscott Lighting Factory.'

Benjamin Roberts appeared in three minutes flat with his hair unbrushed and no socks beneath his black leather shoes. He was six foot four or five and towered over me at just five foot eight.

'You're from the Balscott factory?'

'Is there anywhere quiet we could go and talk?' I asked.

We walked along a gravel path down the side of a building and then up some steps to a dining hall. Benjamin and I sat down across from each other. 'Now,' he said. 'What's all this about?'

'Benjamin—' I said, starting.

'Ben,' he interrupted.

'Sorry, Ben,' I said, corrected. 'I was a friend of your uncle Jolyon.'

He looked down. 'Such a shame,' he said. 'I'll miss him.' He looked up at me. 'But what have you to do with the factory?'

'Your uncle Jolyon told me you'd recently been to Bulgaria.'

'Yes,' he said. 'A group from the skiing club went to Borovets.'

'But your uncle also said you went to see the factory.'

'There isn't any factory, is there?' he said.

'You tell me,' I said. 'You're the one that went to see it.'

He didn't answer but sat looking at me. 'Who are you?' he asked. 'And what are you after?'

'I'm not after anything,' I said. 'Except to be left alone.'

'So why are you here?'

'Someone is trying to kill me,' I said.

'Who is trying to kill you?' he asked. 'And why?'

'I don't know who,' I said. 'Not yet. But I think I may know why. I am Nicholas Foxton, a financial adviser with Lyall and Black. Your uncle approached me because he was worried that the Bulgarian factory project was a scam. He had been shown photographs of the factory buildings, but you then told him that they didn't actually exist. So he asked me to look into it, to check that it wasn't a rotten egg of an investment.'

I went on, 'I think it is a rotten egg of an investment. Your family money was the key to everything because the private finance for the factory triggered the public funding for all the houses. Someone has been defrauding the European Union out of a hundred million euros by obtaining grants towards the cost of building a light-bulb factory and hundreds of homes that don't actually exist, and never will. And that same someone is trying to kill me before I can prove it, and before I find out who they are.'

I paused, and Ben Roberts sat staring at me.

'And,' I said, 'I believe your uncle may have been murdered for the same reason.'

'Uncle Jolyon wasn't murdered, he died of a heart attack,' Ben Roberts said. 'At least, he had a heart attack and then he drowned.'

Ben looked down again. Jolyon Roberts had died only four days previously. It was still very recent—very raw.

'Did you know he was drunk when he drowned?' I asked.

'He couldn't have been,' Ben said, looking up at me.

'Because he didn't drink?' I said.

'Never,' he said. 'He never touched alcohol.'

'Tell me about your trip to Bulgaria,' I said. 'When you went to see the factory.'

'There's nothing there,' he said. 'Nothing at all. The locals have never heard of any plans to build a factory, let alone the houses.'

'Are you sure you were in the right place?' I asked.

He glanced at me. 'Of course I'm sure. I took all the details with me so that I would be able find it.'

'Where was it meant to be?' I asked.

'Close to a village called Gorni, south of Sofia. But, when I saw the site, it was nothing more than a toxic waste dump left over from the Soviet era.'

'So what have you done about it?' I asked. 'Your family has invested a lot of money into the project.'

'Yeah, and lost it all too.' He sounded resigned to the loss.

'Aren't you even going to try to get it back?'

'I don't expect so,' Ben said. 'My father is worried that the family name will be discredited. What he means is that we will be shown up to have been bloody fools—fools that were easily separated from their money. He is furious, but mostly because he was talked into it by Uncle Jolyon and some financial adviser chap.'

'Gregory Black?' I asked.

'He's the one,' he said.

'So your father says to forget five million pounds, just like that?'

'It's only money,' he said almost flippantly. 'Money is fairly easy to replace. It's not like one's family reputation. It can take generations to repair damage to one's family's standing.'

It sounded to me that he was quoting his father.

'But it's not possible to replace your uncle Jolyon,' I said.

'That's surely all the more reason to forget about the whole thing. If the stress of this factory business gave Uncle J his heart attack, then we should let sleeping dogs lie.'

'I believe your uncle was murdered. Don't you want justice?'

'Would that bring him back?' he said angrily. 'Of course it wouldn't. And anyway, I believe that you are wrong.' He stood up. 'What is it you're really after? Money? Money or you'll go to the papers?'

I sat still on the bench. 'I don't want your money,' I said calmly.

He sat down again and stared at me. 'Well, Mr Foxton, what is it that you *do* want?' he asked. 'And why have you come here?'

'I need to find out more about your family's investment in the Bulgarian project,' I said. 'I simply don't have enough information to take my concerns to the authorities. They'd probably laugh at me. All I have are some copies of the original transaction report, some emails between someone in Brussels and a man in Bulgaria, and a sack load of suspicion. And, now that your uncle is dead, I can't ask *him*.'

'So why don't you go and ask Gregory Black?' he said.

'Because I'm not altogether sure that I trust him.'

'OK. I'll speak to my father about it,' Ben said. 'But I can tell you now, he won't like it, and he probably won't talk to you.'

'Ask him anyway,' I said.

'How do I contact you?' he asked.

'Leave a message on my mobile.' I gave him the number.

'I'm going home tonight for the weekend,' Ben said. 'I'll try to find the right moment to speak to him on Sunday afternoon. He's always at his most relaxed after a good Sunday lunch.'

I hoped it would be soon enough.

WHEN I RETURNED to Jan's place in Lambourn at four thirty, I found her, Claudia and my mother sitting round the kitchen table drinking wine.

'Bit early isn't it? I said, declining a glass of Chardonnay.

'Early?' Claudia said with a giggle. 'We started at lunchtime.'

The others giggled with her.

What a fine state of affairs, I thought. I was trying to keep us alive and my mother and fiancée were drunk.

I went upstairs to fetch my computer. I then used Jan's broadband to connect to the Internet, and checked my emails. Nestled among the usual collection from fund managers was one from Patrick Lyall. He had clearly become fed up waiting for me to return his call telling him where to send the letter.

'Nicholas,' he had written, 'as you have not replied to my call asking for your whereabouts, I have no option but to deliver the attached letter to you by email. I hope that you soon come to your senses and start giving the firm the priority it deserves.'

I clicked on the attachment. It was a letter from the lawyer, Andrew

Mellor, acting on behalf of Lyall & Black. The letter was to the point.

Mr Foxton,

In accordance with the Employment Act 2008, I am writing to inform you that your employer, Lyall & Black and Co. Ltd hereby wish to give notice that they consider your recent behaviour to be far below the standard expected from an employee in your position. Consequently, Lyall & Black and Co. Ltd, hereby issue you with a formal warning as to your future conduct. Furthermore, you are requested and required to attend a disciplinary meeting with Patrick Lyall and Gregory Black at the company offices in Lombard Street, London, at nine o'clock on Monday morning.

Yours sincerely,

Andrew Mellor, LLB

It sounded to me that, this time, I really was about to be fired.

Strangely, I didn't seem to care any more.

On Saturday morning I left the three women nursing their hangovers while I went to visit Billy Searle in the Great Western Hospital in Swindon.

'So who knocked you off your bike?' I asked him.

'Don't you bloody start,' he said. 'The fuzz have been asking me nothing else but that since I woke up.'

'So why don't you tell them?' I said.

'I'd rather go on living, thank you very much.'

'So it wasn't an accident?' I said.

'I didn't say that. It might have been.'

'How much longer are you going to be here?' I asked him. He clearly wasn't going anywhere soon as he was firmly attached to the bed by a weights contraption that was pulling on his right leg.

'About another week,' he said. 'At least, that's what they tell me. They need to apply something called a fixator to my leg but they can't do that until the traction has pulled everything straight. Then I'll be able to get up.'

'They thought you were going to die,' I said.

'No bloody chance,' he replied.

'And *I* was arrested for your attempted murder.'

'Yeah,' he said. 'So I heard. Serves you right.' He laughed.

'What for?' I said.

'For being such a boring bastard. You were much more fun as a jock. Do you remember that time we all got thrown out of that hotel in Torquay after your big win at Newton Abbot?'

I remembered it well. 'It was all your fault,' I said. 'You poured champagne into their grand piano.'

'Yeah, well, so maybe I did,' he said. 'But it was a crap piano anyway.'

Billy and I laughed together at the memory.

'Those were the days,' he said. 'Carefree and bloody stupid we were.'

For both of us, it seemed, fun had been on the wane recently.

'So to whom do you owe a hundred grand?' I asked. 'The same guy who tried to kill you?' He didn't answer. He just looked at me. 'Or was he just trying to give you a reminder to pay up?'

'Did the bloody cops tell you to ask me that?' he said crossly.

'No, they don't know I'm here,' I said. 'Billy, I'm just trying to help you.'

'I don't need anyone's help,' he said explosively.

'That's why you ended up in here. Next time, it might be the morgue.'

He lay back against the hospital pillows and said nothing.

'All right,' I said. 'If you won't tell me who, at least tell me why you owe someone a hundred thousand.'

He thought for a while, debating whether or not to tell me. 'I won a race I should have lost,' he said finally.

'What do you mean, a race you should have lost?'

'I told him I'd lose, but then I won it,' he said. 'I did it on purpose. I was so fed up with that bastard Vickers overtaking me in the championship, I was trying to win on everything I rode. Fat lot of good it did me. I was bloody second yet again'

'So who was it that you told you'd lose the race?'

He thought for a moment. 'Sorry, mate,' he said. 'I can't tell you that. My life wouldn't be worth tuppence.'

'Is he a bookie?' I asked.

'No,' he said with certainty. 'He's a bloody nob.'

I expect, to Billy, anyone who spoke the Queen's English without a liberal scattering of swearwords would be classed as a 'nob'.

'Which nob in particular?' I asked.

'I'm not saying,' he said. 'And if I did you wouldn't believe it.'

'And does this nob still want his hundred thousand?'

'Expect so,' he said. 'That's what he lost because I won the race.'

'Tell him you'll enlighten the cops as to the identity of your attacker if he doesn't leave you alone.'

'Don't be bloody naive,' he said. 'That would get me killed for sure.'

'Sounds to me like you're in trouble if you do say who attacked you, and also if you don't.'

'You're right,' he said. 'Once you say *yes* to them the first time, you're hooked for life. There's no way out.' He leaned his head back against the pillows and I thought there were tears in his eyes.

'Billy, there never will be a way out unless you fight back.'

'Well, count me out,' he said adamantly. 'I am not going to be first over the top to be shot down. I value my jockey's licence.'

'So how often have you stopped one?' I asked.

'About ten times altogether,' he said. 'Spread over three years or so. But I decided there would be no more when Frank Miller broke his leg, and I finally had the chance to be champion jockey.'

'But then young Mark Vickers pops up to beat you.'

'The bastard,' he said with feeling. 'It's not bloody fair.'

Life wasn't fair, I thought. Ask anyone with cancer.

JAN SETTER had already left for the races by the time I arrived back at her house at noon.

'How much longer do we need to stay here?' Claudia asked. 'I want to go home.'

'I do too, my darling. We will go home as soon as it's safe.'

I logged on to the Internet and used online banking to check on my personal accounts. Things might get quite tight if I did lose my job at Lyall & Black. While I might handle investments for others of millions of pounds, my own nest egg was much more modest.

If I did get fired, I might need to live off my savings for a while. And then what would I do? Billy had accused me of being boring but it wasn't me that was boring, I decided, it was my job. I needed more excitement in my life, more adrenalin rushing through my veins—but not necessarily due to having a silenced pistol pointed at me.

But what could I do? I was trained and qualified only to be a financial adviser. But what I wanted to be most was a jockey, or a rodeo-rider, or a free-fall skydiving instructor, or . . .

Bugger my dodgy neck.

9

Sunday was a day of rest. 'You stay in bed,' I said to Claudia. 'I'll fetch you some breakfast.'

I brought her a cup of coffee and some muesli. 'Isn't Jan lovely?' she said. 'We had a long chat yesterday while you were out.'

'What did you talk about?' I asked.

'Life in general,' she said obliquely. 'Stuff like that.'

'Did you tell her about . . . you know?'

Why was the 'c' word so difficult to use?

'I started to but then your mother came in, and I'm still not sure it's time to tell her yet.'

'But when will it be time? Now seems as good a time as any.'

'I suppose you're right,' she said. 'I just feel . . .' She stopped.

'What?' I said.

'I suppose I don't want her to be disappointed in me.'

'Don't be daft,' I said. 'She loves you.'

'Only because she thinks I'm her pathway to grandchildren.'

'That's not true,' I said, but I did wonder if she was right.

'She won't love me if I marry you and we find I can't have any babies. She will then see me not as a pathway but as an obstacle.'

She was almost in tears.

'Darling,' I said. 'Please don't upset yourself. OK. If you don't want to, we won't tell her. Not yet.'

But we would have to tell her if, and when, Claudia's hair started falling out.

THE REST OF SUNDAY seemed to drag on interminably with me forever wondering how Ben Roberts was faring with his father. But, as I was still reluctant to leave my mobile phone switched on, I would have no way of knowing anyway.

My mother, with Jan helping, cooked roast beef for lunch with all the trimmings, the wonderful smells even enticing Claudia downstairs in her dressing gown.

'I can't tell you how long it's been since I had a proper Sunday lunch in this house,' Jan said as we sat down at the kitchen table.

Afterwards, I went to make some calls from Jan's office. First I used her land line to access my voicemail remotely. There were four new messages, all from Chief Inspector Flight, and each one threatened me with arrest if I didn't come forward to speak to him. He read out a number where he could always be reached, and I wrote it down on the notepad beside the telephone.

But there was no message from Ben Roberts. Perhaps he hadn't yet found the right moment to speak to his father.

Next, I called DCI Tomlinson's mobile number, taking care to dial 141 first. 'Sorry,' I said, 'if you aren't working on Sunday.'

'I am working,' he said. 'I'm in my office.'

'Do you have any news for me? Was the dead man Bulgarian?'

'We don't know yet. His image and fingerprints haven't turned up on anything. Still waiting for the DNA analysis. But I can tell you one thing. The forensic boys tell me the gun matches.'

'Matches what?' I asked.

'The gun found in the bush outside your mother's cottage was definitely the same gun that killed Herb Kovak, and they're pretty sure the same gun was also used to shoot at you in Finchley.'

'Does that mean Chief Inspector Flight is now off my back?'

'I wouldn't exactly say that,' he said. 'He's still hopping mad.'

'Yes,' I said. 'I know. He's left messages on my phone.'

'Speak to him,' Tomlinson said. 'That's probably all he wants.'

We disconnected. I wasn't going to call DCI Flight from here. Dialling 141 might prevent the number appearing on caller-ID but the police could still obtain it from the telephone company. And while I trusted Chief Inspector Tomlinson not to go to the trouble of finding where I was from the call, I didn't trust DCI Flight.

So, at about five o'clock, I drove into the outskirts of Swindon and parked in a pub car park before switching on my mobile and calling the Gloucestershire detective.

'DCI Flight,' he said crisply, answering at the first ring.

'This is Nicholas Foxton,' I said.

'Ah,' he said. 'And about time too.'

'Have you spoken to DCI Tomlinson and Superintendent Yering?'

'Yes,' he said slowly. 'I have.'

'Good,' I said. 'So who was the man at my mother's cottage?'

'Mr Foxton,' he replied curtly. 'It is *me* who needs to ask *you* some questions, not the other way round.'

'Ask away,' I said.

'What happened at your mother's cottage last Thursday evening?'

'A man with a gun broke in, we had a fight, and he fell down the stairs and broke his neck.'

'Is that all?' he asked.

'Isn't that enough?' I asked sarcastically. 'Oh, yes, and he was trying to stab me at the time he fell down the stairs.'

'We found a knife under the body,' he said. 'What happened exactly?'

'The man cut the power and the telephone,' I said. 'He broke a pane of glass in the kitchen to get in and, as he was climbing through the window, I hit him with a golf umbrella. He dropped the gun, which slid under the fridge. He then took a knife from the block and tried to stab me. I managed to get upstairs but the man followed. As he was attacking me, we struggled and both of us fell down the stairs. He came off worse. End of story.'

There was a lengthy pause, almost as if the chief inspector had not been listening to me.

'Hold on,' I said suddenly. 'I'll call you back.'

I hung up, switched my phone off, drove out of the pub car park and down the road. After about half a mile, a police car with blue flashing lights drove past me, going in the opposite direction.

I went round a roundabout and drove back to the pub, driving straight past without slowing down. The police car, still with its blue flashers on, had stopped so that it was blocking the pub car park entrance, and two uniformed policemen were getting out of it.

Was that a coincidence? No, I decided, it was not.

I obviously hadn't needed to ask DCI Flight if he still wanted to arrest me. I'd just seen the answer.

I made my way back to Lambourn, being careful not to speed or in any way attract the attention of any passing policeman.

I CAUGHT THE TRAIN from Newbury to Paddington just after seven o'clock on Monday morning, leaving the blue hire car in the station car park. As the train slowed to a stop in Reading, I turned on my phone and called my voicemail.

'You have two new messages,' said the familiar voice. The first was from

DCI Flight promising not to arrest me if I came to Cheltenham police station to be interviewed. Why did I not believe him?

The second was from Ben Roberts.

'Mr Foxton, I have spoken with my father,' his voice said. 'He is not willing to meet with you or to discuss the matter further. I must also ask that you do not contact me again. I'm sorry.'

He didn't actually sound very sorry and I wondered if his father had been standing next to him when he had made the call.

My investigating wasn't exactly going very well.

I turned off my phone and sat back in my seat as the train rushed along the metal towards London, and I wondered what the day would bring. I had to admit that I was nervous about the disciplinary meeting with Patrick and Gregory. Lyall & Black had been my life for five years and I had begun to really make my mark, bringing some high-worth clients to the firm. Over the next few years I might have expected to expand my own client base while giving up most of the responsibility of acting as one of Patrick's assistants. I might even have hoped to be offered a senior partner position.

However, I was now in danger of missing out completely.

But why? What had I done wrong? It wasn't me who was defrauding the European Union of a hundred million euros, so why was it me who was attending a disciplinary meeting?

Perhaps the only thing I had done incorrectly was to not go straight to Patrick, or to Jessica Winter, the compliance officer, as soon as Mr Roberts had expressed his concerns over Gregory and the Bulgarian factory project. I should never have tried to investigate things behind their backs.

And I would rectify that mistake today.

I caught the Circle Line tube from Paddington to Moorgate and then walked from there towards Lombard Street.

As I walked alongside the high walls of the Bank of England, I suddenly started to feel uneasy. For four days, I had been careful not to let anyone know where I was staying, yet here I was walking to an appointment at the offices of Lyall & Black, for a meeting with one of those I believed was responsible for trying to kill me.

I really didn't fancy finding another gunman waiting for me in the street outside my office building.

I slowed to a halt with people hurrying past me. I was less than a hundred yards away from the end of Lombard Street. It was as near as I got. I turned round, retraced my path, went into a coffee shop and ordered a cappuccino. I looked at my watch. It was ten to nine. Patrick and Gregory would be expecting me in ten minutes. What should I do?

My instinct at my mother's cottage had been right when I'd prevented Claudia from opening the door to the gunman. But I desperately needed to talk to someone about my suspicions, to set in motion an investigation into the Bulgarian affair. Surely then I would be safe, as killing me would be too late. If Ben Roberts's father wouldn't talk to me, who else should I speak to? It had to be Patrick. I turned on my mobile phone and rang the office number.

Mrs McDowd put me through. Patrick came on the line.

'Patrick,' I said. 'It's Nicholas. I won't be coming to the meeting. I need to talk to you alone, without Gregory knowing.'

'Nicholas,' he said formally. 'I must insist that you come into the office right now. Where are you?'

Where should I say? 'I'm at home. Claudia still isn't well. Where can I speak to you in private?'

'Here,' he said firmly and loudly. 'I will speak to you here, in the office, at the disciplinary meeting.'

'I'm sorry,' I said. 'But I will not be coming to the office today.'

'Listen to me,' he said. 'If you don't come into the office today, there seems little point in you coming back at all.'

He hung up.

I could imagine him going and telling Gregory I wasn't coming. I was just glad I hadn't told him the truth about where I was.

I caught the tube to Hendon Central, walked down Seymour Way to number 45 and let myself into Herb Kovak's flat. Sherri had gone home to America and there were a few letters lying on the mat. I picked them up and added them to the pile on the desk. I sat down on Herb's desk chair and opened his mail.

There were some utility bills and a letter from a building society complaining that they hadn't received the preceding month's interest on Herb's mortgage. It reminded me of the gym that also hadn't been paid. How many others were there? I wondered.

I KNEW PATRICK lived in Weybridge, because Claudia and I had been to his house for dinner. I also knew that his journey home involved catching a train at Waterloo. I planned to join him for some of it.

He usually left the office between six o'clock and half past, but I was at Waterloo waiting by five in case he was early; nevertheless, I very nearly missed him.

By twenty-five past six my eyes were so punch-drunk from scanning so many faces that my brain took several seconds to register that I had glimpsed a familiar one. I chased after him, thrust my ticket into the grey automatic barrier and ran down the platform.

I leapt aboard the train just seconds before the doors slammed shut. As the train pulled out of Waterloo Station I began to work my way along the congested carriages.

Eventually I spotted him sitting in the relatively empty first-class section. He was reading a newspaper. He didn't even look up as I sat down on the empty seat next to him. 'Hello, Nicholas,' he said calmly. 'I was wondering when you would turn up.'

'I'm sorry,' I said, 'but I need to talk to you without Gregory knowing.'

'What about?' he asked.

'Colonel Roberts,' I said. 'He spoke to me nearly two weeks ago at Cheltenham races and again at Sandown a week last Saturday.'

'So, tell me, what did he speak to you about?'

'He was worried about an investment that the Roberts Family Trust had made in a light-bulb factory in Bulgaria. Mr Roberts's nephew had been to the site where the factory should be and there was nothing there, except a toxic waste dump.'

'Perhaps it hasn't been built yet. Or he was in the wrong place.'

'That's what I thought,' I said. 'But apparently Gregory had shown photos of the factory to Mr Roberts, and the nephew is adamant that he was in the right place.'

'You have spoken to the nephew?' Patrick asked.

'Yes, I have,' I said. 'I spoke to him on Friday.'

'And have you approached Gregory about it?'

'No,' I said. 'Gregory was so angry with me last week for all that Billy Searle business that I didn't like to.'

'How about Jessica?' he asked.

'No, not her either. I should have, but I haven't had the chance.'

'So why are you telling me? The Roberts Family Trust is a client of Gregory's. You need to speak to him, or to Jessica.'

'I know,' I said. 'I just hoped you could look into it for me.'

He laughed. 'You're not frightened of Gregory, are you?'

'Yes,' I said. And I was, very frightened indeed.

'Is this what all this being away from the office has been about?'

'Yes,' I said again.

He looked at me. 'Do you realise that you have placed your whole career on the line? Gregory and I agreed at the disciplinary meeting this morning, the one you were supposed to attend, that we would demand your resignation. However, Andrew Mellor advised us that we were obliged to hear your side of any story before we made a decision. So will you be in the office tomorrow so we can sort this out?'

'I would much rather you started an internal inquiry into the Bulgarian investment before I returned,' I said. 'I have reason to think that a multi-million-euro fraud is going on here, and that Gregory may be mixed up in it. I believe that the Bulgaria business may have something to do with why Herb was killed.'

'But that's ridiculous. Next you'll be accusing Gregory of murder.'

I said nothing but just sat there looking at him.

'Oh, come on, Nicholas,' he said. 'That's madness.'

'Madness it may be,' I said. 'But I'm not coming into the office until I'm certain that I'd be safe.'

He thought for a moment. 'Come home with me now and we'll sort this out tonight. We can call Gregory from there.'

The train pulled into Esher Station.

'No,' I said, jumping up. 'I'll call you tomorrow morning.'

I rushed through the door and onto the platform.

I didn't want Patrick telling Gregory where I was—not tonight, nor on any other night.

BY THE TIME I made it back to Lambourn, the ladies were in bed and the house was in darkness save for a single light left on for me in the kitchen. I was hungry and made myself a cheese sandwich.

I then sat eating it at the kitchen table, washing it down with a glass of orange juice.

It had been a good day, I decided. I still had a job and I had finally spoken to Patrick about my concerns. Whether or not he believed me was another matter. But surely he was duty-bound to start an investigation and bring Jessica Winter into the loop.

If Gregory, or whoever, was trying to kill me to prevent an investigation into the fraud being started, then surely I would be out of danger once it had, because killing me then would only reinforce the need for the investigation to continue. Unless he felt he had nothing more to lose and killed me out of revenge for uncovering his scheme.

Either way, I was going to lie low for a few more days yet.

TUESDAY DAWNED bright and sunny. Talking to Patrick had set my mind more at ease and I felt I was getting somewhere at last.

I took the car out to call Chief Inspector Tomlinson. In the light of the episode at the Swindon pub, I decided that calling on the move was the best policy, hence I started to dial the chief inspector's number as I was travelling along the M4 motorway between Newbury and Reading. But the phone rang in my hand before I had a chance to complete the number.

'Nicholas Foxton,' I said, answering.

'Hello, Mr Foxton, it's Ben Roberts.'

'Yes, Ben,' I said. 'How can I help?'

'My father has changed his mind. He'd now like to talk to you.'

'Great,' I said. 'When and where?'

'He wonders if you would like to come to Cheltenham races tomorrow evening as his guest. It's the Hunter Chase evening meeting and he's hired a private box. He says he would like to talk to you at the end of the racing.'

'Will you be there?' I asked.

'I will to start with but I'll have to leave early to get back to Oxford for a club dinner.'

'Can I get back to you?' I said. 'I need to talk to my fiancée.'

'Bring her with you,' he said immediately. 'It's a buffet supper not a sit-down so numbers are not a problem. And I'll be leaving before the pudding so there'll be plenty of that left, anyway.' He laughed.

I couldn't help but like Ben Roberts. 'OK,' I said. 'I'd love to.'

'I'll tell my dad. He'll be pleased,' he said. 'See you then.'

We hung up.

Was it sensible to go back to Cheltenham? I wondered. It was DCI Flight's home patch and the racecourse would be full of Gloucestershire policemen. But why should I worry? After all, I hadn't done anything wrong.

Next I called Chief Inspector Tomlinson.

'Where are you?' the chief inspector asked.

'I'm on the motorway,' I said. 'I want a meeting with you and Superintendent Yering. And DCI Flight, if he wants to be there. As long as he doesn't arrest me. Arrange it for Thursday if you can.'

'What's the meeting for?' he asked.

'So I can tell you why I think Herb Kovak was killed and why our dead gunman was also trying to kill me.'

'What's wrong with today?' he said. 'Or tomorrow?'

'There's someone else I want to talk to first.'

'Who?' he said. 'I told you to leave the investigating to us.'

'I intend to,' I said. 'That's why I want the meeting.' But I also wanted to learn more about the Bulgarian investment before it.

'OK,' he said. 'I'll fix it. How do I contact you?'

'Leave a message on this number, or I'll call you again tomorrow.'

I disconnected. I called the office and Mrs McDowd answered.

'Hello, Mrs McDowd,' I said. 'Mr Nicholas here. Can I speak to Mr Patrick, please?'

'You're a naughty boy,' she said in her best headmistressy voice. 'You mustn't upset Mr Gregory so. His heart can't take it.'

I didn't reply. As far as I was concerned, the sooner his heart gave out the better. I waited as she put me through.

'Hello, Nicholas,' said Patrick. 'Where are you?'

Why was everyone so obsessed with my whereabouts?

'Have you spoken to Jessica?' I asked.

'Not yet. I've been reviewing the file myself this morning. I intend to discuss the matter with Gregory this afternoon.'

'Mind your back,' I said.

'Be serious,' Patrick said.

'I am being serious, very serious,' I replied. 'If I was you, I'd speak to Jessica first and then both of you talk to Gregory.'

'I'll see,' Patrick said.

Patrick and Gregory had been partners for a long time and I couldn't really blame him for checking things himself before he brought in the compliance officer.

'You might need someone who can read Bulgarian,' I said. 'I'll call you again tomorrow to see how you're getting on.'

I hung up and glanced in the rearview mirror. There were no signs of any flashing blue lights. I drove sedately back to Lambourn.

'I WANT TO go home,' my mother said, meeting me in Jan's kitchen as I walked in from the car.

'And you will,' I said. 'Just as soon as I'm sure it's safe.'

'But I want to go home now. We've been here long enough.'

'All right,' I said. 'I promise I'll take you home tomorrow.'

I'd take her tomorrow before I went on to the races. But there was more unrest from Claudia. 'I want to go home,' she said when I went up to our bedroom.

She was standing by the bed packing her things into her suitcase.

'Have you been talking to my mother?' I asked.

'Maybe,' she said.

'Darling,' I said. 'I've arranged a meeting with the police on Thursday to sort everything out. We can go home after that.'

'Why can't you have this meeting tonight or tomorrow?'

'Because I have to talk to someone first and I'm seeing them at Cheltenham races tomorrow evening.'

She sat down on the bed. 'I don't understand. If the man who was trying to kill you was himself killed then why are we still hiding?'

'There may be others,' I said. 'I'll tell you what. I've promised Mum I'll take her back to her cottage tomorrow so why don't we all go back to Woodmancote with Mum around lunchtime, and you can come with me to the races in the evening.'

I WAS WORRIED about finding Mum's cottage sealed up as a 'scene of crime' with 'Police—Do Not Cross' tape across the porch and padlocks on the doors. But when we arrived the only thing different was a new dangling wire that connected the building to a telegraph pole in the lane—the hasty repair to the cut telephone wire.

My mother let us in through the front door using her key.

It was all the same as before, with no evidence to show that a ferocious life-or-death struggle had gone on here less than a week previously. However, none of us could resist staring at the base of the stairwell, at the place where we had last seen the gunman.

The police had even secured the kitchen window, fixing a piece of plywood over the broken windowpane.

Claudia and I left for the races just after four o'clock. 'Who is it we are going to see?' she asked as we turned into the car park.

'A man called Shenington,' I said. 'Viscount Shenington. And he's hired a private box.'

'Very posh,' she replied, making a face.

We might be glad of the box, I thought, as we climbed out of the car. A weather front had moved in, bringing clouds and rain. Evening meetings like this one at Cheltenham, with no floodlighting, relied on bright summer evenings. The last race might be run in darkness.

'And who is this Viscount Shenington exactly?' Claudia asked, as we walked to the entrance huddled together under her minute umbrella.

'He's a racehorse owner and the senior trustee of the Roberts Family Trust. They're clients of Lyall and Black.'

'Oh,' she said, losing interest. Was my job really that boring? 'So why do you need to talk to this man before you see the police?'

I had purposely not told Claudia anything about my suspicions concerning the Bulgarian factory and housing project. She had far too many of her own problems to contend with.

'The Trust,' I said, 'has made an investment in something which I think is a front for fraud. I need to learn more about it before I speak to the police. I have some questions to ask him, that's all.'

'Will it take long?' she asked.

'He wants to speak to me after the racing.'

'Oh,' she said again, this time sounding disappointed. 'So we're here till the bitter end.'

'I'm afraid so,' I said. 'But he has invited us to his box for the whole time, and there'll be food and drink available.'

She perked up when she discovered that the box was a magnificent glass-fronted affair with a wonderful view over the racecourse. It was full of guests. Ben Roberts marched over with outstretched hand.

'Mr Foxton.'

'Ben,' I replied. 'Nice to see you again. My fiancée, Claudia.'

Ben shook her hand. 'I'm Ben Roberts. Come and meet my father.'

He led the way across the room to a group of men standing in the far corner. Ben's father towered above the others by a good six inches. The 'tall' gene was clearly alive and well in all the Roberts family.

'Dad,' said Ben. 'This is Mr Foxton and Claudia, his fiancée.'

'Delighted to meet you,' I said, offering my hand.

He looked down at me and slowly put forward his hand to shake. It was hardly the most friendly of welcomes, but I hadn't really expected anything else. I knew that he didn't truly want to speak to me.

'Good evening, Mr Foxton,' he said. 'Good of you to come.' He turned towards Claudia. 'You too, my dear. Have a drink. And some food.' He waved towards the buffet table. 'We'll speak later.'

He went back to his conversation.

'Good,' said Ben with considerably more warmth. 'What would you like to drink? Champagne?'

'Lovely,' Claudia said.

'Fruit juice for me, please,' I said. 'I'm driving.'

Claudia and I took our drinks out onto the private balcony and I briefly turned on my phone to check my voicemail. There was a new message from Chief Inspector Tomlinson.

'The meeting is fixed for tomorrow morning, Thursday,' his voice said, 'eleven a.m. at Paddington Green police station.'

Not back in their holding cells, I hoped. I'd had my fill of those.

We braved the damp conditions to go down to the weighing room and parade ring after the second race. We went to support Jan, who had a runner in the third.

'Not much chance, I'm afraid,' she said as she emerged from the weighing room with a small saddle over her arm. 'The horse is fine but the owner insists his son should ride it and he's only eighteen. He's still just a boy and this mare needs to be held up to the last. She gets lazy if she's in front too soon.'

She rushed off towards the saddling boxes to prepare the horse. Claudia and I stayed under the cover in front of the weighing room and, presently, Jan's mare came into the parade ring, closely followed by her and the horse's owner.

I scanned my racecard to see who it was and, instead, noticed that one of the other runners was owned by Viscount Shenington. I looked around and spotted him huddling under a large golf umbrella. He was talking to the horse's trainer, the gossip, Martin Gifford.

Claudia and I decided to stay down at the weighing room for the race rather than to go back up to the grandstand box. We could watch all the action on the big-screen television. Also, I thought, I didn't really want to have to talk to Martin Gifford, who would surely go up to the box with his owner to watch their horse run.

But, on that score, I was sadly wrong.

Martin Gifford came to stand on the weighing-room terrace right next to me to watch the race on the television.

'Hi, Foxy,' he said. 'Penny for your thoughts.' He seemed to have forgotten our little spat at Sandown. 'What a horrid day.'

'Yes,' I agreed.

'I'm quite surprised you're here for the hunter chasers,' he said. 'I wouldn't be if I didn't have this damn runner. I tried to talk the owner out of running it but he insisted. It should win, though.'

Now what was I to make of that? Martin Gifford made a habit of saying his horses had no chance, and then they went on to win. I knew that from the last meeting at Cheltenham, when both his horses had won after he'd told me they wouldn't. But was the reverse also true? Was this horse, in fact, a useless no-hoper?

I looked at my racecard again. A rating was printed alongside each horse. The higher the rating the better the horse. Martin's horse had a high rating. Perhaps he really was telling the truth.

We watched on the television as the horses jumped off from the start.

'I could do with this one winning,' said Martin. 'Perhaps then the bloody owner will pay me some of his training fees.'

I turned my head towards him. 'Slow payer, is he?' I asked.

'Bloody right,' said Martin, without taking his eyes from the screen. 'But not so much slow, more like dead stop. Shenington owes me a fortune. Claims he hasn't got it. Says he's nearly bankrupt.'

Interesting, I thought. The Roberts Family Trust, it seems, could happily lose £5 million on an investment in Bulgaria, but the senior trustee couldn't pay his training fees because he was broke.

'But Lord Shenington must have pots of money,' I said.

'Apparently, that's not so,' said Martin. 'Seems his father, the old Earl, still keeps his fingers very tightly on the family purse. And what money Shenington did have of his own, he's lost.'

'Lost?' I said.

'Gambling,' Martin said. 'On the horses, and on the casino tables.'

'So why are you still running his horses?' I asked. 'Did he pay the entry fee for this race?'

'No, of course not,' he said. 'I paid it. He has promised me all the prize money if it wins.'

We both watched on the screen as the horses swung past the grandstand for the first time. The daylight was now so dismal that it wasn't easy to spot which horse was which, but they were all racing closely packed and there was still a long way to go.

The runners passed the grandstand for the second time, and only when the horses swung onto their final circuit was it feasible to tell them apart, from the colours on the backs of the jockeys' silks. Both Jan's and Martin's horses were in the leading group, although even those appeared tired as they swung towards the finishing straight. Three and a half miles was a long way in such heavy going.

Just as Jan had feared, the young jockey on her horse took the lead too soon. Even on the screen, it was clear to see that the horse didn't enjoy being on its own in front and it started to falter and weave about, almost coming to a stop before the last fence. It would have probably refused to jump altogether if another horse hadn't galloped past it and given it a lead.

That horse, too, swung from side to side as the jockey kept looking round, as if he was wondering where all the other horses had gone. The answer was that most of them had pulled up on their way down the hill, figuring, quite rightly, that they didn't have any chance of winning.

Only three of the original fifteen starters actually crossed the finishing line, with Martin Gifford's horse home first. Jan's mare was second, finishing at a walk some twenty lengths behind the winner.

The rain eased a little and Claudia and I made our way over to the white plastic rails that ran across between the parade ring and the unsaddling enclosure, to watch the exhausted horses come in.

Jan wasn't pleased. But Martin Gifford was beaming from ear to ear, which was more than could be said for his horse's owner. Viscount Shenington looked fit to explode, and he gave the victorious rider such a look that I wondered if this young man, like Billy Searle before him, had also won a race which he'd agreed to lose.

And Lord Shenington was certainly a 'nob'.

Perhaps I would look at the records to see if Billy had ever ridden any of Shenington's horses.

'I'm freezing,' said Jan, coming over after the horses had been led away. 'You fancy a whisky mac to warm up? I'm buying.'

As the rain began to fall heavily once again, the three of us scampered over to the Arkle Bar in the grandstand.

'How well do you know Viscount Shenington?' I asked Jan as we sipped our mixture of Scotch whisky and ginger wine.

'I know of him,' she said. 'But not well enough to speak to. His father is a long-standing member of the Jockey Club.'

'He's a client of the firm's,' I said. 'But not one of mine. Do you know if he's got any financial troubles?'

'How would I know anything about his finances?' she said. 'You're the specialist in that department.'

True, but he wasn't my client, and I could hardly ask Gregory.

We watched the fourth race on a television in the bar, the winner again coming in exhausted and smothered in thick mud.

Jan finished her drink. 'I've had enough. I'm going home.'

'Can't we go too?' Claudia asked, shivering.

'Not yet,' I said. 'I've still got to talk to Viscount Shenington. I'm sure Jan could take you back to Mum's place, if you'd like. It's only a mile or so down the road from here.'

'No problem,' said Jan.

'OK,' said Claudia. 'But please don't be long.'

'I won't,' I said. 'I promise.'

SHENINGTON'S BOX was much emptier when I went back up before the fifth race, and there was no sign of Ben. 'He had to go back to Oxford,' explained his father as I removed my Barbour and hung it on a hook by the door. 'He said to say goodbye.'

'He's a nice young man,' I said. 'You should be proud of him.'

'Thank you,' he replied. 'But he can be a bit idealistic at times.'

'Isn't that a good thing in the young?' I said.

'Not always,' he replied, staring at the wall above my head. 'We all have to live in the real world. To Ben, everything is either right or wrong, black or white. There's no middle ground, no compromise, and little or no tolerance of other people's failings.'

It was a statement, I thought, born out of conflict between father and son. Perhaps Ben didn't easily tolerate his father's gambling.

Shenington seemed almost to snap out of a trance.

'Where's your lady?' he asked, looking around.

'She was really cold,' I said. 'A friend of mine has given her a lift to my mother's house.'

'I don't blame her,' he said. 'It's a cold night, and many of my guests have already gone. The rest will probably go before the last race.'

I ventured out onto the balcony and peered through the gloom as another long-distance hunter chase became a test of stamina.

As Shenington had predicted, almost all his remaining guests departed after the race. Finally, there was just Viscount Shenington and two other men in rather drab suits remaining, other than me. Even the catering staff seemed to have disappeared.

Suddenly I felt uneasy. But my concern was too late. One of the two men stood by the door to ensure no one could come in, while the other advanced towards me. He had a gun in his gloved hand.

'Mr Foxton, you are an extraordinarily difficult man to kill,' Shenington said, smiling slightly. 'You usually don't turn up when you're expected, and yet you came here so sweetly, like a lamb to the slaughter.'

He almost laughed.

I didn't.

I'd been bloody careless.

10

'What do you want?' I asked.

'I want you dead,' Viscount Shenington said. 'So you can stop spreading your silly rumour that my brother was murdered.'

'But he was, wasn't he?' I said. 'How could you have killed your own brother? And for what? Money?'

'Everyone's on the make,' he said. 'I just want my share.'

'And is your share a hundred million euros?' I asked.

'Shut up,' he said loudly.

I took a deep breath and the cry for help began in my throat. But that was as far as it got. The man with the gun punched me in my abdomen, driving the air from my lungs and leaving me lying on the floor, gasping for breath. Then the man kicked me in the face, splitting my lip and sending my blood in a fine spray onto the carpet.

'Not in here, you fool,' Shenington said to him sharply.

At least they weren't going to kill me here. It might have been rather incriminating to leave a dead body in the corner of the box among the empty champagne bottles. 'It won't do you any good,' I said through my bleeding mouth. 'The police know I'm here.'

'I somehow doubt that,' Shenington replied. 'My information is that you've been avoiding them over the past week.'

'My girlfriend knows I'm here,' I said.

'Yes, so she does. When I've dealt with you, I'll deal with her too.'

I kept quiet. I'd opened my big mouth enough already. I could hear the public-address system outside. The last race had started.

'Now,' said Shenington to the men. 'Take him down now while the race is running.'

The two men came over and hauled me to my feet.

'Where are you taking me?' I asked.

Shenington said, 'Somewhere dark and quiet.'

The two men walked me past my coat, through the door, across the corridor, and into one of the deserted catering stations. The three of us descended to the ground in the caterer's lift.

The lift stopped and I was marched out of it, and then across the wet tarmac towards the north exit and the racecourse car parks beyond. On a night like this, with only a fraction of the usual crowd, the car parks were deserted.

Somewhere dark and quiet, Shenington had said.

My last, brief journey would most likely come to an end in a far corner of the car park. I tried to slow down but I was being frog-marched forwards. I tried to sit down, but they gripped my arms even tighter.

I'd have to shout for help, I thought, and chance another punch, but the commentator's voice was booming out through the public-address system, so would anyone hear me? There were only a few people about, hurrying home with their collars turned up against the rain.

'Horse!' a voice called loudly off to my right in warning. 'Loose horse!'

There is no doubt that horses have a homing instinct. Ask any trainer who has had a horse get loose and lost on the gallops. More often than not, the horse is found happily standing back in the stable yard, in its own box, and is usually home before the search party. Horses that get loose at the racecourse often dive back towards the place where they came out onto the course.

This particular loose horse came galloping down the horse-walk and attempted to negotiate the ninety-degree turn to get back into the parade ring. A combination of too sharp a bend and too much momentum, coupled with the wet surface, meant that the horse's legs slipped out from beneath it and it fell, crashing through the white plastic railings and sliding across the ground towards the three of us, its legs thrashing about wildly as it tried to regain its footing.

The men on either side of me instinctively took a step backwards, relaxing their hold on my arms. I stepped forwards, out of their clutches, and caught the horse by the reins. In one movement, as the animal managed to stand up, I swung myself onto its back and into the saddle.

I kicked the astonished horse in the belly and we galloped back the way it had come, down the horse-walk towards the racecourse.

'Stop!' shouted an official who was standing in my way, waving his arms about. I glanced behind me. The two men were in pursuit and one was reaching into his pocket for his gun. The official realised that I wasn't going to stop and flung himself aside. I kicked the horse again, and crouched as low as I could to provide the smallest target to the gunman.

I looked ahead. Even though the last race of the day was still in progress, out on the racecourse was definitely the safest place for me to be. Another official saw the horse galloping back towards him and he tugged frantically at the movable rail, closing it across the end of the horse-walk.

But I wasn't stopping. Stopping meant dying.

A rider communicates with his mount in a variety of ways. Pulling on the reins, cajoling with the voice or kicking with the feet. But the most powerful messages between horse and jockey are transmitted by the shifting of weight. Sit back and the horse will slow, but shift the weight forwards over his shoulders and the same horse will run like the wind.

I gathered my feet into the stirrup irons, stood up, shortened the reins, and crouched forwards over the horse's withers. The animal beneath me fully understood the 'go' message.

As we neared the end of the horse-walk, I kicked the horse once more. The animal knew what to do. I shifted my weight again, asking him to lengthen his stride and to jump, and to jump high.

We sailed over the rail with ease. The horse pecked slightly on landing, almost going down on its knees and, for a moment, I feared he was going to fall, but I pulled his head up with the reins and he quickly recovered his balance.

Left or right?

Left, I decided, pulling that way on the reins, away from the grandstand, and towards the safe, wide-open spaces of the racecourse.

The other horses were coming up the finishing straight towards me, but I was well to the side of them. My mount tried to turn, to run with the others, but I steered him away and galloped down to the far end of the finishing straight before stopping and looking back. The grandstand lights appeared unnaturally bright. It was difficult to tell if the two heavies were giving chase but I had to assume they were.

I turned the horse again and cantered up the hill, towards the farthest point on the racecourse away from the stands and the enclosures. What did I do now?

The nondescript blue hire car would be waiting for me in the racecourse car park, but its keys, together with my mobile phone and my wallet, were in the pockets of my Barbour, which I presumed was still hanging by the door in Shenington's box.

I watched as a vehicle turned onto the racecourse from where I had emerged from the horse-walk. I could see the headlights bumping up and down as it worked its way along the grass. Another vehicle followed it onto the grass but turned the other way. Both vehicles moved forwards, slowly driving round the course. If I stayed where I was then the two of them would close on me in a pincer movement.

But I had no intention of allowing a vehicle to come up close to me unless, and until, I knew for certain that Shenington and his heavies were not in it.

At Cheltenham, the racecourse, unlike those in America, was not a simple oval track, but two complete racecourses laid one on top of another, with an extra loop down one end. There was no way that these two vehicles would be able to corner me on their own, not unless I was careless, and I had been careless enough for one day.

I trotted the horse over to the edge of the racecourse property looking for an exit, but a high chain-link fence had been erected along its length.

'With that neck, I wouldn't ride a bike, let alone a horse,' the spinal specialist had said to me all those years ago. Yet here I was on horseback galloping round in the dark, but I felt completely safe and at home. I just had to make sure I didn't fall off.

I cantered the horse right along the fence in the hope there might be a gate. The fence was too high for any horse to jump, let alone a tired-out hunter chaser that should have been warm in his stable by this time of night.

The chain-link fence finally gave way to a hedge. I trotted the horse on along its length and finally found a gap in the undergrowth. The horse and I went through the gap and into a field. By this time, it was an almost completely black night. We moved forwards at a walk, the blind leading the blind. The animal must have been as confused as me as to where we were going, but he had been trained well and responded easily to my every command.

'Come on, boy,' I said quietly into his ear. 'Good boy.'

Suddenly, I thought I heard a man cough. I gently pulled the reins and the horse stopped and stood silently. I listened intently in the darkness. Had I been mistaken?

The man coughed again. Then he called out, in a language I didn't recognise. He was on the other side of the hedge, but I couldn't tell exactly how far away. A second man answered, again in a foreign tongue, and he was certainly further away still.

I held my breath and prayed that the horse wouldn't make a noise or jangle the bit in his mouth. The rain came to my aid, falling in heavy drops. The noise of the rain would mean that they would be unable to hear me moving on. I made some fairly gentle clicking noises and nudged the horse in the ribs with my foot.

We eventually came upon a gate, and it wasn't locked. I dismounted and led the horse through, closing the gate behind us.

A light suddenly came on, flooding the area with brightness and momentarily startling the horse.

Dammit!

The animal tossed his head up and down and neighed loudly. 'Good boy,' I said. The horse neighed a couple of times more.

The light was attached to the gable end of a wooden barn and had a motion sensor below it—a security light. I looked around. We were in a farmyard with more buildings beyond the barn.

I heard a whizzing sound close to my right.

The sound instantly made the hairs on my neck stand upright. I knew that noise because I'd heard it before in Lichfield Grove. It was the sound of a bullet passing by. I could hear shouting, foreign-language shouting.

I pulled the horse forwards and we ran round the corner of the barn away from the direction of the shouting. Another bullet whizzed past me and disappeared into the night.

I pulled myself back up onto the saddle, gathered the reins and set off again. We went across the farmyard and then down a drive that curved away into the darkness. Soon I could see headlights moving from right to left ahead of me, as a car moved along the Winchcombe road at the end of the drive.

We had now left the security lights behind, but I had to take a chance in the dark, as I kicked the horse forwards as fast as I dared.

I neared the road. I knew that I ought to go to the right towards Prestbury village and Cheltenham police station. I'd be safe there, and DCI Flight would finally get his interview.

Instead, I turned left towards Woodmancote, and Claudia.

How could I have been so stupid as to have told Shenington that she had gone to my mother's? If he had been the one who sent the broken-neck gunman there to kill me, and I had no doubt that it had been, he would know exactly where to find my mother's cottage.

I just hoped I would get there first.

Fortunately, at this time on a wet Wednesday, the road was quiet. Only a couple of times did I have to pull off onto the wide grass verge as cars came sweeping past. However, the noise of the metal horseshoes clickety-clacking on the tarmac as we cantered along sounded alarmingly loud in the night air.

I trotted the horse down the road towards the lane where my mother lived. The lane was actually the fourth arm of a crossroads and I was just approaching it from straight ahead when a car came along the other road and turned right into the lane. It had to be going to my mother's cottage as it was the only house down there.

I kicked the horse forwards and followed, keeping to the grass to deaden the noise of the hoofs.

Halfway down the lane, I slid off the horse's back and tied him to a tree, moving forward silently but quickly on foot.

I could now see the cottage. Shenington was standing by the front door, his face brightly lit by the outside light. I crept closer across the grass, towards the gravel drive.

'Viscount Shenington,' he was saying loudly. 'We met earlier at the races.'

'What do you want?' I could hear Claudia shouting from inside.

'I'm returning Mr Foxton's coat,' Shenington said. 'He left it in my box by mistake.' He was holding my coat out in front of him.

Don't open the door, I willed Claudia. PLEASE—DON'T OPEN THE DOOR.

She did, of course. I could hear her turning the lock.

My only chance was to act now. As the front door swung open, I ran for him, crunching across the gravel. He turned slightly towards the noise but I was on him before he had a chance to react.

I caught Shenington just above the knees in a full-blown flying tackle. The two of us crashed to the ground together, the whiplash causing his upper body and head to take most of the impact.

Shenington was in his mid-sixties and I was less than half his age, and I had the strength brought on by desperation and anger. I jumped up quickly and I sat on him, twisting my fingers in his hair and forcing his head down into a rain-filled puddle on the drive. How did he like it, I wondered, to have his face held under water?

Claudia stood, shocked and staring, in the doorway.

'Nick,' she wailed. 'Stop it! Stop it! You'll drown him!'

'This is the man who has been trying to kill me,' I said, not releasing my grip.

'That doesn't mean you can kill *him*,' she said.

I reluctantly let go of his hair and rolled him over. I couldn't tell if he was breathing or not. I didn't care.

'He's got a gun,' Claudia said, fear apparent again in her voice.

He'd been lying on it. I leaned down and picked it up. I left Shenington where he lay and went inside to call Cheltenham police station.

'Can I please speak to DCI Flight,' I said to the officer who answered. 'I want to give myself up.'

'What have you done?' he said.

'Ask DCI Flight,' I replied. 'He's the one who wants me.'

'He's not here at the moment,' the officer said. 'Some bloody lunatic has stolen a horse up at the racecourse and every spare man is out looking for him.'

'Ah, I might just be able to help you there,' I said. 'The horse in question is tied up outside my mother's house in Woodmancote, right outside where I'm standing now.'

'How the hell did it get there?'

'I rode him. I'm the bloody lunatic everyone is looking for.'

DETECTIVE CHIEF INSPECTOR FLIGHT was far from amused. He had spent more than an hour trudging across the dark, muddy racecourse looking for the horse while wearing his best leather shoes.

'How is Viscount Shenington?' I asked. We were in one of the interview rooms at Cheltenham police station.

'Still alive,' he said. 'But only just. They're working on him at the hospital. The doctor says that, even if he does survive, his brain is likely to have been permanently damaged due to being starved of oxygen for so long.'

Shame, I thought.

'You say that you simply tackled him and you didn't see that his nose and mouth were lying in the water?'

'I just thought he was winded by the fall,' I said. 'Only after I'd checked that Claudia was all right did I discover he was face down in a puddle. Then, of course, I rolled him over onto his back.'

'Did you not think of applying artificial respiration?' he asked.

I looked at him. 'The man had come there to kill me. Why would I try to save him? So that he could have another go?'

He looked up at the clock on the wall. It was well after midnight.

'We'll have to continue this in the morning,' he said, yawning.

'I have to be at Paddington Green police station by eleven,' I said.

THE MEETING at Paddington Green lasted for more than two hours. There were four police officers present, Detective Chief Inspectors Tomlinson and Flight, a detective inspector from the City of London Police Economic Crime Department—the Fraud Squad, and Superintendent Yering, who chaired the meeting.

At his request, I started from the beginning, outlining the events in chronological order from the day Herb Kovak had been gunned down at Aintree, right through to those of the previous evening at Cheltenham racecourse, and at my mother's cottage in Woodmancote.

'Viscount Shenington,' I said, 'seems to have been desperate for money due to his gambling losses and provided the five million pounds from the Roberts Family Trust in order to trigger the grants from the European Union. He gave his brother the impression that he had needed to be convinced to make the investment.'

'Perhaps he did to start with,' said DCI Flight, 'until he discovered the availability of the grants.'

'Maybe,' I said. 'But I think it's far more likely that the idea for stealing the EU grants came first and Shenington was simply brought in as the necessary provider of the priming money.'

'So he wasn't the only one involved?' Tomlinson said.

'Not at all,' I said. 'I've seen emails between a Uri Joram in the office of the European Commission in Brussels, and a Dimitar Petrov in Bulgaria.'

'How did you see them?' Tomlinson interrupted.

'On Gregory Black's computer,' I said. 'He was copied in to their correspondence. He's one of the senior partners at Lyall and Black, the firm where I work.' Or where I used to work.

'And what do you think he has to do with this?' he asked.

'I believe that Gregory Black probably found Shenington for Joram and Petrov. They would have needed someone with five million pounds to invest to trigger the larger sum from the EU. Shenington was a client of Gregory's, and who could be better, a man who controlled a wealthy family trust but was himself broke and in dire need of money to pay his gambling debts?'

'But what has all this to do with the death of Herbert Kovak?' asked DCI Tomlinson. That was *his* major concern.

'Herb Kovak had accessed the file with the emails between Joram and Petrov a few days before he was killed. And Gregory Black would have known, because Herb's name appeared on the recently accessed list. I saw it there. Perhaps Herb had asked some difficult questions about the project, questions that got him killed.'

I went on, 'In the last week or so, every time Gregory Black knew where I was, someone tried to kill me there. I now think that Shenington only changed his mind about wanting to talk to me, then asking me to the races, because I hadn't been turning up at my office. He as good as admitted it yesterday. He said I was a difficult man to kill because I usually didn't turn up when I was expected. Well, I was expected at a meeting with Gregory Black on Monday morning, and I'm now certain that I would have been killed if I'd gone to it. I probably wouldn't have even reached the office front door. I'd have been shot down in the street. Murdered in a public place, just like Herb Kovak was at Aintree.'

'It's time I spoke again to Gregory Black,' said DCI Tomlinson.

A total of three police cars made the trip across London to 64 Lombard Street. It was a quarter past two by the time we arrived at my office. Gregory should be just back from lunch.

'Can I help you?' Mrs McDowd said as the policemen entered.

'Can you tell me where I might find Mr Gregory Black?' said Detective Inspector Batten from the Fraud Squad.

At that point Gregory walked down the corridor.

'There he is,' said Mrs McDowd, pointing.

The detective inspector wasted no time. 'Gregory Black,' he said, taking hold of Gregory by the arm, 'I arrest you on suspicion of conspiracy to defraud, and suspicion of conspiracy to murder. You do not have to say anything, but it may harm your defence if you do not mention when questioned something which you later rely on in court. Anything you do say may be given in evidence.'

Gregory was stunned. 'But that's ridiculous,' he said. 'I've done nothing of the sort.'

Then he saw me. 'Is this your doing?' he demanded, thrusting his face belligerently towards mine. 'Some kind of sick joke?'

'Murder is never a joke,' said DI Batten. 'Take him away.'

Two uniformed officers moved forwards, handcuffed Gregory, and led him out through the glass door and into the lift.

'What's going on?' Patrick had appeared in the reception area, obviously summoned by the noise. 'What are these men doing here?'

'They are here to arrest Mr Gregory,' said Mrs McDowd.

'Arrest Gregory? But that's ridiculous. What for?'

'Conspiracy to defraud, and conspiracy to murder,' DI Batten said.

'Fraud? Murder? Who has he murdered?' Patrick demanded.

'No one,' said DI Batten. 'Suspicion of *conspiracy* to murder.'

Patrick wasn't to be deterred.

'So who then is he suspected of conspiring to murder?'

'Me,' I said, stepping forwards.

Patrick said nothing. He just stared at me.

LATER IN THE AFTERNOON, I went into my office for the first time in almost two weeks to find that Rory had moved himself into Herb's desk by the window. Diana was still where she had always been.

At the moment, I couldn't see Lyall & Black surviving as a firm past next week. We had all better start looking for new desks, by another firm's window.

There were nearly a hundred emails for me on the company server, plus twenty-eight messages on my voicemail, including two from Slim Fit Gym reminding me that they wanted Herb's locker back.

I went over to Herb's cubicle. The key was still pinned to the board. I took it off and put it in my pocket.

I sat down again at my desk and started going through the mass of emails but without really taking in any of the information contained in them. My heart simply wasn't in this job any more.

If and when Claudia beat this cancer, we would do something different, something together. Something more exciting. But maybe less dangerous.

I got up to leave. As I walked down the corridor I had to step over some big tied-up polythene bags stacked full of files and computers. The Fraud Squad was busily packing up the stuff from Gregory's office.

THE RECEPTIONIST at the Slim Fit Gym was pleased to see me. 'To be honest,' she said, 'it's beginning to smell a bit. There must be some dreadfully sweaty clothes in there.'

Herb's key fitted neatly into the heavy padlock on the locker, and I swung open the door. I leaned back. It smelled more than a bit.

There was a dark blue holdall in the locker with a pair of training shoes placed on top. I tucked the shoes into the holdall on top of the clothes, and left the receptionist tut-tutting about having to disinfect all the lockers. I walked back towards Lombard Street and dumped the whole thing, together with all the contents, into a City of London-crested street litter bin. I didn't think Mrs McDowd would be very happy if I took that smell back into the office.

I had walked nearly a hundred yards further on when I suddenly turned round and retraced my steps. I had searched everything else of Herb's. Why not that holdall?

Neatly stacked, in a zipped-up compartment beneath the clothes, was over a hundred and eighty thousand pounds wrapped in clear plastic bags. There was also a list of ninety-two names and addresses, all of them in America.

Good old Herb. As meticulous as ever.

'MR PATRICK WOULD LIKE to see you,' Mrs McDowd said to me as I skipped through the door with the bag of loot over my shoulder. 'In his office, now.'

Patrick was not alone. Jessica Winter was also there.

'Nicholas,' said Patrick. 'Come and sit down.' I sat in the spare chair next to the open window. 'We need to implement a damage limitation exercise. To maintain the confidence of our clients, and to assure them that it's "business as usual" at Lyall and Black.'

'And is it "business as usual"?' I asked. Members of the Fraud Squad were still in the next-door room bagging up evidence.

'Of course,' he said. 'We mustn't let this little setback disrupt our work. I will write to Gregory's clients telling them that, for the time being, I will be looking after their portfolios.'

'So how about the Bulgarian business?' I asked.

'Jessica and I have just been looking at it,' Patrick said.

'And?' I asked.

'It's inconclusive,' Jessica said. 'There's no evidence to show the investment was obtained by fraudulent means or that there was any purposeful deception by anyone in this firm.'

She's covering her back, I thought. 'How about the EU grants?'

'They are not our business,' Patrick said. 'Neither Gregory, nor Lyall and Black as a firm, can be held responsible for the actions of people in Brussels. The only matter that affects this firm is the Roberts Family Trust investment, and only then if we were knowingly negligent in brokering it. As far as we can establish, the investment idea was put forward by the senior trustee of the trust.'

I had to admit, it was a persuasive argument, especially as Viscount Shenington was in no state to refute it. Perhaps I had been a tad premature in writing off the future of Lyall & Black.

But that didn't explain what had happened to Herb Kovak, and it didn't explain Shenington's comment about me being difficult to kill, and not turning up where I was expected. The only place I'd been expected had been the offices of Lyall & Black, and the only people who had known had been the firm's staff. Gregory must have at least discussed the matter of my murder with Shenington. That alone would have been enough to convict him.

'What about the photographs that Gregory showed to Colonel Roberts?' I said. 'The ones that purported to prove that the factory and houses had already been built.'

'Gregory told me this morning that he'd been sent those by the developer in Bulgaria, and in good faith,' said Patrick. 'He'd had no reason to doubt their authenticity.'

Jessica stood up and left. I remained where I was.

'Now, Nicholas,' said Patrick when the door was shut, 'your job is still yours if you want it. To be honest, I don't know how we would manage at the moment if you weren't here.'

So was that a vote of confidence in my ability or a decision born simply out of necessity? 'Thank you,' I said. 'I'll think about it.'

'Don't take too long,' Patrick said. 'It's time to get back to work.'

'I'm still not happy about things,' I said. 'Especially the fraud.'

'Suspected fraud,' he corrected. 'If you ask me, it's a shame you ever went to see Roberts's nephew in Oxford.'

'Maybe,' I said.

'Well, go now and get on with your work, I have things to do.'

I stood up and went back to my desk. I was still troubled by Patrick and Jessica's seeming brush-off of such a serious situation.

Herb had accessed the file and then he was killed. Shenington and his gunmen knew more about my movements than they could have done without someone in the firm passing on the information.

Something wasn't right. I could tell because the hairs on my neck refused to lie down. Something definitely wasn't right.

I took out a sheet of paper from a drawer and wrote out again a copy of the note I had found in Herb's coat pocket.

YOU SHOULD HAVE DONE WHAT YOU WERE TOLD. YOU MAY SAY YOU REGRET IT, BUT YOU WON'T BE REGRETTING IT FOR LONG.

I wrote it out in capital letters using a black ballpoint pen so that it looked identical to the original. I picked up my mobile phone and the note, and went down the corridor. I walked into Patrick's office, closing the door.

'Yes?' he asked, showing surprise at my unannounced entrance.

I stood in front of his desk, looking down at him as if it was the first time I had ever seen him properly.

'What did you tell Herb to do?' I asked him quietly.

'What do you mean?' he replied with a quizzical expression.

'You told him that he should have done what he was told,' I said. I laid the note down on the table, facing him, so that he could read the words. 'What was it you told Herb to do?'

'Nicholas,' he said, looking up at me and betraying a slight nervousness in his voice, 'I don't know what you're talking about.'

'Yes, you do,' I said. 'It was *you* all along, not Gregory. *You* devised the fraud, *you* found Shenington to put up the five million from his family trust, and *you* saw to it that you weren't found out.'

'I don't know what you're talking about,' he said again, but his eyes showed me he did.

'And *you* had Herb killed,' I said. 'You even wrote this note to him as a sort of apology. Everyone liked Herb, including you. But he had to die, didn't he? Because he had accessed the Roberts file and he'd worked out what was going on. What did you do? Try to buy his silence? But Herb wasn't having any of that, was he? Herb was going to go to the authorities, wasn't he? So he had to die.'

Patrick sat in his chair looking up at me. He said nothing.

'And it was *you* that tried to have me killed as well,' I said. 'You sent the gunman to my house in Finchley and then, when that didn't work, you sent him to my mother's cottage to kill me there.'

He remained in his chair staring at me through his glasses.

'But that didn't work either,' I said. 'So you arranged for me to come here on Monday for a meeting with you and Gregory.' I laughed. 'A meeting with my maker, more like. But I didn't come. Then I saw you on the train and you said "*come home with me now and we'll sort this out tonight*". But I'd have been dead if I had, wouldn't I?' I paused. He still said nothing. 'So then Shenington invited me to be his guest at the races in order to complete the job.'

'Nicholas,' Patrick said. 'What is all this nonsense?'

'It's not nonsense,' I said. 'I never told you that I'd been to see Mr Roberts's nephew in Oxford. In fact, I'd purposely *not* told you because I didn't want anyone knowing my movements. I just told you that I'd spoken to him. For all you knew, it could have been on the telephone. But Shenington told you that I went to Oxford to meet his son, didn't he? And you repeated it to me just now.'

'You have no proof,' he said, changing his tune.

'Did you know that you can get fingerprints from paper?' I asked, picking up the note carefully by the corner.

He wasn't to know that the original had already been tested by the police and found to have only my and Herb's prints on it.

His shoulders sagged and he looked down at the desk.

'What did Herb say he regretted?' I asked.

'He said he regretted finding out,' Patrick said wistfully with a sigh. 'I was careless. I stupidly left a document under the flap of the photocopier. Herb found it.'

'So what did you tell him to do?' I asked for a third time.

'To accept what he'd been offered,' he said, looking up at me. 'But he wanted more. Much more. It was too much.'

Herb had clearly not been as much of a saint as I'd made out.

'So you had him killed.'

He nodded. 'Herb was a fool,' he said. 'He should have accepted my offer. It was very generous, and you can have the same—a million euros.'

'You make me sick,' I said.

'Two million,' he said quickly. 'It would make you a rich man.'

'Blood money,' I said. 'Is that the going rate these days for covering up fraud, and murder?'

'Look,' he said. 'I'm sorry about Herb. I liked him and I argued against having him killed, but the others insisted.'

'Others?' I said. 'You mean Uri Joram and Dimitar Petrov.'

He stared at me with his mouth open.

'Oh yes,' I said. 'The police know all about Joram and Petrov because I told them. I told them everything.'

'You bastard,' he said with feeling. 'I wish Petrov had killed you at the same time he shot Herb Kovak.'

Throughout the encounter I'd been holding my mobile phone in my left hand. It was a smartphone, with a voice-memo recorder. I'd recorded every word that had been said.

I pushed the buttons and played back the last bit. Patrick sat very still in his executive leather chair listening and staring at me with a mixture of hatred and resignation in his eyes.

'*I wish Petrov had killed you at the same time he shot Herb Kovak.*' It sounded rather metallic out of the telephone's tiny speaker, but there was no doubting that it was Patrick Lyall's voice.

'You bastard,' he said again.

I folded the note, turned away from him, and walked back along the corridor to my desk to call Chief Inspector Tomlinson. But I'd only just picked up the telephone when there was a piercing scream from outside the building.

I stuck my head out through the window.

Patrick was lying face up in the middle of the road, and there was already a small pool of blood spreading out round his head.

He had taken the quick way down from our fourth-floor offices.

Straight down.

And it had been the death of him.

Epilogue

Six weeks later Claudia and I went to Herb Kovak's funeral at Hendon Crematorium, the Liverpool coroner finally having given his permission.

There were just five mourners, including the two of us.

Sherri had returned from Chicago and would be taking Herb's ashes back to the States with her. The previous day, she and I had attended a solicitor's office to swear affidavits for the court to confirm a Deed of Variance to Herb's will, making her, his sister, rather than me, the sole beneficiary of his estate. It would surely have been what he would have wanted. I, however, was to remain as his executor in order to complete the sale of his flat, and to do the other things that were still outstanding.

I had written to all the American names I had found in Herb's dark blue holdall, informing them of his untimely death and that their little scheme to use his credit-card accounts for their Internet gambling had died with him. Then I'd used the cash from the holdall to pay off all the credit-card balances, and used my letter from the coroner to close the accounts.

Detective Chief Inspector Tomlinson had come down from Merseyside for the funeral service, wearing the same ill-fitting suit he'd worn when I'd first met him in the offices of Lyall & Black. That had been less than three months ago but it felt like a lifetime.

Lyall & Black and Co. Ltd was no more.

Gregory Black had been released by the police but he had taken early retirement. I had walked out of 64 Lombard Street before the paramedics had even scraped Patrick's corpse from the pavement.

I still didn't know what I would do, so I was currently living off my savings, and looking after Claudia.

The last six weeks had been difficult for her. She had undergone two sessions of chemotherapy. Her hair had fallen out and today, as usual, she was wearing a headscarf. However, Mr Tomic, the oncologist, was pleased with her progress and reckoned that the two sessions were enough. As he'd said, 'we don't want to jeopardise your fertility now, do we?' We would just have to wait and see. With cancer, there were never any guarantees.

The fifth mourner was Mrs McDowd. I wondered how she had known about the funeral but, of course, Mrs McDowd knew everything.

I stood out at the front to utter a few words about Herb. I made some banal comments about his love of life, and his wish to help others less fortunate than himself, but without pointing out that the others he helped were law-breaking American Internet gamblers.

In all, the service took less than twenty minutes. Then the five of us went outside into the warm June sunshine.

Claudia and Mrs McDowd consoled Sherri while the chief inspector and I moved a little distance away.

'The European Union have started an internal inquiry,' he said, 'into the whole Bulgarian light-bulb factory affair.'

'Any arrests?' I asked.

'Not yet,' he said. 'Between you and me, I don't think there will be. There didn't seem to be the slightest urgency.'

'Any news on Shenington?' I asked him.

'No change,' he said. 'He is in what they call a "persistent vegetative state". In cases of severe brain damage like this, if patients show no change for a year, the doctors usually recommend to their families that artificial nutrition be withdrawn, to let them die.'

Ben Roberts would clearly have some difficult decisions to make in the months ahead.

'Did you identify the dead gunman as Dimitar Petrov?' I asked.

'We're still working on it,' he said. 'It seems that both Dimitar and Petrov are very common names in Bulgaria.'

'Can't Uri Joram in Brussels help you?'

'Apparently he denies any knowledge of anything,' he said. 'Claims his email address must have been used by others.'

'Why am I not surprised?' I said. 'How about Shenington's heavies at Cheltenham?'

'Not a sniff,' he said. 'They vanished into the night.'

It reminded me of Billy Searle, who was now, in fact, out of hospital, recuperating at home with the fixator on his broken leg. Officially, he was still denying any knowledge of who had knocked him off his bicycle, but he had confirmed to me privately that the 'nob' responsible had indeed been Viscount Shenington.

The chief inspector and I rejoined the others.

'Rosemary says she's lost her job,' said Claudia.

'Everyone at Lyall and Black has lost their jobs,' said Rosemary McDowd with bitterness.

Her tone also implied an accusation, and I took it to be towards me. Why was it, I wondered, that the blame often fell not on the wrongdoer but on the person who exposed them? It wasn't me who Mrs McDowd should blame for the demise of Lyall & Black. It was Patrick Lyall.

And I surely had more right to be angry with her than vice versa. After all, it had been she who had told Patrick that I'd been staying at my mother's house, which had then allowed him and Shenington to send a gunman there to try to kill me.

'So what are you going to do now?' I asked her.

'I have absolutely no idea,' she said flatly. 'How about you?'

'I thought I might try my hand at working in the movies, or in the theatre,' I said. 'I've written to a few companies offering my services as a funding specialist, to help them find the production money for films and plays. I think it looks quite interesting.'

'But isn't that a bit of a gamble?' she said.

I smiled at her.

With ovarian cancer, life itself was a bit of a gamble.

Heads you win, tails you die.

felix **francis**

Profile

Born:
1953.

Education:
Degree in physics from
London University.

Siblings:
Older brother Merrick.

Residence:
Oxfordshire.

Unusual Talent:
Can recite opening lines
of all forty-plus Dick
Francis novels.

Previous Jobs:
Science teacher, leader of
Andes hiking expeditions.

With his first solo novel, *Gamble*, Felix Francis proves that he's just as talented as his late father, Dick Francis, who wrote more than forty novels, which sold in their millions worldwide, bringing their creator legions of loyal and devoted fans. Felix, the youngest son of Dick and his wife Mary, clearly has similar skills to those of his late father and readers must hope that he will long continue to write with the same verve and style.

In essence, Felix has been in training for the job of continuing the Francis franchise for many years. 'My father's first novel, *Dead Cert*, was published when I was eight,' he explains. 'I grew up in a fiction factory. The conversation at breakfast wasn't about who was doing the school run, it was about whether Sid Halley would survive the night with a .38 slug in his guts,' he chuckles, referring to one of his father's series heroes, a jockey-turned-sleuth.

Although there were always horses around, Felix didn't follow his father into the saddle. As a teenager he had hip problems, which ruled out any possibility that this might happen. The problems also put an end to his ambition to be a pilot—he was turned down on medical grounds by British Airways. Felix then chose a career in physics, becoming a teacher for several years. 'I loved teaching and I still have a great fascination for science in general and physics in particular,' he says. 'The first thing I had published was an O-Level physics paper for the Oxford and Cambridge Examination Board in 1986.'

So how then can he re-create that other vital element of a Dick Francis book, the insider knowledge of racing? 'Well, I may only have a degree in physics,' he jokes, 'but I do have a good imagination. And I had plenty of practise writing fiction in school reports. But, if I want to check any horse-racing details, I go to my brother Merrick.'

In fact, Felix's physics knowledge led to his first real contribution to his dad's work. 'The first part of a Dick Francis book I ever wrote was the design of the bomb that blew up a plane in *Rat Race* in 1970, when I was an A-level physics student. I wrote the computer programme in *Twice Shy*, the one that had a teacher who was also a marksman, which is exactly what I was. I shot for England—that was thirty-five years ago—and I shot for Oxfordshire till 1996.' But the family business beckoned further, and, having become increasingly involved over the years in helping his father with the 'paperwork', in 1990 Felix quit his job as head of the science department at Bloxham School to manage his father's business affairs on a full-time basis and to help write and research the books.

It was, he says, 'the worst-kept secret in publishing' that while his father had the ideas for the books, and would write the first draft in longhand, his mother, Mary, would give them plenty of polishing and finessing as she typed them up. It was very much a collaboration between the two, but Mary did not want to take any credit. 'My mother always called my father Richard because her sister was married to a man called Dick, so the name Dick Francis was, in a way, a combination of Richard and Mary.'

After Mary's death in 2000, the balance of Felix's partnership with his father turned a corner with *Shattered*, published in 2001 and Dick Francis's thirty-eighth novel. 'I helped finish *Shattered* off, and it was the right title for it, because my father was exhausted. He was eighty years old and he wasn't going to get the deadline.'

As his father aged and became more frail over the years, Felix's contributions increased steadily. The last four Francis novels were co-written by father and son. But when Dick Francis passed away in January 2010, aged eighty-nine, Felix was on his own.

The common ground between *Gamble* and the Dick Francis novels is extensive. The story is set in the world of horse-racing and Felix has used many of his father's creative trademarks, including the first-person narrator and the amateur central character who finds himself inadvertently at the scene of the crime, but who proves more resourceful than the police in solving it. Most of the gambling in *Gamble* is not on the horses, it is gambling where losing means dying, but does Felix like to have a flutter on the horses? 'No. Strangely, I don't like betting. I have met too many rich bookmakers! Occasionally, if I'm with friends at the races, I will have a small flutter to participate in the occasion but I almost invariably lose. And if you bet on a horse then that is the only horse you tend to watch in the race. I prefer to watch them all.'

Felix is delighted to be carrying on the Francis brand. 'When people ask me what I do now, I reply, "I write the Dick Francis novels." It is the biggest joy of my life. I feel as if I have found happiness being an author.'

COPYRIGHT AND ACKNOWLEDGMENTS

THE AFFAIR: Copyright © Lee Child 2011.
Published at £18.99 by Bantam Press, an imprint of Transworld Publishers.
Condensed version © The Reader's Digest Association, Inc., 2011.

DEAD MAN'S GRIP: Copyright © Really Scary Books/Peter James 2011.
Published at £18.99 by Macmillan, an imprint of Pan Macmillan, a division of
Macmillan Publishers Limited.
Condensed version © The Reader's Digest Association, Inc., 2011.

ONE SUMMER: Copyright © 2011 by Columbus Rose, Ltd.
Published at £12.99 by Macmillan, an imprint of Pan Mamillan, a divison of
Macmillan Publishers Limited.
Condensed version © The Reader's Digest Association, Inc., 2011.

GAMBLE: Copyright © Dick Francis Corporation, 2011.
Published at £18.99 by Michael Joseph, an imprint of Penguin Books Ltd.
Condensed version © The Reader's Digest Association, Inc., 2011.

The right to be identified as authors has been asserted by the following in accordance with
sections 77 and 78 of the Copyright, Designs and Patents Act, 1988: Lee Child, Peter James,
David Baldacci, Felix Francis.

Spine: Shutterstock. Front cover (from left): Cultura RM/Alamy, Transtock Inc./Alamy,
Shutterstock and Istockphoto; (centre left): Gerry Penny/epa/Corbis; (centre right):
www.alanayers.com and Dougal Waters/Getty Images; (right): Caro/Alamy and Gareth
Lewis/Alamy. 6–7: images: Shutterstock; illustration: Rick Lecoat@Shark Attack; 160 ©
Johnny Ring. 162–163: images: Shutterstock; illustration: Rick Lecoat@Shark Attack; 310 ©
courtesy of Peter James. 312–313 images: Julian Herbert/Reportage; illustration: David
Ricketts@velvet tamarind; 432 © Alexander James. 434–435 images: Rudy
Malmquist/FlickR, Ben Bloom/The Image Bank; illustration: Amy Eccleston@velvet tamarind.
574 © Debbie Francis.

Printed and bound by GGP Media GmbH, Pössneck, Germany

020-275 UP0000-1